DATE DUE

The Library Store   #47-0103

THE
PUSHCART PRIZE, XXIV:
BEST OF THE
SMALL PRESSES

BEST OF
THE SMALL
PRESSES

The
PUSHCART
PRIZE
2000
XXIV

Edited by
Bill Henderson
with the Pushcart
Prize editors

THE PUSHCART PRESS — WAINSCOTT NY

Note: nominations for this series are invited from any small, independent, literary book press or magazine in the world. Up to six nominations—tear sheets or copies, selected from work published, or about to be published, in the calendar year—are accepted by our December 1 deadline each year. Write to Pushcart Press, P.O. Box 380, Wainscott, N.Y. 11975 for more information.

Acknowledgments

Selections for The Pushcart Prize are reprinted with the
permission of authors and presses cited. Copyright reverts to
authors and presses immediately after publication.

Distributed by W. W. Norton & Co.
500 Fifth Ave., New York, N.Y. 10110

Library of Congress Card Number: 76–58675
ISBN: 1–888889–19–5
       1–888889–21–7 (paperback)
ISSN: 0149–7863

For Ray

INTRODUCTION

by BILL HENDERSON

For almost twenty-five years The Pushcart Prize editors have celebrated new writers, and this edition includes perhaps more new voices than any other in the series. But annually we also honor those who have meant so much to small presses and literary magazines and who have left us recently. In this introduction I honor three people: Andre Dubus, Ray Freiman and Michael Rea.

Andre Dubus spent much of his writing life with little magazines and presses. We reprinted his short fiction starting way back in 1978 with "The Fat Girl" from his David R. Godine story collection *Adultery And Other Choices*. Later selections included the short story "Rose" (from *Ploughshares*) and the essays "Love In the Morning" (*Doubletake*) and "A Hemingway Story" (*Kenyon Review*).

Andre was not only a frequent visitor to my small town on the East End of Long Island—his agent, Phil Spitzer, who was Andre's friend and supporter for many years, lives around the corner—but he was also a cheerleader for small presses and a terrific teacher.

Many years ago, when Andre lost his leg and almost his life while rescuing a boy in an automobile accident near Boston, I was running a small press advertising campaign for the National Endowment for the Arts Literature Program and I had asked Andre to be a judge and commentator for that program. On the night of his accident, even though he was horribly injured, he asked his wife to telephone me and tell me not to worry. He would get the job done. He would be well again. Even his doctors didn't know that: his very survival was in question. But Andre knew he would live. He was a survivor. A tough, loving guy. And one of our great writers. When he died on February 24, 1999, I lost a friend and a man who was brave both physically and morally. He was never bashful about proclaiming his Catholic faith, and he encouraged the rest of us to declare our own faiths publicly and enthusiastically.

My friend Ray Freiman was in charge of the printing of this series from day one. I met Ray when I was just starting an early version of Pushcart Press in a basement in North Plainfield, New Jersey. I was 29 years old, an oft-rejected writer who knew nothing about publishing beyond rejection and here I was starting a press with a tiny list and little money and not a clue about what I was doing. (The press was called Nautilus Books. It folded swiftly.) I had heard of Ray's skills in printing and designing books, and I called him for help. When he showed up in my North Plainfield basement, I was jumpy and nervous. Here was the former Vice-President of mighty Random House in my basement. I didn't even know where to start talking to him. I knew literally nothing about publishing. But Ray was a gentle and generous man. He ignored my nervousness and began to teach me. And for almost 30 years he continued to educate me in the production of books. Ray died on February 1, 1999. He was a good friend. Pushcart will not be the same without him.

I also want to thank Elizabeth Richebourg Rea, whose late husband Michael M. Rea I celebrated in the dedication and introduction of *Pushcart Prize XXII*. Through the Dungannon Foundation, founded by Elizabeth and Michael, this series has continued to receive generous financial support at key times. Some years I did not know how we would ever pay the next Pushcart bill. At such times, Michael and Elizabeth were there to help out. And the sponsorship of the Dungannon Foundation has also been extended to today's outstanding short story writers through the annual Rea Award for the Short Story. Past winners include Cynthia Ozick, Robert Coover, Donald Barthelme, Tobias Wolff, Joyce Carol Oates, Paul Bowles, Eudora Welty, Grace Paley, Tillie Olsen, Richard Ford, Andre Dubus, Gina Berriault, John Edgar Wideman, and Joy Williams.

Without Elizabeth and Michael I wouldn't have survived to write these words. Such goodness and giving deserve a big billboard in the sky somewhere. Quietly, people like them make wonderful things happen in a world where it often seems most people could care less.

A special thanks this year also to Jack Driscoll, who helped me read the fiction. Jack is the author of *Lucky Man, Lucky Woman* (Pushcart Press, 1999) a first novel that not only won Pushcart's Editors' Book Award, but was also selected by Barnes and Noble for their Discovery

Series and by the *Independent Publisher* magazine as the best small press novel of the year. Jack is also the author of the story collection *Wanting Only to Be Heard* (University of Massachusetts Press). To me he is a friend, and a fellow fisherman. With Jack as a guide, I caught a huge brown trout on Lake Michigan this spring and I have photos to prove it. Fiction and fishing, Jack does it all.

Our poetry editors this year are Michael Dennis Browne and Kimiko Hahn. They have done a thankless and impossible job of sifting through thousands of nominated poems and selecting thirty for reprint. Both editors said they could have selected dozens more if space permitted.

Kimiko Hahn is the author of *Air Pocket* (Hanging Loose Press, 1989), *Earshot* (HLP, 1992), awarded The Theodore Roethke Memorial Poetry Prize and an Association of Asian American Studies Literature Award, *The Unbearable Heart* (Kaya, 1996), which received an American Book Award, *Volatile* (HLP, 1998), and *Mosquito and Ant* (W. W. Norton, 1999). Recent poetry can be found in *Kenyon Review, Manoa, Another Chicago Magazine,* and *Best American Poetry of 1996 (Scribner);* her prose has appeared in *Bomb, The Global Review, Tri-Quarterly* and the anthology, *Charlie Chan is Dead* (Penguin). Kimiko is a recipient of fellowships from the National Endowment for the Arts and the New York Foundation for the Arts, and last year she was awarded a Lila Wallace-Readers Digest Writers Award. She is an Associate Professor in the English Department at Queens College, New York City.

Michael Dennis Browne was born in England in 1940 and came to the United States in 1965. A graduate of the creative writing program at Iowa, he has taught at Iowa, Columbia, Bennington, and, since 1971, at the University of Minnesota in Minneapolis, where he is a professor of English and former director of the creative writing program. As a librettist, he has written many texts for music, working principally with Stephen Paulus and John Foley, S.J.; the works include song cycles, operas, cantatas, carols, hymns, and songs for children. He has received fellowships from the National Endowment for the Arts, The Bush Foundation, and the Jerome Foundation. His awards include Discovery '68, the Borestone Prize, a Loft-McKnight Award, and a 1993 Minnesota Book Award for *You Won't Remember This.*

This edition of *The Pushcart Prize* is special in many ways. Not only do we welcome many new authors to the series, as we do every year, we also have reprinted work from 15 presses that are new here: *Art and Understanding,* Avocet Press, *Boston Review, First Intensity, Five Points, Greensboro Review, Zoetrope: All-Story, Many Mountains Moving, Mudfish, Open City, Other Voices, Oyster Boy Review, Solo 2,* Tia Chucha Press, University of Georgia Press and University of North Texas Press—altogether 62 selections from 47 presses, and further proofs (if you needed any) that small presses and little magazines are alive and thriving in conglomerate-dominated, consumer-ridden, computer-addicted America.

THE PEOPLE WHO HELPED

FOUNDING EDITORS—*Anaïs Nin (1903–1977) Buckminster Fuller (1895–1983), Charles Newman, Daniel Halpern, Gordon Lish, Harry Smith, Hugh Fox, Ishmael Reed, Joyce Carol Oates, Len Fulton, Leonard Randolph, Leslie Fiedler, Nona Balakian (1918–1991) Paul Bowles, Paul Engle (1908–1991), Ralph Ellison (1914–1994) Reynolds Price, Rhoda Schwartz, Richard Morris, Ted Wilentz, Tom Montag, William Phillips. Poetry editor: Lloyd Van Brunt.*

CONTRIBUTING EDITORS FOR THIS EDITION—*Wally Lamb, Judith Taylor, Joyce Carol Oates, Andre Dubus, Dana Levin, Edward Hirsch, Pamela Stewart, Ted Wilentz, Barbara Selfridge, Jane McCafferty, Stanley Lindberg, Kirk Nisset, Melvin Jules Bukiet, Laurie Sheck, Tony Ardizzone, Gerald Shapiro, Diann Blakely, Ed Falco, J. Allyn Rosser, Kim Addonizio, Richard Jackson, Dan Masterson, James Harms, Brenda Hillman, Susan Bergman, Mary Peterson, Risa Mickenberg, Jewel Mogan, John Allman, DeWitt Henry, Nancy Richard, Robley Wilson, Tom Paine, Richard Garcia, Robert Phillips, Thomas Disch, P. H. Liotta, Daniel Orozco, Rick Bass, Colette Inez, Lucia Perillo, David Lehman, Tomaž Šalamun, Philip Dacey, Arthur Smith, Eleanor Wilner, Caroline Amanda Langston, Sharman Apt Russell, Rosellen Brown, Brenda Miller, Robert McBrearty, Pattiann Rogers, John Drury, David Jauss, Susan Wheeler, Julia Vinograd, Joan Murray, Thomas Kennedy, George Keithley, Richard Kostelanetz, Sherod Santos, Tarin Towers, Rane Arroyo, Michael Harper, Thomas Frank, Marilyn Krysl, Clarence Major, Carolyn Kizer, Gretchen Legler, Rosemary Hildebrandt, Karen Bender, Marie Sheppard Williams, Morton Elevitch, H. E. Francis, Stuart Dybek, Philip*

Levine, Stephen Dunn, Donald Revell, Bin Ramke, Cleopatra Mathis, Jane Hirshfield, Michael Bowden, Kristina McGrath, Jim Simmerman, Eugene Stein, Katherine Min, Ron Tanner, Jay Meek, Kristin King, Jim Daniels, Carol Snow, Jessica Roeder, Susan Mates, David Baker, Alan Michael Parker, Mike Newirth, Ellen Wilbur, Robert Schirmer, Sigrid Nunez, Fred Busch, Mark Irwin, Thomas Sayers Ellis, Chard de Niord, Antler, Michael Gregory Stephens, Lance Olsen, Michael Heffernan, Grace Schulman, Michael Van Walleghen, Martin Espada, Roger Weingarten, Richard Tayson, Mark Cox, Vern Rutsala, Steve Yarbrough, Stuart Dischell, Josip Novakovich, Robin Hemley, Maura Stanton, Dorianne Laux, Martha Collins, Marianne Boruch, William Olsen, Stephen Corey, Alberto Rios, David Wojahn, Jennifer Atkinson, Jane Miller, Rita Dove, Molly Bendall, Gary Fincke, Ehud Havazelet, Reginald Gibbons, David Rivard, Gibbons Ruark, David Baker, Jeffrey Harrison, Melissa Pritchard, David Romtvedt, Claire Davis, Len Roberts, Robert Wrigley, Pinckney Benedict, Tony Quagliano, C. E. Poverman, Maureen Seaton, Sylvia Watanabe, Laura Kasischke, Arthur Sze, Philip Appleman, Michael Collier, Marilyn Hacker, Emily Fox Gordon, Robert Pinsky, Mariko Nagai, Jack Marshall, Tom Lux, Jean Thompson, Lynne McFall, Katrina Roberts, Christina Zawadiwsky, Christopher Howell, Julie Showalter, Kathy Callaway, Mark Wisniewski, Joan Swift, John Daniel, Carl Phillips, Paul Zimmer, Joe Ashby Porter, Ha Jin, Linda Bierds, Edward Hoagland, Marvin Bell, Sharon Solwitz, Michael Waters, James Reiss, Mark Jarman, Janice Edius, Timothy Geiger, Gordon Weaver, Jim Barnes, Carl Dennis, Billy Collins, Kathy Fagan, Tom Filer, Michael Martone, Lou Mathews, Andrew Hudgins, S. L. Wisenberg, Debra Spark, Susan Moon, Agha Shahid Ali, Erin McGraw, Gary Gildner, Eamon Grennan, Mary Ruefle, Christopher Buckley, Elizabeth Spires, Lee Upton, Lynn Emanuel, Rachel Hadas, Gerry Locklin, Kent Nelson, Henry Carlile, Lois-Ann Yamanaka, Kenneth Gangemi, Toi Derricotte, Tom McNeal.

PAST POETRY EDITORS—Lloyd Van Brunt, Naomi Lazard, Lynne Spaulding, Herb Leibowitz, Jon Galassi, Grace Schulman, Carolyn Forché, Gerald Stern, Stanley Plumly, William Stafford, Philip Levine, David Wojahn, Jorie Graham, Robert Hass, Philip Booth, Jay Meek, Sandra McPherson, Laura Jensen, William Heyen, Elizabeth Spires, Marvin Bell, Carolyn Kizer, Christopher Buckley, Chase Twichell, Richard Jackson, Susan Mitchell, Lynn Emanuel, David St. John,

Carol Muske, Dennis Schmitz, William Matthews, Patricia Strachan, Heather McHugh, Molly Bendall, Marilyn Chin.

ROVING EDITORS—*Rick Moody, Marvin Bell*

EUROPEAN EDITORS—*Liz and Kirby Williams*

FICTION EDITORS—*Jack Driscoll, Bill Henderson*

ESSAYS EDITOR—*Anthony Brandt*

POETRY EDITORS FOR THIS EDITION—*Michael Dennis Browne, Kimiko Hahn*

EDITOR AND PUBLISHER—*Bill Henderson*

CONTENTS

THE
PUSHCART PRIZE XXIV:
BEST OF THE
SMALL PRESSES

THE MANSION ON THE HILL

fiction by RICK MOODY

from THE PARIS REVIEW

T HE CHICKEN MASK was sorrowful, Sis. The Chicken Mask was supposed to hustle business; it was supposed to invite the customer to gorge him or herself within our establishment; it was supposed to be endearing and funny; it was supposed to be an accurate representation of the featured item on our menu. But, Sis, in a practical setting, in test markets—like right out in front of the restaurant—the Chicken Mask had a plaintive aspect, a blue quality (it was stifling, too, even in cold weather), so that I'd be walking down Main, by the waterfront, after you were gone, back and forth in front of Hot Bird (Bucket of Drumsticks, $2.99), wearing out my imitation basketball sneakers from Wal-Mart, pudgy in my black jogging suit, lurching along in the sandwich board, and the kids would hustle up to me, tugging on the wrists of their harried, underfinanced moms. The kids would get bored with me almost immediately. They knew the routine. Their eyes would narrow, and all at once there were no secrets here in our town of service-economy franchising: *I was the guy working nine to five in a Chicken Mask,* even though I'd had a pretty good education in business administration, even though I was more or less presentable and well-spoken, even though I came from a good family. I made light of it, Sis, I extemporized about Hot Bird, in remarks designed by virtue of my studies in business tactics to drive whole families in for the new *low-fat roasters,* a meal option that was steeper, in terms of price, but tasty nonetheless. (And I ought to have known, because I ate from the menu every day. Even the coleslaw.)

Here's what I'd say, in my Chicken Mask. Here was my pitch: *Feeling a little peckish? Try Hot Bird!* or *Don't be chicken, try Hot Bird!* The mothers would laugh their nervous adding-machine laughs (those laughs that are next door over from a sob), and they would lead the kids off. Twenty yards away, though, the boys and girls would still be staring disdainfully at me, gaping backward while I rubbed my hands raw in the cold, while I breathed the synthetic rubber interior of the Chicken Mask—that fragrance of rubber balls from gym classes lost, that bouquet of the gloves Mom used for the dishes, that perfume of simpler times—while I looked for my next shill. I lost almost ninety days to the demoralization of the Chicken Mask, to its grim, existential emptiness, until I couldn't take it anymore. Which happened to be the day when Alexandra McKinnon (remember her? from Sunday school?) turned the corner with her boy Zack—he has to be seven or eight now—oblivious while upon her daily rounds, oblivious and fresh from a Hallmark store. It was nearly Valentine's Day. They didn't know it was me in there, of course, inside the Chicken Mask. They didn't know I was *the chicken from the basement, the chicken of darkest nightmares,* or, more truthfully, they didn't know I was a guy with some pretty conflicted attitudes about things. That's how I managed to apprehend Zack, leaping out from the in-door of Cohen's Pharmacy, laying ahold of him a little too roughly, by the hem of his pillowy, orange ski jacket. Little Zack was laughing, at first, until, in a voice racked by loss, I worked my hard sell on him, declaiming stentoriously that *Death Comes to All.* That's exactly what I said, just as persuasively as I had once hawked *White meat breasts, eight pieces, just $4.59!* Loud enough that he'd be sure to know what I meant. His look was interrogative, quizzical. So I repeated myself. *Death Comes to Everybody, Zachary.* My voice was urgent now. My eyes bulged from the eyeholes of my standard-issue Chicken Mask. I was even crying a little bit. Saline rivulets tracked down my neck. Zack was terrified.

What I got next certainly wasn't the kind of flirtatious attention I had always hoped for from his mom. Alex began drumming on me with balled fists. I guess she'd been standing off to the side of the action previously, believing that I was a reliable paid employee of Hot Bird. But now she was all over me, bruising me with wild swings, cursing, until she'd pulled the Chicken Mask from my head—half expecting, I'm sure, to find me scarred or hydrocephalic or otherwise disabled.

24

Her denunciations let up a little once she was in possession of the facts. It was me, her old Sunday school pal, Andrew Wakefield. Not at the top of my game.

I don't really want to include here the kind of scene I made, once unmasked. Alex was exasperated with me, but gentle anyhow. I think she probably knew I was in the middle of a rough patch. People knew. The people leaning out of the storefronts probably knew. But, if things weren't already bad enough, I remembered right then—God, this is horrible—that Alex's mom had driven into Lake Sacandaga about five years before. Jumped the guardrail and plunged right off that bridge there. In December. In heavy snow. In a Ford Explorer. That was the end of her. *Listen, Alex,* I said, *I'm confused, I have problems and I don't know what's come over me and I hope you can understand, and I hope you'll let me make it up to you. I can't lose this job. Honest to God.* Fortunately, just then, Zack became interested in the Chicken Mask. He swiped the mask from his mom—she'd been holding it at arm's length, like a soiled rag—and he pulled it down over his head and started making simulated automatic-weapons noises in the directions of local passersby. This took the heat off. We had a laugh, Alex and I, and soon the three of us had repaired to Hot Bird itself (it closed four months later, like most of the businesses on that block) for coffee and biscuits and the chef's special spicy wings, which, because of my position, were on the house.

Alex was actually waving a spicy wing when she offered her life-altering opinion that I was too smart to be working for Hot Bird, especially if I was going to brutalize little kids with the creepy facts of the hereafter. What I should do, Alex said, was get into something positive instead. She happened to know a girl—it was her cousin, Glenda—who managed a business over in Albany, the Mansion on the Hill, a big area employer, and why didn't I call Glenda and use Alex's name, and maybe they would have something in accounting or valet parking or flower delivery, *yada yada yada,* you know, some job that had as little public contact as possible, something that paid better than minimum wage, because minimum wage, Alex said, wasn't enough for a guy of twenty-nine. After these remonstrances she actually hauled me over to the pay phone at Hot Bird (people are so generous sometimes), while my barely alert boss Antonio slumbered at the register with no idea what was going on, without a clue that he was about to lose his most conscientious chicken impersonator. All because I couldn't stop myself from talking about death.

Alex dialed up the Mansion on the Hill (while Zack, at the table, donned my mask all over again), penetrating deep into the switchboard by virtue of her relation to a Mansion on the Hill management-level employee, and was soon actually talking to her cousin: *Glenda, I got a friend here who's going through some rough stuff in his family, if you know what I mean, yeah, down on his luck in the job department too, but he's a nice bright guy anyhow. I pretty much wanted to smooch him throughout confirmation classes, and he went to . . . Hey, where did you go to school again? Went to SUNY and has a degree in business administration, knows a lot about product positioning or whatever, I don't know, new housing starts, yada yada yada, and I think you really ought to . . .*

Glenda's sigh was audible from several feet away, I swear, through the perfect medium of digital telecommunications, but you can't blame Glenda for that. People protect themselves from bad luck, right? Still, Alex wouldn't let her cousin refuse, wouldn't hear of it, *You absolutely gotta meet him, Glenda, he's a doll, he's a dream boat,* and Glenda gave in, and that's the end of this part of the story, about how I happened to end up working out on Wolf Road at the capital region's finest wedding- and party-planning business. Except that before the Hot Bird recedes into the mists of time, I should report to you that I swiped the Chicken Mask, Sis. They had three or four of them. You'd be surprised how easy it is to come by a Chicken Mask.

Politically, here's what was happening in the front office of my new employer: Denise Gulch, the Mansion on the Hill staff writer, had left her husband and her kids and her steady job, because of a wedding, because of the language of the vows—that soufflé of exaggerated language—vows which, for quality-control purposes, were being broadcast over a discreet speaker in the executive suite. Denise was so moved by a recitation of Paul Stookey's "Wedding Song" taking place during the course of the Neuhaus ceremony ("Whenever two or more of you / Are gathered in His name, / There is love, / There is love . . . ") that she slipped into the Rip Van Winkle Room disguised as a latecomer. Immediately, in the electrifying atmosphere of matrimony, she began trying to seduce one of the ushers (Nicky Weir, a part-time Mansion employee who was acquainted with the groom). I figure this flirtation had been taking place for some time, but that's not what everyone told me. What I heard was that seconds after meeting one another—the bride hadn't even recessed yet—Denise and Nicky were secreted in a nearby broom closet, while the office phones bounced to voice mail, and were peeling back the layers of our Mansion dress code, until, at day's end, scantily clad and intoxicated by rhetoric and desire, they stole a limousine and left town without collecting severance. Denise was even fully vested in the pension plan.

All this could only happen at a place called the Mansion on the Hill, a place of fluffy endings: the right candidate for the job walks through the door at the eleventh hour, the check clears that didn't exist minutes before, government agencies agree to waive mountains of red tape, the sky clears, the snow ends, and stony women like Denise Gulch succumb to torrents of generosity, throwing half-dollars to children as they embark on new lives.

The real reason I got the job is that they were shorthanded, and because Alex's cousin, my new boss, was a little difficult. But things were starting to look up anyway. If Glenda's personal demeanor at the interview wasn't exactly warm (she took a personal call in the middle that lasted twenty-eight minutes, and later she asked me, while reapplying lip liner, if I wore cologne) at least she was willing to hire me—as long as I agreed to renounce any personal grooming habits that inclined in the direction of Old Spice, Hai Karate or CK1. I would have spit-polished her pumps just to have my own desk (on which I put a yellowed picture of you when you were a kid, holding up the bass that you caught fly-fishing and also a picture of the four of us: Mom and Dad and you and me) and a Rolodex and unlimited access to stamps, mailing bags and paper clips.

Let me take a moment to describe our core business at the Mansion on the Hill. We were in the business of helping people celebrate the best days of their lives. We were in the business of spreading joy, by any means necessary. We were in the business of paring away the calluses of woe and grief to reveal the bright light of commitment. We were in the business of producing flawless memories. We had seven auditoriums, or *marriage suites,* as we liked to call them, each with a slightly different flavor and decorating vocabulary. For example, there was the *Chestnut Suite,* the least expensive of our rental suites, which had lightweight aluminum folding chairs (with polyurethane padding) and a very basic altar table, which had the unfortunate pink and lavender floral wallpaper and which seated about 125 comfortably; then there was the *Hudson Suite,* which had some teak in it and a lot of paneling and a classic iron altar table and some rather large standing tables at the rear, and the reception area in Hudson was clothed all in vinyl, instead of the paper coverings that they used in Chestnut (the basic decorating scheme there in the Hudson Suite was meant to suggest the sea vessels that once sailed through our municipal port); then there was the *Rip Van Winkle Room,* with its abundance of draperies, its silk curtains, its matching maroon settings of inexpensive linen, and the *Adirondack Suite,* the *Ticonderoga Room,* the *Valentine Room* (a sort of giant powder puff), and of course the *Niagara Hall,* which was grand and reserved, with its separate kitchen and its enormous fireplace and white-gloved staff, for the sons and daughters of those Victorians of Saratoga County who came upstate for the summer during the racing season, the children of contemporary robber barons, the children whose noses were always straight and whose luck was always good.

We had our own on-site boutique for wedding gowns and tuxedo rentals and fittings—hell, we'd even clean and store your garments for you while you were away on your honeymoon—and we had a travel agency who subcontracted for us, as we also had wedding consultants, jewelers, videographers, still photographers (both the arty ones who specialized in photos of your toenail polish on the day of the wedding and the conventional photographers who barked directions at the assembled family far into the night), nannies, priests, ministers, shamans, polarity therapists, a really maniacal florist called Bruce, a wide array of deejays—guys and gals equipped to spin Christian-only selections, Tex-Mex, music from Hindi films and the occasional death-metal wedding medley—and we could get actual musicians, if you preferred. We'd even had Dick Roseman's combo, The Sons of Liberty, do a medley of "My Funny Valentine," "In-a-Gadda-Da-Vida," "I Will Always Love You" and "Smells Like Teen Spirit," without a rest between selections. (It was gratifying for me to watch the old folks shake it up to contemporary numbers.) We had a three-story, fifteen-hundred slip parking facility on site, convenient access to I-87, I-90 and the Taconic, and a staff of 175 full- and part-time employees on twenty-four hour call. We had everything from publicists to dicers of crudités to public orators (need a brush-up for that toast?)—all for the purpose of making your wedding the high watermark of your American life. We had done up to fifteen weddings in a single day (it was a Saturday in February, 1991, during the Gulf War) and, since the Mansion on the Hill first threw open its door for a gala double wedding (the Gifford twins, from Balston Spa, who married Shaun and Maurice Wickett) in June of 1987, we had performed, up to the time of my first

28

day there, 1,963 weddings, many of them memorable, life-affirming, even spectacular ceremonies. We had never had an incidence of serious violence.

This was the raw data that Glenda gave me, anyway, Sis. The arrangement of the facts is my own, and in truth, the arrangement of facts constitutes the job I was engaged to perform at the Mansion on the Hill. Because Glenda Manzini (in 1990 she married Dave Manzini, a developer from Schenectady), couldn't really have hated her job any more than she did. Glenda Manzini, whose marriage (her second) was apparently not the most loving ever in upstate history (although she's not alone; I estimate an even thousand divorces resulting from the conjugal rites successfully consummated so far at my place of business), was a cynic, a skeptic, a woman of little faith when it came to the institution through which she made her living. She occasionally referred to the wedding party as *the cattle;* she occasionally referred to the brides as *the hookers* and to herself, manager of the Mansion on the Hill, as *the Madame,* as in, *The Madame, Andrew, would like it if you would get the hell out of her office so that she can tabulate these receipts,* or, *Please tell the Hatfields and the McCoys that the Madame cannot untangle their differences for them, although the Madame does know the names of some first-rate couples counselors.* In the absence of an enthusiasm for our product line or for business writing in general, Glenda Manzini hired me to tackle some of her responsibilities for her. I gave the facts the best possible spin. Glenda, as you probably have guessed, was good with numbers. With the profits and losses. Glenda was good at additional charges. Glenda was good at doubling the price on a floral arrangement, for example, because the Vietnamese poppies absolutely had to be on the tables, because they were so . . . *je ne sais quoi.* Glenda was good at double-booking a particular suite and then auctioning the space to the higher bidder. Glenda was good at quoting a figure for a band and then adding instruments so that the price increased astronomically. One time she padded a quartet with two vocalists, an eight-piece horn section, an African drumming ensemble, a dijeridoo and a harmonium.

The other thing I should probably be up-front about is that Glenda Manzini was a total knockout. A bombshell. A vision of celestial loveliness. I hate to go on about it, but there was that single strand of Glenda's amber hair always falling over her eyes—no matter how many times she tried to secure it; there was her near constant attention to

29

her makeup; there was her total command of business issues and her complete unsentimentality. Or maybe it was her stockings, always in black, with a really provocative seam following the aerodynamically sleek lines of her calf. Or maybe it was her barely concealed sadness. I'd never met anyone quite as uncomfortable as Glenda, but this didn't bother me at first. My life had changed since the Chicken Mask.

Meanwhile, it goes without saying that the Mansion on the Hill wasn't a mansion at all. It was a homely cinder-block edifice formerly occupied by the Colonie Athletic Club. A trucking operation used the space before that. And the Mansion wasn't on any hill, either, because geologically speaking we're in a valley in here. We're part of some recent glacial scouring.

On my first day, Glenda made every effort to insure that my work environment would be as unpleasant as possible. I'd barely set down my extra-large coffee with two half-and-halfs and five sugars and my assortment of cream-filled donuts (I was hoping these would please my new teammates) when Glenda bodychecked me, tipped me over into my reclining desk chair, with several huge stacks of file material.

—Andy, listen up. In April we have an Orthodox Jewish ceremony taking place at 3 P.M. in Niagara while at the same time there are going to be some very faithful Islamic-Americans next door in Ticonderoga. I don't want these two groups to come in contact with one another at any time, understand? I don't want any kind of diplomatic incident. It's your job to figure out how to persuade one of these groups to be first out of the gate, at noon, and it's your job to make them think that they're really lucky to have the opportunity. And Andy? The el-Mohammed wedding, the Muslim wedding, needs prayer mats. See if you can get some from the discount stores. Don't waste a lot of money on this.

This is a good indication of Glenda's management style. Some other procedural tidbits: she frequently assigned a dozen rewrites on her correspondence. She had a violent dislike for semicolons. I was to double-space twice underneath the date on her letters, before typing the salutation, on pain of death. I was never, ever to use one of those cursive word-processing fonts. I was to bring her coffee first thing in the morning, without speaking to her until she had entirely finished a second cup and also a pair of ibuprofen tablets, preferably the elongated, easy-to-swallow variety. I was never to ask her about her weekend or her evening or anything else, including her holidays, unless she asked me first. If her door was closed, I was not to open it. And if I ever reversed the digits in a phone number when taking a message for her, I could count on my pink slip that very afternoon.

Right away, that first A.M., after this litany of scares, after Glenda retreated into her chronically underheated lair, there was a swell of sympathetic mumbles from my coworkers, who numbered, in the front office, about a dozen. They were offering condolences. They had seen the likes of me come and go. Glenda, however, who keenly appreciated the element of surprise as a way of insuring discipline, was not quite done. She reappeared suddenly by my desk—as if by secret entrance—with a half-dozen additional commands. I was to find a new sign for her private parking space. I was to find a new floral wholesale: for the next fiscal quarter, I was to *refill her prescription for birth-control pills.* This last request was spooky enough, but it wasn't the end of the discussion. From there Glenda starting getting personal:

—Oh, by the way, Andy? (she liked diminutives) What's all the family trouble, anyway? The stuff Alex was talking about when she called?

She picked up the photo of you, Sis, the one I had brought with me. The bass at the end of your fishing rod was so outsized that it seemed impossible that you could hold it up. You looked really happy. Glenda picked up the photo as though she hadn't already done her research, as if she had left something to chance. Which just didn't happen during her regime at the Mansion on the Hill.

—Dead sister, said I. And then, completing my betrayal of you, I filled out the narrative, so that anyone who wished could hear about it, and then we could move onto other subjects, like Worcester's really great semipro hockey team.

—Crashed her car. Actually, it was my car. Mercury Sable. Don't know why I said it was her car. It was mine. She was on her way to her rehearsal dinner. She had an accident.

Sis, have I mentioned that I have a lot of questions I've been meaning to ask? Have I asked, for example, why you were taking the windy country road along our side of the great river, when the four-lanes along the west side were faster, more direct and, in heavy rain, less dangerous? Have I asked why you were driving at all? Why I was not driving you to the rehearsal dinner instead? Have I asked why your car was in the shop for muffler repair on such an important day? Have I

31

asked why you were late? Have I asked why you were lubricating your nerves *before* the dinner? Have I asked if four G&Ts, as you called them, before your own rehearsal dinner, were not maybe in excess of what was needed? Have I asked if there was a reason for you to be so tense on the eve of your wedding? Did you feel you had to go through with it? That there was no alternative? If so, why? If he was the wrong guy, why were you marrying him? Were there planning issues that were not properly addressed? Were there things between you two, as between all the betrothed, that we didn't know? Were there specific questions you wanted to ask, of which you were afraid? Have I given the text of my toast, Sis, as I had imagined it, beginning with a plangent evocation of the years before your birth, when I ruled our house like a tyrant, and how with earsplitting cries I resisted your infancy, until I learned to love the way your baby hair, your flaxen mop, fell into curls? Have I mentioned that it was especially satisfying to wind your hair around my stubby fingers as you lay sleeping? Have I made clear that I wrote out this toast and that it took me several weeks to get it how I wanted it and that I was in fact going over these words again when the call from Dad came announcing your death? Have I mentioned—and I'm sorry to be hurtful on this point—that Dad's drinking has gotten worse since you left this world? Have I mentioned that his allusions to the costly unfinished business of his life have become more frequent? Have I mentioned that Mom, already overtaxed with her own body count, with her dead parents and dead siblings, has gotten more and more frail? Have I mentioned that I have some news about Brice, your intended? That his tune has changed slightly since your memorial service? Have I mentioned that I was out at the crime scene the next day? The day after you died? Have I mentioned that in my dreams I am often at the crime scene now? Have I wondered aloud to you about that swerve of blacktop right there, knowing that others may lose their lives as you did? Can't we straighten out that road somehow? Isn't there one road crew that the governor, in his quest for jobs, jobs, jobs, can send down there to make this sort of thing unlikely? Have I perhaps clued you in about how I go there often now, to look for signs of further tragedy? Have I mentioned to you that in some countries DWI is punishable by death, and that when Antonio at Hot Bird first explained this dark irony to me, I imagined taking his throat in my hands and squeezing the air out of him once and for all? Sis, have I told you of driving aimlessly in the mountains, listening to talk radio, searching for the one bit of cheap, commercially interrupted persuasion that will let me put these memories of you back in the canister where you now at least partially reside so that I can live out my dim, narrow life? Have I mentioned that I expect death around every turn, that every blue sky has a safe sailing out of it, that every bus runs me over, that every low, mean syllable uttered in my direction seems to intimate the violence of murder, that every family seems like an opportunity for ruin and every marriage a ceremony into which calamity will fall and hearts will be broken and lives destroyed and people branded by the mortifications of love? Is it all right if I ask you all of this?

Still, in spite of these personal issues, I was probably a model employee for Glenda Manzini. For example, I managed to sort out the politics concerning the Jewish wedding and the Islamic wedding (both slated for the first weekend of April), and I did so by appealing to certain aspects of light in our valley at the base of the Adirondacks. Certain kinds of light make for very appealing weddings here in our valley, I told one of these families. In late winter, in the early morning, you begin to feel an excitement at the appearance of the sun. Yes, I managed to solve that problem, and the next (the prayer mats)—because K-Mart, *where America shops,* had a special on bathmats that week, and I sent Dorcas Gilbey over to buy six dozen to use for the Muslim families. I solved these problems and then I solved others just as vexing. I had a special interest in the snags that arose on Fridays after 5 P.M.—the groom who on the day of the ceremony was trapped in a cabin east of Lake George and who had to snowshoe three miles out to the nearest telephone, or the father of the bride (it was the Lapsley wedding) who wanted to arrive at the ceremony by hydrofoil. Brinkmanship, in the world of nuptial planning, gave me a sense of well-being, and I tried to bury you in the rear of my life, in the back of that closet where I'd hidden my secondhand golf clubs and my ski boots and my Chicken Mask—never again to be seen by mortal man.

One of my front-office associates was a fine young woman by the name of Linda Pietrzsyk, who tried to comfort me during the early weeks of my job, after Glenda's periodic assaults. Don't ask how to pronounce Linda's surname. In order to pronounce it properly, you have to clear your throat aggressively. Linda Pietrzsyk didn't like her surname anymore than you or I, and she was apparently looking for a groom from whom she could borrow a better last name. That's what I found out after awhile. Many of the employees at the Mansion on the Hill had ulterior motives. This marital ferment, this loamy soil of

33

romance, called to them somehow. When I'd been there a few months, I started to see other applicants go through the masticating action of an interview with Glenda Manzini. Glenda would be sure to ask, *Why do you want to work here?* and many of these qualified applicants had the same reply, *Because I think marriage is the most beautiful thing and I want to help make it possible for others.* Most of these applicants, if they were attractive and single and younger than Glenda, aggravated her thoroughly. They were shown the door. But occasionally a marital aspirant like Linda Pietrzsyk snuck through, in this case because Linda managed to conceal her throbbing, sentimental heart beneath a veneer of contemporary discontent.

We had Mondays and Tuesdays off, and one weekend a month. Most of our problem-solving fell on Saturdays, of course, but on that one Saturday off, Linda Pietrzsyk liked to bring friends to the Mansion on the Hill, to various celebrations. She liked to attend the weddings of strangers. This kind of entertainment wasn't discouraged by Glenda or by the owners of the Mansion, because everybody likes a party to be crowded. Any wedding that was too sparsely attended at the Mansion had a fine complement of *warm bodies,* as Glenda liked to call them, provided gratis. Sometimes we had to go to libraries or retirement centers to fill a quota, but we managed. These gate crashers were welcome to eat finger food at the reception and to drink champagne and other intoxicants (food and drink were billed to the client), but they had to make themselves scarce once the dining began in earnest. There was a window of opportunity here that was large enough for Linda and her friends.

She was tight with a spirited bunch of younger people. She was friends with kids who had outlandish wardrobes and styles of grooming, kids with pants that fit like bedsheets, kids with haircuts that were, at best, accidental. But Linda would dress them all up and make them presentable, and they would arrive in an ancient station wagon in order to crowd in at the back of a wedding. Where they stifled gasps of hilarity.

I don't know what Linda saw in me. I can't really imagine. I wore the same sweaters and flannel slacks week in and week out. I liked classical music, Sis. I liked historical simulation festivals. And as you probably haven't forgotten (having tried a couple of times to fix me up—with Jess Carney and Sally Moffitt), the more tense I am, the worse is the impression I make on the fairer sex. Nevertheless, Linda Pietrzsyk decided that I had to be a part of her elite crew of wedding crashers, and so for a while I learned by immersion of the great rainbow of expressions of fealty.

Remember that footage, so often shown on contemporary reality-based programming during the dead first half-hour of prime time, of the guy who vomited at his own wedding? I was at that wedding. You know when he says, *Aw, Honey, I'm really sorry,* and leans over and flash floods this amber stuff on her train? You know, the shock of disgust as it crosses her face? The look of horror in the eyes of the minister? I saw it all. No one who was there thought it was funny, though, except Linda's friends. That's the truth. I thought it was really sad. But I was sitting next to a fellow *actually named Cheese* (when I asked which kind of cheese, he seemed perplexed), and Cheese looked as though he had a hernia or something, he thought this was so funny. Elsewhere in the Chestnut Suite there was a grievous silence.

Linda Pietrzsyk also liked to catalogue moments of spontaneous erotic delight on the premises, and these were legendary at the Mansion on the Hill. Even Glenda, who took a dim view of gossiping about business most of the time, liked to hear who was doing it with whom where. There was an implicit hierarchy in such stories. *Tales of the couple to be married caught in the act on Mansion premises were considered obvious and therefore uninspiring.* Tales of the best man and matron of honor going at it (as in the Clarke, Rosenberg, Irving, Ng, Fujitsu, Walters, Shapiro or Spangler ceremonies) were better, but not great. Stories in which parents of the couple to be married were caught—in, say, the laundry room, with the dad still wearing his dress shoes—were good (Smith, Elsworth, Waskiewicz), but not as good as tales of the parents of the couple to be married trading spouses, of which we had one unconfirmed report (Hinkley) and of which no one could stop talking for a week. Likewise, any story in which the bride or the groom were caught *in flagrante* with someone other than the person they were marrying was considered astounding (if unfortunate). But we were after some even more unlikely tall tales: any threesome or larger grouping involving the couple to be married and someone from one of the other weddings scheduled that day, in which the third party was unknown until arriving at the Mansion on the Hill, and at which *a house pet was present.* Glenda said that if you spotted one of these tableaux you could have a month's worth of free groceries from the catering department. Linda Pietrzsyk also spoke longingly of the day when someone would arrive breathlessly in the office with a narrative of a full-fledged orgiastic reception in the Mansion on the

Hill, the spontaneous, overwhelming erotic celebration of love and marriage by an entire suite full of Americans, tall and short, fat and thin, young and old.

In pursuit of these tales, with her friends Cheese, Chip, Mick, Stig, Mark and Blair, Linda Pietrzsyk would quietly appear at my side at a reception and give me the news—*Behind the bandstand, behind that scrim, groom reaching under his cousin's skirts.* We would sneak in for a look. But we never interrupted anyone. And we never made them feel ashamed.

You know how when you're getting to know a fellow employee, a fellow team member, you go through phases, through cycles of intimacy and insight and respect and doubt and disillusionment, where one impression gives way to another? (Do you know about this, Sis, and is this what happened between you and Brice, so that you felt like you personally had to have the four G&Ts on the way to the rehearsal dinner? Am I right in thinking you couldn't go on with the wedding and that this caused you to get all sloppy and to believe erroneously that you could operate heavy machinery?) Linda Pietrzsyk was a stylish, Skidmore-educated girl with ivory skin and an adorable bump in her nose; she was from an upper-middleclass family out on Long Island somewhere; her father's periodic drunkenness had not affected his ability to work; her mother stayed married to him according to some mesmerism of devotion; her brothers had good posture and excelled in contact sports; in short, there were no big problems in Linda's case. Still, she pretended to be a desperate, marriage-obsessed kid, without a clear idea about what she wanted to do with her life or what the hell was going to happen next week. She was smarter than me—she could do the crossword puzzle in three minutes flat and she knew all about current events—but she was always talking about *catching a rich financier with a wild streak and extorting a retainer from him,* until I wanted to shake her. There's usually another layer underneath these things. In Linda's case it started to become clear at Patti Wackerman's wedding.

The reception area in the Ticonderoga Room—where walls slid back from the altar to reveal the tables and the dance floor—was decorated in branches of forsythia and wisteria and other flowering vines and shrubs. It was spring. Linda was standing against a piece of white wicker latticework that I had borrowed from the florist in town (in return for promotional considerations), and sprigs of flowering trees garlanded it, garlanded the spot where Linda was standing. Pale colors haloed her.

—Right behind this screen, she said, when I swept up beside her and tapped her playfully on the shoulder, —check it out. There's a couple falling in love once and for all. You can see it in their eyes.

I was sipping a Canadian spring water in a piece of company stemware. I reacted to Linda's news nonchalantly. I didn't think much of it. Yet I happened to notice that Linda's expression was conspiratorial, impish, as well as a little beatific. Linda often covered her mouth with her hand when she'd said something riotous, as if to conceal unsightly dental work (on the contrary, her teeth were perfect), as if she'd been treated badly one too many times, as if the immensity of joy were embarrassing to her somehow. As she spoke of the couple in question her hand fluttered up to her mouth. Her slender fingertips probed delicately at her upper lip. My thoughts came in torrents: *Where are Stig and Cheese and Blair? Why am I suddenly alone with this fellow employee? Is the couple Linda is speaking about part of the wedding party today? How many points will she get for the first sighting of their extra-marital grappling?*

Since it was my policy to investigate any and all such phenomena, I glanced desultorily around the screen and, seeing nothing out of the ordinary, slipped further into the shadows where the margins of Ticonderoga led toward the central catering staging area. There was, of course, no such couple behind the screen, or rather Linda (who was soon beside me) and myself *were the couple* and we were mottled by insufficient light, dappled by it, by lavender-tinted spots hung that morning by the lighting designers, and by reflections of a mirrored *disco ball* that speckled the dance floor.

—I don't see anything, I said.

—Kiss me, Linda Pietrzsyk said. Her fingers closed lightly around the bulky part of my arm. There was an unfamiliar warmth in me. The band struck up some fast number. I think it was "It's Raining Men" or maybe it was that song entitled "We Are Family," which played so often at the Mansion on the Hill in the course of a weekend. Whichever, it was really loud. The horn players were getting into it. A trombonist yanked his slide back and forth.

—Excuse me? I said.

—Kiss me, Andrew, she said.—I want to kiss you.

Locating in myself a long-dormant impulsiveness, I reached down for Linda's bangs, and with my clumsy hands I tried to push back her

37

blond and strawberry-blond curlicues, and then, with a hitch in my motion, in a stop-time sequence of jerks, I embraced her. Her eyes, like neon, were illumined.

—Why don't you tell me how you feel about me? Linda Pietrzsyk said. I was speechless, Sis. I didn't know what to say. And she went on. There was something about me, something warm and friendly about me, I wasn't fortified, she said; I wasn't cold, I was just a good guy who actually cared about other people *and you know how few of those there are.* (I think these were her words.) She wanted to spend more time with me, she wanted to get to know me better, she wanted to give the roulette wheel a decisive spin: she repeated all this twice in slightly different ways with different modifiers. It made me sweat. The only way I could think to get her to quit talking was to kiss her in earnest, my lips brushing by hers the way the sun passes around and through the interstices of falling leaves on an October afternoon. I hadn't kissed anyone in a long time. Her mouth tasted like cherry soda, like barbecue, like fresh hay, and because of these startling tastes, I retreated. To arm's length.

Sis, was I scared. What was this rank taste of wet campfire and bone fragments that I'd had in my mouth since we scattered you over the Hudson? Did I come through this set of coincidences, these quotidian interventions by God, to work in a place where everything seemed to be about *love,* only to find that I couldn't ever be a part of that grand word? How could I kiss anyone when I felt so awkward? What happened to me, what happened to all of us, to the texture of our lives, when you left us here?

I tried to ask Linda why she was doing what she was doing—behind the screen of wisteria and forsythia. I fumbled badly for these words. I believed she was trying to have a laugh on me. So she could go back and tell Cheese and Mick about it. So she could go gossip about me in the office, about what a jerk that Wakefield was. *Man, Andrew Wakefield thinks there's something worth hoping for in this world.* I thought she was joking, and I was through being the joke, being the Chicken Mask, being the harlequin.

—I'm not doing anything to you, Andrew, Linda said.—I'm expressing myself. It's supposed to be a good thing. Reaching, she laid a palm flush against my face.

—I know you aren't . . .

—So what's the problem?

I was ambitious to reassure. If I could have stayed the hand that fluttered up to cover her mouth, so that she could laugh unreservedly, so that her laughter peeled out in the Ticonderoga Room . . . But I just wasn't up to it yet. I got out of there. I danced across the floor at the Wackerman wedding—I was a party of one—and the Wackermans and the Delgados and their kin probably thought I was singing along with "Desperado" by the Eagles (it was the anthem of the new Mr. and Mrs. Fritz Wackerman), but really I was talking to myself, *about work,* about how Mike Tombello's best man wanted to give his toast while doing flips on a trampoline, about how Jenny Parmenter wanted live goats bleating in the Mansion parking lot, as a fertility symbol, as she sped away, in her Rolls Cornische, to the Thousand Islands. Boy, I always hated the Eagles.

Okay, to get back to Glenda Manzini. Linda Pietrzsyk didn't write me off after our failed embraces, but she sure gave me more room. She was out the door at 5:01 for several weeks, without asking after me, without a kind word for anyone, and I didn't blame her. But in the end who else was there to talk to? To Marie O'Neill, the accountant? To Paul Avakian, the human resources and insurance guy and petty-cash manager? To Rachel Levy, the head chef? Maybe it was more than this. Maybe the bond that forms between people doesn't get unmade so easily. Maybe it leaves its mark for a long time. Soon Linda and I ate our bagged lunches together again, trading varieties of puddings, often in total silence; at least this was the habit until we found a new area of common interest in our reservations about Glenda Manzini's management techniques. This happened to be when Glenda took a week off. What a miracle. I'd been employed at the Mansion six months. The staff was in a fine mood about Glenda's hiatus. There was a carnival atmosphere. Dorcas Gilbey had been stockpiling leftover ales for an office shindig featuring dancing and the recitation of really bad marital vows we'd heard. Linda and I went along with the festivities, but we were also formulating a strategy.

What we wanted to know was how Glenda became so unreservedly cruel. We wanted the inside story on her personal life. We wanted the skinny. How do you produce an individual like Glenda? What is the mass-production technique? We waited until Tuesday, after the afternoon beer-tasting party. We were staying late, we claimed, in order to separate out the green M&Ms for the marriage of U.V.M. tight end

Brad Doelp who had requested bowls of M&Ms at his reception, *excluding any and all green candies.* When our fellow employees were gone, right at five, we broke into Glenda's office.

Sis, we really broke in. Glenda kept her office locked when she wasn't in it. It was a matter of principle. I had to use my Discover card on the lock. I punished that credit card. But we got the tumblers to tumble, and once we were inside, we started poking around. First of all, Glenda Manzini was a tidy person, which I can admire from an organizational point of view, but it was almost like her office was empty. The pens and pencils were lined up. The in and out boxes were swept clean of any stray dust particle, any scrap of trash. There wasn't a rogue paper clip behind the desk or in the bottom of her spotless waste basket. She kept her rubber bands banded together with rubber bands. The files in her filing cabinets were orderly, subdivided to avoid bowing, the old faxes were photocopied so that they wouldn't disintegrate. The photos on the walls (Mansion weddings past), were nondescript and pedestrian. There was nothing intimate about the decoration at all. I knew about most of this stuff from the moments when she ordered me into that cubicle to shout me down, but this was different. Now we were getting a sustained look at Glenda's personal effects.

Linda took particular delight in Glenda's cassette player (it was atop one of the black filing cabinets)—a cassette player that none of us had ever heard play, not even once. Linda admired the selection of recordings there. A complete set of cut-out budget series: *Greatest Hits of Baroque, Greatest Hits of Swing, Greatest Hits of Broadway, Greatest Hits of Disco* and so forth. Just as she was about to pronounce Glenda a rank philistine where music was concerned, Linda located there, in a shattered case, a copy of *Greatest Hits of the Blues.*

We devoured the green M&Ms while we were busy with our reconnaissance. And I kept reminding Linda not to get any of the green dye on anything. I repeatedly checked surfaces for fingerprints. I even overturned Linda's hands (it made me happy while doing it), to make sure they were free of emerald smudges. Because if Glenda found out we were in her office, we'd both be submitting applications at the Hot Bird of Troy. Nonetheless, Linda carelessly put down her handful of M&Ms, on top of a filing cabinet, to look over the track listings for *Greatest Hits of the Blues.* This budget anthology was released the year Linda was born, in 1974. Coincidentally, the year you too were born, Sis. I remember driving with you to the tunes of Lightnin' Hopkins or Howlin' Wolf. I remember your preference for the most bereaved of acoustic blues, the most ramshackle of musics. What better soundtrack for the Adirondacks? For our meandering drives in the mountains, into Corinth or around Lake Luzerne? What more lonesome sound for a state park the size of Rhode Island where wolves and bears still come to hunt? Linda cranked the greatest hits of heartbreak and we sat down on the carpeted floor to listen. I missed you.

I pulled open that bottom file drawer by chance. I wanted to rest my arm on something. There was a powerful allure in the moment. I wasn't going to kiss Linda, and probably her desperate effort to find somebody to liberate her from her foreshortened economic prospects and her unpronounceable surname wouldn't come to much, but she was a good friend. Maybe a better friend than I was admitting to myself. It was in this expansive mood that I opened the file drawer at the bottom of one stack (the *J* through *P* stack), otherwise empty, to find that it was full of a half-dozen, maybe even more, of those circular packages of *birth-control pills,* the color-coated pills, you know, those multihued pills and placebos that are a journey through the amorous calendars of women. All unused. Not a one of them even opened. Not a one of the white, yellow, brown or green pills liberated from its package.

—Must be chilly in Schenectady, Linda mumbled.

Was there another way to read the strange bottom drawer? Was there a way to look at it beyond or outside of my exhausting tendency to discover only facts that would prop up darker prognostications? The file drawer contained the pills, it contained a bottle of vodka, it contained a cache of family pictures and missives the likes of which were never displayed or mentioned or even alluded to by Glenda. Even I, for all my resentments, wasn't up to reading the letters. But what of these carefully arranged packages of photo snapshots of the Manzini family? (Glenda's son from her first marriage, in his early teens, in a torn and grass-stained football uniform, and mother and second husband and son in front of some bleachers, et cetera.) Was the drawer really what it seemed to be, a repository for mementos of love that Glenda had now hidden away, secreted, shunted off into mini-storage? What was the lesson of those secrets? Merely that concealed behind rage (and behind grief) is *the ambition to love?*

—Somebody's having an affair, Linda said.—The hubby is coming home late. He's fabricating late evenings at the office. He's taking some desktop meetings with his secretary. He's leaving Glenda alone with the kids. Why else be so cold?

41

—Or Glenda's carrying on, said I.

—Or she's polygamous, Linda said,—and this is a completely separate family she's keeping across town somewhere without telling anyone.

—Or this is the boy she gave up for adoption and this is the record of her meeting with his folks. And she never told Dave about it.

—Whichever it is, Linda said,—it's *bad*.

We turned our attention to the vodka. Sis, I know I've said that I don't touch the stuff anymore—because of your example—but Linda egged me on. We were listening to music of the delta, to its simple unadorned grief, and I felt that Muddy Waters's loss was my kind of loss, the kind you don't shake easily, the kind that comes back like a seasonal flu, and soon we were passing the bottle of vodka back and forth. Beautiful, sad Glenda Manzini understood the blues and I understood the blues and you understood them and Linda understood them and maybe everybody understood them—in spite of what ethno-musicologists sometimes tell us about the cultural singularity of that music. Linda started to dance a little, there in Glenda Manzini's office, swiveling absently, her arms like asps, snaking to and fro, her wrists adorned in black bangles. Linda had a spell on her, in Glenda's anaerobic and cryogenically frigid office. Linda plucked off her beige pumps and circled around Glenda's desk, as if casting out its manifold demons. I couldn't take my eyes off of her. She forgot who I was and drifted with the lamentations of Robert Johnson (hellhound on his trail), and I could have followed her there, where she cast off Long Island and Skidmore and became a naiad, a true resident of the Mansion on the Hill, that paradise, but when the song was over the eeriness of our communion was suddenly alarming. I was sneaking around my boss's office. I was drinking her vodka. All at once it was time to go home.

We began straightening everything we had moved—we were really responsible about it—and Linda gathered up the dozen or so green M&Ms she'd left on the filing cabinet—excepting the one she inadvertently fired out the back end of her fist, which skittered from a three-drawer file down a whole step to the surface of a two-drawer stack, before hopping and skipping over a cassette box, before freefalling behind the cabinets, where it came to rest, at last, six inches from the northeast corner of the office, beside a small coffee-stained patch of wall-to-wall. I returned the vodka to its drawer of shame, I tidied up the stacks of *Brides* magazines, I locked Glenda's office door and I went back to being the employee of the month. (My framed picture hung over the water fountain between the rest rooms. I wore a bow tie. I smiled broadly and my teeth looked straight and my hair was combed. I couldn't be stopped.)

My ambition has always been to own my own small business. I like the flexibility of small-capitalization companies; I like small businesses at the moment at which they prepare to franchise. That's why I took the job at Hot Bird—I saw Hot Birds in every town in America, I saw Hot Birds as numerous as post offices or ATMs. I like small businesses at the moment at which they really define a market with respect to a certain need, when they begin to sell their products to the world. And my success as a team player at the Mansion on the Hill was the result of these ambitions. This is why I came to feel, after a time, that I could do Glenda Manzini's job myself. Since I'm a little young, it's obvious that I couldn't *replace* Glenda—I think her instincts were really great with respect to the service we were providing to the Capital Region— but I saw the Mansion on the Hill stretching its influence into population centers throughout the northeast. I mean, why wasn't there a Mansion on the Hill in Westchester? Down in Mamaroneck? Why wasn't there a Mansion on the Hill in the golden corridor of Boston suburbs? Why no mainline Philly Mansion? Suffice to say, I saw myself, at some point in the future, having the same opportunity Glenda had. I saw myself cutting deals and whittling out discounts at other fine Mansion locations. I imagined making myself indispensable to a coalition of Mansion venture-capitalists and then I imagined using these associations to make a move into, say, the high-tech or bio-tech sectors of American industry.

The way I pursued this particular goal was that I started looking ahead at things like upcoming volume. I started using the graph features on my office software to make pie charts of ceremony densities, cost ratios and so forth, and I started wondering how we could pitch our service better, whether on the radio or in the press or through alternative marketing strategies (I came up with the strategy, for example, of getting various non-affiliated religions—small emergent spiritual movements—to consider us as a site for all their group wedding ceremonies). And as I started looking ahead, I started noticing who was coming through the doors in the next months. I became well versed in the social forces of our valley. I watched for when certain affluent families of the region might be needing our product. I would, if required, attempt cold-calling the attorney general of our state to persuade him of the splendor of the Niagara Hall when Diana, his daughter, finally gave the okey-dokey to her suitor, Ben.

I may well have succeeded in my plan for domination of the Mansion on the Hill brand, if it were not for the fact that as I was examining the volume projections for November (one Monday night), the ceremonies taking place in a mere three months, I noticed that Sarah Wilton of Corinth was marrying one Brice McCann in the Rip Van Winkle Room. Just before Thanksgiving. There were no particular notes or annotations to the name on the calendar, and thus Glenda wasn't focusing much on the ceremony. But something bothered me. That name.

Your Brice McCann, Sis. Your intended. Getting married almost a year to the day after your rehearsal-dinner-that-never-was. Getting married before even having completed his requisite year of grief, before we'd even made it through the anniversary with its floodwaters. Who knew how long he'd waited before beginning his seduction of Sarah Wilton? Was it even certain that he had waited until you were gone? Maybe he was faithless; maybe he was a two-timer. I had started reading Glenda's calendar to get ahead in business, Sis, but as soon as I learned of Brice, I became cavalier about work. My work suffered. My relations with other members of the staff suffered. I kept to myself. I went back to riding the bus to work instead of accepting rides. I stopped visiting fellow workers. I found myself whispering of plots and machinations; I found myself making connections between things that probably weren't connected and planning involved scenarios of revenge. I knew the day would come when he would be on the premises, when Brice would be settling various accounts, going over various numbers, signing off on the pâté selection and the set list of the R&B band, and I waited for him—to be certain of the truth.

Sis, you became engaged too quickly. There had been that other guy, Mark, and you had been engaged to him, too, and that arrangement fell apart kind of fast—I think you were engaged at Labor Day and broken up by M.L.K.'s birthday—and then, within weeks, there was this Brice. There's a point I want to make here. I'm trying to be gentle, but I have to get this across. Brice wore a beret. *The guy wore a beret.* He was supposedly a great cook, he would bandy about names of exotic mushrooms, but I never saw him boil an egg when I was visiting you. It was always you who did the cooking. It's true that certain males of the species, the kind who linger at the table after dinner wait-

44

ing for their helpmeet to do the washing up, the kind who preside over carving of viands and otherwise disdain food-related chores, the kind who claim to be effective only at the preparation of breakfast, these guys are Pleistocene brutes who don't belong in the Information Age with its emerging markets and global economies. But, Sis, I think the other extreme is just as bad. The sensitive, New Age, beret-wearing guys who buy premium mustards and free-range chickens and grow their own basil and then let you cook while they're in the other room perusing magazines devoted to the artistic posings of Asian teenagers. Our family comes from upstate New York and we don't eat enough vegetables and our marriages are full of hardships and sorrows, Sis, and when I saw Brice coming down the corridor of the Mansion on the Hill, with his prematurely gray hair slicked back with the aid of some all-natural mousse, wearing a gray, suede bomber jacket and cowboy boots into which were tucked the cuffs of his black designer jeans, carrying his personal digital assistant and his cell phone and the other accoutrements of his dwindling massage-therapy business, he was the enemy of my state. In his wake, I was happy to note, there was a sort of honeyed cologne. Patchouli, I'm guessing. It would definitely drive Glenda Manzini nuts.

We had a small conference room at the Mansion, just around the corner from Glenda's office. I had selected some of the furnishings there myself, from a discount furniture outlet at the mall. Brice and his fiancée, Sarah Wilton, would of course be repairing to this conference room with Glenda to do some pricing. I had the foresight, therefore, to jog into that space and turn on the speaker phone over the coffee machine, and to place a planter of silk flowers in front of it and dial my own extension so that I could teleconference this conversation. I had a remote headset I liked to wear around, Sis, during inventorying and bill tabulation—it helped with the neck strain and tension headaches that I'm always suffering with—so I affixed this headset and went back to filing, down the hall, while the remote edition of Brice and Sarah's conference with Glenda was broadcast into my skull.

I figure my expression was ashen. I suppose that Dorcas Gilbey, when she flagged me down with some receipts that she had forgotten to file, was unused to my mechanistic expression and to my curt, unfriendly replies to her questions. I waved her off, clamping the headset tighter against my ear. Unfortunately, the signal broke up. It was muffled. I hurriedly returned to my desk and tried to get the forwarded call to transmit properly to my handset. I even tried to amplify it through the speaker-phone feature, to no avail. Brice had always affected a soft-spoken demeanor while he was busy extorting things from people like you, Sis. He was too quiet—the better to conceal his tactics. And thus, in order to hear him, I had to sneak around the corner from the conference room and eavesdrop in the old-fashioned way.

—We wanted to dialogue with you (Brice was explaining to Glenda), because we wanted to make sure that you were thinking creatively along the same lines we are. We want to make sure you're comfortable with our plans. As married people, as committed people, we want this ceremony to make others feel good about themselves, as we're feeling good about ourselves. We want to have an ecstatic celebration here, a healing celebration that will bind up the hurt any marriages in the room might be suffering. I know you know how the ecstasy of marriage occasions a grieving process for many persons, Mrs. Manzini. Sarah and I both feel this in our hearts, that celebrations often have grief as a part of their wonder, and we want to enact all these things, all these feelings, to bring them out where we can look at them, and then we want to purge them triumphantly. We want people to come out of this wedding feeling good about themselves, as we'll be feeling good about ourselves. We want to give our families a big collective hug, because we're all human and we all have feelings and we all have to grieve and yearn and we need rituals for this.

There was a long silence from Glenda Manzini.

Then she said:

—Can we cut to the chase?

One thing I always loved about the Mansion on the Hill was its emptiness, its vacancy. Sure, the Niagara Room, when filled with five-thousand-dollar gowns and heirloom tuxedos, when serenaded by Toots Wilcox's big band, was a great place, a sort of gold standard of reception halls, but as much as I always loved both the celebrations and the network of relationships and associations that went with our business at the Mansion, I always felt best in the *empty* halls of the Mansion on the Hill, cleansed of their accumulation of sentiment, utterly silent, patiently awaiting the possibility of matrimony. It was onto this clean slate that I had routinely projected my foolish hopes. But after Brice strutted through my place of employment, after his marriage began to overshadow every other, I found instead a different message inscribed on these walls: *Every death implies a guilty party.*

Or to put it another way, there was a network of sub-basements in the Mansion on the Hill through which each suite was connected to

46

another. These tunnels were well-traveled by certain alcoholic janitorial guys whom I knew well enough. I'd had my reasons to adventure there before, but now I used every opportunity to pace these corridors. I still performed the parts of my job that would assure that I got paid and that I invested regularly in my 401K plan, but I felt more comfortable in the emptiness of the Mansion's suites and basements, thinking about how I was going to extract my recompense, while Brice and Sarah dithered over the cost of their justice of the peace and their photographer and their *Champlain Pentecostal Singers.*

I had told Linda Pietrzsyk about Brice's reappearance. I had told her about you, Sis. I had remarked about your fractures and your loss of blood and your hypothermia and the results of your post-mortem blood-alcohol test; I suppose that I'd begun to tell her all kinds of things, in outbursts of candor that were followed by equal and opposite remoteness. Linda saw me, over the course of those weeks, lurking, going from Ticonderoga to Rip Van Winkle to Chestnut, slipping in and out of infernal sub-basements of conjecture that other people find grimy and uncomfortable, when I should have been overseeing the unloading of floral arrangements at the loading dock or arranging for Glenda's chiropractic appointments. Linda saw me lurking around, *asked what was wrong and told me that it would be better after the anniversary, after that day had come and gone,* and I felt the discourses of apology and subsequent gratitude forming epiglottally in me, but instead I told her to get lost, to leave the dead to bury the dead.

After a long excruciating interval, the day of Sarah Danforth Wilton's marriage to Brice Paul McCann arrived. It was a day of chill mists, Sis, and you had now been gone just over one year. I had passed through the anniversary trembling, in front of the television, watching the Home Shopping Network, impulsively pricing cubic zirconium rings, as though one of these would have been the ring you might have worn at your ceremony. You were a fine sister, but you changed your mind all the time, and I had no idea if these things I'd attributed to you in the last year were features of the *you* I once knew, or whether, in death, you had become the property of your mourners, so that we made of you a puppet.

On the anniversary, I watched a videotape of your bridal shower, and Mom was there, and she looked really proud, and Dad drifted into the center of the frame at one point, and mumbled a strange *harrumph* that had to do with interloping at an assembly of such beautiful women (I was allowed on the scene only to do the videotaping), and

47

you were very pleased as you opened your gifts. At one point you leaned over to Mom, and stage-whispered—so that even I could hear—*that your car was a real lemon and that you had to take it to the shop and you didn't have time and it was a total hassle and did she think that I would lend you the Sable without giving you a hard time?* My Sable, my car. Sure. If I had it to do again, I would never have given you a hard time even once.

The vows at the Mansion on the Hill seemed to be the part of the ceremony where most of the tinkering took place. I think if Glenda had been able to find a way to charge a premium on vow alteration, we could have found a really excellent revenue stream at the Mansion on the Hill. If the sweet instant of commitment is so singular, why does it seem to have so many different articulations? People used all sorts of things in their vows. Conchita Bosworth used the songs of Dan Fogelberg when it came to the exchange of rings; a futon-store owner from Queensbury, Reggie West, managed to work in material from a number of sitcoms. After a while, you'd heard it all, the rhetoric of desire, the incantation of commitment rendered as awkwardly as possible; you heard the purple metaphors, the hackneyed lines, until it was all like legal language, as in any business transaction.

It was the language of Brice McCann's vows that brought this story to its conclusion. I arrived at the wedding late. I took a cab across the Hudson, from the hill in Troy where I lived in my convenience apartment. What trees there were in the system of pavement cloverleafs where Route Seven met the interstate were bare, disconsolate. The road was full of potholes. The lanes choked with old, shuddering sedans. The parking valets at the Mansion, a group of pot-smoking teens who seemed to enjoy creating a facsimile of politeness that involved both effrontery and subservience, opened the door of the cab for me and greeted me according to their standard line, *Where's the party?* The parking lot was full. We had seven weddings going on at once. Everyone was working. Glenda was working, Linda was working, Dorcas was working. All my teammates were working, sprinting from suite to suite, micromanaging. The whole of the Capital Region must have been at the Mansion that Saturday to witness the blossoming of families, Sis, or, in the case of Brice's wedding, to witness the way in which a vow of faithfulness less than a year old, a promise of the future, can be traded in so quickly; how marriage is just a shrink-wrapped sale item, mass-produced in bulk. You can pick one up anywhere these days, at a mall, on layaway. If it doesn't fit, exchange it.

I walked the main hallway slowly, peeking in and out of the various suites. In the *Chestnut Suite* it was the Polanskis, poor but generous— their daughter Denise intended to have and to hold an Italian fellow, A. L. DiPietro, also completely penniless, and the Polanskis were paying for the entire ceremony and rehearsal dinner and inviting the DiPietros to stay with them for the week. They had brought their own floral displays, personally assembled by the arthritic Mrs. Polanski. The room had a dignified simplicity. Next, in the *Hudson Suite,* in keeping with its naval flavor, cadet Bobby Moore and his high-school sweetheart Mandy Sutherland were tying the knot, at the pleasure of Bobby's dad, who had been a tugboat captain in New York Harbor; in the *Adirondack Suite,* two of the venerable old families of the Lake George region—the Millers (owners of the Lake George Cabins) and the Wentworths (they had the Quality Inn franchise) commingled their resort-dependent fates; in the *Valentine Room,* Sis, two women (named Sal and Martine, but that's all I should say about them, for rea- sons of privacy) were to be married by a renegade Episcopal minister called Jack Valance—they had sewn their own gowns to match the cad- mium red decor of that interior; *Ticonderoga* had the wedding of Glen Dunbar and Louise Glazer, a marriage not memorable in any way at all, and in the *Niagara Hall* two of Saratoga's great eighteenth-century racing dynasties, the Vanderbilt and Pierrepont families, were about to settle long-standing differences. Love was everywhere in the air.

I walked through all these ceremonies, sis, before I could bring my- self to go over to the *Rip Van Winkle Room.* My steps were reluctant. My observations: the proportions of sniffling at each ceremony were about equal and the audiences were about equal and levels of whimsy and seriousness were about the same wherever you went. The emo- tions careened, high and low, across the whole spectrum of possible feelings. The music might be different from case to case—stately baroque anthems of klezmer rave-ups—but the intent was the same. By 3:00 P.M., I no longer knew what marriage meant, really, except that the celebration of it seemed built into every life I knew but my own.

The doors of the Rip Van Winkle Room were open, as distinct from the other suites, and I tiptoed through them and closed these great carved doors behind myself. I slipped into the bride's side. The light was dim, Sis. The light was deep in the ultraviolet spectrum, as when we used to go, as kids, to the exhibitions at the Hall of Science and In- dustry. There seemed to be some kind of mummery, some kind of expressive dance, taking place at the altar. The Champlain Pentecostal Singers were wailing eerily. As I searched the room for familiar faces, I noticed them everywhere. Just a couple of rows away Alex McKinnon and her boy Zack were squished into a row and were fidgeting desperately. Had they known Brice? Had they known you? Maybe they counted themselves close friends of Sarah Wilton. Zack actually turned and waved and seemed to mouth something to me, but I couldn't make it out. On the groom's side, I saw Linda Pietrzsyk, though she ought to have been working in the office, fielding calls, and she was surrounded by Cheese, Chip, Mick, Mark, Stig, Blair and a half-dozen other delinquents from her peer group. Like some collective organism of mirth and irony, they convulsed over the proceedings, over the scarlet tights and boas and dance belts of the modern dancers capering at the altar. A row beyond these Skidmore halfwits—though she never sat in at any ceremony—was Glenda Manzini herself, and she seemed to be sobbing uncontrollably, a handkerchief like a veil across her face. Where was her husband? And her boy? Then, to my amazement, Sis, when I looked back at the S.R.O. audience beyond the last aisle over on the groom's side, *I saw Mom and Dad.* What were they doing there? And how had they known? I had done everything to keep the wedding from them. I had hoarded these bad feelings. Dad's face was gray with remorse, as though he could have done something to stop the proceedings, and Mom held tight to his side, wearing dark glasses of a perfect opacity. At once, I got up from the row where I'd parked myself and climbed over the exasperated families seated next to me, jostling their knees. As I went, I became aware of Brice McCann's soft, insinuating voice ricocheting, in Dolby surround-sound, from one wall of the Rip Van Winkle Room to the next. The room was appropriately named, it seemed to me then. We were all sleepers who dreamed a reverie of marriage, not one of us had waked to see the bondage, the violence, the excess of its cabalistic prayers and rituals. Marriage was oneiric. Not one of us was willing to pronounce the truth of its dream language of slavery and submission and transmission of property, and Brice's vow, *to have and to hold Sarah Wilton, till death did them part, forsaking all others,* seemed to me like the pitch of a used-car dealer or insurance salesman, and these words rang out in the room, likewise Sarah's uncertain and breathy reply, and I rushed at the center aisle, pushing away cretinous guests and cherubic newborns toward my parents, to embrace them as these words fell, these words with their intimations of mortality, *to tell my parents I should never*

50

have let you drive that night, Sis. How could I have let you drive? How could I have been so stupid? My tires were bald—I couldn't afford better. My car was a death trap; and I was its proper driver, bent on my long, complicated program of failure, my program of futures abandoned, of half-baked ideas, of big plans that came to nought, of cheap talk and lies, of drinking binges, petty theft; my car was made for my own death, Sis, the inevitable and welcome end to the kind of shame and regret I had brought upon everyone close to me, you especially, who must have wept inwardly, in your bosom, when you felt compelled to ask me to read a poem on your special day, before you totaled my car, on that curve, running up over the bream, shrieking, flipping the vehicle, skidding thirty feet on the roof, hitting the granite outcropping there, plunging out of the seat (why no seat belt?), snapping your neck, ejecting through the windshield, catching part of yourself there, tumbling over the hood, breaking both legs, puncturing your lung, losing an eye, shattering your wrist, bleeding, coming to rest at last in a pile of mouldering leaves, where rain fell upon you, until, unconsciously, you died.

Yet, as I called out to Mom and Dad, the McCann-Wilton wedding party suddenly scattered, the vows were through, the music was overwhelming, the bride and groom were married; there were Celtic pipes, and voices all in harmony—it was a dirge, it was jig, it was a chant of religious ecstasy—and I couldn't tell what was wedding and what was funeral, whether there was an end to one and a beginning to the other, and there were shouts of joy and confetti in the air, and beating of breasts and the procession of pink-cheeked teenagers, two by two, all living the dream of American marriages with cars and children and small businesses and pension plans and social-security checks and grandchildren, and I couldn't get close to my parents in the throng; in fact, I couldn't be sure if it had been them standing there at all, in that fantastic crowd, that crowd of dreams, and I realized I was alone at Brice McCann's wedding, alone among people who would have been just as happy not to have me there, as I had often been alone, even in fondest company, even among those who cared for me. I should have stayed home and watched television.

This didn't stop me, though. I made my way to the reception. I shoveled down the chicken satay and shrimp with green curry, along with the proud families of Sarah Wilton and Brice McCann. Linda Pietrzsyk appeared by my side, as when we had kissed in the Ticonderoga Suite. She asked if I was feeling all right.

51

—Sure, I said.

—Don't you think I should drive you home?

—There's someone I want to talk to, I said.—Then I'd be happy to go. And Linda asked:

—What's in the bag?

She was referring to my Wal-Mart shopping bag, Sis. I think the Wal-Mart policy which asserts that *employees are not to let a customer pass without asking if this customer needs help* is incredibly enlightened. I think the way to a devoted customer is through his or her dignity. In the shopping bag, I was carrying the wedding gift I had brought for Brice McCann and Sarah Wilton. I didn't know if I should reveal this gift to Linda, because I didn't know if she would understand, but I told her anyhow. *Is this what it's like to discover, all at once, that you are sharing your life?*

—Oh, that's some of my sister.

—Andrew, Linda said, and then she apparently didn't know how to continue. Her voice, in a pair of false starts, oscillated with worry. Her smile was grim. —Maybe this would be a good time to leave.

But I didn't leave, Sis. I brought out the most dangerous weapon in my arsenal, the pinnacle of my nefarious plans for this event, also stored in my Wal-Mart bag. The Chicken Mask. That's right, Sis. I had been saving it ever since my days at Hot Bird, and as Brice had yet to understand that I had crashed his wedding for a specific reason, I slipped this mask over my neatly parted hair, and over the collar of the wash-and-wear suit that I had bought that week for this occasion. I must say, in the mirrored reception area in the Rip Van Winkle Room, I was one elegant chicken. I immediately began to search the premises for the groom, and it was difficult to find him at first, since there were any number of like-minded beret-wearing motivational speakers slouching against pillars and counters. At last, though, I espied him preening in the middle of a small group of maidens, over by the electric fountain we had installed for the ceremony. He was laughing good-naturedly. When he first saw me, in the Chicken Mask, working my way toward him, I'm sure he saw me as an omen for his new union. *Terrific! We've got a chicken at the ceremony! Poultry is always reassuring at wedding time!* Linda was trailing me across the room. Trying to distract me. I had to be short with her. I told her to go find herself a husband.

I worked my way into McCann's limber and witty reception chatter and mimed a certain Chicken-style affability. Then, when one of those disagreeable conversational silences overtook the group, I ventured a question of your intended:

—So, Brice, how do you think your last fiancée, Eileen, would be reacting to your first-class nuptial ceremony today? Would she have liked it?

There was a confused hush, as the three or four of the secretarial beauties of his circle considered the best way to respond to this thorny question.

—Well, since she's passed away, I think she would probably be smiling down on us from above. I've felt her presence through the decision to marry Sarah, and I think Eileen knows that I'll never forget her. That I'll always love her.

—Oh, is that right? I said,—because the funny thing is I happen to have her *with me here,* and . . .

Then I opened up the small box of you (you were in a Tiffany jewelry box that I had spirited out of Mom's jewelry cache because I liked its pale teal shade: the color of rigor mortis as I imagined it) held it up toward Brice and then tossed some of it. I'm sure you know, Sis, that chips of bone tend to be heavier and therefore to fall more quickly to the ground, while the rest of the ashes make a sort of cloud when you throw them, when you cast them aloft. Under the circumstances, this cloud seemed to have a character, a personality. *Thus, you darted and feinted around Brice's head,* Sis, so that he began coughing and wiping the corners of his eyes, dusty with your remains. His consorts were hacking as well, among them Sarah Wilton, his troth. How had I missed her before? She was radiant like a woman whose prayers have been answered, who sees the promise of things to come, who sees uncertainties and contingencies diminished, and yet she was rushing away from me, astonished, as were the others. I realized I had caused a commotion. Still, I gave chase, Sis, and I overcame your Brice McCann, where he blockaded himself on the far side of a table full of spring rolls. Though I have never been a fighting guy, I gave him an elbow in the nose, as if I were a Chicken and this elbow my wing. I'm sure I mashed some cartilage. He got a little nosebleed, I think I may have broken the Mansion's unbroken streak of peaceful weddings.

At this point, of course, a pair of beefy Mansion employees (the McCarthy brothers, Tom and Eric) arrived on the scene and pulled me off of Brice McCann. They also tore the Chicken Mask from me. And they never returned this piece of my property afterwards. At the moment of unmasking, Brice reacted with mock astonishment. But how could he have failed to guess? That I would wait for my chance, however many years it took?

—Andy?

I said nothing, Sis. Your ghost had been in the cloud that wreathed him; your ghost had swooped out of the little box that I'd held, and now, at last, you were released from your disconsolate march on the surface of the earth, your march of unfinished business, your march of fixed ideas and obsessions unslaked by death. I would be happy if you were at peace now, Sis, and I would be happy if I were at peace; I would be happy if the thunderclouds and lightning of Brice and Sarah's wedding would yield to some warm autumn day in which you had good weather for your flight up through the heavens.

Out in the foyer, where the guests from the Valentine Room were promenading in some of the finest threads I had ever seen, Tom McCarthy told me that Glenda Manzini wanted to see me in her office—before I was removed from the Mansion on the Hill permanently. We walked against the flow of the crowd beginning to empty from each of the suites. Our trudge was long. When I arrived at Glenda's refrigerated chamber, she did an unprecedented thing, Sis, she closed the door. I had never before inhabited that space alone with her. She didn't invite me to sit. Her voice was raised from the outset. Pinched between thumb and forefinger (the shade of her nail polish, a dark maroon, is known in beauty circles, I believe, as *vamp*), as though it were an ounce of gold or a pellet of plutonium, she held a single green M&M.

—Can you explain this? she asked.—Can you tell me what this is?

—I think that's a green M&M, I said.—I think that's the traditional green color, as opposed to one of the new brighter shades they added in a recent campaign for market share.

—Andy, don't try to amuse me. What was this green M&M doing behind my filing cabinet?

—Well, I—

—I'm certain that I didn't leave a green M&M back there. I would never leave an M&M behind a filing cabinet. In fact, I would never allow a green M&M into this office in the first place.

—That was months ago.

—I've been holding on to it for months, Glenda said.—Do you think I'm stupid?

—On the contrary, I said.

—Do you think you can come in here and violate the privacy of my office?

—I think you're brilliant, I said.—And I think you're very sad. And I think you should surrender your job to someone who cares for the institution you're celebrating here.

Now that I had let go of you, Sis, now that I had begun to compose this narrative in which I relinquished the hem of your spectral bed-sheet, I saw through the language of business, the rhetoric of hypocrisy. Why had she sent me out for those birth-control pills? Why did she make me schedule her chiropractic appointments? Because she could. *But what couldn't be controlled, what could never be controlled, was the outcome of devotion.* Glenda's expression, for the first time on record, was stunned. She launched into impassioned colloquy about how the Mansion on the Hill was supposed to be a *refuge,* and how, with my *antics,* as she called them, I had sullied the reputation of the Mansion and endangered its business plan, and how it was clear *that assaulting strangers while wearing a rubber mask is the kind of activity that proves you are an unstable person, and I just think, well, I don't see the point in discussing it with you anymore and I think you have some serious choices to make, Andy, if you want to be part of reg-ular human society,* and so forth, which is just plain bunk, as far as I'm concerned. It's not as if Brice McCann were a *stranger* to me.

I'm always the object of tirades by my supervisors, for overstepping my position, for lying, for wanting too much—this is one of the deep receivables on the balance sheet of my life—and yet at the last second Glenda Manzini didn't fire me. According to shrewd managerial strat-egy, she simply waved toward the door. With the Mansion crowded to capacity now, with volume creeping upward in the coming months, they would need someone with my skills. To validate the cars in the parking lot, for example. Mark my words, Sis, parking validation will soon be as big in the Northeast as it is in the West.

When the McCarthys flung me through the main doors, Linda Pietrzsyk was waiting. What unfathomable kindness. At the main en-trance, on the way out, I passed through a gauntlet of rice-flingers. Bouquets drifted through the skies to the mademoiselles of the Capi-tal. Garters fell into the hands of local bachelors. Then I was beyond all good news and seated in the passenger seat of Linda's battered Volkswagen. She was crying. We progressed slowly along back roads. I had been given chances and had squandered them. I had done my best to love, Sis. I had loved you, and you were gone. In Linda's car, at

55

dusk, we sped along the very road where you took your final drive. Could Linda have known? Your true resting place is forested by white birches, they dot the length of that winding lane, the fingers of the dead reaching up through burdens of snow to impart much-needed instruction to the living. In intermittent afternoon light, in seizure-inducing light, unperturbed by the advances of merchandising, I composed a proposal.

Nominated by The Paris Review, Robert Phillips

IN SEARCH OF MIRACLES

essay by ANN HOOD

from DOUBLETAKE

THE DAY MY father was diagnosed with inoperable lung cancer, I decided to go and find him a miracle. My family had already spent a good part of that September chasing medical options, and what we discovered was not hopeful. Given the odds, a miracle cure was our best and most reasonable hope. A few weeks earlier, while I lay in a birthing center having my daughter, Grace, my father had been in a hospital across town undergoing biopsies to determine the cause of the spot that had appeared in his mediastinum, which connects the lungs. Eight years before, he'd given up smoking after forty years of two packs a day and had been diagnosed with emphysema. Despite yearly bouts of pneumonia and periodic shortness of breath, he was a robust sixty-seven-year-old, robust enough to take care of my son, Sam, to cook, and to clean the house he and my mother had lived in for their forty-seven years of marriage.

We are a superstitious family, skeptical of medicine and believers in omens, potions, and the power of prayer. The week that the first X ray showed a spot on my father's lung, three of us had dreams that could only be read as portents. I dreamed of my maternal grandmother, Mama Rose. My cousin, whose own father had died when she was only two and who had grown up next door to us with my father stepping in as a surrogate parent for her, dreamed of our great-uncle Rum. My father dreamed of his father for the first time since he'd died in 1957. All of these ghosts had one thing in common— they were happy. A few days later, my father developed a fever as the two of us ate souvlaki at the annual Greek Festival. The X ray they took that night in the emergency room was sent to his regular

57

doctor. Nine months pregnant, I arrived at my parents' house the next morning with a bag of bagels. My father stood at the back door with his news. "The X ray showed something," he said dismissively. "They need to do a few more tests."

For the next month, he underwent CAT scans and -oscopies of all sorts, until, finally, a surgeon we hardly knew shouted across the hospital waiting room: "Where are the Woods?" I stood, cradling my newborn daughter. "Hood," I said. "Over here." He walked over to us and without any hesitation said, "He's got cancer. A fair-sized tumor that's inoperable. We can give him chemo, buy a little time. Your doctor will give you the details." He had taken the time to give my father the same information, even though as he was coming out of anesthesia it had seemed like a nightmare to him.

When someone died in our family, my father pulled out his extra-large bottle of Jack Daniels. It had gotten us through the news of the death of my cousin's young husband, my own brother's accidental death in 1982, and the recent deaths of two of my own forty-something cousins, one from melanoma and one from AIDS. That late September afternoon, my father pulled out the bottle for his own grim prognosis. As the day wore on, we'd gotten more news: only an aggressive course of chemotherapy and radiation could help, and even then the help would be short-lived, if it came at all. "Taxol," the pulmonary specialist had told us, "has given some people up to eighteen months." But the way he bowed his head after he said it made me realize that eighteen months was not only the best we could hope for, but a long shot. My sister-in-law, a doctor, too, was harsher. "Six months after diagnosis is the norm," she'd said.

Sitting in the kitchen that once held my mother and her ten siblings, their parents and grandparents, every day for supper, I did some quick math. Was it possible that the man sitting across from me sipping Jack Daniels would not be alive at Easter? A WASP from Indiana, he had married into a large, loud Italian family and somehow become more Italian than some of his in-laws. At Easter, he was the one who made the dozen loaves of sweetbread, the fresh cheese and frittatas. He shaped wine biscuits into crosses and made pizzelles that were lighter than any my aunts produced. At six-foot-one and over two hundred pounds, cracking jokes about the surgeon, he did not look like someone about to die. He was not someone I was going to let die. If medical science could only give him a year and a half tops, then there was only one real hope for a cure. "There's a place in New Mexico with miracle dirt," I announced. "I'm going to go and get you some." "Well," my father said with typical understatement, "I guess I can use all the help I can get."

A LEAP OF FAITH.   Perhaps for some people the notion of seeking a miracle cure is tomfoolery, futile, or even a sign of pathetic desperation. The simplest definition of a miracle that I know is the one that C. S. Lewis proposes in his book *Miracles:* an interference with nature by supernatural power. But even that definition implies something that many people do not believe—that there is something other than nature, the thing that Lewis calls the supernatural. Without that other power, there can be no miracles. For those who cannot buy into the notion of this other power, miracle healing belongs back in the Dark Ages, or at least in a time before the advent of modern medicine. To believe in miracles, and certainly to go and look for one, you must put aside science and rely only on faith.

For me, that leap was not a difficult one. My great-grandmother, who died when I was six, healed people of a variety of ailments with prayer and household items, such as silver dollars and Mazola oil. The source of a headache was always believed to be the evil eye and was treated by my great-grandmother by pouring water into a soup bowl, adding a few drops of oil, then making circles on the afflicted person's palm while muttering in Italian. Curing nosebleeds involved making the sign of the cross on the person's forehead. Around our hometown of West Warwick, Rhode Island, she was famous for her ability to cure sciatica. In order to do this, my great-grandmother had to go to the person's house on the night of a full moon and spend the night, so she could work her miracle at dawn the next day. There was a time when she had a wait list for her services.

Most miracles occur through the intercession of a saint. If one wants a favor, one prays to a particular saint to act on one's behalf. My great-grandmother was no different. She had prayers to various saints to help find lost objects, answer questions, heal. Her prayers to Saint Anthony could answer important questions, such as, Will I have a baby? Does he love me? Will my mother be all right? The prayer was in Italian. She would go into a room, alone, and ask the question. If she was able to repeat the prayer three times quickly and without hesitation or errors, the answer was a favorable one. But if the prayer "came slow" or she couldn't remember the words, the outlook was dire.

The legend goes that my great-grandmother learned all of these things as a young girl in Italy. She was a shepherdess on the hills of a town outside Naples, near a convent. The nuns took a liking to her and passed on their knowledge. Her faith was sealed years later when my grandmother, her only daughter, was three. On a vacation in Italy from the United States, where they had immigrated, my grandmother came down with scarlet fever. The doctors said she would not live through the night. My great-grandmother bundled up her daughter and walked all the miles to the convent. There, the nuns prayed in earnest to the Virgin Mary to spare this child. By morning, she was completely well except for one thing: her long dark curls fell off at the height of her fever. My great-grandmother took her daughter's hair and gave it as an offering of thanks to the Virgin Mary. When my grandmother's hair grew back, it was red, and it remained red until the day she died, seventy years later.

I grew up with this story, and others like it. I never questioned it. Like the story of the day I was born or the day my parents met, I accepted it as fact. But when I shared the story with a friend recently, he said at its conclusion, "But of course that's not true." Startled, I asked him what he meant. "Why, that never happened," he said, laughing, "It couldn't happen. Maybe her fever simply broke or maybe the doctors thought she was sicker than she was. But she wasn't cured by the Virgin Mary, and her hair probably just turned more red as she got older." Therein lies an important distinction between one who believes in miracles and one who doesn't. A believer accepts the miracle as truth, no questions asked. Although I didn't accept my friend's explanations of our family lore, I also knew I could not dissuade him from believing them.

THE HEALING DIRT. That was how I came to take my ten-week-old daughter an hour northwest of Santa Fe, New Mexico, up into the Sangre de Cristo Mountains, to the little town of Chimayo and its El Santuario. The area had been a holy ground for the Tewa Indians, a place where they believed fire and water had belched forth and subsided into a sacred pool. Eventually, the water had evaporated, leaving only a puddle of mud. The Tewa went there to eat the mud when they wanted to be cured. Sometime around the year 1810, during Holy Week, a man called Don Bernardo Abeyta is said to have been performing the Stations of the Cross in the hills at Chimayo. Suddenly, he saw light springing up from one of the slopes. As he got close to it, he realized the light was coming from the ground itself. He began to dig with his hands and there he found a crucifix. He ran to the Santa Cruz church, which was in a nearby town, and the priest and parishioners went with him and took the crucifix back to their church. The next morning, the crucifix was missing. Somehow it had returned to the place it was found. The same thing happened two more times, so they decided to build a chapel—El Santuario—at the spot. This chapel contains the hole, called *el pocito* (the well)—with the healing dirt.

Like many sites that claim miracles, Chimayo is difficult to reach. Grace and I flew from Boston to Albuquerque, changing planes en route. There, we met my longtime friend Matt, rented a car, and drove for over an hour to Santa Fe. The next morning we rode into the mountains on what is called the High Road to Taos, along curving roads covered with snow. Signs are few, and even getting to El Santuario requires a certain amount of faith. Along the way, we had to stop more than once so I could breastfeed the baby. Despite all of this, I never once grew discouraged. Before I left, my father had hugged me and said, "Go get that dirt, sweetheart." No matter what, I would get it for him and bring it safely home.

Chimayo is called the Lourdes of America because of all the healings that have been associated with it. When one thinks of miracle healing sites, Lourdes is probably the place that first comes to mind. If I hadn't already taken a serendipitous trip there fifteen years earlier, it is probably where I would have gone. In 1982, when I was working as a flight attendant, I was called to work a trip one day while I was on standby. It wasn't until I hung up that I realized the only destination I had been given was "Europe." This was unusual.

I was twenty-five years old and at a point in my life where I had abandoned many of my childhood ways. I had moved from my small hometown in Rhode Island to live in Manhattan. I was working at a job that was not usually associated with someone who had graduated sixth in her high school class and with high honors from college. Instead of the young lawyers I had been steadily dating, I was now madly in love with an unemployed actor. And, perhaps most important, I had given up not just on the Catholicism with which I was raised, but on religion altogether. Like many people I knew at that time, I liked to say that I believed in God, but not in organized religions. The truth is I didn't really think much about God back then, except in sporadic furtive prayers for my immediate needs: Don't let me be late, Please have him call, Help me decide what to do.

61

When I arrived at Kennedy Airport and looked at my flight schedule, I was delighted to see that the first part of the trip involved deadheading—flying as a passenger—to Paris that evening and staying overnight. The next day, at Charles DeGaulle Airport, I spotted several other flight attendants waiting for the same Air France flight. They all looked glum. After introductions, I asked if any of them knew where we were headed. "Didn't they tell you?" one of them moaned. "We're going to Lourdes!"

It was Easter week, when upward of a hundred thousand people go to Lourdes, and the streets were clogged with people with varying degrees of illness and deformity, nurses and nuns in starched white uniforms, tourists with cameras snapping pictures of the dying prone on their stretchers, the cripples atrophied in their wheelchairs, the blind with their white canes. But none of this prepared me for what was to come.

It took us almost four hours to board the flight back because of all the wheelchairs, stretchers, and medical equipment. Already the doctor on board had administered emergency care to a dying man. A mother told me that her daughter, seventeen years old and blind, had a rare disease in which her brain was destroying itself. "There's nothing to be done," she whispered. "This was our last chance." The girl sat beside her, staring blankly from eyes the light blue of faded denim. When I placed a meal tray in front of a sixty-year-old man suffering from multiple sclerosis, he grunted, gathered all his strength, and threw it back at me, his eyes ablaze with anger. "It's not you," his wife apologized, her head bent to hide the tears that streamed down her cheeks. "He's angry at everyone."

I sought out the priest who had led a group of a hundred people from Philadelphia. "Do you believe that any of these people will be cured by a miracle?" I demanded. I was young and jaded and arrogant, a stranger to death or illness.

"A miracle," he said, "is usually instantaneous. But some of these people have things that it will take X rays and tests to see if they are cured."

I looked at the young girl with the brain disease. Certainly then she had not had a miracle.

"The church has physicians," he explained, "who study alleged miracles." He told me about the process, how a miracle case must be proved by a medical history and the records and notes of everyone who has treated the person. Scientific evidence such as X rays and biopsies are examined. "And," he added, with what I interpreted as skepticism, "the cure must be a total cure. No relapses or reoccurrences."

"How many of these instantaneous cures have happened at Lourdes?"

He averted his eyes. "I think three," he said. "But you're missing the point," he said, "This is all they have left to do. Miracles come in unexpected ways."

It seemed to me a sad journey. Especially when out of the approximately forty cases a year investigated by the Consulta Medica, only about fifteen are deemed miracles. (The Consulta Medica is the Catholic Church's official body for investigating miracle claims.) Such a statistic in 1982 would have made me even angrier that these people had gone so far, with such hope, only to be disappointed. But by the time I went to Chimayo, I was a different person, and that statistic actually bolstered my belief that the dirt there might cure my father.

I was no longer the skeptical, arrogant young woman who had left Lourdes in a self-righteous huff. Just three months after my trip there, my brother died unexpectedly, and I found myself wanting to find faith somewhere, to believe in something more solid than my fleeting encounters with Buddhism, the Quakers, Ethical Culture, and the Unitarian Church. Over the years between then and my father's illness, I'd been married and divorced, suffered a miscarriage, lost jobs, changed careers, remarried, given birth to two children, and moved back to my home state of Rhode Island. And I'd returned to church, though not the Catholic Church of my childhood.

When I arrived at El Santuario, I had the fear of my father's death to motivate me and an open heart, a willingness to believe that a cure—a miracle—was possible. Matt had come with me to bring back dirt for his friend, who was dying from Hodgkin's disease. Not even the signs posted everywhere—NOT RESPONSIBLE FOR THEFT—could deter us. Here was a small adobe church with a dirt parking lot, a religious gift store, and a burrito stand called Leona's, which was written up as the best burrito place in New Mexico in all of my guidebooks.

We proceeded under an archway and through a courtyard where a wooden crucifix stood, then into the church where the altar was adorned with brightly painted pictures by the artist known as the Chili Painter. But we hadn't come to see folk art. We had come for a miracle. So we quickly went into the low-ceilinged room off the church in search of the *pocito*. What we found first was a testimony to all the cures attributed to this place. The walls were lined with crutches and canes, candles and flowers, statues of saints, all offerings of thanks for healings. Despite the signs asking people not to leave notes because of the fire danger around the lit candles, and not to write on anything except the guest book, the offerings had letters tucked into their corners. One statue had a sonogram picture pinned to the saint's cloak. Another had a letter in Spanish: "Thank you for the recovery of our little Luis. Our baby boy is now well. Mil gracias."

Against one wall of this room sits a shrine to the Santo Niño, who is believed to walk about the country at night healing sick children and wearing out his shoes in the process. As a result, an offering of shoes is given to him whenever a child is healed. The shrine at Chimayo is full of children's shoes, handmade knit booties, delicate silk christening shoes. Roses and letters of thanks adorn the statue, which is seated and holds a basket of food and a gourd to carry water.

In this small room, I began to tremble. I felt I was in a holy place, a place that held possibility. I had not felt that sense of possibility in the hospital and doctors' waiting rooms that had dominated my life these past few months. Even when a surgeon promised to remove my father's tumor if "the sucker will only shrink some," I didn't get the sense of peace I had as I stood surrounded by these testimonies to faith. One, from Ida P. of Chicago, stated that her husband still had six more radiation treatments to go when, on a Sunday, she brought him the dirt. On Monday the tumor was gone.

Ducking our heads, Matt and I entered the even smaller room that housed the *pocito*. It was just a hole in the dirt floor. The walls here were also covered with offerings, including a note that said: "Within this small room resides the stillness of souls that have discovered peace. Listen to their silence. JK, New York," Matt and I kneeled in front of the *pocito* and scooped the dirt with our bare hands into the Ziploc bags we had brought. I cannot say what Matt was thinking as he dug. But I had one prayer that I repeated over and over: Please let my father's tumor go away.

TO TRUST AND LOVE AGAIN.   Unlike other sites attributed to miracle healings, Chimayo is not associated with any particular saint. At Lourdes, people believe that Saint Bernadette intercedes on their behalf. Four years before my visit to Chimayo, I went on a long weekend trip to Montreal, Canada. One of my stops was a visit to Saint

Joseph's Basilica, where a priest named Brother André was said to have healed people through prayer and oil from a particular lamp. The cures were frequent and often spontaneous. For the year 1916 alone, 439 cures were recorded. "I do not cure," Brother André said. "Saint Joseph cures."

But I did not visit Saint Joseph's Basilica for a cure. I went because the relic displayed there is a particularly gruesome one: Brother André's heart. I've always attributed my love of the more grotesque aspects of Catholicism to my Italian upbringing. My memories of my first trip to Rome are dominated by the various bones and pieces of cloth that churches display. The notion of viewing a heart was especially appealing. However, once I entered the ornate basilica and viewed the heart in its case, I decided I should also see the place where people go to pray to Brother André for a miracle. The walls of this room, too, were lined with offerings, the canes and braces of those who have been healed.

In many ways, I was even more of a cynic than I had been when I'd visited Lourdes. The death of my brother and the emotional havoc it wreaked on my family had left me in a spiritual vacuum from which I had not yet recovered. More recently, a love affair had gone bad, and I was questioning not just my spiritual beliefs, but also my ability to trust and love again.

That day in Montreal, I was not in need of a physical healing, but I had been in turmoil for several months, a turmoil that it did not seem would have an ending anytime soon. For someone who had entered the basilica on a lark—to view a human heart—I was strangely moved by the place, and by the people around me who knelt and prayed. Their conviction was obvious, and in many ways I envied their ability to believe in the power of prayer, or saints, or miracles. I knelt, too, and thought of all the events that had led me to this dark time I was living. At its core was a betrayal in love, a broken promise, a broken heart. A decision—whether to trust this person again—seemed unreachable. I replayed the past months like someone watching a home movie, and then I asked for resolution.

Resolution came. Not that day, or even that month, but many months later. I would not even now claim that the resolution came from the moments I spent praying in Saint Joseph's Basilica. What I gained there was a peace of mind, a calming of the soul, without which I could not have reached a decision. Perhaps more important is that I also began my journey back to faith through that visit. Although the

Catholic Church excludes such healings from consideration for miracles, as they do the cures of any mental disorders or diseases that have a high rate of natural remission, I believe a healing of some sort began there. Three years later, as I stood in El Santuario de Chimayo hoping for a miracle of the physical sort, I remembered that day in Montreal and the feeling that overtook me there. As WK from California wrote after her own visit to Chimayo: "It didn't cure me, but then it's God's will. Peace of mind is sometimes better."

A GRACED WORLD.   Buoyant from our time spent at El Santuario, Matt and I went off to find one of the weavers that live in and around Chimayo. Carefully following the signs for Ortegas, we ended up at a small store that sold carvings and local folk art, not rugs. "Is this Ortegas?" we asked, confused, when we entered. Matt was as certain as I that we had followed the signs exactly and turned in where they pointed. The ponytailed man behind the counter, Tobias, smiled at us. "You've been to get the dirt," he said. Later, Matt and I would both comment on how gentle his face was. Perhaps it was this gentleness that led me to tell him why I had come and the particulars of my father's disease. He nodded. "He'll be cured," he said. "I've seen it myself, the healings."

He told us the story of a couple who had arrived at his door—"like you two!" The man was grumpy, angry at his wife for insisting they come all this way from Los Angeles when her doctors had told her a cure was hopeless. Sympathetic toward the wife's plight, Tobias invited them to dinner. Reluctantly, the man agreed. As they sat eating on the patio of a nearby restaurant, a strange light began to emit from the woman's breast. Soft at first, it grew brighter and larger until it seemed to encompass her entire chest, like a cocoon. Then it slowly dissipated. It was the skeptical husband who spoke first. "Did anyone else see that?" Each of them had. "My tumor is gone," the wife said confidently. Although Tobias did not know what kind of cancer the woman was suffering from, he was certain then that it was breast cancer, and that she had been cured. He was right on both accounts. Back in California, baffled doctors pronounced her completely free of breast cancer.

"It works," Tobias said.

Matt asked him how, with thousands of people visiting the *pocito*, the dirt was never depleted.

"Oh," Tobias said, "the caretaker refills it every day. Then the priest blesses it."

This mundane refilling disappointed me. The story I had heard about the dirt was that it replenished itself in some inexplicable way.

"It's not the dirt," Tobias told us. "It's the energy of all the people who come and pray into that *pocito* that makes miracles happen."

Of course, there is no real explanation for what makes miracles happen. But there are plenty of explanations that attempt to disprove them. Just as my friend gave many reasons why my grandmother lived through her bout of scarlet fever, skeptics use scientific, historical, and geographic data to explain away "miracles." Simply put, people either believe or don't. In my own search to understand miracles, I came across books and articles in support of each side.

Joe Nickell, the senior research fellow for the Committee for the Scientific Investigation of Claims of the Paranormal, has written an entire book debunking everything from stigmatas to the Shroud of Turin. On miracle healings, he believes that some serious illnesses, such as cancer and multiple sclerosis, can undergo spontaneous remission, in which they go away completely or abate for long periods of time. Nickell also cites misdiagnoses, misread CAT scans, and misunderstandings as explanations for miracle healings. He reports that as of 1984, six thousand miracles had been attributed to the water at Lourdes but only sixty-four of those had been authenticated as miraculous. Those sixty-four miracles, he claims, were most likely spontaneous remissions, as in the case of a woman who was "cured" of blindness, only to discover she was suffering from multiple sclerosis and the disease had actually temporarily abated.

In response to such skepticism, Dr Raffaello Cortesini, a specialist in heart and liver transplants and the president of the Consulta Medica, told Kenneth L. Woodward, the religion editor of *Newsweek* magazine and the author of *Making Saints,* "I myself, if I did not do these consultations, would never believe what I read. You don't understand how fantastic, how incredible—and how well-documented—these cases are. They are more incredible than historical romances. Science fiction is nothing by comparison." Believers in miracles do not even need such substantiation.

Still, advances in medical science have made the number of accredited miracles decrease over the years. Pope John Paul II, in his address to a symposium of members of the Consulta Medica and the

Medical Committee of Lourdes in 1988, agreed that medicine has helped to understand some of these miraculous cures, but, he added, "it remains true that numerous healings constitute a fact which has its explanation only in the order of faith . . . " Because proving miracle cures has become so difficult, the church has lightened its requirements on miracles for canonization. It is true that historically, miracles were much more commonplace. In the thirteenth century, Saint Louis of Anjou was responsible for a well-documented sixty-six miracles, including raising twelve people from the dead. Obviously, today's doctors might easily disprove not only many of Louis of Anjou's miracles but also a good number of those that came before and after him. That still leaves us with the ones that no one—not even Joe Nickell—can explain that have occurred since the advent of modern medicine.

Other skeptics point to geography as a factor in alleged miracles. Since many miracles depend on the intervention of saints, and since most saints are European, a higher number of miracles occur there. Certain countries, such as Italy, boast more miracles than others. Physicians from Italy—southern Italy in particular—believe so strongly in miracles that they are more willing to accept a cure as miraculous. The culture there is such that saints and miracles are a part of everyday life. As I drove through southern Italy recently I was struck by how common statues of saints were. They appeared on roadsides, hanging from cliffs, in backyards, on city street corners, virtually everywhere. Almost always there were offerings at the statue's feet, flowers, bread, letters. This was where my own ancestors came from, and I can attest to our family's openness about letting miracles into our lives.

But other cultures share this openness, this willingness to recognize the miraculous. Rather than disproving miracles, I wonder if it doesn't support their existence. It was Augustine who claimed that all natural things were filled with miracles. He referred to the world itself as "the miracle of miracles." I saw this acceptance of daily, small miracles when I visited Mexico City during the Feast of the Virgin of Guadalupe. It was there, in 1531, that a local man named Juan Diego, while walking outdoors, heard birds singing, saw a bright light on top of a hill, and heard someone calling his name. He climbed the hill and saw a young girl, radiant in a golden mist, who claimed to be the Virgin. She told him she wanted a church built on that spot. When Juan Diego told the bishop what he had seen, the bishop asked him to go back and demand a sign as proof that this was really the Virgin. When he returned, the apparition made roses miraculously bloom, even though it was December. Convinced, the bishop allowed a cathedral to be built there. More than ten million people annually visit the shrine in Mexico City, making it the most popular site, after the Vatican, in the Catholic world.

Although it was an impressive sight to behold when I made the walk to the Basilica of the Virgin of Guadalupe along with people, many on their knees, who had come from all over Mexico, that spectacle of adoration was not what struck me about Mexico and its relationship to the miraculous. Rather, it was the way the culture as a whole viewed miracles that impressed me. Street vendors everywhere sold *milagros,* the small silver charms that mean, literally, "little miracles." The charms take the shape of body parts—arms, legs, hearts—and are pinned to saints in churches, to the inside of people's own jackets, everywhere. When I told a vendor that my mother had recently broken her hand, he gave me a *milagro* in the shape of a hand, at no charge.

Throughout Mexico one can also view *retablos,* paintings made on wood or tin that request favors for everything from curing someone of pneumonia to asking that children not fall out of windows or that a woman have a safe childbirth or that a house not catch on fire. Although many churches have glorious collections of *retablos,* these paintings also adorn the walls of shops and homes, humble requests for miracles large and small. "Oh, yes," a friend of mine who lives in San Miguel d'Allende told me, "here in Mexico it is a miracle if someone's oxen do a good job or if it doesn't rain on a special day. Miracles happen every day here."

As if to prove her point, we encountered one such miracle the night before I left Mexico City. Several of us climbed into a cab to go to a restaurant, but the driver was unfamiliar with the address. Everyone studied the map and planned the route, but still we couldn't find the street. Several times we stopped and asked directions. We still couldn't find it. After forty minutes and yet another set of directions, the cab came to a screeching halt. "We're here!" our driver exclaimed happily. "It's a miracle!"

Perhaps, then, part of understanding what a miracle is comes from one's openness to the possibility that they exist and occur regularly. It could be argued that one has to be Catholic to have this ability, since predominantly Catholic countries and cultures claim to have such an attitude. There are many Catholics who would agree that they believe in miracles simply because of their religion. Since I haven't actively participated in Catholicism since I was a young teenager, I would not have credited Catholicism with my own belief in the miraculous. But in retrospect, the roots of that belief must be in my Catholic and Italian upbringing, a combination that certainly indoctrinated me into believing of a general kind.

In fact, the connection between miracles and healing stems largely from the miracles attributed to Jesus. One could, then, broaden the definition of who more readily accepts miracles to include all Christians. Yet I suppose that someone could believe in miracles without believing in the teachings of Christ, or even without believing in God. Conversely, one can believe in God without believing in miracles. What seems most likely is what Kenneth Woodward explains: "To believe in miracles one must be able to accept gifts, freely bestowed and altogether unmerited." Once one has the ability to do that, it is a small leap to then accept that these gifts have come because someone has intervened on your behalf. Woodward goes on to say that "in a graced world, such things happen all the time." If one presumes that the world is without grace then one cannot accept any gifts, especially those that come from prayer.

When I made my pilgrimage to Chimayo, I had reached a point in my life where I believed in a graced world. I believed that the birth of my son was miraculous, that the love I shared with my husband was a gift, as was my ability to shape words into meaningful stories. Of course I credited hard work, talent, and character, too. But I had come to believe in Augustine's view of the world as the "miracle of miracles." When I arrived back in Rhode Island with the dirt from El Santuario, I felt that anything could happen.

Twenty-four hours after my father held the dirt, he was in respiratory failure and was rushed to the hospital by ambulance. It was Christmas Eve, three months after his diagnosis. Although it would have been a perfect time to have a crisis of faith, quite the opposite happened. I simply believed that he would survive. What happened next surprised me more than his bad turn of health.

While he was in the hospital, his recovery from what turned out to be pneumonia deemed unlikely, his doctor performed a CAT scan, assuming the tumor had grown. My father had only had two treatments of chemo and he needed five before there was any hope of the tumor shrinking. Visiting him, I asked if he was prepared for a bad CAT scan.

"Oh, no," he said with great confidence, "the tumor is gone." "Gone?" I said. He nodded. "I sat here and watched as cancer left my body. It was black and evil-looking and came out of my chest like sparks, agitated and angry." I was willing to believe the tumor might disappear, but such a physical manifestation was more than I had considered. True, Tobias had told us of a light enveloping a sick woman's chest, and it had seemed miraculous. But here was my father, a practical, no-nonsense midwesterner, telling me a story that hinted of science fiction.

The next day my mother called me from the hospital. "Ann," she said, awed, "the CAT scan shows that the tumor has completely gone. It's disappeared." In the background I heard my father chuckling, and then my mother made the doctor repeat what he had said when he walked into the room with the results: "It's a miracle."

AN ANSWERED PRAYER. Here is the part where I would like to say that my father came home, tumor-free, cancer-free, miraculously cured. The part where I would like to tell you that, well again, he traveled with me to New Mexico, to El Santuario de Chimayo, to leave his CAT scan results in the little low-ceilinged room beside the baby shoes and notes of thanks and crutches and braces and statues and candles.

Instead, my father went home, had one more dose of Taxol, and the next day was once again rushed by ambulance to the hospital in respiratory failure. He spent almost two weeks in intensive care, diagnosed with double pneumonia. From there, he was moved onto the cardiac ward for a week and then into rehab. Weakened by his near-death illness, he moved around using a walker and had no memory of his days in the ICU. My family remembered it all too well, however: the all-night vigils by his side, sleeping on chairs, waiting for doctors and tests and change. Once he was in rehab, his doctor repeated the CAT scan, suspecting a recurrence of the tumor. But there was none, and a date for his release was set.

Two days before he was to come home, he spiked a fever and acquired a cough that proved to be the onset of yet another bout of pneumonia, this one a fungal pneumonia common in patients undergoing chemotherapy, and usually fatal. The doctors prepared us for the worst. "He will never leave the hospital," his pulmonary specialist told us. His health failing, my father instructed us on how to prepare the Easter breakfast specialties that he had been in charge of for the last

71

twenty-five years—how to turn a frittata so it doesn't break, the secret to making light pizzeles.

The day before Easter he began to die. His oxygen supply was so low that his legs grew blue and mottled. A priest was called and administered the last rites, now known as the sacrament of the sick. But when the priest walked away, I grabbed my father's hand and sought a miracle yet again: "Daddy," I said, "please come back. For me and Sam and Grace." At the sound of my children's names, my father struggled not only to open his eyes, but to breathe, a deep life-sustaining breath. By that evening, he was sitting up. "I thought I was a goner there," he joked. Easter morning he told my mother that her frittata was too dry. I stayed with him all day. We watched a movie that night, and then he went to sleep.

The doctor suspected the cancer was back and had spread to my father's brain. He did CAT scans on his bones, lungs, and head. But my father remained tumor-free and cancer-free. Despite this, he died a week later, from the pneumonia he'd caught because of a compromised immune system. More than once since then I have found myself wondering not *if* I got a miracle or not, but whether I prayed for the wrong thing. Should I have bent over the *pocito* and asked for my father to live rather than for the tumor to go away? What I am certain of is this: I got exactly what I prayed for on that December afternoon at El Santuario de Chimayo.

Around the world, at Lourdes and Fatima, on the Greek island of Tinos and in a municipality called Esquipulas on the far eastern part of Guatemala, in Montreal and Chimayo, people are making pilgrimages, asking for miracles to save their lives or the lives of their loved ones. At least, that is what they believe they want, and they will settle for nothing less. After my father died, I still wanted to find someone whose miracle had happened, who had prayed for God to spare their loved one, and for God to have answered.

In my search I traveled to the remote Italian town of San Giovanni Rotondo on the Monte Gargano, the "spur" of the Italian boot that divides the plains of Apulia from the Adriatic Sea. There, a Capuchin monk known as Padre Pio is said to have performed miraculous cures, even after his death in 1968. No ordinary man, Padre Pio had the stigmata, the gift of transverberation (a wound in his side like the one Jesus had), and the ability to bilocate—to be in two places at the same time.

On our way from Naples to San Giovanni Rotondo, an all-day car ride through mountains and rugged terrain, I read the story of Padre Pio aloud to my husband and our eight- and four-year-olds. My husband kept rolling his eyes. More than once he whispered to me, "The guy was a kook." But when I'd finished, I asked the children if they believed that Padre Pio was capable of everything the book said. Did they believe he could heal people, too? "Oh yes!" they both said without hesitation. He was, they concluded, a very special person.

It was a brutally cold March afternoon when we arrived at the cathedral there. The wind blew at over fifty miles an hour. But still the church was packed. I made my way downstairs to Padre Pio's tomb, where the kneelers around it were full of pilgrims with offerings of roses. A father stood beside his young son, who sat hunched and twisted in a wheelchair. As they prayed, the father lovingly stroked the boy's cheek. Watching them, I was convinced that the boy would not walk out of here, leaving his wheelchair behind. I did not believe that the boy would ever walk. But rather than feeling anger at this, as I had years earlier at Lourdes, I felt a sense of peace, a certainty that the boy and his father would leave here spiritually stronger, that they would somehow have the courage to deal with the disease the boy had been given.

True, Padre Pio has been given credit for many miracles. In one, a young girl was born without pupils in her eyes. Her grandmother prayed to Padre Pio without any results. A nun urged her to make a pilgrimage from her small town to San Giovanni Rotondo. There, the monk touched the girl's eyes, and she could see. On their way home, they stopped to visit a doctor who, upon examining the child, was puzzled. The girl could see, but she still had no pupils. As in all places where miracles are said to happen, the legends of the healings are whispered among those who go. They are written about in the small brochures one can buy for a few dollars at the church. But it is only the hopeful, the desperate, who crowd around the water, the dirt, the heart, the tomb.

As I stood to leave Padre Pio's tomb, a middle-aged man and his mother hurried into the room. The woman held a statute of the Virgin Mary, an offering. But what I saw on their faces was a look that I recognized too well, a look I wish I was not familiar with. They wore the shocked and grief-stricken expressions of those who know they are about to lose someone they love. Perhaps they had just received the news. Or perhaps the person had taken a turn for the worse. They had come here because the doctors had told them there was nothing else that could be done. It was a matter of days or weeks or months. The only thing left to do was ask for a miracle.

ANOTHER MIRACLE.   Despite the fact that I am a woman who is firmly rooted in the physical world, practical and realistic and skeptical about many things in life at the end of the twentieth century, I still traveled across the country with my newborn daughter, believing I could bring home a miracle for my dying father. Almost a year to the day that my father died, I went back to El Santuario de Chimayo. Father Roca, who has been the parish priest there for forty years, talked to me in his tiny office inside the church. I had written to him months earlier and told him my story. In person, he is a man who dispenses smiles and stories as easily as holy water; several people came in while I was there and, without missing a beat, he blessed their medals and crucifixes, sprinkling holy water, murmuring prayers.

"I have reread your letter many times," he told me. "I am so happy for your family." Thinking he was confused, I said, "But my father died." Father Roca shrugged. "It was God's will. The tumor went away, yes?" I nodded. "Do you know who came here one month before he died? Cardinal Bernadin. From Chicago. He came here and asked me to take him to where the dirt was. I led him to the *pocito* and then left. Fifteen minutes later he emerged, smiling, at peace. 'I got what I came for,' he said." "He wasn't cured," I said. Father Roca smiled. "I know."

I spent about twenty minutes with Father Roca. He told me about the crucifix that was found here. He told me about the miracles he had personally witnessed: the woman who was so sick that her son had to carry her to the *pocito* but who walked out on her own; the young man who came to pray en route to throwing himself off the mountain in despair, but after praying at the *pocito,* decided to return to his wife and baby. To Father Roca, the miracles of El Santuario de Chimayo are not just physical. Rather, they are miracles of inner transformation. "There is," he told me, "something very special about this place."

Later, I returned to the small room with the offerings, and the smaller room with the *pocito* that the caretaker refilled every day. I prayed there, a prayer of thanks for the miracles that had come my way since I'd last visited Chimayo: good health, the love of my children and my husband, the closeness of my family, and, finally, the courage to accept what had come my way. If someone at the shrine on my first visit

74

had told me the miracle I would receive was peace of mind, I would have been angry. But miracles come in many forms, both physical and spiritual. Before I left El Santuario, I again removed a Ziploc bag from my pocket and filled it with dirt. Back at home, my aunt had recently been diagnosed with lung cancer. She needed a miracle, too.

Nominated by Doubletake

BUILDING A PAINTING A HOME

by BOB HICOK

from THE IOWA REVIEW

If I built a barn I'd build it right into the sky

with windows twice as large as walls and ringed
with theoretical pines, clumps of green on simple sticks

and doors cut from the ocean, doors that wave
and doors that foam and shadows inside to eat

every cow I own because I'm afraid of cows,
two stomachs imply that aliens are involved,

moo is what the brain-washed say, my fields
would be green until yellow and yellow

until white, acres of albino wheat
for the manufacture of weightless bread,

I only eat what floats in a house that spins
as the weather vane turns, a house that follows

a rooster in love with wind, the sky
and my barn are blue and the sky also floats,

there's nothing to hold anything down,
even eternity's loose and roams the erotic

contortions of space, even my children
recognize tomorrow better than they remember

today, if I built a barn I'd build the land
and the sun before that, I'd spread the canvas flat

with my hands and nail it to the dirt, I'd paint
exactly what I see and then paint

over that until by accident something habitable
appears, until the kettle screams on the stove,

until the steam is green and the sound is gold.

Nominated by Kathy Fagan, Edward Hirsch, Jane Hirshfield, William Olsen, Robert Wrigley

SEED

fiction by MARY YUKARI WATERS

from SHENANDOAH

THE NAKAZAWAS were in China barely a week when they first heard the drumming of a prisoner procession. They were sitting side by side on the hard seat of their new Western-style garden bench. Though it was twilight and turning cool, the ornamental wrought iron retained the sun's rays, reminding Masae of a frying pan slowly losing heat. Turning her head toward the sound, she stared at the concrete wall as if seeing through to the dirt road on the other side.

Clearly a small drum, it lacked the booming resonance of *taiko* festival drums back home. *Tan tan tantaka tan, tan tan tantaka tan*, it tapped in precise staccato, flat and almost toy-like, as if someone were hitting the drumhead with chopsticks. Moments later, like an afterthought, came the scuffling sound of many feet, and a man's cough less than ten meters away. The Nakazawas sat unmoving in the dusk. Out of habit, Masae's thoughts darted out to their baby girl: Indoors . . . noise didn't wake her . . . good. Above the wall, in sharp contrast to the black silhouette of a gnarled pine branch, the sky glowed an intense peacock blue. It seemed lit up from within, some of the white light escaping through a thin slit of moon.

"Ne, what'll they do to them?" Masae asked her husband Shoji once the drumbeats began to fade.

"Shoot them, most likely," Shoji said. He shifted forward on the hard iron seat and leaned down to tap his cigarette with a forefinger, once, twice, over his ashtray in the crabgrass. "Some might get sentenced to hard labor."

Masae turned her entire body to face her husband's profile. Its familiar contours, now shadowed by nightfall, took on for an eerie instant the cast of some other man: hollowed cheeks, eyes like strong brush strokes. "Araaaaa—" she sighed with a hint of reproach. Granted, these things happened in occupied countries and they had known about the prison camp before their move; still, they could do without such reminders while relaxing in their own garden. Masae wondered what people back home would think of this. In their old Hiroshima neighborhood, mothers went to great lengths to shield their children from unpleasantness, even pulling them indoors so they wouldn't watch two dogs circle each other in heat. Last winter, naturally, the neighborhood children had been spared any specific details of the Pearl Harbor incident. "I think," she now told her husband, "this is not a good location."

"H'aa, not so pleasant," Shoji said. He sounded humble; normally he would have been quick to point out that the company had chosen this house. They sat silent in their walled-in garden, on the bench which had, by now, lost all its heat. Masae could sense a faint shift in their relations. The drumbeats still rang faintly in her ears, like the aftermath of a gong. In the mock orange bushes behind them, a cricket began to chirp—slow, deliberate, unexpectedly near.

"Ochazuke might taste nice," Masae said, "before bed." Comfort food from home: hot green tea poured over leftover rice, flavored with salty flakes of dried salmon and roasted seaweed.

"Aaah! Masae, good thinking!" Shoji said, rising. His hearty exclamation was absorbed efficiently, like water by a sponge, into the silence of the Tai-huen plains.

The Nakazawas lived two kilometers from the main town, which was so small it had only six paved streets. If Masae looked out from the nursery window on the second floor (for she rarely ventured past the garden walls), she saw the dirt road leading straight into town. To her left were hills: wheat-colored, eroded over centuries to low swells on the horizon. Dark wrinkles wavered down their sides, as if the land had shriveled. Right behind those hills, the Japanese Army had built a labor camp for Chinese prisoners of war. On the other side of the dirt road, a flat expanse of toasted grass stretched out to a sky which faded in color as it approached the earth, from strong cobalt blue to a whitish haze. And somewhere past that skyline was the great Pun'An Desert.

Shoji was not in the Army. He managed a team of surveyors. His company back home, a construction conglomerate, had targeted this area because there was talk of building a railroad; Tai-huen might become a crucial leg in the Japanese trade route. Similar foresight in the Canton and Hankow provinces, which had come under Japanese rule three years ago in 1939, was paying off now in housing commissions. "The faster we take the measurements," Shoji kept repeating to Masae, as much for his own benefit, she felt, as hers, "the faster we go home. Next April, that's the goal. Maybe June, no longer than that." He worked late most nights in the Japanese tradition, flagging a bicycle-ricksha in town to bring him home over the long dirt road in the moonlight.

Each night Masae watched for her husband from the nursery window as she sang their daughter Hiroko to sleep. Hiroko, two years and nine months come the end of summer, was already developing her own idiosyncrasies. She fell asleep in one position only: curled up on her left side, right arm slung over the right half of her tiny bean-stuffed pillow, head burrowed under its left half. Masae didn't see how she could breathe, but she knew better than to tug away the pillow even if Hiroko was asleep.

Tonight, cranking open the window to feel the night breeze, Masae drew in a deep breath. With the climate so dry, the air had no real smell other than that of the dusty wooden sill over which she leaned. But Masae loved that instant when her face, dulled from the heat of day, first came into contact with the night air. She savored it so fully that if the cool breeze were a feather brushing her cheek, she could have counted its strands.

Two months ago, after the first enemy prisoners passed by, Masae had kept all the windows locked. Since then her vigilance had waned, but only slightly—enough to open a window, but not to leave it unattended. Even Koonyan, their heavy-set maid who came two afternoons a week, still unnerved her; the girl never spoke, merely taking in Masae's Japanese orders without any expression. Recently Masae dreamed that Koonyan turned toward her and revealed a face without features, as smooth and blank as an egg. She admitted this to Shoji, with a self-deprecating little laugh. "Nothing to be afraid of," he told her. "Hoh, behind that face she's busy thinking about her little pet birds!"

Shoji's wry comment referred to a company function two months ago, which they had attended shortly after the prisoner procession. It was a Western-style welcome dinner held in their honor, at someone's home in the main town. Masae was seated beside the company interpreter, an elderly Japanese man who had studied Chinese classics at Kyoto University. Shoji sat across the table from them, his chin partially obscured by a vase of thick-petaled indigenous flowers. Last year a prisoner had escaped, the interpreter told them with a lilting Kansai accent. This Chinese man had hidden in the dark on someone's pan-tiled roof, lying flat as a *gyoza* skin while the Army searched for him in the streets; he might have gone free if not for the Army's German shepherds. "See," Masae told her husband across the flowers, "it pays to play it safe!"

"But they're not overly antagonistic toward us," the interpreter had reassured them, "compared to occupied provinces I've seen. Tai-huen's been under one warlord or another for dynasties. Here their fo-cus is on small things, pet birds for example. Every household has a pet bird in a bamboo cage."

"Aaa, well, they're peasants," Shoji said benevolently. He had stud-ied global geological theory at Tokyo University, which held as much prestige as the interpreter's alma mater, and he was proud of his large-scale understanding of things.

"True, but it's not just that, I think. Sometimes the small focus is necessary. I myself find it crucial."

"Yes—no doubt." Shoji shot Masae a quick glance of confoundment over the flowers. It occurred to her that these fleshy petals might be indirectly related to a cactus species.

"Yes, it's crucial." A quality of sorrow in the interpreter's voice, deeper somehow than mere sympathy for the Chinese, threaded its way to Masae's sensibility through the muted clinks of silverware around her. "The immensity of this land. . . ."

At her window now, looking out over the darkening plain for the jig-gling light of Shoji's ricksha lantern, Masae's thoughts drifted out to-ward the great Pun'An Desert. She had never seen a desert; she imagined it much like these plains except hotter and bleaker, stripped of its occasional oak trees and the comforting motion of rippling grass. An endless stretch of sand where men weakened, and died alone. Masae, being from Hiroshima, had grown up by an ocean which had drowned thousands in storm seasons. Yet as a child she had sensed the water's expanse as full of promise—spreading out limitless before her, shifting, shimmering, like her future. She and her schoolmates had linked elbows and stood at the water's edge, digging their toes into the wet sand and singing out to sea at the tops of their voices: songs such as "Children of the Sea" or, if their mothers weren't around, the moun-taineering song that Korean laborers sang, "Ali-lan." She remembered the tug of her heart when, on the way to school, she had followed with

81

her eyes a white gull winging a straight line out to sea. But those were the impressions of youth. Masae was now at mid-life, mid-point—Hiroko had been a late child—and for the first time she sensed the inevitability of moving from sea to desert.

THE NEXT NIGHT, for the third night in a row, Hiroko demanded that her mother read *Tomo-chan Plants her Garden*. Masae sat on a floor cushion before the dark nursery window, while Hiroko perched on her lap and turned the pages when told. Each page showed, with predictable monotony, yet another brightly colored fruit or vegetable ballooning up magically from its seed, hovering above it like the genie in their *Arabian Nights* book. They certainly looked nothing like the meager produce their maid brought home from the open-air market: desert vegetables, Masae thought. The big *daikon* radishes, for example. She was serving them raw as all Japanese women did in the summer, finely grated and mounded on a blue plate to suggest the coolness of snow and water. But these radishes had no juicy crunch. They were as rubbery as boiled jellyfish and required rigorous chewing. Shoji didn't seem to notice—he was often exhausted when he came home—and Masae fancied lately that he was absorbing the radishes' essence. Since they had come to Tai-huen, something about him had shrunk in an indefinable way, as if an energy which once simmered right below the surface of his skin had retreated deep within his body.

Yet Shoji denied having any troubles, and laughed shortly at what a worrier she was. As long as Masae could remember, Shoji's laughs had been too long—about two ha-ha's past the appropriate stopping point. They had always irritated her, those laughs, but lately Shoji stopped way before that point as if to conserve them. She missed his long laughter now, the thoughtless abundance of it.

"The End," Masae concluded, slowly closing the book. Hiroko squirmed on her lap, and Masae could sense the wheels in her mind starting to turn, thinking up new questions about the story in order to postpone her bedtime. To deflect the questions, Masae picked her up and carried her to the window, upon which their faces were reflected in faint but minute detail, as if on the surface of a deep pool. The child's head gave off the warm scent of shampoo.

"Way out past those lights," she told her daughter, cranking open the window with her free hand, "is the desert, *hora!*" Their reflections twisted and vanished; coolness flowed in around them. A coyote howled in the distance.

"What's a dizzert?"

"Lots of sand, nothing else. No people. No flowers."

"Ne, how come?" This, turning around to squint up to her mother.

"It's too dry for anything to grow."

Hiroko digested this in silence; then, "Are there rice balls?"

"No. There's nothing out there in the desert."

"What about milk?"

"No."

"What about—" she twisted in Masae's arms to peer back at the nursery—"toys?"

"*No.*"

"How come?"

Masae drew a deep breath. At such times she felt like she was floundering in a churning river. She longed for Shoji—or any adult, for that matter—with whom she could follow a narrow stream of rational thought to some logical end.

"Mama told you why, remember?" she said. "You already know the answer. Yes, you do."

"The dizzert lost all its seeds!" Hiroko cried, tonight's story fresh in her mind. "You got to get some seeds. And then you can grow things." Masae left the matter alone.

After Hiroko fell asleep, she returned to the window. The stars neither glimmered nor winked; they lay flat on the sky in shattered white nuggets. The town lights were yellower, a cozy cluster of them glowing in the distance with a stray gleam here and there. She imagined blowing the lights out, with one puff, like candles.

Seeds. As a girl Masae had read a book on deserts, how it rained once every few years. After the rain, desert flowers burst into bloom only to die within two days, never seen by human eyes. Such short lives, ignorant of their terrible fate. She had wondered at the time how a seed could be trusted to stay alive in the sand; wouldn't it just dry up from years of waiting? In the driest, bleakest regions of the desert, who was checking whether flowers still bloomed at all? Aaa, Masae thought, this is what comes of keeping company with a child.

But one fact was indisputable: the Pun'An Desert was expanding. Shoji had mentioned it, only last night—spreading several centimeters each year, according to the latest scientific report. Killing the grass in its path like a conquering army. Wasn't it reasonable, then, that seeds were actually dying in this part of the world, leaving fewer and fewer of them to go around? An inexplicable sense of loss overwhelmed Masae. When Shoji's ricksha lantern bobbed into view, its light refracted through her tears and gleamed brighter than any evening star.

A PRISONER PROCESSION was coming. Masae heard its faint *tan tan tantaka tan* from the living room, where she sat on the floor reading a letter from her mother. She had assumed, since that one procession in the beginning of summer, that prisoners would always come by after sunset. But it was still afternoon. Koonyan, the maid, was still here—her blank, egg-shaped face had just peered in at her mistress as she glided silently down the hall—so it wasn't even five o'clock yet.

Masae was aware of the strange picture she must make to Koonyan, sitting in the middle of the floor while surrounded by perfectly good imported furniture. The company representative who arranged their move must have been an Anglophile; he had stocked the house with a modish array of brocaded ottomans and chaise lounges, even the bench made of black iron out in the garden. The Nakazawas could not relax in such chairs. They installed *tatami* matting on the concrete floors, and Masae had Koonyan sew floor cushions for all the rooms. Shoji bought a saw and shortened the legs of the Western style dining table so they could sit at ease during meals.

Don't you worry so much, her mother's letter said. Masae noted the slowness of the mail; the letter was dated August 10, 1942, more than four weeks ago. *We're all just fine. There've been only those two air raid alarms—not a single hit. Rationing, though, has gotten much more inconvenient, and not having nice meals on the table can be demoralizing, especially for your father! But I am confident in my heart that all this will have blown over by the time you sail back. I can imagine how Hiro-chan will have grown. . . .*

There was the heavy click of the back entrance doorknob turning, then Hiroko's high-pitched voice: "Mama—Mama, the festival's coming—" To Hiroko, who had experienced the Koinobori Festival just before moving to China, drums always meant festivals.

Masae followed her child as she ran toward the garden gate, passing through the flickering shade of the pine tree. When Hiroko got excited, her right arm always swung harder than her left. The habit had started back in Hiroshima. She had been carried about so often on the arm of one relative or another, her left arm curled around the back of someone's neck, that when she was set down she forgot to move her "neck" arm. "Mama, I want to go!" Hiroko wailed without turning

84

around. An image flashed through Masae's mind of a man pouncing, catlike, from the roof. But it faded. And she felt a sharp need to gaze at other living faces, even Chinese ones. She turned to Koonyan, who had followed her out, and nodded. Koonyan leaned a hefty shoulder into the solid weight of the wood, face impassive above her navy mandarin collar; Hiroko imitated her movements, grimacing. The rusty hinges yielded with a prolonged creak.

About forty men, dressed in khaki uniforms, shuffled toward them in three columns. Long shadows stretched out behind them, narrow and wavery like floating seaweed. Herding the prisoners were four Japanese guards with German shepherds at their heels, dogs as tall as Hiroko. "*Wan wan!*" shrieked Hiroko in delight, mimicking dog barks and leaning forward as far as Masae's grip on her hand would allow. "*Wan wan!*" The dogs' ears—huge black-tipped triangles of fur— flicked to attention, but otherwise the German shepherds ignored her, stalking past with the controlled intensity of wolves. One Japanese guard, noticing Masae's kimono, gave a curt nod; she acknowledged it with a slight bow. The Chinese stared ahead, their brown faces blurred with exhaustion and the dust of the plains.

Tan tan tantaka tan, tan tan tantaka tan, beat the little drum at the head of the line. Hiroko, eyes crinkled up with joy, let out a loud excited squeal. She began dancing; standing in place, bending and straightening her knees in jerks which didn't quite match the drum's rhythm. Her ponytail flopped limply on the top of her head.

One tall prisoner about Shoji's age looked over at Hiroko, brighteyed in her red sundress. The corners of his mouth stretched out in a wistful smile. One by one the others began to grin, and Masae had a jumbled impression of teeth: stained teeth, buck teeth, missing teeth. The prisoners turned their heads and kept looking at the dancing child as they passed by, wrists bound behind them with strips of cloth; Hiroko beamed back, thrilled by the attention of all those adults.

And as the columns of men grew small in the distance, Masae felt this moment shrink into memory, shriveling and gathering into a small hot point in her chest. A stray seed, she thought. It could have so easily been lost. Hiroko would not remember this, nor would the dead prisoners. *The immensity of this land. . . .* Ancient land, stretching out to desert beneath the blank blue sky of late summer.

Nominated by Tomás Filer

A MURDER OF CROWS

essay by DANIEL HENRY

from NORTHERN LIGHTS

THE CROW'S writhing body throws diamonds in the rare rainforest sunlight. The bird flies crazily—twisting, twirling, hiccuping—as if warning us or clowning out a declaration of war. It careens to the buffer-forest's edge and clings to a treetop where it screeches for hours. As the summer dusk gathers at midnight, the bird suddenly ceases its racket, ushering an undertow that tugs at our dreams through the night. So ends the first day of a siege that offers new insight into the collective term for crows—murder.

False Island is forty miles north of Sitka, Alaska, as the crow flies. The camp was built at the toe of what local foresters claim was once the largest clearcut in the world. A battered swath two to ten miles wide persists across 60 miles of Chichigof Island, on the northwestern coasts of the Tongass National Forest, where towering spruce were clearcut and replaced by tightly woven thickets of devil's club and red alder. Before it became a Forest Service retreat for the young and restless in 1979, False Island was a logging camp made up of a dozen herky-jerky ATCO trailers connected by a mile of solder. Standing apart from these aluminum worm-casings were a little red schoolhouse, a generator shed, a log house sewage plant, and assorted second-thought outbuildings.

Served by a whopping roadbuilding budget, the Forest Service built a web of roads which allowed loggers living at False Island to haul out enough trees to supply a boggling number of upscale Japanese subdivisions. But because they still liked the sound of wind rushing through trees and the way moss-piled carpets grew deep in a mature forest, the boys kept 20 acres of old growth "buffer" adjacent to one side of camp

86

and called it "the woods." The woods still shelter the mouth of Clear Creek into which hundreds of thousands of salmon replay their genetic destiny every summer.

This postage stamp forest hugs the pebbly shores of Jingleshell Cove on the Chichigof side of Peril Strait, a timid reminder of what was once an uninterrupted rainforest sprawling from northern California to the Alaska Peninsula. The squared-off patch of trees is a ghost of what struck naturalist John Muir as the "tropical luxuriance" he saw in the seamless woods. Nonetheless, its relative isolation and fecundity make the remnant grove a haven for animals. Shaggy brown bears still stroll and feed among fellow fauna in this hallowed space: mink, wolf, marten, deer, coyote, porcupine, birds, fish. Look. There, a dozen bald eagles glower over the broad tideflat from the mossy outstretched branches of the remaining 700 year-old Sitka spruce trees. There, four adult bears scoop humpies out of the creek while a sow leads a pair of cubs along a beach not sixty feet from employee quarters. Breathy explosions of killer whales prowling offshore ring among the surviving members of this token arboretum, still standing witness to the brief, reckless conquests exacted upon the neighborhood by itinerant humanity.

It is a dead calm midsummer's afternoon when a couple of pals and I watch the first crow barrel down Main Street, squawking out its primal alarm. Late lunch on a cable spool picnic table outside the cookshack. On this day most of the 80 workers in the Young Adult Conservation Corps camp are scattered throughout the Tongass on spike camps. Our ten-day missions are to build log picnic shelters and fish ladders, muck out the cross-Admiralty Island canoe trail, plant trees or survey the inventory trails in pristine stands being readied for harvest. In the end, we will return to False Island for a few days of showers, friends, and hot grub, then light out again for the backcountry. My official title is "Group Living Specialist," meaning that when the crews are in, I organize capture the flag, film fests, kayak trips, and community gardening; when they're out, I head up whoever's left to work on camp maintenance, hustle supplies off floatplanes and barges, stir sewage, and otherwise sustain camp survival on the island's remote shores. Crows are common visitors to camp, but not like the crazy one swooping by us, screeching its apocalyptic warning.

Two sounds of the second morning stand clear in my memory. The first is of the solitary crow perched in a treetop raucously cawing over and over in a clipped, repetitive cadence that comes to resemble the safety beep of a commercial truck backing up. The second sound is the harsh scrape of coarse feathers raking the air to interrupt our morning coffee before we could even see the squadron of a hundred crows turn a corner onto Main Street and blow past us. They scatter when they hit the trees, then join the sentinel bird in its tightly paced call. But the birds cry in different rhythms, creating a demonic clatter that builds throughout the day.

By midnight, enough crows have arrived to put one or more birds on all spruce boughs outsweeping into the camp fringe and along the beach. I hunch around a driftwood fire with friends swatting no-see-ums and appraising the shadowed crow streaks over our heads. In an hour's time, the crows' congregation assumes evolving forms: flying monkeys from Wizard of Oz, jet fighter packs, insect swarms. Isabel pokes the coals with her stick. Weird, she says. A convention without joy, like a funeral. But why—who's it for? She jabs her sword in the glowing eye, then retreats into murky light and a mounting barrage.

The raucous symphony builds to a stadium roar on the third day when camp director Pete and I walk one end of the grove to the other. Tens of thousands of crows have transformed our solemn woodland asylum into a clamorous, stinking squalor. Shit flies everywhere, as do feathers, piss, and corvid epithets screamed at full volume. When we get back to camp, a visiting green-shirter from the Sitka district office asks Pete if he thinks that there's anything we should do. Pete snorts. What? Call the cavalry?

Others around camp are letting the birds get to them. Quinn takes half of her lunchbreak to caw loudly and throw beach pebbles at the blaring black mass in the trees. Jay Blazo (so named after he dowsed a cooking fire with a half-can of Blazo white gas, then rolled away while his co-workers beat the flames out of his clothing) reports that he's acquired a headache from the ruckus. His friend, Whitebird, vouches for him by grimacing on demand. Whitebird is in camp recovering from an injury sustained while lighting his farts in threadbare jeans. Blazo's crew sneaked out of camp without him. They are my camp crew assigned to erecting a cement incinerator not far from the woods, so close-up exposure to the birds has prompted paranoia of cinematic proportions. Big Jim overhears their complaints and beams his ample, mischievous grin. He turns to show the shit-streaked barcode on the back of his jacket.

We are not alone in our preoccupation with this screeching black tide. Lone ravens and eagles perch on the periphery. A marten makes its rare appearance one morning in a bristling patch of wild celery at the forest's edge. Red-tailed hawks ride updrafts a thousand feet over the trees. Dozens of Steller's jays sit watching from the smaller trees in camp, oddly silent.

The favorite subject for breakfast discussion on the fourth day is the effect the crows are having on our sleep. One of two cooks, Michael, is as grouchy and sullen as the bald eagle we watched swoop down on a beached salmon that morning and, missing it, slam into a rootwad. He says that the crows' commotion last night even drowned out a Grateful Dead jam he'd cranked up on his Walkman. Michael's scowl is a sou'easterly slamming up the ragged coast to rip away any memory of blue sky. He's drunk a gallon of coffee since getting up at 4:30; his harangue is especially honed as we trancewalk within earshot. The upshot of Michael's compulsions is that his bad days are the camp's best. Our reward from his anger is a sumptuous spread: French toast in teetering columns, troughs of steaming home fries, fruit salad, link and soy sausage, fresh-squeezed grapefruit juice. Michael leans over the food, mumbling about having to eat crow to win back sleep. We nod our tacit agreement, bleary and irritated at the rising ranks of crows in the woods. The food helps. What happens after breakfast helps even more.

Big Jim is the first to leave the mess hall to face the day's work. Moments later the door opens and his shaggy blond head reappears. There's that smile again. Check it out, he says.

The rest of us, including Michael, do.

Drizzle leaks from a pregnant cloudbank scraping the treetops. There is a faint drumming on the ATCO roofs. A raven lands nearby, chuckling softly. We are swallowed in a sudden hush. The crows have vanished.

Or so we think. Closer inspection reveals thousands of muted black birds filling in the spaces of the forest like notes in a manic symphony score. Songbirds pick at berries and bugs in the clearcut tangle, gulls mew and scream over fish left on the tideflats, but the crow-ladened trees remain reticent until a few minutes before lunch.

Whitebird's face is ashen under his black bristles when he comes in for the lunchbreak. It's evil, come words between waxen lips. Consciously or not, he imitates the askew glare that Hitchcock commanded from Tippi Hedron's eyes in *The Birds,* pinned open in horror during a slashing winged attack. Evil, he repeats. Totally outta control. We listen. Pandemonium roars from the stand of old trees. We run into the woods for a closer look.

It is a hell-fight beyond our imagination.

Bodies rain from the trees. Dying birds hit the forest floor screaming like warriors startled by their final vulnerability. Their black breasts' normal gloss fades under blood and duff, pierced to the heart by beaks bearing ancient regards. We watch with grotesque fascination as silent cries issue from the twisting jaws of birds whose heads are attached to their bodies only by a strand of sinew. Many of the feathered shadows writhing on the ground are composed of two or three crows pinned to each other by their beaks and claws. Eyes hang by bloody bits of gristle. Some birds spin in silly circles as they attempt flight without one or both wings. Eviscera showers us with the life essence still wriggling out of it.

We carefully pick a route from treetrunk to treetrunk to avoid being hit by the shrieking black death clusters. Despite our caution, though, we can't escape splatters of blood flying everywhere, staining crimson Rorschachs into our clothing. It is the price for satisfying our morbid curiosity, to cloak ourselves in the blood of this killing place. When I realize that in my revulsion I've stopped breathing, I turn and beeline back to camp. Leave the birds to their own dark rituals.

The mad cacophony of bird battle continues in diminishing waves until late. After a while, we hear individual death cries over the white noise of war, punctuated by kamikaze bursts of discovery and destruction. Then, in the grey of Northern midnight, a feeble line of crows straggles out from the grove, crossing the Strait and away to other forests on other islands.

The victors leave us with death and ringing silence until a varied thrush breaks into burred fluting at the brightening dawn. The hush lulls me into the deepest sleep of the week, swaddled in a blanket of aural relief. Even Michael sleeps in, so breakfast comes late on the fifth day of this story. Whitebird refuses to work at the incinerator on account of vibes. I walk out with him to inspect the scene.

The few bent carcasses littering the worksite are clues which lead us into the big trees. A palpable stench punches us as we step into spruce cover. Usually viridescent, the mossy floor is heaped with black, broken bodies. In some places the dead are piled up nearly two feet deep. We daintily pick a route through the mounds until it is impossible to move without crushing carcasses underfoot. Before long, we're kicking them like autumn leaves, raising clouds of feeding insects in our wake. Two hawks swerve in from the beach to pick through the remains. We become aware of a bloody slick accumulating on our rubber boots. Whitebird pulls back, turns and heaves. We head back for breakfast.

Throughout the day, people sneak away to the woods to inspect the aftermath of the showdown. Isabel and Pete return with a story about a family of mink they had watched scampering among the bodies. The mother was dragging stiffened remains to her brood of youngsters who would emerge from under a deadfall to shred their gifts. Blazo claims to have watched a boar brown bear cuffing crow drifts like a novice golfer in a sand trap.

Big Jim nudges me awake on the morning of the sixth day. Michael is chopping onions to Creedence Clearwater in the kitchen, but no one else stirs. You gotta see this, Big Jim insists. What is it? He slits his eyes like a secret buddha and turns towards the woods. Gotta see it for yourself.

I've reflected on that morning many times over the years. It was a humbling glimpse into the tireless life force that binds us beyond species, habitat, motivation, or income. Epiphanies such as this one come in sudden, startling surprise packages; the shock of recognition lingers a lifetime. Whether I analyze or re-examine the event in the context of wildlife phenomenon, timber practices, life cycles, or cosmic connectedness, I keep coming back to this scene:

The site of a horrific massacre has been transformed into a verdant, glowing forest floor. Even the puddles of body fluids pumped out in the crows' last mortal moments have been sopped up by the deep moss. The occasional ink-hued feather scuttering in a whispered breeze contains the only clues to the week's carnage. Big Jim and I sit, mouths open, wordless.

Nominated by Northern Lights

MITCH

by ROBERT CREELEY

from SOLO 2

Mitch was a classmate
later married extraordinary poet
and so our families were friends
when we were all young
and lived in New York, New Hampshire, France.

He had eyes with whites
above eyeballs looked out
over lids in droll surmise—
"gone under earth's lid" was Pound's phrase,
cancered stomach?

A whispered information over phone,
two friends the past week . . . ,
the one, she says, an eccentric dear woman,
conflicted with son?
Convicted with ground

tossed in, one supposes,
more dead than alive.
Life's done all it could
for all of them.
Time to be gone?

Not since 1944–45
have I felt so dumbly, utterly,

in the wrong place at
entirely the wrong time,
caught then in that merciless war,

now trapped here, old, on a blossoming earth,
nose filled with burgeoning odors,
wind a caress, sound blurred reassurance,
echo of others, the lovely compacting
human warmths, the eye closing upon you,

seeing eye, sight's companion, dark or light,
makes out of its lonely distortions
it's you again, coming closer, feel
weight in the bed beside me,
close to my bones.

They told me it would be
like this but who could
believe it, not to leave, not to
go away? "I'll hate to
leave this earthly paradise . . ."

There's no time like the present,
no time in the present. Now it floats, goes out like a boat
upon the sea. Can't we see,
can't we now be company
to that one of us

has to go? *Hold my hand, dear.*
I should have hugged him,
taken him up, held him,
in my arms. I should
have let him know I was here.

Is it my turn now,
who's to say or wants to?
You're not sick, there are
certainly those older.
Your time will come.

In God's hands it's cold.
In the universe it's an empty, echoing silence.
Only us to make sounds,
but I made none.
I sat there like a stone.

Nominated by Pamela Stewart

THE FIRST MEN

fiction by STACEY RICHTER

from MICHIGAN QUARTERLY REVIEW

I'M RIDING UP an escalator with Roxy explaining how she's the worst mother in the world. Some of my students, I say, have really bad mothers, but she takes the cake. Roxy, who's a real cunt, says something along the lines of "you ungrateful whore" and storms off to Ship and Shore, which is retailese for Fat and Ugly.

I go to the Ladies Lounge and vomit then proceed to Lingerie to buy a couple of push-up bras on credit. Look, it isn't my fault that Teddy drinks too much, okay? I just want to say that. EVERYBODY ACTS LIKE EVERYTHING IS MY FAULT AND IT ISN'T MY FAULT. I hate it, hate it, hate it. And I wanted that perfume, that's why I lifted it. What do you want me to say? That it's a disease? I have news for you baby. Greed is not a disease.

A little later, an ugly clerk at The Sunglass Hut is explaining why these three hundred dollar glasses are ultimately *me* when Roxy swoops past with her nose in the air, jingling her car keys so I'll notice she's leaving without me. I can tell she wants me to run after her, but I'm not going to give her the satisfaction—I mean, is this any way to treat your own daughter? I'm stranded with no nutritional options but corn dogs and frozen yogurt and giant cinnamon buns that stink up all the stores west of The Gap. I've maxed out most of my cards. I am not drunk, I haven't scored in several days, nor have I been laid. I'm considering trying to go easy on drugs because of the children. Think of the children! That's what Roxy says, but give me one good reason why I should listen to her.

Besides, I do think of the children. Right now I'm thinking of Roger Wells, everyone calls him Pig Pen—cute. He's in my third period Health Ed class, and he sells me downers at a reduced rate in exchange for a guaranteed B+. This was a good deal for everyone until Pig Pen started skipping class entirely. How am I going to buy drugs when he won't fucking come to class? "It's no big deal, Miss Roberts. Whatever you say, Miss Roberts." That kid is a liar and a degenerate—B+ or not, I'm filling in the negative comment bubbles with a number two pencil on that one. I am TRYING to teach a unit on reproduction, very touchy vis à vis the school board, the PTA, the textbook company, and there are only so many things I'm authorized to say according to state law—the curriculum on this date is fully legislated. I keep repeating *abstinence, abstinence* when Pig Pen slinks in late and tosses a note on my desk that says I owe him big money. Through the window, I get a peek at his drones circling. This kid is a really bad kid.

You want to know how they get that bad? Some are born bad. Some of them have bad parents. Some of them watch too much MTV and it spoils them. You can spot the ones that have been corrupted by heavy metal music from the slogans on their t-shirts and their constant, vulture-like slouch. Some of them have been in accidents and received blows to the head. When they wake up, they're bad. Pig Pen may have been bad due to any of these influences, or he may have gone bad during a gym class trauma—getting picked last for a year, pantsing, taunts concerning penis size. It's been known to happen. One day they're little boys and girls, and the next they're criminals and drug addicts.

So after the bell rings I tell Pig Pen I need a few days to get the money together, and would he please get me some more of those good downers? For a while he had a pharmaceutical source and could obtain the best, best shit, and when I looked at him I swear I almost started to drool. Pig Pen said okay Miss Roberts.

God's honest truth, I was going to pay the kid. Good, bad, I didn't care, he had what I needed. Unfortunately I had to go and drop in on Roxy and have my entire head screwed up, a task that took her about twenty minutes. She's sitting in her kitchen, in a warm-up suit patterned after the British flag, trying to make me eat a pound cake. She's accusing me of having an eating disorder and keeps saying, "Let me look in your mouth, let me look in your mouth," as though I'm a farm animal she's thinking of buying. Then she puts a slice of cake with whipped cream and strawberries in syrup in front of me—a sort of witch test. If I don't eat it, I'm mentally sick. If I do, I'll turn into a fat slug like her.

I pick up the fork. Roxy informs me that I am a heathen, and that I have picked up the wrong fork. I pick up another fork. She sighs and wedges her lumpy hips more firmly in her chair, but after thirty-two years of this I'm certain that this fork is the one. I cut the cake into bite-sized pieces. I consume it daintily. I wait until she's running the insinkerator before I duck into the bathroom to vomit.

After that, she starts whining that we never go anywhere together so we make a date to go to the mall on Saturday. My friend Wanda won't talk to me anymore, but when she did, she used to say WHY DO YOU SPEND SO MUCH TIME WITH THAT WOMAN IF SHE DRIVES YOU CRAZY? But what she doesn't understand is that Roxy has accused me of taking her boyfriend Teddy out drinking when the truth is Teddy is an alcoholic and doesn't need anyone to "help" him drink. We went to the Golden Nugget once or twice, but HE called ME and asked for a ride. Shit. Do you want to know why I'm bad? My mother made me this way.

The upshot is that after the cake incident I was so stressed out I went to Rossingham's and bought four gold chains and a cubic zirconia tennis bracelet with instant credit and a small down payment and have Roxy to thank for this little spree. The next thing I know it's already Saturday and I'm broke, stranded at the mall, pausing in the food court to watch captive sparrows pecking crumbs off the floor. I think the smell lures them through the automatic doors and the poor things are too stupid to figure out how to get back out. Or, I don't know, maybe it's the greatest deal; maybe for a sparrow the mall is the lap of luxury, like living in the Hyatt for a human.

So I'm bird watching and calmly sipping my Diet Coke when I look up and who should be approaching? Not Pig Pen, thank God, but one of his worker drones, Seymour Jackson, to whom I'd given a D the year before in Biology. Seymour Jackson is a big white kid with a military crew-cut and arms that reach almost to his knees. He has the deadened, blank face of a jock but Seymour is not a jock because he's a bad boy and a drug dealer who smokes cigarettes incessantly. In class, he'd chew tobacco and spit into a Big Gulp cup that he liked to balance on the edge of my desk on his way out. Those of Seymour's peers not too frightened to refer to Seymour at all, refer to Seymour as "Action."

The way it goes for high school teachers these days is you generally don't want to chitchat with kids you've given a D, particularly strapping lads who work for an organization to whom you owe money for narcotics. Nevertheless, Action Jackson comes right up and looks at me—just looks. Very mean. Very tall.

"Miss Roberts?" He seems confused.

"What can I do for you, Seymour?"

"You're at the mall?"

Let me tell you a little bit about these kids. They're not bright. They sniff nail polish remover and drive around with handguns tucked under their registration slips. They wear sunglasses in the rain and get gum stuck in their braces. In my class they think it's really funny to act like a retarded mental idiot when I call on them. There are no class clowns anymore—the youth of today are too dim-witted for wisecracking. When I see the instructions "shake and pour" on a carton of orange juice I think thank God, because these kids are in desperate need of instructions. So I say to Action, enunciating clearly: "Yes, Seymour. I am at the mall."

He's drumming his hands on his stomach, rolling his head around in a weak imitation of Stevie Wonder. Teenage boys, Jesus Christ. They can't hold still for a second and they can't look you in the eye. You can practically smell the hormones steaming from them—it's repellent, but at the same time it's a struggle not to take them home and fuck their brains out. I AM NOT referring to Brandon Murray here. Brandon Murray is a pathological liar who is "at risk" and any charges he's made against me should be regarded as impeachable fantasy.

Then Action wants to sit down. "Miss Roberts, Miss Roberts, can I sit here a minute?" What am I supposed to say? I am thinking this kid might have a gun in his jeans. I owe seven bills and some change to Pig Pen, which isn't all that much, considering these guys drive Camrys and carry cell phones in their backpacks, but they watch a lot of TV, a lot of movies, and they've picked up all manner of bullshit about loyalty, manhood, honor, prompt payment.

"Miss Roberts," he tosses a pack of cigarettes on the table, then his backpack, then a clump of keys with a little pot pipe on the ring. "That book you made me read, the one about the cave men. . . ."

"They're called *Homo erectus*, Seymour."

"Homo whatever. Look, I know I didn't pay attention in class, but I keep thinking about it. The whole thing about him hunting giant tree sloths and adapting and working in groups. . . ." Action's foot is going up and down as if it were electrified. It's possible he's on speed, but he's so hyper to begin with it's difficult to tell. He's puffing a cigarette too, pinching the filter really hard, like he wants to prevent something from escaping. "I keep thinking," he's saying, "about the acquisition of language."

"Hey Action. Do you have anything for me?"

"Like what?"

"Something powdered. Or in capsule form."

Action drums on the tabletop. He's moving so much of his body in such a fitful manner that looking at him is like watching something under a strobe light. "I can't do it Miss Roberts," he finally says. "Pig Pen says you gotta pay up first."

"What are you on right now? Can you get some for me?"

"Right now?"

"Yeah, right now."

"Okay," he says. "Wait here."

Action walks around to the other side of the carousel, by the booth where they sell personalized Barbie books imprinted with your child's name. It looks like he's talking on his cell phone, but I'm not sure. I'm thinking that if I manage to escape with my life, I might go to Dillard's and buy some Lancome eye shadow in smoky gold. Also, if I manage to escape with my life as well as score some drugs, I'll buy a pound of chocolates and eat them without vomiting.

After a few minutes Seymour comes back with a styrofoam cup in each hand. As he walks across the food court, I detect a bulge under his left arm, through his warm-up jacket. This is bad news. Seymour occasionally seems nice and vulnerable, like a kid, but the truth is he's also young in the sense that he doesn't understand how dangerous he is. It's too bad Roxy ditched me, because I'm thinking it might be a good idea to have already made an exit myself.

"Here you go, Miss Roberts." Seymour places one of the styrofoam cups in front of me and tucks his long arms under the table. The cup is half full of black liquid.

"What the hell is it?"

"Espresso. Rocket fuel of the gods."

"That's all you've got for me?"

"Hey. It's stronger than you think."

"Seymour, I have to go now." I gather my bags. Action scoots his chair over to my side of the table and touches my arm—very gentle. Very soothing.

"You can't go just yet, Miss Roberts. You gotta wait a while."

"Because. . . ."

"You gotta answer me about *Homo erectus,* okay? I read that First Man book and it was freaking me out." He's leaning toward me, suddenly calm, patient. There's something almost paternal about him and if you knew Action you would be terrified by this also. "I mean, it says that in monkeys, feelings go straight into the brain, right? Like an injection."

"There's something called the limbic system, Seymour. Fear, pleasure, pain."

"The reptile brain!"

"Sorta, right. Seymour, I have to go."

"Wait." His hand is on my knee, not in a sexy way, but in an anchoring way. "*Homo erectus*—he added another step. Like, a filter, right?"

"More or less. Speech centers. Symbolic thinking. Like, if I say the word 'cup' you can think of a generic cup, this cup on the table, whatever, and your brain sorts through the possibilities and figures out what I'm talking about. Ta da, you've got language. You and I communicating. Understand?"

"And this is like, an amazing leap, right? That book said it took a million years."

"Fuck, Seymour. I don't know how long it took. I wasn't there."

Seymour's big face goes slack. He's disappointed, but what do you want me to say? I'm not even trained in science but the district is so strapped that half of us cross-teach. My field is Spanish and I'm a licensed family counselor. For some reason the district has declared I'll teach Health, Biology, and Remedial Math. I am, however, familiar with the book Seymour is referring to, *The First Men,* a title in the Time-Life series I assign as extra credit when a student is failing because it has a lot of pictures. It also happens to have been written by Edmund White, father of the gay literary renaissance and author of a great biography of Jean Genet, a bad boy if ever there was one. If he could ever learn French, I'm sure Seymour would have gotten along great with Jean Genet.

His cell phone is ringing. "Will you please excuse me?" The more polite Action is, the more I figure I'm in trouble. He turns away but keeps his foot on top of my shoe—I have to pretend to ignore this. The more I act like everything is cool, the more likely it is that everything WILL be cool. I'm beginning to think, however, that I'm not going to score any drugs off Seymour on this particular day.

100

He's on the phone saying *uh huh, uh huh*. The way he looks at me with one eye, his body tense but motionless—it's giving me a chill. It's as though every trace of the little boy has been precipitated out of him and what remains is cool and gray. He reminds me of a pair of stiletto heels I tried on in Dillard's. When was that? Less than an hour ago.

"Okay," he says, hanging up the phone. "You're going to have to come with me, Miss Roberts."

"I have a lot of people waiting for me upstairs. My ex-husband. He's a cop."

"You're going to have to hook up with them later, Miss Roberts. I'm really, really sorry about this."

There's a car and then another car parked by a dumpster. Action nods at a pair of kids I haven't had in my class and urges me into the back of an Econoline van, license plate PMD 525. The two guys in front look like brothers—weak chins, slicked hair, sunken cheeks smothered in clumps of cystic acne. Both are so thin that their bones show through their clothes, but it's not like I could take them. They would have weapons.

"You boys," I ask, "do you go to Salpointe?"

They are not saying anything to me. They are not even turning around and acknowledging that I've spoken.

Action climbs in the back beside me and encourages me to buckle up. I feel he wants this not for safety, but to hold me immobile.

"Hey," I say, "I can get some stuff for your face that'll give you the complexion of a baby—my esthetician makes it. You can't buy it in stores."

The boy in the passenger seat twists around and fixes me with dull, sleepy eyes. His face looks like it got pinched by the forceps on the way out, and right where the tongs would have gone, there's a particularly nasty jumble of welts and pus.

"Miss Roberts," says Action, "would you mind keeping quiet?"

"This stuff is a miracle. If you boys hurt me, you'll throw away any chance of ever clearing up your skin."

"Hey, Miss Roberts. . . ." Action sounds pissed.

"And I know how devastating acne can be for kids your age. Okay. I'm through."

The boys start up the van and it feels like we're driving in circles. I can't see outside because the windows are covered with aluminum foil, though I could see through the windshield if Action would scoot over.

Action is on the cell phone again. He's calm, gliding in his movements, and I know this isn't good. He whispers something to the driver, then turns to me.

"We've gotta go see Pig Pen, okay Miss Roberts? You've gotta give him the money now, today."

"Give me the phone, Seymour."

"I'm not allowed."

"Give it to me or else you're expelled."

"I got expelled already."

"I can get you back in. Seymour. Are you listening to me?"

"It's not my choice, Miss Roberts. We got certain agreements between us. We use language to make agreements in order to do business. We're working together like *Homo erectus* did to hunt the wooly mammoths. I'm right about that, aren't I?"

"Yes, Seymour."

"You didn't know I was smart, did you?"

"You're a very bright boy."

"Then why'd you give me the D?"

"Because you didn't do the reading, you didn't take the tests, you didn't come to class. You left tobacco spit on my desk and bothered that girl Shelly, by always asking her if she was wearing a wig. Seymour, look at me." Seymour has started to vibrate again, subtly, in the fingers and feet. "I don't have the money."

The van is no longer traveling in circles. We could easily be out in the desert. People die in the desert all the time—hikers, thieves, Mexicans dodging immigration. They find them days, weeks or years later, beneath palo verde trees, huddled in pathetic disks of shade.

"Do you want to go to the prom? I could get you back into school. Take whoever you want. You could take Shelly."

Action scratches his ear and stares at the foil over the window. After a minute he lights up another cigarette. "Miss Roberts," he says, "I gotta ask you this thing about evolution. Millions of years of things building up—fire, language, hunting, society. I mean, all those stone tools, people trying to form words and their mouths aren't big enough or something. It all builds up to what? To me, like, riding in this van, talking to you?"

"Listen, Seymour. I don't have the money."

He looks away and pats at his hair cautiously, as though it were a toupee. "I know that, Miss Roberts."

"Call my mother—Roxy Ingram. She'll pay Pig Pen."

"Pig Pen already spoke to Roxy, Miss Roberts. She said she wasn't going to pay your debts no more. She said to tell you."

The van makes a right. After a while the ride turns bumpy and I'm almost certain we're on a dirt road. The sun pouring in the windshield is very bright. We all rock from side to side in our seats, the four of us looking very crisp, all the stains on our clothes visible, all of our wrinkles and pimples standing out in the light as though we were under a microscope, being examined for the defect that keeps our mothers from loving us.

"The thing that bothers me though," Action's eyes list sideways to some pensive arena, "is what it means. You know? Man evolving from guys with big jaws and shit—is that, what, science? x = y or whatever? Or is it some kind of miracle?"

Action is a handsome kid. His skin is dewy and he works out at the gym, I guess, because his arms are big and he doesn't have that inchoate, half-formed look a lot of juniors have. There's something oddly beautiful about the way he can't sit still and can't complete a thought and can't finish exhaling before he inhales, and even though it's likely he'll spend most of his life in jail, and fucking deserves it, at this point in his development it seems entirely obvious that he's a wonder of creation anyway—graceful and predatory, like a shark.

"Yeah, Seymour, I think it's a miracle. I think it's a miracle and a marvel that you've evolved to the point where we can sit here discussing evolution, even as you're driving me out to the middle of nowhere to stab me or shoot me or suffocate me with a couch cushion."

"Ha!" He sucks on his cigarette with deep satisfaction. "I thought so. I thought I was a miracle."

Action leans against the door so I can finally see outside. We're in the desert, clipping past saguaro and cholla, weird plants that look like freaks of evolution themselves. At least I can see the sky, rushing toward us, so blue I feel like if I took a swipe at it, pigment would come off on my hand.

"It's not just you, Seymour," I say. "It's me. I'm a miracle too."

He isn't listening. He's making funny noises with his mouth that are probably meant to mimic the sounds an electric guitar makes on the radio. I think the song is *Back in Black*. Also, he's playing a set of air drums and vibrating his knees, both of them, up and down with astonishing speed. I rip the foil off the window. We're moving through a valley carpeted with beautiful, thorny plants, about half of them dead. It's sleepy and still. There's a different time scale in the desert; things

103

move slowly. Saguaro cacti don't sprout their first arms for a hundred years, and even then they're just adolescents.

The van rolls to a stop. The two boys in front twist around and look at me eagerly, like I'm suddenly going to put on a big show or something. Action opens the door and ushers me out to a place that's saved from being described as the middle of nowhere by very little—just the foundation to a house that was either never built or burned to the ground long ago. There's a border of concrete with four steps leading up a dirt lot—a rectangle filled with weeds and some bleached beer cans. It's an island of nothing in the middle of the desert, which is, as always, surprisingly green and filled with motion. I used to like to play in the desert when I was a kid but now I'd rather stay indoors; out here, without any people, everything seems strangely removed, like I'm taking in the view through a veil. The wind reminds me of other times I've felt the wind. The sun could be on film. And all the different plants growing in the dirt. They all have names.

"Is he going to?" The driver says this as though I'm not there.

"Could you do me a favor, Miss Roberts?" Action, again, is smooth and steady, taking my hand as the wind blows his shirt tight against his torso. In other times he would have been the model for a Greek statue, a Roman foot soldier, a quarterback, the one who invented the spear. Even now I can see that he's in his element, gliding. Nothing, for him, is veiled. "Could you go up there?" he says to me. "Would you mind please climbing up those steps now?"

I watch the wind blowing around scrub and trash on the little platform. Above, white clouds drift.

I start climbing. These boys aren't going to hurt me. These boys are good boys. These boys will let me go.

Nominated by The Michigan Quarterly Review

THE SHERIFF GOES TO CHURCH

fiction by ROBERT COOVER

from CONJUNCTIONS

THE STREETS OF THE TOWN are empty and silent and hotly burnished by the noonday sun. Into them on a coalblack horse now rides a lone figure all outfitted in black with silver spurs and sixshooters and a gold ring in one ear. Former sheriff and bandit, a drifter, now a man on a mission. The woman he loves has been condemned to hang at high noon on the morrow, and he cannot let it happen. From under the broad brim of his slouch hat he warily watches, feeling watched, the windows and rooftops, the corners of things. Expecting trouble. The mare seems edgy, too, rolling her head fretfully, biting at the bit. Well, she's an outlaw horse, has likely never set hoof in this town before except on illegal business, she probably has good reason for unease.

In the center of town across from the saloon, a fat mestizo with a missing ear and a tall squint-eyed man with droopy handlebars and a bald head tattooed with hair are testing the trapdoor of the gallows, using a noosed goat, not by the appearance of it for the first time. Yo, sheriff! the man with the tattooed hair calls out, dragging the goat into position. Howzit hangin?

He nods at them and watches the limp goggle-eyed goat drop, then walks the mare cautiously over to the jailhouse. So he's the sheriff again. Yes, he's wearing his silver badge once more, he discovers. The one with the hole in it. Must have found it somewhere. Stands out on his black shirt in a way it never did on his white one.

105

There's a poster outside the jailhouse door announcing the hanging, with a portrait, where his portrait used to be, of the schoolmarm staring sternly out at all who would dare stare back. He is shaken by the intensity of her gaze, and the pure gentle innocence of it, and the rectitude, and he knows he is lost to it.

He hitches the mare to the rail there, and though she is skittish and backs away, her eyes rolling, tugging at her tether, he needs her for what he must next do. He unhooks his rifle from the saddle horn. I'll jest be a minnit and then we'll hightail it outa here, he says softly, stroking her sweaty neck to calm her, and he enters the jailhouse ready for whatever happens.

But nothing does. The jailhouse is empty, except for an old codger with an eyepatch, slumped in the wooden swivel chair, wearing a deputy's badge on his raggedy red undershirt. There is a thick river of scar running through his gray beard, darkly stained with tobacco juice, and his lone eye is red with drink. Hlo, sheriff, he drawls, trying to stand. Glad yu're back. Yu're jest in time t'hang that rapscallious hoss thief yerself. He chortles, then falls back into the swivel chair, takes a swig from a whiskey bottle, belches, offers it out. Yer health, sheriff!

Whar is she? he says.

The prizner? They tuck her over t'the saloon t'shuck her weeds offn her'n scrub her down afore her hangin.

The saloon?

Yup, well they got soap'n water over thar and plentya hep in spiffyin her up. The boys wuz plannin t'rub her down good with goose grease'n skunk oil after, polish her up right properlike. He's already at the door and there's a pounding in his temples that's worse than snakebite. Hey, hole up, sheriff! Ain't that a outlaw hoss out thar?

Mebbe. I'll check into it. Yu stay here'n keep yer workin eye on that whuskey bottle.

I aim to.

The mare is wild-eyed and frothing, rearing against her hitching rope, so he lets her go. Stay outa sight, he whispers to her as he unties her. This wont take long. I'll whistle yu when we're set t'bust out. The horse hesitates, pawing the ground, whinnying softly, but he slaps her haunches affectionately and, glancing back over her shoulder at him, she slips away into the shadows behind the jailhouse.

The object of his quest is not in the saloon either. It's quiet in there, four men playing cards, a couple more at the bar, a puddle of water in the middle of the floor where a bucket of soapy water stands, a lacy

106

black thing ripped up and hung over its lip. The men at the bar are laughing and pointing at the bucket or else at the wet long-handled grooming brush beside it. That goddamn humpback! one of them says, hooting.

Hlo, sheriff, grins the bartender, a dark sleepy-eyed man of mixed breed with half a nose. Wellcum back. Whut's yer pizen?

An argument breaks out at the card table, the air fills with the slither of steel coming free of leather, shots ring out, and a tall skinny man with spidery hair loses most of his jaw and all else besides, slamming against the wall with the impact before sliding in a bloody heap to the floor. Looks like they's a chair open fer yu, sheriff, says the man who shot him, tucking his smoking derringer back inside his black broad-cloth coat. Set yer butt down and study the devil's prayerbook a spell.

I aint a sportin man. Whut's happened t'the prizner?

Yu mean that dastardly hoss thief? Haw. Caint say. He lets fly a brown gob of tobacco juice at a brass spittoon, and it crashes there, making the spittoon rattle on its round bottom like a gambling top. She might be over t'doc's fer a purjin so's t'git her cleaned up inside as smart as out, though after her warshin in here, I misdoubt she needs it.

The others laugh at this. Naw, I think doc musta awready seed her, says the barkeep. He was in here a spell ago sniffin his finger.

Probly then, laughs another, they tuck her up t'the schoolhouse fer a paddlin.

Whut's that got t'do with bein a hoss thief?

Nuthin. It's jest fer fun. Give her summa her own back. And they all whoop and howl again and slap the bar and table.

He pushes out through the swinging doors, his blood pounding in his ears and eyes. Can't recollect where the doctor lives, if he ever knew, so he heads for the schoolhouse. On his way over, he hears a banging noise coming from a workshop back of the feed store. It's a tall ugly gold-toothed carpenter knocking out a pine coffin. Howdy, sheriff, he says, lifting the coffin up on its foot. Jest gittin ready t'cut the lid. Inside, on the bottom, there is a crude line drawing of a stretched-out human figure, no doubt done by tracing around a person lying there. One of the faces from the hanging posters has been cut out and pasted in the outline of the head and nails have been driven in where the nipples would be. The arms go only to the elbows (probably her hands were folded between the nails) but the legs are there in all their forked entirety. I reckon it should oughter fit her perfect. Whuddayu think?

107

I think yu should oughter burn it.

The schoolhouse is not where he remembered it either. Instead, he comes on a general dry goods and hardware store in that proximate neighborhood and he stops in to ask if she's been seen about.

Sheriff! Whar yu been? cries the merchant, a round bandylegged fellow with a black toupee and his nose pushed into his red face. They's been a reglar plague a hellraisin bandits pilin through here since yu been gone! Jest look what they done t'my store! Shot up my winders, killt my staff, stole summa my finest goods'n splattered blood'n hossshit on all the rest! Yu gotta do sumthin about this! Whut's a sheriff fer ifn honest folk caint git pertection!

That's a question I aint got a clear answer to, he says, staring coldly into the fat merchant's beady eyes. Right now I'm trying t'locate a missin prizner.

Whut, yu mean that ornery no-account barebutt hoss thief? She aint missin. Yer boys wuz by here a time ago with her, plumb cleaned me outa hosswhips'n hoe handles, she was in fer a grand time. I think they wuz headed fer the stables. Yu know. Scene a the crime. He turns to leave, but the merchant has a grip on his elbow and a salacious grin on his round red face. I gotta tell yu, sheriff, I seen sumthin I aint never seed before. He leans toward him, his cold fermented breath ripe with the stink of rot and mildew. She wuz, huh! yu know, he snickers softly in his ear. She wuz cryin!

He tears free from the merchant's greasy grip and strides out the door onto the wooden porch, his spurs ringing in the midday hush. They could be anywhere. There's a dim shadowy movement over in the blacksmith's shed, but that's probably his horse pacing about. He should probably just go back to the jailhouse and wait for them. But then the white church steeple beckons him. She gave him a Bible once, he recalls. They'll have to take her there sooner or later if she wants to go, and she surely will. There's probably a law about it.

He is met inside the church doors by the parson, or a parson, standing in a black frock coat behind a wooden table with a Bible on it, a pair of ivory dice (REPENT, says a tented card beside them, AFORE YU CRAP OUT!), a pistol and a collection plate. Howdy do, sheriff, he says, touching the brim of his stovepipe hat. He's a tall ugly goldtoothed man with wild greasy hair snaking about under the hat and a drunkard's lumpy nose, on the end of which a pair of wirerimmed spectacles is perched like two pans of a golddust balance. Wellcum t'the house a the awmighty. Yu're jest in time fer evenin prayers!

I aint here fer prayin. I'm lookin fer a missing prizner.

Yu mean that jezebel hoss thief? She gone missin? A leather flap behind the parson blocks his view but he can hear the churchgoers carrying on inside, hooting and hollering in the pietistical way. Well she's probly in thar, ever other sinner is.

Thanks, revrend, he says, and heads on in, but the parson grabs him by the elbow. The pistol is cocked and pointed at his ear. Whoa thar, sheriff. I can't let yu go in without payin.

I tole yu, I aint here fer the preachin, I'm on sheriffin bizness.

Dont matter. Yu gotta put sumthin in the collection plate or I caint let yu by.

I aint got no money, he says firmly, staring down the gun barrel. And I'm goin in thar.

Dont hafta be money, says the parson, keeping the pistol pointed at his head but letting go of his elbow to tug at his reversed collar so as to give his Adam's apple more room to bob. Them sporty boots'll do.

No. Gonna need them boots. If he just walked on in, would the preacher shoot him in the back? He might.

Well how about that thar beaded injun scalp then? He hesitates. He doesn't know why he wears it. For good luck maybe. Like a rabbit's paw. But he's not superstitious. And it doesn't even smell all that good. Awright, he says, and he cuts it off his gunbelt with his bowie knife and tosses it in the collection plate, where it twists and writhes for a moment before curling up like a dead beetle.

Now I'll roll yu fer them boots, ifn yu've a mind to, grins the parson goldenly, picking up the dice and rattling them about in his grimy knobknuckled hand, but he pushes on past him under the flap into the little one-room church, the preacher calling out behind him: I'm sorely beseechin the good lawd that yu localize that snotnose gallows bird, sheriff! Dont wanta lose her at the last minnit and set all hell t'grievin!

Veiled gas lamps hang from blackened beams in the plank-walled room, the air hazy with smoke and smelling of stale unwashed bodies and the nauseous vapors of the rotgut whiskey—drunk, undrunk and regurgitated—being served like communion from boards set on pew backs. Hanging in the thick smoke like audible baubles are the ritual sounds of singing spittoons, dice raining upon craps tables, the clink of money, soft slap of cards, the ratcheting and ping of fortune wheels and slot machines, the click click click of the roulette ball, and amidst the zealous cries of the high rollers, oaths are being sworn and glasses smashed and pistols fired off with a kind of emotional abandon. Are yu all down, gentamin? someone hollers, and another cries out: Gaw-damighty, smack me easy! Somewhere in the church, behind all the smoke and noise, he can hear the saloon chanteuse singing about a magical hero with a three-foot johnnie, now hung and gone to glory, her voice half smothered by the thick atmosphere. Sweat-stained hats hang in parade on hooks along the walls under doctrinal pronounce-ments regarding spitting and fair dealing, mounted animal heads, dusty silvered mirrors which reflect nothing and religious paintings of dead bandits and unclothed ladies in worshipful positions, but the only sign anywhere of the one he's looking for is one of the posters an-nouncing tomorrow's hanging nailed up over a faro table, the portrait obscenely altered. BUCK THE TIGER! it says, and a crude drawing shows where and how to do so.

He turns a corner (there is a corner, the room is getting compli-cated) and comes upon a craps table with strange little misshapen dice, more like real knucklebones, which they likely are. Set down, sheriff, and shake an elbow, says the scrubby skew-jawed fellow in dun-colored rags and bandanna headband who is working the table, a swarthy and disreputable character who is vaguely familiar. His bro-ken arm is in a rawhide sling, its hand fingerless, and there's a fresh red weal across his rough cheeks, the sort of cut made by a horsewhip. Here, he can no longer hear the chanteuse; instead, at the back by the big wheel of fortune, there is a choral rhythmic rise and fall of drunken whoops, so it's likely she's back there somewhere. Not someone he cares to see just now. Go ahead'n roll em, sheriff, says the wampus-jawed scrub, wagging the stump at the end of his broken arm. Them sad tats is mine. Wuz.

Aint got no stake. But dont I know yu from sumwhars? With his good hand, the halfbreed flashes a bent and rusty deputy's badge, hid-den away in his filthy rags. Whut? Yu my deppity?

I wuz. But I lost my poke'n then some in that wicked brace over by the big wheel. I hafta work fer this clip crib now.

Whar's the prizner then?

Well we lost her, too.

Lost her—?!

T'that hardass double-dealin shark over thar, the dodrabbid burglar whut operates this skin store. He's the one whut give me this extry el-bow and my own bones t'flop when I opened my big mouth after ketchin him with a holdout up his sleeve. He sees him now, enthroned behind a blackjack table under a glowing gas lamp, over by a tall wheel of fortune, an immense bald and beardless man in a white suit and ruffled shirt with blue string tie and golden studs, wearing blue-tinted spectacles smack up against his eyes. He sits as still and pale as stone, nothing moving except his little fat fingers, deftly flicking out the cards. The rhythmic whooping is coming from there and may be in response to the cards being dealt. The motherless asshole tuck us fer all we had, sheriff. Got the prizner in the bargain.

Yu done wrong. She warnt a stake.

I know it.

What's he done with her?

Well. His ex-deputy hesitates. It aint nice. He glances uneasily over his shoulder. Best go on over thar'n see fer yerself.

There's an icy chill on his heart and a burning rage at the same time and he feels like he might go crazy with the sudden antipodal violence of his feelings, but he bites down hard and collects himself and sets his hat square over his brow and drops his hands flat to his sides and straightens up his back and lowers his head and, with measured strides, makes his way over toward the glowing fat man at the blackjack table. The room seems to have spread out somewhat or to be spreading out as he proceeds, and there are new turns and corners he must bear around, sudden congestions of loud drunken gamblers he must thread his way through, and sometimes the blackjack dealer seems further away than when he first set out, but he presses on, learning to follow not his eyes but his ears (those whoops and hollers), and so is drawn in time into the crowd of men around the blackjack table. What is provoking their rhythmic hoots, he sees when he gets there, is the sight of the schoolmarm stretched out upon the slowly spinning wheel of fortune, her black skirts falling past her knees each time she's upside down. He tries not to watch this but is himself somewhat mesmerized by the rhythmic rising and falling, revealing and concealing, of the schoolmarm's dazzling white knees, the spell broken only when he realizes that she is gazing directly at him as she rotates with a look compounded of fury, humiliation and anguished appeal. It is a gaze most riveting when she is upsidedown and the whoops are loudest, her eyes then blackly underscored by eyebrows as if bagged with grief, her nose with its flared nostrils fiercely horning her brow between them, the exposed knees above not unlike a bitter thought, and a reproach.

He steps forward, not knowing what he will do, but before he can reach the table, a tall bald man with tattooed hair pushes everyone

111

aside and, tossing down a buckskin purse, seats himself before it. Dole me some paint thar, yu chislin jackleg! he bellows with drunken bravado, twirling the ends of his handlebar moustache. He's seen him before, testing out the gallows, except that since then he's acquired a wooden leg. His partner, the one-eared mestizo, now wearing a bearclaw in his nose and an erect feather in a headband, hovers nearby with his pants gaped open. I'm aimin t'win summa that gyrating pussy fer my bud'n me, and I dont wanta ketch yu spikin, stackin, trimmin, rimplin, nickin, nor ginnyin up in no manner them books, dont wanta see no shiners, cold decks, coolers, nor holdouts, nor witness no great miracles a extry cards or a excess a greased bullets. Yu hear? So now rumble the flats, yu ole grifter, and cut me a kiss.

The dealer, holding the deck of cards in his soft smooth bejeweled hands as a sage might clasp a prayerbook, has sat listening to all this bluster with serene indifference, his hairless head settled upon his layered folds of chin like a creamy mound of milkcurd, eyes hidden behind the skyblue spectacles which seem almost pasted to them. The tinted spectacles, he knows, are for reading the backs of doped cards, the polished rings for mirroring the deal, a pricking poker ring no doubt among them, and his sleeves and linen vest are bulked and squared by the mechanical holdout devices concealed within. When, so minimally one can almost not see the movement, he shuffles, cuts and deals, he seems to use at least three different decks, crosscutting a pair of them, and the deal is from the bottom of the only deck in view at any one time, or at least not from the top.

The squint-eyed man with the tattooed hair rises up and kicks his chair back with his wooden leg. I jest come unanimously to the conclusion yu been cheatin, he shouts as the dealer calmly slides the man's leather purse into his heap of winnings, then takes up the deck to reshuffle it, so smoothly that the deck seems like a small restless creature trapped between his soft pale hands, his own child perhaps that he is fondling. Behind him, the schoolmarm, bound to the fortune wheel, grimly turns and turns, though now, with the bald man on his feet, or foot, the rhythmic whooping dies away.

Easy, podnuh, whispers the one-eared mestizo, his hand inside his pants. He spits over his shoulder, away from the dealer. He's awmighty fast, that sharper. Don't try him. It aint judicious.

Shet up, yu yellabellied cyclops'n gimme room! the bald man roars. He stands there before the bespectacled dealer, legs apart and leaning on his pegleg, shoulders tensed, elbows out, hands hovering an inch from his gunbutts. I'm callin yer bluff, yu flimflammin cartload a hossshit!

A hole opens up explosively in the bald man's chest like a post has been driven through it, kicking him back into the crowd, the dealer having calmly drawn, fired and reholstered without even interrupting his steady two-handed shuffle of the cards. He sets the deck down and spreads his plump palms to either side as though to say: Anyone else care to try their luck?

He makes certain his sheriff's badge is in plain view, tugs at the brim of his hat, hitches his gunbelt and steps into the well-lit space just abruptly vacated by the peglegged man with the tattooed hair. He picks up the fallen chair, watching the dealer closely, and sets it down in front of the blackjack table, but remains standing. I'm askin yu t're-turn me back my prizner, he says quietly. He has a hunch about the dealer now, something he grows more convinced of the longer he stands there studying him. She warnt a legal bet. Yu knowed that. I may hafta close this entaprize down.

His weedy ex-deputy with the busted arm leans close to the dealer who seems, though his thick lips do not move, to whisper something in his crumpled ear. He sez he dont spect that'll happen, says the ex-deputy out the side of his mouth. Behind the mountainous fat man, the revolving schoolmarm's white knees rise into view like a pair of ex-pressionless stockingcapped puppets, then fall into curtained obscurity, over and over, but he steels himself to pay them no heed, and to ignore as well her burning gaze, for now he must think purely on one thing and one thing only. He sez ifn yu want back that renegade hoss thief, yu should oughter set yerself down'n play him a hand fer her.

Caint. Aint got no poke. Yes, he's sure of it now. It's why he sits so still. Listening. To everything. His ears thumbing the least sound the way his pink-tipped sandpapered fingers caress the cards. Behind those spectacles, the man is blind.

Well whut about yer boots? suggests the ex-deputy. Or yer weep-ons? He shakes his head. The ex-deputy whispers something in the fat man's ear, then tips his own ear close to attend to the reply. Well awright, he sez. Yer life then, he sez. Yer'n fer her'n.

Hunh. Shore. He shrugs, and sits down on the edge of the chair to get his voice into the right position. Aint wuth a plug nickel nohow. A flicker of amusement seems to cross the fat man's face, the reawak-ened cards fluttering between his hands like a caged titmouse, or a feeding hummingbird. He removes his spurs so they will not betray him, and then, leaving his voice behind, rises silently from the chair to slip around behind the dealer. Reglar five-card stud, his voice says. Face up. Dont want nuthin hid. The dealer offers the deck toward the chair. No cut, mister. Jest dole em out. The room has fallen deadly silent as he circles round, nothing to be heard but the creaking and ticking of the wheel of fortune, all murmurs stilled, which may be perplexing the fat man, though he gives no sign of it. With barely a visible movement, he deals the empty chair a jack and himself a king. I reckon yu're tryin t'tell me sumthin, his voice says from the chair, keeping up the patter to cover his movements. Something an old deerhunter once taught him as a way of confusing his prey. It was a simple trick and so natural that, once he learned it, he was amazed he had not always known how to do it. But a pair a these here young blades'll beat a sucked-out ole bulldog any day, his voice adds cockily when a second jack falls, a second king of course immediately following on. Uh oh, says his voice. Damn my luck. Pears I'll require a third one of them dandies jest t'stay in this shootout. Which he gets, it in turn topped by a third king. He is behind the dealer now, gazing down upon his bubbly mound of glowing pate. Well would yu lookit that, says his voice as the fourth jack is turned up. I reckon now, barrin miracles, the prizner's mine. Stealthily, as the fourth king falls, he unsheaths his bowie knife. The dealer's head twitches slightly as though he might have heard something out of order and were cocking his ear toward it, so his voice says from the chair: Aint that sumthin! Four jacks! Four kings! But we aint done yet, podnuh. Yu owe me another card. Yu aint doled out but four. The fat man hesitates, tipping slightly toward the voice, then, somewhat impatiently, flicks out a black queen which falls like a provocation between the two hands of armed men. Well ifn that dont beat all, his voice exclaims. How'd that fifth jack get in thar? The dealer starts, seems about to reach for his gun or the card, but stays his hand and, after the briefest hesitation, flips over a fifth king. Haw, says the voice. Nuthin but a mizzerbul deuce. Got yu, ole man! And as the gun comes out and blasts the chair away, he buries the blade deep in the dealer's throat, slicing from side to side through the thick piled-up flesh like stirring up a bucket of lard.

The man does not fall over, but continues to sit there in his rotundity as before, his head slumping forward slightly as though in disappointment, his blue spectacles skidding down his nose away from the puckery dimples where eyes once were. His gunhand twitches off another shot, shattering an overhead lamp and sending everyone diving

114

for cover, then turns up its palm and lets the pistol slip away like a discard. A white fatty ooze leaks from his slit throat, slowly turning pink. He wipes his blade on the shoulders of the man's white linen suit, triggering a mechanical holdout mechanism that sends a few aces flying out his sleeves, and then he carefully resheathes it, eyeing the others all the while as they pick themselves up and study this new situation. He's not sure how they will take it or just who this dealer was to them, so to distract them from any troublous thoughts they may be having he says: Looks like them winnins is up fer grabs, gentamin.

That sets off the usual crazed melee, and while they are going at it, he arrests the wheel of fortune to free the schoolmarm. When he releases her wrists, she faints and collapses over his shoulder, so that he has to unbind her hips and ankles with the full weight of her upon him. It is getting ugly in the churchroom, guns and knives are out and fists and bottles are flying, so he quickly sidles out of there, toting her beamhigh over his shoulder like a saddlebag, the room conveniently shrinking toward the exit to hasten his passage. At the door, before darting out into the night, he glances back over his free shoulder at the mayhem within (this is his town and for all he knows the only people he has ever had and he is about to leave them now forever) and sees through the haze the dead dealer, still slumped there under the glowing lamp like an ancient melancholic ruin, his hairless blue-bespectacled head slowly sinking away into his oozing throat.

Nominated by Conjunctions

LIZARD

by SUSAN HAHN

from SOUTHWEST REVIEW

You grew so thin your bracelet slipped
off your wrist. We couldn't find it
in the windblown sand—
our eyes encrusted, almost blind—
combs that once lifted your thick hair fell
and were buried there. The lizard slid

along and was adorned with many ornaments—
throat fans, tail crests, casques on its head,
spines and frills around its throat.
It grew so large and corpulent
as it ate you up. We knew
no chant to drive it out.
On our knees

we watched it probe and dig.
Straightened, we raced after it.
It was so capable of rapid acceleration.
We chased it through the hospital.
Then, in June they scanned you
with their enormous machines
and it was nowhere to be seen.
We picked huge bouquets of summer

flowers and you smiled. We shopped
for new clothes to cover your delicate translucent

bones. In the dressing room I saw your soul.
The lizard had chewed away all fat and left you
luminous. The three-way mirror
almost captured it. But in the fall

its venom began to spew again
from the longitudinal groove
on the inner side
of each mandibular tooth.
O I knew its body well—
its chameleon ways were no
surprise—the hell in

all its designs. The last
time it rose up on the screen
I wept and screamed. Cold-
blooded, how it craved your hot, dry
body—your fever that it sunned itself

under. Gorged, it's gone on hidden
folds of skin—sails to glide it
through the air. No one knows exactly where
it will land.

Nominated by Mark Irwin, Carl Phillips, Southwest Review

THE BEST GIRLFRIEND YOU NEVER HAD

Fiction by PAM HOUSTON

from OTHER VOICES

A PERFECT DAY in the city always starts like this: My friend Leo picks me up and we go to a breakfast place called Rick and Ann's where they make red flannel hash out of beets and bacon, and then we cross the Bay Bridge to the gardens of the Palace of the Fine Arts to sit in the wet grass and read poems out loud and talk about love.

The fountains are thick with black swans imported from Siberia, and if it is a fine day and a weekend there will be wedding parties, almost entirely Asian. The grooms wear smart gray pinstripe suits and the women are in beaded gowns so beautiful they make your teeth hurt just to look at them.

The Roman towers of the Palace façade rise above us, more yellow than orange in the strengthening midday light. Leo has told me how the towers were built for the 1939 San Francisco World's Fair out of plaster and papier maché, and even though times were hard the city raised the money to keep them, to cast them in concrete so they would never go away.

Leo is an architect, and his relationship to all the most beautiful buildings in this city is astonishing given his age, only five years older than I. I make my living as a photographer; since art school I've been doing magazine work and living from grant to grant.

The house Leo built for himself is like a fairy tale, all towers and angles, and the last wild peacock in Berkeley lives on his street. I live in

118

the Oakland Hills in a tiny house on a street so windy you can't drive more than ten miles per hour. I rented it because the ad said this: "Small house in the trees with a garden and a fireplace. Dogs welcome, of course." I am dogless for the moment but it's not my natural condition. You never know when I might get overwhelmed by a desire to go to the pound.

It's a warm blue Saturday in November, and there are five Asian weddings underway at the Palace of the Fine Arts. The wedding parties' outfits do not match but are complementary, as if they have been ordered especially, one for each arch of the golden façade.

Leo reads me a poem about a salt marsh at dawn while I set up my old Leica. I always get the best stuff when nobody's paying me to shoot. Like the time I caught a bride waltzing with one of the caterers behind the hedgerow, his chef's cap bent to touch the top of her veil.

Then I read Leo a poem about longing in Syracuse. This is how we have always spoken to each other, Leo and I, and it would be the most romantic thing this century except that Leo is in love with Guinevere.

Guinevere is a Buddhist weaver who lives in a clapboard house on Belvedere Island. She makes cloth on a loom she brought back from Tibet. Although her tapestries and wall hangings have made her a small fortune, she refuses to use the air conditioner in her Audi, even when she's driving across the Sacramento Valley. Air conditioning, she says, is just one of the things she does not allow herself.

That Guinevere seems not to know Leo is alive causes him no particular disappointment, and that she forgets—each time she meets him—that she has met him several times before only adds to what he calls her charming basket of imperfections. The only Buddha I could love, he says, is one who is capable of forgetfulness and sin.

Guinevere is in love with a man in New York City who told her in a letter that the only thing better than three thousand miles between him and the object of his desire would be if she had a terminal illness.

"I could really get behind a relationship with a woman who had only six months to live," was what he wrote. She showed me the words as if to make sure they existed, though something in her tone made me think she was proud.

The only person I know of who's in love with Leo (besides me, a little), is a gay man named Raphael who falls in love with one straight man after another and then buys each one a whole new collection of CD's. They come, Leo says, as if from the Columbia House Record Club, once a month like clockwork, in a plain cardboard wrapper, no return address and no name. They are by artists most people have never heard of, like Cassandra Wilson and Boris Grebeshnikov; there are Andean folk songs and Hip Hop and Beat.

Across the swan-bearing lake a wedding has just reached its completion. The groom is managing to look utterly solemn and completely delirious with joy at the same time. Leo and I watch the kiss, and I snap the shutter just as the kiss ends and the wedding party bursts into applause.

"Sucker," Leo says.

"Oh, right," I say. "Like you wouldn't trade your life for his right this minute."

"I don't know anything about his life," Leo says.

"You know he remembered to do all the things you forgot."

"I think I prefer it," Leo says, "when you reserve that particular lecture for yourself." He points back across the lake where the bride has just leaped into her maid of honor's arms, and I snap the shutter again. "Or for one of your commitment-phobic boyfriends," Leo adds.

"I guess the truth is, I can't blame them," I say. "I mean if I saw me coming down the street with all my stuff hanging out I'm not so sure I'd pick myself up and go trailing after."

"Of course you would," Leo says. "And it's because you would, and because the chance of that happening is so slim, and because you hold out hope anyway that it might . . . that's what makes you a great photographer."

"Greatness is nice," I tell him. "I want contact. I want someone's warm breath on my face." I say it as if it's a dare, which we both know it isn't. The flower girl across the lake is throwing handfuls of rose petals straight up in the air.

I came to this city near the ocean over a year ago because I recently spent a long time under the dark naked water of the Colorado River and I took it as a sign that the river wanted me away. I had taken so many pictures by then of the chaos of heaved-up rock and petrified sand and endless sky that I'd lost my balance and fallen into them. I couldn't keep separate any more what was the land and what was me.

There was a man there named Josh who didn't want nearly enough from me, and a woman called Thea who wanted way too much, and I was sandwiched between them, one of those weaker rock layers like limestone that disappears under pressure or turns into something shapeless like oil.

I thought there might be an order to the city: straight lines, shiny surfaces and right angles that would give myself back to me, take my work somewhere different, maybe to a safer place. Solitude was a straight line too, and I believed it was what I wanted, so I packed whatever I could get into my pick-up, left behind everything I couldn't carry including two pairs of skis, a whole darkroom full of photo equipment, and the mountains I'd sworn again and again I couldn't live without.

I pointed myself west down the endless two lanes of Highway 50— *The Loneliest Road in America* say the signs that rise out of the desert on either side of it—all the way across Utah and Nevada to this white shining city on the Bay.

I got drunk on the city at first the way some people do on vodka, the way it lays itself out as if in a nest of madronos and eucalyptus, the way it sparkles brighter even than the sparkling water that surrounds it, the way the Golden Gate reaches out of it, like fingers, toward the wild wide ocean that lies beyond.

I loved the smell of fresh blueberry muffins at the Oakland Grill down on Third and Franklin, the train whistle sounding right outside the front door, and tattooed men of all colors unloading crates of cauliflower, broccoli and peas.

Those first weeks I'd walk the streets for hours, shooting more film in a day than I could afford in a week, all those lives in such dangerous and unnatural proximity, all those stories my camera could tell.

I'd walk even the nastiest part, the blood pumping through my veins as hard as when I first saw the Rocky Mountains so many years ago. One night in the Tenderloin I rounded a corner and met a guy in a wheelchair head on who aimed himself at me and covered me with urine. Baptized, I said to my horrified friends the next day, anointed with the nectar of the city gods.

I met a man right off the bat named Gordon, and we'd drive down to the Oakland docks in the evening and look out at the twenty-story hydraulic boatlifts which I said looked like a battalion of Doberman pinschers protecting the harbor from anyone who might invade. Gordon's real name was Salvador and he came from poor people, strawberry pickers in the central valley, two of his brothers stillborn from Malathion poisoning. He left the valley and moved to the city when he was too young by law to drive the truck he stole from his father's field boss.

He left it double-parked in front of the Castro Theater, talked a family in the Mission into trading work for floor space, changed his name

121

to Gordon, changed his age from 15 to 20 and applied for a grant to study South American literature at San Francisco State.

He had his Ph.D. before he turned twenty, a tenure-track teaching job at Berkeley by 21. When he won his first teaching award his mother was in the audience; when their eyes met she nodded her approval, but when he looked for her afterwards, she was nowhere to be found.

"Can you believe it?" he said when he told the story, his voice such a mixture of pride and disappointment that I didn't know which was more unbelievable, that she had come or that she had gone.

"If one more woman I used to date turns into a lesbian," Leo says, "I'm moving to Minneapolis."

The wedding receptions are well under way and laughter bubbles toward us across the lagoon.

"It's possible to take that as a compliment," I say, "if you want to bend your mind that way."

"I don't," he says.

"Maybe it's just a choice a woman makes," I say, "when she feels she has exhausted all her other options."

"Oh, yeah, like you start out being a person," Leo says, "and then you decide to become a car."

"Sometimes I think it's either that or Alaska," I say. "The odds there, better than ten to one."

I remember a bumper sticker I saw once in Haines, Alaska, near the place where the ferries depart for the lower forty-eight: *Baby*, it said, *when you leave here you'll be ugly again.*

"In Alaska," I say, "I've actually had men fall at my feet."

"I bet a few men have fallen at your feet down here," he says, and I try to look him in the eye to see how he means it, but he keeps them fixed on the poetry book.

He says, "Aren't I the best girlfriend you never had?"

The last woman Leo called the love of his life only let him see her twice a week for three years. She was a cardiologist who lived in the Marina who said she spent all day with broken hearts and she had no intention of filling her time off with her own. At the start of the fourth year, Leo asked her to raise the number of dates to three times a week, and she immediately broke things off.

Leo went up on the Bridge after that. This was before they put the phones in, the ones that go straight to the counselors. It was a sunny day and the tide was going out, making whitecaps as far as he could see into the Pacific. After a while he came down, not because he felt better but because of the way the numbers fell out. There had been 250 so far that year. Had the number been 4 or 199 or even 274 he says he might have done it, but he wasn't willing to go down officially with a number as meaningless as 251.

A woman sitting on the grass near us starts telling Leo how much he looks like her business partner, but there's an edge to her voice I can't identify, an insistence that means she's in love with the guy, or she's crazy, or she's just murdered him this morning and she has come to the Palace of the Fine Arts to await her impending arrest.

"The great thing about Californians," Leo says when the woman has finally gotten up to leave, "is that they think it's perfectly O.K. to exhibit all their neuroses in public as long as they apologize for them first."

Leo grew up like I did on the East Coast, eating Birds Eye frozen vegetables and Swanson's deep-dish meat pies on TV trays next to our parents and their third martinis, watching *What's My Line* and *To Tell the Truth* on television and talking about anything on earth except what was wrong.

"Is there anyone you could fall in love with besides Guinevere?" I ask Leo, after he's read a poem about tarantulas and digger wasps.

"There's a pretty woman at work," he says. "She calls herself The Diva."

"Leo," I say, "write this down. I think it's a good policy to avoid any woman who uses an article in her name."

There are policemen at the Palace grounds today handing out information about how we can protect ourselves from an epidemic of carjackings that has been taking place in the city for the last five months. The crime begins, the flyer tells us, with the criminal bumping the victim's car from behind. When the victim gets out of the car to exchange information, the criminal hits her—and it's generally a woman—over the head with a heavy object, leaves her on the sidewalk, steals her car and drives away.

The flyer says we are supposed to keep our windows rolled up when the other driver approaches, keep the doors locked, and say through the glass, *"I'm afraid. I'm not getting out. Please follow me to the nearest convenience store."* It says under no circumstances should we ever let the criminal drive us to crime scene number two.

"You couldn't do it, could you?" Leo asks, and slaps my arm like a wise guy.

"What do you think they mean," I say, "by crime scene number two?"

"You're evading the question because you know the answer too well," he says. "You're the only person I know who'd get your throat slit sooner than admit you're afraid."

"You know," I say to Leo, to change the subject, "you don't act much like a person who wants kids more than anything."

"Yeah, and you don't act like a person who wants to be married with swans."

"I'd do it," I say. "Right now. Step into that wedding dress, no questions asked."

"Lucy," Leo says, "seriously do you have any idea how many steps there are between you and that wedding dress?"

"No," I say. "Tell me."

"Fifty-five," he says. "At least fifty-five."

Before Gordon I had always dated the strong silent types, I think, so I could invent anything I wanted to go on in their heads. Gordon and I talked about words, and the kind of pictures you could make so that you didn't need them and I thought what I always thought in the first ten minutes: that after years and years of wild pitches I'd, for once in my life, thrown a strike.

It took me less than half a baseball season to discover my oversight: Gordon had a jealous streak as vicious as a heat-seeking missile and he could make a problem out of a paper bag. We were asked to leave two restaurants in one week alone, and it got to the point, fast, where if the waitperson wasn't female, I'd ask if we could go somewhere else or have another table.

Car mechanics, piano tuners, dry cleaners, toll takers, in Gordon's mind they were all out to bed me and I was out to make them want to, a honey pot, he'd called me once, and he said he and all other men in the Bay Area were a love-crazed swarm of bees.

When I told Guinevere how I'd fallen for Gordon she said, "You only get a few chances to feel your life all the way through. Before—you know—you become unwilling."

I told her the things I was afraid to tell Leo, how the look on Gordon's face turned from passion to anger, how he yelled at me in a store so loud one time that the manager slipped me a note that said he would pray for me, how each night I would stand in the street while he revved up his engine and scream *please Gordon, please Gordon, don't drive away.*

"At one time in my life I had breast implants just to please a man," she said. "Now I won't even take off my bracelets before bed."

Guinevere keeps a bowl of cards on her breakfast table between the sugar and the coffee. They are called Angel Cards and she bought them at the New Age store. Each card has a word printed on it: *sisterhood* or *creativity* or *romance,* and there's a tiny angel with her body in a position that is supposed to illustrate the word.

That morning I picked *balance,* with a little angel perched in the center of a teeter-totter, and when Guinevere reached in for her own word she sighed in disgust. Without looking at the word again, without showing it to me, she put the card in the trashcan and reached to pick another.

I went to the trashcan and found it. The word was *surrender,* and the angel was looking upwards with her arms outstretched.

"I hate that," she said, her mouth slightly twisted. "Last week I had to throw away *submit.*"

Guinevere brought me a cookie and a big box of Kleenex. She said that choices can't be good or bad. There is only the event and the lessons learned from it. She corrected my pronunciation gently and constantly: the *Bu* in Buddha she said is like the *pu* in pudding and not like the *boo* in ghost.

When I was twenty-five years old I brought home to my parents a boy named Jeffrey I thought I wanted to marry. He was everything I believed my father wanted: He had an MBA from Harvard. He had patches on the elbows of his sportcoats. He played golf on a course that only allowed men.

We spent the weekend drinking the wine and eating the paté Jeffrey's mother had sent him from her *fermette* in the southwest of France. Jeffrey let my father show him decades worth of tennis trophies. He played the piano while my mother sang her old torch songs.

I waited until I had a minute along with my father. "Papa," I said— it was what I always called him—"How do you like Jeffrey?"

"Lucille," he said, "I haven't ever liked any of your boyfriends, and I don't expect I ever will. So why don't you save us both the embarrassment, and not ask again."

After that I went back to dating mechanics and river guides. My mother kept Jeffrey's picture on the mantel til she died.

The first time I was mugged in the city I'd been to the late show all alone at the Castro Theatre. It's one of those magnificent old movie

125

houses with a huge marquee that lights up the sky like a carnival, a ceiling that looks like it belongs in a Spanish Cathedral, heavy red velvet curtains laced with threads that sparkle gold, and a real live piano player who disappears into the floor when the previews begin.

I liked to linger after the movie finished, watch the credits and the artificial stars in the ceiling. That Tuesday I was the last person to step out of the theater into a chilly deserted night.

I had one foot off the curb when the man approached me, a little too close for comfort even then.

"Do you have any change you can spare?" he said.

The truth was I didn't. I had scraped the bottom of my purse to put together enough quarters, nickels and dimes to get into the movie, and the guy behind the glass had let me in thirty-three cents short.

I said I was sorry and headed for the parking lot. I knew he was behind me, but I didn't turn around. I should have gotten my keys out before I left the theater, I thought. Shouldn't have stayed to see every credit roll.

About ten steps from my car I felt a firm jab in the middle of my rib cage.

"I bet you'd feel differently," the man said, "if I had a gun in my hand."

"I might feel differently," I said, whirling around with more force than I intended, "but I still wouldn't have any money."

He flinched, changed the angle of his body, just slightly back and away. And when he did, when his eyes dropped from mine to his hand holding whatever it was in his jacket pocket, I was reminded of a time I almost walked into a female grizz with a nearly grown cub. How we had stood there posturing, how she had glanced down at her cub just that way, giving me the opportunity to let her know she didn't need to kill me. We could both go on our way.

"Look," I said. "I've had a really emotional day, O.K.?" As I talked I dug into my purse and grabbed my set of keys, a kind of weapon in their own right. "And I think you ought to just let me get in the car and go home."

While he considered this I took the last steps to my car and got in. I didn't look in the rearview mirror until I was on the freeway.

By mid-afternoon Leo and I have seen one too many happy couples get married and we drive over the Golden Gate to Tiburon to a restaurant called Guymos where we drink margaritas made with Patrón tequila and eat ceviche appetizers and look out on Angel Island and the city—whitest of all from this perspective, rising like a mirage out of the blue green bay.

We watch the ferry dock unload the suburbanites, then load them up again for the twice-hourly trip to the city. We are jealous of their starched shirts and brown loafers, how their clothes seem a testament to the balance in their lives.

The fog rolls over and down the lanyard side of Mt. Tamalpais, and the city moves in and out of it, glistening like Galilee one moment, then gray and dreamy like a ghost of itself the next, and then gone, like a thought bubble, like somebody's good idea.

"Last night," I say, "I was walking alone down Telegraph Avenue. I was in a mood, you know, Gordon and I had a fight about John Lennon."

"Was he for or against?" Leo says.

"Against," I say, "but it doesn't matter. Anyway, I was scowling, maybe crying a little, moving along pretty fast, and I step over this homeless guy with his crutches and his little can and he says, 'I don't even *want* any money from you, I'd just like *you* to smile.'"

"So did you?" Leo says.

"I did," I say. "I not only smiled, but I laughed too, and then I went back and gave him all the money in my wallet, which was only eighteen dollars, but still. I told him to be sure and use that line again."

"I love you," Leo says, and takes both of my hands in his. "I mean, in the good way."

When I was four years old and with my parents in Palm Beach, Florida, I pulled a seven-hundred-pound cement urn off its pedestal and onto my legs, crushing both femurs. All the other urns on Worth Avenue had shrubs in them trimmed into the shapes of animals, and this one, from my three-foot point of view, appeared to be empty.

When they asked me why I had tried to pull myself up and into the urn I said I thought it had fish inside it and I wanted to see them, though whether I had imagined actual fish, or just tiny shrubs carved into the shape of fish, I can't any longer say.

The urn was empty, of course, and waiting to be repaired, which is why it toppled over onto me. My father rolled it off with some of that superhuman strength you always hear about and picked me up—I was screaming bloody murder—and held me until the ambulance came.

127

The next six weeks were the best of my childhood. I was hospitalized the entire time, surrounded by doctors who brought me presents, nurses who read me stories, candy stripers who came to my room and played games.

My parents, when they came to visit, were always happy to see me and usually sober.

I spent the remaining years of my childhood fantasizing about illnesses and accidents that I hoped would send me to the hospital again.

One day last month Gordon asked me to go backpacking at Point Reyes National Seashore, to prove to me, he said, that he could take an interest in my life. I hadn't slept outside one single night since I came to the city, he said, and I must miss the feel of hard ground underneath me, must miss the smell of my tent in the rain.

Gordon borrowed a backpack, got the permit, freed the weekend, studied the maps. I was teaching a darkroom workshop in Corte Madeira on Saturday. Gordon would pick me up at four when the workshop ended; we'd have just enough time to drive up the coast to Point Reyes Station and walk for an hour into the first camp. A long second day would take us to the beach, the point with the lighthouse, and back to the car with no time again to spare before dark.

I had learned by then how to spot trouble coming and that morning I waited in the car with Gordon while first one man, way too young for me and then another, way too old, entered the warehouse where my workshop was going to be held.

I got out of the car without seeing the surfer, tall and blond and a little breathtaking, portfolio under the arm that usually held the board. I kept my eyes away from his but his handshake found me anyway. When he held the big door open I went on through. I could hear the screech of tires behind me through what felt like a ton of metal.

That Gordon was there when the workshop ended at 4:02 surprised me a little. Then I got in the Pathfinder and saw only one backpack. He drove up the coast to Point Reyes without speaking. Stinson, Bolinas, Dogtown and Olema. The white herons in Tomales Bay had their heads tucked under their arms.

He stopped at the trailhead, got out, threw my pack into the dune grass, opened my door and tried with his eyes to pry me from my seat.

"I guess this means you're not coming with me," I said, imagining how we could do it with one pack, tenacious in my hope that the day could be saved.

What you're thinking, right now, is why didn't I do it, get out of that car without making eye contact, swing my pack on my back and head off down the trail. And when I tell you what I did do, which was to crawl all the way to the back of the Pathfinder, holding on to the cargo net like a tornado was coming, and let go with one ear-splitting head-pounding scream after another till Gordon got back in the car, till we got back down the coast, back on the 580, back over the Bridge, and back to Gordon's apartment, till he told me if I was quiet, he'd let me stay, you would wonder how a person, even if she had done it, could ever in a million years admit to such a thing.

Then I could tell you about the sixteen totalled cars in my first fifteen winters. The Christmas Eve my father and I rolled a Plymouth Fury from meridian to guardrail and back four full times with nine complete revolutions, how they had to cut us out with chainsaws, how my father, limber from the Seagram's, got away unhurt. I could tell you about the neighbor girl who stole me away one time at the sound of my parents shouting, how she refused to give me back to them even when the police came with a warrant, how her ten-year-old hand must have looked holding my three-year-old one, how in the end it became a funny story that both sets of parents loved to tell. I could duplicate for you the hollow sound an empty bottle makes when it hits formica, and the stove is left on and the pan's started smoking and there's a button that says off, but no way to reach.

I could tell you the lie I told myself with Gordon. That anybody is better than nobody. And you will know exactly why I stayed in the back of that Pathfinder, unless you are lucky, and then you will not.

"Did I ever tell you about the time I got mugged?" Leo asks me, and we both know he has but it's his favorite story.

"I'd like it," I say, "if you'd tell it again."

Before Leo built his house on the street with the peacocks he lived in the city between North Beach and the piers. He got mugged one night, stepping out of his car fumbling for his house keys; the man had a gun and snuck up from behind.

What Leo had in his wallet was thirteen dollars, and when he offered the money he thought the man would kill him on the spot.

"You got a cash card," the man said. "Let's find a machine."

"Hey," I say when he gets to this part, "that means you went to crime scene number two."

The part I hate most is how he took Leo's glasses. He said he would drive, but as it turned out he didn't know stick shifts, and the clutch burned and smoked all the way to Nob Hill.

"My name's Bill," the man said, and Leo thought since they were getting so friendly, he'd offer to work the clutch and the gear shift to save what was left of his car. It wasn't until Leo got close to him, straddling the gear box and balanced against Bill's shoulder, that he smelled the blood under Bill's jacket and knew that he'd been shot.

They drove like that to the Marina Safeway, Bill's eyes on the road and his hands on the steering wheel, Leo working the clutch and the shifter according to feel.

At the cash machine Leo looked for help but couldn't get anyone's eyes to meet his, with Bill and his gun pressed so close to his side.

They all think we're a couple, he thought and laughter bubbled up inside him. He told Bill a lie about a hundred-dollar ATM limit, pushed the buttons, handed over the money.

They drove back to Leo's that same Siamese way, and when they got there Bill thanked Leo, shook his hand, asked one more favor before he took off.

"I'm going to give you a phone number," Bill said. "My girlfriend in Sacramento. I want you to call her and tell her I made it all right."

"Sure," Leo said, folding the paper.

"I want you to swear to God."

"Sure," Leo said, "I'll call her."

Bill put the end of the gun around Leo's belly button. "Say it, motherfucker, say, I swear to God."

"I swear to God," Leo said, and Bill walked away.

Back in his apartment Leo turned on Letterman. When the shaking had stopped he called the police.

"Not much we can do about it," the woman at the end of the line told him. "We could come dust your car for fingerprints, but it would make a hell of a mess."

Two hours later Leo looked in a phone book and called a Catholic priest.

"No," the priest said, "you don't have to call her. You swore to God under extreme circumstances, brought down upon you by a godless man."

"I don't think that's the right answer," I had said when I first heard the story and I say it again, on cue, today. The first time we had talked about the nature of godlessness, and how, if a situation requires swearing to God, it is—by definition—extreme.

But today I am thinking not of Bill or even of Leo's dilemma, but of the girlfriend in Sacramento, her lover shot, bleeding and hijacking architects, and still remembering to think of her.

And I wonder what it was about her that made her stay with a man who ran from the law for a living, and if he had made it home to her that night, if she stood near him in the kitchen dressing his wounds. I wonder how she saw herself, as what part of the story, and how much she had invested in how it would end.

"I'm so deeply afraid," Gordon had said on the docks our first night together, "that I am nothing but weak and worthless. So I take the people close to me and try to break them, so they become as weak and worthless as me."

I want to know the reason I could hear and didn't hear what he was saying, the reason why I thought the story could end differently for me.

Things ended between Gordon and me in a bar in Jack London Square one night when we were watching the 49ers play the Broncos. It was Joe Montana's last year in San Francisco; rumors of the Kansas City acquisition had already begun.

It was a close game late in the season; the Broncos had done what they were famous for in those days, jumped out to a twenty-point lead, and then lost it incrementally as the quarters went by.

The game came right down to the two-minute warning, Elway and Montana trading scoring drives so elegant it was like they shook hands on it before the game. A minute twenty-seven left, ball on the Niners' twenty-two: Joe Montana had plenty of time and one last chance to shine.

"Don't tell me you're a Bronco fan," a guy on the other side of me, a late arrival, said.

"It's a tough job," I said, not taking my eyes off the TV set. For about the hundredth time that evening the camera was off the action and on a tearful, worried or ecstatic Jennifer Montana, one lovely and protective hand around each of her two beautiful blonde little girls.

"Geez," I said, when the camera came back to the action several seconds too late, "you'd think Joe Montana was the only football player in America who had a wife."

The guy next to me laughed a short choppy laugh. Joe took his team seventy-eight yards in seven plays for the win.

On the way to his Pathfinder, Gordon said, "That's what I hate about you sports fans. You create a hero like Joe Montana just so you have somebody to knock down."

"I don't have anything against Joe Montana," I said. "I think he throws the ball like an angel. I simply prefer watching him to watching his wife."

"I saw who you preferred watching," Gordon said as we arrived at the car and he slammed inside.

"Gordon," I said, "I don't even know what that man looked like."

The moon was fat and full over the parts of Oakland no one dares to go to late at night and I knew as I looked for a face in it that it didn't matter a bit what I said.

Gordon liked to drive the meanest streets when he was feeling meanest, and he was ranting about me shaking my tail feathers and keeping my pants zipped, and all I could think to do was remind him I was wearing a skirt.

He squealed the brakes at the end of my driveway and I got out and moved toward the dark entryway.

"Aren't you going to invite me in?" he asked. And I thought about the months full of nights just like this one when I asked his forgiveness, when I begged him to stay.

"I want you to make your own decision," I said over my shoulder, and he threw the car in second, gunned the engine and screeched away.

First came the messages taped to my door, the words cut out from ten different typefaces, held down with so many layers of tape it had the texture of decoupage. Then came the slit tires, the Karo syrup in my gas tank, my box set of Dylan's Biography in a puddle at the foot of my drive. One day I opened an envelope from a magazine I'd sent for to find my paycheck ripped into a hundred pieces and then put back in the envelope, back in the box.

Leo and I trade margaritas for late-afternoon lattes, and still the fog won't lift all the way.

"What I imagine," I say, "is coming home one night and Gordon emerging from between the sidewalk and the shadows, a Magnum 357 in his hand, and my last thought being, 'Well, you should have figured that this was the next logical thing.'"

"I don't know why you need to be so tough about it," Leo says. "Can't you let the police or somebody know?"

I say, "This is not a good city to be dogless in."

132

Leo puts his arm around me; I can tell by the way he does it he thinks he has to.

"Do you wish sometimes," I say, "that you could just disappear like that city?"

"I can," Leo says. "I do. What I wish more is that when I wanted to I could stay."

The ferry docks again in front of us and we sit quietly until the whistles are finished and the boat has once again taken off.

"Are you ever afraid," I say to Leo, "that there are so many things you need swirling around inside you that they will just overtake you, smother you, suffocate you till you die?"

"I don't think so," Leo says.

"I don't mean sex," I say, "or even love exactly, just all that want that won't let go of you, that even if you changed everything right now it's too late already to ever be full?"

Leo keeps his eyes fixed on the city which is back out again, the Coit Tower reaching and leaning slightly like a stack of pepperoni pizza pies.

"Until only a few years ago, I used to break into a stranger's house every six months like clockwork," he says. "Is that something like what you mean?"

"Exactly," I say. A band of fog sweeps down, faster than the others and takes away the city, even the site of Leo's mugging, even the apartment where Gordon now stays.

When I was eighteen years old I met my parents in Phoenix, Arizona to watch Penn State play USC in the Fiesta Bowl. I'd driven from Ohio, they'd flown from Pennsylvania, and the three of us—for the first time ever—shared my car.

My father wanted me to drive them through the wealthy suburbs, places with names like Carefree and Cave Creek. He'd been drinking earlier in the day than usual, they both had, and he got it into his head that he wanted to see the world's highest fountain shoot 300 gallons of water per minute into the parched and evaporative desert air.

We were halfway through Cave Creek, almost to the fountain, when the cop pulled me over.

"I'm sorry to bother you", he said, "but I've been tailing you for four or five minutes, and I have to tell you, I really don't know where to start."

The cop's nameplate said Martin "Mad Dog" Jenkins. My father let out a sigh that hung in the car like a fog.

"Well, first," Officer Jenkins said, "I clocked you going 43 in a 25. Then you rolled through not one but two stop signs without coming to a safe and complete stop, and you made a right hand turn into the center lane."

"Jesus Christ," my father said.

"You've got one tail light out," Officer Jenkins said, "and either your turn signals are burned out too, or you are electing not to use them."

"Are you hearing this?" my father said to the air.

"May I see your license and registration?"

"I left my license in Ohio," I said.

The car was silent.

"Give me a minute, then," Officer Jenkins said, "and I'll call it in."

"What I don't know," my father said, "is how a person with so little sense of responsibility gets a driver's license in this country to begin with."

He flicked the air vent open and closed, open and closed. "I mean you gotta wonder if she should even be let out of the house in the morning."

"Why don't you just say it, Robert," my mother said. "Say what you mean. Say *daughter, I hate you.*" Her voice started shaking. "Everybody sees it. Everybody knows it. Why don't you say it out loud?"

"Ms. O'Rourke?" Officer Jenkins was back at the window.

"Let's hear it," my mother went on. *"Officer, I hate my daughter."*

The cop's eyes flicked for a moment into the back seat.

"According to the information I received, Ms. O'Rourke," Officer Jenkins said, "you are required to wear corrective lenses."

"That's right," I said.

"And you are wearing contacts now?" There was something like hope in his voice.

"No sir."

"She can't even lie?" my father asked. "About one little thing?"

"O.K. now, on three," my mother said. *"Daughter, I wish you had never been born."*

"Ms. O'Rourke," Officer Jenkins said, "I'm just going to give you a warning today." My father bit off the end of a laugh.

"Thank you very much," I said.

"I hate to say this, Ms. O'Rourke," the cop said, "but there's nothing I could do to you that's going to feel like punishment." He held out his hand for me to shake. "You drive safely now," he said, and he was gone.

When the Fiesta Bowl was over, my parents and I drove back up to Carefree to attend a New Year's Eve party given by a gay man my mother knew who belonged to a wine club called the Royal Order of the Grape. My father wasn't happy about it, but he was silent. I just wanted to watch the ball come down on TV like I had every year of my childhood with the babysitter, but the men at the party were showing home movie after home movie of the club's indoctrination ceremony, while every so often two or three partygoers would get taken to the cellar to look at the bottles and taste.

When my father tried to light a cigarette he got whisked outside faster than I had ever seen him move. I was too young to be taken to the cellar, too old to be doted on, so after another half-hour of being ignored I went outside to join my father.

The lights of Phoenix sparkled every color below us in the dark.

"Lucille," he said, "when you get to be my age, don't ever spend New Year's Eve in a house where they won't let you smoke."

"O.K.," I said.

"Your mother," he said, as he always did.

"I know," I said, even though I didn't.

"We just don't get love right, this family, but . . ." He paused, and the sky above Phoenix exploded into color, umbrellas of red and green and yellow. I'd never seen fireworks before, from the top.

"Come in, come in, for the New Year's toast!" Our host was calling us from the door. I wanted more than anything for my father to finish his sentence, but he stabbed out his cigarette, got up, and walked inside. I've finished it for him a hundred times, but never to my satisfaction.

We pay the bill and Leo informs me that he has the temporary use of a twenty-seven-foot sailboat in Sausalito that belongs to a man he hardly knows. The fog has lifted enough for us to see the place where the sun should be, and it's brighter yet out by the Golden Gate and we take the little boat out and aim for the brightness, the way a real couple might on a Saturday afternoon.

It's a squirrelly boat, designed to make fast moves in a light wind, and Leo gives me the tiller two hundred yards before we pass under the dark shadow of the bridge. I am just getting the feel of it when Leo looks over his shoulder and says, "It appears we are in a race," and I look, too, and there is a boat bearing down on us, twice our size, ten times, Leo tells me, our boat's value.

"Maybe you should take it, then," I say.

"You're doing fine," he says. "Just set your mind on what's out there and run for it."

At first all I can think about is Leo sitting up on top of the bridge running numbers in his head, and a story Gordon told me where two guys meet up there on the walkway and find out they are both survivors of a previous jump.

Then I let my mind roll out past the cliffs and the breakers, past the Marin headlands and all the navigation buoys, out to some place where the swells swallow up the coastline and Hawaii is the only thing between me and forever, and what are the odds of hitting it, if I just head for the horizon and never change my course?

I can hear the big boat's bow breaking right behind us, and I set my mind even harder on a universe with nothing in it except deep blue water.

"You scared him," Leo says. "He's coming about."

The big boat turns away from us, back toward the harbor, just as the giant shadow of the bridge crosses our bow. Leo jumps up and gives me an America's Cup hug. Above us the great orange span of the thing is trembling, just slightly, in the wind.

We sail on out to the edge of the headlands where the swells get big enough to make us both a little sick and it's finally Leo who takes the tiller from my hand and turns the boat around. It's sunny as Bermuda out here, and I'm still so high from the boat race that I can tell myself there's really nothing to be afraid of. Like sometimes when you go to a movie and you get so lost in the story that when you're walking out of the theater you can't remember anything at all about your own life.

You might forget, for example, that you live in a city where people have so many choices they throw words away, or so few they will bleed in your car for a hundred dollars. You might forget eleven or maybe twelve of the sixteen-in-a-row totaled cars. You might forget that you never expected to be alone at thirty-two or that a crazy man might be waiting for you with a gun when you get home tonight or that all the people you know—without exception—have their hearts all wrapped around someone who won't ever love them back.

"I'm scared," I say to Leo and this time his eyes come to meet mine. The fog is sitting in the center of the Bay like it's over a big pot of soup and we're about to enter it.

"I can't help you,' Leo says, and squints his eyes against the mist in the air.

When I was two years old my father took me down to the beach in New Jersey, carried me into the surf until the waves were crashing onto his chest and then threw me in like a dog to see, I suppose, whether I would sink or float.

My mother, who was from high in the Rocky Mountains where all the water was too cold for swimming and who had been told since birth never to get her face wet (she took only baths, never showers) got so hysterical by the water's edge that lifeguards from two different stands leapt to my rescue.

There was no need, however. By the time they arrived at my father's side I had passed the flotation test, had swum as hard and fast as my untried limbs would carry me, and my father had me up on his shoulders, smiling and smug and a little surprised.

I make Leo drive back by the Palace of the Fine Arts on the way home, though the Richmond Bridge is faster. The fog has moved in there, too, and the last of the brides are worrying their hair-dos while the grooms help them into big dark cars that will whisk them away to the Honeymoon Suite at the Four Seasons, or to the airport to board planes bound for Tokyo or Rio.

Leo stays in the car while I walk back to the pond. The sidewalk is littered with rose petals and that artificial rice that dissolves in the rain. Even the swans have paired off and are swimming that way, the feathers of their inside wings barely touching, their long necks bent slightly toward each other, the tips of their beaks almost closing the "M."

I take the swans' picture, and a picture of the rose petals bleeding onto the sidewalk. I step up under the tallest of the arches and bow to my imaginary husband. He takes my hand and we turn to the minister, who bows to us and we bow again.

"I'm scared," I say again, but this time it comes out stronger, almost like singing, as though it might be the first step—in fifty-five or a thousand—toward something like a real life, the very first step toward something that will last.

Nominated by Other Voices

THE HOUSES OF DOUBLE WOMEN

fiction by JULIAN ANDERSON

from THE KENYON REVIEW

It was not my idea to sell the farm and buy a moldy Cape Cod in town. A lot of people lived with cancer, I told Rita, without turning their lives inside out like this. We were country people, not used to lawns and sidewalks. Our dog, our woods, our privacy—we were giving them all up. Was moving really necessary? Rita got her way, of course, and come April there I was, just turned sixty, unloading a wing chair from a U-Haul as if I truly believed I could become someone's neighbor.

Rita held open the door as I heaved the chair through. "You obviously haven't taken things into account," I puffed as I set it down.

"What things?" she said.

The jauntiness of the orange scarf she wore like a turban to hide her hairlessness provoked me. "Holland," I said. Could she not feel the eyes watching from behind mini-blinds? "They like tulips around here," I said. "Let's hope they won't mind two old dykes."

Rita's eyes suddenly filmed. "Grace," she said.

"OK, OK," I said.

Home maintenance was going to be important. I bought a rotary pushmower and began walking it over the grass. Out on the farm I had swathed through high weeds on top of the tractor every few days, as the mood took me. Rita had transplanted forest flowers around the house—Michaelmas daisy, hepatica, running cedar—not bothering much with nurseries or seed catalogs. She grew the flowers and I handled the vegetables. Asparagus ran riot like ragweed. In late summer I'd haul in zucchini the size of small dolphins. Tomatoes we couldn't give away just rotted in bountiful mounds and deer feasted after sunset on low-hanging pears.

Our public work—portfolio management for a major investment company—had taken us out to other people's homes. In hefty suits and briefcases, we conveyed ourselves like Chicago gangsters into town and sat with the clients in air-tight living rooms. Rita, a touch vain and naturally formal, had always enjoyed the chance to dress up, but I was relieved to get back home, change into sweats and, like a hound home from the vet, dig around in the dirt till the smell was gone. On weekends we got down to what we loved the most: hiking with the pups.

Our dogs were our true and steady company. Few people ever came out to see us, just hunters looking for lost beagles, the mailman in his mufflerless Chevy, someone asking directions to a church revival. Otherwise we were pretty much on our own. This was not hard for me, brought up by an aunt and uncle working opposite shifts in a cigarette factory. But Rita, lovely Rita, only child of the Smithsons of Smithsonville, South Carolina, who had spent her summers drinking root beer and braiding her cousins' hair under the shade of mulberry trees— she always expected visitors with happy news. No one ever came.

In our first months together, all those long years ago, Rita had sunk into a gully of remorse. She lay on the sofa, the only piece of furniture in our rented rooms, convinced she had behaved outrageously in running off to me. Let the record show, however, that I did *not* steal Rita from her own wedding despite what the Smithsons subsequently claimed. She had been engaged when we met—that is true—but I played no part in breaking it off.

I was teaching a lower-level math class at the time, finishing up my own M.B.A. No one expected me to marry which, if unflattering, at least freed me up. I knew I could succeed at business. A photograph from that time shows me hard-eyed, bleak-mouthed, fully armed with ambition, dressed to kill.

In the spring semester a junior showed up in the second row of my three o'clock class. She was given to wearing hot pink sleeveless shells—this was the mid-sixties—tucked a leg under herself and took careful notes. I needed all the time I could get to keep up with my own course work, but Rita Gwendolyn Smithson began taking full advantage of my office hours. She had a knack for choosing moments when my officemates were out. I tried to answer her questions succinctly and move her out, but she sat on and on in the hard wooden chair at the end of my desk, a man's gold and blue-glass class ring on a chain knocking her sternum as she flipped through notes. "The exam is pure review," I said. I opened a book as a signal.

"I just want to make sure," she explained, holding the gigantic ring still with one hand as she leafed through papers on her knees. I noticed the many shades of gold in her glossy page-boy cut.

"You have an affinity for math," I remarked.

Voice low, she confessed, "I want to be the best in your class." Then she blushed so deeply I had to rummage in some drawers.

I found a sharpener and turned it hard around my red pencil. "You'll do fine," I assured her.

This happened daily for a week. Finally I could take it no longer. I got up, closed the office door, turned the lock by suspicions till it caught, walked to the window and lowered the venetian blinds. They skied down fast, doing the snowplow in a dust cloud, but neither of us smiled. Turning, I faced her, bristling like a cat. I strode the four steps to where she sat. Leaning over, eyes not daring to meet hers, as though this were a kindness, I set my seal.

In the subsequent silence that roared, Rita picked up her things and closed the door. I sat on for a long time at my desk, staring at my typewriter, unable to put my spinning mind to my work, wondering what I'd done. I'd had crushes, I'd known the comfort of older women, but this felt peculiar, off-balancing, not of my choosing, dangerous to my future plans and yet all the while tasting of nothing more than sweetness and salt, Palace Pink lipstick, the olives an undergraduate had had for lunch that Tuesday noon in a smooth Johnson-administration April of 1965.

At my suggestion we played a game of tennis. I felt heavy with the half hour's exertion, aware of how out of shape I'd become over the winter. Rita, on the other hand, returned every service with a nice slice, placing the ball consistently in a corner, making me run, enjoying the volley. After the game, as we cooled down with Cokes at a picnic table, she looked fresher than ever, full of bounce.

Her grin displayed perfect teeth. "I'll see you Monday for more homework help."

I prickled at the implications. "Anyone might have come in."

"People aren't always coming in," she insisted.

I pushed her a little. "You think I'm stodgy? You're hoping for some B-grade romance? You'd like me to rush down a staircase and enfold you?"

Her head bobbed to sip from her straw. "That sounds good. That would do it."

"Exactly *what* would it do?"

She glanced away, confused. "Look," I said, tapping a finger gently on the back of her hand. "I'm sorry to speak to you this way, but life is brief. You have to give it your soul, play right, or you don't live at all. There's no time to fool around, with your heart or anyone else's."

She met my eyes with the look of a puppy shamed by a training mistake.

The problem I ran into right away was that Rita would not come clean. I was wracked with a sense of behaving dishonorably, toying with a coed, an *engaged* coed, but I could not get her to stay away.

"You're a tease," I told her when she next came to the office.

"I'm not, I'm *not*," she insisted, suddenly busy with erasing. She was unused to challenges, to someone as hard as me.

"What about Bev McGee?" I pressed. "I thought you'd set a date."

I knew Bev McGee, a senior engineering major. He'd been in my calculus class as a freshman and done fairly well. He was a nice boy from southern Virginia, of medium height, a trusting face, shoulders broadened by the V-necked sweaters he tied around them, a slow way of walking that told you he could fix a tractor if he had to. He continued to escort her—to ball games, to parties—where she hung on his elbow, the chaste and lovely girlfriend.

"What about him?" Rita said.

"You tell me."

"Well, Grace, for goodness sake, I can't break it off, just like that!"

"You're wearing his ring."

She shifted in my chair. "It doesn't necessarily mean anything."

"It necessarily means something to me."

She took hold of the chain around her neck, lifted it over her head and handed it to me. "Take it."

"I don't want it." I jerked my hand back.

"I'm throwing it away," she said, and walked toward the open window.

"Stop," I said. "You can't do that! What would you tell him?"

"That I lost it in the forsythia."

I led her back by the arm to the wooden chair. "You've got to end it honorably."

141

She looked frightened. "But not just yet."

"Why not?"

"My shower's next Saturday. Aunt Nadine's already sent the invitations. I couldn't do that to her!"

I closed my face in my hands.

She patted my shoulder. "Do you forgive me?"

"Rita," I whispered, "I don't know, I don't know." Then, looking up, I caught her eye and without meaning to, I smiled, and the way she glowed back hooked me like a magnet.

Between the lobster bisque and chicken breasts of her luncheon, Rita ran away—and turned up at my back door.

"I couldn't do it," she panted, slipping like a frantic cat into my kitchen, abashed and elated. She gave a lopsided smile. She scraped at a smudge of luncheon on the bodice of her yellow shirtwaist. She began picking up a row of sea shells on my window sill.

"Listen," I said, speaking very quietly in case we could be overheard by my landlord who had the rooms at the front of the house. "Go back this instant and tell them whatever lie you must, but you're not going to treat them this way." She was edging along my kitchen cabinets. "Get, now. Go on. Scoot." I held the screen door open wide.

Glancing back at me for that moment, she looked aged with panic. I was hard, but I was not going to play finder's keepers. I wanted her to come to me clean.

Taking the ethical high road may free you from guilt, of course, but it did nothing to cheer me up that tedious afternoon spent marking exams, imagining the household tips exchanged over pistachio ice cream at the luncheon, Rita like some unicorn trapped by hunters and walled in by silver-ribboned gifts.

But Rita always got her way. She has never in her life done anything but exactly what she wanted—except now, on account of her illness. One midnight a month before the wedding, when I opened my door to a knock, I found her bossing around a taxi driver with a load of suitcases he was heaving onto my stoop. She looked pale but fully in charge. "This is it," she said, paying him, turning to me without a smile. "Let's go in. I'm freezing." I held the door open and stared in silent wonder at my love, taking off her shoes.

"Make yourself at home," I offered, after the fact but sincere.

"Ha!" she said and bounced onto the couch. "Well! I will!"

Then she broke down. For days she lay on that sofa, sobbing into her arms. Unnerved by the sight of her, I demanded, "Did I ask you to come here? Did I make you break off your engagement?"

"Yes, you did."

"I did nothing of the kind."

"You implied, Grace, that you wouldn't love me if I married him!"

"You are impossible!" I shouted. I brought her iced tea with gin and found her staring into space. "You don't have to stay," I risked reminding her.

"Oh!" she cried. "How could you!" Her eyes looked like the giant orbs of a praying mantis, swollen and red.

"I just meant," I said. "If you're in any doubt, don't mind me."

I felt rebuffed by her misery, unwanted, unable to comfort. I found her suffering childish, in fact, but then, I was not so sensitive as Rita. And I had never been on the verge of a normal life.

Tossing about for ways to please her, I drove out to the pound and brought her home a collie puppy with an eager bark. Rita was laying out a game of solitaire on the floor when we came into the house. The pup scrambled over to her, slipping on the cards. Half-grown, no manners but much natural enthusiasm, he spiraled around, licking her face, shoving his shoulder against hers, then, suddenly, dropped his head onto her lap. Rita slowly smoothed the spot between his eyes. He blinked up into her face; he knew he was her man.

"Is he supposed to look like Bev or something?" she finally said, but she seemed alive for the first time in weeks.

"Call him McGee," I said lightly. She did. McGee became the first of the dynasty of collies who shared our life on the farm. We had seven over the years. Our last, a hefty fellow with especially golden fur, we had to give up in the move. Our life would hold no place for him, a dog accustomed to fields and rabbits. I could not imagine constraining him with a leash, scurrying behind with a scoop and baggie. There are things you can't explain to an animal, though he sensed that Rita was ill. His voice strained on a high note as he watched her angle her walker across treacherous rugs. We placed him through the vet's with a man who hunted. You try not to worry, just hope for the best.

At the end of our new street, I felt self-conscious. Our old furniture wouldn't fit the tight rooms. Rita's walker got hung up on the foot of a Chippendale wing chair and tipped her into a highboy, bruising her cheek. I brought her some ice for her face, and poured us some gin.

Holding both pack and glass to her face, she remarked, "Our neighbors must think us so foolish—all this clutter."

The neighbors, if they thought so, kept it to themselves. For weeks we met no one to speak to. We could only speculate about the inhabitants of those freshly painted houses. We saw them occasionally out there, at it: trimming hedges, weeding borders, painting lampposts. I began to feel some pressure. "We have to rake the lawn," I said to Rita, who was fighting with the child-proof cap on her new pills.

Rita puffed, "Keep it fun."

She mail-ordered one of those straw wreaths for our front door. I spotted it while raking and broke out in a laugh. "From the outside at least," I told her, when she answered my knock at the door, "we look quite harmless."

She studied me, hurt, over the top of a history book she'd borrowed from the library. "We *are* harmless. We are *friendly*. We are *perfectly* nice."

"Jeez," I muttered, but returned to my work, knowing I mustn't protest.

During that first week, while I was out edging our sidewalk, people looked at me once in a while from their cars. Our sidewalk had a hump from a root and their overtures made me conscious I needed to get to that, too. A thirtyish woman who smelled of sunscreen walked over, introduced herself as Janice Gibbs, and pointed out her house three doors down. She said they were adding on an extension for their twins. "Twins," I said, smiling widely to convey how easy we would be as neighbors.

In our third week, more people congregated on our sidewalk to watch the enigmatic man in the house next to ours, number 47, move out. We'd seen him occasionally, watering petunias in his business suit. He was relocating to Houston, someone said. He saluted us all in the rear-view mirrors of his pickup, his tiger-striped cat Hanover hanging halfway out the window.

The little crowd from the street lingered on our sidewalk for a while after he had pulled away. I felt that his departure had promoted Rita and me up a notch from newcomers. Janice Gibbs, whose two identical crew-cut little boys were wrapping themselves around her legs, remarked to Rita, "Bob never had time for upkeep. That house needs TLC."

"It does," Rita agreed, flushed. "I wonder who'll move in next, Janice," she offered, but got no response. Maybe Rita had rushed the first-name thing. Also, in the back of your mind, you wonder if this had something to do with who you were, who they thought you were.

The house stayed empty for just three weeks. Janice had made me notice how undertended it was. Squat, polka-dots painted on its shutters, a mole-ridden lawn, it seemed to disdain propriety or household economy. I admired it a little for that.

Then one Friday morning the first week of July we were awakened early by the slamming of car doors hard. From the bathroom window we watched what was happening next door: a young woman with a ponytail tied in a puffy red bow and another woman, in khaki shorts and tank top, were carting in boxes, lumber, paint cans, rollers. They looked serious about their intentions.

"Did you see that?" I whispered to Rita who was standing on tiptoe to get a better view. "They're women. Both of them."

She whispered with a happy smile, "Don't they just make you tired?"

I took heart at their energy. I knew they were under pressure from the block. In solidarity with our new neighbors, when we got home from a blood check and Rita was napping, I found my screwdriver and tightened up all our garden chairs. It took the better part of my afternoon, but I felt inspired by those young people, their hopes, their dreams.

The story of an individual life plays out like the history of the universe, expanding and contracting. You start as a speck, grow larger, spread wide, gather possessions, follow world events and sports results, then without recognizing the exact moment, you suddenly start to shrink; the future no longer looks so good, you realize how little anything matters, and you give up more and more till you part with your own home, that piece of acreage that made you *you*. If you move, what is left? Just yourselves and a bowlegged highboy lurking darkly in the hall like some displaced great-aunt. Not that we disliked our new house. But it was hard to get serious about sidewalk humps in a life that seemed a bad dream. I kept thinking: Was this really how we'd ended up?

The young people next door took it all in earnest. They threw themselves into upkeep. We didn't see them to speak, they were so busy coming and going, but on the second Saturday following their arrival a carload of people emptied itself onto their front yard. Girls in shorts were yanking weeds, raking, picking up black walnuts while sweating, middle-aged women hauled more things out of the house to the curb and dug holes in the lawn with spades.

145

Who were these people? It was so unusual. When I went out to pick up the newspaper in our drive, I gave them a wave. No one looked my way. I braced myself and walked over. The short-haired young woman in the khaki shorts we knew lived there stopped work and nodded, tight-jawed.

"We're next door," I said. "Grace Watson. My friend Rita's inside." I wanted them to know about us, women together.

"Kelly," she said, extending a muddy hand. "Kelly McGee." She kept her hand firmly in mine and seemed not to notice my surprise at hearing the name. She motioned to the other woman. "My partner— Lynn." The partner looked over. "Neighbor," Kelly said.

Lynn gave an identical smiling nod. "Got to get these dandelions out," she said. "Some friends from our community are helping out."

"Oh," I said, trying to understand all this. To keep her talking, I said, "Did I see tennis rackets?"

Lynn grinned. "We hit the ball around. How about you?"

"We used to play quite a bit," I said. "Years ago."

"We're pretty serious about it," Kelly admitted.

"It's wonderful exercise." I couldn't think of anything more. Somehow I had wished they'd have had a little more time to spare me, but I understood if they were busy. I watched a little embarrassed as one of their friends gathered pine cones that had fallen from our tree.

Lynn called over to me as I was turning toward our house, "I called Traffic yesterday to get a speed bump in."

"Oh," I said, startled. "Well. Thank you. For your civic interest."

"It's a precaution, what with the children on the street, and when school starts up, waiting for the buses."

The day's warmth was beginning to oppress and I badly wanted cool and silence. "I guess, since we don't have children. . . ."

Lynn flashed a bright smile. "We're adopting."

"Oh. Congratulations."

She and Kelly shared a grin. "Kelly Lynn is due in six months."

"Named it already," I said. "That's wonderful." I felt at a loss. "We certainly appreciate your efforts. In the neighborhood, I mean." I waved as I crossed the drive to our yard, but my heart wasn't in it.

I had mixed feelings about my encounter. Afraid that Rita would take the woman's name McGee as a good omen, I didn't mention it, but at dinner I did remind her of the hump in their sidewalk. "It's their responsibility now. If one of us trips on it, I'm going to sue big time."

146

"Then we'd better fix ours first," Rita countered.

I speared up the olives in my chef's salad fast.

In the morning when I was ready to organize boxes in the basement as planned, Rita was still in a robe that kept sliding open. I saw it was one of her bad days. She had applied thick green eye shadow and marked out her mouth in two shades of pink; it alarmed me, all that surface color and the glimpse of bluish skin underneath.

"Keep back from the window," I warned as I pushed the lever on the toaster.

"They're not even home," she interrupted, turning abruptly away. "They left for work at six." I could tell from the stiffness of the way she poured that I was in arrears for some reason. I escaped to tasks in the yard.

Some nights later, Janice Gibbs and I met on the street, waiting for the eclipse, like Girl Scouts. I was beginning to feel like an old-timer now, what with the new kids next door. Over there at 47 a power drill whined softly and Kelly's silhouette worked by a sawhorse in the lighted garage. "Busy beavers," I remarked to Janice. I was interested in what she might say.

Looking up at the sky, Janice paused and then remarked, "It's good for property value. They're always kept up, the houses of double women."

I stood thinking about this—double women as good homeowners. It did not sound like a slur, and yet I felt disqualified from agreeing or disagreeing. In the dark of the eclipse, our heads identically upward, she added, "Those two will burn out."

I clenched a smile at the moon.

Rita had fallen asleep early, so I thought about the comment on my own as I turned off the air conditioning and locked things up. At the bathroom window I paused to feel the night air. The crickets were chatting in the pine tree, and down below I could see busy shadows passing across the blinds in the house next door. Watching, feeling a tightening within, I realized I had been here little more than a month and already I detested our neighbors.

The next project at 47 was to paint over the polka dot shutters with a conservative pine green. "That's a nice choice," said Rita from behind the curtains, unsure. "They've got my vote."

"Why so drab?" I said. My dander was up. I picked out two pints of red and white at the paint store and spiraled barber stripes around our lamppost in front.

Rita hobbled out on her walker to see what I was up to.

"We're exciting people to know," I warned her.

Her face went flat with alarm.

Which was not the expression that met me when I came in muddy from weeding around the viburnum later that afternoon. "They've got a puppy," she whispered. Her voice sounded panicky, as though I should call the police, as though she was going to cry. My boots in hand, I pressed next to her at the window. We caught just a glimpse of Kelly and a flash of fur disappearing behind the garage.

"It's a collie!" Rita said. "Not more than six months old."

The next afternoon we saw Lynn walk the dog past our house. Neither looked our way.

"They call it Trevor," Rita reported later, sitting down to our little supper of eggs. "Maybe for Hugh Trevor-Roper?"

I gave the salt shaker some firm taps from below to loosen it. "I don't know," I told her gently.

Rita positioned herself by the sidewalk on a cushion in a posture of gardening. When Trevor passed on his walks, she lured Lynn into conversation. Soon I knew something of our neighbors' doings.

"They're on the civic association," Rita informed me. "They're getting the curbs repainted because the yellow near the hydrants is worn off. I never noticed that. Did you?"

"No, I didn't." I added, "That's not the sort of thing I would notice."

"But it's wonderful that they have," Rita reminded me.

Our neighbors scheduled their free time down to the minute. I had to endure their weekend itinerary. "They're having a picnic with others from their community. Everyone has to bring something red and something white. It could be an apple pie—that's red and white, you see—or a tablecloth, or cups and plates."

"Red and white," I said. "Just what is this community?"

Rita looked hopeful. "We could join. I think."

The suggestion was beneath my contempt. I said, "Just see what happens when the bundle of joy moves in. That'll shake things up."

"They've got her enrolled in pre-school, prenatally," Rita told me with pleasure. "They're down for Suzuki violin, too."

"For the baby or the dog?"

Rita ignored me. "There's pumpkin cheesecake for dessert, Grace."

I looked at her, surprised. Cheesecake was one of her specialties but she had not had baking energy for months.

"Lynn," she explained. "I gave her the recipe. I told her how it was your favorite. She said she'd updated the recipe by adding ginger and cardamom."

I felt my blood rush to my eyes. "She has the nerve to tell you that your baking is out-of-date?"

"She was just being helpful. Try a piece."

There it sat, nicely humped in its pottery dish with country geese, and I knew it would have the smooth, subtle flavor I liked, but my gorge rose at the thought of Lynn's updating. "I'm full," I said. I skewered my napkin through its ring.

I heard them all next door, dog and owners, that night when I was taking the garbage out. Shadowed by the garage, I paused near their window. The blinds were halfway up and I could see their matching country-coordinated furniture with the stenciled pattern around the ceiling Rita had told me about and the needlepointed chair cushions. They had pushed the sofa and chairs back and were tossing a tennis ball around. Of course they didn't understand that a dog like that needed much more exercise than they could provide. It whined for the toss in soft barks, and through the rectangle of my view I could see its tail wave like a wind-driven flag.

When I had rolled the cans to the curb and come back inside, I found Rita asleep over an acrostic. She heard me shooting the bolt and woke with a start. As I helped her get into her nightgown, I didn't mention what I'd seen or remember out loud what I was thinking about: the loamy smell of our last McGee returned from the woods, fur matted with puddle mud and burrs, softly whining to be dried and let inside, his long snores.

Next door they planted a dogwood. They pointed their chimney. Then one Friday Kelly, of the biceps, who seemed to have no end of know-how, got out a jackhammer and began ripping up their sidewalk. She was taking on the hump.

I was just grilling our swordfish, wondering about our own sidewalk, when she started mixing cement. Rita arched a freshly-plucked eyebrow. She was unfolded lengthily in a chaise, working the acrostic. Her new, fuzzy growth of hair she had clipped back in girls' plastic barrettes from the drugstore. She must have thought she looked good, but it twisted me to see her so.

"I'll fix the damn hump this weekend," I promised out loud. I knifed a steak and flipped it. Next door they had such command, I thought, such engagement and control. And we? We had lived in the shadow of our early risks. We had pursued our private passions. And it was all being taken from us. Next door they had no idea of what we endured.

Dinner was enjoyed to the melodious strains of nearby jackhammer, and I spent the unpleasant minutes thinking: it was not fair to make your neighbors feel like slouches. It was not right to flaunt your industry. "I hope they move," I said to Rita as I stacked the plates.

"They won't move for seven years," she told me, "in order to recoup points and closing costs."

"Good lord," I said. I felt something pulling zippers inside me.

Rita remarked with strained off-handedness, "Lynn was telling me about an assisted living community. But there's a waiting list."

I could not hide my anger. "What is that supposed to mean? I'm assisting you. Right here. You don't have a community; you have me. And there's no waiting—you're in. Did you tell her that?"

Rita looked hesitant. "I didn't. I told them we'd invite them over."

"You're not serious."

"I told them you'd arrange a time."

"Why would we want them in our house?"

Rita's voice was soft but firm. "Because they're young and brave and friendly. Because they're just starting out and because they are better neighbors than we could ever have dreamed of and we owe them our support." Her face seemed lopsided from the force of her feeling. It filled me with self-loathing.

I looked toward our dividing fence. "When do you propose we do this?"

Rita shifted herself upright and tapped her pen against her lips. "They have tennis Tuesday and Thursday. Maybe Friday? Brown cows and cake."

I admired the spirit of Rita's gesture, but something I could not quite articulate would not leave me alone. Rita watched our neighbors as if they were a television commercial, and she was all set to buy them: their squeaky-clean, time-managed, child-paid-for, double-woman way of life. Our own world, with its shadows and tangles felt to me murky but richer. I envied our neighbors their clarity, but some half-tamed creature of the undergrowth pawed inside me, whining in falsetto, yearning to strike out.

After drying the dishes, I set off to issue the invitation. I feared if I phoned my coolness might come through; I could fake it better in person, and I was curious to get a look inside, too. Crossing to knock at

150

47, though, I found my way blocked. The whole area in front of their house was blockaded by sawhorses with blinking yellow lights on top, everything neat and official, and exaggerated, as if our neighbors were barricading a major traffic accident, not four wet feet of cement.

I stopped and looked at the house. The collie pup on the porch, chewing something between its paws, sat up. I could hear its watchful growl in the dark. My pulse beat hard in my temples as I edged through the sawhorses, stepped across the lawn and up the first of their porch steps.

"Good boy," I whispered. "Nice Trevor." Dogs have always trusted me, so I had no fear of its barking. "Let's take a little walk, boy," I coaxed.

Nervous, unsure, it shivered as I untied the leash from the wrought iron support. Its tennis ball rolled to my feet, so I took that, too. "Come, boy," I urged.

Whining lightly still, the dog let me guide it down the steps, across the lawn. It waited as I lifted aside one of the barricades, heavier than I'd expected. When I held out the ball, he pulled upward, ready, intent.

"Fetch!" I whispered and tossed the ball a short distance toward the sidewalk. The leash slipped through my hands as Trevor obliged, plodding forward, sinking paws into the wet cement, slipping and sliding as he rummaged with his nose.

"That's enough," I called after a minute. "Bring it back." My assistant, ball in mouth, surprised, let me catch him by the collar and lead him back up to the porch. "Good dog," I assured him. "Perfect." I pulled up a hosta leaf and wiped between his toes. The few beads of cement came easily off his fur.

Inside the house all was quiet. Trevor tugged the fuzz off the ball while I replaced the sawhorse. Then I inspected the sidewalk. By streetlight, the paw prints looked craterous.

The next morning, Rita was sitting at the desk in the living room so I staked out the bathroom window upstairs. Around nine o'clock our friends walked down to check their cement. They lifted aside the sawhorses and stopped short. I kept a chuckle in check—they had spotted the alterations.

Watching, I saw them turn their heads toward the puppy snoozing on its side, tied up to the porch. Then Lynn ran a hand down Kelly's arm. The tops of their heads revealed nothing as they strode back into the house. My spirits sank as I saw they were unified; they were in it together. I listened for Rita. "I'm just making the beds," I called down to her, though I stayed by the window. Ten minutes later Lynn was squatting streetside by a wheelbarrow, chopping into new cement, smoothing it level on the walk. Nothing, nothing could stop them, said the motion of her trowel.

I heard Rita knock against a table. I hurried to the landing, calling down, and she looked up at me with hazy confusion. She seemed to be preparing to go out somewhere. Her shoulder bag dragged behind her on the carpet. Her hair, loose, dropped around her eyes. Her face suddenly crumbled. "I've lost my pink barrettes," she said and began to sob, still standing, but listing to one side like a trawler capsizing.

I hurried down to her and pulled her close. "Rita," I said.

"I keep losing things," she said against my shoulder.

I patted her faster. "What's this about?"

She gave a raspy sigh. "I've been making out a will. Lynn said—" She broke into a sob. "Grace," she said. "I've made you come here where you hate it, and I'm not getting better, and I don't even have anything to leave you."

I closed my eyes. Her bones jutted within my arms like broken wings. Her skin smelled sour beneath the strawberry of her soap. The clean truth of her words cut and muted me. Outside on that sunny Saturday, I could hear the chopping. The wonderful women next door were repairing the damage I'd done; they were going strong. As they bumped their barricades around, Rita and I held fast to each other inside our own dark house.

Nominated by The Kenyon Review, Kristin King

THE DOG YEARS

by TONY HOAGLAND

from MANY MOUNTAINS MOVING

when it seemed every girl I dated
had a friend—
a Sheena or a Scoop, Jerome or Mr. Bones—
a four-legged, longtime furry pal

whose single-minded, tail-shaking
devotion to his mistress
caused me a certain pang,
knowing his relationship with her

would outlast mine;
that he would still be here,
jumping on the furniture
long after I was just a memory

beside the toothbrush rack, another
anecdotal mugshot
in the history book of non-commitment.
Still, that animal and I would often,

of a sunny afternoon, promenade together,
sniffing at the pants of strangers,
one of us pausing
while the other peed,

having in common both
a short attention span
and an insatiable appetite
for the love of womankind.

How perplexing for that dog
it must have been
when at the midnight hour
it was me, not him,

admitted to the fresh
bower of her bed—
and more than once,
in the warm, aromatic dark

full of animal mysteries
and spiritual facts,
I myself felt baffled by my luck,
like a sinner who has woken up

inexplicably in heaven,
while far off in the background
some poor wretch
who had lived by all the rules

howled and scratched at the shut door.

Nominated by Lynn Emanuel, Laura Kasischke, Pamela Stewart, Marilyn Krysl

THE ILLUSTRATED ENCYCLOPEDIA OF THE ANIMAL KINGDOM

fiction by DAN CHAON

from WITNESS

ON THE SECOND FLOOR of an old Victorian house which has been converted into tiny apartments, Dennis dreams that he is holding a baby. The infant in the dream is wrapped in a gray-blue blanket, with only its round face peeking out. Dennis can feel its limbs squirming beneath the swaddling as he smoothes his palm lightly over the infant's cheek. When his hand touches the baby's skin, he wakes up.

Above him, he hears the woman on the third floor walking. Her floorboards—his ceiling—sigh as she goes, as if she's stepping over shifting ice. He is aware, even as he opens his eyes, that the dream is partially hers, a seed she had planted. He doesn't know her really, but he thinks about her often. She walks across his ceiling at all hours of the night. In certain rooms he will occasionally hear a radio playing above him, and on some evenings if he sits by the radiator in his bedroom he will hear her stumbling, sweetly awkward monotone as she reads her son a story. Dennis believes that her husband has left her. Perhaps he is dead. Perhaps there never was a husband to begin with.

It is the woman upstairs, or the dream, or maybe simply the fact that it is a new town and he knows no one and he is twenty-five years old and spends far too much time (he thinks) in his own head, too much time lying on his bed in his underwear with a beer growing warm on his chest as he listens. It is a combination of all of these things, no doubt. Something makes him decide to call the hospital, which is located in the city that he lived in before he moved to this new one. He is aware that it is foolish to call the hospital. But he just wants to see what they will say.

So he calls one morning from work during his lunch when his co-workers are out, they all seem to have places to go, etc. He calls and is transferred several times. While he waits, classical music that seems somewhat familiar is played for him through the phone lines.

The lady who finally answers is very professional about the whole thing, very administrative. He has signed a contract which is legally binding, she says, and (hundreds of miles away) he nods earnestly into the receiver. I know that, he says. He explains that he doesn't want to cause trouble, he's just sort of curious, and she says, "That's sweet," in a condescending voice that suggests that she is probably pretty, probably used to turning men down quickly and cheerfully, a tight fake smile reducing them to a speck. Dennis feels himself shrinking. "You must get calls like this all the time," he says apologetically, and she says, "No, frankly, I don't."

Well, he thinks when she hangs up the phone. He can feel himself blushing, though of course no one knows who he has called, and he certainly won't tell anyone. He feels stupid.

Maybe it is strange to wonder, he thinks: Odd. It wasn't as if there were love involved, not even physical contact, just an easy fifty dollars he'd heard about through a friend who was in the first year of medical school. The friend had been doing it about once a week and he got Dennis in, though Dennis's vital statistics, his looks and IQ and extracurricular activities were probably not as impressive as most of those medical school boys. So maybe they didn't even use his. He'd only done it because he really had needed the cash at the time—it was his senior year in college.

When he went in he'd felt very embarrassed. The nurse was not much older than he—a short, stocky girl who wore her hair in a way that made him think that maybe she'd had an unhappy childhood. She couldn't look at him. She just gave him some forms to fill out on one of those clipboards with a pen hanging on a beaded metal chain like the kind that are attached to bathtub drain plugs. He turned in the pa-

156

perwork and the nurse led him down a hospital-smelling corridor, both of them shy, silence trailing down the long hallway until they came to a halt in front of a little bathroom. She gave him a kind of test-tube with a screw-on lid and cleared her throat, shifting her weight in those chunky white shoes, and she opened a door and said that there were some magazines he could look at if he wished. She might have used the word "peruse."

He glanced in and there were some old *Playboy* and *Penthouse* magazines on the table next to the toilet. He nodded, not meeting her eyes. What was there to say? The nurse was trying to be professional about it, but he could see she was secretly mortified behind her nurse facade, and when he tried to smile ironically she just cleared her throat again and left in a hurry. Poor girl, he thought.

It was strange, because it was she, the nurse, who he ended up thinking of, rather than the centerfolds with their tawny unreal shapes and unmarked expressions. When he brought his test-tube out and gave it to her he felt a sort of regret shudder through him. Her eyes were so sad that he was sure for a moment that she knew he'd been thinking of her. He sometimes thought that any baby that came out of it must be as much that nurse's as it was his own.

He finds it difficult to truly believe that there is a baby, but it's something he thinks about, sometimes. It's interesting imagining someone—maybe an infertile couple or perhaps a single woman who has some money—someone, going through those pages of descriptions and deciding on him. Maybe he has the nationality they are looking for, the color of hair or eyes, or one of the accomplishments he's written down—his winning the state spelling bee in high school, his abilities in baseball, his college major—attracts them in some way, and they say, "This is the one." He wonders if that's how it works. He likes to imagine that there is the possibility of a person out there. They might have a certain shape of face or fingers, or a certain way of smiling. They might even eventually have certain moods—a particular vague and watery melancholy feeling, sometimes—because of him. He doesn't know why he wants so badly for this to be true.

It's summer. Cicadas fill the air with an intermittent static, and in the weeks that follow he often sees them in the morning, in the tiny back yard out behind their apartment house, his upstairs neighbor and her son, who must be about four, a thin, deep-eyed kid with a head like a baby bird. Dennis gazes down at them, watching as the boy builds

OUACHITA TECHNICAL COLLEGE

something with mud and sticks in the corner by the fence; watching as he reads his book: *The Illustrated Encyclopedia of the Animal Kingdom.* On the cover, there are drawings of a snake, a zebra, a parrot, a beetle, all the same size.

The woman sits quietly, smoking. She runs her fingers thoughtfully along the side of her bare foot, that curling-iron hair she has crushed flat in the back where she's slept on it. When he thinks of her face in his mind, it looks hard and melancholy and almost cruel because of the traces of make-up that remain around her lips and eyes. She exhales smoke.

On the day he made his phone call to the hospital, he happened to be walking home from work and he found a box of books. The box had been put out by the curb for the trash man to pick up, right outside a big old house that looked something like his except it hadn't been split up into apartments. There was nothing wrong with the books that he could see—an old set of children's encyclopedias, not a complete set but nice nonetheless, with beautiful photographs. It didn't even look like they'd been read! He glanced around to see that no one was looking, and then he lifted the box and carried it home.

After dinner that evening, he had gone up the stairs with the box and knocked on the woman's door.

"I found this," he said, showing her the books and smiling sheepishly. "I've heard you reading to your son and I thought it would be something he would enjoy."

He'd practiced this short speech several times, but after it left his mouth he realized that it was a mistake to say that he'd heard her reading. Her eyes narrowed a bit, suspiciously, and when she leaned down to look at the titles of the books, she wrinkled her nose. He was aware that they smelled a little like a basement.

"He's a little young for encyclopedias," she said, and Dennis shifted his weight. The books were heavy.

"Well," he said, "they've got nice pictures."

"Hm," she said. She looked him over again, and he saw her eyes come to a decision. If they were to fall in love, Dennis thought, it would never work out. She saw something essential about him that she could never learn to like. He didn't know what it was, exactly, but he could feel it in the air around him, like a smell—a particular trigger which he lacked—a winking type of confidence, or body hair, or a temper. Whatever it was.

"If you want to leave them," she said, "that's okay. I mean, he'll prob-ably just wreck them. Color in them and stuff. You could sell them." She shrugged, and put a hand against her hair. "You don't have kids of your own," she said.

"No." He smiled, hesitating because she made no move to take the box. He braced it against his hip. "No, not really," he said thoughtfully. And then, after a second he realized that this was an odd thing to say. "I guess I might have kids," he said, "but none that I know of."

"Oh," she said, and then she laughed shortly. "You're one of those, huh?" She looked at him for a moment with something like, what? Flirtation? Sarcasm? Something familiar but not quite friendly. He couldn't tell, but it made him blush. He set the box down.

"No," he said. "No, it's . . ." and for a moment he actually considered telling her about the hospital and the rest, though he knew that would be worse, at this point, than just letting her think what she wanted.

"It's complicated," he said.

"Uh-huh," she said. She gave him that same look again, and he watched her thinking, a whole complex set of things was passing through her mind. She did not believe that he was the type, and she wondered, briefly, why he would say such a strange thing, what he re-ally meant. She thought of her son's father, or maybe she didn't. She opened the door a little more, and Dennis could see the boy inside, sitting cross-legged in front of the television, his face lit unnaturally as he trotted a plastic elephant along the carpet. It would have been neat if the boy suddenly turned to look at him, but he did not.

"Well," the woman said. "Thanks."

When Dennis first moved into the apartment, the little boy upstairs was going through a period of having nightmares. The child would wake up screaming, and of course Dennis would awaken as well. "Help me!" Dennis thought he could hear the child crying. "Help me!" At last, Dennis would hear the woman's footsteps, and then her voice, gentle and tired. "Hush," she was probably saying. "It's okay. It's okay. Be still now." And then, after a time, she would be-gin to sing.

He doesn't know why this had affected him so, the sound of her singing, but he can remember shuddering. He had curled up a little more, thinking, "What is it? What's wrong with me?" and trying to de-cide that it was simple, that it was ordinary loneliness, being disori-ented in a new place, boxes still not unpacked, his family far away, his own father, dead a few years now, buried in a cemetery some thousand miles distant.

But it had felt, at that moment, that there was something wrong with the world itself. He could have sworn, he knew in his heart that something terrible had happened to the world, and that everyone knew it but him.

Nominated by Martha Collins, Reginald Gibbons, Joyce Carol Oates, Sylvia Watanabe, David Jauss

BORROWED FINERY

memoir by PAULA FOX

from THE THREEPENNY REVIEW

A PUBLICITY STILL of the actress Zasu Pitts, crouching half-naked among heaps of gold coins, an expression of demented rapacity on her face—an advertisement for the movie *Greed,* made in 1923, the year I was born—epitomized my childhood view of American banking and American business. As I grew older, my attitude toward money changed, but not by much. In my mind's eye, Zasu Pitts still holds out handfuls of coins, but she is not offering them, she is gloating over her possession of them.

The minister who took care of me in my infancy and earliest years saw to it that I didn't look down and out. Twice a year, in spring and in fall, he bought a few things for me to wear, sparing whatever he could from his yearly salary. Other clothes came my way donated by mothers in his congregation whose own children had outgrown them. They were mended, washed and ironed before they were handed on.

In early April, before my fifth birthday, my father mailed the minister two five-dollar bills and a written note. I can see him reading the note as he holds it and the bills in one hand while with the index finger of the other, he presses the bridge of his eyeglasses against his nose because he has broken his left stem.

This particularity of memory can be partly attributed to the rarity of my father's notes—not to mention enclosures of money—or else to the new dress that part of the ten dollars paid for. Or so I imagine.

The next morning the minister drove me in his old Packard car from the Victorian house on the hill where we lived in Newburgh, a Hudson Valley town half an hour distant and a few miles north of the Storm King promontory, which sinks into the river like an elephant's brow.

We went to Schoonmaker's department store on Water Street. The minister took my hand as we walked down the aisle. It was the first time he'd taken me to a big store. When we emerged onto the sidewalk, he was carrying a box that contained a white dotted Swiss dress. It had a Peter Pan collar and fell straight to its hem from smocked shoulders. He had written a poem for me to recite at the Easter service in the Congregational church where he preached. I would have something new to wear, to stand before all the people and speak his words. I loved the minister and I loved the dotted Swiss dress.

Years later when I read through the few letters and notes my father had sent to the minister, and that he'd saved, I realized how he had played the coquette in his apologies for his remissness in supporting me. His excuses were made with a kind of fraudulent heartiness, as though he were boasting, not confessing.

Unlike the meaning that lurked in his words, his handwriting was beautiful, an orderly flight of birds across yellowing pages.

WHEN I was ten or so, living with my Spanish grandmother in a one-room apartment in Kew Gardens, Long Island, with a Murphy pull-down bed in which we both slept, and that emerged in the evenings like a mastodon from the closet where it lived, I was the recipient of a paper sack stuffed with discarded clothes from my cousin, Natalie. Stained slips, wool stocking worn thin at the heels, garter belts with flaccid suspenders, and ragged brassieres were all wound about each other like sleeping snakes. At the very bottom of the sack was a folded print dress made of slippery material, rayon perhaps. It had a rope-like belt with tasseled ends that looped twice around my waist. I wore it to the public school I attended, though it was far too big, and its pattern of large ugly green flowers made it, somehow, unseemly.

Natalie, several years older than I, lived in a railroad flat in a Spanish Harlem tenement with her parents, a grown-up sister, and a yellow mongrel that bit everyone—or threatened to—except her father, my uncle Fermin. My grandmother and I made periodic visits to the flat. It was a long subway journey from Kew Gardens, long enough for my apprehension to deepen as we neared the end of the trip. Would Uncle Fermin be at home wearing a hat that hid his eyes? His skin was so white, his nose so like the blade of a knife!

On the long-ago Saturdays when one of us managed to scrape up money for tickets, Natalie and I would spend afternoons at the Bluebird movie house on Broadway and, I think, 158th Street. Cartoons preceded the feature film and were greeted with patches of wild applause. Along with Olive Oyl and her long feet and tiny head, I especially recollect Mickey Mouse, thin and worried-looking in those days as though he'd just eluded a laboratory technician's grab, not as he looks today, plump, smug and bourgeois.

And what movies we saw! The radiance of the actors and actresses, their eyes, their faces, their voices and movements. Their clothes! Even in prison movies, the stars shone in their prison clothes as if tailors had accompanied them in their downfall.

In the Bluebird, it was as though a woman sang stories larger than lives, about fate and love and evil enacted in shadowed rooms I couldn't enter, only glimpse from where I sat, rapt.

Some Saturdays as we returned to the tenement where Natalie lived, we heard thumping and could feel through the soles of our feet the vibrations of sound from my uncle's radio, all the way down from the fifth floor to the sidewalk where we had halted. On Natalie's face would appear a distressed, complicit smile, as though she held herself responsible for the noise.

It was not an ordinary radio. My uncle had built a plywood screen that covered the two narrow windows of the tiny parlor and had nailed or glued to it all the radio components, added two loudspeakers and, whenever he was in the flat, would turn up the volume as high as it would go.

The room felt ominous, as though something lived in it that might bring down the whole building. In summer, what breezes made their way down the street were shut out by the plywood screen, and in winter wind and cold leaked around its edges. My uncle sat in his coat and hat in the only armchair in the room, submerged in the uproar as though stupefied, the yellow dog at his feet growling, no doubt in baffled protest.

Neighbors stopped by the local police precinct to complain—only a very few tenants had telephones in those days—but the police never came. My grandmother would retire to one of the cell-like bedrooms and lie on a cot, one arm flung across her eyes and brow.

My uncle's wife, Elpidia, was a peasant woman from a Cuban village, and he had married her, I was told by my grandmother, to protest his engagement to the daughter of a plantation owner, an arrangement made by his father when Fermin was only a bad-tempered boy. She had married him out of dazzlement and some kind of love, and had come with him to the United States.

163

To escape the awful radio racket in the parlor as best I could, I used to go to the kitchen to watch Elpidia iron on a spindly board that resembled a wooden grasshopper. Grimly, as thought she were trying to kill it, she struck at it with a small black iron she had heated on the stove. Whatever garments were spread on the board's surface frequently bore scorch marks.

On other days on our visits to the flat, I would find my aunt slumped on a stool drawn up to the sink, weeping, silently, one hand supporting her chin as she stared down at the cockroaches that came and went with their hideous broken speed, now a pause, now a rush.

I don't recall her wearing anything but a faded, stained brown house dress. Her breasts looked like poorly stuffed small pillows. In one of them her death began. She developed cancer before her forty-fifth birthday and, after months of suffering, died of it.

When I was eight, I had lived in Cuba with my grandmother on a sugar plantation that belonged to an ancient relative, Tía Luisa, who was not my aunt at all but a distant cousin. Because of that and because of my grandmother's broken English—even after decades in the United States, she spoke with a heavy accent—which obliged me to speak to her in Spanish, I was fluent by then.

One later winter afternoon when it began to grow dark around four, I stood in the kitchen a few feet away from Elpidia, watching her. At last, I ask her why she cried so.

"no sé, mi hija," she answered, turning toward me her kindly, utterly miserable face. "No sé . . ." I don't know, my daughter. I don't know.

MY PARENTS returned from Europe, after a sojourn of three or four years, when I was eleven. They slid into my sight standing on the deck of a small passenger ship out of Marseilles that docked in New York City on the Hudson River alongside a cavernous shed. They were returning home after their adventures, the most recent being their flight from the Balearic Island of Ibiza during the Spanish Civil War.

My mother had draped a polo coat over her shoulders—I supposed because it was a cool spring day—and she smiled down at my grandmother and me where we waited in the shadowed darkness of the shed. Sunlight fell in daggers through holes in the roof high above us.

It had been years since I'd seen either of them. They were as handsome as movie stars. Smoke trailed like a festive streamer from the cigarette my mother held between two fingers of her right hand. When she realized we had spotted her, she waved once and her head was momentarily wreathed in smoke. The gangplank was lowered thunder-ously across the abyss between the ship's deck and the pier. Passengers began to trickle across it. Suddenly my parents were standing in front of us, a steamer trunk like a third presence between them.

"Hello . . . Hello . . . Hello," they called to us as though they were far away. They pointed out pieces of their luggage for porters, speak-ing to my grandmother and me in voices that were deep, musical—not everyday voices like those I heard in Kew Gardens—but of unbroken suavity as though they had memorized whole pages written for them on this occasion of their homecoming.

They spoke of shipboard life, about a cave in Ibiza outside of which my father had crouched for hours, humiliated by the fit of claustro-phobia that had paralyzed him not two feet from the entrance, while my mother hid inside along with other refugees before escaping the next day to the ship that carried them to Marseilles, and about the fact, ruefully acknowledged by both of them with charming smiles, that no troops from either side had especially wanted to capture them, about the behavior of the French, and British filmmaking, and such a myr-iad of subjects that although I stood motionless and listening raven-ously, I felt I was tumbling down a mountain side, an avalanche a few yards behind me.

Unlike her brother, Fermin, my mother had not a trace of a foreign accent. But in the middle of a sentence, she switched to Spanish and bent suddenly to embrace my grandmother with nearly human warmth as if she'd all at once recalled that the elderly woman stand-ing so submissively before her, a stunned smile on her face, was her own mother, who, with her poor grasp of English, would not have un-derstood even a part of what was said.

My mother's eyes stared at me over my grandmother's shoulder. Her mouth formed a cold radiant smile. My soul shivered.

My father leaned toward me, reaching out a hand to push a clump of my hair behind my ear. The tips of his fingers were damp. He laughed. He murmured, "Well, pal. Well, well . . . here we all are . . ."

I HAD been told by some relative that my father wrote for the movies. During the month that followed their return from Europe, he sold a script to a Hollywood studio for $10,000, a sum beyond my comprehension.

After two days, they left the small Manhattan hotel that they'd gone directly to from the ship, and took a room at the Half-Moon Hotel on the boardwalk at Coney Island, a ramshackle pile at the best of times that burned down long ago. My father said they were too "broke" to afford the first place. Something about his tone of voice suggested to me that being "broke" was only a temporary condition, and that it was different from being poor.

He also told me that he'd written the entire movie in a week while Elsie, my mother, handed him Benzedrine tablets from the bed upon which she lay doing crossword puzzles and lighting cigarette after cigarette. My grandmother and I visited them there one afternoon. During the hour we spent with them, my father presented me with a typewriter, a Hermes baby featherweight, saying, "Don't hock it. I may want it back," and only a few days later took it back with a muttered explanation I couldn't quite make out.

During that same visit, he asked for the loan of a bequest left to me two years earlier by "la Señora Ponvert," swearing he would repay me—all this spoken as though we both understood what tomfoolery it all was, the old lady leaving it to me, the amount itself, fifty dollars, and, further, that the people in the room, my grandmother and I, he and Elsie, even the room itself, were all manifestations of a larger truth than reality could ever be—and at this vertiginous moment my mother spoke from the chair where she was sitting, looking though the pages of a magazine. "Tía Luisa," she said without glancing up at me. I had forgotten, not that it was the same person they both had mentioned to me by different names, but that there had been a bequest. I looked over at my grandmother, who was nodding her head rapidly and saying, yes, yes, in a nearly inaudible voice as though she had been considering that very matter and had arrived at the fortunate conclusion that she and I would make the journey to the bank and withdraw the money at once.

When my father sold the movie in a week or so—it was easier in those days, simpler—he didn't offer to pay me back my fifty dollars, or to return the typewriter. And I, feeling that both matters would be judged by them as trivial, never mentioned them. I hadn't cared about the money but I had liked the typewriter.

Once my father was paid for the movie, he arranged for me to meet Elsie at De Pinna's department store on 5th Avenue to buy me some clothes. There was little danger in the subways and on the streets in those days, and a child was safer, except for an occasional flasher lurking at the end of a station platform. But as I rode into the city from Kew Gardens, I felt an alarm pervading me I couldn't name.

166

I saw Elsie before she saw me. She was moving indolently toward the glove counter near the store entrance. She looked so isolated yet so complete in herself.

Then she seemed to sense my presence. She turned around as I neared her. "Oh. There you are," she said formally. Her smile was meant for great things.

The shoe department was on the second floor, and we were going to begin there. We went to the elevator, my mother keeping a distance between us. From time to time, she glanced at my shabby footwear. I felt ashamed, as though it were I who had made them unfit for her eyes.

She bought me two pairs of beautiful shoes, one black, one green suede. During the time we were together, it was as if we were continually being introduced to each other. I was conscious of an immense effort—to start anew every time I began to speak.

It took less than twenty minutes. She smiled brilliantly at me. "Can you get home by yourself?" she asked me as though I had suddenly strayed into the path of her vision. I nodded wordlessly. The shopping was over.

I watched her walk away up Fifth Avenue with her peculiar stride, so characteristic of her that in the relatively few weeks she'd been back in the United States, I'd already learned it. Half the time she would tip-toe as though she were ready to fly off the earth. For years afterwards I thought about that stride of hers, and now and then I would imitate it. It had been an expression of her strangeness, her singularity, even, if remotely, of her glamour.

I tried wearing the green suede shoes with Natalie's print dress, which, as I'd grown taller, fit me better. But they didn't work. And I had no other clothes to match the elegance of those shoes. They gathered dust in my grandmother's closet. When I left for good, I left the shoes there too.

Nominated by The Threepenny Review, Sigrid Nunez

FAITHFULNESS

by FORREST GANDER

from FIRST INTENSITY

That we can never explain the experience.

To say: Certain ganglion cells were excited
by stimulation of the red cones.

To say: I saw the goldfinch peck a dandelion.

To say: Go to the Street of Bleating Toads.
West of town by a trail,
we come to the foot of Jump Mountain
and the grave of Major John Hayes, of Daniel
Morgan's Riflemen, who requested his burial
near the Indian mound, that on Judgment Day
when God's writing reversed, he might
know if the Massawomee
dead rose too.

Radiant opacity.
What will he see when his eyes are tongued open?

Apparent world, the holy book insists,
not the only one. Or is this a vulgar translation?

The pitcher plant swallowed a wren.
Each point of smooth space overlies
a tangent of Euclidean space
endowed with striated dimensions, swoons, and suspenses.

To say, *I have lost the consolation of belief*
but still have the ambition to worship.

To recognize the smell, mixed with pine-combed wind,
of mucus inside one's own nostrils.

How then adjust to the other's stride
but by being possessed
by what one came to possess?

So the hominid bones were gouged
in exactly the locations that might be expected
if someone had used a stone tool
to extract meat from a corpse.

Nominated by Brenda Hillman, Agha Shahid Ali, David Rivard, First Intensity

ALSO LOVE YOU

by REGINALD SHEPHERD

from THE GETTYSBURG REVIEW

for Chris

I think of you when I am dead, the way rocks
think of earthworms and oak roots, tendrils
that break them down to loam and nutrients,
something growing out of every
disappearance. I will be simpler then, sheer
molecule, much easier to understand:
steam rising from sidewalk vents, rain
accumulating on ailanthus leaves
after the rain has ended, the lingering smell
of rain and rotting leaves. (*Look for me,
I'll be around,* that's every song: I'll be that
too.) I will you kites unraveled from their tangled lines
(so far up you can't tell what they want to imitate),
weather balloons and evening stars, easily
mistaken objects of luminosity; observation
satellites to record you just out of sight
and tell you what you've missed. I will be
the lichen bubbling from a crack in the
Belmont Rocks, where you don't go,
between the brilliant men loitering
in their temporary beauty. You will. I will
you every artificial slab that makes a beach

170

if you think hard enough, anchored
fronds of blue-green algae bobbing
in the surface motion just like kelp
weaving in waves on Long Island Sound,
like, come to think of it, sirens' hair combed out
to tourmaline and emerald. I could be this fallen
branch across your path in Lincoln Park, marker: grasp it
and push it aside. I will you people bicycling
just past sunset and joggers straying from
their path, whole evenings of various exercise,
and this first of a whole series of lampposts
burned out, blocks of them. I will be the wind
that messes up your hair, you've just
gotten it cut, pollen, pawn of light and
light winds, air sultry and somehow
sexual, those men still sunning themselves,
giving themselves up to light and passing
eyes, your eyes perhaps. I'll be the things
left behind for you, I'll be much kinder
then. I'll kiss the drowsing atmosphere
all of a summer's afternoon, and that's not all.

Nominated by Marilyn Hacker, Rachel Hadas, Maureen Seaton

NACHMAN

fiction by LEONARD MICHAELS

from THE THREEPENNY REVIEW

IN 1980, RAPHAEL NACHMAN, a visiting lecturer in mathematics at the university in Cracow, declined the tour of Auschwitz, where his grandparents had died, and asked instead for a tour of the ghetto, where they had lived. The American consul, Dirk Sullivan, arranged for a guide to meet Nachman at his hotel, and hoped to have nothing more to do with him. He thought Nachman was a contrary type, too full of himself. As for Nachman, he thought Sullivan was officious.

At eight o'clock, the morning of his tour, Nachman left his room and passed through the small lobby on his way to the still smaller dining room for coffee. He noticed a girl standing alone beside the desk. Her posture and impassive expression suggested she was waiting for somebody, but she didn't glance at Nachman as he approached, so he assumed the girl wasn't his guide. He asked anyway, "Are you waiting for me, Miss? I'm Nachman."

The girl looked as if he'd mildly disturbed her reverie, and said, "How do you do? I'm Marie Borokowski, your guide."

She didn't smile, but Nachman told himself Poles aren't Americans. Why should she smile? She was here to do a job. She'd been sent by the university, at the request of the American Consul, to be his guide. Perhaps she'd have preferred to do something else that morning. So she didn't smile but neither did she look unhappy.

They shook hands.

Nachman invited her to join him for coffee. She accepted and followed him into the dining room.

Nachman wasn't inspired to make conversation at eight o'clock in the morning, but he felt obliged, though Marie looked content to sit and say nothing. After sipping his coffee he said, "I like Cracow. A beautiful city."

"People compare it to Prague."

"From what I've seen, there has been no destruction of monuments and buildings."

"Russian troops arrived sooner than the Germans expected."

Nachman expected her to tell him the story of Cracow's salvation, but she stopped there. Again, he was disconcerted, but the girl was merely terse, not rude. Her soft voice gave Nachman an impression of reserve and politeness.

"How fortunate," he said. "The city remained intact."

"There was plunder. Paintings, sculptures . . . Is 'plunder' the word?"

"Indeed. Are you a student at the university, Marie?"

"Yes. I study mathematics."

"Of course they sent me someone in my field. I should have thought so."

"I attended your lectures."

"You weren't too bored?"

"Not at all."

"That's kind of you to say."

"You talked about the history of problems, which is not ordinarily done. A student might think all problems were invented the day of the lecture. I wasn't bored."

"Your English is good. Do you also speak Russian?"

"I was obliged to study Russian in high school."

"So you speak Russian?"

"I was unable to learn it."

"English came more easily?"

"Yes."

"What else were you obliged to study?"

"Marxism."

"Did you learn it?"

"I'm afraid not."

"Why not?"

"I'm not very intelligent."

Nachman smiled. She'd said it so seriously.

"How old are you, Marie?"

173

"Nineteen."

"Are you from Cracow?"

"No. A village in the country. The nearest city is Brest Litovsk."

"I've heard of Brest Litovsk."

"You would never have heard of my village."

It was easier to study the girl if she talked and he listened, but Nachman asked questions mainly because he felt uneasy. It was a defensive approach. The American Consul had warned Nachman about Polish women and the secret police. It seemed unlikely that the secret police had employed this girl—less than half Nachman's age, and with such a solemn peasant face—to compromise him and make him vulnerable to their purposes. Besides, she was a student of mathematics. Nachman could have asked her specific questions about mathematics, and, in less than a minute, he'd discover if she were lying, but it would be awkward and unpleasant if she were. She didn't seem to be lying about her failure to learn Russian or Marxism.

So Nachman lit a cigarette and sipped his coffee. He didn't test her knowledge of mathematics, and he decided not to ask about her failure to learn Russian and Marxism. He understood that Marie was telling him, indirectly, that she hated the Russians. She was neither a spy nor a village idiot.

The American Consul had unsettled Nachman during their interview. The memory lingered strongly.

Nachman had said, "My field is mathematics. Nothing I do is secret, except insofar as it's unintelligible. I'm of no conceivable interest to the secret police. If they want to ask me questions, I'll give them answers. I'd do the same with anyone."

"You know many people, Professor Nachman. Isn't that true?"

"They are all mathematicians. Our work means nothing to the majority of the human race. I invent problems. If I'm lucky, I solve them and publish the solutions before some other mathematician. My publications are available to anyone who has access to a library and understands numbers."

"You're modest, Professor Nachman. You were invited to Cracow because your work has important implications for computer science. But be that as it may, a casual remark about any person you know is recorded and filed. There are listening devices everywhere. Even in my car. I'm sure they are in your hotel room."

"I don't gossip, and there is no one in my hotel room but me. I don't talk to myself."

"I believe you, but if you were to say in conversation at a cocktail party, in all innocence, that so-and-so is a homosexual, or a heroin addict, or badly in debt, your comment would enter his file at the headquarters of the secret police. With other such innocent comments, which are gathered in different cities—not only in Poland—a detailed picture of so-and-so is eventually developed."

"For what purpose?"

"Who knows what purpose will emerge on what occasion?"

"I never heard of a homosexual mathematician. Could you name one?"

"Of course, but my point is we are not to name any. As for Polish women, they have destroyed American marriages—more often than you imagine."

"Are you married?"

"My marriage is in no danger, but thanks for your concern, Professor Nachman. The allure of Polish women is considerable. They are the most gorgeous women you will ever meet. I'm sure you noticed Pamela, the receptionist."

"Does she destroy marriages?"

"With her, a man could fall in love. It has been known to happen in Poland. Even a tough, cold, sophisticated, executive type falls in love, and forgets the distinction between matters of the heart and corporate information of the most privileged kind. Every word he says is reported. The fate of his marriage is incidental."

"I'm not married. I have no secrets. I don't gossip. I didn't come to Cracow for romantic adventures. It's arguable that I'm a freak. You're wasting your time, Mr. Sullivan, unless you want to make me self-conscious."

"My job is to welcome American visitors and mention these things. Bear in mind that your value to the secret police is known to them, not you. By the way, I have your ticket for the tour of Auschwitz. Compliments of the State Department."

He held the ticket across his desk toward Nachman.

"Thank you. I don't want to tour Auschwitz. I would like to see the ghetto, particularly the synagogue."

MARIE SAID they could walk, after breakfast, from the hotel to the ghetto. She added, as they left the hotel, "On the way, we can visit an ancient church."

It was an extremely cold morning. Marie walked with a long stride, easily and steadily, as if she could walk for hours and hours, and was indifferent to the cold. Nachman found himself adjusting to her rhythm, though he was hunched up in his overcoat, and didn't walk as smoothly as Marie.

"Do you go to church regularly?"

"I haven't been inside a church since I was a child," she said. "This one is famous, visited by many foreigners. I thought you might want to see it, but we can go directly to the ghetto. The church isn't important."

"Do you want to visit the church?"

Marie seemed to wonder if she wanted to or not. Then she said, "Do you want to visit the ghetto?"

It wasn't an answer. Nachman supposed Marie felt she'd answered enough questions. He'd been reproached, but not undeservedly. The girl had a strong character.

"My grandparents lived there," said Nachman. "I want to see the synagogue. My grandfather was known for his piety. I suppose he worshipped in that synagogue."

The way they walked in the cold seemed to shape his remarks, each sentence the length of a stride, more or less.

"You suppose?"

"I know little about him. We never met."

"He didn't go to America with your parents."

"My parents never forgave themselves. He died in Auschwitz. As a child, I was told almost nothing about family history. My parents didn't care to remember Poland, and preferred that I didn't think about it."

"As a result your life has been spared bitter memories."

"As a result, not a day passes that I don't think about it."

"You're more than curious about your grandfather. You want very much to know."

Nachman said lightly, "It is why I do mathematics."

The words surprised him. They sounded as if he meant what he said.

Marie glanced at Nachman, but she didn't ask the question she had in mind. Nachman didn't give her the opportunity. He continued, "As for my grandfather, he was frequently mentioned, but always in a mythical way. I heard that he was consulted by Polish nobility for his business acumen—what business, I don't know—and respected by the Jews for his piety and learning."

"He must have been an interesting person."

"He was also a musician, he was good at numbers, he could speak well in public. I was told he was witty. But all of this is mythology.

When I asked what instrument he played, I was told, 'Many instruments.' When I asked what he did with numbers, I was told, 'He did everything in his head and never used pencil or paper.' I don't know what he spoke about in public, or on what occasions. I was told that I look like him. I inherited his name, Raphael Nachman."

"They didn't destroy Cracow, only your family history. That's why you came to Cracow."

"Not really. I was invited to lecture at the university. I wouldn't be here otherwise. What I want to know, I discover with a pencil and paper. My grandfather could do everything in his head. I'm not as good as he was. Maybe the problems have become more complex. I'll tell you something strange. Ever since I arrived, I've had an uncanny sensation. It's as if I'd been here before. When I walk around a corner I expect to know what I'll see. I couldn't tell you in advance, but when I see it—a small square with a church and a restaurant or a theater—I feel I've seen it before. It's a small city, but one could get lost walking around. I've walked around several times, in different directions. I have no sense of direction, but find my way back to the hotel without trouble. I get lost in Los Angeles, where I was born, yet I am incapable of getting lost in Cracow. Even the pavement has a strange familiarity. It seems to recognize me. It pulls at my feet."

"You don't need a guide."

"But I do. I don't know where things are."

"We will go directly to the synagogue."

"No, no. Take me to the church first. The synagogue can't tell me anything about my grandfather, at least not what I would care to know. We'll go first to the church, then to the ghetto and the synagogue."

Nachman was aware that he'd talked extravagantly, precisely what the American consul had warned him against, but Nachman wasn't in love, and he was talking more to himself than to Marie.

She seemed to listen with the most serious concentration, her expression so intense it was almost grim. She respected Nachman as a mathematician, no doubt, and she was perhaps fascinated by his personal revelations. Maybe she felt privileged to hear such things, but her feelings were of no consequence to Nachman. Marie was a Polish kid from the countryside, not a world-class Polish beauty like the receptionist at the American Consulate. Nachman wasn't in love, except with his own voice. After today, he'd never see the girl again. He felt free to talk.

The truth is that Nachman had never been in love. He'd had girl-friends, but the idea of love had never appealed to him. He played the violin and he solved problems in mathematics. His need for ecstasy was abundantly satisfied. He was a sensual man only in very limited ways. He didn't, for example, enjoy eating. Two or three bites took care of hunger. The rest was nutrition. He also didn't care about clothes, or cars, or entertainment, or social life, or other common pleasures. He didn't care about money. As for sex, he could live without it, though he'd been born and raised in Los Angeles. He'd always had girlfriends, and they'd always been friends.

He described himself as a congenital conservative, one who feels no lust to consume the world, and isn't enlarged by experiences. This was his first trip to Europe. He'd been outside the United States only once before, to attend the funeral of an aunt in Toronto. He didn't yearn to travel. He didn't even go to movies. Every morning he made the bed in his hotel room, and cleaned up after himself in the toilet, so the room looked as if he'd never been there. It was a touch compulsive, but that's how Nachman wanted his room to look, as if he weren't guilty of existence.

If you said he was dull, many others would agree, especially his American colleagues at UCLA. They were rarely excited by Nach-man's mind, even when discussing his specialty in mathematics. He demanded tedious repetition while others were flying toward solu-tions. Unusual for a mathematician, but Nachman was slow. His pub-lished work, however, was amazing, as much for his solutions as for the fact that Raphael Nachman, The Slow And Repetitious, had arrived at them. This annoyed his colleagues. They suspected that he was kid-ding, and not really slow. He was perverse, secretly laughing at every-one. Like a crab, he seemed to go backwards when others rushed forward, yet he arrived before them.

His Polish colleagues had looked forward to his visit. They expected thrills from the man in person. But Nachman provided no thrills. The brilliant Poles occasionally forgot the problem as they waited for the laborious Nachman to finish discussing its history, and then writing out the solution on the blackboard. Could they have done it themselves, quickly or slowly? Few mathematicians were as good as Nachman. Perhaps few were as desperate. Nachman had solved a thousand prob-lems, and needed to solve more. Marie seemed to have appreciated his lectures, but what else could she say? Nachman didn't believe her. He knew he was considered boring, if not infuriating.

"Here we are," said Marie.

"This is a church?"

"This is the synagogue. We'll go to the church later."

Nachman shrugged. Marie was willful. She did what he wanted, though it wasn't what he said he wanted.

The building looked old, very old, and yet not the same as what might be officially designated as ancient. It looked old in the sense of having long been used, and as if it were still being used, as opposed to being preserved in static and sterile temporality. An empty old building, heavy with abiding presence rather than history, and the presence was human rather than divine. Even the large flat soot-blackened stones that formed a rough path to the door had the quality of presence, not history. The hollow interior, which reminded Nachman of the inside of a wooden ship, a caravel with a spacious hold, and which made an effect of stunning emptiness, seemed to have been recently abandoned by the mass of passengers, who would soon return and fill the big, plain, wooden space with the heat of their bodies and their chanting. The congregation was certainly gone, annihilated at a specific date which is memorialized in books, but Nachman, overwhelmed by a nameless sensation, felt he had only to wait and the books would be proved irrelevant, the Jews would return and collect in this room, his grandfather among them.

Nachman entered deeply into the space, and stood there with Marie beside him, neither of them speaking. Then they heard a noise, a cough or a sneeze, and turned toward the rear of the room. A man stood not far away, partly in the shadows, looking at them. He was less than average height, and had a large head and broad shoulders. His neck was bound in a red silk scarf. It had once been an elegant scarf. The color still lived but the silk was soiled by sweat and grease, and it was frayed. His gray wool coat seemed barely able to contain his bulk, and his arms were too long for the sleeves. Presumably, the caretaker. He walked toward them, authority in his stride. Though he was far from young, there was vigor and strength in his torso and short bowed legs.

Marie spoke to him in Polish. He answered in a rough and aggressive voice, so much unlike hers that he seemed to speak a different language. Then Marie said to Nachman, "He says there is no fee. It is all right for us to stay until he closes the building in the afternoon."

Nachman said, "Ask him questions."

"What questions?"

179

"Anything you like."

Marie spoke to the man again, and a conversation ensued that was not the least intelligible to Nachman, but he listened to the words as if he could follow them, and he heard his name mentioned by Marie. After a few moments, Marie said, "He has been the caretaker of the synagogue for more years than he can remember, from before the war. He said he remembers your grandfather. You look like him."

"You told him who I am?"

"I mentioned the name Nachman. He said he remembered such a man, and you look like him."

"Ask him more questions."

Marie spoke to the man again. He seemed increasingly to liven as he answered, and he made gestures with his thick hands to emphasize what he said. His face took on different expressions, each of them swiftly replacing the last. There was so much motion in his features that Nachman wasn't sure what he looked like, only that it was a big dark face with bulging blue eyes, the nose of an alcoholic with burst capillaries along its length, and an exceptionally mobile mouth. He was full of talk, full of memories. They seemed to push at his eyes from behind, as if they intended to push straight through and be seen.

Nachman waited and watched. He listened hard. He was dizzy with anticipation, fearfully anxious to know what the man was saying. He hesitated to ask Marie anything until the man said as much as he wanted. Marie finally turned back to Nachman and said, "I think we should go."

"But what did he tell you?"

"He told me that Nachman was gifted. People would cross the street to touch his coat. They came to him for advice, often about money matters, but also about love affairs and sickness."

"He had some kind of medical knowledge?"

"He knew herbs that could cure skin diseases. He helped Poles and Jews, but it was dangerous for him. He was afraid of his powers. This fellow himself, the caretaker of the synagogue, says he once came to Nachman with a broken leg that wouldn't heal. The pain was indescribable. He says Nachman went into a trance. Nachman suffered, as if his own leg were broken. In his trance, he made strange sounds, as if he were talking to somebody, but not with words. Let's go, Professor Nachman. We've heard enough."

Nachman didn't want to go.

180

"What happened? Did his leg heal?"

"Yes."

Nachman stared at the man, much taken by him. He wanted to hear more details of the event, but Marie was insistent.

"We can come back, if you like. Let's go now."

"What else did he say?"

"I'll tell you later."

"I must give the man something."

Nachman pulled bills from his pants pocket.

"Is American money acceptable? I have fifty dollars."

"Give him a dollar."

"That's not enough."

"He'll be happy with a dollar. Give it to him and let's go."

Nachman was trembling. Was this girl a guide, or some kind of despot? He'd felt her strength of character, and he'd liked it, but at the moment it seemed more like obstinate determination. Nachman recalled the way she walked, with that long tireless stride. He thought suddenly it was consistent with her whole character. Her voice was soft, but she was abrupt and terse. Her figure was lean as a fashion model's, but not languid. It had stiffness, military tension, as if built to endure. She was willful; pigheaded. He'd asked for a guide, not a leader.

Nachman gave the man five dollars, and then shook his hand. The man grinned and nodded thanks. Then, to assert himself against Marie's desire to leave, Nachman suddenly smiled at the man and embraced him.

Marie sighed. "He's not a Jew, Professor Nachman."

Nachman was startled by the remark.

Walking away from the synagogue, again with her rhythm, Nachman said, "I didn't care if he was a Jew. He was eager to talk about my grandfather. I learned something. I was grateful to him. What else did he say?"

"He said your grandfather could play musical instruments, and he could sing Polish folk songs. He said a few other things."

"What other things?"

"He could juggle."

"Juggle? My grandfather was a juggler?"

For the first time that morning Marie raised her voice. "He said your grandfather could bend nails with his teeth. He could fly."

Nachman looked at her and understanding came to him slowly, against resistance in feeling.

Nachman was then silent for several blocks, upset and confused. The morning felt colder to Nachman, though the sun was bright. The long walk hadn't warmed his body. When they came to the ancient church, he followed Marie inside, as if without personal will. It was less cold, but far from warm.

The church was small and unusually dark, thought Nachman, despite the tall windows which glared with color. There was a great deal of elaborately wrought gold and brass. It seemed to writhe and it gave off a dull shine. The darkness wasn't dispersed, but rather intensified by the dazzling flames of candles along the walls and in niches. A priest was conducting a service. Some elderly men and women were gathered in the pews before him, a few of them on their knees, others standing. Nachman wandered away from Marie, immersing himself in the general darkness, absorbing the sensation of deep shadows and scattered brilliance of flame and metal, all of it enclosed in heavy stone. He felt his isolation, his separateness within the church. He settled into the feeling as if into the obscurity of a great cloak. Long minutes passed before he remembered Marie and looked about for her. She was standing near the door, leaning against a pillar, looking at the priest, apparently absorbed by the ritual. Nachman approached her slowly and stopped a few feet away, waiting for her attention. She looked at him finally, and then moved toward him. As they walked together toward the door, she said, "Maybe I'll return. I don't know." Nachman understood, from the weight of her voice, that she meant return to the religion of her childhood.

Outside, Nachman lit a cigarette, his second of the day. It freed him of his memories of the past hour. He said, "Would you like to eat? You must be hungry."

"There are no luxurious restaurants."

"Anyplace with heat will do. I'm cold."

"It's still early, but I know where we can have vodka. Eel, too, maybe. The owner is a distant relation. Would you like vodka? You can pay him in dollars."

"In this cold, vodka would be excellent. I never felt so cold."

The restaurant, a fair-sized, square room with pretty wallpaper, was warmer than the church. The two waiters wore dinner jackets and ties. But there were no customers aside from Nachman and Marie. He had the impression the waiters were sustaining a ritual for lack of knowing what else to do. The menu was printed on large sheets of good, thick paper, and it announced a considerable variety of dishes, but Marie told him not to bother ordering any of them. It would embarrass their waiter. The dishes didn't exist. She would ask what they could order, and then repeated what she'd suggested earlier.

"Vodka and eel. All right?"

"All right."

Nachman cared much less about the food than sitting inside a fairly warm room, at a table with a clean white table-cloth. A glass of vodka was set before him and Marie. Nachman picked up his glass and drank. The vodka went down in a delicious searing flow. He wanted another glass almost immediately. Two plates of eel, chopped into small sections, were then set before them. Nachman ate a section. It tasted good, but he ate mainly to justify drinking vodka.

Marie finished eating before he did. She sipped her vodka slowly. Nachman urged her to take what remained of his plate of eel. She accepted. With his third glass Nachman became high, and felt almost good. His vision seemed to improve, too. Marie's plain face took on a glow and looked beautiful. What is plain, anyway? he asked himself. Her features were nicely proportioned. Nothing was ill-shaped. Others wouldn't call her beautiful or pretty, but it was a real face. Beautiful enough for him. Where you expected a nose, she had a nose, and a mouth, a mouth. All right, so she wasn't beautiful. Her face looked good to him. It was a good face, normal and undeformed, however plain. He was sure he would remember it with affection. Her brown eyes were intelligent and kind. What more could a man want? But why was he thinking this way? In a city where his grandparents had been murdered, his family history annihilated. This was a problem, too, wasn't it? But Nachman felt no obligation to solve it. For an instant Nachman wished only that he could love Marie, feel what a man is supposed to feel for a woman, but not for the sake of ecstasy. He would have liked something real, true, consistent with his nature, like the vodka, maybe. Pain, but a good pain. After today he'd never see Marie again. He already felt the poignancy of loss. She'd been a good guide. He wanted to kiss her.

"Would you like another vodka?"

"No, thank you." Her voice was soft and polite as usual. He remembered how she'd raised her voice to him in the street, walking away from the synagogue. She'd known what he was feeling in the synagogue, under the spell of the caretaker, and had wanted to protect Nachman. But from the way she looked at him now, he could tell that she had no idea what he was feeling. For her, ordinary life had resumed. She simply looked, as if even in her personal depths she was polite. She accepted what was there, didn't wonder. It wasn't in her to be intrusive, to wonder about his soul, and yet when it mattered she'd understood and been with him. Nachman knew that he was being sentimental, indulging a feeling. It was partly due to the vodka, but Nachman was awed by her, and it didn't seem at all unrealistic or foolish or morally dubious, and he knew the feeling would outlast this moment.

Nominated by The Threepenny Review, Jessica Roeder

THE SERENITY PRAYER

essay by ELISABETH SIFTON

from THE YALE REVIEW

> *God, give us grace to accept with serenity the things that cannot be changed,*
> *courage to change the things that should be changed, and the wisdom to distin-*
> *guish the one from the other.*
>
> Reinhold Niebuhr

AMERICANS CALL it the "serenity prayer," which is how it's known
to all those who encounter it as a mantra of Alcoholics Anonymous.
The reassuring calm of the word *serenity* is soothing, though to call
it the "grace" or "courage" or "wisdom" prayer might better empha-
size the demanding spiritual effort it recommends. People often pre-
sume that it's very old, for its stringency and spiritual clarity seem
unusual in our soupy, compromised modern times. And they facilely
presume a typical postmodern skepticism as to its precise authorship:
it's surely rabbinical in origin, or Stoic, derived or translated from
Latin or Hebrew, maybe Scottish? Oh well, even if some latter-day
pastor thinks he composed it, it's more likely that he pulled it from his
ragbag of accessible holy thoughts first set forth in a century with a
better prose style than ours, like the seventeenth, and rejigged it for
all of us now.

In Germany false confidence about the prayer's venerable antiquity
has gone further. And it is superbly centered on the presumption that
of course the prayer is German. Not long ago after the country's de-
feat in 1945, when its ruined provinces were still divided among the
occupation forces of the victorious Allied powers, when its economy

was all but destroyed, never mind its spirit, the prayer began to be cited as expressive of the true greatness of the German Christian soul. Within a few years newly confident politicians in the Federal Republic quoted it as such in morale-building speeches, and it still crops up in books and articles as a wonderful eighteenth-century Swabian Pietist guide to wisdom. How dramatic the irony, then, that the prayer's actual author was an American of German descent whose public work for thirty years had been in the sharpest possible opposition to religious and political life in Germany, whose family for generations had kept a sometimes strict, always careful distance from the fatherland, who considered that modern German Pietism was all too often "shallow" and "irrelevant," as weak as the bland hypocrisies of religion in his own country, and who wrote the prayer in the United States in 1943, at the height of the war against Germany.

My father composed the prayer in a place and context I knew well and remember vividly. For almost twenty years we spent our long holidays—Memorial Day to Labor Day, it was, for a family of academics—in a village in northwestern Massachusetts with an unusual summer colony. In Heath's Union Church, more or less Congregational, July and August Sundays often found visiting clerics in the pulpit, and my father was one of them; the rest of the service was in the hands of the parish's familiar year-round figures. Mrs. Burrington played the organ as she always did; "Holy, Holy, Holy" was the opening processional hymn as it always was; Miss Dickinson and Mrs. Gleason and Mrs. Stetson arranged the flowers—mountain laurel from the woods, hydrangeas and peonies and phlox from nearby gardens; Charlie Packard passed the plate. I can't remember which of the men joined him in passing around the wooden trays at the monthly communion service, but I remember the cubes of fresh-baked white bread, the little shot glasses of grape juice, and the wooden racks on the pew backs where you put the empties, next to the shelves for prayer and hymn books. Light streamed through the big rectangles of clear glass windows into the spare, monochrome hall: this was quintessential rural New England at its Sunday best. It was at a service in this Heath church in 1943 that my father first spoke his new prayer, as he did many others; he regularly preached there to its congregation of year-round parishioners, mostly farmers, and its sprinkling of summer people.

Our fetching up in Heath was due, mostly, to Ethel Paine Moors and her amazing politics. This splendid Boston lady was herself from

186

a grand family and married to the impeccable John Cabot Moors, Nonconformist and banker, member of the Harvard Corporation, classmate and friend of Harvard's president A. Lawrence Lowell. She presided over a predictably important house in Brookline and a huge "cottage" in Cohasset, on the South Shore, but she had a special fondness for The Manse, a squarish eighteenth-century Heath farmhouse on a remote hillside several miles north of the Deerfield River, which her father had bought for her in 1906. Mr. Moors didn't much care for The Manse, and rarely visited this rural pocket of Massachusetts *profond*, but Mrs. Moors loved it, and loved Heath. She was right to: its high meadows and pastures, its long views out over the Berkshire hills, its deep snowy winters and brilliant summers were superb. During the 1920s and 1930s she encouraged friends to come to Heath, too; abandoned old houses were then almost affordable as summer places for the impoverished clerics and scholars she favored. But unconventional iconoclasm and radical devotion to social justice were the unspoken requirements.

This was also true for an overlapping circle of Heath enthusiasts who learned of the place from Louise and Howard Chandler Robbins. Dean Robbins—of the Episcopal cathedral in Washington, D.C.— came from a family with deep roots in the region. Chandlers had been among the Deerfield residents carried off to Ontario by the Algonquins who raided the valley in the fearful massacre of 1675; Robbinses and their Malone and Landon cousins lived all over that corner of Massachusetts. We called him Uncle Howard, as we called his wife Auntie Lou and Mrs. Moors Aunt Ethel, and spent a lot of time in his wonderful old house with its big, dramatic garden. Auntie Lou liked building and rebuilding places: she had properties in Santa Barbara, California; of course in Washington; at Sneden's Landing, on the Hudson River above New York City; and she looked after several in Heath. I thought her a marvel for having fashioned or discovered such character and wit in all these houses, but my mother cautioned me about their damp cellars. "Louise has a gift, but a curious weakness about water." More important, she had congenial political convictions.

My parents met Ethel Moors in the early 1930s—I don't know the precise circumstances, but they surely involved left-wing politics and surely concerned Harvard, where my father preached several times a year and Mr. Moors was a Major Force. Aunt Ethel was fiercely radical-progressive, and she approved of my father's politics: critical from the left of the New Deal until after the 1936 elections, then

187

supportive of FDR's challenges to political and economic conservatism; emphatically philo-Semitic; vigorously internationalist as against the pacifism of the left and the bigoted isolationism of so much of America's political classes.

It may be hard for some of us now to recognize just how strongly entrenched and wary those prewar political classes were, how hostile to change, indifferent to social justice, and devoted to class privilege. But in their context Ethel Moors's warmhearted, effervescent enthusiasm made her a blithe presence in a grim landscape. She never forgot how dangerous and difficult it was, and would be, to challenge the status quo. "Yes, yes, I suppose she approves," my father once conceded about Aunt Ethel's praise, but, he chuckled, "she'd like me even more if I were black and Jewish and socialist." Aunt Ethel had every good reason to believe that among blacks and Jews and socialists she was likely to find brave, decent people willing to risk their lives to improve the world.

The Moorses had become friends of Felix Frankfurter during the uproar over the Sacco-Vanzetti case in 1928, when Aunt Ethel had embraced the cause of those unlettered Italian anarchists, on whose innocence of murder charges Frankfurter, then a Harvard Law professor, robustly insisted. This earned him praise in many quarters but pitted him against heavy (eventually victorious) opposition that was personified above all by President Lowell, who chaired the commission reviewing the notoriously political case after the two had been convicted. Moors remarked astringently of his classmate that he was "incapable of seeing that two wops could be right and the Yankee judiciary could be wrong." He might have added that Lowell was especialy vehement in the Sacco-Vanzetti matter precisely because Frankfurter was on the other side: they had exchanged vitriolic letters when in 1923 Lowell had tried to impose a quota on Jewish students at Harvard, a policy Frankfurter tore into; relations were frosty at best. (In the circumstances of that earlier time, a highminded person was supposed to prefer the overt quota at Harvard over the covert one Nicholas Murray Butler had rigged at Columbia. FF and the Moorses thought both were disgusting.) No surprise, anyway, that the Frankfurters could be found in a pretty white house by the waterfall in Dell, a cluster of dwellings near an old mill on a brook road that led from Heath down to Charlemont, on the Deerfield River.

A good part of Dell, including the Frankfurters' house, belonged to Bishop Charles Gilbert of New York, one of several "left-wing" Episcopal bishops who summered in the township. A most conservatively mannered cleric, he was, but he favored the laboring poor and was broadminded enough to have once welcomed the Patriarch of Moscow in his cathedral, so the upper crust considered him out of line. I still have the pretty china teacups my mother got at an auction after the death of yet another cleric whose house and belongings were in Bishop Gilbert's charge. The plethora of bishops could be confusing: "No, not Bishop White's china," she'd explain. "It's china from Bishop Gilbert's white house."

Uncle Felix arrived every year in late June, promptly after the Supreme Court term ended, along with his beautiful clever wife, Marion, and many book cartons. Boxes of Court papers were couriered to him all summer long, which I thought very grand. All summer long he worked hard in his study, enjoying Heath's solitude and beauty, recharging his batteries. There were bridge games with the bishops, long walks. He liked the sharp, richly flavored local ginger ale, so much so that he ordered cases shipped to Washington in the winters; we all agreed it was far superior to any old Canada Dry. My family didn't bother to get the ginger ale in New York, where we lived during the academic terms in a big faculty apartment at Union Theological Seminary, but throughout the war years square cartons arrived from Heath with reinforced brass corners and "Fragile" stamped in purple on the top, each with seventy-two eggs in cushioned gray cardboard rows within; we stored them on a cool shelf in the back pantry, along with the Heath jams and my mother's Anglo-Indian spices.

In his unique way FF epitomized the Cambridge-Washington axis in Heath. There were plenty of well-known Yale clerics further south, like Henry Sloane Coffin in Lakeville, Connecticut (he was president of Union Seminary), or north, like the Lovetts and Sherrills, Episcopal bigwigs who summered in New Hampshire (in a neighborhood also thick with Princeton Presbyterians), but thanks to Aunt Louise and Aunt Ethel, Heath seemed to be dominated by Harvard pedigrees or by no pedigrees at all. In tone Uncle Felix was proudly law-professorial years after he'd left Cambridge, proudly Viennese Jewish a half-century after his arrival at Ellis Island, and proudly Washingtonian in his huge appetite for political dispute. He fizzed and bubbled. He argued and asked questions. He snorted like a schnauzer when he laughed, which was often, he chortled when he told stories, and he literally slapped his thigh at his own jokes. He liked edge, and precision, and seriousness, and he hated solemnity. When Archibald

MacLeish and his wife came over from Conway for tea one afternoon, Uncle Felix trounced him at badminton on our lawn, and then, I'm afraid, we gently trashed the visitor, of whom we were all very fond, in a postmortem after supper. MacLeish took himself too seriously, wanted you to recognize his Significance as a Poet, had poor political judgment. None of this went over in Heath.

Uncle Felix, being decisively agnostic, was amused to find himself in a nest of clergymen. Not only in Dell, with Bishop Gilbert and Sherman Johnson, a New Testament scholar at the Episcopal Theological School in Cambridge, not only his Washington friend Dean Robbins and my father in Heath Center, but a contingent on the road to North Heath. There, Mrs. Drown, the eccentric, outspoken widow of another E.T.S. gentleman, commanded the slopes of Plover Hill— "my pasture," she called it—where she lived in a handsome old house with her spaniels, her maids (unusual in Heath, if not unique), and her opinionated bluestocking ways. I believe she's the only nineteenth-century person I ever met who actually wore *blue* stockings. We used to have Sunday lunch with her after my father preached; she'd argue with him over fine points of New Testament interpretation, complain if the strawberries were soggy, and generally carry on in a spirited, eccentric Bostonian way. Behind the swinging door to the kitchen, I could see her maids parking the porcelain plates on the floor so the spaniels might enjoy the leavings before the dishes were taken to the sink. It was said that Mrs. Drown was tactful when it mattered.

Further along the road came William Wolf, who as an E.T.S. student had been one of Mrs. Drown's "boys" who drove for her; he was now a faculty member himself, a marvelous rangy man with an infectious sense of hilarity in most things and a shrewd, energetic intellectual style. William Kirk, another selfless man of the cloth, rented a place on the Colrain road—he'd directed a settlement house in Saint Louis and later moved to New York to run another one—where he summered with his tall wife and three daughters: they were all so handsome, with Bill's red hair and Mary's impeccable "good bones"! I can't imagine Heath without their ever-flowing generosity of time and of heart. Later there were Sydney Thomson Brown and her husband, Robert McAfee Brown; just after the war this missionary's daughter came with us to Heath as a kind of "au pair" girl for the summer, and Bob was a student of my father's; the Browns married under Heath auspices, as it were, and then became regular summer residents. Not to mention Worcester Perkins, rector of the Church of the Holy Communion in Manhattan, which is now a nightclub.

Last, Heath enjoyed the serene, powerful presence of Angus Dun, Episcopal bishop of Washington, another decorated soldier on the social justice front. Early in the 1920s Auntie Lou had built a cottage across the road from the Robbinses' brown-shingled prerevolutionary house, a barn-red place with a porch facing west for the best view (this was frequent in Heath) and overlooking a swimming pool that was its raison d'être: she lured Angus and Kitty Dun to the Red Cottage knowing the pool would be a beneficence for the bishop, who was painfully paralyzed by polio.

Somehow the town endured all these men of the cloth. Others would have found it too ecclesiastical. My parents' good friend W. H. Auden, who visited us in Heath in 1946 while he was teaching at Bennington, not far away, wrote the next summer from Cherry Grove, Fire Island, a very different sort of summer colony, exchanging theological views and commiserating about the unpleasant respiratory illnesses from which my mother suffered because of seasonal allergies. Perhaps it wasn't the meadow pollen, he asked in his brotherly way, "but a surfeit of clerics?"

Auntie Lou had cabins and cottages all over the place. One summer, I recall—it may have been 1951 or so—a hushed and whispered plan eventuated in our climbing into our 1939 Ford and driving off to see someone to whom she had loaned a hideout in the woods twenty or forty miles away. It was important for this friend and my father to talk, she felt, and also important that we tell no one of the man's presence in the countryside or of our seeing him. The gentleman in the cabin hidden in pine woods was pleasant, tense, rather gray: it was the famous radical William Remington, a government economist who was one of the McCarthy period's first victims. He had been twice convicted of perjury in testifying before a grand jury trying to ascertain just how communist he was—he'd been fingered by the dreadful Elizabeth Bentley. The grand jury's conduct had appalled Judge Learned Hand; on the Second Circuit Court of Appeals he twice voted to reverse the convictions, the second time unsuccessfully; the Supreme Court refused to hear the case. Perhaps it was all hush-hush because of FF's proximity. Soon Remington went to jail, and only a few months later he was murdered there by an anti-communist fanatic who believed he was helping to save the Republic.

191

Auntie Lou also designed and built a guest house right next door to the Robbinses' own beautiful place. Between, a sloping flower-filled field was bisected by a brook that gurgled out from a culvert under the road and ran, plashing and burbling, through beds of wild watercress to one of three ponds that Uncle Howard contrived along its course. My parents first rented this little house from Louise and then bought it at just about the time the war broke out.

The rather clumsy but charming design of the Stone Cottage featured a westerly view (of course) toward Mount Greylock, eighty miles away; the middle-distance prospect, like all those dutiful American copies of Claude, had forest on the left, a few big trees on the right, and water in the center—the first of Uncle Howard's ponds, where my brother and I raised ducks to show at the Heath Fair. (We missed one summer, when our poodle took advantage of a drought that gave easy access over caked mud to the little puddle left in the center of the pond and killed the ducklings. Her water retriever's blaze of accomplishment and the ruff of white feathers belied her phony, poodly innocence. The poodle was left-liberal, too, naturally: she came to us via a network of ardent poodle enthusiasts who were staunch New Dealers and anticonventional skeptics, including the drama critic Louis Kronenberger and his wife, Emmy; June and Jonathan Bingham—this was before Jack went to Congress, when he was working for Averill Harriman; and the superb Swiss scholar Arnold Wolfers, Yale professor of international affairs, and his wife, Doris. Decades later I learned from Daniel Aaron—a man of the left for certain—that he, too, had poodles from the Puttencove Kennel, like ours. I told him that after my father's death my mother had confessed about a very Republican conversation she'd had with the gentleman in Boston whose wife owned the kennel, in order to establish her bona fides as a poodle owner. She never dared tell my father that Mr. Putnam had enquired as to "the race of your servants, Mrs. Niebuhr?" a question that would have scandalized Pa as indeed any Heath resident and put the kibosh on her getting the dog.)

The Stone Cottage was built into the meadow hillside on two levels and surrounded by terraces that my mother turned into a lovely garden; you entered at the back, on the second floor, and were supposed to descend via a circular staircase to a living room below, which looked out across the lawn and terraces to the Berkshire vista beyond. But since Auntie Lou had characteristically built the house right on top of—or anyway very near—a spring, the living was always moldy, so we

192

used it for ping-pong and for storing bicycles, and lived entirely up-stairs. Visiting divinity students or their girl friends were my babysit-ters. A local friend taught me how to swim in the Duns' cold, cold swimming pool. I and my pals went on bicycle trips organized by Bill Kirk while our parents wrote books. At the Kirks' house, too, we had feisty weekend hymn sings. And from the Stone Cottage we walked every Sunday morning to the Union Church in the village center.

Two centuries after its founding, Heath retained its original sparse, spread-out, hilly-frontier feeling, so the village green wasn't one of those declared, willed, communal architectural announcements that New Englanders make when they feel truly settled. But it had an aus-tere, windswept sweetness, this isolated, brave place, with its library, its grocery store with the post office in the back, and the steepled white clapboard church that one approached, as one does so many New England public buildings, on the broad, shallow flagstone steps made of local granite. Bishops Dun and Gilbert, my father, Dean Rob-bins, Mr. Perkins, Professor Johnson, and the Bills (Wolf and Kirk), along with various young seminarians who were students of one or other of them, all conducted services in that church—an astonishing summer invasion.

These ecumenical gentlemen got along easily—the plainspoken Nonconformists, the Episcopal divines, and my father, who belonged to the Evangelical and Reform Synod, a small denomination which, by the way, his own father had been active in helping to organize (later to merge with the Congregationalists in the United Church of Christ); "E & R" was a child of the old Church of the Prussian Union, therefore theologically Lutheran but presbyterially struc-tured. (Secular Americans always presume that Christian Germans are Lutheran or Catholic, more's the pity.) Small wonder you could find four of these Heath clergy as delegates to the founding meeting of the World Council of Churches in Amsterdam in 1948, and two as observers to Vatican Council II. They knew how not to have needless liturgical or doctrinal disputes, and they were brave, conscientious people. I thought of them as typical American clergy: how wrong I was! Little did I know how unusual was their sturdy broadminded-ness, how atypical their devout modesty. I grew up well insulated from the barbarous, self-congratulatory sloth of what journalism now calls Mainstream American Protestantism, and it took me decades to realize this.

Once, Uncle Felix, who'd come up the hill to hear my father preach despite his marked distaste for going into a church, but who had found the service rather cheering and not offensive to his skeptical ears—he even joined in singing the hymns—said to him after the service, "May a believing unbeliever thank you for your sermon?" to which my father replied, "May an unbelieving believer thank you for appreciating it?"

All the summer people were great fans of Heath's permanent citizens. Ethel Moors knew them best since she'd been there longest: her father's Norwegian coachman had loved the Berkshires and the Paines had settled him on a farm adjacent to The Manse; his son, Oscar Landstrom, married one of three daughters in a long-established local farming family, and by the 1940s the cousins Landstrom, Dickinson, Gleason, and Burrington dominated South Heath; lucky Aunt Ethel had them all as neighbors. But the Robbinses, too, knew everyone. Uncle Howard's nephew Dana Malone farmed year-round in Heath: son of a Deerfield lawyer who had been Massachusetts's attorney general, he lived first in The Creamery, up behind the church, then in yet another capacious white clapboard farmhouse with a handsome porch, this one on the South Heath road. He had unconventional new ideas about dairy farming that he liked to put into practice, but science or no science, people raised their eyebrows at his milking his cows at 9:00 A.M. and 9:00 P.M. instead of the standard early hours.

No exclusive social functions or patterns defined the summer group—that would have been frowned on, anyway—and we all simply joined in regular Heath activities. Charlie Packard, an accomplished man-of-all-trades who "kept an eye on the place" for some of us in the winter, prepared our plots in the spring so we could plant our Victory Gardens as soon as we arrived, throughout the summer tried to drum sense into us, and fixed our ailing cars. I remember him, wrinkled and darkly tanned, like a walnut, trying to be patient with our stupid questions—about the vegetables, about carpenter ants, or snakes in the well, or busted iceboxes, or the history of Heath. We borrowed books from the village library every Tuesday and Friday—for me it was yards and yards of Albert Payson Terhune, Gene Stratton Porter, Frances Parkinson Keyes, and how many other three-named writers? At church, my Niebuhr grandmother, an accomplished teacher of small children, helped out Mrs. Landstrom in the Sunday school, Eleanor Wolf spelled Mrs. Burrington at the organ, the Kirk girls and I sang in the choir. We bought our milk and eggs not from valley stores

194

in Charlemont or Shelburne Falls but from our neighbors, and we all pitched in to prepare for the Heath Fair, in late August.

The rhythm of summer farm and road work kept the Heath men busy, and not many of them were regularly seen at church. I recall my father easily accepting their grave, polite regrets that rain or sun, planting or haying, dispersal or retrieval of pastured heifers was commanding immediate attention on the coming Sunday. But of course. Still, my father knew—after all, he'd been a working pastor for a dozen years and was the son and grandson of pastors—that women, not men, are often the ligaments that hold parishes together and that plenty of men, like these fine friends, tick the box marked "Christian" on polls inquiring as to their religious affiliation yet most of the time simply tip their hats to their wives' devotions.

The farmers' politics were also paradoxical. Heath had sent a few dozen men into the Union army the century before, and like all good Massachusetts country people since the Civil War, they were staunch Republicans, invoking the predictable clichés of New England individualism to inveigh against FDR's "socialistic meddling" in the economy. Yet their lives had been immeasurably improved by the New Deal's social and economic programs (not least by Rural Electrification) and by postwar developments like the G.I. Bill; and, my father noted, the actual structure of their working lives was far from individualistic. "They're communists, actually," he'd say cheerfully, wondering how they might react if he told them so. Pre-1848 communists. For much of the year whole sections of the township pooled resources—financial (to rent extra equipment in the summer or to lease ice-locker space in the winter) and human (when all hands went into the fields together to bring in the hay and to process the corn harvests)—and couldn't possibly have managed otherwise.

My father had grown up among very different farms in the villages and towns of Missouri and southern Illinois—along that great swathe of the German-speaking, German-thinking, German-farming Middle West whose richer soils allowed people to prosper as few of our New England neighbors could, where single grain companies tended to dominate whole counties, and where the feel of community life was very different—certainly in the years before the Great War, which inevitably ruptured the solid German-American tone and tossed the farmers into spiritual and political confusion. The checkerboard Ralston signs on grain elevators all across the prairie were as much a feature of my father's childhood memories as his father's

195

Saturday-morning Hebrew and Greek lessons to his children (conducted in German, of course); or the small-town streets that ended in walls of corn; or the infinite flat fields beyond, where one could watch on the horizon for the horsetails of approaching tornadoes; or the itinerant workers who came so often to the back door, offering to "help around the place," and were given shelter and board until they landed a job; or my grandmother's calmly virtuoso cooking of the bounty of provisions—hams, turkeys, geese—with which his parishioners paid my grandfather for baptisms, weddings, and funerals (and for his expert dowsing, a useful, nicely pagan sideline in a rural parish). So these harshly rocky pastures, these New England fields whose boulders and obstructions it had taken two centuries to clear, these old farms tucked into sheltered dales and mill houses perched over tumbling forest brooks (Uncle Felix's was like that)—these were exotic for my Middle Western father. But he felt at home, for he admired the intelligence and deep modesty of his Yankee friends, their stoic liveliness and easy democratic spirit. I don't know what Mr. Landstrom or Mr. Stetson, say, thought of Mrs. Moors's politics or my father's, if they bothered to consider them, but there was affectionate respect all around.

High spirits marked the most exciting of Heath's festivities, the annual fair and its parade, held in August, across from Dana Malone's place, next to an oak grove above the Dickinsons' farm, half under the shade of the dark, high trees, half in an open, mowed field. Yeasty, sugary fragrances suffused the milk-white air in the canvas tents, where tables arranged in a spacious oval displayed constellations of cakes, breads, and cookies; others glowed with a rich tapestry of jellies and jams, pickles and relishes, flawless vegetables, perfect fruit. Outside, under the oaks, calves and piglets, chickens and ducks (my brothers' and mine among them) fussed and preened in their pens, awaiting blue, red, or no ribbons. All morning Susan Kirk and I would mill about admiring the displays, eating snacks—no fast food here! no imported generic carnival junk from non-Heath hands!—and drinking root beer or celery tonic in bottles pulled from the sloshy metallic depths of big red Coca-Cola iceboxes. Our mothers schmoozed with Mrs. Landstrom and Mrs. Stetson, and tried to decide which of the beautiful rugs to buy—braided or rag? Or the padded dress hangers covered in gingham? Or cross-stitched table linens? Quilts? Soon the ox-draws began, and the hammer-throw competitions.

As the fair wound down, the parade started up, and here the summer and winter people collaborated in truly deranged nonsense. On the farmers' familiar flatbed trucks or horse-drawn haycarts marvelous floats were mounted depicting all kinds of wondrous scenes: Bishop Dun was a big hit one summer as the Wild Man from Borneo, hairily nude from the waist up, waving his powerfully muscled arms about, munching leaves and bellowing nonsense syllables in a lusty, booming voice that usually carried across vast cathedral naves; one of the Gleason boys was his "keeper."

In the evening we all went to, or acted in, a play at the Town Hall. I have a picture of my father in a star role as a circus barker, with a shiny top hat and striped red-and-white pants; skinny young Ken Stetson, whose vegetables always won blue ribbons and whose farm was famous as a statewide gold-star winner, played the Fat Lady, flirting goofily with the barker. A few years before, about the time he wrote the serenity prayer, Pa had the lead as the "toff" of a jewel-thieving gang: I can't remember the play, but I recollect how much he enjoyed memorizing its Runyonesque lines. Another summer we did *Our Town*—Mary Kirk directed, Bill Wolf was the Stage Manager, Susan Kirk had a nifty role as the hero's sister, and I had a little part, too; Mrs. Burrington played the hero's mother. Everyone thought the production was ace, and Uncle Felix claimed that Thornton Wilder himself would have preferred it to more famous ones.

My idyllic Heath images come from after the war, mostly, but it wasn't radically different in 1943, when my father wrote his beautiful prayer—Heath, I mean. The world was of course completely different. His prayer's postwar life in America has been so bound up with the Twelve-Step Program that most people construe its hopes as expressing principally what, in our self-help culture, we think we must aim for in our personal self-improvement projects. And like all prayers it *is* about one's own soul. But there is more to it than that. The first-person plural is theologically conventional for prayers in many a Christian tradition, and here it is expressly intended to go to the heart of the possibilities and impossibilities of *collective* action for *collective* betterment. And that is how his Heath friends and colleagues understood it.

This was a prayer composed by an ex-Marxist who was still a vehement antifascist, by a pastor deeply at odds with the leadership of most Protestant and Catholic churches, which had failed and were failing, he thought, to give heed to the present dangers and to the hideous threats posed to democracy and freedom by totalitarian forces

197

everywhere. It was a prayer written by an American whose first language was German, whose earliest childhood memories were intensely German, who had grown up in an America whose single largest ethnic group was of German origin (as it still is), an America that had not yet demonized the "Kraut," but a German-American for whom the ancestral home had now become a spiritual and political disaster zone. It was a prayer written by a teacher and writer who had spent a decade speaking out against Hitler and against the implicit support or condoning of his regime throughout Europe and the United States, and was now all the more committed in his opposition to the Nazis and his support of the war effort. It was written by a Zionist who, with like-minded colleagues, was continuing his unremitting efforts to help Europe's Jews; the German fascists were, it was clear, in the process of exterminating them. It was written by an active skeptic about conventional liberal optimism, an active opponent of conventional conservative disregard for social justice, a deeply devout man who wrestled daily with the problem of how to relate his innermost religious commitments to the public life of the community; he had become famous for a book he'd written a decade earlier called *Moral Man and Immoral Society*, whose analyses he was already rejecting as simplistic.

In 1930, he and his brother Helmut, also a theologian, had broken off relations with their German cousins in Lippe Detmold, after getting letters from them reporting contentedly on Hitler's electoral victory there and on the cousins' consequent hopes for a positive, better future for Germany. My aunt Hulda, a teacher of religious education, and my grandmother—we called her Mütterchen—continued to send Christmas and birthday greetings, keeping up a modicum of family news-exchange, but my father and uncle demurred. They had their hands full, their spirit committed elsewhere, their minds preoccupied.

My father had first visited the German Niebuhrs in 1923, when he was a young pastor facing the brutally complex human problems of a parish in Detroit, then the locus of tremendous strife, racial tension, and class misery boiling up around the new automobile industries. In Detroit he and his widowed mother lived and worked in the shadow of the mighty Henry Ford—that much-praised admirer, indeed distributor of the *Protocols of the Elders of Zion*—and of the ranting anti-Semitism that would soon find braying voice in the weekly national radio shows of Father Charles Coughlin, a brazenly bigoted Catholic radio star. He was getting involved in the community's struggles to obtain better working conditions and to unionize the factories (he invited

American Federation of Labor spokesmen to talk at his church), struggles that pitted the working people of Detroit against the automobile companies that were bent on extracting their labor with as little recompense, respect, or regard as possible. And along with a few others, he felt the urgency of not only improving the lives of the blacks newly arrived from the South in search of work in northern cities but altering the unacceptable hostility that whites showed toward them.

In Lincoln, Illinois, where he had succeeded his father as pastor of Saint John's Evangelical Church in 1914, plenty of hard problems had needed attention (one of the first he'd faced as a twenty-two-year-old newcomer to the pulpit was the issue of what language to worship in: all across the Middle West, the patriotism and decency of millions of Americans accustomed to a bilingual German-American life were suddenly in question), but nothing like this inferno of difficulties in newly industrialized Detroit. What would induce people to resolve their deep and painful differences when they seemed, if they had any kind of stability or security, anxious merely to protect their settled "way of life"? How was one to counter capitalism's ruthless inhumanity, its greed-power nexus, which that mediocrity Henry Ford so well represented? Pa like many American pastors had studied for the ministry with German-trained theologians—so had his father and several generations of his mother's family before him—and now he thought much of what they had taught was irrelevant. Still, his cousins in Lippe Detmold welcomed him, and he imagined that somehow he would be at home in the intellectual and spiritual cultures of his family's two homelands.

The big old farm in Hardissen, whence his father, Gustav, had fled in 1872 to escape the mindless tyranny of an autocratic father, charmed and amazed him. It was a comfy, self-confident place, handsome, effective, dull. He could see why the American Niebuhrs had wanted to leave (his father hadn't been the only one). He felt uncomfortable with its complacency; it distressed him to see the authoritarian tone with which the farmhands were relegated to a lower table away from the family, with its rigid hierarchies, its pious conventions, its implicit autocracy still. Things hadn't been like that in Illinois. Gustav Niebuhr had come to America a half-century before in part because he so admired Abraham Lincoln as a truly great national leader, and he had cheered Teddy Roosevelt's sturdy invectives against the robber barons' predatory greed and cruel indifference to working people. But the Lippe Niebuhrs admired the intense conservatism of Germany's business and political leaders. It seemed that the

199

cousins had responded very differently to the challenges of the twentieth century.

His aunt Henrietta gave a reception where he could meet the local pastor, "a 'pietist' in the classical sense of the word," my father wrote later, whose political ignorance he found repellent, not to mention his "sublime knowledge of his own salvation." He had a run-in with a fellow on another matter: the *Pfarrer* attributed Germany's recent woes to the presence of a Jew in the cabinet, by which he meant Foreign Minister Walther Rathenau, one of my father's heroes, who had been murdered by right-wing German nationalists only months before. "I spoiled my aunt's party," remembered Pa.

On that same trip he searched out progressive Evangelical pastors to discuss with them the future of the church, of Christianity, in the Weimar democracy. It was a time of edgy, complex, but thrilling new possibilities. The German clerics were guardedly pessimistic, but one of the best and brightest of them confided that nothing would improve until "we get the Jews out of politics." This kind of thing made one's heart sink. My father found it outrageous: he did not believe there was any serious theological or cultural basis for a Christian to consider such bigotry permissible, however customary it might have been, however condoned or even encouraged. We were in the twentieth century, after all, and it was not too much to expect decent people to try to move beyond the murky medievalism of Christianity's worst moments. Granted, such anti-Semitism was widespread and often flagrant, a sign of the moral bankruptcy and tawdry superficiality of churches everywhere, but that made it only all the more important to uphold the central Christian doctrines that found it sinful.

Yet German theological faculties and German churches were filled—as organized religion so often is—with all too many banal, corrupted, thoughtless people. And so certain of their own godliness! "These kinds of people are ruining our world," my father wrote. "If the world will go down, it will go down not by the hands of criminals, but by the hands of those that were so conscious of their righteousness." Come 1933, it's no surprise that he and my uncle and quite a few of their American colleagues did not expect Germany's "official Christendom" to oppose the godless rantings of Nazi demagogues and terrorists.

Not that American churchmen were much better. As tense, anxious seasons passed in Detroit, my father became ever more impatient with the bland irrelevance of his fellow pastors' "Christian thought," as impatient as he was grateful for the rare but fervent civic energies of a Jewish businessman and one or two other activists who worked with him on the city's race-relations board and with whom he'd become friends. "There were only two Christians in Detroit then," he liked to quote the city's Episcopal Bishop Williams as saying, "and they were both Jews."

The apathy and indifference of most clergymen to the crisis of the Depression, not to mention their prejudiced, reactionary selfishness, are shocking to consider, though not surprising. The churches' vacuity and vapidity during the Roaring Twenties gave ample warning. Soon millions of people—some 15 percent of the labor force—were out of work and destitute, their morale and health broken; war and fascism threatened everywhere; the economy was in advanced chaos; and most Americans were living without insurance, without hope, without sustenance. They deserved some straightforward clarity about moral "priorities." But the pastoral leaders of American Catholics, Episcopalians, Lutherans, and Congregationalists remained, on the whole, silent or evasive about the desperate inequities threatening the nation's spiritual and social life. When the pleasantly optimistic Reverend John Haynes Holmes opined in 1931 that Europe was "slowly but surely approaching the longed-for goal of harmony and peace," the Niebuhrian rebuke thundered back: "Let Liberal Churches Stop Fooling Themselves!" Among the far from "liberal" Presbyterians, Baptists, and Methodists—divided between North and South, the racist southern wings of each being rigidly segregationist (sadly, the color line still holds in Southern churches)—it was if possible even worse.

Bishops, archbishops, pastors, editors in the church press, elders, rectors, and wardens—most of these big shots devoted their energies to preserving their positions, augmenting their safety, insulating their precincts from each other's doctrinal "impurities." Is it surprising that virtually none of them spoke out on the subject of the Nazi assault on Jews? and almost no rabbis either? The few voices heard were those of scholars at divinity schools teaching only a tiny percentage of America's clergy, and they did not command ecclesiastical power structures.

Still, one must be grateful for the steadiness of tone in the pronouncements of those who *did* understand the dangers. The theologian Paul Lehmann and Wilhelm Pauck (a great church historian and Luther scholar, trained in Berlin and teaching in Chicago) and my father—to name a few of the few—were outspoken in their denunciation of the theological inadequacy of Christian double-talk about

201

Jews and the sinister connection between incipient antidemocratic indifference and piously anti-Semitic imprecation, whether in Germany or in the United States. This was a key issue already in the 1920s, and they knew it.

In 1927–28 and again in 1930, my father was back in Germany on further trips, the third time coming not from Detroit but from New York City, where he had gone to teach at Union in 1928. The stock market crash just a few months before was soon to bring the economies of the West crashing to a halt; pastors and teachers, like everyone else, were facing unprecedented chaos. How did one extract meaning from this? My father reported that while most of his observations supported the view that American church life had at least potential vitality and an attentiveness to ethical and social issues that the German churches lacked, yet in Germany "an organization of religious leaders calling themselves 'religious socialists,' in which, among others, the young philosopher of religion Paul Tillich is active, has been working on the problem of religion and labor with a thoroughness and honesty which no American religious organization has yet approached." Would that those brave efforts in Germany had had time to bear fruit! They were soon struck down, ruthlessly.

He also deplored the deep conservatism and self-satisfaction of the theological faculties in the "mother-nation of theological liberalism." (What would he think now? The somber complacency of German's church-academia was all too often untouched by the cataclysms of 1933–89.) If only, he cried, their sense of things was "more relevant to the desperate moral situation which a modern industrial nation faces!" He thought most of Germany's official church was living as if in the pre-1914 epoch—indeed, in their dishonesty and reaction, as if Germany had not been defeated in 1918—and he compared its "thoughtless identification of *Christentum und Deutschtum*" to the "naive nordicism of our Klan-infested churches in the Deep South." It was sinister, wrong, dangerous.

Clayton Morrison, founder of *The Christian Century,* was an earnest, good man who completely failed to see this sinister danger. His views had long been at odds with my father's, though he was a shrewd enough magazine editor to get Pa to write a regular column for him, in which my father inveighed against *CCs'* neutralist, pacifist, and anti-Semitic editorial line—this was all no doubt good for circulation. In 1931, Morrison gave my parents a set of beautiful Chinese embroi-

202

dered linen placemats as a wedding present—I still use them, thinking of all this as I do—telling them in a note that he admired but could not share their brave optimism at a time so dark and full of foreboding. Such gloom, my father thought, rested on sloppy foundations, on inadequately reasoned Christian faith.

This was a matter his new English bride understood immediately. Ursula Keppel-Compton had turned up in one of his courses at Union in 1930—she and a young German named Dietrich Bonhoeffer were the two foreign students around that year—and she had a razor-sharp, very well-trained mind; she had just come down from Oxford with an honors degree (a "double first") in theology and history. When she was awarded the fellowship to Union, Coffin had objected to having this honor go to a woman; the Regius Professors of Theology at Oxford and Cambridge, whose decision was final, insisted. Her wit and clarity—like her intense blue-eyed blonde beauty—were soon well-known to his political, secular friends and to her fellow seminarians. And she brought to my father's personal intellectual life—he already had a bent for British, especially Labour Party, history and politics—a welcome dose of English skepticism, with her dislike of woozy German profundity and academic pretension. Also, she had interesting friends in the English clerical establishment, both Nonconformist and Anglican, whom he was shortly to come to know. Her family forgave him for publishing an article entitled "Great Britain in Second Place" just as they became engaged, and they married in Winchester Cathedral in December 1931, she in tea-dipped ecru lace, he impressed into a morning suit (he drew the line at spats and refused to wear them). "We stood on either side of the tomb of a Saxon king," my father would tell us. "Can you imagine a Yahoo like me from a farm in Missouri in such a situation?"

My mother never thought Bonhoeffer was much of a theologian, though she bowed to no one in her deep respect for his spiritual and personal courage. Perhaps it would be more accurate to say that she was in a position to witness how much he changed and grew from the conceited classmate he'd been in 1930, when he was snobbishly dismissive of his fellow students, seemed rather conventionally indifferent to the ethical inadequacies of Karl Barth's theology, and with comprehensive European arrogance dismissed the lectures he heard, along with most American intellectual life, as "shallow." So easy for him to say! He was so much more densely and seriously educated than the other students! He was so well attuned to religion as the "transcendent experience of Goodness, Beauty, Truth, and Holiness"! But Bonhoeffer didn't yet know what Aunt Ethel already knew, what some of his "naive" fellow students in the United States already knew: that putting one's faith to the test of lived experience was to prepare to put one's life on the line.

The summer after Bonhoeffer left Union Seminary and returned not to Germany but to a temporary, perhaps temporizing, job in England, young pastors who had been in class with him were in the South and Middle West trying to help black farmers and white workers: within years Myles Horton's efforts in Tennessee were firebombed (later he founded the Highlander School there, one of the first interracial educational institutions in the South); other seminarians were jailed on charges of criminal syndicalism; Jim Dombrowski got into trouble in Pennsylvania, which didn't stop him from moving on to Mississippi. "We cannot save our civilization at all except we change its whole basis, nothing less," wrote my father in *The Unemployed,* a magazine put out by the League for Industrial Democracy. Unemployed people then numbered close to thirteen million in the United States, but the point was not just them but everyone.

Few German pastors or theologians would have gone along with my father's despairing radicalism of 1931, let alone of 1933 or 1936. And there certainly weren't many like-minded American clergy: even twenty or thirty years later my father was still viewed as dangerously left-wing; the pastors of most churches didn't want to have anything to do with him. True, exciting new thinkers were transforming a few seminary classrooms, and they were welcomed in university chapels all over the country—my father rode circuit from campus to campus throughout the academic year—but you hardly ever encountered them in ordinary parishes, whatever the denomination, and this never changed. Countless people have told me their memories of hearing Pa's sermons in college, the way he excited their seriousness, challenged their conventions, stirred up their faith or lack of it; he was not easily forgotten. (Alan Paton, who encountered him in London in 1946, called him "the best speaker I heard in my life; he spoke for an hour without notes, and he had us in the hollow of his hand.") But beyond the college chapels where he was a hardy perennial, only two or three churches welcomed him. One was Saint George's, in New York, where he preached on the second Sunday in January for many years and we lunched afterward with the chief warden, Uncle Felix's old pal the legendary liberal lawyer C. C. Burlingham. But then, how many among us are willing and able not just to argue but to work for a complete restructuring of our postmodern, postindustrial, but alas not post-unjust society? It was rare then, and rarer now.

The tone, the atmosphere, of those radical seminarians was wonderfully astringent and clear-headed. When I was growing up in Heath, after the war, they were still my family's dear friends and heroes. Their mix of practical political courage, social energy, spiritual depth, and cultural vivacity was intoxicating, and I miss it. Again, it took me far too long to recognize how unusual they were: I made the happy, stupid mistake of thinking lots of Americans were like them. In the 1970s, I happened to turn on the television set one Saturday afternoon in New York—I was housebound painting bookcases on the afternoon of the Kentucky Derby, and I hoped to catch it—and as the TV flickered on, I saw Bill Moyers interviewing an old gentleman in a rocking chair. They were on a porch, and you could see behind them a sublime landscape of wooded mountains. "Mah political gaahds?" the old gentleman was repeating Moyers's question in a beautiful Southern voice. "Oh, Ah'd say Shelleh." My Yankee ears couldn't catch this, and I had to listen more carefully. "Yes," he went on, "Shelleh, Mox, and Reinie Neebah."

Tears of happiness bolted from my eyes. It was Myles Horton, bless him. To hear his wonderful voice touched my heart, but my nostalgia for his robust, unprententious political courage nearly broke it. That was just what I remembered from my childhood—these intrepid, marvelous people! The crucible that was the Great Depression had been an experience that for some had forged real character: as my father always insisted, the important distinction was, or should have been, not between *which* formulas for improvement one fought but that one fought at all: altogether too many people took no position and defended this fatuity as respectable caution. To have no position was to be prey to fascism: that's the way we saw it. Anyway, thirty years later, to hear this fine Southern schoolteacher naming Niebuhr, Marx, and Percy Bysshe Shelley as his guides to a lifetime of dangerous opposition to entrenched segregationism! Now, in the 1970s, with Martin Luther King, Jr., and Robert Kennedy dead, and with Americans sourly, grimly, yet eagerly settling for the criminal malefactions of a bigoted reactionary like Richard Nixon! You can bet Horton's continuing practical optimism, sitting there on his porch overlooking the glorious Cumberland Mountains, was a true reproach. I watched the Derby, but it's Myles Horton I remember.

205

Clayton Morrison, however, like so many other American clergymen, frowned on such activism—it was too radical, distastefully upsetting. He did not want to acknowledge that it related to a larger issue: to the threat of fascism everywhere—in the United States as in Europe—and he lingered, in a hand-wringing posture of anguished Christian uncertainty, a distance away from the trouble, decrying the use of force against evil, drawing back from active commitment to a curriculum of true social justice. As for the Jews, they ought, surely, to be more clearly whatever it was they wanted to be, less "hyphenated," more assimilationist, frankly, or else how could one be sure of their loyalty? This was lousy theology and ridiculous politics, Pa thought. And the insensitivity about Jews was not only in itself deeply repugnant but a sign of general moral sloth. "The Christian Church in America has never been upon a lower level of spiritual insight and moral sensitivity than in this tragic age of world conflict," he wrote in 1934.

By then two enormous transformations had occurred that changed the political culture from the one that Bonhoeffer, Keppel-Compton, Niebuhr, and the others had discussed in 1931. Franklin Roosevelt had won election in 1932, had given his stupendous first inaugural speech, and had initiated the New Deal. Felix Frankfurter, still at Harvard, energetically went about helping his best law students find jobs in the new government agencies that were going to get America back on its feet. (That now ex-President Lowell disliked FDR, "a traitor to his class," even more than he disliked FF gave this work an extra, exhilarating punch.) My father was skeptical: Teddy Roosevelt's progressivism hadn't been enough; his cousin's New Deal wasn't going to be, either. Still, it was a great deal better than elsewhere. In Germany, Hitler had been appointed chancellor of a coalition government ten days after FDR moved into the White House and in March 1933 gained by parliamentary vote the dictatorial powers he craved. Within months he had destroyed political opposition to his regime and soon had laws enacted that banned Jews from the German polity.

And 1934 was the year that in Germany saw a group of Protestant pastors who had been antitotalitarian from the start, Bonhoeffer among them, unite in signing the Barmen Declaration in opposition to the Nazified policies that most German clergy were willing to accept. That was a political decision of some courage, and who could but welcome it? Yet several seasons had already gone by during which all potentially effective challenges to Hitler's terrorist state had been quashed, and it was late in the day to be fussing over a theory of church-state relations that would satisfy both Calvinists and Lutherans and not rattle the Third Reich *too* much (this was what most of Barmen was about); the theological underpinnings of the Confessing Church, as well as its realization of the huge dangers about to engulf it, was at best wobbly and unreliable, at worst accommodationist. Its most heroic heroes, like the Lutheran pastor Martin Niemöller, or Bonhoeffer himself, did not yet decisively recognize the urgency: the sand was running through the glass.

Many Christians in Germany and America, as elsewhere, glossed their cultural and social bigotries with a patina of churchly double-talk about Jews being, as it were, theologically challenged ought-to-be Christians, people who, if they stopped to think about it for a moment, would surely see that they had been stalling for millennia at a point more than halfway on the road to inevitable Christianity. Devout German Pietists especially, it should be noted, found one of the most obnoxious things about Jews to be their resistance to conversion, which, they noted, was already an issue in the Gospels. Of course, if one kept on with this subject, one could avoid examining one's own spiritual and moral failures to attend to the Gospels' instructions, and ignore the poison of one's own inhumane prejudices. When still in his twenties, in one of his earliest printed pieces, my father had denounced this influential nonsense about Converting the Jews—and he did so with strong biblical arguments. For Christians, the covenant with the Lord does not begin with Jesus Christ and there is not a break, or crack, dividing the Old Testament of law from the New Testament of love: the covenant for us all begins with Abraham. Moreover it was from Jews that Christians had learned, and should be learning still, that the imperishable moral wisdom of the Prophets has as much to do with the institutions of the nation as with the heart of a single person.

This way of understanding it—which has a pedigree easily as distinguished, as antique, as well represented in the historical library of Christian thought as that of any other ways of interpreting the hyphen in the word "Judeo-Christian"—was, in the 1930s, scarcely attended by Jews or Christians in positions of ecclesiastical authority. But I believe many good people, reading their Bibles, instinctively understood it, as they continue to do today. Hardly any bishops or deans, very few professors and pastors, said it out loud, which left the way open for the most degraded kinds of "rationality" to invade debate on such political-theological issues. For my father and his like-minded theologian friends, the grotesque efforts made in Germany during the Third Reich to pretend that one could have a de-Judaized Christianity were beneath contempt and did not merit consideration, but one had to note that the rise of fascism was bringing out latent poisons in doctrinal disputes all over the place. It was vitally important to be very clear on the theological points, which were, as they had been for centuries and are still, matters of life and death.

Hitler's luridly pagan fascism, preying as evil will on human weakness, not strength, encouraged Christians in Germany and elsewhere in their unexamined social and cultural misgivings about Jews. But this is not to say that Christian Germans, who may have been predisposed to this bigotry, were doomed to promote or succumb to it. (Most of my secular American Jewish friends, whether or not they'll admit it, believe that Germans *are* so doomed, an attitude as prejudiced as the anti-Semitism they rightly loathe, for heaven's sake.)

Take Paul Tillich, that fine "Aryan" holder of the Iron Cross First Class, who had written not only a good book on *The Religious Situation* (which my uncle Helmut translated) but another in 1932 on *The Socialist Decision* (which my father admired). He instantly got in trouble with the National Socialists in good part because of his unwavering pro-Semitism. When Storm Troopers indeed stormed into Frankfurt University in April 1933, where Tillich was chair of the philosophy faculty ("Paul among the Jews," Max Horkheimer called him), and after the black and brownshirts had burned books in a great bonfire in the square in front of the Römer—"the ancient building where German emperors were crowned," as he noted poignantly—he was suspended from his post. Uncertain months passed, so he went to the Ministry of Culture to ascertain for himself what his future might hold. And what did he and the callow young official there talk about? They discussed the relation between the Old and New Testaments, Tillich insisting unequivocally that the Jewish Bible was a fundament of Christian faith.

By June of that terrible year Union Seminary was ready with a job offer for Uncle Paulus, and the Tillichs—broken-hearted but relieved, in anguish but in hope—left Germany in September. His friends remember that at the train station he "was strained, tense, quiet, almost desperate . . . more concerned about the fate of his Jewish friends than for his own." When the Tillichs got to New York, my mother was at their new apartment to greet them, and my father found a German-speaking student to coach Uncle Paulus in English (as it happens, Carl Voss, great-grandson of the Johann Voss who first translated Homer into German). Like my father and many others, over the next few years as the persecution of Jews grew more violent, Tillich found himself breaking off friendships and severing bonds with former colleagues in Germany who disagreed with his views. In America, though, Pauck in Chicago was bending the ear of Robert Hutchins, as others were bending the ears of James Conant at Harvard and Alvin Johnson at the New School for Social Research, on behalf of beleaguered German dissidents. "Tillich emphasized over and over again that not the Jews alone but Christianity and humanism were also being put to death," Pauck said. As the world knows, Germans did not see it that way—or see it clearly enough, or see it in time.

So the situation in Germany and for Jews everywhere was among the many things that I believe my father thought one should pray to have the courage to change—the wrongful public policies and, if necessary, the errors of one's own heart. That he saw that Hitler was "bent upon the extermination of the Jew" and had destroyed the basis for political opposition to him did not alter this commitment as the decade wore on. What dark and terrifying times! He did not himself return to Germany and so could not report directly to American readers on the church situation there during what Germans call the Nazi Time, but he had secondhand news from academic and clerical friends and from ecumenically-minded clerics in other European countries who were doing their best to help Jews, indeed all victims of Fascism. Alas, there were so very, very few of them! But he organized or joined groups devoted to these aims and continued to write regularly on the fate and nature of Jewry; this theological and political commentary was one of his "most fundamental contributions," as his friend the scholar Franklin Littell had written, "much appreciated by Jewish spokesmen and one that shoots an arrow straight into the golden center of American *Kulturprotestantismus.*"

By 1936 he had settled in the Berkshires for the summers with his growing family—my brother had been born two years before. The typewriter clattered all morning and afternoon (in 1920s two-index-fingers ratatat style) as he worked on his torrent of articles and books. (He never wrote out the sermons for which he was most admired, however; these were extempore, with a few words scribbled on the back of an envelope and hurriedly thrust into a breast pocket at the last Sunday-morning moment, just before he ambled up the chapel aisle behind the choir and other clerics, singing the processional hymn with great gusto and completely off-key. "I like to preach," he acknowledged. "I'm a preacher.") And he prepared for his classes at Union, where the academic work was excitingly rigorous.

The Union Seminary faculty was, like the summer colony in Heath in this respect, a marvelously high-spirited group then. I remember well its remarkable scholars, characters of real force and consequence; uniformly white and male, they came from strikingly diverse backgrounds and their personal styles were almost comically varied. They taught their students with enormous energy, intelligence, and what appeared to be an implacable indifference to race, class, or gender— men and (some) women, whites and (some) blacks, Americans and foreigners—preparing them for "callings" to pastoral work, scholarship, teaching, and a well-instructed Christian life in a whole range of unpredictable settings. Students called the close-knit, rather conservative social cohesion of the place "strangling fellowship," but the intellectual liberality was palpable.

The Union scholars included, by the way, well-known authorities on prayer and liturgy, many of them compilers or revisers of prayer books, hymn books, and "guides to worship." Between them—English, French, German, and American Protestants of almost every denomination—they knew all the prayers that had ever been perpetuated in any liturgical document, a scholarship they shared generously with their students and colleagues. To use the thin, dry vocabulary of today's academy, they knew how to deploy many types of discourse: they could lecture or write monographs, surely, but they knew how to preach and knew how to pray. I mention this because people don't fully recognize how detailed and comprehensive can be a cleric's command of prayers, homilies, and liturgical practice. Working teacher-pastors know very well the difference between composing a brand-new prayer and ringing a change on an old one: the Union scholars did both all the time; they had mastered with real virtuosity this technical skill that Protestant clergy must have (even Episcopalians, though along with their Anglican brethren they sail the course set by the incomparable 1549 *Book of Common Prayer*, surely one of the greatest books of the English language). We came to know their prayers well at the seminary's daily and weekly services. Thus in my father's case his prayers came not out of nowhere but out of a richly complex somewhere—of Heath, of Union, of austere American-German

210

evangelicism, of deeply studied biblical theology, of a closely considered style of worship.

During that summer of 1936, my parents left the Berkshires for long enough to have a working holiday in England, where they saw a great deal of their friend Stafford Cripps, whose Socialist League was admirable but perhaps not efficacious? (Cripps was my godfather, and Winston Churchill's famous putdown of his political foe notwithstanding—"There but for the grace of God goes God himself"—I remember him as kindly, lively, approachable. He was a hero to me because, like a cleverer and more powerful Aunt Ethel, let's say, having easily disregarded the privileges of place, class, and personal safety in the interests of a larger social betterment, he got right to work. His shrewd legal maneuvers on behalf of the miners of Durham in the 1920s made for a story that I liked hearing my father tell.) Pa preached all over the place, although not, of course, in Anglican churches, where he was verboten in those pre-ecumenical times. How could churchmen help to create a polity that would attend to the often conflicting imperatives of economic health, social justice, and political strength, not to mention spiritual decency? And what would the church's role be in such a society? Religion and the state: the balance between them was uncertain, as it is still—and murderously dangerous to adjust or challenge.

It has been said that when Archbishop William Temple of York met my father, he exclaimed as they shook hands, "At last, I have met the disturber of my peace." I have a nice picture of them together: Temple with his broad, wise face and impressive mien, wearing his lordly working uniform with its gaiters and swinging black coat over episcopal purple, my father taller and rangier, in Nonconformist mufti, with his bald head and eagle-y profile, his genial smile. Other friendships were consolidated that summer—with the great historian R. H. Tawney, whose very name evokes to me bracing intelligence, intrepid morals, modest courage. And with the pacifist Bishop George Bell of Chichester, who was in touch with many German resisters and was a friend of Bonhoeffer's; with John Strachey, D. S. Cairns, the great Kant scholar Norman Kemp Smith; with Maurice Bowra and a clutch of other Oxford scholars, including that formidable giant of biblical scholarship C. H. Dodd. Harold and Phyllis Dodd were treasured personal friends—my mother would have been his assistant in 1930 if she hadn't come to America—but for their students the

211

Dodd-Niebuhr axis was theological. The first commandment, Temple suggested, should be "Thou shalt love the Lord thy Dodd and thy Niebuhr as thyself."

Merriment aside, Germany was never far from the thoughts of any of these people that summer. My father reported at second hand that the Nazi regime had still not "succeeded in quieting the religious opposition to its totalitarian claims"; he predicted that further conflict would come, since the Nazis were obviously determined "more than ever to subject the German youth to an anti-Christian education," which at least some church elements were determined to resist. The situation was frighteningly bleak, and he despaired of the "pessimistic and negative character" of Germany's "prevailing Lutheranism," which lacked the "certain degree of mature disillusionment required for appreciation of the Christian religion in its more classical form, with its skeptical attitude toward the ideal pretensions of every political panacea." Yet seven hundred pastors in the Confessing Church had been imprisoned for their political opposition to the regime—a lot of pastors if you look at it one way, or no way near enough if you consider that Germany then had seventeen thousand pastors: it depends on your expectations of principled heroism. A thousand or so Catholic priests besides. Thirty-four thousand people had signed petitions for the release of the anti-Nazi activist Carl van Ossietzky several years earlier, but he was still in jail, and the Nazis kept him there even (especially?) when he won the Nobel Peace Prize that same year. My father wrote eagerly about the Confessing Church's big conference and protest meeting, where delegates cited the large increase in the attendance at churches directed by Confessional pastors. He was proud of the Hamburg pastor Paul Humburg, who that summer called on "Christians everywhere" to "resist the government's youth program"; though the regime had denied him the right to speak anywhere but in his pulpit, so that he couldn't attend the conference, his parishioners printed and circulated the sermon in hundreds of thousands of copies.

I don't think it's presumptuous to imagine that papal policy in the 1930s and 1940s would be one thing my father prayed to have the serenity to accept, since obviously one couldn't change it. His ardent comments on that subject have a cool analytical rigor that does not bely his appalled scorn—for the Vatican's praise of Mussolini's conquest of Ethiopia, for the Spanish cardinals' support of General Franco, for the servility of the French bishops who later collaborated

212

with Vichy, in general for the Vatican's support of its hierarchy, as he put it, as against the congregants, its devotion to its own power structure, and its neglect of ordinary people. A good example was its support of Catholic Action groups, directly responsible to the bishops, and its withdrawal of support from local priests who were active in political movements that expressed "the common man's discontent with the status quo"; the political tendencies of these movements "would be difficult to give an exact description of," but quite clearly they were "economically more liberal and politically more daring than anything ventured by the hierarchy."

What, he asked in 1937, was the motive force behind "the intimate alliance between Catholicism and fascism"? He found the oft-cited answer that they shared a common enemy in godless bolshevism inadequate, even hollow, clearly showing "a certain pathos." As if Mussolini and Hitler and Franco were the only alternative to Stalin?! The new pope, whom he correctly predicted would be Cardinal Pacelli, would hardly make a difference, though, not only because Pacelli had had such a formative influence on papal policy earlier in the decade but because "the total situation is determined by forces on both sides too deeply rooted in history and too inexorable in their logic to permit the hope that a change in reigning popes will greatly affect the issue." It was a tragedy, he thought, if opposition to fascism were to come more reliably from those who derived "moral self-respect" from Soviet communism and who appropriated the "moral prestige of Lenin's disinterestedness" than from true Christians. His cordial friendships and affectionate but fierce doctrinal disputes with Father John LaFarge and, later, with Father John Courtney Murray—two Jesuit giants now remembered with awe but then dismissed and frowned upon by the callow, reactionary power elite of American Catholicism—only deepened his distress about the tragic inability of even the church's greatest minds to alter their doomed acceptance of the Vatican's *raisons d'état,* and of the ludicrous doctrine of papal infallibility that hovered over the enterprise.

In 1937 and 1938 and 1939, summers at Heath were partial ones, islands of recuperative rest in a sea of ever-intensifying work. It was this way for everyone. In London in the summer of 1939, only weeks before the War broke out, Pa preached a sermon on a Saint Paul text— "Perplexed, but not unto despair"—to a big meeting of the Student Christian Movement, which many of the young people remembered with gratitude in the fierce seasons ahead. He met with Bonhoeffer, who was in anguish: Pa helped to arrange a temporary appointment for him at Union, but Bonhoeffer then decided he must return to Berlin, a decision my father honored. They prayed together. And I was christened in a little church in Sussex: my godmother, who was to become one of my favorite heroines, was the redoubtable Margaret Wedgewood-Benn, later Lady Stansgate—the daughter, wife, and mother in notable families of Nonconformist left-wing parliamentarians. My mother liked to speculate that perhaps she was the shrewdest politician in the family and told me many stories about her subtle political energies: there was no doubt as to my luck in having such a fairy bestow a wish over my cradle.

Peggy Benn was as deeply committed a Zionist as my father was becoming—which is not to say that she was a "Christian Zionist," a type of mild bigot who thought the real solution to the Jewish Problem was to send all the Jews to "the Holy Land" and thus avoid the question of what to do about them in the countries where they plausibly or implausibly wanted to be normal citizens. This issue was more than urgent, since the unspeakable Nazi assault on Jews was intensifying, while a British White Paper suspended further Jewish immigration to Palestine. These matters were a high priority for her and other political activists and ecumenical clerics. And my father was also working hard on his Gifford Lectures, which he delivered at the University of Edinburgh later that autumn. The tone that is now so famous in the serenity prayer radiates throughout this immense theological text: the work of true spiritual contrition, and the labor of true justice, never ceases. Many of its most difficult passages were presented to an audience who couldn't hear the words above the din of anti-aircraft artillery; he revised the text for publication as the first volume of *The Nature and Destiny of Man* in the dark winter that followed. Soon Holland, Belgium, and Denmark were conquered, Norway invaded. The second volume, written in 1942, ends:

> Wisdom about our destiny is dependent upon a humble recognition of the limits of our knowledge and our power. Our most reliable understanding is the fruit of "grace," in which faith completes our ignorance without pretending to possess its certainties as knowledge, and in which contrition mitigates our pride without destroying our hope.

214

Meanwhile, what were American clergy doing? In 1940, a few months after war broke out, the Federal Council of Churches, a big umbrella organization of official U.S. Protestantism, issued an appeal for neutralism (written by some of my father's students, among others, he wryly noted). Espousal of the doctrine of radical noninvolvement, let us call it, in the war to save democracy—I can't credit it with "pacifism"—was not limited to his pals in the Fellowship of Reconciliation. This was five years after the Aryan decrees had robbed Jews of their rights as citizens in Germany, seven years after Tillich had left for the United States and six after Karl Barth had returned to his native Switzerland and Confessing pastors had joined thousands of Nazi opponents in the concentration camps, two years after the annexation of Austria and the Nazi Party–sponsored atrocities of Kristallnacht, a year after Hitler's invasion of Bohemia; Poland had been trampled; France and the Lowlands had fallen; the Battle of Britain was in full swing; even in Congress the Neutrality Act had been amended. The churchmen's appeal, my father observed simply, was "completely divorced from all political realities." Americans today, who proudly boast of their country's vital contribution to the Allied victory, should not forget that this eerie divorce from reality continued for almost two years while F.D.R. tried to bring public opinion around and Britain continued its desperate, solitary struggle against a triumphant Hitler.

And what of the churches there? England was fighting nobly, and alone, against the fascist threat, but, Pa observed despairingly, what could be expected from an Anglican establishment in which the Archbishop of Canterbury had praised the Anschluss for being "achieved without bloodshed"? Temple and Bell were exceptions to the low-grade rule. Of course, there were skeptics who had deplored Neville Chamberlain and were "full of self-righteousness about the sins of the British Empire which a good Christian must disavow," but this wouldn't do, either: "every empire is full of sin; not the least sin of the British Empire is its playing the game of power politics so badly in recent years. . . . I do not find much virtue in the kind of moral sensitivity which gags at [these] sins and leans over backward to appreciate Nazis."

In June 1940, my father noted, not for the first time, that the morning mail was bringing "reports of disaster everywhere." Also in the post was a Socialist Party letter chiding him for deviating from its platform

215

in his urgent interventionism about the war against Hitler. He resigned from the party with this comment:

> The Socialists have a dogma that this war is a clash of rival imperialisms. Of course they are right. So is a clash between myself and a gangster a conflict of rival egotisms, and there is a perspective from which not much difference may be perceived between these egotisms. But from another perspective there is an important difference. "There is not much difference between people," said a farmer to William James, "but what difference there is, is very important." That is a truth which the socialists have not yet learned. They are right in insisting that the civilization which we are called upon to defend is full of capitalist and imperialist injustice, but it is still a civilization.

On the same day *The Nation* published a letter he wrote for a group he helped to put together called the American Friends of German Freedom, about

> a group of almost forgotten men and women in the catastrophe enveloping Europe, . . . the anti-fascist Germans who were fighting Hitler long before the armies went into the field. Driven from their own country, shunted about from one place of refuge to another, they have persisted in the courageous work of building the anti-Hitler underground movement. Some have been lost already . . . others are in danger of being . . . caught, and have no chance of survival; the firing squad or decapitation will be their fate. We owe it to these people who have sacrificed themselves to carry on the fight for freedom—most of them could have emigrated to safety, but have elected to continue their work—to exhaust every possibility to effect their rescue.

Recent writers have referred sarcastically to this minute number of valiant people as the "much-vaunted German resistance," but this is unfortunately a slander: the resisters were never vaunted at all, not then and not since, indeed scarcely remembered and massively ignored, as Bishop Bell or Bill Pauck or Uncle Paulus could easily have attested. (The slanderers have perhaps not much lived experience of being in physical danger and don't seem to know what moral danger is. Their easy condemnations smell of the lamp.) Some of the resisters were church people, but of course many were not; there were good, bad, brave, less brave, atheist, *dévoué*, left-wing, right-wing resisters— they came in all stripes, but never in quantity. In November 1941, in a book review of Niemöller's sermons, my father praised their "thrilling note of immediacy and urgency," but Niemöller (with whom he had grave differences of opinion) had been imprisoned in solitary confinement for more than four years on Hitler's orders, even though the judges had given him a light sentence when convicting him of the Nazis' trumped-up charges against him.

My father wrote many such book reviews, as well as almost weekly editorials urging all-out support of the war effort, and in summertime he wrote them in the Stone Cottage, for by now our family was settled there. My wonderful aunt Hulda and Mütterchen came often, too, and Uncle Helmut and his family soon found a holiday place in nearby Rowe. Those glorious summer days with fragrant strawberry meadows and dappled forests, mist over the brooks and sunsets blazing behind Mount Greylock! How amazing that the kindly adults around me—I think especially my grandmother—somehow preserved a happy routine of calm normality during those war-torn months.

Pa finally resigned from *The Christian Century*, fed up with its holier-than-thou neutralism and continuing anti-Semitism, its advocacy of "completely perverse" policies, and he started a rag of his own, *Christianity and Crisis*. And by now the summer friendship with Uncle Felix became colored by a shared anxiety about the same issues that so troubled Peggy Benn and that had to be addressed in the United States, too: getting the U.S. government to increase the emigration of Jews to America and to favor if not support outright the project of a Jewish state in Palestine. In the summer of 1941, Frankfurter and my father were visited in Heath by an old friend of Felix's and a new friend of my parents—the then thirty-one-year-old Isaiah Berlin—Zionism, not badminton, was the order of the day.

Berlin was in the United States awaiting word on taking up a position Guy Burgess had organized for him at the British embassy in Moscow, where Stafford Cripps was now ambassador. Although the Soviets had OK'd it, given that he was hardly a conventional accredited F.O. type, to say the least. Pa said he'd put in a good word for him when he next wrote Stafford: Cripps's reply contained the useful tip that this was the first he'd heard of the plan, and he didn't know if there was indeed a job for Isaiah to do. Berlin went on to the British embassy in Washington, where his range of social and political friendships became characteristically enormous, and his dispatches on what was being said and done in the wartime capital, duly considered by Churchill's War Cabinet, became legendary.

Naturally, Uncle Felix and Isaiah and my parents had a million things to talk about, the collision course on which Zionism and British policy were set being one, the strained relations between Chaim Weizmann and the dying Louis Brandeis being another. But the major theme concerned "what is to become of the Jews in the postwar world," as my father wrote a few months later, which "ought to engage all of us, not only because a suffering people has a claim upon our compassion, but because the very quality of our civilization is involved in the solution." All too often, they thought, the debate was being conducted at a hopelessly low level: a symposium on "Jews in the Gentile World" published around this time, for example, was exasperating in its silliness, with "learned men" trying to "illumine a vexing problem" by "holding up the candle of the obvious to the daylight of common experience," talking pretentious nonsense, offering specious reasoning, idiotic psychobabble, or poor contrasts between Jewish and Christian ethics that slandered the first and misapplied the second.

Yet it is true that the situation in the United States regarding local anti-Jewish prejudices, Nazi persecution of the Jews, and the Zionist ideal—issues that Hitler's evil had now inextricably linked—was extremely complex. Hours of talk in Heath and New York were devoted to it. Everyone knew that earlier efforts of far-sighted Catholics, Prots, and Jews to encourage interfaith cooperation in order to discourage anti-Catholic and anti-Jewish bigotry had been coming apart since the rise of Hitler. The National Conference of Christians and Jews, for example—founded in the 1920s by an energetic Yalie named Everett Clinchys who roped in Wilson's secretary of War, Newton Baker; a leading Reform Jew, Roger W. Straus; and the Columbia historian Carleton Hayes, a well-known Catholic layman—was foundering because of Hitler's policies, some of its members claiming that the NCCJ should take no position at all on Nazi racial laws, that it should not have "for its object the importation into our American life of controversies engendered by the domestic policy of foreign nations." Well! When this

218

attitude was linked with Reform Jewry's long-standing skepticism about Zionism, it induced a kind of do-nothing trance, while other American Jews rancorously squabbled about whether and where to secure a haven for their persecuted cousins in Europe. Alas, these disputes allowed bigoted Christians to equivocate, saying cynically, sanctimoniously, that they could hardly go out on a limb for Jews or for Israel when Jews themselves couldn't make up their minds. So disputatious, those Jews!

Plenty of hypocritical Christians, and not a few Jews, had viewed the events of 1938–40—Kristallnacht, the riots in Jerusalem, the British White Paper, the sudden rush of desperate Jewish refugees fleeing the Wehrmacht as it advanced across Europe—as, somehow, deadly confirmation that Jews were rather tiresome and might well even have been fomenting some of the trouble from which they then suffered so grievously. It was rumored that Mr. Sulzberger, of *The New York Times,* had wondered whether it wouldn't be better simply not to mention Jews in the paper, in the hopes that the fuss would die down? But by 1941 it was different. The blessed combination of Governor Herbert Lehman and Mayor Fiorello LaGuardia, also in New York, encouraged a counterforce alliance of Zionists ranging from Harold Ickes to Herbert Hoover to pressure Roosevelt to support the idea of Israel (The British government, amazingly, tried covertly to stop them from organizing a fund-raising dinner).

At *The Nation,* which had often published his pieces, my father was encountering resistance to his views on this subject and reluctance to publish them. Uncle Felix urged him to persevere, thinking that "too many liberals are still enslaved by their romantic illusions and cannot face your clean, surgeon-like extradition of reality." When the articles finally appeared, on "Jews After the War" and on the stake that all good Christians and democrats should consider they had in the state of Israel, FF wrote, "I would give a cookie to see the letters you have had. I know nothing in print that faces the Jewish problem more trenchantly and candidly."

It was not such a huge compliment: the silence on "the Jewish problem" was noticeable. Archbishop Temple (now of Canterbury) was a lone, noble voice supporting the World Jewish Congress in an otherwise pointless debate in the House of Lords. Church leaders and *The Christian Century* went on warning their flocks not to succumb to "Jewish propaganda." But plenty of people, including the leadership of the AFL and Wendell Willkie, were beginning at least to see the point of favoring the establishment of a state for Jews in Palestine.

One interesting person in the tragic tumult was the Methodist bishop of Pittsburgh, Francis McConnell, a clearheaded brave man who had cut his political teeth trying to help the steel workers during their famous strike in 1919 (he was sniped at from the left by William Z. Foster and from the right by steel-industry titans). In December 1942 he and my father were at a key conference where McConnell insisted on the urgency of action, since "between five and six million Jews are now being subjected to a deliberate program of extermination," a point that had been made for some months by Gerhart Riegner of the World Jewish Congress, by Willem Visser't Hooft of the World Council of Churches, and by Rabbi Stephen Wise, who in August had finally persuaded Sumner Welles, in the State Department, of the truth of the horrible reports filtering out of Central Europe. Yet the people who Didn't Want to Know were prevailing.

I remember well my parents' joint reminiscences, after the war, with Frankfurter and Berlin, about those terrible, terrible times, and their fierce, sometimes uproarious comments about those prevalent people. We all knew who the friends were—but oh the guffaws and acerbic dismissals of the enemies: the undependable appeasers, the reactionaries, the anti-Semitic Jews, the isolationists, the Nazi sympathizers, the bad Germans, the Germans who thought they were "good" but weren't! The speed and hilarity with which my mother and Isaiah would staff the imagined Establishment of a postinvasion Vichy England! would invent *Times* of London editorials about the importance of Keeping Order! would mimic the postures of famous Jews who were really "Trembling Amateur Gentiles," as Lewis Namier called them! My goodness, Uncle Felix really loathed Walter Lippmann, and Arthur Krock wasn't even worth talking about! Who, at All Souls' high table during a German occupation of Oxford, would have been most obsequiously enthusiastic about the new regime? What had Cardinal Spellman in common with Charles Lindbergh? Oh the merciless drubbing of pious do-gooders who prayed for their own salvation and never risked their safety! Oh the mocking of Germans' weaknesses for the often phony depths of *Innerlichkeit*! My father, who did not hate easily, was discomfited by the merriment, but he would not have denied that many of these targets were contemptible. Moreover, like Uncle Felix and Isaiah, he had a good nose for the stench given off by that "unstable compound of materialist bombast, philistine rage and provincial sentimentality" which, as one historian has described it, is fascism's vile but widely distributed source.

In April 1942, my father mused aloud, in a *Nation* article, about the historical roots of Nazism (then as now a safer subject than the future of the Jews) and about the curious truth that "for some strange reason" people seemed to "find satisfaction in regarding the present evil course of the Germans as the consequence of congenital defects." He correctly, in my view, saw this "strange" habit as a simple clear inversion of Hitler's master-race theory, a temptingly easy "opportunity to discover that Germans are and always have been a race of sadists, monsters, and rebels against civilization." He called it Vansittartism, since the position had been well expressed by Sir Robert Vansittart, the anti-appeasement British politician. He also rejected Emil Ludwig's theory of "good German culture and bad German civilization," because, he thought, it too easily separated thought and action, word and deed, which in real life were richly and inextricably connected. Still, it was true that "German culture has been as profound in measuring the ultimate problems of human existence as it has been perverse in dealing with the proximate problems of human society, particularly the problem of justice."

Equally, he rejected facile attributions of Nazi energies to Prussia, or to German romanticism, or to simple anti-Semitism. All these interpretations were inadequate because "they induce complacency about our own sometimes comparable, sometimes contrasting vices," which included, he thought, "moral sentimentality" and "senseless confidence in discarnate reason, emancipated from the vitalities of history." "No simple theory of German depravity squares with the complex facts of history," he concluded. "It is important to remember this so that the hatreds of war will not lead us into a draconic peace." It is important to remember this for many other reasons. Yet few people today, either Christian or Jew, of either the left or the right, would acknowledge that after all, "Hitler is a brother to all of us in so far as his movement explicitly avows certain evils which are implicit in the life of every nation." A half-century later, the spiritual candor of this remarkable sentence has lost none of its shocking power.

My father routinely continued to review books on Germany during the war years, work he did for the usual obvious reasons (including the money), but a deeper motive was surely that the assignments allowed him to vent his opinions about problems he was always brooding on

221

with special intensity, given his own background and given the breadth and depth of his associations with Germany. Like how many other German-Americans who hated Hitler and were giving their lives in battle against him?—he thought long and hard not only about the "unpolitical" Germans he so distrusted but about the anti-Nazi ones, whose hearts might well be torn, he thought, "when they contemplate the consequences of German defeat. The most stout-hearted among them still find defeat preferable to victory and continued enslavement; but it is idle to regard this choice as an easy one, or to deny the reality of the[ir] dilemma." The observation has his characteristic respect for the spiritual life of compromised and weakened opponents.

He wondered about the effectiveness of Thomas Mann's 1942 book of radio addresses, *Listen, Germany*. Mann "allows himself to taunt the German people for their political ineptness," which might be "justified, but that does not make it helpful to a people facing such desperate alternatives." Great as Mann was, his political rhetoric tended to be naive: "sometimes he assures the Germans that 'if you are defeated the vindictiveness of the whole world will break loose against you.' Since Dr. Goebbels strikes the same note, one may question its value as propaganda against Nazism."

After four years of war, vindictiveness was darkening people's hearts everywhere—how could it have been otherwise?—though anger could not lessen the pain. In 1943 my father was again denouncing Vansittartism as "a rationalized form of vindictiveness which . . . leads to silly miscalculations of complex political factors." And he marked the tragedy of the once "very considerable democratic elements in Germany . . . which were the first to defy tyranny, some of whom tried in vain to persuade the democratic world of the peril which Hitlerism represented, and of the necessity to meet this threat with outside as well as inside resistance. The outside resistance did not materialize until after the internal resistance had been crushed." How terrible the irony, he thought, that "some of the appeasers of yesterday are proponents today of the idea that there are no democrats in Germany."

This false idea was very popular by 1943–44, especially as the tide of war turned against Germany and Japan, when Americans became as fierce and indifferent to nuance as any people will be whose men and women are winning hard-fought battles against an evil enemy—and they had no doubt the enemy was evil. Distinctions were not being maintained, and sinful anger could be seen in excess everywhere, with clear policy effects. My father, like quite a few of his clergy friends, inveighed against saturation bombing, for example, and opposed the shrieking public enthusiasm for the American government's insistence on unconditional surrenders—on grounds obvious to any well-trained Niebuhrian who understands that sin is in the heart of all of us, that pretensions to power and omnipotence delude even the saintliest dispositions. But these were grounds that most Americans didn't want to hear about just then, and certainly not most American clergymen.

Dean Robbins was not "most American clergymen." As what Germans like to call a "major animal" in Washington and in the Federal Council of Churches, as a neighbor who had heard my father in the Heath church during that summer service in 1943, he thought the little prayer about grace, courage, and wisdom should be included in material the FCC was preparing for army chaplains. At the time, I didn't know that Uncle Howard was a "big beast," of course; I knew him only as a melancholic gentleman with a passion for wooded country. Uncle Howard, who spend a lot of time in Heath, devoted attention not only to the churches' work for the war effort but to the forests that covered much of his property.

How lucky I was to have been able to roam around those glorious woods! The Robbins land ran south of our house for many acres— spruce, pine, oak, birch, maple—well-managed and harvested, healthy, exciting woodlands. One could start from our meadow pond and its waterfall, then go on below the Robbins's opulent garden to the next pond, around which Auntie Lou nourished beds of marsh marigolds and evening primroses, whence the brook meandered into the woods. Mushrooms, Indian pipes, ground pine, ferns, granite outcroppings, bogs, and little trout hollows in the brook. Eventually, after waterfalls, the third pond. If you kept going long enough, you emerged from the woods into high meadows and pastures on an abandoned road with abandoned cellar holes on either side: lilacs and roses growing lustily in this pretty wilderness were signs of the earlier domestic precincts there. You came, eventually, to a windswept hilltop that featured the South Heath Cemetery and one of Heath's world-class skyfilled mountain views.

When my parents were away, which was often, I would bicycle along a different road to this same high point, thence down a further road to the Landstroms' farm, where I would stay with the family until my parents returned. I'd try to help with the chores—the haying, or putting up vegetables—but I probably just got in the way. I liked best helping Mr. Landstrom to feed and milk the cows in the late afternoon, after hours of shelling beans or baking biscuits or chasing after lost heifers; he treated me, as he treated everyone, with generous courtesy, and he taught me whatever he thought I needed to know as I trailed after him up and down the stanchions with the milking equipment, up and down the aisle between the cows with the feed scoop; into the haybarn above, where I would dive from the highest hayfilled sections down fifteen or twenty feet to the lower ones, though he thought this foolish; into the stone-lined separator room, with its amazing dairy fragrance of very, very fresh cream; around the corner to the pigpens. Restless, powerful animals, pigs: they made me nervous. Much more fun to swing on the swing hanging from the enormous sugar maple on the Landstroms' front lawn, or to learn cross-stitching or jam-making from Mrs. Landstrom, whom I adored, or to play with their benign German shepherd, Smokey, or, at home, with our terrier, Topsy; she had puppies in the last year of the war—we named the greedy one Goering and the long-legged one Halifax.

The Robbins forests were magical to me, and I peopled them with Algonquin warriors and their families—Deerfield was only eighteen miles away, after all, and the massacre had happened only recently, at least in my dreams—with Pooh and Piglet, with all the beasts of India and of Sussex that I learned about in the Rudyard Kipling books my English mother gave me. Mütterchen taught me how to collect princess pine to garnish the church decorations, how to make sunprints of ferns, find ladyslippers in the hidden sunlit glens, sew clothes for my dolls, and distinguish among mushrooms. Aunt Hulda and I would go for long woodland walks and picnics in Dell, have adventures on the abandoned Oxbow trail after an afternoon of blueberrying on Burnt Hill, across from Mrs. Drown's house (named for some now-forgotten Indian blaze two centuries before); and I drew pictures of Jesus at Galilee in my Sunday school coloring books. I knew where Galilee was: I had heard talk about it.

Meanwhile, my father gave Dean Robbins a copy of the prayer, and in 1944 it was indeed included in the *Book of Prayers and Services for the Armed Forces, Prepared by the Commission on Worship of the FCC and the Christian Commission for Camp and Defense Communities.* It was translated into German—presumably because the booklet's compilers foresaw the use of their work in an occupied Germany. At some point Alcoholics Anonymous started using it as their oft-cited prayer. My father of course never copyrighted it, because like most clergy he presumed that prayers were not private property and it was inconceivable to construe them as a source of revenue.

Not that other people haven't made money from the prayer. There was a postwar fashion for pairing it with Albrecht Dürer's drawing of praying hands—this was deemed aptly pious. Examples cropped up on bookends, tea towels, pieces of etched stained glass to stick in library windows. Former students or distant admirers sent these trophies to my father—they meant to be kind—and he shook his head in wonderment. My caustically anti-pious (though very devout) mother, who considered that one's taste in certain matters signified one's spiritual condition, would raise an expressive eyebrow and mutter about vulgarity of the soul. (In contrast, really close friends—and these were not coincidentally secular Jews, agnostic ex-Catholics, or cheerfully irreverent Prots—would send along the worst samples precisely to induce gasps of disbelieving wonder. Painted trays or crocheted hymn-book covers, say). These artifacts keep turning up. I met someone recently who swore she'd seen the prayer painted on the side of a Swiss chalet (with the false German attribution, of course), and only the other day I came across bookplates inscribed with its words. AA encourages its appearance on coffee mugs, naturally enough: I wonder whether it's on ashtrays?

After half a century, there are plenty of riffs done on the prayer, and some of them are ghastly, others quite cheery. I like a goofy one that turned up in *Calvin and Hobbes.* Calvin says to Hobbes, "Know what I pray for?" Hobbes: "What?" Calvin: "The strength to change what I can, the inability to accept what I can't, and the incapacity to tell the difference." Hobbes: "You should lead an interesting life." Calvin: "Oh, I already do!"

A friend of mine recently discovered in a local Barnes & Noble a "Folding Screen Book" entitled "The Serenity Prayer," with eight panels of pretty pictures to go with a simplified version of the text, like a children's picture book: the "wisdom" panel has a nice photo of a waterfall, and "to know the difference" features a bird in flight. I suppose it looks spiritual? Does the bird "know the difference"? Is it flying away from the waterfall? This little booklet costs eight dollars. But of course making aerosol spray cans of spiritual whipped cream out of public-domain "virtue" is a well-respected custom in the American marketplace, as the vile William Bennett with his ghastly *Book of Virtues* has demonstrated.

In 1946, after another idyllic Heath summer, my father returned to Germany for the first time in sixteen years. I had a typically terse note from Stuttgart: "I wrote [your brother] a letter but have not written you. But you haven't written either. . . . The children here are all hungry. They do not have enough to eat. Almost all the buildings were destroyed by bombs. We must pray for these children and help them."

As a member of a government commission investigating the occupied territories, he met with university chaplains, big shots in the Social Democratic Party and Christian Democratic Union, theologians and poets at a conference at Bad Boll (where his father's favorites, the earliest Christian Socialists in Germany, the two Blumenhardts, had founded a retreat), with Niemöller, Bonhoeffer's father, and Bishop Otto Dibelius in Berlin, with dozens of others. Again he encountered brave, sensible men and women, including clergy, but more often the German pastors seemed completely oblivious, somehow, to the landscape of death and social dismemberment, physical torment, spiritual chaos, and moral confusion around them. "They walk as if in a dream . . . a whole nation writhes in agony."

In that same year, an inconsequential German pedagogue in Kiel named Theodor Wilhelm received a copy of the serenity prayer, in English, from some Canadian friends who sent it to him "as a first sign of postwar reconciliation," he wrote later; they had called it an "old little prayer." For reasons known only to himself, Wilhelm then incorporated it in a book he wrote, which was published in 1951 under the pseudonym Friedrich Oetinger. Why Wilhelm chose to use this name as a nom-de-plume, when the historical figure of F. C. Oetinger, a Swabian Pietist of the eighteenth century, was not only well known in Germany but an ancestor of his wife's, is a mystery. Wilhelm's book had nothing whatsoever to do with that trivial and obsolete theologian, and vice versa.

Nevertheless, the serenity prayer—though not the book—somehow quickly became accepted throughout Germany as written by the earlier Oetinger. This double mistake was then and is now astoundingly strange, and I find it indigestible. For anything written by a Niebuhr to be attributed—with such speedy complacency—to an exemplar of sentimental German religious fervor! It bears out my father's hunch that sometimes Germans are just amazingly self-absorbed and uncomprehending.

226

By the 1970s the dreadful Wilhelm 'fessed up, though he got most of the story wrong, and few Germans could have known the "true facts": by now the prayer was in general circulation as a Swabian one. The eighteenth-century Oetinger, he acknowledged, was

> a preacher to the birds in the woods, and his books are full of mystical sentimentalities. Anyone with even a little knowledge of Swabian pietists, of their special mixture of sectarianism, mystical eccentricity, and apocalytic frenzy, must know that such a sober reflection [as in the prayer], such a pragmatically argued distinction between the possible and the unchangeable, even more the challenge of active social change, could never grow in the soil of Swabian conventionality. But the prayer, cloaked with this Pietist godliness, made its way in the Federal Republic and became a favorite ending for solemn talks. It became the motto of the Bundeswehr's academy, and General Speidel began using it to characterize the spirit of Germany's new military leadership. In Koblenz the false attribution is carved in stone and surrounded by flags.

Belatedly, Wilhelm put his students on to the obligatory task of checking everything the real Oetinger had ever written. Nowhere did they come upon even a single phrase that resembled any in the prayer. Wilhelm and his wife went to an officer at the military academy and talked to him about the mistaken attribution. "His response was as sensible as it was grateful," he reported: "to leave the text intact but erase the name Oetinger. I hope it has been done."

Well, yes, I don't know whether it was done, but why would the only solution be to give no source citation at all? The rich paradoxes here are worth preserving. Why not acknowledge the German-American author?

Wilhelm himself resisted the idea that Niebuhr had written the prayer, and he could only rather sleazily suggest that my father, "even if he is not the composer of the text, is the one who introduced it to the wider American public." This condescending smear was accepted by the "wider German public." Goodness, how easily they armor themselves with the weird, awful presumption that in the Profound Spirituality ball game they must surely have been the first to get on base.

Imagine the prayer now, chiseled on a rock and surrounded by proud black, red, and gold banners, at the very place where–at the end of this incredible century in which German armies have gone into battle in two horrific world wars–German officers must, in a wholly different frame of mind, train young German soldiers in a wholly different world:

> Gib mir die Gelassenheit, Dinge hinzunehmen, die ich nicht ändern kann. Gib mir den Mut, Dinge zu ändern, die ich ändern kann; und gib mir die Weisheit, das eine vom ändern zu unterscheiden.

For the German army! My father was a connoisseur of irony in history, but I believe that this is so bizarre and poignant as to surpass even his expectations. What a startling end to the story, given his family background and his life work, given that he spent his best years in what he later assessed as doomed and fruitlesss efforts to convince his American and German colleagues of the follies inherent in their pieties, given his deep misgivings about the Germans' overly developed respect and enthusiasm for military power.

He had willingly allowed the widespread use of his prayer by the American army during wartime, but he did not know about the prayer's new life in peacetime, postwar Germany, nor about its new renown in the upper reaches of the Federal Republic, a state that officially honored him a few years before his death only when his old friend and ally the Social Democrat Willy Brandt became chancellor. This was after decades of government by Christian Democrats, who had inherited and still espoused so much of the conventional German worldview that American Niebuhrs had been opposing for three generations. West Germany was a state whose spirit my father still found dangerously flawed by the same pious hypocrisies he had deplored all his life in both the United States and Europe; East Germans, meanwhile, were showing equally dangerous, equally pious German tendencies to cede moral authority to the state and thereby compromise their freedom.

My father died in 1971, and is buried in Stockbridge, Massachusetts, where he resided during his last years, not far from the Heath woods that his mother and sister and he and I explored together. Stockbridge is famous in American history as the town where the great Jonathan Edwards—an eighteenth-century Protestant giant if ever there was one, another of my father's heroes and about as different from a Swabian Pietist as you can get—preached to a tiny congregation of frontier people and Indians:

> Gracious and holy affections have their exercise and fruit in Christian practice. I mean, they have that influence and power upon him who is the subject of 'em that they cause that [it] should be the practice and business of his life. This implies . . . that he persists in it to the end of life; so that it may be said not only to be his business at certain seasons, the business of Sabbath days, or certain extraordinary times, or the business of a month, or a year, or of seven years, or . . . under certain circumstances; but the business of his life, it being that business which he perseveres in through all changes, and under all trials, as long as he lives. The necessity [of this] in all true Christians is most clearly and fully taught in the Word of God.

My family still has the German Bible Reinhold Niebuhr was given by his German schoolteachers in Illinois when he graduated in 1910, inscribed to a "truly good German." And I still have the King James Bible he gave to me when I was confirmed, and the American history books in which he wanted me to study the Founding Fathers. A bust of Abraham Lincoln in his study reminded us always of his profound admiration for this Middle Western biblical democrat who, if ever any political leader did, understood the perils and dangers of righteous indignation and who truly had the wisdom to distinguish what had to be changed from what could not be changed.

Recently Missouri honored Niebuhr as a distinguished native son, and his bust stands in the statehouse rotunda, along with those of Omar Bradley and Scott Joplin, Pearl Buck, and Charlie "Bird" Parker; he's opposite Josephine Baker and just around the corner from Harry Truman. This might have pleased but would have embarrassed him—he thought such memorials only showed the vanity of the eternal human wish to claim immortality, and he had an instinctive dislike of graven images. On his daily walks in New York City with our sinful poodles, he would observe the old stone and bronze statues of now-forgotten heroes that decorated Riverside Drive. "See what I mean?" he'd exclaim to his class in Christian ethics. "Look at that fellow across the street whom you pass every day on the way to International House.

229

Do you know who he is or why his statue is there? I ask you, Who the hell is Butterfield`?" (This was considered shockingly blasphemous for a Rev. to say.)

And yet, he was happy to have his prayers used in whatever context people wanted or needed them—and he respected the intense gratitude that AA members had for the serenity prayer. He would, I am sure, have also respected the very different phenomenon of the Bundeswehr's admiration of it. Indeed, seeing it at the military academy might have moved him to hope that yes, Germany has in some ways definitely changed.

Still, though he might demur, I know I prefer the idea of the memorial in Jefferson City, Missouri, to the falsified route by which his wonderful words ended up carved in stone for the cadets in Koblenz.

Nominated by The Yale Review and Pat Strachan

ALL THE APHRODISIACS

by CATHY HONG

from MUDFISH

blowfish arranged on a saucer. Russian roulette. angelic slivers.
ginseng. cut antlers allotted in bags. dogs on a spit, a Dutch girl

winking, holding a bowl of shellfish.

white cloth, drunkenness. a different language leaks out—
the idea of throat, an orifice, a cord—

you say it turns you on when I speak Korean.

the gold paste of afterbirth, no red—

Household phrases   -pae-go-p'a   (I am hungry)
                                -ch'i-wa   (Clean up)
                                -kae sekki   (Son of a dog)

I breathe those words in your ear which makes you climax,
afterwards you ask me for their translations. I tell you it's a secret.

gijek niin tigit rriil—the recitation of the alphabet, guttural
   diphthong, gorgeous.

what are the objects that turn me on, words—

han-gul, the language first used by female entertainers, poets,
   prostitutes—

the sight of shoes around telephone wires,
   pulleyed by their laces, the blunt word cock

little pink tutus in F.A.O. Schwarz,
they used to dress me as a boy when I was four.

white noise, white washed. The whir of ventilation in the library.

Even quarantined amongst books, I tried to kiss you once. Tried to
    touch your cock.

strips of white cotton, the color of the commoner, the color of virtue,
the color that can be sullied—

my hand pressed against your diaphragm, corralling your pitch—

a pinch of rain caught between mouths,

analgesic tea. poachers drawing blood—

strips of white cotton I use to bind your wrist to post, tight
enough to drawl vein, allow sweat—

sweat to sully the white of your sibilant body,

the shrug of my tongue, the shrug of command, ssshhht.

Nominated by Mudfish

SNOW DREAMS

fiction by TOM BAILEY

from DOUBLETAKE

I

THE SIDE DOOR cracks open. I expect my eldest—dark, curly-headed Gary David—but it's my eighteen-year-old, blond Kevin, who slides in from outside, red-eyed and sheepish. I look him up and down as I hold the bowl and beat the batter. He's standing, hands pocketed, casting around the kitchen, glancing at the sink, the clock, the floor, the beamed ceiling, the smoking Upland. I've tried to raise my boys like I've managed to train every dog I've ever owned—with a biscuit in my left hand and a switch in my right—and I'm burning now to smack this son of mine with the accusation of what he knows is right, because I brought up both of them to know better than to drink and ever handle a gun. I wait for Kevin's eyes to finally meet mine and then, using a firm gaze, I give him a spank-hard look. He glances away, ashamed, I think, and I go back to pouring out our pancakes, reach for the boiling coffee.

There's a low scuff-kick at the door and Kevin has to unstick his hands from his Carhartts to open it for Gary David loaded up past his chin with split wood. To see my two grown sons standing side by side, I imagine folks could get the idea my Susan's made a practice of visiting long, lazy afternoons with the postman—summer day to winter night different as these two boys are. Kevin's more simply the spitting image of who I used to be before I suddenly, at the age of nineteen, while serving my time in Nam, split out of my issue with a last thirty-seven pound, three-and-a-quarter inch growing spurt, before I rolled over forty-five and my own bright blue eyes dimmed, and I got fixed with these squarish, silver-rimmed bifocals, when I still had all of my own straw-blond, thick, and wavy hair. Standing next to him, Gary David—both in looks and in his shyness and care—mirrors his grand-daddy, Susan's black-headed, part Onondaga daddy, as if he'd sat up in the grave and lurched back out into the world for one more tall, stiff try at things.

Another, bigger, difference between them is that my youngest, Kevin, is the first of us Hazens to go on to school past the twelfth grade, taking classes now down at the local junior college in Canton. Next year, though, he wants to transfer full time to Cortland State. He wants to live over three hours away and have us pay for him to earn himself a *real* degree. The first two times he mentioned this I felt the pressured dollar sign of it ticking bomb-big behind my left eye. The third time I exploded, yelling out before Susan could grab my knee and squeeze, *You just want to be on the parental dole your whole god-damn life! You don't want to have to ever work for a living!* Gary David, who's more sensible about these things, is going to be a car-penter after me. He'll find himself a nice girl like that Anne Burke whose family's lived outside Sebattis near long as we Hazens have. He'll marry and name his first boy Gary. But what I find most curious in their natures is that while Gary David was born with the heart and desire, born with the *belief* in the building, his brother Kevin has the better hands, a sharper eye for the truths of wood grains and the ab-solute honesty of plumb lines. Though perhaps even more strange still is that these two boys—these *two men*—aged a good five years apart and night and day opposite as they are, can be such good friends.

Gary David's sniffing strong over Kevin. "You leave any at the brew-ery?" he asks. "Who was it over, not that Jeanie Prescott again?" By not answering Kevin convicts himself. "Aw, Kev . . . ," Gary David starts and gently sets down the wood like you wouldn't expect a boy to—even while he's talking to Kevin—being considerate of his mother sleeping upstairs. Kevin simply stands with his hands in his pockets, blinking, red-eyed. He's brought this girl around once or twice, and I guess she's green-eyed cute enough for dating. But she's from *New York City* of all places, just going to school up here in our North Coun-try so she can ski seven months of the year, and she's not one of us or even remotely of our kind.

Two weeks ago Kevin asked me if he could skip his buck this season, and when I asked and eyed him why, he confessed it was because this Jeanie didn't *like* it. She didn't want him to go because she didn't think hunting was *right*. "No," I said to him, "no, you can't *skip* it," and stood up and left him standing there, more abrupt with him than I'd meant to be I guess, but too full of the voice-shaking responsibility of it right then to speak reasonably. This responsibility which was my father's responsibility before mine and his father's responsibility before him: the necessity of fulfilling our tags toward stocking three freezers to get us through one of these no-fooling winters again. If we want to eat that is.

For us, deer season's not a matter of plaqueing a staring head or congratulating ourselves over a rack of horns. For us, hunting's as crucial as surrounding every inch of spare space under our extra-wide porch and eaves with carefully cut, dried, and split wood—never imagining, not even able to imagine nor capable of comprehending in the blistering chainsaw heat of summer, that we could ever in twelve straight hard winters use all we've stacked, and then and again stumped equally as incredulous every May when we have to scramble up the last skinny sticks and shavings of bark to heat the freezing kitchen at 5 A.M. This one single and unforgiving truth, out of which the responsibility I'm speaking was born: that it's already time to start the dragging and sawing and splitting again that very same afternoon if we're going to be ready for the first freeze come September. It's all about living up here—*surviving*—and so far as I'm concerned there *is* no difference between the two, but it's the huge *difference* between us Hazens and a lot of other folk who don't know or have any idea at all about the cold.

I cut my eyes at the clock. It's already three minutes past our 2:30 A.M. time to have left and be gone. I get up with my plate, rinse it off in the sink. My boys follow behind me doing the same, and then we grab our gear, ease out the door, and crunch across the crust of snow to the truck.

• • •

It's a thirty-minute drive in to our spot, winding back through the preserve and up and across Big Cloud Mountain, onto a half oval of road bordered to the east by an icy brook. Having wound and humped to be there by three, we sit silently in the truck and stare through the glare of our headlights. A teal-colored Chevy and a brown Impala squat in our space. A neon-pink bumper sticker on the truck shouts: THIS BUCK HUNTS! We pop the doors and climb out into the shadow dark, and it doesn't take a flashlight to show us by the heavy frosted glass that these fellows must've come in last night, before gun season started.

I'm quick to anger, but only a few things make me mad. If these men have broken one rule to get their deer, they won't hesitate to break another or another after that. They're the kind of men who, I know, *will do what it takes.* I knew their kind in Nam, and I could tell you some stories of things they're capable of that would make your hair go straight. I've known their kind here at home, too, watched them do carpentry, say, on a government job like HUD. You'd tear out that already straightened hair to see the work these men do, screwing everyone but themselves. When I have nightmares of evil in this world, it always comes to me in this man-shape of sloppiness and a too-easy, unearned return. And it's this evil that I'm constantly on guard against— my mission I guess—what in the passing on of an honest way of living this life I hope to give the strength of to my two sons, a strength which they'll have to call upon to fight against it long after I'm gone.

Gary David breaks off the cold snap of silence. "What do you think, Dad?"

I try to put the best face on it I can. I tell myself: *There are 20,000 acres in front of us.* We'll turn our backs on their tracks and head the other way.

"Get the rifles, Gary David," I say.

The moon's up, spotlight bright. I lead and Gary David and Kevin follow. We walk down a gentle slope and then we begin the climb. The hill goes steep, mountains suddenly steeper. With all the clothes and the silly shell bag I've got slung over my shoulder I feel heavy and robotic, old. Gary David and Kevin pitched in and bought the bag for me last Christmas, and though to me it seems worse than useless with rifles on a one-day hunt, the least I can do to avoid the waste is to put it to work and carry it for them. It's unscuffed, though off-colored by dust, too stiff and strangely new and—for my comfort anyway—a little too close to the size and shape of a woman's purse. My own .30–.06 shells I still keep safe in looped elastic over my breast pocket the way my father did, the same way my grandfather carried his. My boys stay right behind me the whole while, young, walking easily, their breath lightly silvering.

Shots ring out into the moonlight at 3:53 A.M. They slap, *bang bang bang bang bang bang,* and then echo booming between the rows of hills. Then there're two guns, three. The first one's reloaded and starts in again, *bang bang bang bang bang bang.* All of them rage away. There are a few distinct cracks. A pop. Then there's silence, a harder and stiller silence now it seems for having been disturbed so violently. Waiting crouched in the aftermath of the ambush, my body's tensed tight, reminded of war. It's against the law to shoot until first light, but from our right, from the east, we hear a thin but distinct, "Ya-*hooooo!*" Weekend blasters, sons-of-a-goddamn-bitches, crazy men. We angle even more sharply southwest away from them, push on, marching faster, in deeper, and then on faster and farther and in deeper still.

On the down side of a saddle-humped mountain, in a circled clearing, we stop for a coffee break, eat the sugared pancakes we pocketed along, the close winter sky graining a hint of light. Sitting in the dark, under a brightening sky, the cold surrounding us hard and crisp and clear as a shield, warm deep down inside our Carhartts, I think how it's times like these, moments like this pure still moment, that make me glad of who I am and that I've got two sons to remind me of it, to line the path and keep me on it, sons who'll carry on this life and the respect for it long after I'm gone. And it's in this simple flash of living that I can see the war and the killing I did clearly, the good it did for me, perhaps the only good it did for any of us: it helped me to recognize moments like this one, to note and appreciate them in a way and feel them with a white-flared intensity I would never've known if I hadn't ever cared and feared so for life, and not just my own.

I take a sip of the hot coffee and glance at my sons. In this sudden second I nearly manage to tell them I love them—-both of them—different as they are and always will be for me, and that I'm glad they're here with me now, but even thinking to blurt out *I love you* shrinks my throat tight to strangling. I think, *This is what it means to be out here more than anything, deeper even than the professed and hammered-home responsibility.* And I suddenly realize the obvious untold reason I snapped at Kevin for not wanting to come hunting with us this season. The truth I know deep down's I couldn't live without either one of them. I cast back the dregs of my coffee and snuff my sleeve, manage to croak a harsh, "We'll never get a goddamn deer if you girls keep lollygagging." They shuffle to their feet and then we start again on our mission march.

· · ·

The country we now find ourselves in has changed from fat oak and maple. Now it's rock-rugged, spruce-filled, and shale-scaled. A tremendous valley opens out to our left and in the speck bottom of it there's an iced-blue mountain lake sparkling silver with the first rayed flashings of sunshine. We'll never hound down a buck like this, and ready or not it's time for me to plan a strategy and split us up. I pick the first suitable tree for Kevin, a curiously forked spruce with a wide view of this expanse, the natural path ridgeline coming up and the new day. We leave him there, looking sleepy-headed, but safe in the knowledge that the hard march has sweated the last of the alcohol out of him, and then Gary David and I push on and up and over the long slope. I place him at the top of the next piney ridge. Then I push on up and down and around along the same ridge for another halfmile.

The single beech I find has a great sky-reaching spread of limbs, and I squirm out a comfortable way to wedge myself in, sweeping the open V-sights of my Remington .30-.06 over the maze of thickets and snow below. It's winter's dawn and we're ready and waiting, the opening daylit hour of the first day of hunting season each year when the most bucks are shot, before they've been alerted to the fact they're in season again, and we're far enough out in these woods that I don't think we'll have any trouble with idiots and their carelessness. I think how I would've driven myself and my boys another five miles simply to escape them and the threat of some stupid accident.

Then I hear the shaking of the brush, a racked buck stumbling toward me through the thick-tangling scrub. *Impossible,* I think, but know, too, from all the stories I've ever heard or even told, the statistics I can quote, that it's exactly this unexpected moment which I should expect and for which I should be ever-vigilant. I finger a cartridge out from the elastic above my chest pocket, feed it in and gently lock home the bolt, flick off my safety and snug my cheek, seat the sights, pointing the aimed V upwind. The buck's sixty yards off. He stops and sneeze-snorts a warning and I feel the hollow hurry in my chest, the fevered, hot-to-cold itching sweat that he's somehow caught my scent or simply *sensed* me in this tree, but then he starts crashing carelessly forward toward me again—the new morning's icy light catching the flash of his huge brushlike rack.

There's an impact thump like kicking a plump pumpkin, the shot echoing crisply, and then a rush as the buck tumbles bagged heavy into a white-staticed silence. And I'm breathing hard, raspily recovering from a full dose of buck fever as I shimmy fast down the beech. My rifle seared empty, the bolt thrown open, I jump from five feet up, climb to my feet, dust the snow quickly off, and then I chamber another round.

The buck's fallen just behind a tall drift, inside a mess of thickets. Just last year my sons and I sat around the kitchen table shaking our heads over the unbelievable newspaper story of an experienced hunter who'd been gored nearly to death by a big buck he'd wounded crazy, how he'd had to crawl himself out of the woods holding onto his own spilled entrails. From where I am I can see the flecked red shining brilliantly. There's a flailed path back where he sprinted and then fell.

I tiptoe in, safety off again, finger on the trigger, use the barrel to press aside the buck-colored brush, and peek carefully in.

II

The first shot slapped Kevin straight up out of an uneasy sleep where he'd been dreaming Jeanie had him pinched by the nose and was fussing and fussing at him like a crow. He staggered, grabbed the branch in front of his face, feeling the uncomfortable ache of having wedged himself by the crotch into the crotch of the odd, hairy tree, and touched the cold hurt of his exposed nose, ran the drip of it onto his sleeve.

He heard Jeanie's cawing again and then he looked straight up to see the crow alone on the top branch, laughing at him. He pointed his levered .30-.30 up at it and watched it flap slowly up and wheel away within easy reach of his sights. Rings of sound continued to bind then ripple by him, smoothing out and out until the snow cushioned the woods silent and peaceful again. Kevin wondered who had taken the shot, his father or Gary David? If either of them had taken a shot, he knew neither had missed. He himself hadn't even bothered to load his rifle. Then he heard a second flat slap. It shocked sharply past, the echoed ripples touching lightly by him again. *Good,* he thought, *because if they get two we can leave. We'd have to leave,* he thought, *or we wouldn't be able to carry out all the meat.* Though if he knew his father, *Mr. Gary Hazen,* they *would* carry out every single slab and scrap of venison and usable hoof and horn, regardless if they *could* carry it or not. His father made a special carpenter's glue from the hooves, rigged gunracks with the wired forelegs. He even took the incredible time necessary to hand-buff indestructible knife handles from the horns. So Kevin sat cramped and cold in the tree, hoping they had gotten two, but hoping just as hard they wouldn't get three.

239

The thing was, leaving Jeanie's dorm room the night before, he had promised—in fact he had *sworn* to her—that he would tell his father that morning. He had just found out himself that Friday night, but he had promised he would have it out *before* they went hunting. But, of course, he hadn't. He had meant to. On the way home he had stopped in at The Lantern and had eight beers to pump himself up for it and, sitting at the bar glowing gold, he had felt cocksure, strong, thinking how maybe he'd just kick his goddamned father's ass, tell him to fuck the hell off and mind his own business—and not just about this either, but about transferring down to State when Jeanie did to earn a four-year degree, about hunting, cutting and splitting all that ridiculous firewood year in and year out, about becoming a carpenter, the whole bullshit dump truck load full of it—but when he'd climbed out of his beaten Dodge in front of the house at 2 A.M., he'd felt the cold. He'd felt suddenly too tired to hash or duke it out. Somehow he'd scratched at the door and had stepped into the warm kitchen without saying anything. Then they were in the truck and then, head down, paying for the beers and no sleep with every uphill step, he'd hiked way the hell out here, and now he was in this tree and now he was hoping his father and his brother both had gotten their precious bucks so he could go the hell home and get some sleep.

Kevin glanced at his watch. Nearly two and a half hours had passed since his father and brother had left him. The morning sunshine flashed, glittering gold. It was amazingly cold for that time of year, but after three winters of hardly any snow or any serious North Country cold, the old men at the diner had predicted last week's November blizzard far back in the strangest wet, chilly August any of them had ever seen or even heard tell about. Kevin himself had to admit he liked the snow. There was something blanket-comfortable about it. And in the snow he didn't mind the cold so much. Jeanie was from the city, from Queens actually, and she didn't like the cold. She did like to ski, though, and so the snow had grown up as a bond between them.

Snow.

Kevin closed his eyes against the four-walled whiteness, but felt her setting up on an elbow again, watching him for his reaction. She was touching up a single hair on his chest, slowly curling it around her perfect red fingernail, queuing up the question mark of it. He'd wondered then if she wanted him to yell at her or just scream or maybe whoop for some sort of joy. But the news had knocked him out.

240

TKO'd, his dream-self stood up out of his floored body and walked out the door and down the hall and down and around the steps, out onto the perfect, snow-covered campus lawn. Then, as if he were a kid again, he was angeled out in the snow, on his back waving his arms— his wings—his legs, the sweep of his robe, and the snow was falling softly down, down and down, blanketing him, his whole body down to his tingling toes, his chest icing ice-solid, blueing his lips, sticking white to his eyelashes, softly white, padding white, and the growing weight of it white-pressing his eyelids past zigzagging reds into a deep, dark-sliding blackness: avalanched alive. That's when he'd opened his eyes to find Jeanie still staring down at him. In this snow dream his planned life died, school and a degree froze and then melted that easily away and he saw himself getting up and out of the bed of some house which his smiling father and his happy goddamned brother would help him build, getting up every single morning at 5 A.M. to go work off the loan he was meeting every month on some new stupid shiny red, big-tired truck, working every available odd overtime job just as his father had always done, frugal with every spare second of his whole life, just to keep the baby (then babies) in diapers, in bonnets, in pureed pears. He saw a gray lunch-boxed lunch, his own coffee thermos (bought on sale), then back to sawdust in his boots, the always aching shoulders, earning his father's calluses, wearing his father's chosen life as if it were his own.

Then, though, he'd felt Jeanie's lips burn straight down to kiss his naked chest, reawakening him, his desire rising through the cold to hardaching reality again. He'd rolled up from underneath it all slowly then, and their lips had met and he'd tasted her tears, arched up to her as she gripped him, and they'd made love again and then again before he went to face him, his promise, their bond, sealing it, sealed: their future lives.

"Just goddamnit," Kevin said to himself. He scraped away from the tree and peeled back his sleeve to check his watch. It had been nearly three hours now since they'd split up. There hadn't been any more shots, but neither had his father sent Gary David back to fetch him so that he could help them clean and strip the carcasses. He glanced around his assigned clearing. His eyes stung, felt sandpapered bald from lack of sleep. He circled them wet and then, the unloaded rifle slung over his shoulder, he worked himself loose from his set stand, and started down the tree. He'd use the shots as an excuse to go see.

241

• • •

The two sets of boots tracked an easy path through the snow, his father's footsteps bigger, pressed deeper, and then Gary David's smaller and lighter, pressed just inside the trail breaking bigger tracks, his older brother trying unsuccessfully—or so it seemed to Kevin, it had always seemed this way to Kevin—to fill them. And as he trudged on after them, purposefully stepping just off their beaten path, making himself do the harder work of breaking new snow, he couldn't help but think to himself that as much as he loved his big brother, when it came to their father he also thought of him as a bit of a strung puppet, a dummy for the things their father wanted him to think and say.

Inside a stand of wind-strafed pine, Kevin stopped where he could see his father had set Gary David to give him a view of the entire valley. He saw where the tracks stopped to go up, but Gary David wasn't there. He circled the tree. On the other side, his father's bigger boots trudged off, and then he saw where Gary David had jumped down into them, sinking into his tracks again. Kevin's first panged thought was that his father had come back for his brother but not for him. Then he noticed both sets of tracks headed out. Neither set pointed back. And then standing under the pine puzzling down, Kevin grinned, and then standing under the tree in the snow patting over his pockets to confirm it he laughed out loud: his *father* had been carrying the shell bag!

In their marched hurry, and because it was not the way the Hazens had *always done things*—not the way *his father's father* had done it and *his father's father's father* before him—not a fixture, in the way dad had orchestrated, ordered, and directed every hunt for the past eight years that Gary David and he had been traipsing through these woods after him—he'd simply and ridiculously forgotten to dole out their ammo to them.

But Kevin saw his own caught dilemma, too: it was as obvious as it could be that for the past three hours he hadn't even tried to load his rifle. He'd been sitting in his stand, sound asleep, dreaming. *Unforgivable.* And his father wouldn't forgive or let him forget about it either—not ever. Kevin could hear the told story of it over and over again during their clinking breakfasts at the diner, the head shaking and chuckles it would always get.

Gary David must have realized the mistake as soon as he'd gotten himself good and safely situated and, of course, it had been his older brother who had climbed all the way back down and who had fallen in behind their father and who was probably trudging back toward Kevin right now, sacrificing his own precious hunting time for his younger brother who hadn't even tried to load his rifle and who didn't even give a damn. Kevin felt pretty shitty about that. But he still couldn't help but smile—no matter what the consequences. The whole forgetful episode reminded him of a mistake he himself might easily have made any hour of any day of any week, but it delighted him no end his father had done such a typical, stupid thing. He *is* human, Kevin thought, pleased and amazed. It was a good feeling, and he stored the warmth of it away, thinking how he might very well need it sometime later that day.

He started off after them, feeling almost happy, feeling better, at least, than he had felt all day. He followed the two sets of tracks for a long while, uphill and through the snow. The first thing Kevin caught sight of was a caution road-sign flag of safety orange. He stopped, seeing, but in the harsh glare unable to imagine or make out at all what it was exactly he saw. It looked to him as if he'd caught his father scraping and groveling. He was on his knees, bowing low, inchwormed up as if he were praying in the snow, the brand-new shell bag strapped on his back. Then, from ten yards, Kevin saw his brother Gary David sprawled flat, the snow red-mapped tell-tale around him. He heard his own howl. Shocked still, he saw the rifle barrel choked-off in his father's mouth.

III

It was late afternoon: twelve hours since they'd stepped out of the truck in the clearing beside the frozen stream at 3 A.M. The temperature had risen in the earlier, full, clear sunshine, but now with the long winter's night around them, the cold was closing in. Kevin stoked the fire and the flames jumped wild, hissing. His father lay close beside the fire covered as warmly as Kevin could imagine to make him. When Kevin had first recognized what had happened, he'd felt his world physically tilt, heave, then slither from beneath his feet He'd landed, clutching snow, felt his stomach lurch and roll—he couldn't help this and it wouldn't stop—then, still stringing spit, he'd crawled quickly forward toward them, patting blindly over the crushed and blinding snow. Kevin had to let go of his brother's pipe-cold arm and had reached out and touched his father's wrist to feel a thin pulse hiding just below the skin. With the realization that his father was still alive, he'd forced himself to shove his brother's death aside and had pulled himself up through the horror of it with one single-minded, numbed-stupid but saving thought: *fire.*

After he had kindled the wet sticks and built the flames hot enough to support the frozen limbs and had scavenged and carried back armload after armload of wood from beneath snow drifts to keep the flames going strong, Kevin had taken the careful time necessary to wrap his father's sticky head, torn cheek, and blown jaw in his own T-shirt before realizing he, too, was starting to chill, to chatter danger-ously himself.

Of course Kevin had no idea just how seriously cold it would get that night. If his father had ever allowed them to pack along a radio, he would have heard the flurried broadcast of warnings and if he had he might have pushed on through the dark toward the heater in the truck without waiting for his mother to get worried enough to send the Rangers out after them, knowing that if there was no chance of mak-ing it there was also very little choice but to try. The coming cold, sweeping into the snow left by the blizzard in the mountains that night was expected to break every record for November, but then the actual temperature of 17 below would exceed even those record-breaking ex-pectations. What Kevin could sense, though, even without a weather advisory on the radio, was the increasingly still and silent razor-edge of the air. Even the fire seemed to be having more and more trouble breathing, the flames going thickish and slow, glowing blue, low and close over the orange coals. Kevin looked to his father then, but his fa-ther's eyes were rolling uncontrolled, between snapping suddenly open to out-cold closed. Kevin felt a sudden futile flaring. No matter what happened to them then, he wanted his father to know that what had happened to Gary David that morning hadn't been his fault. It had obviously been an *accident,* and accidents happened no matter how carefully you planned or dreamed or wished for something else. *Didn't he know something about that?* He wished then he had told his father that he was going to marry Jeanie, about the baby they were go-ing to have. He'd planned to stand up and say to him: *I will live my own life, make decisions as my own man, but I will respect you and the way you raised me always.* And that's when he heard himself say out loud: "I love you, too, Dad," Kevin felt rushed through blue space. He trailed his father back to find himself seated beside him before the fire again, overwhelmed by the aftershot, shocked understanding of what, all along, his father had really been trying to teach Gary David and him about surviving in the cold. Then, without his having to think further about it or even plan, Kevin angeled his stored warmth over his father. He closed his eyes and dreamt the Rangers stumbled upon them just before dawn.

Nominated by Andre Dubus

AT NIAUX

by LAURIE SHECK

from THE IOWA REVIEW

Fists and wounds of light, battlements and ranks of light: we
        leave them outside, wander in with flashlights
whose beams flirt and shiver on the walls. Here is the
        clay floor, slippery, soft, and here
the anxious dark I carry within me as I walk.

The ground bulges as if it did not want
        our footsteps. The drawings of animals are almost a mile
in. Each morning my dreams disintegrate, coming unstuck
        from their sleepy frame, the canvas in flame,
or a film's edges melting and curling as it burns,

but these walls dream their animals unceasingly,
        the chargers, the mothering, the injured ones, the gravid,
the gaping nest of each eye fiercely open.
        We walk on and on.
These flowers are like the pleasures of the world,
        but there are no flowers here. The walls loom up,

half flash-lit, half in dark. *A headless man? The garments*
        of Posthumous? This is his hand, his foot mercurial,
his mortal thigh. . . .
        The walls conspire, make up stories. No. They're murder
without plot, betrayal without motive, the aura of crime
        but not the crime, the humming of it like shockwaves
through water.

Who walks ahead of me? And stops, as if by a river
        whose surface holds the stark
reflected autopsy of stars, or his own face
        lying in its watery distortions,
mouth slightly open, as if wanting to speak. . . .

We have come a long way. We put down our flashlights,
shut them off
        to conserve battery power, the guide writing in a book
the time of our arrival in this far chamber
        of the cave, her light the only light now,
the black air behind us crawling over itself
        and over itself,

while the animals rise up beneath her light, streaked and fleshed
        onto the walls, fetlocks, horns, candor of unchained
instances, graceful summations
        in this velvety unyielding hiddenness,
not roughed-up by doubt or vertigo.

I remember, *Twas but a bolt*
        of nothing, shot of nothing. . . . the dream's still here.
But this is not a dream. Most delicate and fiercest venturing,
        how did you come to make these animals that do not
fade? Reindeer, bison, and horses moving off
        into the blackout that won't kill them,

the blackout advancing, caressing the wreckage and the leaping,
        whatever is brought to it, anything at all, our hands
our faces, anything,
        the blackout singing, taking it all in.

Nominated by Rita Dove, Susan Wheeler

MISS FAMOUS

fiction by ROBERT BOSWELL

from THE COLORADO REVIEW

HE WAS BLACK, too tall to be a dwarf, too short to be normal. Monica had to show her driver's license before he would let her into his condominium. She liked to think her DMV photo was alluring, her mouth showing a little pout, head tilted at a tough-girl angle, bangs falling just right across her forehead. She generally liked to be carded, but not during work.

"I have my own vacuum," he said, wanting her to leave the Merry Maids Hoover in the carpeted hall. "Follow me, please." His voice had the melodic lilt of strangeness, and there was something in his walk, a tiny wobble, as if the floor beneath him were shifting. Monica's daughter, Sally, not quite three years old, ran with that same rocking motion, her arms lifted and flailing at the air.

Monica regarded all black men as personally threatening, but she knew this about herself and tried to compensate. There weren't that many blacks in Albuquerque, but she had dated one for a while. His lips had touched the soft skin below her ribs, his tongue had explored her belly button. But while they were together, she found herself suggesting barbecued ribs, Kentucky Fried Chicken, even watermelon. "I love the blues," she had said and then found herself unable to name a single performer. "The one Diana Ross played in that old movie," she had appended. She would have been humiliated, but he'd had no interest in the blues, which she found annoying. He had been disappointing, hardly black at all. However, she hadn't trusted him with her daughter. There was that.

The black man she now followed down the hall went by the name of Mr. Chub. He intimidated her: his blackness, his shortness, the swaggering teeter of his walk, the cut of his expensive clothes—pants ballooning at the waist, tapered at the ankle, as if to emphasize the brevity of his torso, and his white shirt, buttoned to the collar, cuff links (cuff links!) in the shape of gold coins.

"This is your first house of the day?" he asked, his voice smooth, like someone from the radio, like Brian, her lover. Not actually her lover at the moment. Brian was her former and, she was confident, her future lover. A smooth voice like Brian's, but Mr. Chub's voice was strange, too, haunting.

Monica assured him this was her first stop of the day. He paused before a closet, his hand on the brass knob, thin brows arching. Above his large head, a tight nest of dark, curly hair. *Natty* was the word that came to mind—natty hair and nattily dressed—but she thought it might be a racist word. Her mind seemed to insist that she was a bigot, but she didn't feel it in her heart.

His big head nodded slightly. "And you . . . pardon me, but you did bathe this morning?"

"You don't have the right to ask me that," she said, suddenly defiant, fearless, then immediately afraid. She had showered and shampooed her hair. She bought shampoo from her hair stylist. She didn't scrimp on her hair.

"I apologize," he said and removed the vacuum from the closet, a Kirby Deluxe with a chrome case, brand new and gleaming like a car just waxed.

"It's beautiful," Monica said.

"Sis-sis-sis," he stammered. "Sis-sis." He looked away, composed himself, his shoulders rolling mechanically. "I . . . have . . . a . . . stutter," he said, as if announcing royalty. "Rarely," he added.

"My husband stutters," she said, dismissive, half shutting her eyes, imagining it was true. She could almost picture him, his hair rumpled, his sweet and naked mouth unable to fix on a word. "I'm used to it," she said.

Mr. Chub seemed charmed by this. His smile grew large and rectangular, teeth white and perfect. From the neck up he was movie-star handsome, a peaked mustache feathering his full upper lip. "If you have any questions you may call me," he said and showed her the intercom mounted low on the wall—his level, the Chub plane. "This button is tricky," he warned, pushing it with his black thumb, pink in the creases. Not really black, of course, a shade of brown, with some red in it, like a dark oak stain, a tobacco color. The black man she had dated had been a waiter in a seafood restaurant. He had been getting a degree in economics. Uncircumcised. He preferred V-neck sweaters. She made a mental note to look through Mr. Chub's clothing.

She stripped the bed, bundling the expensive pinstriped sheets, imagining this man's life, then imagining her own—a woman with a husband, a woman whose husband stuttered, a woman who cleaned condominiums as a way to get close to the mysterious Mr. Chub. She could write an article on him or even a book, either exposé or biography, depending. When Brian finally reappeared in her life, she would reveal that she had begun a biography, but she would refuse to divulge her subject's name. He insists on anonymity, she would say.

She vacuumed the big closets first, noting the shirts, identical except for color, all facing the same way and evenly spaced, like marching men in a parade. They would fit her, she thought, and wished she could try one on. There were only two sweaters, crew necks, folded and stacked on a shelf, but many belts—twenty-six—wide ones with enormous buckles, thin ones with elegant latches, belts made of metal, belts ringed with turquoise, a crude leather belt with little silver figures on it—milagros. She had a cross at home covered with milagros, silver shapes that healed whatever was broken—damaged arm, chronic headaches, bad marriage. In the center of Monica's cross was a silver heart milagro; she would rub her finger over it daily and ask that her heart be healed. On Mr. Chub's belt were silver legs in a pair, one leg longer than the other. Monica touched the silver image to her lips. She would put a photo of this belt on the cover of her book. Maybe an actual milagro could be pounded into the cover of the hardback.

She knelt to inspect his footwear: six pairs of identical black shoes, polished and mounted on sloping wooden blocks. The soles of the left shoes were an inch thicker than the soles of the right. Custom-made, she thought, imagining a man kneeling and measuring her bare feet, then stretching the cloth tape to calibrate her legs, her thighs, to make shoes that would balance her perfectly, even her keel, flatten the world.

She would not sleep with Mr. Chub. No matter how grave his pleading, his crooked legs bent beneath him. She inhaled sharply as she pictured it. On his knees, he would only reach her thighs, his natty hair blending with her pubis, his enchanted voice humming through her torso.

Monica cleaned houses most thoroughly when they were not dirty to begin with. Mr. Chub's spare condominium looked as if it had been cleaned the day before. She concentrated on grout in the tile lining the shower stall, grime on the chrome legs of the sink, dust at the base of the porcelain toilet.

He entered the bathroom while she knelt before the toilet, which made her gasp.

"I didn't mean to startle you," he said.

She clutched her heart, panting convincingly, "I'll be all right." She offered him a smile, which he returned.

"You work very intently," he said in that rhythmic singsong—so smooth. How would she ever find words to describe it?

The Man with the Magical Voice, a working title.

"I just thought I'd look in on you," he said.

"I'm fine," she assured him. On her knees, she was only an inch or two shorter than he. She was on the Chub plane, the world around her instantly altered.

"You know how to reach me," he said. "Don't hesitate." He might have looked down her blouse. He turned too quickly for her to be certain.

———

Dear Chub, the letter began, *Have you forgotten the way to El Paso?* Monica found the letter in the trash, slipped it into her basket of cleansers, touched it several times to be sure it was still there. Even as he commended her work and promised he would ask for her again, she had slid a finger past the plastic bottle of Lysol to feel the crinkled texture of the paper. An unauthorized biography, and here was the first clue. Each week she would add to her store of knowledge about him.

She drove directly to her next customer—her next John, she used to say, as if she were a hooker, but no one had found the term provocative or funny. She parked in front of the Stalker's house, a red brick bungalow inhabited by a middle-aged man who followed her about, watching her clean, a computer genius, she guessed from the mess he kept, who lived alone. "My wife died of a strap infection," he had said slyly, expecting her to be curious, a stupid joke hiding in the mispronunciation, in his watery eyes, but she had refused to ask. She thought of him as a Heffalump, a stalker, a creep; he had, however, given her a set of china, unchipped and almost complete. "I've no need for it," he had said hiding his secret motives so well she still could not name them. "I'd appreciate your taking it all."

She sat in the front seat of her blue Corolla, under the shade of the Stalker's giant sycamore, and flattened Mr. Chub's crumpled letter against her knee.

Dear Chub,

Have you forgotten the way to El Paso? We all would like to see your ugly self some of these days soon. Does anyone there call you WaterBoy? Have to come home to hear the words that go straight to the heart. I am doing alright. Really, I am. I know you heard they cut out that lump I had that you did not know about. Which is why I am writing, because I know somedumbody told you. Which I didn't want. My own way of telling you would have been more fun for the both of us. Anyhow, it is out, and there is a little cut like a smiley face under my nipple. You will like it.

Come see the girl who loves you no matter what. Hear me? I love WaterBoy. I love Chub. As for Mr. Chub, he is a stranger I don't or even want to know.

Don't step on my heart.

Your Only One,
Missy

Monica pressed the letter to her chest. The book would write itself. It would win all the prizes. She and Brian would cruise to Hawaii, Greece, Fiji. Sally would need a private tutor.

The curtains in the Stalker's house parted. She would keep him waiting another few minutes. The suspense would be good for his heart.

———

There was no question whether Brian would show up, only when. Fate being what it was, she guessed it would happen soon. His wife was already so explosively large, Monica could hardly bear to watch her wade into Casa Azul and drop onto her chair. Their baby was not due for two more months. Brian would come to Monica, appear at her trailer door, just before the baby was born or shortly thereafter. He would resurface in her life, like a man in a boating accident who has held his breath too long: gasping and clutching, weeping over the good fortune of merely being alive.

Monica didn't volunteer at Casa Azul in order to see Brian's wife. It was important work. She had gone there the first time to gawk at her, but then she saw what they were doing. Food for the hungry. Shelter for the abused. A woman and her baby had spent one night in Monica's trailer. She had forgotten their names, but they had been dark skinned, and the woman spoke with an accent. Monica had let them have the bed, while she slept on the sofa, next to Sally's crib—which was too small for her now. Brian would buy Sally a new bed when he came back.

Monica lunched in Waffle Park, sharing a picnic table with a guy in a black suit, red tie. His chin was too strong, pulling his face out of proportion, but Brian might be jealous anyway—this man was younger than Brian, closer to her age, and his suit was pressed and creased. If she showed any interest at all, Brain would be jealous—if he had some way to know about it.

"Are you through with that section?" she casually asked the man with the chin, lightly touching the folded newspaper at his elbow.

"Help yourself," he said, pushing it her way.

Business section, but she glanced over it.

"Investments?" the Chin asked her. "Checking on your money?"

"Just looking. I like to be informed," she said. Her tone was brush-off, but not too brush-off. She didn't ever want to see him again, but she didn't want him to know that yet.

He returned to his lunch—a sandwich, no vegetables at all. She gave up on the business section, pulled her book from her bag. Poetry. Monica had studied poetry for a while, taken classes at the community college and through the library. She had published two poems in the college magazine. But she had given up poetry to write fiction and then given that up to paint. She sold two paintings, one for twenty-five dollars to a boyfriend, the other for fifty to a man in Santa Fe who wanted her to pose in the nude. She had been surprised when he didn't make a pass at her. Just painted. She had spent hours at his house naked, even after he had paid her. She watched the *X-Files* naked on his couch, the artist beside her but not touching her. His painting had included the slight stretch marks on her stomach, the memory her body held onto of being pregnant, the way her hair remembered the hot iron with its curl.

She read her book:

> A nervous smile as gaze meets
> gaze across
> deep
> river.

She glanced up at the Chin, who was studying the sports section now, his newspaper folded down to a little square. "Are you nervous about something?" she asked him.

"Me?" he said, lowering the paper and beginning, then, to appear nervous.

"You look nervous," she said.

"How can you tell?" He flicked one eye oddly, a tic in the early stages.

"I bet I know your nickname," she said. "Do you have a nickname?"

"When I was a kid, I had one," he said. "What's your name?"

"That's not important," she said.

"I've seen you, though. Before. You bring your lunch here often?"

"I used to," she said, which was true. Before Brian, she had come to Waffle Park twice a week, directly from the Stalker's house on Tuesdays and from the Colonel's on Fridays. Then she met Brian, and he had wanted to take her out so much, ethnic food, expensive places, once a hotel in the middle of the day. He had been crazy for her, and she had quit coming to Waffle Park.

It wasn't really called Waffle Park, of course. She gave things names.

"So what do you think my nickname was?" The man with the chin shoved the paper aside. She had his complete attention.

"Water Boy," she said, smiling, cocking her head.

"Water Boy?" He sounded shocked, or tried to, then attempted a smile, but he was disappointed, that much was clear. What she said to him mattered.

"You were hoping I'd say Romeo or Mr. Beautiful?" She rolled her eyes dramatically.

"Well, no, but Water Boy?" Flicked, and flicked again, that nervous tic.

"Did I get it right?" she asked.

"Skeeter," he said. "My father—"

"I had a nickname, too," she said, though she had not yet thought what it might be.

He hesitated. His eyes wandered over her chest. "I bet I know. I bet it was Foxy," he said, eyes bright now and zeroed in on her.

"Oh, please." She made a face to convey disgust. "My mother started it—the nickname—then my sister used it, my girlfriends. It was a female kind of nickname."

"So?" he said, "what was it?"

"Sting," she said. "Mostly. I mean, my mother would say, 'My little Sting,' and my sister would call me Stinger, and the girls called me The

254

Sting." She made a bridge of her fingers and let her chin rest there, happy with her invention.

"How . . . why'd they call you Sting?"

"They called me Sting because I have a big nose. It is big, isn't it?"

"I think you have a great nose," he said.

"My ex-husband used to say that. He loved me for my nose."

"What did the boys call you?"

"Some called me Sting, the rest used my name."

"You're not going to tell me your name?"

"I come here twice a week," she said. "I'll tell you another time."

The Chin smiled again, a knowing smile, which she didn't like, and no tic. She could read him already. She would not come here again for at least a month. This idea pleased her, and she raised her book, as if she had forgotten about him.

"You must like the Police," he began. When she lowered her book and frowned, he added, "The band, you know. Sting is the lead singer, or was. I don't guess they're a band anymore."

"I hate them," she said. "They're so insipid. I quit going by that name when that band came out. That, and the last boy who called me Sting stepped on my heart."

"I have to go," the Chin said, gathering together his paper and lunch bag. "But you'll have to tell me how he did that, how he broke your heart."

"I didn't say he broke it. He stepped on it."

"Durable heart. I like that." His smile was full of self-appreciation. "See ya," he said. "I'll be looking for ya."

She gave him only a twist of her head to indicate goodbye. Already, she could hear herself telling Brian that he, Brian, had stepped on her heart, which he had, after all. He would know as much if his wife hadn't intentionally gotten pregnant. Blinding him. The idea of a baby, of becoming a father again, blinded him. Monica had meant to tell the Chin that her ex-husband stuttered, that she liked men who stuttered but she didn't like facial tics.

One time Sally's father had said to her, "What you don't know would sink a ship," which had made her think love was dependent on what you didn't know—a kind of blindness. Myopia, glaucoma, amblyopia, heterotropia, esotropia—she'd written a poem about it, eons ago, back when she had loved Sally's father and had been seeing a guy named Eddie, not sleeping with him, just seeing him. Eddie had been to Nicaragua, right when it was interesting to go. He had been desperate to screw her, which was why she had not let him. She had seen him twice week for almost a year. Just petting, a little hand play.

Petting, what a funny word. She took her notebook out and wrote down the word *petting* and then made a list of the things that one might pet, starting with dogs and then describing the places on her own body that men liked to touch.

———

Her last house of the day was Mrs. Nighetti, whose apartment was as cluttered as Mr.Chub's was empty. Photographs of her nine sons lined the mantle of her fireplace, black and white photographs of beautiful young men.

"And only Vincent makes his mother happy with a grandchild," she told Monica, as she did every week. "Nine of them. Boys the girls go silly over, my phone never stopped ringing. Now their papa's dead, the phone is quiet, and what do I have to show? Only Vincent makes his mother happy with a grandchild, a girl, no less, Carlotta, which you may not know, but Carlotta is my name. Names her after his mother, my Vincent." She did not look like a woman who had borne and raised nine sons, did not really look old, except for the bags beneath her eyes. Monica doubted she would permit someone to clean her apartment if she weren't confined to a wheelchair.

"Do you have any new pictures?" Monica asked her.

Mrs. Nighetti, from her wheelchair, showed Monica her palms. "You'd think that wife of his would know I want new pictures of my Carlotta every week, but she's too busy getting famous. 'I'm going to be a famous model,' she tells Vincent. To hear her talk, the baby set her back years." Mrs. Nighetti waved her hands as if to push the very idea away. "But I may have some old ones you haven't seen."

Of the two hours Monica spent weekly at Mrs. Nighetti's, half of it would be in conversation—often over cups of hot tea.

Mrs. Nighetti handed Monica a photograph. "Here's my girl sitting in the lap of Miss Famous."

Miss Famous. Monica liked that. She felt sort of famous herself, a private sort of glory. A secret celebrity. It was the one real thing she knew, while the rest of the world was ignorant. She recalled, for an instant, the trip her senior class had made to Disneyland, how she had liked to pause behind people while their relatives snapped photos. All over the country, she appeared in pictures, the mystery woman in dark glasses at the border of the photos.

"So tell me," Mrs. Nighetti said, "this Brian, has he come to his senses yet? Has he come rushing to you with an armful of roses?"

"Not a word," Monica said and sipped her tea.

"I've written my Pauly, my youngest boy. Handsome like Clark Gable, but with better skin. An electrical contractor with his own truck like they've got to have, and dating a woman whose name he won't remember in a year. Trash, forgive me for saying it." She quickly made the sign of the cross, touching her fingertips to her lips at the beginning and again at the end.

"I forgive you," Monica said, which made Mrs. Nighetti flap her big hands and laugh. Monica let her eyes roam the photographs for the one that might be Pauly. She had never met him, but his mother had written to him about her. No doubt he pictured Monica in his mind, thought about her, imagined her body, her life. What was that if not fame? The Chin was picturing her right now, she guessed. Not to mention the Stalker and Mr. Chub. Brian. She touched her fingers to her lips and crossed herself in the quick, solemn manner that Mrs. Nighetti had taught her.

————

Sally ran her slow gallop, arms flailing across her father's grassy yard to Monica's open arms. "She took a nap," the new girlfriend called out, sitting on the steps, keeping her distance. "'Bout an hour and a half."

A frightened bird, Monica thought, eyeing the girlfriend. Chirp. Chirp. "Thanks," she yelled, her voice as vibrant and happy as she could make it. She lifted her daughter into the car, buckled her into the car seat Brian had given them. "What did you do today, Sweetie?"

"We play," she said, taking on her car personality, the sweetly quiet child who stared out the window and clapped for dogs and trucks. Brian would be upset about the car seat in the front—the instruction booklet recommended the rear—but Monica thought it only fair to Sally to let her ride beside her mommy. What did Brian know about raising children, anyway? His own daughter was a mess. A fat, moody adolescent with pimples and an attitude. It occurred to Monica, as she pulled into traffic, that his daughter, when she'd been tiny, had probably seemed as sweet and perfect as Sally. It was not possible that Sally could turn out so badly. Monica had gotten high with Brian's daughter a few times. All after Brian had left her. It was a way to keep in contact with him; although he didn't know about it, and his daughter didn't know who Monica was. "I'm the love of your father's life," she imagined herself saying.

From her car seat, Sally clapped at a passing Ryder truck, saying, "Big."

Her life is in my hands, Monica thought, steering them down the freeway, her hands resting at the bottom of the steering wheel. *My hands,* she thought, picturing a close-up of them: her fingers fill the screen, the delicate bones almost visible beneath the skin. Some actresses had stand-ins for their bodies, she'd read. It was never Jane Fonda's breasts you saw, but some perfect girl without a face. Did her lover know that her breasts were famous?

Monica planned her evening as she drove. She would stop at Casa Azul briefly to see how big Brian's wife was, to see if his daughter wanted a ride somewhere. She would stop at Alpha Beta to get milk and Pampers. She would drive by Brian's house without even glancing at it. She would get to the trailer in time for *Sesame Street.* She would read Mr. Chub's letter again. She might begin the biography. Notes about his condominium, the way he walked, the way his beautiful, breathless voice rode the air. He had wanted to know whether she'd bathed, which meant he had pictured her naked. She would mention the shiny vacuum, and the belts in his closet, the custom-made shoes that gave him balance. And his shirts, all those shirts, the way they all faced the same direction, one after another, identical but for color, one spaced perfectly after the next, like promises kept, like a series of snapshots all the same, like the days of a life.

Nominated by Stuart Dischell, Alan Michael Parker

GRAVITAS

by ELIZABETH ALEXANDER

from THE AMERICAN VOICE

Emergency! A bright yellow schoolbus
is speeding me to hospital. My pregnant belly bulges
beneath my pleated skirt, the face
of my dear niece Amal a locket inside my stomach.

Soon she will be born healthy,
and after, her sister, Bana.
Labor will be tidy and effortless.
In fact, I will hardly remember it!

All of this is taking place in Kenya, where they live.
This is my first dream of pregnancy
since I have been actually pregnant,
therefore I dream in reality, not metaphor.

I am gravid, eight weeks along.
My baby, I have read, has a tail
and a spine made of pearls,
and every day I speak to her in tongues.

Nominated by Maureen Seaton, The American Voice

CARLOS

by THEODORE DEPPE

from POETRY

My first day leading the prison writing workshop: Carlos
complimented my choosing the chair nearest the door.

I read a poem by Whitman that once sent me hitchhiking
and Carlos stood up, asked to read a section from his four-
    hundred-page work-in-progress,

a poem that turns on his first finding Neruda's "One Year Walk";
he said it *lit up the night like a perfect crime, so I left everything—*

I had no choice—walked three thousand miles to the Pacific.
From memory he recited a passage in which his father
left the family

a small fortune, all counterfeit: though I doubted the facts, I can
    still see
that worn briefcase, almost-perfect hundreds stacked neatly in
    shrink-wrapped packs.

I was young, it took me two weeks to accept that I could teach this
    lifer
nothing. World of concrete floors and everlasting light:

he was grateful to God who gave him *a blazing mind not granted to
    anyone living or dead,*
and wouldn't have changed a word anyway.

Nominated by Jeffrey Harrison, Wally Lamb, Katherine Min

NEON EFFECTS

essay by EMILY HIESTAND

from SOUTHWEST REVIEW

> *At times all I need is a brief glimpse, an opening in the midst of an incongruous landscape, a glint of lights in the fog, the dialogue of two passersby . . . and I think that, setting out from there, I will put together, piece by piece, the perfect city, made of fragments . . . of signals . . .*
>
> —Italo Calvino, Invisible Cities

"Do you want to know what I think?" Tommy asks, mildly and not rhetorically but offering his customer the small window of free will, the chance to *not know* what already burdens Tommy's superior automotive mind.

What Tommy Hoo thinks has rarely been apparent in the eight years that he and Steve Yuen and their pals at Nai Nan Ko Auto Service have cared for my Subaru three-door coupe. No, normally one must urge Tommy and Steve to say what they think, posing brutally direct questions: "Do I need a new battery before winter or not?" "Is the gurgle in the transmission trouble or not?" Even when Tommy and Steve do answer, they convey a sense that the jury is still out on the beloved Western idea "cause and effect." They have a bone-deep respect for the contingency of all things, and have never before actually volunteered a definitive opinion. It is an unprecedented moment in our relationship.

"Do you want to know what I think?"

"Yes, yes," I murmur.

Encouraged, my mechanic declares, firmly and unambiguously, "Don't put it on your car."

261

What I want to put on my car came as a gift from my husband, Peter, who was with me the palmy summer night that I saw a medium-size UFO floating down Brighton Avenue, hovering on a cushion of clear blue light that came billowing from underneath the craft—an airy, etherealizing light, shedding a serene glow over the asphalt road and its scurrying film of detritus. Some of us have been half-hoping for this all our lives, those of us who as children crept out after bedtime on summer nights, who stood in our backyards barefoot in the mowed grass to look up at the implacable dark glittering. And we have been well prepared for the moment in the close of darkened movie theatres; the special effects teams of Spielberg and Lucas have taught us, shown us, how to experience an encounter. We grow quiet, we suspend yet more disbelief, we feel a naïve awe and a shiver of fear as the Mother Ship appears, huge and resplendent with lights beyond our ken, and again when the fragile, more-advanced-than-us beings step out into our atmosphere. But we think it will happen far away—if it happens at all—in a remote desert, on some lonely country road, to someone else. We are not prepared for this astonishment to visit our own city street, to glide publicly past the Quickie Suds and Redbone's Bar-B-Que. Now Peter has pulled up close to the hovercraft and I can see inside its glowing body. There, not abducted, are two teenage boys such as our own planet produces.

"It's a Camaro," Peter says.

It is. A late model silver Camaro to which the boys have Done Something—something that washed over me, as Philip Larkin said of jazz, the way love should, "like an enormous yes."

And now Tommy has said, "Don't put it on your car," pronouncing where Tommy has never before pronounced.

"It" is two neon tubes which mount on the underside of a car and create a ravishing fusion of color and light whenever you flick a switch on the dashboard. The effect—"The Ultimate Effect" it says on the package—is produced by an underbody lighting kit that consists of the neon tubes, mounting hardware, and a fat wad of wiring. This kit is one of the thousands of devices collectively known as "automotive aftermarket products": sound systems, sunroofs, drinkholders, mudflaps, seat covers, carpeting, coats for nose grills, and ice machines. (And, I like to think, bud vases.) One nice thing about the genre of aftermarket products is that it opens up what might have otherwise seemed closed and finite. Implicit in every aftermarket product is the idea that

262

a vehicle is never a *fait accompli;* rather, its manufacturer has merely stopped fabrication at a reasonable point and has delivered a work-in-progress—a canvas.

The present canvas has the contour of a lithe sedan, but within that contour lies a hatchback that gives the sleek sedan the carrying capacity of a pickup truck. The rear window is a marvel of the glassmaker's art, an immense, gently curving expanse that arcs snugly over the chassis like the canopy of an F-16 over its Blue Angel. I have come with this car and the kit to Tommy and Steve because I trust them, and because their shop is so nearby that I can walk over whenever Tommy calls to say "You *cah* is ready," in his crisp, then soft, muscular speech that accents unexpected syllables, often with a faint gust of air—the sounds and emphases of Chinese overlaying English and giving it a gently pneumatic texture.

It helps to be able to *walk* to the garage of an auto mechanic whose wall is covered with letters of praise and satisfaction. It is one of the village-scale civilities that can be found in the urban world, a place that can be an impersonal tale, not least because of the automobile itself, the ways it reconfigures lives, flattens the depth of space, blurs time. So I don't want to go to another mechanic across town. I want to work with Tommy and Steve on this. When we talked over the telephone, Tommy had said, "No, we don't do that." And then he paused and asked, "Is it a *pinstripe?*" and, as always, his tone conveyed that we were only beginning, together, to enter into another automotive mystery.

Seeing the opening, I replied, "Oh no, it's not a pinstripe, it's just a couple of neon tubes mounted on the undercarriage. I could almost do it myself." (An outrageous lie if taken literally, but Tommy took my meaning: that the operation would be child's play for his shop.) "But there *is* some wiring to hook up, and I wouldn't want to mess with the electrical system."

"No, we don't do that."

I didn't say anything, and then Tommy said, "Why don't you bring over. We will take look."

One look at the kit, however, and Tommy and Steve are dead against it, and the reason is rust. "Rust," they intone together, as clerics of old must have said "Grim Reaper"—capitals implied in bitter homage. Here is the problem: to install the Ultimate Effect, a row of holes must be drilled on the undercarriage of the car, and this, my clerics believe, is an open invitation to the corroding enemy. Moreover, on this car the rocker panels offer the only site on which to mount tubes, which fact gives us reason to say "rocker panels" several times (and me to remember a charged scene in *The French Connection*), but it must not be a good thing because the faces of Tommy and Steve remain glum.

The men also point out that the kit instructions say: IF YOUR AREA EXPERIENCES SNOW AND ICY CONDITIONS, YOU MUST REMOVE THE SYSTEM BEFORE THE WINTER SEASON. Needless to say, New England experiences these conditions, yet it would seem simple enough to remove neon tubes each November and re-mount them in April (dark when Persephone descends, illuminated when she rises). But Tommy notes that no quick-release clamp system is provided with the kit, and points out that he is not inclined to jury-rig one.

"Half-hour to take off, half-hour to install. Each time," he says funereally.

The two mechanics and I stand and look at one another politely, the current automotive mystery now fully declared. After another moment Tommy says softly, kindly, "Miss *Hies*tan', this will not add to the *value* of *you cah.*"

After a long moment peering at each other as across a gulf, I venture an explanation.

"It's for fun," I say.

"For fun," Nai Nan Ko's mechanics repeat slowly, skeptically. And then, nimbly, before my very eyes, they begin to absorb the new concept.

"For fun," they say to each other. And now they are smiling and trying very hard not to smile, nearly blushing and bashful, and unable to look at me directly. We have unexpectedly stepped over into some new and intimate territory.

Upon reflection, one knows why these men did not consider fun at the first. Commonly I appear, as all their customers do, in a stoic, braced attitude awaiting the estimate, or later in miserly ponderings: Can the brake repair be put off a few weeks? (No.) Would a less expensive battery be okay? (No.) Fun has not come up during our eight years of dealings, not once. And now optional tubes that cost a bundle to install, tubes that tempt fate, that add no value, do not strike Tommy and Steve as barrels of it.

In the new silence that steals over us as we stand about the neon kit, I mention that it is a gift from my husband, that I will have to talk with him about the rust problem. At this piece of information, the situation transforms. Immediately, Tommy and Steve are smiling at me directly and sympathetically, relieved to be able to believe that I am on a wifely errand of humoring. In a near jolly mood, Steve stows the kit in the trunk of my car, and when last I see the two mechanics they are huddled, brooding happily under the raised hood of a banged-up Civic.

I am also left to brood. Here is dull old duality, posing its barbaric polarity: radiant swoon or structural integrity. Shrinking from the horrible choice, it occurs to me that someone must know how to do this, that the fine mechanics of Nai Nan Ko may simply not know the tricks that New England's custom shops have devised to deal with neon and rust, neon and winter, even as MIT's particle physicists do not necessarily know how to keep a cotton-candy machine from jamming. Sure enough, Herb, at the Auto Mall in Revere, knew all about neon effects.

"Four tubes or two? For two tubes, lady, that will be three hours, a hundred and fifty to install." And he is emphatic about rust, roaring out "No problem!" One of America's mantras and a phrase that wants a whole essay for itself.*

"None at all?" I persist. "Won't the holes allow water to seep in, especially during the winter when the tubes are out?"

"Well, sure," Herb replies peevishly, "a little water is going to get in, but it's not going to rot out right away, maybe in the *future* or sometime. Hold on a minute, lady. Eddie!" Herb calls into his shop. "That guy with the black Saturn gets his CD-changer installed in the trunk." Then back to me. "Where were we?"

"About the underbody rusting," I prompt, but greatly savoring the sound of Herb's Future—a place where rust *does* occur but whose temporal locus is so indeterminate as to make precautions about it absurd.

"See," says Herb, "I use a non-acid silicon sealant and we prime the holes with a primer."

Pressing the harried Herb one more degree, I ask if he has devised a quick-release system for the tubes for winter removal.

"Naah," Herb replies. "I've never taken one off. They just leave 'em on."

"Really?" I ask. "But these instructions say that ice and snow destroys the neon tubes."

*Glancingly, one can say of "No problem!" that its subtext is often a radical laissez-faire-ism, the speaker's Mr. Magoo-esque state of mind, which triggers a semantic backfire, making you think, This guy may not only *not* solve any existing problem, he may cause an entirely new one. The term is also used now in situations where previously a speaker would have been expected to say "You're welcome." And this second usage creates a curious sensation, introducing into the exchange of simple courtesies the idea of some problem, albeit one that is, for the moment, absent.

"Yeah, maybe," says Herb. "But I've never taken them off for anybody. *Nobody* takes them off in the winter." As an afterthought, he adds, "And that's when they get wrecked."

And that's when they get wrecked. In a tone that means, Winter is the time, lady, when neon tubes on cars are *supposed* to get wrecked, Ecclesiastically speaking.

"Anything else?" Herb asks.

A hard frost comes to the old Puritan city, and then winter, and the *tubos de neon* lie in their box along with the manual in Spanish and English, the high-voltage transformer, the rocker switch, fifty feet of black cable, six nylon clamps, six black *tuberia termocontrabile,* eight hex screws, and *la cable de energia rojo.* There is a time for everything: a time for seeking a neon mechanic, and a time to just read the manual instead and wait for spring, even as gardeners all over our region are curling up under quilts with the Book of Burpee. The first instruction, printed in large capital letters at the top of page one, is SOLO PARA EL USO FUERA DE LA CARRETERA O EN EXHIBICIONES / FOR OFF-ROAD OR SHOW USE ONLY.

Taken seriously, it would void the whole project.

The scroll of warnings continues. *El transformador para el Sistema de Luz de Neón produce un voltaje muy alto. Proceda con cautela durante la instalacion para evitar una descarga electrica o heridas.* Meaning, you can die of electrical shock doing this, so seriously listen up: Do not mount the effect at all on vehicles with antilock braking systems. Do not install the wiring too close to the gas tank, in consideration of the five-to-nine-thousand *voltaje muy alto.* Always always turn off the effect at gas stations when refueling. In the same large, all-caps typeface used for its death-warnings, the manual stresses one crucial aesthetic pointer. KEEP THE NEON UNITS ABOVE THE LOWEST POINTS OF THE CHASSIS TO HIDE THEM, the manual instructs. YOU WANT JUST THE GLOW TO BE SEEN, NOT THE UNITS THEMSELVES. This is first-rate advice that the Luminists and the Hudson River Valley School would recognize at once—all those painters who knew to locate the source of their bathing light just *beyond* the dark sail, the looming crag, the fringe of native firs.

I look up from page three (how to use a cigarette lighter to melt the *tuberia termocontrabile* to make a watertight seal), and the only thing aglow outside is a streetlight in the dull gray cowl of a cold January. And yet there is a somewhere where the neon season never ends:

South Florida, whose tropical climate and car culture, whose fancy for sheen and the night were destined to have brought neon and cars together at some point in the twentieth century.

The provenance of neon on wheels is traceable to Hialeah and the dragsters who first began to substitute neon tubing for the wiring on their distributors—Whoa! That lights up the whole engine block! Maybe Steve Carpenter saw that, the photographer who rigged up some temporary tubes under a Ferrari Testarossa and took a picture of the result for the album cover of a *Miami Vice* soundtrack. The general idea had gotten into the air, and the air was being inhaled, and all awaited the brothers Efrain and Roberto Rodriguez.

During one of the boreal storms that shoulder into our region, I place a long-distance call to their shop in Miami. Deirdre Rodriguez answers the telephone and over the next twenty minutes tells me that her husband, Efrain, is out in the warehouse right now overseeing a shipment to Tokyo; that the fire-loving countries of Latin America, China, and Japan are her best new customers; that, of *course* she has neon on her car! ("What do you think, darling?!"); that she has a special pink-to-purple-to-magenta spectrum, and that her mother has one too! Mrs. Rodriguez, who speaks in the clipped accent of her native England, remembers the hour of advent.

"I will tell you a woman-to-woman comment," she says, lowering her voice. "This is how it really happened. One night, we were lying in bed reading, and my husband said, 'Deirdre dear, I am going to put neon under cars.' Well, neon is so very fragile, isn't it? Sometimes our installers cannot even transport the tubes to the job sites without breaking them. So I said to him, 'Darling, go back to sleep.' Poor thing, I thought, he has completely snapped."

But within a week, says Mrs. Rodriguez (nibbling a little crow), the brothers had one tube of purple neon installed under Roberto's car. "Incredible!" Mrs. Rodriguez recalls of the sight. "We were speechless." On the spot, she says, her husband and his brother understood that "they must do something." Over the next months, Efrain and Roberto spent hours experimenting in their sign shop, where they invented a way to encase neon tubes in heavy-gauge plastic cylinders, figured how to bundle the tubes with a compact transformer and how to lay out the wiring system under a chassis. By spring they were ready, and at the Miami Grand Prix the Rodriguez brothers presented the Glow Kit.

Miami saw and Miami approved in a citywide supernova of enthusiasm, which was to be expected. In less warm-blooded places, neon has been a symbol for a garish modernity: "The neon glow from those technological New Jerusalems beyond the horizons of the next revolution," sniffs Aldous Huxley. But Miami knows better. She seems always to have known, intuitively, that this emanation from a gas both noble and rare belongs most intimately to her own streets. Although Las Vegas and Tokyo both have more ostentatious neon than Miami, and Paris long ago enfolded the bright gas into the evening cascade of her amorous boulevards, no city does neon with Miami's style. Mere days after the Rodriguez invention was unveiled, Miami's salt-free vehicles had begun to glow with the same radiance that nuzzles its old Deco façades. A native Miamian muses to me that her city's neon must be a human signal back to the glossy subtropical landscape—a semaphore sent to roseate spoonbills, to pink flamingos and lurid sunsets—a friendly, natural wave, a wish to belong.

Soon after the debut at the Grand Prix, the neon effect began to migrate from South Florida westward to Texas and California. It moved northward up the Eastern Seaboard until it reached the Mid-Atlantic coast, where it began to bog down. In Maryland and Virginia, the effect was declared illegal, possibly because underbody lighting tends to wash out painted highway lines, possibly because the police are a jealous police. (Especially the police do not care for other vehicles using blue light, which is their own color.) Of all regions, New England has been slowest to respond; to find my peers I must travel to the warmer, Latin quarters of our city, undimmed by the flinty northern palette.

❧

Naturally, I am aware that a good many people are not only *not* putting neon on their cars, they have sold these cars and are going about on bicycles and subways, mentioning holes in the ozone layer. Who does not take their point? The automobile was once our superdense icon of protean motion, of independence; was once made sensible by vastness; was a soulful chamber, its highways songlines. It was deliverance for Okies driving through dust. And then its Faustian appetite overtook farmlands and estuaries, dissolved the city in sprawl, fumed the air, spurred malls and Valhalla Villages. The car and its beds of tarmacadam possessed planners to trade in the boulevards of memory for cloverleaves and concrete ramps. It has nearly ruined the railroads (our Zephyrs, Crescents, and Coast Starlights).

The usual erasure of places—all the vanishing places that can be carried only as Baudelaire's great swan carries its natal lake through the poultry market—has been painfully accelerated by the automobile's demands. I know that. And yet I wish to adorn the suspect thing. It is one of the small canvases of a fragmented people. I know that too. And there is a credibility problem here for me, who has for years railed about the Commodification of Everything, saying, Lookyhere, Marx was right. Marx *was* right, consumer culture does insidiously invite us to think of everything, even our very own lives, as "product." And yet I am gladly shelling out $154.99 for a box of high-grade glam. Perhaps it is because these underbelly lights, while admittedly not a totally worked-out policy for transformation of culture, seem finer, truer, more heartfelt than one president's let-them-eat-cake "thousand-points-of-light" nonprogram. Because the gonzo extraterrestrial fireflies feel like descendants of Baudelaire's *movements brusques* and *soubresauts,* the strange and quick new ways of moving in the city. Because they are nite lights, sending the kind of signals—"affectionate, haughty, electrical"—of which Walt Whitman spoke. We can easily guess that the poet of the urban world would go for neon lamps: "Salut au monde!" Whitman calls across the mobile century, "What cities the light or warmth penetrates I penetrate those cities myself . . . I raise high the perpendicular hand, I make the signal."

Maybe too it is because these glow pods are a shard of the sublime, the old aesthetic of exaltation, so chastened over this century by a well-known catalogue of horrors. Maybe the sublime has turned hypermodern, calibrated its energies, and bolted the idea of ecstatic transport onto Trans Ams—is lurking underneath things. Maybe I shouldn't say much more. Maybe the ultimate effect is, after all, just fun and flash, a sassy way of saying "I'm here." But it turns a mass-produced object into a carriage of light, and the light these youths bring into the city also seems to work a little as safe passage, as a visa across the often guarded lines of urban and ethnic territory. "*Es como una familia,*" one young man will say of the fraternity of neon.

∽

About the time that our ground begins to relax into spring, Annie, the tango dancer, tells me about Bigelow Coachworks. Annie has a leonine shock of gold hair, a closet full of swirly skirts, and a collection of vintage

Fiestaware. She dances the slow Argentine-style tango and I felt sure that her word about neon customizers would be trustworthy. The first thing I notice about Bigelow Coachworks (other than it being named coachworks) is that the shop is immaculate. Not one oil-soaked rag. Inside the office there is a counter and a young woman behind it whose strawberry blond hair has been teased and sprayed into what used to be called a beehive. For neon, the young woman says, I must talk with Jim Jr.

No sooner have I said the word "neon" than Jim Jr., who has the palest kind of amber eyes, has plunged into the issues: First, the switch and ways it can be wired—into the headlights or parking lights, or independently onto the dash. The independent switch is a problem, Jim says, because you can forget to turn it off and drain your battery. Next, do I want two tubes or four? Two is plenty in Jim Jr.'s opinion; in fact, having no rear-mounted tube avoids the messy matter of plastic cases melted by the exhaust pipe. Now the mounting. Am I aware that the tubes aren't really made for New England winters? And do I know that the kits don't come with dismounting hardware? Do I know that Jim has engineered custom clamps that stay in place and make it easy to pop the tubes in and out with the seasons? As for rust, a touch of silicon on each screw will suffice.

It is a virtuoso romp, all the nuts and bolts of the neon sublime known and mastered by Jim, who has installed some fifteen systems, including, he says with a shy smile, the one on his own truck. My man. Jim Jr. levels with me about the thirty-six-inch tubes.

"These are going to give a *lame* effect," he says, examining the kit. "There isn't enough *juice* here for the effect we want."

Fortunately, the fifty-four-inch tubes for the effect we do want can be had right up the street, at Ellis The Rim Man's Auto Parts store, a temple to the aftermarket product where a beefy salesman shows me the selection (all made by the Rodriguez brothers) and then says, in the tone of a man who wants to have a clear conscience,

"You know, it's really dying out."

"Dying?"

"I think the kids just got tired of being harassed by the police." The salesman now pauses, glances at the two young salesclerks at the counter, and clues me in: "It's only boys who buy this stuff—you know, ethnics, Hispanic boys."

As the present contradiction occurs to him, he studies me evenly.

When the young men at the counter see what I am buying, one of them asks politely, "Is this for your son?"

270

My son, I think, not the least insulted, only feeling the sudden sensation of having one, and being the kind of mother who would get a top-of-the-line neon kit for him.

"No, it's for me," I say, smiling.

"Al-*right*," the boys say, and shoot me the hubba-hubba look. Now they want to talk neon.

"*Si, si,*" of course they have it on their *caros*. Enrique has green and José has aqua. They have neon *inside* their cars too—under the dash, on their gear shift knobs. The store has a demonstration model. José gets it out, plugs it in; we stand around it to ogle the colored coils zooming around inside the clear plastic handle.

What do Enrique and José like about having neon on their cars? What *don't* they like! It's way *chevere*, way cool, it's like being inside a nightclub! Man, it lights up your whole body and everything you go by, and makes things look really, really bright. When José and Enrique hear that I saw my first neon car near the store, they cry out in unison.

"That was *us!*"

"You drive a silver Camaro?"

"Oh, no" they cry again, just as pleased. "Oh, no, that *wasn't* us, that was Alberto. That's Alberto's spaceship!"

Now they want to tell me something way-way *chevere*: the festival is coming. That's where we can see all the best neon cars and also the low-riders slow-dancing their cars down the road, each spotless vehicle also booming with salsa.

"So neon hasn't died out?"

"No way," gapes Enrique, incredulous at the thought. Wait and see! Much lighting-up in the streets before summer is over.

The boys hold the door as I exit the showroom—carrying a long cardboard box of glass, transformer, and rare gas under my arm. They step out with me onto the broad sidewalk of our city's Commonwealth Avenue. It is about nine at night, July, prime time, and while we are standing there a boy that Enrique knows comes billowing by in a Cougar with some brand-new magenta light to spill. He creeps almost to a stop.

"*Hola!*" he calls.

"*Hola!*" the boys call back. "*Que lindo se ve.* How nice it looks. *Que bufiao! Miraeso.* Look at that. *Ooouuu, la luz.*"

Nominated by Southwest Review, *Grace Schulman*

THE GARDENS OF KYOTO

fiction by KATE WALBERT

from DOUBLETAKE

for Charles Webster, 1926–1945

I HAD A COUSIN, Randall, killed on Iwo Jima. Have I told you?

The last man killed on the island, they said; killed after the fighting had ceased and the rest of the soldiers had already been transported away to hospitals or to body bags. Killed mopping up. That's what they called it. A mopping-up operation.

I remember Mother sat down at the kitchen table when she read the news. It came in the form of a letter from Randall's father, Great-uncle Sterling, written in hard dark ink, the letters slanted and angry as if they were aware of the meaning of the words they formed. I was in the kitchen when Mother opened it and I took the letter and read it myself. It said that Randall was presumed dead, though they had no information of the whereabouts of his body; that he had reported to whomever he was intended to report to after the surrender of the Japanese, that he had, from all accounts, disappeared.

I didn't know him too well but had visited him as a young girl. They lived near Baltimore, across the bay outside Sudlersville. No town, really, just a crossroads and a post office and farms hemmed in by cornfields. Theirs was a large brick house set far back from the road, entirely wrong for that landscape, like it had been hauled up from Savannah or Louisville to prove a point. It stood in constant shadow at the end of an oak-lined drive and I remember our first visit, how we drove through that tunnel of oak slowly, the day blustery, cool.

272

Sterling was not what we in those days called jovial. His wife had died years before, leaving him, old enough to be a grandfather, alone to care for his only child. He had long rebuked Mother's invitations but for some reason had scrawled a note in his Christmas card that year—this was before the war, '40 or '41—asking us to join them for Easter dinner.

Mother wore the same Easter hat and spring coat she kept in tissue in the back of the hallway linen closet, but she had sewed each of us a new Easter dress and insisted Daddy wear a clean shirt and tie. For him this was nothing short of sacrifice. Cynthia said he acted like those clothes might shatter if he breathed.

Daddy turned off the engine and we all sat, listening to the motor ticking. If Mother had lost her determination and suggested we back out then and there, we would have agreed. "Well," she said, smoothing out the lap of her dress. It was what she did to buy time. We girls weren't moving anyway. We were tired enough; it was a long drive from Pennsylvania.

"Wake me up when it's over," Cynthia said. She always had a line like that. She curled up and thrust her long legs across Betty and me, picking a fight. Betty grabbed her foot and twisted it until Cynthia shrieked *For the love of Pete*. Mother ignored them, reapplying the lipstick she kept tucked up the sleeve of her spring coat. I looked out the window. I'm not sure about Daddy. No one wanted to make the first move, Betty twisting Cynthia's foot harder and Cynthia shrieking *For the love of Pete get your gosh darn hands off me* and Mother jerking around and telling Cynthia to stop using that language and to act her age.

The last reprimand struck Cynthia to the core. She sat up quickly and yanked the door open.

•   •   •

Did I say oak? It might have been walnut. I believe at that point, standing outside the car, we heard the comforting thwack of a walnut on a tin roof, the sound popping the balloon Cynthia had inflated, releasing us to walk, like a family, to the front door, where Randall already stood, waiting.

He had some sort of sweet-smelling water brushed into his hair. This I remember. It was the first thing you would have noticed. He also had red hair, red as mine, and freckles over most of his face. He stood there, swallowed by the doorway, his hand out in greeting. His

273

were the most delicate fingers I had ever seen on a boy, though he was a teenager by then. I have wondered since whether he polished his nails, since they were shiny, almost wet. Remember he was a son without a mother, which is a terrible thing to be, and that Great-uncle Sterling was as hard as his name.

Anyway, Cynthia and Betty paid him little mind. They followed Mother and Daddy in to find Sterling and we were left, quite suddenly, alone. Randall shrugged as if I had proposed a game of cards and asked if I wanted to see his room. No one seemed much concerned about us, so I said sure. We went down a water-stained hallway he called the Gallery of Maps. It was after some hallway he had read about in the Vatican, one that has frescoes of maps from before the world was round. Anyway, he stood there showing me the various countries, pointing out what he called trouble spots.

I can still picture those fingers, tapering some, and the palest white at the tips, as if he had spent too long in the bath.

We continued, passing one of those old-fashioned intercom contraptions they used to have to ring servants. Randall worked a few of the mysterious oiled levers and then spoke, gravely, into the mouthpiece. "I have nothing to offer but blood, toil, tears, and sweat," he said. Churchill, of course, though at the time I had no idea. I simply stood there waiting, watching as Randall hung up the mouthpiece, shrugged again, and opened a door to a back staircase so narrow we had to turn sideways to make the corner.

"They were smaller in the old days," Randall said, and then, perhaps because I didn't respond, he stopped and turned toward me.

"Who?" I said.

"People," he said.

"Oh," I said, waiting. I had never been in the dark with a boy his age.

"Carry on," he said.

We reached a narrow door and pushed out, onto another landing, continuing down a second, longer hallway. The house seemed comprised of a hundred little boxes, each with tiny doors and passages, eaves to duck under, one-flight stairways to climb. Gloomy, all of it, though Randall didn't seem to notice. He talked all the while of how slaves had traveled the underground railway from Louisiana here, and how one family had lived in this house behind a false wall he was still trying to find. He said he knew this not from words but from knowing. He said he saw their ghosts sometimes—there were five of them—a mother and a father and three children,

274

he couldn't tell what. But he'd find their hiding place, he said. He had the instinct.

I'm not sure whether I was more interested in hearing about slaves in secret rooms or hearing about their ghosts. This was Maryland, remember, the east side. At that time, if you took the ferry to Annapolis, the colored sat starboard, the whites port, and docking felt like the flow of two rivers, neither feeding the other. In Pennsylvania colored people were colored people, and one of your grandfather's best friends was a colored doctor named Tate Williams, who everybody called Tate Billy, which always made me laugh, since I'd never heard of a nickname for a surname.

Anyway, Randall finally pushed on what looked like just another of the doors leading to the next stairway and there we were: his room, a big square box of a room filled with books on shelves and stacked high on the floor. Beyond this a line of dormer windows looked out to the oaks, or walnuts. I could hear my sisters' muffled shouts below and went to see, but we were too high up and the windows were filthy, besides. Words were written in the grime. *Copacetic,* I still recall. *Epistemological, belie.*

"What are these?" I said.

"Words to learn," Randall said. He stood behind me.

"Oh," I said. This wasn't at all what I had expected. It felt as if I had climbed a mountain only to reach a summit enshrouded in fog. Randall seemed oblivious; he began digging through his stacks of books. I watched him for a while, then spelled out H°E°L°P on the glass. I asked Randall what he was doing, and he told me to be patient. He was looking for the exact right passage, he said. He planned to teach me the art of "dramatic presentation."

Isn't it funny? I have no recollection of what he finally found. And though I can still hear him telling me they were smaller then, ask me what we recited in the hours before we were called to the table, legs up, in his window seat, our dusty view that of the old trees, their leaves a fuzzy new green of spring, of Easter, and I will say I have no idea. I know I must have read my lines with the teacher's sternness I have never been able to keep from my voice; he with his natural tenderness, as if he were presenting a gift to the very words he read by speaking them aloud. I know that sometimes our knees touched and that we pulled away from one another, or we did not. I wish I had a picture. We must have been beautiful with the weak light coming through those old dormers, our knees up and backs against either side of the window seat, an awkward W, books in our hands.

• • •

It became our habit to write letters. Randall wrote every first Sunday of the month. He would tell me what new book he was reading, what he'd marked to show me. I might describe a particular day, such as the time Daddy flooded the backyard with water to make an ice-skating pond, though we told Mother the pump had broken and it was all we could do to turn the thing off before the rain cellar flooded. Of course, once the sun wore down our imagined rink and we found ourselves blade-sunk and stranded in your grandmother's peony bed, Daddy had to tell her the truth.

She loved her peonies, as you may remember, and fretted all that winter that we had somehow damaged the roots, that spring would come and the pinks she had ordered, the ones with the name that rhymed with Frank Sinatra, would have no company. But everything grew and blossomed on schedule, and we ended up calling the peony bed our lake and threatening to flood it every winter.

Randall sent me back a letter about a book he had found on the gardens of Kyoto, how the gardens were made of sand, gravel, and rock. No flowers, he said. No pinks. Once in a while they use moss, but even their moss isn't green like we know green. No grass green or leaf green but a kind of grayish, he wrote. You can't even walk in these gardens because they're more like paintings. You view them from a distance, he wrote, their fragments in relation.

That line I can still recall, though at the time I was baffled. I knew we were at war with the Japanese; we were repeatedly given classroom instruction on the failings of the Japanese character. We had learned of crucifixions and tortures; we understood the Japanese to be evil—not only did they speak a language no one could decipher, but they engaged in acts of moral depravation our teachers deemed too shocking to repeat. I understood them to be a secret, somehow, a secret we shouldn't hear. Now, oddly, I knew something of their gardens.

• • •

The last time I saw him was the Easter of 1944. He was not yet seventeen—can you imagine? the age of enlistment—but would soon be, and he understood that it would be best if he went to war, that Sterling expected him to, that there were certain things that boys did without question. He never spoke of this to me; I learned it all later. Instead, his letters that winter were filled with some tremendous discovery he had made, a surprise he intended to share that Easter, not beforehand. You can imagine my guesses. Daddy had barely shut off the engine when I opened the door and sprang out. I might have bypassed all those narrow rooms and passageways altogether, scaled the tree and banged on one of those filthy windows, but I could feel Mother's eyes. She wanted me to slow down, to stay a part of them. In truth, the drive had been a sad one—Cynthia newly married and stationed with Roger in California, Betty oddly silent. Our first visit seemed light-years past, an adventure far more pleasant than it had actually been, a family outing when we were still family. We had grown into something altogether different: guests at a party with little in common.

I stood, waiting for everyone to get out of the car, waiting until Mother opened the door and yelled, Hello. Then I ran to Randall's room. I knew the way, could find it blindfolded—through the passageways and up the flights of stairs. I touched the countries in the Gallery of Maps, the danger spots, the capital cities. I picked up the mouthpiece and recited my Roosevelt impression—"I hate war, Eleanor hates war, and our dog Fala hates war"—just in case anyone was listening.

When I got to Randall's door I saw that it was ajar, so I went in without knocking. He stood facing the line of dormers, his back to me, something so entirely unfamiliar, so adult, in his stance that for an instant I thought I might have barged into the wrong room, that for all this time a second, older Randall had lived just next door.

"Boo," I said. I was that kind of girl.

He turned, startled, and I saw he had been writing my name on the window grime.

Have I told you he was thin? Rail thin, we called it. A beanpole. Just legs and arms and wrists and neck. I imagine if he had been permitted to live his life, he might have married someone who would have worried about this, who would have cooked him certain foods and seen that his scarves were wrapped tight in winter. No matter. He crossed the room to me.

"Any guesses?" he said.

"None," I said, blushing. Of course, this was the age of movie star magazines, of starlets discovered at soda fountains. I had plenty of guesses, each sillier than the next, but I knew enough to keep them to myself.

He marched me out of his room to the cook's stairway, a long narrow corridor down to the foyer, then pushed on a second door I'd always assumed led to the pantry. It took us back to the Gallery of Maps, where he paused, as if expecting me to react. "So?" I said. He ignored me, taking my hand and leading me to the darkest continent in the Gallery—an hourglass stain near the far end tucked behind the door to the musty unused parlor.

Randall swung the door shut and pointed to a few shredded cobwebs collected in the corner, where Antarctica would have been.

"*Look,*" Randall said. And then I saw: a tiny black thread, horizontal, a hairline fracture dividing time remaining from time spent unlike the other cracks in the walls, the vein-like fissures that ran through that old house. "A *clue,*" Randall said.

• • •

Sometimes, when I think about it, I see the two of us there, Randall and me, from a different perspective, as if I were Mother walking through the door to call us for supper, finding us alone, red-haired cousins, twins sketched quickly: bones, hair, shoes, buttons. Look at us, we seem to say. One will never grow old, never marry. One will never plant tomatoes, drive automobiles, go to dances. One will never drink too much, disappoint his children, sit alone, wishing, in the dark.

No matter. Randall knocked on the wall and I heard a strange hollowness. "Right here," he said. "Right beneath my nose."

He pushed and the wall flattened down from its base like a punching bag. He held it there and got down on all fours, then he crawled in. I followed, no doubt oblivious to the white bloomers Mother still insisted I wear with every Easter dress.

The wall snapped shut, throwing us into instant black. It was difficult to breathe, the sudden frenzied dark unbearable. And cold! As if the chill from all those other rooms had been absorbed by this tiny cave, the dirt floor damp beneath my hands, my knees.

"Randall?" I said.

"Here," he said. Then, again, "Here."

His voice seemed flung, untethered; it came from every direction and I began to feel the panic you know I feel in enclosed places. I would have cried had Randall not chosen that moment to strike a match. He was right there beside me, touchable, close. I sat as he held the match to a candle on the floor. It wasn't a cave at all, just a tiny room, its walls papered with yellowed newspaper, the words buried by numbers. Literally hundreds of numbers had been scrawled across the walls, the ceiling. Everywhere you looked. The strangest thing. Some written in pencil, others in what looked like orange crayon, smeared or faint, deep enough to tear the newsprint. There seemed to be no order, no system to them. Just numbers on top of numbers on top of numbers.

I could hear Randall breathing. "What do you think they were counting?" I said.

"Heartbeats," he said.

It was the slaves' hiding place, of course. I crawled to the far corner, my palm catching on something hard: a spool of thread. Red, I remember, its color intact. There were other things to look at. Randall had collected them, and now he showed me, piece by piece: a rusted needle, a strand of red thread still through its eye, knotted at the end; a leather button; a tin box in which were cards with strange figures printed on them, an ancient tarot, perhaps; a yellow tooth; a handkerchief—the initials BBP embroidered in blue thread on its hem; a folded piece of paper. Randall unfolded it slowly, and I believed, for an instant, that the slaves' story would be written there. Another clue. But there was nothing to read, simply more numbers, a counting gone haywire.

Randall held the paper out to me and I took it, feeling, when I did, the brush of his soft fingers. "It must have been the only thing they knew," I said, staring at the numbered paper, my own fingers burning.

"Or had to learn," Randall said.

"Right," I said, not fully understanding.

"Look," he said. He held a comb, its wooden teeth spaced unevenly. "I bet they played it," he said.

"I bet they did," I said. Even then I knew I sounded stupid. I wanted to say something important, something that might match his discovery. But all I could think of was the dark, and the way the candlelight made us long shadows. I pulled my legs beneath me, still cold, and pretended to read the numbers. After a while, aware of his inattention, I looked up. He was bent over, holding the needle close to the candlelight, sewing, it appeared, the hem of his pant leg with a concentration I had only witnessed in his reading.

I leaned in to see. *BB*, he had embroidered, and now he stitched the straight tail of the *P.*

He was startled. I'm not sure we had ever been that close to one another, eye-to-eye, my breath his breath. The candlelight made us look much older than ourselves, eternal, somehow, stand-ins for gods. "I thought I'd take him along," he said, by way of explanation.

We remained in the slaves' hiding place until supper, sitting knee-to-knee, trying to count the numbers. We gave up. Randall read some advertisement for Doctor something-or-other's cure-all, which worked on pigs and people, and we laughed, then he took the stub of a pencil he always kept knotted in his shoelaces and wrote three numbers across the advertisement—5, 23, 1927—the date and year of his birth. He stared at the numbers a minute, and then drew a dash after them, in the way you sometimes see in books after an author's name and birthdate, the dash like the scythe of the grim reaper.

"Don't," I said, licking my finger and reaching to erase the line. I may have smeared it a bit, I don't know. I know at this point Randall grabbed my wrist, surprising me with the strength in those fingers. It was the most wonderful of gestures. He brought my hand to his cheek and kissed my palm, no doubt filthy from crawling around on that floor. He seemed not to care. He kept his lips there for a very long time, and I, as terrified to pull away as I was to allow him to continue, held my breath, listening to my own heart beat stronger.

• • •

There was one other, actually. Visit, I mean. The morning Randall came through Philadelphia on his way out. He was going to ride the Union Pacific, in those days a tunnel on wheels chock full of soldiers stretching from one end of the country to the other—some heading east to Europe, others heading west to the Pacific. Your grandmother would tell me stories of worse times, during the Depression, when she said that same train took children from families who could no longer feed them. She said she remembered a black-haired boy walking by their farmhouse, stopping with his parents for a drink of water. They were on their way to the train, the orphan train, they called it, sending the boy east, where someone from an agency would pick him up and find him a new place to live. She said it was a terrible thing to see, far worse than boys in bright uniforms heading out to save the world from disaster. She said children in trains, sitting high on their cardboard suitcases to get a view out the window, their eyes big as quarters, their pockets weighted down with nothing but the few treasures their parents had to give them—first curls, nickels, a shark's tooth, ribbons—things they no doubt lost along the way. That, she'd say the few times I tried talking to her of Randall, is the worst thing of all. Children given up for good.

But I don't know. I remember the look of Randall stepping off the train. His uniform indeed bright, his leather shoes polished to a gleam shiny as those fingernails. It was a terrible sight I can tell you. Mother and I had driven to meet him at the station. I believe it was the only time I ever saw him when I wasn't in an Easter dress. You would have laughed. I wore a pink wool skirt and a pink cashmere button-down, my initials embroidered on the heart. A gift from Cynthia. I was so proud of those clothes, and the lipstick, Mother's shade, that I'd dab with a perfumed handkerchief I kept in my coat pocket.

But the look of Randall stepping off the train. He had grown that year even taller, and we could see his thin, worried face above the pack of other soldiers. The morning was blustery, and it felt like there might be snow. Other girls were on the platform slapping their hands together, standing with brothers, boyfriends. It seemed we were a collection of women and boys. Mother stepped forward a bit and called out to him, and Randall turned and smiled and rushed over to us, his hand extended.

But that was for Mother. When I went to shake it, he pulled me into a hug. He wore the regulation wool coat, and a scarf, red, knotted at his neck, and I tasted the scarf and smelled the cold, and the lilac water, and the tobacco smoke all at once.

"Look at you," he said, and squeezed me tighter.

Mother knew of a coffee shop nearby, and we went, though we had to stand some time waiting for a table, the room swamped with boys in uniform. I became aware of Randall watching me, though I pretended not to notice. I had come in to that girl age of boys finding me pretty, and I felt always as if I walked on a stage, lighted to an audience somewhere out in the dark. Mother chattered, clearly nervous in that big room with all those soldiers, waiters racing to and fro, splashing coffee on the linoleum floor, wiping their foreheads with the dishrags that hung from their waists, writing checks, shouting orders to the cooks. Yet all the while I felt Randall's gaze, as if there were something he needed to tell me, and that all I had to do was turn to him to find the clue.

But I don't know. There wasn't much time. Too soon there came upon the place that feeling of leaving. Soldiers scraped back their chairs, stood in line to pay their checks. Everyone had the same train to catch. Mother smoothed her skirt out and said she believed we should be heading back ourselves. Then she excused herself, saying she'd rather use the ladies' room there than at the train station.

Randall and I watched her weave her way around the other tables, some empty, others full. We were, quite suddenly, alone.

Have I told you he was handsome? I didn't know him well, but he had red hair, red as mine, and a kind, thin face. He might have had the most beautiful thin face I have ever seen. I should have told him that then, but I was too shy. This is what I've been thinking about: maybe he wasn't waiting to tell me anything, but waiting to hear something from me. No matter. I may have taken another sip of coffee, then. I know I did anything not to have to look at him directly.

"On the train up I sat next to a guy from Louisville," he finally said. "His name was Hog Phelps."

"Hog?" I said.

"Said he wasn't the only Hog in his family, said he was from a long line of Hogs."

I looked at Randall and he shrugged. Then he laughed and I did, too. It seemed like such a funny thing to say.

• • •

I received only one letter from Randall after that. It was written the day before he sailed for the Far East, mailed from San Francisco. I remember that the stamp on the envelope was a common one from that time—Teddy Roosevelt leading his Rough Riders up San Juan Hill— and that Randall had drawn a bubble of speech coming from his mouth that said, "Carry on!" I opened the letter with a mixture of trepidation and excitement. I was too young and too stupid to understand what Randall was about to do. I imagined his thoughts had been solely of me, that the letter would be filled with love sonnets, that it would gush with the same romantic pablum I devoured from those movie star magazines. Instead, it described San Francisco—the fog that rolled in early afternoons across the bay, the Golden Gate Bridge, and how the barking sea lions could be heard from so many streets, and the vistas that he found, as if painted solely for him, on the long solitary walks he took daily through the city. He wrote how he seemed to have lost interest in books, that he no longer had the patience. There was no *time*, he wrote, to sit. He wanted to walk, to never stop walking. If he could, he would walk all the way to Japan by way of China. Hell, he wrote (and I remember the look of that word, how Randall seemed to be trying out a different, fiercer Randall), when I'm finished with this I'm going to walk around the entire world.

I tried to picture him writing it, sitting at a large metal desk in the middle of a barracks, like something I might have seen in *Life*. I pictured him stooped over, with a reader's concentration, digging the pen into the regulation paper in the way he would have, if we were face-to-face talking, stressed a word. I saw him in civilian clothes, in the dress pants he wore every Easter. The same ones, as far as I could tell—a light gray wool, each year hitched up a little higher and now, leg crossed across one knee, entirely ill-fitting, the *BBP* far above the ankle. He might have, from time to time, put the pen down and leaned back to think of a particular description, fingering those initials he had stitched in red. It was clear to me even then that he had worked on the letter like a boy who wants to be a writer. Certain words broke his true voice, were tried on, tested for fit. They were a hat too big for him— the Randall I knew interrupted again and again by the Randall Randall might have become. The *Hell*, as I have mentioned. A line from some dead poet—*I would think of a thousand things, lovely and durable, and taste them slowly*—I had heard him recite in his room a hundred times, and other words I recognized as words still left to learn. It seemed he wanted to cram everything in.

Still, it is a beautiful letter. I have saved it for years. It finds its way into my hands at the oddest times, and when it does I always hold it for a while, rereading the envelope. Teddy shouts, Carry on!, and I curse him. All of them. Then I pull out the paper, one folded sheath, and unfold it as slowly as I would a gift I'd never opened. My fear is that somehow in my absence, his words have come undone, been shaken loose, rearranged, so that what I will find is no more than a page of randomness, letters shuffled into forms with no meaning, indecipherable, foreign.

But there! My name in salutation, the sweetness of the attendant *Dear*. I'm again as I was, as he may have pictured me—writing at that desk beneath the window, the metal newly polished, the air fresh, eucalyptus-scented, the sea lions barking—when he signed *Love, Randall,* and underlined it with a flourish as elegant as a bow.

Nominated by Doubletake

THE LOOP, THE SNOW, THEIR DAUGHTERS, THE RAIN

fiction by LIZA WIELAND

from THE JOURNAL

THEIR DAUGHTERS SAY Grandma. Their daughters say door, chair, spoon. Their daughters say no. Their daughters say, Cut my hair with a raisin. They once said, Let's play orchestra, and they will soon say, Everybody here has a chair except I have a step stool. They say, Because I might not be able to get out. The snow is coming down loud. They say, I want to do it all by myself.

They are not yet forty, and their daughters are not quite three. They are sisters, Louise and Lana, and their daughters are cousins, Hannah and Sarah. Their husbands, who work together, are about to go on a business trip to Chicago and take their daughters. At the airport, their daughters say bye bye plane, and at the last minute, Louise and Lana decide they will not be able to bear the silence in the house, and so they go too.

In Chicago, the forecast says rain. It's Saturday in the Loop. On the plane their fathers taught Hannah and Sarah to say loop, and now their mothers prompt them. Loop. They say, Where's Daddy, and their mothers say, At his meeting. Hannah and Sarah have learned to say the last three words of any sentence they hear. *Sentence they hear.* All morning long, it has been *back soon dear, back soon dear,* like a species of forest animal, their mothers think, white-tailed and always just de-

284

parted. The husbands said, Don't forget your umbrellas, and so their daughters point at the umbrellas everyone carries so unwillingly: *for-get your umbrellas.* Then they just say ella. The sky over Lake Michigan is glowering and restless, full of clouds that can't seem to get away fast enough. In Marshall Field's there are checked umbrellas, lost umbrellas, cheap and expensive umbrellas, umbrellas swinging from wrists and elbows like odd useless appendages. Ellas everywhere.

Their mothers take them upstairs to see the dolls, the ones with complete wardrobes and trousseaux, with glittering eyes that open and shut: Mary Poppins, Scarlet O'Hara, Sleeping Beauty, whose green eyes are set with tiny lead weights and so are particularly slow to open. Of all dolls, their daughters say *Ella,* as in Cinder-, the girl who starts out as a silent scullery maid and then gets to talk to the prince. In odd, still moments, their mothers have wondered about that. What would you say to a prince? Nice coat. Hey, you're a real good dancer.

Outside again, their daughters say lake. Michigan is too much to ask. Their daughters say *swimming?* And so against their better judgment, the mothers wheel them, carry them down to the beach at Grant Park. Chilly water, their mothers say, about lake water the color of cold. If they could open up this wind blasting their faces, peel it down to the center, the color of chilly water is what they would find. From out of their backpacks and their strollers their daughters look east across the lake and their eyes deepen into black. Their mothers notice but keep silent. How would you say to a daughter, I see you becoming bottomless, so you can be filled up. Stop it before you go too far. Plenty of time for that later. If the fathers were here, they would put a stop to it, they would be able to say, No, come back up to the Loop. Loop, they would say; loop, their daughters would say, not really frightened at all, like a French child crying wolf. *Loup.* A false alarm. Like rain that never comes when it is expected, like a child talking. Their mothers look up, and it is raining, their daughters are talking, and no one can say how or when it began.

On Sunday, they all go to church, where because it is so quiet, their daughters say everything that comes into their heads. An unfamiliar church, somewhere on the south side. The lake is still not far away, and their daughters can hear its beating against the shore, its play-acting, *I am an ocean, I am the sea,* over and over, its wet shoulders falling forward onto the sand.

St. Philip Neri, it's his church. Their daughters say Flip and then they laugh. They can see him on one side of the altar. It's his church, their mothers say. Their daughters say *house?* At communion they watch their mothers chew the communion host and say *have some?* Holding out their tiny hands. When their mothers grow quiet and drop their faces into their open palms, their daughters watch without moving. They don't blink their impossibly long eyelashes. There is an old woman in the pew behind them, so old she is wearing a lace veil like a skullcap, the kind of veil no woman has worn into St. Philip Neri in twenty years. She believes the daughters are contemplating the nature of the soul. She trusts that small children can do this, believes hers did it before they started to grow up, her children who have now moved far away. If they can't, she asks her husband in her prayers that night, who can? She believes he answers *you*.

Outside St. Philip Neri, it begins to snow. Their daughters, in their still-infant wisdom, feel this before they see it. They see the statues in the church pull their stone cloaks closer. They touch the knees of their tights, glad for covering, not yet knowing anything of pantyhose. Outside the snow announces itself with a few flakes blown in over Lake Michigan like feathers from some wintering gull. On Lake Shore Drive, people are dazzled. It's only September, some say and check their pocket calendars. It's too early, some say, close to tears, the easily betrayed. No, some say. No, their daughters say. Global warming, some say, the armchair meteorologists. Falling, the sidewalk acrobats say. Each one is different, some say, tourists coming out of the Art Institute.

Their daughters say no, which of course means snow. The snow comes harder, and their fathers pack them into their car seats. Why don't they cry when we do this? the mothers wonder as they help pull the harnesses over their daughters' soft, small heads, pull their tiny arms up from under the padded bar, unbend the stick legs. Their daughters say *go! Go now!* Their daughters say *Costco,* which is what a car trip often means. The snow comes at the car windshield in heavy, white blots. Their mothers point and say cotton. Like cotton. Next week, their daughters will say cotton and wowder, when they are discovered cleaning the floor with talcum powder, cotton, water. Now they say wowder, which means both thunder and water.

Their daughters look out at snow falling on Calumet Park and Riverdale and Blue Island. No, no, no, they say over and over, refusing weather, refusing southward travel, all travel. But no, the fathers have driven in the wrong direction, they don't have the map, and so it's back up north through Cicero, Schiller Park, Des Plaines, all those new languages, and the snow like a blanket over them, over all lan-

286

guage. Binkie, they say, for blanket. *Look!* Their mothers say. *Can you say snow like a blanket?* Their fathers glance in the rear-view mirror, watch the disappearance of the sooty Loop, and they ask, *Can you say heavy industry?* Their daughters think their fathers are silly and miraculous. They cannot bear to lose them. They know this even now but will never be able to say it.

Their daughters say Grandma, which is where they are driving now, to Grandmother's house we go, west from the Loop, out to Hoffman Estates. They will have lunch, their daughters' foods brought in glass jars, glowing, and lustrous like the windows at St. Philip Neri. Their mothers will leave several of these jars for dinner, *foof,* they say, for food, as if eating were magic, *foof!* And then they will drive back to Chicago with their husbands and go out to dinner and disappear into their hotel rooms early, into each other's arms. Already they are dreaming of a night, a whole long night during which their daughters will say nothing. That is how they look forward to it: silence. Their daughters will, for one night, stop learning the language at this alarming rate, stop pulling words out of their mothers' bodies the way they once did breast milk. Their daughters will forget Ernie, whom they love beyond reason, and far more than Bert. They will forget babba and chilly water. They will forget no, and the mysterious Ada, the goddess of used-upedness, whose name must mean *all done.* For one night, they will be too shy to ask anyone to take them outside into the front yard to look for the moon. They'll forget to cry *balloom, balloom,* and point into the heavens and wait.

Their mothers are thinking of the silent night of the body, what they have never had words for. They know some women have words for it, they've read such words in books, heard them spoken, remember a few of them, water, heat, blossom, open. They have a shard-like memory of a woman saying, *It feels like you were born there.* From the movies, they think, maybe. Translated in a subtitle. For themselves, though, the point is no talk, casting themselves adrift and going back so far that they come to a time before words, before that kind of need. To speak is to need, they think. To speak is to admit how lonely a place the world is. They wish they could save their daughters from it, hush them up tight against loneliness. They wish it with the part of themselves that is fierce and aboriginal and always silent.

At Grandma's the television is on. One of the cousins does this, turns the television on and leaves the room, gets the sound going so he can hear it all over the house. All of the young cousins do it, mostly for the

287

channels that play music. Like the radio. Their daughters stand in front of the television and rock their tiny hips from side to side. They say *dance?* and when nobody will, they say *help?* When any group of four musicians appears—three guitars, one drum kit—their daughters say *Hootie.* An old clip of the Beatles runs, and they pause to count and then they say *Hootie.* All the younger cousins laugh. These cousins have come to the age of first sly thoughts, and so they want to teach Hannah and Sarah how to say *Mom, could you get me a beer? A pack of Marlboro reds, please.* The young cousins want to teach them to say *fire truck,* hoping that the whole shiny long word will prove too much for their little mouths and collapse into obscenity. The cousins have come to a place that might as well be across the whole world from Hannah and Sarah. They know all the words for what they want to say, these young cousins do, and they know what the words mean and this knowledge has made them mute.

Their daughters say *outside,* and Louise and Lana put them into the arms of the college-aged cousins. The snow has stopped falling, gathered behind clouds and held its breath. There is in the afternoon air north of Hoffman Estates toward South Barrington the sense that something or someone has asked a question of great moment and is waiting for an answer to be spoken. From Grandma's they walk, the mothers, the daughters and the college-aged cousins, beside Poplar Creek. Sometimes there are deer nosing the deadfall at the water's edge, and the college-aged cousins would love to see Hannah and Sarah get their first glimpse of deer. They walk all the way out to the lake, a pond really, drying up smaller every year, not big enough to name, and so everyone has, privately, like wishing. Louise and Lana ask the cousins what they are learning, and the cousins tell them, the words for business, the words for economics, anthropology, genetics, literature. They ask, so what do you do for fun, and then their daughters repeat the cousins' words, catch them up in the thin nets of their voices so they will not fall into the lake and be lost, or roll away into Poplar Creek. Their daughters repeat, *lover, field hockey,* they say *glee club,* and the sound rises and drops over the lake like a shiny penny to wish on, *glee, glee, glee.*

The wind blows in a strange, aching gust, like a scratch, like a tear in fabric and it begins to snow again. Their daughters recognize it now—they say *no* and then they say *Daddy.* The six women walk back to Grandma's, two cousins, the mothers and their daughters. The older four say to each other, *It's so good to see you. It's so long between visits,* the oldest two say, *next thing we know, you'll have daughters of your own.* The snow makes them speak this way, as if through the window of a departing vehicle, with the breathlessness of departure. They feel this hurry but they don't know why. There are no words for it, this quality of snow, snow too early, in the suburbs, their backs to the nameless lake, water of wishes and promises, so dark below the surface.

The fathers and husbands and lovers watch from the picture window, thinking also without words, how beautiful the women are, with their chapped faces and their dark hair struck with snow. They say nothing, each alone with his breaking heart. Something about those flecks of snow—the word *proximity,* the word *ease*—how the women let snow rest in their eyelashes, in the fine hairs in front of their ears, places they hardly ever let the husbands and lovers touch, something feels like it will drive them into a fury. A fine needle of anger rises up through their bodies. They wonder why a woman would take a baby out into the snow without a hat.

Meanwhile, the snow turns to rain, and then after a time, the temperature drops again. The west suburbs will be trussed up in ice, then covered again with snow. In September. Even among the real meteorologists, there are no words for what is happening.

The mothers know they must say goodbye to their daughters so they can drive back to Chicago in time for dinner. There are reservations, but first the ritual of dressing, and talk, drinks sent up from the hotel bar. It is an hour more private than any other, more inviolable, a word the husbands love, but would never say, a word outdated, a word that not much is anymore.

And so the mothers look all over Grandma's house for their daughters, find them in a corner of the big cousin-filled room, playing with a bicycle pump. Their daughters take turns with the needle of the pump, one pressing it gently into her navel while the other works the pump's plunger. The mothers stand still and watch and wonder what it is their daughters want from their game, how they remember this old connection site. When they kiss their daughters goodbye, the game is barely interrupted. The daughters look up at their mothers with a great unfathomable knowledge in their eyes. The blue seas of iris swim. Their mothers have the sense of being seen through, seen beyond. Their daughters say *bye bye,* they say *night-night, see you in the morning time.*

On the way back to Chicago, the husbands talk business, they say *investment,* they say *securities,* they say *prime rate,* they say *Greenspan.* They talk about the World Series, *underdog, Atlanta in six, Wohlers,* and the wives look up at that, a beautiful name, mysterious, a word for something warm and smooth-edged. *Don't know what that is, don't know what you'd use them for, but wohlers would be nice to have around. Like Justice.* Sometimes the mothers, the wives feel this way, that when people talk, they don't understand the language, don't know where they are. Suddenly now they're wives again. What do the words mean? How should they act, like wives and not like mothers? They sneak looks at their husbands, the fathers. Twenty minutes ago, they were the fathers, but now they're the husbands, and it doesn't seem to confuse them at all. The mothers think about the car seats in the trunk, lying on their sides, looking vaguely prosthetic that way, and dangerous. They are driving east around the northern rim of O'Hare Airport, where the atmosphere trembles full of air traffic, the frenzy of de-icing, the spew of it, and inside the splintering of families. *Bye bye.* A grown daughter and her parents in the airport bar. They saw this once, pieced together the story. She had a lay-over, the grown daughter did. She was catching a flight to Los Angeles. A couple of beers apiece. Her father bought her a new carry-on bag. She and her mother talked. Louise and Lana watched them, then without discussion, got up and followed them to the departure gate. At the last moment, embracing her mother, the daughter began to weep. The mother said, *Don't worry, you'll get your . . .* and then murmured something they couldn't hear. The father wiped his eyes. The daughter got in line with the other passengers and then when she turned to look again, she saw that her parents had gone. This made her weep more; she reached into her bag, found her sunglasses and put them on. Louise and Lana clasped hands. Each wondered, privately, why the whole world did not fall apart, did not drown in tears like this, sadness that could never be soothed, only diminished for a time by a cocktail, an in-flight movie, distance, time, speed, weather.

Now they are mothers missing their daughters in a darkening landscape made even more insubstantial by snow. They wish it could happen somehow that their husbands would pull the car off the road and, there behind the cover of evening and snowfall and increasing fog on the inside of the windows, make love to them. It has happened before, once coming home from a funeral, once after a long, mean, smoldering argument. It is a place to go when words fail, a capitulation, a bargain, truce, condolence, code, sign, shorthand. And of course impossible now, surrounded by the husbands, the fathers, the wives, the mothers, this car crowded with people who, like everyone all over the world, cannot put even their smallest griefs into words.

At Grandma's their daughters say, *The snow is coming down loud.* The young cousins argue, telling them that the point of snow is quiet, that it never makes any noise, never. Their daughters shake their heads in the young cousins' reddening, bulge-eyed faces. *Loud,* they say, and the young cousins, who cannot disagree with anyone else in this house, and win, take Hannah and Sarah by the shoulders and shake them, hard. They know this will make for a huge outcry, and an adult will come running into the room, and there will be trouble, but they cannot help themselves. What are these babies doing here anyway, the young cousins think, they are ruining everything, and it's all because they were wrong about snow and we were right, and it always happens like this. Why would anyone think snow is coming down loud? At that instant, the young cousins' mothers hurry into the room. *What on earth have you done,* they are saying, *can't you see they're just babies.* And precisely in that moment, the young cousins hear it, in the silence after their mothers' question, in the gesture of a mother bending to pick up a child, their mothers bending to pick up someone else's children and not them. They hear the snow loud on leaves, creaking the invisible hinges of tree limbs, snow clumping like shoes on the walkway, *ding ding* loud on the slate roof, snow sorrowing itself into the wind. *What have you done,* these mothers say, and the young cousins want to tell them, *Oh Mother, we have grown too big for you to carry. That's what we have done. We have grown up.*

And in that same moment, everyone looks outside to see that darkness has fallen. Everyone has a word for it: *dinner, porchlight, 60-Minutes-is-on, make-Zachy's-lunch,* for tomorrow is Monday, a school day. Hannah and Sarah twist out of their rescuers' arms and go to the picture window. *Balloom,* they say, *balloom.* But all they see are their own faces, and then far in the distance, a secret glittering, all the wishes in the nameless lake risen to carry the weight of the snow. Behind them, aunts and uncles and cousins pass back and forth carrying plates to the table, silverware and cups that catch the light and fling images against the darkened window. The prongs of a fork, the bevel of a drinking glass make stars; the curve of a white plate makes a gibbous moon.

Their daughters have come to expect that the heavenly bodies are not visible some nights, and some nights they are, and then these bodies stay still while their mothers lift them up and say *look, balloom.* But it is never this way, a flash, then gone, an idea, an image half-remembered. Never this close. Hannah and Sarah can feel some force building in the room behind them, a loud noise growing even louder, an insistence, *Yes,* the warm air presses against their backs, *yes,* the smells of roast chicken, garlic; they smell without seeing the buttery ooze of mashed potatoes. *Louise forgot to leave it,* they hear, *Oh, well. They can eat what we're having. They're big girls. Aren't you big girls?* Grandma says.

Yes. In the dark window, they are big girls. The wind is blowing huge wet snowflakes in at them. No, they say, pointing. They could say snow, but they like the baby word, the economy of it. *Aren't you big girls?* The fire in the fireplace says *yesss;* the spit from a pot on the stove says it too. What is that gleam on the lake, snow piling at its edge, ice creeping toward its dark, nameless heart? *No.* Where are their mothers? *No.* Grandma tries to draw them away from the window. *No.* Oh yes, she says, come away from there. *No.* If they turn from the window, they will understand that their mothers have gone and left them here. They will realize. If they could only get out to the lake. *Glee club,* they remember, *glee, glee, glee.* If they could only get to the lake. Their mothers would be there, saying *no like a blanket.*

Snow on the fields between Hoffman Estates and The Loop. Snow on the highway. On the broken backs of corn, on the planes at O'Hare, on the Ten o'Clock news. Unaccountable, unbelievable, in September.

Somewhere, their daughters are inconsolable. Their mothers can feel it. In the Palmer House, on the fourth floor, they sit up in bed, they loose themselves from the tangle of their husbands' arms. They listen. There is a streetlamp outside the window, and snow falling inside the yellow tent of light it casts down to the sidewalk. Someone is calling. A man by himself, a failed meteorologist, is whistling. He has lost his job tonight because he stood before his maps and charts and blowing clouds and couldn't say a word. Dead air. Snow in September? the sportcaster prompted. The producer snapped his fingers, cursed under his breath. The pretty news anchor, who knew people whispered she was a bubblehead, she said, Bill? But the meteorologist couldn't think what to say. Somewhere there was a teleprompter, he knew that much, the words running down like a waterfall. Somewhere.

Snow in September? Absolute silence in the studio, inside a million homes. And then finally, he turned to camera one and said, *Do you people know there really aren't any maps up here next to me? There aren't any maps. I just sweep my arms around and pretend.* He thought about his years of training, weather school, clouds and patterns. Natural disasters. Unspeakable, all of it. And then he walked right off the set, walked off through the curtain of snow, walked until he came to the Palmer House and went into the bar. There was a trio playing jazz. He watched two couples having brandy, jewel-like after-dinner drinks, saw the sleepy drift of each woman toward her husband. He sat down at a table next to them. Tourists, he believed, who would not recognize him, would not have seen what just happened on the Ten o'Clock news. He listened to them talk about two women, Hannah and Sarah, who were not there, and gradually he realized those two women were their young daughters. Their mothers said, *The boys tried to get them to say fuck.* And the meteorologist thought of telling them, You try to keep it at bay, but you can't. The unspeakable. The truth. That there aren't any maps. He had children, out in the great wide world. A CPA, a carpenter, a jazz singer. He would go hear her, the next time he was in St. Paul, sit in the dark and listen to her tremble through all those nonsense syllables. *It will rain,* he said out loud, but to no one in particular. *It will turn to rain, all of it.*

Now, hours later, he is leaving the Palmer House and whistling, and the mothers hear him, and they think, unaccountably, those old sayings, *whistling in the dark, whistling past the graveyard.* They think of their daughters, and it feels like a million miles between this room and Grandma's house in Hoffman Estates. Their daughters may be frightened, and they haven't yet learned how to whistle. Their daughters may be inconsolable. And like a shot, the telephone rings, like a whistle driven out of a man by a hard fall on ice.

It's Grandma, sputtering, tired out, at the end of her rope. There's crying in the background, wailing, long choking sobs. Their daughters won't go to sleep. They've been crying for hours. At first it was words, *go home now? Where's Mommy? Where's Daddy and the car?* The college-aged cousins tried to put them to sleep, in the back room, together in the bottom bunk. *No no no,* they said, and the cousins asked *why not,* and Hannah and Sarah pointed to the top bunk looming above them and said, *Because we might not be able to get out.*

You can hear them, Grandma says, listen. For two hours, wailing, like this, no words. We ask what they want, and they can't tell us. We

293

just asked if they want to talk to you, and they cried harder. Then one of the college-aged cousins comes on the extension. She says, They can't talk. We don't know what happened. They were looking for the moon and then they just lost it.

The mothers put their palms over the phone's mouthpiece. They explain to the husbands. Do you think they'll just quiet down and go to sleep? But the husbands, fathers again, say, No, let's go. Already, they're out of bed, switching on the bathroom light. Already they're into their clothes, out the door, down to the front desk, the parking garage, revving the engine, blasting the heat. All ready, already. The husbands say that all the time, in all situations, all tones of voice. The fathers say it even more, constantly, like the breath that's behind words, all words, every single one.

And so they drive out from the Palmer House, out from between Wabash and State, past Monroe, Madison, snow slices like wedding cake balanced an inch high on top of the street signs. But in this pre-season emergency, the authorities have come through, that's what the radio says. And truly. The streets are newly plowed so that the just-now dusting of snow looks like sugar, and the car rides sweetly over it. The fathers drive. The mothers are in the backseat, leaning into each other, the warm line where their bodies meet like a language, but better. *What a relief,* it says. *Of course,* it says. *We knew all along.*

The fathers are tired but jovial, their voices low, murmurous, back and forth, signal and return. The mothers don't listen, and then they do, and they hear the fathers saying lines from movies, from old television, back and forth, each finishing the other's sentences, lines about driving, lines about snow, lines about darkness, lines about nothing. In the fathers' voices, it all becomes a song, the radio going on low, like an orchestra, under the words. *Let's play orchestra,* their daughters said, just last week. The mothers shut their eyes. Close around them are machinery, darkness, men, all the places where words are said to fail, but really almost never do.

The snow is coming down as it always has, its inescapable erasure of language, all language, the words we need and the spaces between them. This is what the mothers see behind their closed eyes, spaces between themselves and their daughters growing greater tonight and every night to come. This is what the mothers hear, half-asleep, traveling toward their daughters: their daughters say, *I want to do it all by myself,* and their mothers must let them. Their daughters will say *bye bye.* The nonsense syllables of Ella Fitzgerald crackle on the radio, like

294

the sound a body makes when it is standing still, trying to decide which way to turn, where to go next. When it is waiting for the heartbreak which will surely come and from which no mother can save it.

Up ahead, ten more miles now, is Grandma's house, the house these daughters turned mothers grew up in, before they met their husbands and went so far away with them. Inside their own daughters will be sleeping, finally. But their mothers will lift them gently out of the bottom bunk, and their fathers will follow with yellow and pink canvas bags and toys. The mothers will carry their daughters out to the car and hold them in their laps, rolled in blankets, belted in awkwardly to their bodies. This kind of carrying is dangerous in snow, Grandma says, dangerous in any weather. Not dangerous, the fathers say, just not lawful. Remember how we rode like this as children, without any kind of special seat, and worse, entirely unbelted, punching each other, all talking at once into the driver's ear?

Their daughters whimper, but do not awaken. Though maybe they have. Maybe they are listening with their eyes shut tight, listening to their parents talk about tomorrow and breakfast and the airplane home. How the snow may cause delays. Their lips move obscurely against their mothers coats. They are dreaming the sentences they will say in the morning. They are naming the lake out behind Grandma's house. The little breaths out of their mouths sound like *wish*. The mothers say, *So much for our big night*, and the fathers smile a little and shake their heads. From out of the roadside darkness, a deer driven in by the snow steps onto the highway, concludes who knows what, but wisely, and steps back. The mothers and fathers see it all, thrill and calm in nearly the same instant. Their daughters feel the big highway lights on their faces, then the interval of darkness between, like heaves of storm. In their sleep, their daughters say *wowder*, then with an exhale and the last sob, they say *rain*.

Nominated by Steve Yarbrough, The Journal

OLYMPIC RAIN FOREST

by JANE COOPER

from FIELD

I left the shutter open, the camera
flooded with light, the negatives
were abstract and damp as the undersides of leaves.

So much greenish light, I had never
imagined a transfusion of so much tenderness.

Why can't it all be printed? How can I stand here
holding in one hand a fossil fern, in the other
a colored guide from the Sierra Club?

Travel isn't originality. I
left the shutter open.

What I need is a new medium, one that will register
the weight of air on our shoulders, then
how slowly a few hours passed,

one that will show
the print of your heels that morning on the spongy forest floor,
there, not there.

Nominated by Philip Levine

THE DISAPPEARING TEAPOT

memoir by ALICE MATTISON

from THE THREEPENNY REVIEW

IHAVE MACULAR degeneration: the centers of my retinas—the maculae—are coming apart. The condition affects both eyes, but the right eye is worse. The words "macular degeneration" name a symptom, not a disease. Usually they refer to an ailment of older people that occurs when the eye's blood vessels burst. My difficulty, "dry" macular degeneration, runs in families. No one else in my family has ever had it, to my knowledge, but photographs of my sister's retinas look like photographs of mine, though she has only slightly flawed vision.

My difficulty in seeing began in 1983, when I'd just made a change in my working life. I was teaching part-time, looking after my children, and writing. I'd written poetry all my life and had been writing short stories, not very well, for seven years. I'd begun to feel that if my fiction was ever to be any good, I'd have to turn my back on poetry, at least for a time. I was afraid that if I looked away from poetry, it would disappear (and eventually that happened; I no longer write poems). Nonetheless, I decided to give all my writing time to poetry or fiction but not both. From then on I would write fiction during the warm months and poetry during the cold months. In May 1983, I began writing fiction exclusively, and soon felt a new, violent, scary delight in it.

That August, I noticed that I was having trouble reading. The letters danced and jumped, and I thought I needed new reading glasses, but before I had a chance to visit the eye doctor, I read a newspaper article about macular degeneration. The article explained that someone with partial sight in one eye might not notice because the other eye would fill in. It urged the reader to check each eye in turn, covering one eye and looking at something that was straight—anything at all—with the other. To learn more precisely what was going on, one might look at a grid with a dot in the middle. The paper had printed one, just a box marked off like a crossword puzzle without black spaces but with a central black dot: the reader was told to note, while looking at it with each eye in turn, whether the dot in the middle was missing or whether any of the lines was distorted.

I didn't suspect anything. I thought I was just joining all the other newspaper readers as we teased ourselves with fear of a disease we'd never heard of: first worrying that we might have it, then discovering with satisfaction that we didn't. I covered my left eye and looked out the window at a telephone pole. Halfway down its length, several feet of it curved like the edge of an ear. Disconcerted, I looked at the grid with my right eye. Half of the central dot was missing and the lines near it were curved. Thirteen years later, part of the telephone pole has dissolved into its background as if someone had smudged part of a watercolor painting while it was wet, and the dot and lines at the center of the grid—they're called Amsler grids, and we macular degenerates often look at them—are gone as well. When I close my left eye, objects vanish: a pile of books across the room, a car half a block away.

In the next weeks I saw an ophthalmologist, who sent me to a second ophthalmologist, and on and on. The doctors said I had a disease, I had it in both eyes, it wouldn't get better, it might get worse, and nothing I did would make any difference. They all finished up cheerfully saying they had good news, and the good news was always that this disease would never make me completely blind. "At worst," they would say, "you'll lose your central vision entirely and won't be able to read or sew." I'd stumble from their offices biting back rage—not at my problem but at the doctors' notion of good news.

For a few weeks, in fact, I lost the ability to read at all unless I covered one eye with a patch. My two eyes, so different from each other now, would not form a single image. I think I was afraid to force my eyes to work together, or maybe my brain needed time to figure out how to do it. Gradually, reassured by learning that reading wouldn't make my eyes worse, I began to try again, though I had to stare at the page for a while each time I began, forcing my eyes to form one image.

Reading had become tiring and troublesome, nothing like the effortless absorption of phonemes, images, and ideas I'd taken for granted since I'd first learned how. These days I see an optometrist, William Padula, who studies vision and the brain. With the reading glasses he has prescribed, which magnify letters far more than would be required simply for me to recognize them, I am able to read more easily, and when bits of opaque tape are stuck in the inner corners of the lenses, for reasons that Dr. Padula can explain and I can't, the letters stop moving. During the hard first year of the disease I didn't undertake to read anything as long as a novel, but now I read novels and write them. Still, I can't read the way I did before. When I'm tired I'd rather not read, and I grow edgy and cranky reading italics, glossy paper, handwriting, varied font sizes, dot matrix print, light print, smudged print, and clever graphics. People think I must have trouble with small print but I don't if it's clear and the margins are wide. I have trouble with big print, and often take in the words or letters in a headline in the wrong order. In the housewares section of the supermarket I once noticed a sign, SAUL BELLOW; it was SHALLOW BOWL.

Light doesn't damage my eyes but it hurts. In that brilliantly lit supermarket, I wear sunglasses and a cap pulled down low, but I'm in pain in the central aisles, where light glints off jars of spaghetti sauce and tops of tin cans. A friend suggested a beekeeper's helmet. Why not? I'm famous for baseball caps, I never go out without sunglasses, and I wear amber-tinted distance glasses or amber-tinted reading glasses indoors when confronting candles, fluorescent lights, or halogen lights. On the other hand, I seem to need *more* light than other people to see detail. I don't drive at night. There's a lamp near my stove. Things that move quickly make my eyes hurt or make me seasick. I keep the cursor on my computer at its lowest speed.

When I keep both eyes open, I'm not aware of any flaws in my vision because the left eye fills in the right eye's gap, but I don't recognize people coming toward me until after they recognize me—and sometimes not at all—nor can I read signs placed where I'm expected to read them. I don't seem to sort out unfamiliar places as well as other people. Sometimes I think maybe my vision is fine, and I'm imagining all these problems. But I can't remember how things used to look.

The ophthalmologists I consulted wanted badly to diagnose what I have. Hereditary macular degeneration takes various forms. One disease is called Best's Macula, and each doctor in turn looked through an instrument at the back of my eyes and said, "Has anybody ever mentioned Best's Macula to you?" Then, looking again, each of them said, "No, you don't have Best's Macula." I was proud of my disease's rarity (apparently it's terribly rare), but I didn't care what it was called any more than a bird cares what kind of warbler it is. There was nothing to be done about it, everyone assured me, no matter what its name. I did want a word of my own, however. I wanted a word to express the correct degree of awfulness of what had happened to me, and I thought about that a lot. My lousy vision did not constitute a *tragedy,* I felt, nor a *catastrophe,* nor a *disaster.* But it was much more than a *nuisance.* Finally I decided it was a *burden,* because that word suggested a practical problem that was also upsetting. "It's a burden," I'd tell people.

But sometimes I think it's a catastrophe and sometimes I think it's only a nuisance. After thirteen years, I don't know how much my eye trouble troubles me, or how bothersome it objectively is, how it compares to other troubles. Occasionally I am envied—because I have a good husband, good children and parents, or because I publish fiction. When someone expresses envy toward me, I feel guilty. Later I remember my crumbling maculas! Yeah, I imagine myself saying, but I'm losing my central vision.

When I think about my eye trouble, mostly I am interested in it; I think it's fascinating. I sit in the rocking chair in my kitchen and look at what I've come to call The Ophthalmological Teapot, a red ceramic teapot on a shelf across the room over the stove. When my problem started I could make the knob on the lid of the teapot disappear by closing my left eye. Now I can make the whole teapot disappear, and some of the area around it as well. Why should this feel like an accomplishment, like sleight of hand or even witchcraft?

When my eyes went bad, for a few months I was downcast all day every day. Then my mood improved. Sometimes I'm irritated at having to change glasses constantly. Sometimes I get annoyed with friends who can't learn to stop while I switch into or out of my sunglasses at doorways, or with waiters in restaurants who relight the candle I've blown out twice already. But I don't remember being seriously upset about my eyes since those early months, except for a week in February of 1985, when having lost some of my central vision felt like the worst thing that could happen to me.

For six years, I had taught freshman English on Saturday mornings at a small Catholic college near where I live. Most of the Saturday students were women in their forties or fifties: humorous, sensible people coming back to school, scared of books and writing, but easily won over. I loved teaching them, but sometimes I had twenty-eight students, all of whom wrote every week. Few had typewriters and computers were rare. Once my eye ailment started I asked them to print and skip lines, but teaching them became exhausting, and the room where I taught was lit by wicked fluorescent lights.

Finally I decided I had to quit. One Saturday in February, I stopped off to see the director of continuing education, a friendly nun named Sister Jane. When I told her I was going to stop teaching at the end of the term, we both cried. I walked upstairs to my classroom, late; the students were all inside. I leaned for a long minute on the tile wall, soothed by the feel of the cool tiles on my forehead and the rough grout between them. Then I went in and taught that class.

All weekend I felt awful. On Monday morning my kids went to school and my husband went to work. Since it was the cold time of the year, I was writing a poem. When I got hungry I went downstairs. In the refrigerator I found some leftover vegetables and rice, put them into a pot, and turned on the stove, standing near it because I was cold. The vegetables included white slices of Jerusalem artichokes. Staring at them as they heated up, I saw that they were discolored. The food had begun to spoil. I was disgusted, and disgusted with myself for not noticing before. I threw the food in the garbage. I would never teach at a college again, I thought, and nothing was so much fun as teaching. My stupid eyes had ruined my life.

The phone rang. I assumed it was Sister Jane, who had the knack of calling when I felt low. She said the Holy Ghost told her when to do it. "I'm not in the mood," I said aloud to the Holy Ghost. I picked up the phone. A light, pleasant, rather excited male voice I didn't know said my name. I said yes, I was Alice. The man was Roger Angell, from *The New Yorker,* and he was calling to accept a story I'd sent him.

I'd sent stories to *The New Yorker* years before, then stopped when I read an article about the odds against getting published there. The previous fall, though, friends had bullied me into trying again. I'd pointed out that publishing in the literary magazines was likelier and just as respectable—not that I was publishing fiction anywhere. But I had always wanted to have something printed in a magazine my parents had heard of. I sent a story to Roger Angell because someone had told me he was a fiction editor, and I liked his baseball pieces. Mr. Angell had rejected that story but to my amazement sent an encouraging letter instead of the familiar rejection slip. The next story elicited a form letter with one handwritten sentence by Roger Angell at the bottom. A week before the phone call, I'd sent him another story, then forgotten about it, not expecting a reply for a long time.

When we hung up I called Edward, my husband, and said, "I got a story into *The New Yorker*." Then I called my friend Sandi, but by the time I reached her, what I said was, "A man called who *claimed* to be Roger Angell, and he *says* they're accepting my story." Something that now seems quite nutty had happened to me: I had begun to doubt my own memory of what had just occurred, and I continued to wonder whether to trust myself for a long time. While my friends congratulated me on my luck, I was just worried. Sometimes I thought a practical joke had been played on me. Much of the time, I was sure I had merely *imagined* Roger Angell's call, though we had discussed the story in some detail. I had trouble talking about the acceptance, especially on the phone. I expected some wild screw-up of phone lines to cause someone from the magazine to overhear my conversation and learn that I had the mad fantasy that they wanted to print something I'd written. Visiting a friend in New York, I fled when she mentioned my forthcoming story to a friend of hers we met in the street. I was sure what my friend had said was untrue.

Proofs in *New Yorker* type didn't help; letters and phone calls didn't help. Just before the story was scheduled to come out, I was frantic with the fear that I'd imagined everything—and had told so many people!—and was reassured only briefly when it really did appear. More stories were accepted. Every now and then I'd have a burst of certainty: my work was appearing in *The New Yorker*. That was *good*. Mostly, I just wasn't sure it was true, or, if it was, I was convinced that anything that happened, good or bad, would make the magazine decide not to print me anymore. More than a year after that first acceptance, when *The New Yorker* had printed six of my stories (and turned down many more), I was interviewed on a local radio show and refused to talk about getting published there. It wasn't that I was so modest. I was afraid, once again, that I had imagined the whole thing. I think that was the end of the fear, though. The magazine didn't take anything for a year, and by the time it accepted another story, I was fine. I was happy.

Maybe my feelings about *The New Yorker* had nothing to do with my unreliable sight. I was forty-three when that first story came out. Maybe if you don't get what you want by the time you're forty, your mind just rejects it. But I don't think so. On other surprising occasions, my mind has worked reasonably well. Even at that time, I wasn't completely overwhelmed, though of course I was damned pleased. I wasn't afraid to disagree with the famous thorough *New Yorker* editing. I knew I'd had a stroke of luck, but I continued to think—I still think— that the judgment of some small literary magazines meant as much. I didn't think publishing in *The New Yorker* proved I was a good writer—I'd come across stories there I didn't like. I didn't even *read* much of *The New Yorker* because my fussy eyes objected to its glossy paper. Still, I badly wanted those acceptances to have happened—and I couldn't stop thinking that maybe they hadn't. I'd check, and there my stories would be. Then I'd grow unsure again. I was ashamed to tell my friends that I didn't always believe something demonstrably true, and when I did tell them, I don't think they understood that I meant what I said literally. People often say something is "unbelievable," but they don't usually mean they don't believe it. My uncertainty marred my pleasure in what had happened; I disliked my own mind those months.

When I told this story recently to a new friend, she suggested that what I didn't believe in was the diminution of my vision, not the publication of my stories. I think she was wrong, but almost right: when she spoke, I felt sudden excitement. Sometimes I think I couldn't believe in the acceptances because I wanted to go back to being unhappy about my eyes. That first call interrupted my grief and I never could return to it. For years, my attention was elsewhere. Or maybe the *New Yorker* acceptances seemed like a new version of the eye trouble; what the two experiences had in common was unlikeliness, and yet they had happened.

Not long ago I heard a lecture by Elizabeth Cox about writing fiction. She said that a fiction writer must learn to look just to the side of what he or she wants to describe, that if we look right at it, it disappears. I think she meant something I've heard from other people and have thought myself: that the blurred, self-contradictory understanding required for writing fiction comes at us unexpectedly and indirectly, and is not the product of deliberate fact-finding. I'd never come upon her metaphor before. And sure enough: when I look directly at something, at least with my right eye, it most certainly disappears. It was when that gap in my vision occurred that I began to be able to write publishable fiction. Of course one can write decent fiction with two good eyes (though maybe I couldn't). But perhaps a new fiction writer could profit from an exercise something like the game I play, looking at the teapot with one eye. Maybe it would be helpful to look at the red teapot and imagine it black, or imagine it gone.

Now that I've written these pages, I know I wanted to write this essay for the same reason I write fiction: what happened to me makes a story. I like to tell lighthearted stories about my eyes. I point out to listeners that my fractured central vision is only slightly more noticeably my own than anybody's vision is his or her own. "All *vision* is solitary," I say. I describe my six pairs of glasses, discomfiting friends who complain that they've turned forty and can't read the phone book. At one point my glasses had names: Ann, Bessie, Coco, Delilah . . .

One day I heard "One Art" by Elizabeth Bishop read aloud, and the poem struck me more forcibly than before. I realized for the first time that when Bishop says, "The art of losing isn't hard to master," she doesn't mean, as I had always thought, that the art of losing *is* hard to master unless we deny our feelings. She means what she says, that the art of losing can be learned, and I realized that I've learned how to lose vision. Yet the ending of the poem, when she makes herself admit that loss can look like disaster, is also true. Like the losses Bishop wrote about, mine might be a disaster to me. Possibly.

All conscientious people worry that they are making more of a trouble than it deserves; I think about that—and maybe I am making less of it than it deserves. Or maybe it's not possible to say how much of a loss my flawed vision represents. Sometimes I think I'd miss the eye ailment if it miraculously went away, or miss having something to mention to the gods of fortune when life felt too good. My disease, as diseases go, has advantages: it doesn't show, it affects an unembarrassing part of the body—neither digestive nor sexual—and I can't be accused of having caused it.

The main advantage of the eye trouble, though, might be its disadvantage. I can make a teapot disappear. You probably can't, whatever your own persnickety body has given you to think about. Sitting at my computer, I can see copies of a novel I wrote piled on a shelf in a closet. If I close my left eye, they vanish, but then I must think—sometimes I *have* to think—that maybe they never existed. I know that my left eye sees correctly and my right eye sees wrong—but what if it's the other way around? Maybe I didn't write the novel. Surprised at a vulnerable moment, I thought that I might well have imagined an entire complicated part of my life. We are accustomed to using our eyes to learn the truth about what's around us, but my two eyes seem to tell two different truths.

However, I'm writing not about whether the world is real or imagined but about fiction. The essence of fiction is not that it isn't true but that it might not be true. In the current enthusiasm for memoir and autobiographical fiction, I've sometimes heard people talk as if it didn't matter what you called a piece of writing that was based on your life but partly made up. I think it does matter what you call it. Once we call something fiction—even if it's true—it changes. It becomes a house with its back door unlocked.

It's unpleasant—though impressive—to make a teapot or a pile of books disappear by closing one eye. It's even more unpleasant to start wondering whether what you think is your life might be imagined. But at least I live where the real meets the unreal. The books that may or may not lie on the shelf in my closet, depending on which eye I use to look, contain a story I believe I invented. The characters in that book used to show up while I was writing it and scream at me for getting things wrong. They'd tell me they were real and *I* was imaginary. This sort of experience is a little like seeing a ghost: it sounds romantic and charming until it happens, when it's terrifying. That's what I have to say about my eye trouble. I am grateful to it because it makes it easier for my mind to swivel from the real to the unreal. And it's terrifying.

Nominated by The Threepenny Review

SAND, FLIES & FISH

by MÔNG-LAN

from QUARTERLY WEST

1

I take a glass of the expiring sun, sipping it.
Cambodia's terse mountains to my right. the Gulf
of Thailand in front of me. the border police in their
rumpled uniforms are still as backdrop characters.
the hot sun mats their hair down in neat sweat lines.
a white gull pecks at the black sand. the sand is so
black you think you're close to hell. I wait for the
sun to come down on the sea. the nausea for it. in
the evenings the national Vietnamese news blares
from the loudspeakers. the world's slow motions.
fires' haze. sky's blood draining over the boneless
ocean.

2

even if I described detail by detail to you, the whole
would escape you. how can you see
the southern edge of the continent— what would
that matter? or the black sand grading into the
blueness of the sea, or the vigilant Cambodian

mountains. what would it matter if I told you ships
dock in front of my window. that when not in my
room, I wander through villages eating dirt, whatever
I can beg. it happens to a woman. these things
happen. these accidents. I watch my stomach
bloat with the seed of a man who was a shadow. I
pick at the salt crop gleaming in evening light, and
steal whatever I can to sell in the markets. the
land's lungs are strong. it fills my baby's ears
with its tenor.

3

this edge of the world is a knife. the motorcycle taxi
drivers wait humped, clocks on the dock, that dulled
look for a customer. everything an illusion of
another.

4

salt fields glisten from ocean light. there is so much
light here you could die from it. bamboo houses
stilted on black sand. houses so close they share
the same reflection on the water. pepper fields like
black eggs dry in the sun. here I became pregnant
and had my first child. his fingers learned to
quicken at the touch of sand. he let fish swim in
and out of his lungs and bloodstream. the ocean and
sky, one medium to him, he walked in both. one
day I let him go too far, and the black waves came
down and took him.

5

fishermen, wrapt in another world. their harvest
dries on large metal nets laid aslant—dust settles on
the squid's splayed arms. squatting, smoking,
noticing every ripple on the road. their skins
sinewy, pasty as clay. lying on their hammocks,
crowns of mosquitoes and flies over their heads.
they know your real name without asking.

6

her rat's nest hair. she peels it from her face. the
children pound her with fists. she sweeps her cane,
left and right, screaming something. the children
laugh. hysteria in her eyes. bobbing up and down,
she slaps down money at a cafe stand to buy food.
they laugh. in a tremor she throws the food at the
crowd. they laugh again. her clothes are ragged,
shirt torn at the seams, her skirt dusty, feet thick
and calloused. more fists at her. jab of her cane. a
man scoops the children away from her. clasping
the seams of the crowd, she exhales something
orange and white. eyes pierce her back. in her
drunken momentum she crosses the floating bridge
without paying toll. frothing fire down her chin, her
rat's nest hair blazes to the skies.

7

they watch the land, watch the air. the dust
gathering. strips of white ghost-cloth tied across
their foreheads. the grey-haired, heads down, talking.

the young with round eyes full of fruit, rice, cradles
of incense, yellowing black & white photos of
grandparents, great-grandparents. they dress him up,
the resemblance of him. powdered, rouged, his hair
combed back. what he was in life, more so in death.
my baby died a quiet death. except for the birds,
there was no one to witness.

8

the ocean curves around the land like a fish caught
on a hook, murmuring something to itself. bodies
crooning. stark bamboo houses. the women beat
shrimp into dust, after they're laid out in perfect
pink squares to dry. bowels unload, unweave into
the Gulf of Thailand.

9

pigs arrive at the dock each morning squealing for
their lives. rows of squid drying on nets like
ghosts. the whole village is well preserved smelling
of dried fish and squid. Vietnamese boys watch
Cambodian TV. the black sand wet under my feet
speaks too in another language, teeth chafing against
teeth sound against sound, tongue buckling north
and south into the land. what country is this. it
used to be my home. it was where my child was
born, where he died. it was probably best that he
didn't see anything else but this sun.

Nominated by Jane Miller

WHAT I EAT

fiction by CHARLOTTE MORGAN

from OYSTER BOY REVIEW

I BEEN STANDING HERE beside her car trying to figure out whether to go ahead with the food test.

If "you are what you eat," as the dumb-ass commercial goes, then I'm a bag of salted peanuts, a foot-long chili dog from 7-Eleven, a six-pack of Rolling Rock, a strip of red-hot jerky. Ain't that a typical bit of sucker foolishness, though: "You are what you eat." What does that make the president? A lobster tail? Or how bout the pope? Fish on Fridays, something else every other day of the week? Hey, maybe I'm a special-recipe kick-butt brownie. That's a hoot.

See, if that saying was true, I'd be one thing today, right this minute, but you can sure as hell bet if I won the lottery I'd be something else faster than you could say Jack Rabbit: surf and turf, barbecued ribs, imported brewskie. See how that's so stupid? You'd have to be a feeb to buy it.

And what about this squirming skinny girl in the trunk? This CeCe? What would she be? I ain't give her nothing to eat in almost two days. Heck, she ain't eat a thing. So, looking at it that way, she'd be nothing. Zip. Zero-ski. Or what I eat on the road, which is a baloney sandwich, the last thing I give her two days ago when I picked her up. That'd make us the same. See, I said it don't make sense. But people sell that stuff to the television and make a fortune and go out to fancy restaurants and order whatever the hell they please. Thinking they're better than the rest of us dumb shits.

I been in reform school, where everybody eats the same thing. It ain't like high school, where they give you a choice: the tuna cold plate or the hot plate, the pizza or the meat loaf. Or even the hot-shit salad bar. No way. Inside everybody gets the same plate with the exact same slop. Canned peas running into mashed potatoes from a box (with that stuff mixed in to keep guys from wanting sex all the time; don't work), mystery meat, a cold roll, a pat of fake butter on a piece of cardboard. The exact same plate. So does that make every asshole in there the same? Answer that one.

I'd like to try that out on a judge, see his face. "As you know, sir, I am what I eat, sir. And my Mama, she never give me breakfast ten times in seventeen years, less you count times I was at the tit, which I gather from her won't long. Claims I bit, which I know is one a her bald-faced lies. And lunch won't much better: as a matter of fact, judge sir, that's why I started my life of crime—for something to eat. Started out taking bag lunches from the prissy-ass Mama's boys in my class in third grade. Some of the best food I ever eat. In all due respect, did that make me them, sir, when I wolfed down them lunches? Roast beef sandwiches with lettuce and mayonnaise, oranges cut in wedges and wrapped in aluminum foil, homemade brownies with chocolate chips *and* nuts. When I ate all that did that make me them? Then I took to taking lunch money. You know pretty much how things went downhill after that. I don't hardly grasp it, given the fact I was eating better than ever at the time, judge sir. But that's the long and short of it."

Wonder if I could find a lawyer willing to try the food defense. That's a hoot.

Now this CeCe in the trunk, if she is what she eats she was in a lot of trouble before she run into me in the mall parking lot. I don't get girls: skinny as a rail, you can tell she probably don't eat enough to keep a snake alive, but she ain't got zit one, and her hair looks like one of them commercials, shiny as a creek at night. Or it was when I first seen her. Last time I looked, yesterday evening, it was scraggly as mine, clumpy-like. Vomit in it. But you can be sure that ain't how it looks on a regular day. How you figure it? Clear as day she don't eat right, but her skin and hair look like some health food nut's.

See, if she'd a eat right she'd a put up more of a fight, I bet. She's near bout as tall as I am, though that ain't saying much; but she ain't got a bit a muscle. Just went all limp when I put the gun up to her chest, like a flat tire. I thought she'd fall out there in the parking lot and somebody'd see us and I'd be caught for damn sure. But she gimme them keys like she was handing over a piece a pizza, slid over in that front seat smooth as syrup, didn't make a peep. Eyes staring at me like two pissholes in the snow. Hot damn.

That second or two when she caved in, that was the only sweat of the whole damn deal. The rest has been a snap, if I do say so myself. Easy to drive to this ol shut down barbecue before anybody even recognized this CeCe girl was missing. Them fast foods drove everybody out of business, half the damn places out here on 60 shut down. You could yell your fool head off out back here, behind this old rusty Dempstey Dumpster, wouldn't nobody know. Only she didn't yell once. Whimpered, sorta, like my cat that time she was having them kittens but one got stuck. I give CeCe that baloney sandwich, she took a bite and gagged like it won't fit to eat. That won't right. That's why I took her by the hair and made her get down on the ground. To eat up that piece of sandwich she spit out. Ain't right to waste food. Damn if I ain't heard that about a half-million times. Don't I know it ain't right. Damned straight.

"What in God's name are you up to?" she finally asked me, after she threw up all over the gravel. I seen that look on her face, I seen it a half-million times, the one gets guys punched in the face, slapped into the hole. The one the ass-kissers call defiant.

"You think you're too good to eat baloney, girl? You oughta eat what's put in front of you, be grateful."

You can look at her and see she don't eat right. I wadn't trying to slap her around, just aiming to teach her some proper respect for food. Shit, girl like her, she ain't never had to hustle for food. Who's gonna let her know about that, I ask you? Bet she don't even reward herself with a cream donut when she's done something right. Bet she wouldn't even eat one if I give it to her this minute, hungry as she's bound to be. Skinny Minnie. Hot damn, I'm a poet and don't know it.

Truth is, once I got her out here I didn't have no plan. Won't like that. Can't nobody say it was. That's why I had to put her in the trunk. That and to wipe that smartass look off her face. I says, "You sit tight, you hear, I'm gonna go get us something else to eat." Had to get a little shuteye, catch a few Zs, so I could think clear; needed to go somewhere, get a bite, try to figure my next step. Bout the best place for that is 7-Eleven; I can get two chili dogs and all the mustard and onion I want for 99 cents, on special. You can count on 7-Eleven, even if they don't have the special. They always got the foot-long for that price. And no matter what town I'm in, see, the 7-Eleven is always the same. Plus they got papers I can look at, cause the clerks 19 times out of 20 don't give a shit whether you read the paper or not, no matter what the friggin sign says. That's how I come to find out her name was

CeCe. From the paper. I didn't need to read no paper to know she's a rich bitch. I got eyes.

So I slept in the front seat a while, seat smelled like the stuff my Mama used to spray to get rid of cat piss. Then I walked to 7-Eleven, bought her a chili dog. And one a them Long Johns. They cost the most, got the most cream filling of any at the 7-Eleven. I oughta know. I only get em for myself on a rare occasion. Here's what I'm thinking: if you are what you eat, like the assholes say, and she eats what I eat, then she's me. Or at least like me. No better'n me. Don't make no difference. The food test. If she passes, then I'll take her along, say she's my sister. Or my squeeze. She'd be like my road woman. She'd sit up by me in the car, lean over my way to point out signs and shit, say "Let's stop at the next McDonald's, get us a apple pie." If she don't pass the food test BINGO, she ain't the right one. That simple. She ain't a bit of good to me. Call it a scientific experiment, like when they cut open them frogs in school to see what they's like inside.

SHE'S ALL CURLED UP like one of them grub worms when I open the trunk. I got the gun in my hand, case she gets some notion of jumping out, but she don't so much as turn her head at first.

"CeCe. You want something to eat?" I flash the gun—it ain't loaded, see, but she don't know that—but the bag a food's on the front seat.

Her head moves, then, turns facing the sky stead of me, like a blind person might do. I think, damn, she thinks she's too good to even look at me, but in a second I can tell she's more confused than snobby, like she's trying to figure where the sound come from, even though it's broad daylight. Maybe all that dark, then the light, she can't see good till her eyes adjust. Maybe.

"I brought you some food, CeCe. You better eat something."

Now her eyes light on me, register, and she curls up even tighter, only that face staring up at me. She starts shaking her head, blubbering.

"You don't want nothing to eat? You gotta eat." Maybe it's a trick—people been tricking me all my life. Maybe she thinks I'll feel sorry for her, go get the bag a food, and she'll make a run for it.

"Come on out. I had to go get ya something to eat, that's all. I didn't mean to stay gone so long. I had to eat myself, think this thing through. And the walk took longer than I thought, see. You can come on out now. I ain't planning to use this." I hold the gun up so she can see it, then drop my hand down to my side so it ain't pointing at her.

She don't make a move, though, still stares and cries, tears running all down her face, which is now dirty like she got some oil or black grease on it. I don't know how. This is one clean car.

"Come on CeCe. I planned a little test for you. I'd bet my boots you're good at tests, ain't you? Come on eat something, I'll explain." She don't know, see, that the food IS the test. That wouldn't be right, giving her a hint. I ain't gonna take no chances. This experiment's gotta be one hundred percent fool proof. I laugh at that idea, "fool proof." Hot damn.

She still don't get up outa the trunk, so I gotta grab her arm. It's bony like I expected, and the skin's all damp, I don't know why. When I give a little tug—nothing rough, mind you, just enough to let her know I mean business—she kinda pulls in the opposite direction, like she don't want to come with me. This gets me mad for a minute—I ain't got much of a temper, but something like that gets me mad.

"That the way you want it? Okay, have it your way." And I slam the trunk again. "Your food's gonna get cold. Ain't right, wasting good food." Miss Priss.

Another thing that makes me mad, besides her acting so high and mighty, is that maybe this means she's already failed the food test, before she even got started good. I mean, ain't that what I planned: if she don't eat my food, she ain't the one? BINGO. But she ain't even seen it yet, ain't had a chance to turn up her nose at my two favorites, a chili dog and a cream dream. Hot damn. So does it count, her refusing to get out of the trunk, not even looking at the food? I decide it don't. Fair's fair.

I can't remember ever turning down food, not once in my whole entire life. All's I remember is gobbling down whatever come my way. Some I liked better than others, but I ain't never turned up my nose at none of it.

Glenn used to come over at night, this guy my Mama hung out with for a while. A good while. Longer than any of the others. I won't but five or six then. He'd bring these skin flicks, they'd sit in the dark and watch. I'd lay on the floor there with them, they'd be drinking beer and smoking joints, and I'd lay there on the floor and watch too, all that touching on the TV. Mama and Glenn wouldn't eat anything, wouldn't talk, wouldn't hardly move themselves, except to lift the can to their mouths or pass the joint or drag into the kitchen for another beer. I'd say, "I'm hungry, Mama," and Glenn would say, "Get the kid some chow, Gwenn." I liked that, Glenn/Gwenn. Him calling food chow. She'd go into the kitchen, come back with a bag of pretzel pieces or a can of vienna sausages. I'd lay there and eat those vienna sausages, lick the tomato sauce off my fingers, watching them movies of naked people while my Mama and Glenn hardly moved. My Mama won't much of a cook. I always eat what we had.

Reform school, that's the first time I eat where everybody set down at the same table at the same time and eat the same thing, like them pretend families on TV. I always figured nobody really did that, see, not in real life. Them guys inside, they'd just as soon knife you as look at you if you messed with their grub, too. One time this new kid took a Hershey bar from one of the longtimers. That kid had a bad accident, fell down some steps, broke a bunch of ribs and banged up his face pretty bad. He got smart fast, said them steps was wet. We all knew what went down. You don't mess with nobody's food stash.

so I'm gonna see if this CeCe's got enough sense, enough plain long manners, to eat what's put in front of her. That baloney sandwich was old, won't hers. Fair's fair. I got her her own chili dog, her own cream donut. Each one wrapped separate, in its own paper. Ain't nobody else touched it. Even got a packet of mustard so she can fix it the way she wants. Same for her as for me. See, if she sits there and eats with me, means she knows she ain't a bit better than me. Means she's got respect. "You are what you eat." What a hoot. The food test.

It ain't like some people probably think, that dirty stuff written all over the bathroom walls at school, "Eat me." Hell no. I ain't never been like that. I ain't never forced a girl to do nothing like that. I seen it plenty of times in them skin flicks, more times than I could count, and I heard the guys talking about it enough when I was on the inside. Hell, sometimes seems like that's all they talked about, eatin pussy, she eat me till I like to died, all that. I wanted to yell at them to shut their nasty mouths, to quit talkin like that day and night. My Mama would've smacked me from here to kingdom come if she ever heard me talkin like that. Sometimes they'd even talk like that while we was eatin our meals. Some people ain't got a grain of sense, sure as hell ain't got no manners. That place won't a good place, even if they give me three squares.

AF FIRST I don't know what that "clonk, clonk, clonk" is, then I realize it's coming from inside the trunk. CeCe must've come to her senses, decided she wanted to get out after all. Have some fresh air.

315

Cooperate. That's a good sign for the food test, I figure. I ain't never been one to hold grudges, so I go over and open the trunk and sure enough she uncurls soon as I do, raises a hand up like she's reaching around for something to hold onto. She finds the edge of the car, pulls up slow, looks around with these zombie eyes like those creatures coming out of the pods in that movie, what was it, *The Body Snatchers?*

"Want a hand, CeCe?" This time I don't go over and pull on her, but I do keep the gun down by my side. I don't want to spook her again.

She don't answer right away, sits up more. She looks down at her arms, her clothes, feels her hair, like she don't believe they're for real.

"How'd you know my name?" That voice don't match the weak way she looks: that voice sounds right bossy, if you ask me. Makes me nervous, jumpy. Her purse was in the trunk with her all along. I reckon she knew that. I didn't look through it or nothing before I put her back there. I ain't no robber. That must be why she can't figure how I know her name. Takes me for some kinda dummy.

"Papers. It's all over the front page of this morning's paper." I ram the gun into my back pocket, quick. She ain't lookin directly at me no way, so she don't notice.

"My Daddy would give you a lot of money. If that's what you want. I've got a little in my pocketbook. But he'd give you a lot."

"That's what the paper said."

"You could call, tell him where to leave the money. He's got a beeper. I know the beeper number, if you're worried about the police and the phone and all."

She climbs over to the edge, slow, like she strained a muscle. I go over and sit on one side of the trunk, she sits on the other. Not touching. We sit there on the bumper, like kids who've maybe been camping or hiking or looking for something with one a them metal detector things. Except she's kinda messy looking, with that dirty face and that scraggly hair and her clothes looking like she slept in them. She don't look so pretty-perfect no more. "You gonna hurt me?" Now that voice ain't so high and mighty.

I don't answer.

"You want me to do something kinky, is that what you want?" She loops a piece of her hair behind one ear. When she takes her hand down she looks at it, like she expects to see something on it.

"It's like I told you before, I got some food for you. In the front seat. Let's eat, okay?"

"What's your name?"

"I ain't gonna tell you my name."

"Please don't put me back in that trunk."

"I told you. I had to think. I had to get us some chow." I use Glenn's word.

"Please, I'll do what you want. Just don't put me back in that trunk."

"Come on and get in the front seat. Let's eat."

She stands, slow, like she don't trust her legs; they are right skinny, I can tell in them fancy tight jeans, and I follow her around to the passenger side of the car. She ain't wiggling that butt like she was when I come up on her in the parking lot, no siree. The door's locked. I forgot about that.

"This here's a sharp car. Your Daddy buy it for you?" When I saw that special-order red Honda on the parking lot, I figured it had to belong to some ritzy girl. Wouldn't no guy be driving this thing.

"It belongs to the dealership. He owns a dealership."

"That why it's so clean?" By now I've unlocked her door, opened it like she was my date for friggin dinner, and she sits. The bag of food's on the driver's seat. Them chili dogs're cold by now, but that don't matter to me. I ate beanies and weenies cold from the can my whole growing up. She probably ain't never eat no beanies and weenies at all, one way or another, but it ain't my fault the food's cold.

I beat it around to my side—I know she ain't gonna make a run for it now, but I still don't like to leave her alone in the front. When I stick my head in I can see she's crying for the first time, but she ain't makin no noise. Just wet tracks running down her dirty cheeks; she don't even reach up to wipe her face, just lets them tears run off her chin. That strikes me as weird. I ain't never seen nobody do that. I open my door.

"You like chili dogs?" I pick up the bag, slide into my seat, put it on my lap.

She stares down at her own lap. "What are you planning to do to me?"

"Here." I hand the hotdog, all wrapped, across the seat. "Take it. You want mustard?"

She don't look up, don't make a move to take the chili dog.

"You're not going to call my Daddy are you? You would've done that already if that's what you wanted, right?" Them tears are pouring.

"Eat this. Please." I haven't moved. She hasn't moved. I'm starting to sweat. I don't want to get the wrapper all sweaty.

"If you're going to do something with that gun I wish you'd go ahead and do it." She raises her head and looks at me now. Them brown eyes

317

look like Mama's dog Porter, after Glenn kicked him for taking a crap on the kitchen floor.

"I ain't kicked you, have I?" I put the hotdog on the dash. She ain't doing too hot on the food test, I gotta admit. I'm getting kinda worried.

"What do you want with me?"

"How bout a Long John? Would you rather have that first?" I open the bag, pull out the wax paper with the donut. "I call it eatin backwards."

She goes wild on me. That's the only way I know how to describe it. I'm sitting here, trying to get her to take the Long John, offering it to her calm as you please, and she goes wild on me, knocks it outa my hands, starts screaming and flailing around and clawing at me like some kinda animal. I never laid a hand on her up to this point except to get her outa that trunk. Then I won't rough, just firm you might say. She don't have a mark on her.

I try to grab her hands, but she's everywhere, pulling my hair, scratching my face, kicking my chin. I didn't notice she's wearing these half-cowboy boots some of the rich girls wear until I get one smack up under my chin. Hurts like holy hell. Plus this nasty smell like some old dirty gymsuit or diaper gets real strong. I'd sorta noticed it when I got in the car, something smelling kinda off, but it won't that bad, what with the hotdog in my lap and the spray stuff. Now, with her all over me, it's like that nasty smell's all over me, too. It makes me gag; it ain't like she shoulda smelled, girl like that. She's yelling, too, foul stuff not a bit better than them dirty-mouthed guys in reform school. "Filthy fuckin creep, asshole," stuff like that.

Caught off guard, I get shoved up against the car door for a second. That gun in my pocket, it grinds into my butt, like to kills me. I ain't got a bit of meat on my bones, not even my bony butt. Hurts like hell, gets me mad, her calling me names, going after me when I been trying to give her something to eat. Give her a fair chance. Wild as she is, she ain't all that strong, it don't take much for me to get her off me, once I get over being so surprised. Still, her kickin and scratchin, that gun rammed into my backside, I lose my cool. Ain't no two ways about it.

"Where's your manners, bitch? Ain't you got no manners?" I have to duck my head, grab out with my arms, get her shoved back against the seat. She's slobbering now, spit running out of her mouth, her hair wild around her head. She don't look a thing like the fancy-pants girl walking all cocky to her shiny red car. No siree bob-tail cat she don't. She's breathing hard, too, like she can't hardly get the next breath. I have to

318

hold her down with both my arms, straddle on top of her, and still she's pushing and shoving with that skinny body of hers like she could get somewhere if she just wiggles hard enough. That's a joke. She ain't going nowhere. She ain't even come close to passing the food test.

"You should eat my chili dog like I said, CeCe."

She looks at me frantic-like, shaking her head back and forth, but at least she don't say nothing, I'll give her that. Glenn used to climb on top of me like this, tickle me till I cried, but still I wouldn't say Uncle for him.

"See, you shoulda eat what I brought you. It ain't right, you turnin down my food, like it won't good enough. Didn't your Mama ever tell you about all them hungry children in China?" She goes limp on me when I say this, but she don't look me in the face, don't apologize or say nothin. "Well, didn't she?" I pull her hair to make her look at me, but she don't answer still.

She's not struggling no more. She's sniffling, but she's give up fightin me. I look around and see the white wax paper on the floor, by her feet. The donut's bound to be squished. I pick it up, unwrap the paper, and the cream's all over the outside, it's a broken mess.

"Eat this. Eat every bit of this and then we'll talk."

She don't look up at me, don't say a word.

"I said eat this and we'll talk."

Still she don't move, so I grab her hair again and force her face up. That is one stubborn face. I take the donut and jam it to her mouth, but she holds her lips closed. I push it right into her teeth, but still she won't take a bite, so I end up smearing it onto her face. What with the grease from the trunk and her snot and spit her looks was pretty messed up anyway. She don't look a bit like Miss Priss no more, that's for damn sure. My mama wouldn't be caught dead looking like that. She always did keep herself fixed up, even if she won't much for cooking. That sticky glaze stuff and the white cream filling get all over my hands, but there ain't much I can do about it. I wish she'd taken one bite, just one teeninesy bite. But she didn't, and that's a fact. Fair's fair.

I sit back on her thighs. I ain't heavy, but I'm bound to be hurting her some. Still she don't say a word, don't make a move to wipe the cream and crumbs and pieces of donut off her face.

"I told you, you shoulda eat what I brought you when you had the chance." But she don't speak to me.

"Well, I guess that's that, then." I wipe my hands on her jeans, but they're still all sticky. I gotta wash up, get this crap offa me.

319

She stares at me, finally speaks. "What do you mean, 'that's that'?" Her voice sounds more like a kid's now. That CeCe sure has lost the wind in her sails, that's for damn sure. She shoulda eat something. She could at least wipe her face. It's damn amazing to me how somebody raised like she's bound to have been raised ain't got a bit better manners.

"Come on, stand up, let's go outside a minute." I shove the door, let myself out on her side, pull her along behind me, but she don't resist. That fresh air is a relief, even if it is muggy as hell.

The trunk's still open, see; I ain't never closed it from when I got her out for the food test.

"Please. Please, I'll do whatever you say. Call my Daddy. Please."

"CeCe, this don't have a damn thing to do with your Daddy. Had to do with me and you. Ain't you figured that yet? I thought all you rich bitches was supposed to be brains. You shoulda eat with me."

"Please. I'll do whatever you say." She reaches up, rubs some of that goo off her cheek into her mouth. That little pink tongue comes licking out. It's downright disgusting. I wouldn't kiss that mouth if it was the only one in town.

"You shoulda thought of that, CeCe, you shoulda thought of that when you had the chance."

I'm sick of this girl, sick of looking at her nasty face with food smeared all over it, sick of looking at her matty hair. For the first time I shove her hard. I'm skinny, but I'm strong. Wiry little shit, Glenn used to call me. I shove her into that trunk and slam the lid so fast she don't know what's happened to her. This time I don't hear no slow "clonk, clonk, clonk" coming from inside; this banging's more like the racket at a shooting range.

But I ain't interested. I want to go to 7-Eleven, wash my hands, get a cup of fresh-brewed. They got a clean bathroom, make coffee about every five minutes. It's always hot and fresh. You can count on it, real civilized. Hell, thinking about a girl like that CeCe, it could ruin my appetite.

I walk past that rusted-out dumpster, past that old Bar-b-q sign with Peggy's Pit-Cooked and that pink pig hanging out front, past the entrance to the parking lot, on to Rt. 60 headed back towards town. I walk fast, till I can't even hear that banging noise from the trunk no more, till cars are whizzing past me so quick I got to concentrate on where I'm going. They all going someplace besides here, that's for damn sure.

I put my hand up to my mouth, lick as much of the sticky sweet off as I can. Maybe I'll get a Slim Jim, too, get that sugar taste outa my mouth. I shoulda known a girl like that CeCe wouldn't pass the food test. Next time, I won't pick somebody so snooty toot. Hot damn. Next time, I'll look for somebody who ain't so full a herself, somebody with some manners. Maybe a girl driving a pick-up. High ridin. That's the ticket.

I can't hardly wait to wash my hands. I'm hustling down this old highway. Yessiree, I can't hardly wait to get back to 7-Eleven.

Nominated by Barbara Selfridge, Oyster Boy Review

FROM THE PRADO ROTUNDA: THE FAMILY OF CHARLES IV, AND OTHERS

by ALICIA OSTRIKER

from AMERICAN POETRY REVIEW

Francisco José de Goya y Lucientes
Wishes to inform the universe that it can eat his name.
That it can kiss his finger. He stuffs
The Spanish arrogance of his name
Between your teeth.
Like the ugly royal bodies, it is a stiff sponge of blood,
Gold-beaded. Immobilized by garments. Streaks of stupidity
And pride marble it like meat. You chew and grimace.

He desires the form of this painting to be that of a boa constrictor
Swallowing a Pekingese. He desires the lumps to be visible
And the digestion difficult.

Is it not, remarked Hemingway, *a masterpiece of loathing?*
Look how he has painted his spittle into every face.
How wan the attendant courtiers of such monarchs,

322

A king corpulent and hesitant, a queen whose large arms
Stand akimbo, poodle teeth grinning, called by Gautier
The corner baker and his wife after they have won the lottery,
Whose fatuousness blinds them from seeing flesh, face, form
As very signifiers of the painter's disgust

—with his own ambition?
Himself at work in corners of society portraits
Painting like a courteous animal, despising retouching, forcing
Their homage. What a man will do to possess the respect
Of the gilded worm. Do their commissions choke him?
Is it that hope itself wishes to melt? Whose flesh? What ceremony?
Viscera, witchery, whippings.
The silent shriek of a man in *The Madhouse*
Flees from an oval aperture black as doubt
To re-embody itself a century later
In bourgeois Norway.

Inaudible owls crowd the sleep of Reason,
Saturn devours children
In fact. Fact.

The densest element in the periodic table is lead.
Attempting to lift a box you might hemorrhage.
The painting of Goya is denser than lead,
The painting is insupportable.
If he is leading us by the hand like babes
To worship the abject monstrous because it exists, to sniff
Hysteria from within like an infection
Among the tambourines and the fans and the mantillas,
If Goya's lascivious Maja
Nude and clothed in the duplicity
Native to woman
Makes your mouth water—
If her pale legs flow strangely together
As if glued to a board they cannot bend at the knee,
As if returning to fishtails—

The painting is never what is *there,*
It throbs with the mystery
Of your own sick-to-death soul
Which demands, like everything alive,
Love.

Nominated by Marilyn Krysl

OBLIVION, NEBRASKA

fiction by PETER MOORE SMITH

from THE MASSACHUSETTS REVIEW

1. Frankfurt

Early one gray morning in 1967 PFC Edward Roland Emille, my father, touched down at the Frankfurt International Airport and was paraded with a contingent of other young G.I.'s to a personnel carrier which careened onto the German highway. They call it the *Autobahn*. There is no speed limit on this highway, and the American military vehicle he rode in accelerated maniacally, squealing rocketlike and dangerous across the landscape. Eddie, a simple Nebraska boy accustomed to the yellow monotony of the plains, stuck his head out of the carrier like a dog and marveled at the looming countryside. He opened his eyes and mind wide to the sloping fields of sugar beets and asparagus, the endless orchards of apple and plum, the rolling Taunus mountains dark green and misty on the horizon. He even tried to read the peculiar German road signs, like "Wiesbaden," "Bad Wilbul," and "Prungescheim," as they blurred swiftly past the little flap of canvas he poked his head out of. One sign in particular, Eddie noticed, said, "Ausfahrt," and he saw it again and again. They must have passed this sign fifty times, as a matter of fact. What is this place? he wondered. It must be enormous with all of those exits leading to it. A city? Or a whole state like Montana or New Hampshire, only for Germany? So how come he'd never heard of it?

Checking in at the barracks, Eddie felt bleary from the nine-hour flight in the back of the C-5 military cargo plane; the truth was, he could barely see straight from fatigue; but how often did he find himself in a foreign country? Plus, there were nearly 48 hours of free time before he had to report for duty. The thing to do, naturally, was rent one of those zippy little blue Opals he'd noticed at the rental place just around the corner from the barracks and steer it out onto the sky-is-the-speed-limit Autobahn.

Out there, he thrilled at the Mercedes and Porsches zooming by, swerving and merging recklessly in and out of the passing lane like streaks of color and light. A dark spot would appear in his rear view mirror, and within seconds a sports car would reveal itself in front of him. It was exhilarating. And when he came to one of those Ausfahrt signs, you can bet he followed it, thinking, hey, what the heck? Oddly enough, it led him into a little town with twisty cobblestone streets, tiny biergartens, and gast-hauses. Is this Ausfahrt? Eddie thought. It can't be. He stopped at a corner, momentarily took in the alien German weirdness, then rolled his window down and asked an old man hobbling by, "Ausfahrt?" Eddie could only hope he was pronouncing it correctly. (He wasn't. It's not *fart*, it's *fay-ert*.) The old man understood anyway, and with his walking stick, waved Eddie back in the direction of the highway.

Okay, Eddie thought, and he turned his zippy blue Opal around.

Not long after was another Ausfahrt sign, only this one led him into farmland that stretched into rolling hills, and further, into the mountains he'd seen earlier. Almost instinctively, Eddie knew Ausfahrt wasn't there. So, once again he got on the Autobahn, once again he saw a sign that said, "Ausfahrt," and once again he followed that sign. It led him through suburbs, then into an ever-more-populated region of taller and taller buildings, some old, some new. He was in the city of Frankfurt now, quite a distance from the barracks in Kaiserslaughtern where he had started. To hell with it, he thought, and made his way inside.

Many of the streets were narrow and curvy, and the Germans drove quickly, lurching and gunning their engines fitfully. Eddie was debilitated with fatigue now and getting hungry, so he searched for a place to park, and he pulled over. He saw a cafe and wandered up to the maitre'd. A *zaftig* young blonde woman in a red-and-white-checked apron—Katrina Fischl, my mother—smiled warmly at him.

"Do you speak English?" Eddie asked.

In her *Hoch Deutsch* accent, Katrina answered, "Yes, of course, right this way." She placed him at a small table near the door and handed him a translated menu.

"Can I ask you a question?" he said.

Katrina looked at him expectantly, eyebrows arched.

"I'm looking for Ausfahrt."

"What?" she said. "You're looking—"

"I've been driving all day looking for Ausfahrt, but every time I see a sign for it I am led elsewhere."

"Ausfahrt?"

It was the first time Eddie heard it pronounced correctly.

"Yes," he said. "That's it."

"Exit," she said.

Eddie blinked, wondering if she wanted him to leave.

And then Katrina understood. "Ausfahrt is not a *place*," she said, and she started to laugh. "It's a *word*. It means *exit*. It is the German word for *offramp*." There must have been something in the embarrassed, pathetic look on my father's face that made my mother soften, though, because she told him then, still laughing, "We close at eleven," and asked if he could meet her.

2. Fayetteville

THEY NAMED ME FREDERICK. And by the time I was five my father had been promoted to E-6 Sergeant and was stationed in Fayetteville, North Carolina. We lived in a comfortably furnished duplex on the shady side of the street in base housing with thousands of other families. One winter day in 1973, a Saturday, our street was wet with rain, the sky filled with clouds, and all the children of the neighborhood were inside. I remember boredom like a disease creeping inside me. My mother had been baking a plum torte, letting me gobble the extra sticky-sweet slices she'd cut into a metal bowl. She had also been talking on the phone all day, the receiver cradled against her ear, to her friend Rita, another army wife from Germany. I loved to hear my mother speak *Deutsch*. I didn't understand it. My parents had decided learning two languages would confuse me. But her voice rose and fell familiarly, as though it was the melody of a song I knew but whose words I'd forgotten.

In the living room my father had been trying to get me to play Monopoly, but it seemed too complicated. I liked to grab the little silver car and run around the house with it instead, making zooming engine noises. My father pointed to the yellow hundreds, blue fifties, and pink five-dollar bills. "Look," he motioned, "think of the great stuff you can buy with all this cash."

"Daddy," I giggled, "It's not real."

"Sure it's real," he said. "Absolutely it's real."

That evening my parents would go dancing at the NCO club. My mother's friend Rita was coming over to babysit. She was lenient, and I was excited, hoping to stay up past my eight o'clock bedtime, which Mom rigidly enforced. I remember being shooed out of the kitchen when my mother finally took the plum torte from the oven and got off the phone.

"Freddy," she cautioned, "go bother your father," and she started clumping up the stairs. Then she said to Dad, "I'll be getting ready. You watch this race car driver."

My father, a tall man with a virtually black crew cut, his jaw long and square, his eyes gray as rain, was absolutely, one-hundred-percent *for* the war in Vietnam. He served one tour the year I was born, developed a jungle infection and was sent home. He hated hippies. They should get the hell to Russia, he'd say. Who needed them, anyway? He did like to smoke marijuana, though, which grew wild all over Nebraska when he was a kid. He walked with a swagger. He wore aviator sunglasses. His skin had a permanent pink hue from too many summers husking corn in the Nebraska sun. He had a stamp collection which he painstakingly brought out almost every night, arranging and re-arranging. He loved Monopoly, and he played to win.

Physically, Mom was his complete opposite—blonde, blue-eyed, and round. Everything about her was full and soft. Her hair fell in golden corkscrew curls on her head. Her cheeks were puffy. The next time I saw her, however, she'd been transformed. She wore a shimmering black dress, her hair was sprayed and swirled above her head, her face was made up in eye-shadow, lipstick and rouge. "Kiss me here," she said, pointing to her puffy cheek. I placed a small peck right where she pointed and breathed in the acrid smell of an entire can of hair spray. Her round body balanced expertly on those pointy high heels. Every Saturday I saw her get dressed up like this, but every time it was thrilling, and this time in particular is special to my memory because it is the last time I ever saw her at all.

When my parents were leaving the NCO club that night, my father stopped to talk to Sergeant Juan Perez, a buddy of his from the motor pool. Mom, having had a few drinks, leaned against a car which sat at the curb. It was a Chevy Nova. Apparently, someone had bent and broken off the radio antenna of this Chevy Nova halfway, and my mother's coat, an old short-haired mink she'd inherited from my German grandmother, got caught on it by the sleeve. Anyway, the guy who sat in the driver's seat, Spec-4 Frank L. Mancini, a field cook, didn't even notice Mom was there. He was drunk. They were all drunk. This car, Frank L. Mancini's pride and joy, had mag wheels. Frank L. Mancini gunned his engine and took off squealing, and it dragged my mother down beside it. My father and a bunch of other people stood at the entrance of the NCO club and watched as my mother's body was pulled along the pavement flipping and flopping like a rag doll for half a block. Supposedly, she did not scream until she slid under the car. That's when Frank L. Mancini thought something might be wrong and turned his steering wheel sharply to the right.

My mother's head, the rear right tire.

Picture it.

When I woke in the morning and padded downstairs in my socks and found Rita still in the living room, I knew something wasn't right. "Where's Mom and Dad?" I demanded.

Rita said, "Your father's coming."

She had asked me to stay quietly in my room, and I remember that I was playing with my G.I. Joes on the floor when my father came in and stood in the doorway. I saw his eyes were weirdly swollen and red and I knew something terrible had happened. But Dad smiled, and so I also knew that I mustn't admit that I knew. In as unafraid a voice as I could manage at age five, I asked him, "Where's Mom?"

My father took me downstairs to the kitchen, fed me plum torte for breakfast, and told me in a voice broken with sorrow that my mother had gone home.

3. Lincoln

"My mother is the Duchess of Ausfahrt," I told Nessa, "who lives in a castle in Germany near the greater metropolitan Ausfahrt area." I was nine. We sat in the tall grass of a field which stretched from my grandmother's house in Nebraska to infinity. As far as I was concerned, my father was somewhere beyond infinity, guarding freedom in Korea. He had left me with his mother, my grandmother, who treated me like delicate porcelain, an imported figurine, as though I might break.

"That is crap," Nessa sneered. "Pure garbage." Sandy blonde hair, sun-freckles across the bridge of her nose, Sears tough-skin blue jeans rolled up to her knees, Nessa was serious and mean, with dark eyebrows that arched cruelly when she spoke. She had that Elvis lip curl, too. When she laughed it was pitiless and mocking. She was a savage who turned sweet as rock candy when a grown-up came around.

329

I loved her.

"Why would I lie?" I said. "What could I possibly have to gain by lying?" I looked her directly in the eye.

Suspiciously, Nessa eyed me back.

"Ausfahrt is one of the leading capitals of Europe," I told her.

"So how come your mother never comes to Nebraska?" Nessa said.

"She's busy with the government. Plus they don't recognize royalty in this country."

"Your father is—"

"In the army," I said. "He has important government work himself right now in the Far East."

"If you're lying," Nessa said.

"Can I tell you a secret?" I asked.

She nodded.

"My parents are spies."

"Exactly where in Germany is Outfart?" Nessa wanted to know.

"Ausfahrt," I said, "It's kind of in the middle. Its leading export is plums."

"Plums?"

"And carrots."

"Yeah?"

"And gold. It is a city of ten million," I told her, "surrounded by mountains." At that instant I saw in Nessa's face what I hadn't even been counting on. I saw that some detail—the plums?—had convinced her. I lay back in the grass and kept going, something having snapped loose inside me. I informed her of the river which coursed through the city of Ausfahrt. I pronounced words in the special dialect of the region. I enumerated the industries and agricultures. And a month and a half later, when my fourth grade class was asked to give an oral report on one of the world's capitals, I didn't need to consult the Atlas or the Encyclopedia Britannica like the rest of the kids. I needed merely to state what I already knew.

"The city of Ausfahrt," I said to this group of nine-year-olds, "has a population of ten million. Its leading exports, plums, carrots, and gold, account for 30 percent of Germany's gross national product. The architecture of Ausfahrt is a combination of modern skyscrapers and ancient European buildings. Most notable," I went on, "is the Ausfahrt Cathedral—"

"Freddy?" Mrs. Johanson said.

"—which was designed in the Medieval period but wasn't finished until early this century."

"Freddy?" she said again.

I remember a brilliance of dust floating in the sunlit air of the classroom. I remember Karen Billslaughter coughing and Arnie Fleck shuffling his feet. I can still see the heavily waxed tile floor and the orange molded plastic desks. Vivid to me even now are the maple and oak fall leaves of construction-paper and that cut-out Thanksgiving turkey stapled to the bulletin board. The schoolroom clock, its red second hand whirring in a smooth trajectory toward the unknown, possesses the clarity of something I saw five minutes ago. I looked at my teacher, her lime green polyester pantsuit and pink-tinted glasses, and meant to say, respectfully, "Yes, Mrs. Johanson?" But something got caught in my throat, and when I opened my mouth, nothing came out.

Later that afternoon, from the field behind my grandmother's house, I would watch Mrs. Johanson's metallic green Mercury Monarch pull softly into the driveway. I'd see her remove herself carefully from the car, take a moment to adjust her artificial cashmere coat, and walk toward the front door. I would turn my face to the sun and squeeze my eyes shut tightly against the light.

4. Oblivion

CLOSE YOUR EYES. The first image you see, of course, is a black emptiness, a picture of nothing. Now imagine a horizontal line cutting through the middle of it. Give it a slightly downward-sloping arc. Fill in the space above the line with blue. Fill in the space below the line with green. Now you're getting somewhere. Add textures, like white, cottony clouds in the blue, and dark forests and pale yellow fields in the green. You can put a highway in the distance. You can place an airplane in the sky. Can you hear its jet engines whirring? You might try adding a river which leads in an ever-more-populated direction toward a metropolitan and dazzling city of marble edifices and glass reflections. See how easy this is? Use your mind's eye. This city requires government, history, industry. It needs factories, warehouses, and businesses. Imagine it all. From its sides the suburbs must spiral out. Give it an airport with arrivals and departures. Provide it with hospitals to manage the births, broken bones, diseases, and deaths. Invent bars with alcoholics slumped in the darkened booths. Include parks where lovers endear by the fountains, where junkies shoot up in the bushes, where young mothers push their babies in carriages. Create schools for the children, fields for baseball and football and soccer. There must be a public works, a power station, and a cemetery filled with the city's dead.

Now move west, over the suburbs of this city, toward a flat, open plain. Move past subdivisions and farms until you reach a single road leading toward the remote distance you haven't completed yet. At the far end of this road create a white house. In front of this house put a light blue Ford Grand Torino and a metallic green Mercury Monarch. Move in through the window of this house, where there is a room. In this room place a blue velvet couch, matching arm chairs, and two women, one young, one old, drinking tea. "Your grandson," make the young say, "has a very active imagination."

"Yes," the old woman should smile nervously.

The young woman says this like a question: "Perhaps a little too active?"

"Hmmm," says the old woman.

"Do you know about the assignment?"

"The assignment?"

"Didn't Freddy tell you? I asked my students to give an oral report to the class on an important foreign capital."

"Freddy didn't say anything about it."

"Freddy did a wonderful job—"

The old woman smiles again.

"—but he did it on an imaginary city."

"Imaginary?"

"He made it all up. He said his mother lives there."

"Oh."

"Freddy's mother is—"

"Deceased," the old woman says.

"I'm sorry, that's what I thought, I just had to, you know—"

They sip their tea.

Imagine a silence passing through the room like a person.

Finally, the old woman says, "Thank you, Mrs. Johanson." She walks the young woman to the front door. Then she follows the silence through the house, passing a yellow kitchen, to the back. Beyond a screen door she sees a field which stretches so far outward that there is nothing. There *is* nothing. You haven't created anything there.

"Freddy!" she calls. "Freddy, come inside!" Follow the direction of her voice out into the field. At the edge of a downward slope toward infinity, put a boy. The grass he sits in is tall and dry. Eyes closed, he holds his face toward the sun. He does not move. Make him so still that a pheasant walks by him, that a family of mice scurry unafraid around his folded legs. Far off, the old woman is still shouting. Have her get louder. Have the boy start to tremble. Make it happen so softly that it is almost not there at first, then let it intensify, until the boy is shuddering with the knowledge of exactly where in the universe he is.

Nominated by The Massachusetts Review

ODD COLLECTIONS

essay by ALEXANDER THEROUX

from THE YALE REVIEW

I HAVE THE OCCASION, thankfully not too often, of looking peculiar in my own eyes when, entertaining guests, I never seem able to give a logical reason, when they ask, for my ice-cream scoop collection. And not only looking peculiar, but feeling so, muddles me enough that I'm never quite able to mount the fertile enough explanation for it, at least to me, that when I was growing up, and we went out for ice cream, there was never a cone or dish of the delicious stuff served to me that matched for excitement the singular device that dug out, dispatched, and dished it. Oh, how I wanted one! Wasn't it Freud who insisted that we spend our entire lives basically trying to fulfill those first three or four wishes of ours? Odd collections, my guests notwithstanding, I suppose indicate odd people. But my goodness, how many of us there are.

Helmut Kohl, chancellor of Germany, collects rocks. Emperor Hirohito collected Mickey Mouse watches. Dave Winfield collects marbles. Sir Richard Burton, the Victorian explorer, collected languages; at the end of his life he was believed to speak and write no fewer than twenty-nine. (At one stage he lived with thirty monkeys in order to study the noises they made, eventually compiling a short monkey-vocabulary.) His *Wit and Wisdom from West Africa* is a collection of some 2,859 proverbs. And he had an equal passion for collecting dialects, like Thomas Jefferson, let me add, who collected American Indian dialects and vocabularies. There is also an American Pencil Collectors Society, with more than three hundred active members and a monthly newsletter. Old pencils are apparently valuable, and collectors prize advertising pencils, especially if never sharpened, never used; souvenir pencils, novelty pencils, pencil cases, pencil holders, and so on. One pencil collector in North Dakota has amassed over 25,000 examples in seventy-five years. A man in Texas has a million *stubs,* his hobby.

Barbed wire is a collectible. There are in fact more than a thousand members in the Barbed Wire Collectors of America. (According to an old Texas adage, a barbed wire fence is of no value whatsoever unless it is "horse-high, bull-strong, and pig-tight.") A barbed-wire festival swap and sale is annually held in LaCrosse, Kansas, "The Barbed Wire Capital of the World." Incidentally, Punishing Dodge "Star" wire, patented in 1881, is the most sought-after wire by collectors.

There have been some wonderfully eccentric collections. John Aubrey, England's first serious biographer—and the man who left us the only dirty anecdote about Burbage and Shakespeare—actually collected gossip. "What are the English like?" it might be asked. A worse answer might be given than "Read Aubrey's *Lives.*" H. L. Mencken collected strange given names, like Minnie Magazine and Dr. Gargle and Justin Tune and Ima Hogg, incidentally Houston's greatest collector of American furniture. Cardinal Ippolito Medici collected people who spoke different languages—he kept at his court a troop of barbarians who spoke no fewer than twenty tongues, "each of them perfect specimens of their races." Elsa Maxwell, the big-bummed, loud-voiced, understrapping society gossip-columnist for the *New York Journal-American* who knew only the wealthiest and most influential people in the world, actually collected them for profit—making introductions. It was a service. She was in great demand by lackeys for these all-important connections and charged quite a fee for making them.

A New York workman in the 1940s collected distances, donning a pedometer and going on walks he carefully measured. His notebooks contained such entries as "Walked from home to the fire station. 9 miles, 2 hours 16 min." and "Walked to Wall St. 5 miles, 1 hour, 4 min." He took special walks to the oldest tree, the oldest house, the World's Fair. He even kept a record of how many pairs of socks he ruined on the way. And what about the phenomenon of tulipomania in Holland? The crutches and trusses at Lourdes? Limericks? Indian *scalps?* Don't these also qualify?

A behavioral scientist at Brown University, Lewis Lipsitt, collects coincidences, specifically names that just happen to match occupations. *Aptonym* is the definitive term for such a name. Larry Speakes, for example, was a White House spokesperson, Sally Ride an astronaut,

Felicity Foote a dance teacher, James Bugg an exterminator, and indeed Dan Druff is a barber. Some other real, and choice, ones: Lionel Tiger and Robin Fox, who both write about animal behavior; Mr. Fish, who founded the University of Rhode Island Graduate School of Oceanography; Mr. Hawkes, head of the Rhode Island Audubon Society; Armand Hammer, a frequent American diplomat to the Soviet Union. And photographer Ralph Eugene Meatyard, who had one himself, also kept a looseleaf notebook of thousands of grotesque and absurd names.

A medical student, Joel Silidker, collects condom tins from the thirties and forties. The tins, containing usually three or four, were durable and had to be, since you never knew when you were going to need one. Some former brand names are *Le Transparent, Royal Knights, Duble-Tips,* and *Three Merry Widows.* A certain Russian countess paid fabulous sums for bedpans that once belonged to historical personages. Louise Nevelson collected used coffee filters, washing them, drying them, filing them away. Lizzie Borden, of forty whacks fame, collected birdhouses and feeders. A man in an Arturo Vivante story—*Of Love and Friendship*—collects lichens. There are collections made up of laurel leaves pinpricked with the Sign of the Cross. Jivaro Indians collect shrunken heads as trophy-fetishes. At the New York City morgue, there can be found nose bones saved that have been salvaged from victims of crimes, plane crashes, and various accidents. Then there is Wilson A. Bentley of Jericho, Vermont, who when he died in 1952 left a photo collection of more than 5,300 snowflakes, no two alike, which are on display in town. He took the pictures through a microscope. According to a report, "The flakes, caught on a cold board covered with black velvet, were photographed in Bentley's refrigerated camera room." A Vermont farmer all his life, Bentley is regarded as one of the pioneers of photomicrography.

Is that strange? There's a man in Pittsburgh who collects moist towelettes, a woman in Philadelphia who collects funnels. A man named Hanks in London collected spiderwebs, pressing them between panes of glass. E. Thomas Hughes of Washington has a passion for potatoes and potatoabilia: potato banks, potato poems, potato peelers. We shouldn't forget of course that J. Wellington Wimpy from the *Popeye* comic strip not only mooches hamburgers but collected college degrees—he had twenty-four. Elizabeth Tashjian collects nuts and runs the Nut Museum in Old Lyme, Connecticut (admission, through the eight-foot nutcracker, is one nut per person).

336

Writer Barry Paris collects the lids of non-dairy creamer containers. Francis Johnson, a haybaler from Darwin, Minnesota, has a collection of over seventeen hundred nail aprons, gathered from all fifty states. Old John McSorley, owner of the now-famous McSorley's Ale House on East Seventh Street in New York for many years collected wishbones of holiday turkeys and hung them on a string over the bar, where they are still gathering dust.

Child prodigy William Sidis (1898–1944), a mathematical wizard who entered Harvard at the youthful age eleven and had an I.Q. estimated at fifty to a hundred points higher than Einstein's (the highest, in fact, ever recorded or estimated), collected street-car transfers. He published transfer-collecting newsletters to correspond with other enthusiasts and to run a "transfer deposit bank" called the "Transfer X-Change," whereby collectors could make deposits and withdrawals through the mail. His own collection consisted of more than two thousand items. Several other correspondents claimed collections as large as five thousand transfers, representing more than a thousand cities.

Amenophis III of Egypt had an uncontrollable passion for things that were colored blue, and found in the ruins of his villa were blue cups, blue bowls, blue ampullae, blue amulets, blue jewels. The wise Solomon, we are told in First Kings, knew three thousand proverbs—surely a case of collecting. Jonathan Swift went around collecting jokes. A person in Southold, New York, collects nothing but videos of hockey fights. Members of the American Coaster Enthusiasts (ACE), a national club, collect roller-coaster experiences. And in his house at Talcottville, New York, Edmund Wilson collected autographs on windowpanes, asking famous poets to write verses from their work and sign their names with a diamond pen. Then there were the irrepressible Plaster Casters, several girl groupies from the hip sixties who went around collecting as memorabilia realistic impressions in plaster of their favorite rock stars' phalluses. Their favorite "rig" was Jimi Hendrix's.

King Farouk hid the world's greatest collection of erotic objects in the cellars of the Koubbeh Palace. Poet Philip Larkin supposedly collected pornography, too. And persistent rumors say the same of Sophia Loren and even Arturo Toscanini. There have been a good many sexual hunter-gatherers down through the years. Turkish sultan Abdul Hamid II, deposed in 1909, collected wives—he had 370. Victor Hugo, who was sexually insatiable, often made love to three or four women a day. Sarah Bernhardt, who was raised in a convent and died at eighty-one, had more than a thousand affairs in her lifetime. Rubens, Diego Rivera, Modigliani—all slept with thousands of women. (One of those women, in Modigliani's case, Suzanne Thiroux, distantly related to our family, had a child by him.) Most of their models sat for them in the nude and before any painting sessions usually made love with them. Satyriasis or nymphomania may be considered to be a form of collecting until we stop to realize that it's quite the opposite, noncollecting, shedding in fact, *repudiation*.

There are prostitutes in the Far East—I am not making this up—who collect fluff from the navels of their clients. And a chambermaid in Louisville, Kentucky, according to Liberace, who recounted this story, collected—in matchboxes, and kept like relics on tiny pieces of cotton—the pubic hairs of the rich and famous. "When I make up the bed, I look on the sheets and I know who they belong to," she said (in Bob Thomas's 1987 biography *Liberace*). "It's a very valuable collection." Among others, she has Rudolf Valentino's, Mickey Rooney's, and of course Liberace's. Manfred Klauda has collected eight thousand chamber pots, including Roman glass flasks from the second century B.C., English "Non-Splash Thunder Bowls," a fifty-thousand-dollar eighteenth-century Bourdalou, and many other varieties. Alfred Kinsey collected penile measurements and had more than 2,500 graphics of erections on paper. And didn't the prophet Elijah purportedly collect the prepuces of Jewish boys?

Legend has it that the classic rake Giovanni Casanova, a man tall, dark, and powerfully built, was capable in his prime of having sex anywhere, with anyone, and in any position, with particular reference to the positions described by the sixteenth-century satirist Pietro Aretino. In fourteen years of life in the NBA, with almost one hundred different teammates, there was only one man, according to basketball star Wilt Chamberlain, among all those players—Paul Arizin—who was content with his marriage and didn't use road trips to cheat on his wife. So are we talking about collecting here in any way, shape, or form? Can Casanova's attitude toward sex be described as anything but wastrelism? Or Errol Flynn's? Or Alma Schindler's, who "collected" celebrity husbands—Gustav Mahler, Franz Werfel, Oskar Kokoschka (she merely lived with him three years), Walter Gropius? No, no, no. Collecting is having to hold.

Collecting can frequently give way to mania. Charles Lindbergh was so beleaguered by trophy-seekers that he could not send his shirts to the cleaners and expect to get them back. Franz Liszt's cigar butts were snatched up in the street, and on one occasion an admirer cut out and preserved his chair seat as a relic. Many collectors are pilferers—candid thieves who pillage hotels, dining cars, and steamships of linen, soaps, ashtrays, and silver. Depredations. Outlawry without penalty. And it has given way to madness. A fifteen-year-old high school boy from New York with otherwise perfect deportment found his valued collection missing only the rare penny orange Mauritius, worth $20,000, and became so unstrung in the knowledge that he could never possess it that he got a gun, went out, and proceeded to hold up the shop.

Thwarted in hope, the average collector usually takes defeat reasonably well. However, in extremis the desire can become sheer obsession, almost a disease. The Bluebeard of bibliophilia was a Spanish ex-monk named Don Vicente who murdered twelve other collectors in order to acquire various "unique" volumes. During his trial he remained calm until his lawyer, seeking to prove him innocent, revealed that another copy of one of the books he'd killed to acquire was for sale in Paris. Vicente became hysterical and until the moment he mounted the scaffold did nothing but bellow, "Alas! Alas! Alas! My copy is not unique!" The king of Thrace once broke an exquisite vase deliberately so that it could not be broken by accident. And Matsunaga Danjo, a sixteenth-century constable, intentionally smashed his favorite teapot to smithereens rather than let it fall into the hands of a rival collector.

King Charles I understood the passionate collector's psychology (he never went anywhere without miniature copies of his paintings). When Sir Robert Cotton, a zealous book collector himself, fell into the king's disfavor, Charles forbade him to enter his own library. It was an effective punishment—Cotton died of the deprivation. An interesting sidelight. On the day Oliver Cromwell had the king beheaded in what is now Trafalgar Square, sympathizers—collectors, in a manner of speaking—steeped their handkerchiefs in his blood and they are now considered saintly relics. I once saw a painting of the king with a glowing halo set off in the reliquarial niche of an Anglican church in London's East End.

Speaking of royalty, Prince Charles has admitted to collecting more than a hundred toilet seats. Prince Philip, his father, has a large collection of contemporary cartoons of himself, many of which hang in the lavatory at Sandringham. And Queen Victoria was known for collecting photographs and sketches of friends who had died (indeed, anyone with whom she was even remotely connected who had died), often *immediately* on hearing of their death.

The cartoonist Saul Steinberg seems to have a penchant for collecting telephone books. Waitress Marlow Freeman has a collection of more than 2,300 refrigerator magnets. James Lowe, "Mr. Postcard of America"—"deltiology" is the name given to postcard collecting—has around 400,000 of them. ("The picture postcard's golden age," he says, "was from 1907 to 1915.") Singer Jackie Wilson collected comic books, especially Marvel Comics and Conan the Barbarian, virtually the only kind of reading of which he was capable. David and Cynthia Walsh of Murphysboro, Illinois, collect Pez holders. And Andy Warhol collected semi-used perfumes ("by having smells stopped up in bottles, I can be in control and can only smell the smells I want. . . . I realized [also] I had to have a kind of smell museum so certain smells wouldn't get lost forever." He added, "I used to be afraid I would eventually run through and use up all the good colognes and there'd be nothing left but things like 'Grape' and 'Musk.'") And actor Douglas Fairbanks, Sr., had more than thirty-five overcoats, mostly of camel's hair—he loved overcoats!

Who are those who collect? And why? Is it a hopeless addiction? A preoccupation only for the crack-pated, the antiquarian mind simply schooled in the ways of the census? Some sort of misguided compulsion for finality? (English prime minister and passionate bibliophile Lord Melbourne pronounced upon the death of the poet George Crabbe, "I am always happy when one of those fellows dies, for then I know I have the whole of him on my shelf.") The unavoidable fact is that a good many of us collect. This queer fascination, far older than cabinets and shelves, is as elemental and has universal appeal. As novelist Laurence Sterne observes in *Tristram Shandy*, "Nay, if you come to that, Sir, have not the wisest of men in all ages, not excepting Solomon himself,—have they not had their Hobby-Horses;—their running horses,—their coins and their cockle-shells, their drums and their trumpets, their fiddles, their pallets,—their maggots and their butterflies?"

Madame de Pompadour had more than fifty varieties of orange trees. Liberace had forty-four candelabra and twenty-two pianos. Jean-Baptiste D'Albert de Luynes, born in 1670 in Paris, owned upward of sixty urns filled with different kinds of snuff and, as a logical adjunct, five hundred dozen handkerchiefs. Speaking of handkerchiefs, Bette Davis is said to have had a great many and to have been very persnickety about the way they were ironed. Catherine de Medici had a superb collection of fashion dolls, as does Romanian gymnast Nadia Comaneci. Janine Montupet, French novelist and author of *The Lacemaker*, collects heirloom lace. Poet Rod McKuen collects T-shirts.

340

Gangster Mickey Cohen collected—hoarded—socks. In their western-style museum in Victorville, California, can be seen Roy Rogers' and Dale Evans's collection of taxidermy, not only Trigger, Buttermilk, and Bullet—Roy and Dale's famous horses and dogs—but hundreds of other specimens. (There are also hundreds of guns, two captured from the Vietcong, presumably not by Roy.) Hank Williams also collected guns and lugged them everywhere. Entrepreneur Scott Bruce collects metal lunch boxes (a 1954 Superman Robot model goes for two thousand dollars) and has launched *Flake,* a newsletter for cereal box collectors. And I've heard that Warren Beatty has closets full of bathrobes from Tokyo's Imperial Hotel.

The Secret Archives of the Vatican constitute the world's largest collection of primary sources for almost two thousand years of history, both religious and secular. Each pope, from Saint Peter on, added to the vast treasures until today the archives occupy twenty-five miles of shelves. Among the extraordinary collection of documents are the records of the trials of Giordano Bruno, Galileo, Pico della Mirandola, and Savonarola for heresy; Beatrice Cenci's murder of her father; the conversion of Queen Christina of Sweden; and a good deal of the diplomatic gossip of the Renaissance, reflected in the reports of the papal nuncios. So vast is the collection that many objects remain unindexed and have not been looked at for centuries.

Relics, incidentally, which are a large part of the Church's collections, have been maintained in an attempt to assure the continuation of its common life, of the living with the dead. There were 19,013 relics in a sixteenth-century church in Wittenberg. And a church in Halle in 1521 supposedly had 21,483. (Among the most famous relics of the church are those of the apostle James, Saint Peter's bones, the so-called *sudarium* of Saint Veronica, and the bodies of the three kings, which were brought from Milan to Köln in 1164 by the emperor Frederick I.) The sultans in Istanbul's Topkapi Palace have a silver footprint of the Prophet Mohammed and several hairs from his beard. There's a tooth in a temple in Ceylon. And the Shwedegon Pagoda is built over . . . a femur of the Buddha?

Harold E. Burtt, a professor emeritus at Ohio State, collects and classifies moss. Illustrator Durell Godfrey collects stitched mottoes on linen. Novelist Umberto Eco collects rare books on science and the occult, "as long as they're wrong," he once pointed out. And Owen Evan-Thomas of London owned more than a thousand pieces of treen, wood utensils, once the common ware of the people—saltcellars, mortars, drinking vessels, mazers (bowls), molds, and mills. The most primitive, and the rarest, specimens are the earliest used dinner plates, simple squares of sycamore hollowed in the middle. The oval meat platter, with a well for gravy, is on lines that have never been improved upon. *Thinking* involves collecting. Bertrand Russell's "Theory of Types," which postulates a hierarchy of types of objects, gatherings grouped to form sets (where, say, the first type is individuals, the second classes of individuals, and the third classes of individuals), becomes a collection in itself.

Fin-de-siècle dandy and decadent Count Robert de Montesquieu collected strange out-of-the-way treasures. In one of his residences on the rue Quai d'Orsay he owned, among other things, the bullet that killed Aleksandr Pushkin, a cigarette partially smoked by George Sand, a tear (dried) once shed by Alphonse de Lamartine, the slippers of Lord Byron's great passion, the Countess Guiccioli, and a birdcage that had once housed Jules Michelet's pet canary, along with a jewel box containing a single hair from the beard of the same historian. In his garden he kept Madame de Montespan's pink marble tub overflowing with rambler roses. One of his favorite objects was a bedpan used by Napoleon after Waterloo. He had also acquired a plaster cast of the knees of Madame de Castiglione, the femme fatale of the Second Empire court who in her prime had had herself photographed 190 times. (Montesquieu, not to be outdone, had himself photographed 199 times.)

Goethe collected minerals. Tony Hyman of Elmira, New York, collects cigar boxes and owns four thousand. Ernest Reda of San Jose, California, has a collection of more than three thousand crucifixes. "You'd be surprised," he said, "you can find crosses everywhere." A barber gave him a cross made of human hair; a prison inmate sent a cross made of Camel cigarette packs; someone in Mexico contributed clippings from a bush that grows in the shape of a cross and has thorns where the hands and feet go. Roy Cohn, an avaricious lawyer with a distinctly saurian appearance, collected frogs. And yet, in what dark way do these collections conjure up our anti-selves?

Ghoulishness has cast its dark shadow across the world of collections. The Japanese samurai of the sixteenth century collected the noses and ears of Koreans they killed, and there's a mountain in Nara, the Mimidzuka, or "Ear-Mound," where 38,000 pairs of ears and the noses to match are buried. The Iban tribes of Borneo collect trophy heads and wear them as ornaments from their belts. Charles Semsen, a seventeenth-century Parisian hangman, collected paintings depicting torture and death. William Rosetti, who went after anything "odd, Chinese, or sparkling," was famous for a collection that included, along with the lantern of murderer Eugene Aram, hangman's nooses and executioner's axes. Artist Jean Dubuffet had a large collection of what he called *art brut* (raw art), much of it produced by psychotics. Nancy Reagan's pal Jerry Zipkin collects snakelike objects, stuffed snakes, lamps like cobras, and so on. Artist Fritz Scholder collects mummies, but what he prizes most in his collection his wife gave him, a vial of mummy dust, seriously considered the ultimate nostrum during Victorian times. And I've several times been to Edward Gorey's attic in Yarmouthport, Massachusetts and seen his collection of skulls—iron skulls, ivory skulls, beanbag skulls, skull watches, drawings of them, shelf after shelf. He also collects, along with fur coats— and will only wear—iron jewelry. This collection of cast-iron claw feet from antique bathtubs sit like Cycladic busts on his bookshelves.

Anton La Vey, founder of the International Church of Satan, has a vast collection of Satanabilia, including an ancient Egyptian skull, two crossbows, a stuffed wolf, shrunken heads, and a reproduction of King Tut's sarcophagus. One of Ezio Pinza's passions was collecting Florentine poison rings. During the eighteenth and early nineteenth centuries many collectors in England were desperate for pieces of rope from hanging victims, and hangmen made money by improvising longer ropes, which they cut into souvenir lengths and sold after executions.

To try speculating on what informs the collecting mind is intriguing. In essence, there are two kinds of collectors: those who find the One in the Many, and those who find the Many in the One. (There's a legend that Joseph Stalin had copies of the same room constructed in buildings all over Russia so that no matter what town he was in, he'd always feel at home—an odd example both of collecting and of *refusing* to collect at the same time!) Collectors spend their lives like Hawthornian protagonists turning over rocks and looking for absolutes. Many people, for instance, grow insensibly attached to what gives them a great deal of trouble. The mere challenge of collecting may generate the impulse, the impossibility of success like the inevitability in high-jumping of failure guaranteeing a strange kind of buoyancy, because it is endless.

But the truth is closer to the heart, and surely far less complicated.

The need for an individual to be complete—and odd collections are, if anything, *specific* collections, as close to a person's personality as a name, a fingerprint, the shape of a nose—is often behind the seemingly fun-filled and off-handed accumulation of one kind of object, which is in too many instances nothing less than an ontological drive, a quest for identification. W. B. Yeats writes in his poem "Ego Dominus Tuus" of the need in a person for "the vision of reality" that the poet defines as art, writing, "By the help of an image/I call to my own opposite, summon all/That I have handled least, least looked upon." It is arguably no different for the collector than for Ille in his dialogue with Hic in this seminal poem on the nature of identity between artist and nonartist when he insists, "These characters [antiselves], disclose all that I seek." Artifice, I am not the first to assert, can establish adequacy. And could we not argue that, as Freud once pointed out regarding the first four or five earliest wishes of a child, we remain incomplete all our lives until and unless they are fulfilled? How else may we characterize the otherwise seemingly innocuous object, like Valjean's candlesticks? Charles Foster Kane's sled? The rookie Mickey Mantle card that Bob Costas obsessively carries in his wallet as much to recall his youth as his baseball idol? There is no empirical reason, no strong, salient autobiographical disclosure in Jerry Lewis, a miserable child and social pariah growing up, even to his parents, later owning eighty-eight tuxedos, more than the duke of Windsor? In Nancy Cunard's horde of African bracelets? In biologically childless Joan Crawford's having in a secret bedroom of her house a collection of two thousand dolls, or Amelia Earhart, who dressed very plainly, keeping in a private closet, found only after her death, closets full of high-fashion clothes?

Collecting is confession, just as clearly (and obviously) as taking a choice is making a disclosure. In our assemblages we repeatedly show what for us stands as the summum bonum, an "axis of bias," if you will, regarding objects that, as we gather them, paradoxically give us away. It is all of it less an aspect of acquisition than it is ambition. Ambition is rarely found in its healthy form.

Nominated by The Yale Review, Sherod Santos

ERRATA MYSTAGOGIA

by BRUCE BEASLEY

from THE GETTYSBURG REVIEW

(*Summer Mystagogia*, University Press of Colorado, 1996)

There, in the misprints and vacant
pages, garbled
syntax of the proofreaders' spoils,

even the word *disfiguring* disfigured,
in the trail of twelve misspellings,
where adjectives cling to the wrong
nouns (*woodwasps*
instead of *dogwoods*
made pink),

I track the unfixable

world, its slippery
letters, lessons
no one wants to know how to learn. . . .

Where Augustine poses his question
so emphatically
it takes *two* question marks
to get it right:
All these lovely but mutable

345

things, who has made them
but Beauty immutable??

This mutable
book, its muted
voice, goes out to its warehouses and bookshops
with three pages gone,
second half of "The Reliquary Book"
(beginning "its passages
unmovably bound")

left blank, bound—
by the printwheels' skip—
to oblivion.
So I write this

errata sheet
for the uncorrectable proof
of the world: initiation
into the half-

hearted and bungled, *jug*
become *jog, beaks*
transfigured to *breaks,*
the *aggrsseive month for the ova,*
ellipses
inserted in the middle of a word
as though the lacuna
of language
couldn't help but bleed through. . . .

If Wallace Stevens had won the Colorado Prize,

a friend tells me, *we'd be reading*
"Anecdote of the Jog. . . . "

October, no apology from the editor,
no answer at all, word
of a relative
with water surrounding her heart, rain

dribbling from a birdbath where hollyhocks
shed the last of their pink
(woodwasps? erratum: blooms)

over a gash in the ground where a shallow-
rooted forsythia collapsed in a squall—
On the news, the usual
botch: dull scrub of clearcut hills, hacked
groves of juniper and fir, cheery
senator posed over the saplings:
READY FOR HARVEST IN 2035—

Then a man
with a hatchet
left permanently in his head, its blade
too close to the brain

to remove . . .

The book
broken

in a mutable world, errata
inserted in the place of every page.

> *for David Milofsky*

Nominated by Linda Bierds, Robin Hemley

THE DEAD BOY AT YOUR WINDOW

fiction by BRUCE HOLLAND ROGERS

from THE NORTH AMERICAN REVIEW

IN A DISTANT COUNTRY where the towns had improbable names, a woman looked upon the unmoving form of her newborn baby and refused to see what the midwife saw. This was her son. She had brought him forth in agony, and now he must suck. She pressed his lips to her breast.

"But he is dead!" said the midwife.

"No," his mother lied. "I felt him suck just now." Her lie was as milk to the baby, who really was dead but who now opened his dead eyes and began to kick his dead legs. "There, do you see?" And she made the midwife call the father in to know his son.

The dead boy never did suck at his mother's breast. He sipped no water, never took food of any kind, so of course he never grew. But his father, who was handy with all things mechanical, built a rack for stretching him so that, year by year, he could be as tall as the other children.

When he had seen six winters, his parents sent him to school. Though he was as tall as the other students, the dead boy was strange to look upon. His bald head was almost the right size, but the rest of him was thin as a piece of leather and dry as a stick. He tried to make up for his ugliness with diligence, and every night he was up late practicing his letters and numbers.

His voice was like the rasping of dry leaves. Because it was so hard to hear him, the teacher made all the other students hold their breaths when he gave an answer. She called on him often, and he was always right.

Naturally, the other children despised him. The bullies sometimes waited for him after school, but beating him, even with sticks, did him no harm. He wouldn't even cry out.

One windy day, the bullies stole a ball of twine from their teacher's desk, and after school, they held the dead boy on the ground with his arms out so that he took the shape of a cross. They ran a stick in through his left shirt sleeve and out through the right. They stretched his shirt tails down to his ankles, tied everything in place, fastened the ball of twine to a button-hole, and launched him. To their delight, the dead boy made an excellent kite. It only added to their pleasure to see that owing to the weight of his head, he flew upside down.

When they were bored with watching the dead boy fly, they let go of the string. The dead boy did not drift back to earth, as any ordinary kite would do. He glided. He could steer a little, though he was mostly at the mercy of the winds. And he could not come down. Indeed, the wind blew him higher and higher.

The sun set, and still the dead boy rode the wind. The moon rose and by its glow he saw the fields and forests drifting by. He saw mountain ranges pass beneath him, and oceans and continents. At last the winds gentled, then ceased, and he glided down to the ground in a strange country. The ground was bare. The moon and stars had vanished from the sky. The air seemed gray and shrouded. The dead boy leaned to one side and shook himself until the stick fell from his shirt. He wound up the twine that had trailed behind him and waited for the sun to rise. Hour after long hour, there was only the same grayness. So he began to wander.

He encountered a man who looked much like himself, a bald head atop leathery limbs. "Where am I?" the dead boy asked.

The man looked at the grayness all around. "Where?" the man said. His voice, like the dead boy's, sounded like the whisper of dead leaves stirring.

A woman emerged from the grayness. Her head was bald, too, and her body dried out. "This!" she rasped, touching the dead boy's shirt. "I remember this!" She tugged on the dead boy's sleeve. "I had a thing like this!"

"Clothes?" said the dead boy.

"Clothes!" the woman cried. "That's what it is called!"

More shriveled people came out of the grayness. They crowded close to see the strange dead boy who wore clothes. Now the dead boy knew where he was. "This is the land of the dead."

"Why do you have clothes?" asked the dead woman. "We came here with nothing! Why do you have clothes?"

"I have always been dead," said the dead boy, "but I spent six years among the living."

"Six years!" said one of the dead. "And you have only just now come to us?"

"Did you know my wife?" asked a dead man. "Is she still among the living?"

"Give me news of my son!"

"What about my sister?"

The dead people crowded closer.

The dead boy said, "What is your sister's name?" But the dead could not remember the names of their loved ones. They did not even remember their own names. Likewise, the names of the places where they had lived, the numbers given to their years, the manners or fashions of their times, all of these they had forgotten.

"Well," said the dead boy, "in the town where I was born, there was a widow. Maybe she was your wife. I knew a boy whose mother had died, and an old woman who might have been your sister."

"Are you going back?"

"Of course not," said another dead person. "No one ever goes back."

"I think I might," the dead boy said. He explained about his flying. "When next the wind blows. . . ."

"The wind never blows here," said a man so newly dead that he remembered wind.

"Then you could run with my string."

"Would that work?"

"Take a message to my husband!" said a dead woman.

"Tell my wife that I miss her!" said a dead man.

"Let my sister know I haven't forgotten her!"

"Say to my lover that I love him still!"

They gave him their messages, not knowing whether or not their loved ones were themselves long dead. Indeed, dead lovers might well be standing next to one another in the land of the dead, giving messages for each other to the dead boy. Still, he memorized them all. Then the dead put the stick back inside his shirt sleeves, tied everything in place, and unwound his string. Running as fast as their leathery legs could manage, they pulled the dead boy back into the sky, let go of the string, and watched with their dead eyes as he glided away.

350

He glided a long time over the gray stillness of death until at last a puff of wind blew him higher, until a breath of wind took him higher still, until a gust of wind carried him up above the grayness to where he could see the moon and the stars. Below he saw moonlight reflected in the ocean. In the distance rose mountain peaks. The dead boy came to earth in a little village. He knew no one here, but he went to the first house he came to and rapped on the bedroom shutters. To the woman who answered, he said, "A message from the land of the dead," and gave her one of the messages. The woman wept, and gave him a message in return.

House by house, he delivered the messages. House by house, he collected messages for the dead. In the morning, he found some boys to fly him, to give him back to the wind's mercy so he could carry these new messages back to the land of the dead.

So it has been ever since. On any night, head full of messages, he may rap upon any window to remind someone—to remind you, perhaps—of love that outlives memory, of love that needs no names.

Nominated by Joyce Carol Oates, Robley Wilson

INVISIBLE MAN

by JAS. MARDIS

from KENTE CLOTH (University of North Texas Press)

Too often
the sun rises and retreats
and I am no one
not even me

and the world's eyes
pass through me over me
and the heavy shouldered walking
that I do
and the swagger in my steps
doesn't matter
doesn't matter
and the rise of air in my chest
and the full barrel of my chest
doesn't matter

and the heavy fisted pounding
of my words and ideas and feelings
doesn't matter
doesn't matter
and the hurried shouting of my blood
through my veins
through my veins
doesn't matter
and the jagged resolve of my anger
the constant checking of my anger

and the constant/steady checking
of my angers
doesn't matter
and the, and the, and the
sadness of my life
the daily sad nest of my life
being seen
being looked upon and not seen
or heard
or had
or noticed
beyond anything
other than being in the way
being seen
only to be avoided
only to be watched
only to be ignored
replaced
dismissed
Dis—
Dis—
Dis—

I never read Ellison's "Invisible Man"
or Wright's "Black Boy"
or John Howard Griffin
and his "Black Like Me"
as anything more
than
life guides
because I knew long ago
somewhere
in the womb
where the wall of blood
and birth mucus flowed
I knew
while floating in that sack
that swollen sanctuary
I knew
even then

with that tiny hole of daylight
calling me
I knew then—even then

as I churned into becoming a child
as I swelled my mother's womb
and pushed her belly outward
into the round pleasure
that pregnancy brings the world

I knew then
that
as far as the world was concerned
I was making
my most visible
mark

Nominated by The University of North Texas Press

DEAR MOTHER

fiction by HARRY MATHEWS

from DENVER QUARTERLY

for James Tate and in memory of William Cullen Bryant

THIS IS WHERE I once saw a deaf girl playing in a field. Because I did not know how to approach her without startling her, or how I would explain my presence, I hid. I felt so disgusting, I might as well have raped the child, a grown man on his belly in a field watching a deaf girl play. My suit was stained by the grass and I was an hour late for dinner. I was forced to discard my suit for lack of a reasonable explanation to my wife, a hundred dollar suit! We're not rich people, not at all. So there I was, left to my wool suit in the heat of summer, soaked through by noon each day. I was an embarrassment to the entire firm: it is not good for the morale of the fellow worker to flaunt one's poverty. After several weeks of crippling tension, my superior finally called me into his office. Rather than humiliate myself by telling him the truth, I told him I would wear whatever damned suit I pleased, a suit of armor if I fancied. It was the first time I had challenged his authority. And it was the last. I was dismissed. Given my pay. On the way home I thought, I'll tell her the truth, yes, why not! Tell her the simple truth, she'll love me for it. What a touching story. Well, I didn't. I don't know what happened, a loss of courage, I suppose. I told her a mistake I had made had cost the company several thousand dollars, and that not only was I dismissed, I would also somehow have to find the money to repay them the sum of my error. She wept, she beat me, she accused me of everything from malice to impotency. I helped her pack and drove her to the bus station. It was too late to explain. She would never believe me now. How cold the house was without her. How silent. Each plate I dropped was like tearing the flesh from a living animal. When all were shattered, I knelt in a corner and tried to imagine what I would say to her, the girl in the field. What did it matter what I said, since she wouldn't hear me? I could say anything I liked.

Next day after eating lunch out of a plastic container I went back to the field. I'd found my stained suit on the floor of the closet where I'd dumped it. The added rumpling and dirt made it look even worse. I put it on anyway—I'd been wearing it at the beginning of this misadventure, and I wanted to be wearing it at the end. I do not know if this was a mistake or not. The little girl was playing not far from where I'd seen her the first time. I stood at some distance inside the edge of the field and spoke to her in a voice neither loud nor soft. I said that my wife's lawyer had called earlier to say that she was filing for divorce, but that I would never blame her, the little girl, for that. I told her that she was beautiful, that in a way I loved her, that even though I was utterly unhappy I would remember the scene of her in the field without bitterness. I had more to say, but the girl had stood up and turned to me as though she had heard me, which it soon transpired she had. She was not so little, either, but rather tall and, as she approached me, plainly of a more nubile constitution than I had conceived from afar. She pointed toward me and in a confident voice cried, "That's him!" to persons that were out of my sight for the good reason that they were standing behind me, three men and two women dressed in serious garb, whom I took to be officials of some sort. I then sank into such torment that I suffered a kind of seizure, from whose effects I have taken several months to recover. It turned out that I could not have fallen into better hands, for those five strangers were medical people, and they have tended me, I assure you, with extraordinary care. My indisposition nevertheless has kept me from writing to you sooner, and that is why now, before recounting the most recent events, dear Mother, I hasten to send you the melancholy intelligence of what has recently happened to me.

Early on the evening of the eleventh day of the present month I was at a neighboring house in this village. Several people of both sexes were assembled in one of the apartments, and three or four others, with myself, were in another. At last came in a little elderly gentleman, pale, thin, with a solemn countenance, hooked nose, and hollow eyes. It was not long before we were summoned to attend in the apartment where he and the rest of the company were gathered. We went in and took our seats; the little elderly gentleman with the hooked nose prayed, and we all stood up. When he had finished, most of us sat down. The gentleman with the hooked nose then muttered certain cabalistical expressions which I was much too frightened to remember, but I recollect that at the conclusion I was given to understand that I was married to a young lady of the name of Juniper Simmons, whom I perceived standing by my side, and I hope in the course of a few months to have the pleasure of introducing to you as your daughter-in-law, which is a matter of some interest to the poor girl, who has neither father nor mother in the world.

I looked only for goodness of heart, an ingenuous and affectionate disposition, a good understanding, etc., and the character of my wife is too frank and single-hearted to suffer me to fear that I may be disappointed. I do myself wrong; I did not look for these nor any other qualities, but they trapped me before I was aware, and now I am married in spite of myself.

Thus the current of destiny carries us along. None but a madman would swim against the stream, and none but a fool would exert himself to swim with it. The best way is to float quietly with the tide.

Nominated by Denver Quarterly

THE GIRLS LEARN TO LEVITATE

by ADRIENNE SU

from THE GREENSBORO REVIEW

At last, they are not girls.
They were not born to a house of wailing.
The housekeeper, who owns one pair of shoes, did not look upon
  them with pity.

As the sun sinks, they no longer inhabit their bodies.
Their bodies did not inhabit their mother's body.
Their mother did not waste her blood.

They are lighter, lighter;
they did not fail at suicide.
Little souls escaping, they drift to the kitchen ceiling like steam.

From above, they watch the bodies
pour cups of tea, eat pork dumplings,
fold and refold lace napkins.

They watch the boys push the bodies around;
they watch the parents plot their fates:
a profitable marriage, a caretaker in age.

Although the bodies protest, the girls feel nothing.
Out on the balcony, concentrating on the release
of earthly burdens, they rise unsteadily to the orange sky.

Nominated by Rita Dove

THE MARCH OF THE NOVEL THROUGH HISTORY: THE TESTIMONY OF MY GRANDFATHER'S BOOKCASE

essay by AMITAV GHOSH

from THE KENYON REVIEW

As a child I spent my holidays in my grandfather's house in Calcutta, and it was there that I began to read. My grandfather's house was a chaotic and noisy place, populated by a large number of uncles, aunts, cousins, and dependents, some of them bizarre, some merely eccentric, but almost all excitable in the extreme. Yet I learned much more about reading in this house than I ever did in school.

The walls of my grandfather's house were lined with rows of books, neatly stacked in glass-fronted bookcases. The bookcases were prominently displayed in a large hall that served, among innumerable other functions, also those of playground, sitting room, and hallway. The bookcases towered above us, looking down, eavesdropping on every conversation, keeping track of family gossip, glowering upon quarreling children. Very rarely were the bookcases stirred out of their silent vigil: I was perhaps the only person in the house who raided them regularly, and I was in Calcutta for no more than a couple of months every year. When the bookcases were disturbed in my absence, it was usually not for their contents but because some special occasion required their cleaning. If the impending event happened to concern a weighty matter, like a delicate marital negotiation, the bookcases got a very thorough scrubbing indeed. And well they deserved it, for at such times they were important props in the little plays that were enacted in their presence. They let the visitor know that this was a house in which books were valued; in other words, that we were cultivated people. This is always important in Calcutta, for Calcutta is an oddly bookish city.

Were we indeed cultivated people? I wonder. On the whole I don't think so. In my memory my grandfather's house is always full—of aunts, uncles, cousins. I am astonished sometimes when I think of how many people it housed, fed, entertained, educated. But my uncles were busy, practical, and, on the whole, successful professionals, with little time to spend on books.

Only one of my uncles was a real reader. He was a shy and rather retiring man, not the kind of person who takes it upon himself to educate his siblings or improve his relatives' taste. The books in the bookcases were almost all his. He was too quiet a man to carry much weight in family matters, and his views never counted for much when the elders sought each other's counsel. Yet despite the fullness of the house and the fierce competition for space, it was taken for granted that his bookcases would occupy the place of honor in the hall. Eventually, tiring of his noisy relatives, my book-loving uncle decided to move to a house of his own in a distant and uncharacteristically quiet part of the city. But oddly enough the bookcases stayed; by this time the family was so attached to them that they were less dispensable than my uncle.

In the years that followed, the house passed into the hands of a branch of the family that was definitely very far from bookish. Yet their attachment to the bookcases seemed to increase inversely to their love of reading. I had been engaged in a secret pillaging of the bookcases for a very long time. Under the new regime my depredations came to a sudden halt; at the slightest squeak of a hinge, hordes of cousins would materialize suddenly around my ankles, snapping dire threats.

It served no purpose to tell them that the books were being consumed by maggots and mildew, that books rotted when they were not read. Arguments such as these interested them not at all: as far as they were concerned the bookcases and their contents were a species of property and were subject to the same laws.

This attitude made me impatient, even contemptuous at the time. Books were meant to be read, I thought, by people who valued and understood them: I felt not the slightest remorse for my long years of thievery. It seemed to me a terrible waste, and injustice that nonreaders should succeed in appropriating my uncle's library. Today I am not so sure. Perhaps those cousins were teaching me a lesson that was important on its own terms: they were teaching me respect; they were teaching me to value the printed word. Would anyone who had not learned these lessons well be foolhardy enough to imagine that a living could be made from words? I doubt it.

In another way they were also teaching me what a book is, a proper book, that is, not just printed paper gathered between covers. However much I may have chafed against the regime that stood between me and the bookcases, I have not forgotten those lessons. For me, to this day, a book, a proper book, is and always will be the kind of book that was on those bookshelves.

And what exactly was this kind of book?

Although no one had ever articulated any guidelines about them, so far as I know, there were in fact some fairly strict rules about the books that were allowed onto those shelves. Textbooks and schoolbooks were never allowed; nor were books of a technical or professional nature—nothing to do with engineering, or medicine, or law, or indeed any of the callings that afforded my uncles their livings. In fact, the great majority of the books were of a single kind; they were novels. There was some poetry, too, but novels were definitely the mainstay. There were a few works of anthropology and psychology, books that had in some way filtered into the literary consciousness of the time: *The Golden Bough,* for example, as well as the *Collected Works of Sigmund Freud,* Marx and Engels's *Manifesto,* Havelock Ellis and Malinowski on sexual behavior, and so on.

But without a doubt it was the novel that weighed most heavily on the floors of my grandfather's house. To this day I am unable to place a textbook or a computer manual upon a bookshelf without a twinge of embarrassment.

This is how Nirad Chaudhuri, that erstwhile Calcuttan, accounts for the position that novels occupy in Bengali cultural life:

> It has to be pointed out that in the latter half of the nineteenth century Bengali life and Bengali literature had become very closely connected and literature was bringing into the life of educated Bengalis something which they could not get from any other source. Whether in the cities and towns or in the villages, where the Bengali gentry still had the permanent base of their life, it was the mainstay of their life of feeling, sentiment and passion. Both emotional capacity and idealism were sustained by it. . . . When my sister was married in 1916, a college friend of mine presented her with fifteen of the latest novels by the foremost writers and my sister certainly did not prize them less than her far more costly clothes and jewelry. In fact, sales of fiction and poetry as wedding presents were a sure standby of their publishers. (155)

About a quarter of the novels in my uncle's bookcases were in Bengali—a representative selection of the mainstream tradition of Bengali fiction in the twentieth century. Prominent among these were the works of Bankim Chandra, Sarat Chandra, Tagore, Bibhuti Bhushan, and so on. The rest were in English. But of these only a small proportion consisted of books that had been originally written in English. The others were translations from a number of other languages, most of them European: Russian had pride of place, followed by French, Italian, German, and Danish. The great masterpieces of the nineteenth century were dutifully represented: the novels of Dostoevsky, Tolstoy, and Turgenev, of Victor Hugo, Flaubert, Stendhal, Maupassant, and others. But these were the dustiest books of all, placed on shelves that were lofty but remote.

The books that were prominently displayed were an oddly disparate lot—or so they seem today. Some of those titles can still be seen on bookshelves everywhere: Joyce, Faulkner, and so on. But many others have long since been forgotten: Marie Corelli and Grazia Deledda, for instance, names that are so little known today, even in Italy, that they have become a kind of secret incantation for me, a password that allows entry into the brotherhood of remembered bookcases. Knut Hamsun, too, was once a part of this incantation, but unlike the others his reputation has since had an immense revival—and with good reason.

Other names from those shelves have become, in this age of resurgent capitalism, symbols of a certain kind of embarrassment or unease—the social realists, for example. But on my uncle's shelves they stood tall and proud, Russians and Americans alike: Maksim Gorky, Mikhail Sholokhov, John Steinbeck, Upton Sinclair. There were many others, too, whose places next to each other seem hard to account for at first glance: Sienkiewicz (of *Quo Vadis?*), Maurice Maeterlinck, Bergson. Recently, looking through the mildewed remnants of those shelves, I came upon what must have been the last addition to that collection. It was Ivo Andrić's *Bridge on the Drina,* published in the sixties.

For a long time I was at a loss to account for my uncle's odd assortment of books. I knew their eclecticism couldn't really be ascribed to personal idiosyncrasies of taste. My uncle was a keen reader, but he was not, I suspect, the kind of person who allows his own taste to steer him through libraries and bookshops. On the contrary, he was a reader of the kind whose taste is guided largely by prevalent opinion. This uncle, I might add, was a writer himself, in a modest way. He wrote plays in an epic vein with characters borrowed from the Sanskrit classics. He never left India and indeed rarely ventured out of his home state of West Bengal.

The principles that guided my uncle's taste would have been much clearer to me had I ever had an interest in trivia. To the quiz-show adept, the link between Grazia Deledda, Gorky, Hamsun, Sholokhov, Sienkiewicz, and Andrić will be clear at once: it is the Nobel Prize for Literature.

Writing about the Calcutta of the twenties and thirties, Nirad Chaudhuri says:

> To be up to date about literary fashions was a greater craze among us than to be up to date in clothes is with society women, and this desire became keener with the introduction of the Nobel Prize for literature. Not to be able to show at least one book of a Nobel Laureate was regarded almost as being illiterate. (156)

But of course the Nobel Prize was itself both symptom and catalyst of a wider condition: the emergence of a notion of a universal "literature," a form of artistic expression that embodies differences in place and culture, emotion and aspiration, but in such a way as to render them communicable. This idea may well have had its birth in Europe, but I suspect it met with a much more enthusiastic reception outside. I spent a couple of years studying in England in the late seventies and early eighties. I don't remember ever having come across a bookshelf like my uncle's: one that had been largely formed by this vision of literature, by a deliberate search for books from a wide array of other countries.

I have, however, come across many such elsewhere, most memorably in Burma in the house of Mya Than Tint, who is perhaps the most eminent novelist writing in Burmese today.

Mya Than Tint is an amazing man. He has spent more than a decade as a political prisoner. For part of that time he was incarcerated in the British-founded penal colony of Cocos Island, an infamous outcrop of rock where prisoners had to forage to survive. On his release he began to publish sketches and stories that won him a wide readership and great popular esteem in Burma. These wonderfully warm and vivid pieces, have recently been translated and published under the title *Tales of Everyday People.*

When I went to meet Mya Than Tint at his home in Rangoon, the first thing he said to me was, "I've seen your name somewhere." I was taken aback. Such is the ferocity of Burma's censorship regime that it seemed hardly possible that he could have come across my books or articles in Rangoon.

"Wait a minute," Mya Than Tint said. He went to his study, fetched a tattered old copy of *Granta,* and pointed to my name on the contents page.

"Where did you get it?" I asked, openmouthed. He explained, smiling, that he had kept his library going by befriending the ragpickers and papertraders who picked through the rubbish discarded by diplomats.

Looking through Mya Than Tint's bookshelves, I soon discovered that this determined refusal to be beaten into parochialism had its genesis in a bookcase that was startlingly similar to my uncle's. Knut Hamsun, Maksim Gorky, Sholokhov, all those once familiar names came echoing back to me, from Calcutta, as we sat talking in that bright, cool room in Rangoon.

I also once had occasion to meet the Indonesian novelist Pramoedya Ananta Toer, another writer of astonishing fortitude and courage. Of the same generation as Mya Than Tint, Pramoedya has lived through similar experiences of imprisonment and persecution. Unlike Mya

Than Tint, Pramoedya works in a language that has only recently become a vehicle of literary expression, Bahasa Indonesia. Pramoedya is thus widely thought of as the founding figure in a national literary tradition.

At some point I asked what his principal literary influences were. I do not know what I had expected to hear, but it was not the answer I got. I should not have been surprised, however; the names were familiar ones—Maksim Gorky and John Steinbeck.

Over the last few years, unbeknown to itself, the world has caught up with Mya Than Tint and Pramoedya Ananta Toer. Today the habits of reading that they and others like them pioneered are mandatory among readers everywhere. Wherever I go today, the names that I see on serious bookshelves are always the same, no matter the script in which they are spelled: Garcia Marquez, Vargas Llosa, Nadine Gordimer, Michael Ondaatje, Marguerite Yourcenar, Günter Grass, Salman Rushdie. That this is ever more true is self-evident: literary currents are now instantly transmitted around the world and instantly absorbed, like everything else. To mention this is to cite a jaded commonplace.

But the truth is that fiction had been thoroughly international for more than a century. In India, Burma, Egypt, Indonesia, and elsewhere this has long been self-evident. Yet curiously this truth has nowhere been more stoutly denied than in those places where the novel has its deepest roots; indeed it could be said that this denial is the condition that made the novel possible.

The novel as a form had been vigorously international from the start; we know that Spanish, English, French, and Russian novelists have read each other's work avidly since the eighteenth century. And yet, the paradox of the novel as a form is that it is founded upon a myth of parochiality, in the exact sense of a parish—a place named and charted, a definite location. A novel, in other words, must always be set somewhere: it must have its setting, and within the evolution of the narrative this setting must, classically, play a part almost as important as those of the characters themselves. Location is thus intrinsic to a novel: we are at a loss to imagine its absence no matter whether that place be Mrs. Gaskell's Cranford or Joyce's Dublin. A poem can create its setting and atmosphere out of verbal texture alone; not so a novel.

We carry these assumptions with us much the same that we assume the presence of actors and lights in a play. They are both so commonplace and so deeply rooted that they preempt us from reflecting on how very strange they actually are. Consider that the conceptions of location that made the novel possible came into being at exactly the time when the world was beginning to experience the greatest dislocation it has ever known. When we read *Middlemarch* or *Madame Bovary* we have not the faintest inkling that the lives depicted in them are made possible by global empires (consider the contrast with that seminal work of Portuguese literature, De Camoens' *Lusiads*). Consider that when we read Hawthorne we have to look very carefully between the lines to see that the New England ports he writes about are sustained by a far-flung network of trade. Consider that nowhere are the literary conventions of location more powerful than in the literature of the United States, itself the product of several epic dislocations.

How sharply this contrasts with traditions of fiction that predate the novel! It is true, for example, that the city of Baghdad provides a notional location for the *One Thousand and One Nights*. But the Baghdad of Scheherazade is more a talisman, an incantation, than a setting. The stories could happen anywhere so long as our minds have room for an enchanted city.

Or think of that amazing collection of stories known as the *Panchatantra* or *Five Chapters*. These stories too have no settings to speak of, except the notion of a forest. Yet it is reckoned by some to be second only to the Bible in the extent of its global diffusion. Compiled in India early in the first millenium, the *Panchatantra* passed into Arabic through a sixth-century Persian translation, engendering some of the best known of Middle Eastern fables, including parts of the *One Thousand and One Nights*. The stories were handed on to the Slavic languages through Greek, then from Hebrew to Latin, a version in the latter appearing in 1270. Through Latin they passed into German and Italian. From the Italian version came the famous Elizabethan rendition of Sir Henry North, *The Morall Philosophy of Doni* (1570). These stories left their mark on collections as different as those of La Fontaine and the Grimm brothers, and today they are inseparably part of a global heritage (Dimock).

Equally, the stories called the *Jatakas*, originally compiled in India, came to be diffused throughout southern and eastern Asia and even further with the spread of Buddhism. The story, both in its epic form as well as its shorter version, was vital in the creation of the remarkable cultural authority that India enjoyed in the Asia of the Middle

Ages; not until the advent of Hollywood was narrative again to play so important a part in the diffusion of a civilization.

Everywhere these stories went they were freely and fluently adapted to local circumstances. Indeed in a sense the whole point of the stories was their translatability—the dispensable and inessential nature of their locations. What held them together and gave them their appeal was not where they happened but how—the narrative, in other words. Or, to take another example, consider that European narrative tradition that was perhaps the immediate precursor of the novel: the story of Tristan and Isolde. By the late Middle Ages this Celtic narrative, which appears to have had its origins in Cornwall and Brittany, had been translated and adapted into several major European languages. Everywhere it went the story of Tristan and Isolde was immediately adapted to new locations and new settings. The questions of its origins and its original locations are at best matters of pedantic interest.

In these ways of storytelling, it is the story that gives places their meaning. That is why Homer leaps at us from signs on the New York turnpike, from exits marked Ithaca and Troy; that is why the Ayodhya of the Ramayana lends its name equally to a street in Benaras and a town in Thailand.

This style of fictional narrative is not extinct: far from it. It lives very vividly in the spirit that animates popular cinema in India and many other places. In a Hindi film, as in a kung fu movie, the details that constitute the setting are profoundly unimportant, incidental almost. In Hindi films, the setting of a single song can take us through a number of changes of costume, each in a different location. These films, I need hardly point out, command huge audiences on several continents and may well be the most widely circulated cultural artifacts the world has ever known. When Indonesian streets and villages suddenly empty at four in the afternoon, it is not because of Maksim Gorky or John Steinbeck: it is because of the timing of a daily broadcast of a Hindi film.

Such is the continued vitality of this style of narrative that it eventually succeeded in weaning my uncle from his bookcases. Toward the end of his life my book-loving uncle abandoned all of his old friends, Gorky and Sholokhov and Hamsun, and became a complete devotee of Bombay films. He would see dozens of Hindi films; sometimes we went together, on lazy afternoons. On the way home he would stop to buy fan magazines. Through much of his life he'd been a forbidding, distant man, an intellectual in the classic, Western sense; in his last

368

years he was utterly transformed, warm, loving, thoughtful. His brothers and sisters scarcely recognized him.

Once, when we were watching a film together, he whispered in my ear that the star, then Bombay's reigning female deity, had recently contracted a severe infestation of lice.

"How do you know?" I asked.

"I read an interview with her hairdresser," he said. "In *Stardust*."

This was the man who'd handed me a copy of *And Quiet Flows the Don* when I was not quite twelve.

My uncle's journey is evidence that matters are not yet decided among different ways of telling stories: that if Literature, led by a flagship called the Novel, has declared victory, the other side, if there is one, has not necessarily conceded defeat. But what exactly is at stake here? What is being contested? Or to narrow the question: what is the difference between the ways in which place and location are thought of by novelists and storytellers of other kinds?

The contrast is best seen, I think, where it is most apparent: that is in situations outside Europe and the Americas, where the novel is a relatively recent import. As an example, I would like to examine for a moment a novel from my own part of the world—Bengal. This novel is called *Rajmohun's Wife*, written in the early 1860s by the writer Bankim Chandra Chatterjee.

Bankim Chandra Chatterjee was a man of many parts. He was a civil servant, a scholar, a novelist, and a talented polemicist. He was also very widely read, in English as well as Bengali and Sanskrit. In a sense his was the bookcase that was the ancestor of my uncle's.

Bankim played no small part in the extraordinary efflorescence of Bengali literature in the second half of the nineteenth century. He wrote several major novels in Bengali, all of which were quickly translated into other Indian languages. He was perhaps the first truly "Indian" writer of modern times in the sense that his literary influence extended throughout the subcontinent. Nirad Chaudhuri describes him as "the creator of Bengali fiction and . . . the greatest novelist in the Bengali language." Bankim is also widely regarded as one of the intellectual progenitors of Indian nationalism.

Bankim Chandra was nothing if not a pioneer, and he self-consciously set himself the task of bringing the Bengali novel into being by attacking what he called "the Sanskrit School." It is hard today, looking back from a point of time when the novel sails as Literature's flagship, to imagine what it meant to champion such a form in nineteenth-century India. The traditions of fiction that Bankim was seeking to displace were powerful enough to awe its critics into silence. They still are: what modern writer, for example, could ever hope to achieve the success of the *Panchatantra*? It required true courage to seek to replace this style of narrative with a form so artificial and arbitrary as the novel; the endeavor must have seemed hopeless at the time. Nor did the so-called Sanskrit School lack for defendants. Bankim, and many others who took on the task of domesticating the novel, were immediately derided as monkey-like imitators of the West.

Bankim responded by calling for a full-scale insurrection. Imitation, he wrote, was the law of progress; no civilization was self-contained or self-generated, none could advance without borrowing. He wrote:

> Those who are familiar with the present writers in Bengali, will readily admit that they all, good and bad alike, may be classed under two heads, the Sanskrit and the English schools. The former represents Sanskrit scholarship and the ancient literature of the country; the latter is the fruit of Western knowledge and ideas. By far the greater number of Bengali writers belong to the Sanskrit school; but by far the greater number of good writers belong to the other. . . . It may be said that there is not at the present day anything like an indigenous school of writers, owing nothing either to Sanskrit writers or to those of Europe.

How poignantly ironic this passage seems a hundred years later, after generations of expatriate Indians, working mainly in England, have striven so hard to unlearn the lessons taught by Bankim and his successors in India. So successfully were novelistic conventions domesticated in the late nineteenth and early twentieth centuries that many Indian readers now think of them as somehow local, homegrown, comforting in their naturalistic simplicity, while the work of such writers as G. V. Desani, Zulfikar Ghose, Salman Rushdie, Adam Zameenzad, Shashi Tharoor, and others appears, by the same token, stylized and experimental.

Yet Bankim's opinions about the distinctiveness of Indian literature were much more extreme than those of his apocryphal Sanskrit School. In 1882 Bankim found himself embroiled in a very interesting controversy with a Protestant missionary, W. Hastie. The exchange began after Hastie had published a couple of letters in a Calcutta newspaper, *The Statesman.* I cannot resist quoting from one of these:

> Notwithstanding all that has been written about the myriotheistic idolatry of India, no pen has yet adequately depicted the hideousness and grossness of the monstrous system. It has been well described by one who knew it as "Satan's masterpiece . . . the most stupendous fortress and citadel of ancient error and idolatry now in the world. . . . " With much that was noble and healthy in its early stages, the Sanskrit literature became infected by a moral leprosy which gradually spread like a corrupting disease through almost all its fibres and organs. The great Sanskrit scholars of Bengal know too well what I mean. . . . Only to think that this has been the principal pabulum of the spiritual life of the Hindus for about a thousand years, and the loudly boasted lore of their semi-deified priests! Need we seek elsewhere for the foul disease that has been preying upon the vitals of the national life, and reducing the people to what they are? "Shew me your gods," cried an ancient Greek apologist, "and I will show you your men." The Hindu is just what his idol gods have made him. His own idolatry, and not foreign conquerors has been the curse of his history. No people was ever degraded except by itself, and this is most literally so with the Hindus. (192–93)

Bankim responded by advising Mr. Hastie to "obtain some knowledge of Sanskrit scriptures in the *original*

> . . . [for] no translation from the Sanskrit into a European language can truly or even approximately represent the original. . . . The English or the German language can possess no words or expressions to denote ideas or conceptions which have never entered into a Teutonic brain. . . . A people so thoroughly unconnected with England or Germany as the old Sanskrit-speaking people of India, and developing a civilization and a literature peculiarly their own, had necessarily a vast store of ideas and conceptions utterly foreign to the Englishman or the German, just as the Englishman or

the German boasts a still vaster number of ideas utterly foreign to the Hindu. . . . [Mr. Hastie's position] is the logical outcome of that monstrous claim to omniscience, which certain Europeans . . . put forward for themselves. . . . Yet nothing is a more common subject of merriment among the natives of India than the Europeans' ignorance of all that relates to India. . . . A navvy who had strayed into the country . . . asked for some food from a native. . . . The native gave him a cocoanut. The hungry sailor . . . bit the husk, chewed it . . . and flung the fruit at the head of the unhappy donor. . . . The sailor carried away with him an opinion of Indian fruits parallel to that of Mr. Hastie and others, who merely bite at the husk of Sanskrit learning, but do not know their way to the kernel within. . . ."

He added: "I cheerfully admit the intellectual superiority of Europe. I deny, however . . . that intellectual superiority can enable the blind to see or the deaf to hear." (192–93)

By the time he wrote the passages quoted above, Bankim was already an acclaimed novelist and a major figure in the Bengali literary world. But Bankim's experiments with the novel had begun some twenty years before, and his earliest efforts at novel writing were conducted in English. *Rajmohun's Wife* is the first known fictional work written by Bankim, and it was written in the early 1860s.

It will be evident from the above passages, abbreviated though they are, that Bankim wrote excellent English: his essays and letters are written in a style that is supple, light-handed, and effective. The style of *Rajmohun's Wife,* on the other hand, is deliberate, uncertain, and often ponderous. What intrigues me most about this book, however, are the long passages of description that preface several of the chapters, bookending, as it were, some extremely melodramatic scenes. Here are some examples:

The house of Mathur Ghose was a genuine specimen of mofussil magnificence united with a mofussil want of cleanliness.

From the far-off paddy fields you could descry through the intervening foliage, its high palisades and blackened walls. On a nearer view might be seen pieces of plaster of a

372

venerable antiquity prepared to bid farewell to their old and weather-beaten tenement. . . .

A mazy suite of dark and damp apartments led from a corner of this part of the building to the inner *mahal,* another quadrangle, on all four sides of which towered double-storied verandahs, as before. . . . The walls of all the chambers above and below were well striped with numerous streaks of red, white, black, green, all colours of the rainbow, caused by the spittles of such as had found their mouths too much encumbered with paan, or by some improvident woman servant who had broken the *gola-handi* while it was full of its muddy contents. . . . Numerous sketches in charcoal, which showed, we fear, nothing of the conception of (Michael) Angelo or the tinting of Guido (Reni), attested the art or idleness of the wicked boys and ingenious girls who had contrived to while away hungry hours by essays in the arts of designing and of defacing wall. . . .

A thick and massive door led to the "godown" as the *mahal* was called by the males directly from outside. . . . (*Rajmohun's Wife* 52–53)

A kitchen scene:

Mudhav therefore immediately hurried into the inner apartments where he found it no very easy task to make himself heard in that busy hour of zenana life. There was a servant woman, black, rotund, and eloquent, demanding the transmission to her hand of sundry articles of domestic use, without however making it at all intelligible to whom her demands were addressed. There was another who boasted similar blessed corporal dimensions, but who thought it beneath her dignity to shelter them from view; and was busily employed broomstick in hand, in demolishing the little mountains of the skins and stems of sundry culinary vegetables which decorated the floors, and against which the half-naked dame never aimed a blow but coupled it with a curse on those whose duty it had been to prepare the said vegetables for dressing. (17)

373

The questions that strike me when I read these lengthy and labored descriptions is: What are they for? For whom are they intended? Why did he bother to write them? Bankim must have known that this book was very unlikely to be read by anyone who did *not* know what the average Bengali landowner's house looked like—since by far the largest part of the literate population of Calcutta at that time consisted of landowners and their families. Similarly anyone who had visited the Bengal of his time, for no matter how brief a period, would almost inevitably have been familiar with the other sights he describes: fishermen at work, cranes fishing, and so on.

Why then did Bankim go to the trouble of writing these passages? Did he think his book might be read by someone who was entirely unfamiliar with Bengal? The question is a natural and inevitable one, but I do not think it leads anywhere. For the fact of the matter is that I don't think Bankim was writing for anyone but himself. I suspect that Bankim never really intended to publish *Rajmohun's Wife:* the novel has the most cursory of endings as though he'd written it as an exercise and then thrown it aside once it had served its purpose. The book was not actually published until a decade or so after he'd stopped working on it. For Bankim, *Rajmohun's Wife* was clearly a rehearsal, a preparation for something else.

It is here, I think, that the answers lie. The passages of description in the book are not, in fact, intended to describe. Their only function is that they are there at all: they are Bankim's attempt to lay claim to the rhetoric of location, of place—to mount a springboard that would allow him to vault the gap between two entirely different conventions of narrative.

It is for a related reason, I think, that Bankim conducted his rehearsal in English rather than Bengali. To write about one's surroundings is anything but natural: to even perceive one's immediate environment one must somehow distance oneself from it; to describe it one must assume a certain posture, a form of address. In other words, to locate oneself through prose, one must begin with an act of dislocation. It was this perhaps that English provided for Bankim: a kind of disconnected soapbox on which he could test a certain form of address before trying it out in Bengali.

This still leaves a question. Every form of address assumes a listener, a silent participant. Who was the listener in Bankim's mind when he was working on *Rajmohun's Wife?* The answer, I think, is the bookcase. It is the very vastness and cosmopolitanism of the fictional bookcase that requires novelists to locate themselves in relation to it; that demands of their work that it carry marks to establish their location.

This then is the peculiar paradox of the novel: those of us who love novels often read them because of the eloquence with which they communicate a "sense of place." Yet the truth is that it is the very loss of a lived sense of place that makes their fictional representation possible.

Works Cited

Bankim, Chandra Chatterjee. *Essays and Letters.* In *Bankim Rachanavali.* Calcutta: Sahitya Samsad, n.d.

————. *Rajmohun's Wife.* In *Bankim Rachanavali.* Ed. Jogesh Chandra Bagal. Calcutta: Sahitya Samsad, n.d.

Chaudhuri, Nirad. *Thy Hand, Great Anarch!* New York: Addison-Wesley, 1987.

Dimock, Edward C., Edwin Gerow, C. M. Naim, A. K. Ramanujam, Gordon Roadarmel, J. A. B. van Buitenen. *The Literatures of India, an Introduction.* Chicago: U of Chicago P, 1974.

Nominated by The Kenyon Review

A MEDITATION

by GAIL N. HARADA

from BAMBOO RIDGE

A man contemplates the distance
to the horizon from the place he stands
on the reef in the break and surge
of seawater and foam.
He fathoms the near water,
searching through its infinite shifting
for the lightning glimmer of fishscales
or the teal blue turning of an *uhu*
or the fluid shadow of a school of mullet
gliding like one body, quick and elusive,
poised to cast his throw net
into the encroaching twilight tide
on the edge of Waikīkī.
What do the waves tell him?
How does the wind speak?
When does the universe hum inside a man?
A woman listens for something true
in the waves and wind,
trying to discern words which could resonate
in her body and heart, like lines
of an ancient chant, a *mele kahi* moving her
beyond the tranquility of green tea and grapefruit
into a caldera of molten, fearless clarity.

Nominated by Sylvia Watanabe

Note: *uhu* is a parrotfish
    mele kahi is a place chant

THE TALKING CURE

fiction by FREDERICK BUSCH

from THE MISSOURI REVIEW

LOVE IS UNSPEAKABLE.

Consider the story of the older brother who went off to school, the brilliant, tall mother and wife who hunched herself shorter, curved at her tilted drafting table as if around the buildings she planned for her clients. Consider the husband, son of a bankrupt Hudson Valley apple grower, who made a living as a junior high school principal. And then consider me, fifteen years old and up to my wrists in vomiting dogs and hemorrhaging cats, and the darkening drift and dismay of my parents.

We lived in an old house surrounded by the ruins of the orchards. The air pulsed, in autumn, with the drunken dancing of wasps that had supped on the tan, rotted flesh of English Russets and Chenangos. We walked on the mush of the orchard's decay, and in winter some one of us never failed to be surprised by the glowing red or golden apples which continued to hang, as snow started falling, on the gray-black trunks of dozens of trees. Apple trees aren't peaceful. The trunks and limbs look like tensed or writhing hands.

My mother commuted from the farm to Manhattan by car or train, and she designed the structures that held people's lives. And my father continued to fail her, despite what I would have described, if asked, as pretty sizable efforts to win her approval. And my big brother, Edwin, who had escaped, as I saw it, to Ohio, shone over the plains and through the forests, lighting up my mother's face and causing her to say to friends, "Yes, my baby's gone away."

She looked truly sad—and therefore beautiful and fragile—and she looked highly pleased, and both at once. Apparently, she was proud but also bereft. Something had been stolen from her life, and she knew that she would never retrieve it. This is what I thought I learned, spying— younger siblings tend to live sub rosa lives—from around the corners of our rooms, or simply from my place at the kitchen table where I sat in my life and took note of them in theirs while they failed, mercifully often, to notice me. I was like the furniture. I was a shape your eye slid over. You get used to it—to me—and then you say what you wish I hadn't heard. That's how it is with younger brothers when the genius goes to Oberlin and writes home his observations on existentialism and a man my parents referred to as *Sart!* They sneezed or barked it with a powerful emphasis on the final two letters they didn't pronounce.

My father wished to replace her Edwin, and he never could. And, anyway, that led to competition. And who ever heard of a father competing with his son? It was cannibalistic. It was barbaric. It was Freudian.

That was the last word I heard through the screen windows one hot Sunday afternoon, while I was about to use the back door to report in the cool kitchen, shaded by tall, old maples, not runty apple trees, that I had mowed the lawns and could be found in front of our vast, boxy Emerson, watching the New York Yankees stumble and whiff. Freudian. I knew a bit about Freud. He was the specialist in women who wanted penises. I could not imagine my mother ever wanting a penis, nor could I fathom why my father might wish her to develop one. It took several days for further investigation to suggest that Freudian meant having to do with dreams, and with wishes you didn't know you wished. That made sense, given our family. There were a lot of secret wishes flying around.

I was pretty sure that several of them had to do with Dr. Victor Mason, the veterinarian who took care of our terrible cat until she died, and who hired me to work on weekday afternoons and Saturday mornings. My job was to be the big kid who comes into the examination room with the vet and holds your Yorkshire terrier down while Dr. Mason gives him his inoculations. I talked to the animals and rubbed them and made gitchy-goomy noises to keep the animals from realizing what was happening to them, and to keep the owners from realizing what was happening to their animals.

"Court jester of the household pet," my father called me when Dr. Mason was over for dinner on a Sunday night.

"Valuable assistant," Dr. Mason said. "Peter earns his pay. You know what he has to clean up, some days?"

378

As usual, I sat behind my camouflage screen and the words went over and around me. I ate my cauliflower because it was my policy to attract as little attention as possible, even if the cauliflower was a bit hard to chew. My mother liked to cook, she insisted, and she did it very badly. If she had asked me what I thought of it, I would have told her how colorful the paprika looked on top of the cauliflower stems. I wouldn't have called the paprika pasty or described the stems as wood.

My mother said, "You're talking about Peter behind his front again."

Dr. Mason smiled an enormous grin. He had a broad face in a big square head, and his cheeks and jaws seemed full of muscles. He was taller than my mother, which meant he was bigger by several inches than my father, and he could lift a Great Dane with ease or kneel with some goofy Labrador pup and prod him in the belly with his big head, then kind of jump up to his feet and continue being a vet. Working with him, I felt like the magician's assistant, except I never knew what the trick was going to be. I thought my father was right, the way he described me, and I thought my mother was looking for another night-time fight.

"That was very clever," Dr. Mason said, "'talking behind his front.' You managed to say two things at once." Dr. Mason held the patent on telling people what they might have thought they had just finished saying.

"Well, she's a great rhetorician," my father said.

"That's a compliment, Teddy, am I right?" Dr. Mason said.

"Not at all," my mother said.

"Well, of *course* it is," my father said, a little loudly.

So there was a silence that got uncomfortable, and I began to file a flight plan with myself. I needed to get upstairs to my room and do homework, but not only because I had homework to do. When my mother began to wash the dinner pots before she poured their after-dinner coffee, I knew there was more to come than dessert.

"Peter's doing a first-class job for me. You ever think of a career involving medicine, Peter? Some aspect of the biological sciences?" Dr. Mason rubbed his short gray hair as if he were stroking one of his patients. He asked me the question once or twice a week, and I figured it was just another of his routine queries like, "Hey, Pete, what're you doing smart these days?" At first I had labored to answer him, describing in some detail a melancholy Hammond Innes book about the wreck of the *Mary Deare,* or the poems I wrote in those days—a *rhyme* to *mime* the *crime* of *time*—or my efforts to bring my grades

379

up by sporadically reading several pages in the dictionary. He didn't listen, I realized, so finally I answered his questions by smiling or shrugging, and then changing into my pale blue veterinarian assistant's laboratory coat and mopping up the latest deposit of a nervous dog.

"Peter?" My mother was reminding me of my manners.

"Yes, sir?" I said. "I've been reading about this German guy in World War II. He got to the Forbidden City in Tibet by accident. It's called Lhasa. I've been reading about him, and he got me going to other mountain climbers. This Englishman named Whymper? He tried to climb Mount Everest. He fell off."

"Isn't it funny," my father said. "You could have gotten interested in Tibet. Or Germans. Or foreign languages. Or the way the Communist Chinese took Tibet over. And you ended up interested in mountain climbing. Or is it mountains?"

"I don't know," I said. "Climbing, I guess. But I also read one called *The Rose of Tibet*. There's a lot of all that stuff in it."

"Wonderful," my father said. "I think that's wonderful." He smiled at me as if I had done something noteworthy. That was why he was such a good junior high school principal. He discovered about eleven times a day that people were commendable, and they knew he thought so. He wasn't very good about law and order, and he'd ended up hiring a former state policeman to be in charge of lateness and smoking in the parking lot. He called him an acting assistant principal, but he was the man who chewed your butt if you bothered the seventh grade girls on school property or even *thought* about fighting.

"Dreaming your way up mountains," my mother said, happy again because she was discovering a possible reflection of Edwin's distant light. "You dream about it, don't you, darling? Or write poems about it. It's a part of your interior life."

Perhaps you could hang out road maps to my interior life, I didn't say. But Dr. Mason was watching me, and I felt as though he had a rough idea of what was on my mind. He nodded once, as if we had finished a discussion. I saw that my father was looking at my mother. As she saw him watching, she tried to keep her smile a second longer, but it shimmered on her face, and you could tell she was making an effort. I didn't know precisely what my father knew about how things were, and I wondered how much of my curiosity was Freudian.

On the job, Dr. Mason was trying to extend my days at school by offering me lessons in nothing less than all of life. He seemed to feel he owed me such advancement. There was a home, of course, though I

380

didn't know where, and there was a wife, I knew, but she was not mentioned by my parents, and only referred to in passing by Dr. Mason. His office was a small white clapboard cabin at the end of a curving dead-end lane, and I walked from school—there wasn't a team or club that sought me, or one to which I could offer a skill—unless we were under a blizzard or a rainstorm, when he came to give me a lift in his scuffed tan, noisy Willys pickup truck. It said *Jeep* on the back and it had four-wheel drive, and I loved it because it made me think of adventures among soldiers on landscapes not to be found in New York State. I was happy in the smell of animal hair and chemicals and disinfectant, pleased to have my hands on so much life, and glad to often enough be the object of its uncomplicated affection. But whether I was mopping or scooping, pinioning to the floor or raising to the stainless-steel examination table, I was made uncomfortable by the weight of Dr. Mason's obligation.

He had to put a golden retriever down. Her master, a bulky man in a dark brown business suit covered with his dying animal's hair, came into the examination room and stood, drifting back and forth over his planted broad feet. He wouldn't set the dog on the table or the floor. You could smell her dying, a kind of sour vegetable odor that came off her scrawny shanks and her motionless tail, her unreflecting eyes, her long, gray, bony muzzle.

"Tony," Dr. Mason said to him, "it's the right time."

"Don't *feel* right, Doc," the owner said. His round, fat face would have been red, I realized, on any other day. But it was a kind of gray-white, and I wondered if his shaky stance meant that he was going to keel over or get sick. I didn't know if I could get through that kind of cleaning up.

"Let's set her on the table, Peter." I stepped closer to the owner and pushed my hands alongside his. "Let Peter take the weight, Tony."

Tony was crying now. He kept shaking his head. I couldn't tell if he was trying to stop the tears or say how sorry he was to let her go. In any case, he didn't let her go, and I stood in front of him, smelling his sad old dog and something spicy, perhaps salami.

"Tony, let Peter take the weight."

"Damn it, Doc."

"Now take it, Peter."

She slid onto me, against my chest and I braced myself, for though she looked weightless, she was surprisingly heavy. I took another step back, and then I set her on the table and slowly rubbed her behind the ears. She looked at me sideways and her tail moved twice, and then she was still.

"Now what should I do?" Tony asked him.

"You could wait outside," Dr. Mason said. "If you want to. You could wait, and then I could come and talk to you in a minute."

"Just go outside?" Tony said.

"If that's what you want," Dr. Mason said.

"I hate to leave her."

"Yes," Dr. Mason said.

"Doc," Tony said, and he turned to face the door, and then he leaned at it, pulled his shoulders back, and then slammed his forehead on the door. I think he almost knocked himself out, for he slumped against the door a second or two before he started rubbing his head. The dog might have been used to this trick of his because she moved her tail on the table once. Then Tony opened the door. He said, "Bye, darlin."

Dr. Mason loaded his syringe, and I waited. He said, "Touch her, Peter."

"You mean pet her?"

"So she isn't alone."

I rubbed her ears and waited.

"She gave that man all the company he ever had. I kind of hoped he would want to stay with her. But it was obvious he couldn't. And do listen to me, sounding ever so slightly like John Fitzgerald Kennedy." Or Billy Graham, I thought. Or Jesus Christ Almighty.

I was rubbing the head of the dog and I was waiting.

"You just make your decision," Dr. Mason said. And, by now, he sounded to me like a slide trombone. He said, "Oh, shit." She breathed a little more, and I rubbed her, and then she stopped. Her tongue slid out, and she looked silly.

I felt his big hand on top of mine. He said, "You don't have to rub her anymore."

That night, my mother stayed late at the office and my father and I made hamburgers and agreed to meet at the Emerson once I'd finished my homework, to see if the Yankees managed to field nine men who could run. I did my assignments, more or less, and I tried to write something about what happened at Dr. Mason's office. It was an entirely failed poem, I knew, full of words like *sorrow* and *suffering*, and the only rhyme I could find for *suffering* was *Bufferin*. When I surrendered, when I admitted I had slammed, like Tony into the door, against a situation in which my feelings didn't matter and my words had no meaning, I went downstairs to find my father snoring in front

382

of the set, which was full of Yankees disgracing themselves. I was outside before I knew that I wanted to be. And though I wasn't any kind of athlete, I was a boy, and boys run, and so I ran.

It was May, a dark, mild night, and we lived on a hardpan lane, so I had good footing, and I made progress, even if I'd no idea toward what, and soon I began to enjoy myself, growing aware of my location, striking a pace that I could keep with comfort, beginning to think about Tony and his dog, and the way she suddenly was still beneath my hand. I thought of Dr. Mason's little lesson on mortality or decision-making, and I realized I thought of it in two ways. It was pretty piss-poor, I thought. And it was desperate. All of his lessons were. Why did he feel that he had to teach me? He never taught my parents, and he hadn't much of a lesson plan for poor Tony. It was me. The teaching was for *me*.

I ran out of breath and out of isolated road for running. The next turn would take me onto a county highway that went toward the hamlet where we bought our milk and eggs and bread and newspapers. I stopped and panted a while, and then I began the long walk back. I knew most of the very large old trees I passed, for I had played among them. I knew the giant clumps of brush, the multiple stems of willow near the streams and marshes, and the patches of berries that were good for eating or for collecting in a jar to please your mother. I hadn't pleased her recently, although she approved, apparently, of the fact that I lived more or less inside of my head. My father didn't seem to have pleased her either.

I pretended in those days that our road was the path that Ichabod Crane had taken, pursued by the terrible horseman. Whenever I was alone on that road and I thought of the headless rider, I had to force myself to not look back, to walk instead of run, to inspect the night-time forest without telling myself, *He is right behind me. He is **here.***

Dr. Mason, I thought, had pleased her. And as I thought, I realized he had come to mind because I had just now seen him, and only a few hundred feet from me, ghosting by in his truck. Another road ran parallel to ours, but at a considerable distance. You couldn't hear its traffic during the day, and only at night if there wasn't much wind. Because of a pond it had to circle, the road dipped close to ours where a sycamore, blasted by lightning, had taken down several smaller trees and made a clearing. Looking across thoughtlessly, I had seen a truck that might have been Dr. Mason's. But surely I hadn't seen a Karman Ghia too? I stopped and closed my eyes, but I could only see a memory of an empty road. I opened my eyes and took a couple of steps. I waited for an owl to start in terrorizing me with its screeches, or something silent and big to rustle in the brush. But there was only the ten- or twelve-foot stump of the charred sycamore, and not a vehicle in hearing or sight. Then I closed my eyes and I saw the truck again, and then the little car, and I took off down the road toward home like Ichabod.

My father had gone up to sleep. The house was silent, and I was a fifteen-year-old boy who needed a shower and then was going to bed. I lay there not reading, because I didn't want to attract attention with my light, when I heard my mother's car slowly roll on the gravel outside our back door. I listened to her footsteps in the kitchen, and then in the living room, and I fell asleep—waking astonished the next morning that I had—as her steps approached my sleeping father, as I imagined him opening his eyes and rising, as she said he always did, to say hello.

The kinds of lessons you get from someone like Dr. Mason, or from people like my parents, are the sort you really can't repeat. If you asked me what I learned from being a vet's assistant, I don't think I could set it out in sentences, although there was plenty going on and, whether it seemed exciting or not, Dr. Mason was of course constantly instructing me. It's like those sessions of show-and-tell we had to endure in elementary school. Edwin always found something profitable in his daily events, and he could bring a shed snakeskin, or sassafras he claimed the Indians used to make tea from, or the history of wonderful events that I had seen as simply the damming of a stream or the spinning off of a hubcap from the Good Humor ice cream truck. Edwin and my mother could live a year and end up with an almanac. I was always left with a headful of worries and words that didn't quite rhyme.

I remember the day Dr. Mason clipped the nails of an excited seven-month-old puppy, a bunchy English setter. He wriggled and then began to yelp—it was a scream, almost—because the clippers nicked the artery behind the claw. There was a jet of blood before Dr. Mason got it under control, and he kept laughing and saying, "You're all right. You're all right." But the dog didn't believe him, and neither did the woman who had brought him in. The dog heaved and slobbered, and I went out for the mop. And when she had gone, before we went into the examination room, Dr. Mason said, "You saw the anger in the owner's face? Did you see how I parried her anger? I understood it, of course. She was frightened, and her fear made her angry. Nine times out of ten, Peter, it's the fear. You understand?"

The Dalai Lama of Dogs and Cats, his heavy head and bloody hands, turned to leave the room, and I was spared having to ask *what* was the fear.

We were about to deal with a combination, I swear it, of some kind of retriever and dachshund. He had a big head with a real grin, and he was close enough to the ground to get his belly wet if it rained. He didn't seem to know that he had an abscessed wound on his flank and that he was going to get lanced, cleaned out, and loaded with antibiotics. Then we were doing a booster distemper shot, and then Dr. Mason changed rooms while I stayed behind to clean up. By the time I came in, the man had set his carton of puppies on the examination table, and he had retreated to the corner. Dr. Mason was leaning on the table, one fist on either side of the box.

"Look at this, Peter. Stick your nose in there and tell me what you see."

There were eight or nine puppies, shifting in their sleep, blind and all but hairless. They whimpered as they slept.

"Mr. Leeth's Irish setter bitch produced these puppies yesterday."

Mr. Leeth was small and sturdy and bald. He had a sad, stubbly face and red nose and cheeks. His pale blue eyes were rimmed in red.

"He needs us to kill them today."

"It's my job," Mr. Leeth told me. I felt myself flush. I was embarrassed that he would think to explain himself to a kid. "They're moving me, and I have to live in a hotel for a month or two while I hunt for a house. The hotel won't let me keep them. I can't even take my old dog with me."

"This is the fruit of an unplanned pregnancy, Peter. Some randy dog crept into the doghouse under the fence and *voilà!* A number of very inconvenient puppies."

"Well, now, just a minute there," Mr. Leeth said. "I don't need a sermon, Doc Mason. I need some service. I know where to go for sermons. If you don't want my business, I imagine I can go look a vet up in the Yellow Pages and then pay *him.* Since when did you start dispensing judgments while you pushed your pills?"

I heard Dr. Mason breathe in, then out. He said, "Have you ever seen me pushing a pill around, Peter? Or bullying a bulldog? Or leaning on a Labrador?" He breathed deeply again. He said, "Tim, you *should* go get your Yellow Pages. If I have a feeling about this, I should keep it to myself. I'm not only a medical man, I'm a businessman, and if I take your money I can damned well keep my mouth shut. I apologize. You're right."

Though Mr. Leeth was about to reply, I knew the little lesson was for me.

He answered, "No, Vic. We both got strung out on this. It's a terrible thing to do. Would you—Please take care of it for me." Dr. Mason nodded right away. Mr. Leeth said, "Thank you."

"Do you want to bury them?"

"Oh, Christ," Mr. Leeth said, "nine little graves?"

"You could do one and tumble them all in. We'll have them in a bag for you later in the day. Just dig yourself a pit and lay the whole deal into it."

Mr. Leeth shook his head. He rubbed and rubbed at his mouth. "Do it for me, Vic?"

"Incineration."

"Please."

"They charge by weight for that. But I can't imagine these little things weigh anything at all. We'll go the minimum fee, and you can pay us later."

Mr. Leeth nodded. He said to me, "What do you think my granddaughter will say?"

I actually tried to think of what she would say.

Mr. Leeth left, and Dr. Mason went out for a small bottle of clear liquid and he began to load his syringe. He looked down into the box. I didn't.

"I can do this," he said.

I said, inviting him to play the Dalai Lama of Dogs and Cats—no, *needing* him to—"Do you think I should stay here?"

He looked at me and let his head sag, as if he wanted to lay it on his own shoulder and rest. He slumped, then made his chest expand and his head rise slowly on his thick neck. "No," he said, "but that was a good question, and I'm glad you asked it. But no."

I moved very quickly so I wouldn't see him dip his hands into the carton and lift up four or five inches of dog and kill it with a jab of his thumb. I didn't want to hear the boxful snuffling and hear a puppy squeal if the needle woke it for only an instant. They smelled like cereal, like grain, and I wanted to get something else inside my nostrils, I explained to my father that afternoon.

Of course, I did not make it out of the room without instruction.

"Peter," Dr. Mason said.

I stopped at the door.

"I had hard feelings for a man I'd known for years and years. I'd served him, and I'd profited from the service."

"Yes, sir."

"I wasn't supposed to have any feelings about all the dying he requested I dump down into that carton he brought in. He needed me to do my professional work, and I had feelings that weren't wrong, mind you. I think I was right to feel anger. But I was wrong to *express* my feelings. You see? So I forced them away. By the time he left this room, I was purged. I was professional again. Understand?"

I absolutely did not. I heard a whimper from the carton. I said, "Thank you."

His voice was surprised when he said, "Well, sure."

"I think he should have booted the guy in the ass," I told my father.

"Watch your mouth, now."

"*Ass?*"

"Well, you know. Anyway, I'm used to dealing with younger students. It's a habit. And I believe you're wrong. Booting that poor man in the ass would have made no difference in anybody's life."

"But they were little *puppies*. It wasn't their *fault*. And this Leeth guy brings them in so Dr. Mason can swoop down into the box like the Angel of Death because it isn't convenient to let them live."

"That's nice," my father said, "that Angel of Death."

I shrugged modestly.

"How do you think people *my* age feel in their lives, then, Peter?"

I had a vision of a lesson plan, and maybe a poem I would not be able to keep myself from trying to write, about boxes and dead ends and life-and-death and how the carton of puppies could be a lesson to us all. I was afraid that my father would say something about the puppies that would tip me over into that lesson.

So I answered him by saying, "Dad, I wonder if you would do me a favor and not tell me about the older people, and lives and feeling, and all of that? I don't mean to be disrespectful or anything, but I think I just got too many thoughts to deal with today. Would that be all right?"

He looked at me, and he got those dimples around his nose and mouth before he smiled, but he was absolutely wonderful about not letting it get past that. He nodded, he touched me on the leg above my knee and he squeezed, then let me go.

"I'm trimming privet," he said.

"I'll get the mower out in a while."

387

"Deal," he said. Then he said, "It must have been goddamned tough."

"Language," I tried to joke.

"Seeing the last thing in the world you wanted to see."

I nodded, but he wasn't looking at me. It took me a while, but I did understand that he looked past his kid, and past the night his kid had thought to sneak into, and other nights and afternoons. He was seeing, I understood, the country road along which his tall and sorrowing wife, bereft of her older son and much of motherhood and satisfaction, she might have thought, had driven her Karman Ghia. I figured he saw it follow the Willys pickup truck, and I figured, when I let myself, that he had either witnessed or deduced the last thing in the world he had wanted to see.

For the rest of the years of my life at home, I feared his deciding to tell me. He mercifully didn't. I feared for him the moment she or Dr. Mason decided my father was owed what one of them, doubtless, would describe as the Truth. I don't know whether they did. He outlived my mother, and his heart stopped while he was sleeping. Who is to say what shuts down a heart? I am unable to keep myself from seeing my mother—on the seat of a pickup truck or in a white clapboard cabin smelling of animal fears and wastes—as she bucks in her nakedness beneath the man who administers death. *Freudian,* she'd say. Edwin doesn't know. It's a story I try not to tell.

Nominated by Rosellen Brown, David Jauss, Missouri Review

PROVENANCE

by JOSEPH STROUD

from BELOW COLD MOUNTAIN (Copper Canyon Press)

I want to tell you the story of that winter
in Madrid where I lived in a room
with no windows, where I lived
with the death of my father, carrying it
everywhere through the streets,
as if it were an object, a book written
in a luminous language I could not read.
Every day I left my room and wandered
across the great plazas of that city,
boulevards crowded with people and cars.
There was nowhere I wanted to go.
Sometimes I would come to myself
inside a cathedral under the vaulted
ceiling of the transept, I would find
myself sobbing, transfixed in the light
slanting through the rose window
scattering jewels across the cold
marble floor. At this distance now
the grief is not important, nor the sadness
I felt day after day wandering the maze
of medieval streets, wandering the rooms
of the Prado, going from painting
to painting, looking into Velázquez,
into Bosch, Brueghel, looking for something
that would help, that would frame
my spirit, focus sorrow into some

kind of belief that wasn't fantasy
or false, for I was tired of deception,
the lies of words, even the Gypsy violin,
its lament with the *puñal* inside
seemed indulgent, posturing.
I don't mean to say these didn't
move me, I was an easy mark,
anything could well up in me—
rainshine on the cobblestone streets,
a bowl of tripe soup in a peasant café.
In my world at that time there was
no scale, nothing with which
to measure, I could no longer
discern value—the mongrel eating
scraps of garbage in the alley
was equal to *Guernica* in all its
massive outrage. When I looked
in the paintings mostly what I saw
were questions. In the paradise
panel of *The Garden of Earthly Delights*
why does Bosch show a lion
disemboweling a deer? Or that man
in hell crucified on the strings of a harp?
In his *Allegory of the Seven Deadly Sins:*
Gluttony, Lust, Sloth, Wrath, Envy, Avarice,
Pride—of which am *I* most guilty?
Why in Juan de Flanders' *Resurrection
of Lazarus* is the face of Christ so sad
in bringing the body back to life?
Every day I returned to my room,
to my cave where I could not look out
at the world, where I was forced into
the one place I did not want to be. In
the Cranach painting—behind Venus
with her fantastic hat, her cryptic look,
behind Cupid holding a honeycomb, whimpering
with bee stings—far off in the background,
that cliff rising above the sea, that small hut
on top—is that Cold Mountain, is that where
the poet made his way out of our world?

My father had little use for poems, less use
for the future. If he had anything
to show me by his life, it was to live
here. Even in a room without windows.
One day in the Prado, in the Hall
of the Muses, a group of men
in expensive suits, severe looking,
men of importance, with a purpose,
moved down the hallway toward me,
and I was swept aside, politely,
firmly. As they passed I glimpsed
in their midst a woman, in a simple
black dress with pearls, serene, speaking
to no one, and then she and the men
were gone. *Who was that?* I asked,
and a guard answered: *The Queen.*
The Queen. In my attempt to follow
to see which painting she would choose,
I got lost in one of the Goya rooms
and found myself before one of his
dark paintings, one from his last years
when the world held no more illusions,
where love was examined in a ruthless,
savage anger. In this painting
a woman stood next to Death, her beauty,
her elegance, her pearls and shining hair
meant nothing in His presence,
and He was looking out from the painting,
looking into me, and Death took my hand
and made me look, and I saw my own face
streaming with tears, and the day
took on the shape of a crouching beast,
and my father's voice called out in wonder
or warning, and every moment
I held on made it that much harder
to let go, and Death demanded
that I let go. Then the moment
disappeared, like a pale horse, like
a ghost horse disappearing deep inside
Goya's painting. I left the Prado.

I walked by the *Palacio Real* with its
2,000 rooms, one for every kind
of desire. I came upon the *Rastro,*
the great open-air bazaar, a flea market
for the planet, where everything in the world
that has been cast aside, rejected, lost,
might be found, where I found Cervantes,
an old, dusty copy of *Don Quixote,*
and where I discovered an old mirror,
and looking into it found my father's face
in my face looking back at me,
and behind us a Brueghel world
crowded with the clamor of the market,
people busy with their lives, hunting,
searching for what's missing. How casual
they seemed, in no hurry, as if they had all
of time, no frenzy, no worry,
as the Castilian sun made its slow
arch over us, the same sun
that lanced the fish on crushed ice
in the market stalls, fish with open mouths,
glazed stares, lapped against each other
like scales, by the dozens, the *Madrileños*
gaping over them, reading them
like some sacred text, like some kind
of psalm or prophecy as they made
their choice, and had it wrapped in paper,
then disappeared into the crowd.
And that is all. I wanted to tell you
the story of that winter in Madrid
where I lived in a room with no windows
at the beginning of my life without my father.
When the fascist officials asked Picasso
about *Guernica:* "Are you responsible
for this painting?" He looked back
at them, and answered slowly: "No.
You are." What should I answer
when asked about this poem?
I wanted to tell you the story of that winter
in Madrid, where my father kept dying, again

and again, inside of me, and I kept
bringing him back, holding him for as long
as I could. I never knew how much
I loved him. I didn't know that grief
would give him back to me, over
and over, I didn't know that those
cobbled streets would someday
lead to here, to this quietude,
this blessing, to my father
within me.

Nominated by Jane Hirshfield, Jack Marshall

VERY, VERY, RED

fiction by DIANE WILLIAMS

from BOSTON REVIEW

I HAVE TOO MUCH of a sense of myself as a man to be reckless. I tell myself, "Get it done!" Robert and Buster have volunteered to help me, but I am not an invalid, Mary.

I have asked myself this question. "What does she need?" Mary, I am not ashamed she is naked in the bed, waiting for me. I told her I knew how to behave. This time, however, when I became bored, I had a very, very, very, very long conversation with Diane, Mary.

She says "Remember who you are. Remember what you do." She promises me that I will be pleasantly surprised. She promises. Sometimes, afterward, I hate her. She pities me. *You poor thing* is what she says.

I will yawn significantly after dinner. "Diane," I will say, "isn't it time that we went up to bed?"

Mary, you say to ask Diane to give me one of her fancy handjobs. Will you be home on Saturday?

I thanked Diane for petting me.

These days Diane's skin is waxy, cold. She fell off of the Chesterfield. She was weary from swimming. I did not try to help her. I was afraid, so this is sad. I unfastened her belt. My hand was strong enough, capable enough. I remember. I remember my enjoyment of our happy home.

We went into the dining room, and Gretch came over to us and Gretch said, "You can have whatever you want!"

Gretch is another one. I am going to sleep with Diane and I am going to sleep with Bill's wife.

Buster said he didn't like Diane as much as he liked our other girlfriend.

"Better eat up those peaches," Buster said.

I said, "Buster, right."

Buster, Buster, Buster.

Perhaps, Mary, I just want to see what will happen to Buster. One would not know why any of this is, if this is a drama or if this is a pageant.

Mary?—could you be with me here, Mary? This would not make things easier for me. I just wanted somebody like you to change her mind.

I don't have to say everything I could say about Diane. The doctor asked Buster to carry Diane in. Her skirt was short. She had bobbed her hair.

She accepted a cigarette from Buster once she was back up on the Chesterfield. She also accepted an ashtray from Buster, and she did a lot of throat-clearing. The doctor treated her like a friend.

"Do you have a sore throat?" the doctor asked her.

She'd be perfectly capable of that. I think Diane did have a sore throat! Diane is life-like.

"I'll have a cup of tea!" Diane said.

They all agreed with her about that.

"She can always make me laugh," Mother said. "She is the smartest person I know!"

I will tell you this—I had the shivers and my neck hurt from sitting in my chair. "I love you with all of my heart," I told Diane. I think it is thrilling to hear people say that.

Diane said she would not mind if I told you how she and I do it—I am top of her, then a little on the side of her.

What a night! I thought I saw you and somebody else, high up on our wall, tiny-sized, getting ready to fuck each other, or you were just finishing up. Together, we had here great rivals in a house.

There are many imitations of Diane here, made of horn and rubber and plastic.

I merely tapped Harriet and she broke.

I wonder what this is. Diane was wearing crazy clothes. Her hat fell off of the Chesterfield where she had set it.

She had sprung back into a curled position. We washed the girl carefully.

You think to yourself, I slept with that thing. What Diane still needs is what I need. She said that after the party she had sobbed and sobbed and sobbed. I have heard her tell that story before.

I gave a little tap tap to the vagina of Diane—where there was a sizable stain on it—ink—still wet. I thought she would go around like this.

It was so easy when I took Diane to the bed. "Isn't this a nice ruffle?" I said.

For your information I said, "What did they do to you Diane? Did they sew you up? Look how little you have made it!"

Aren't I a lucky boy?

Diane gave me something which looks like Honorene. Diane fixed it so that I could wear it on my little finger. It's a little chipped. It's a little uncomfortable. It's tight on me.

Diane said, "I think I got that in Burma." When Diane asked me for it, I threw it across the room. Just joking.

I had expected I would be sympathetic to Diane. I woke up sexy and frightened, thinking about the girls in the window stacked up on top of each other, and thinking about you, you frightening person.

I have been expecting a nice compliment from you. When Buster tried to protect Diane, they threw Buster across the room. That that is.

They pointed at Diane, and Buster tried to protect Diane. They threw Buster across the room.

Diane had her hat on and Diane said, "Where are we going?" and I said, "What do you mean where are we going?" and Diane said, "I am going with you."

I said, "Oh, Diane! Diane, oh, no!"

One day she just left town and she went out West. She called me, she said, "I won the lottery."

Diane—the girl—she was not running away from me! I did a dumb thing! I did such a dumb thing! My hair is sticking out of my head because I did such a dumb thing!

Buster returned here with Diane, saying that he had not had much fun with her. He carried Diane back to the hiding place after we had eaten our dinner with Betty.

Diane's vulva is a bit better now. She wears lip rouge. She wears a necklace of pearls. She wiped her hands.

She can climb in, she can climb out of an automobile. She can drive an automobile up onto, up on top of a roadway. She will do the cutest little trick. We are going to have to touch her vulva. We were not wrong in believing that she had been a full-fledged girl at one point. We thought of touching the vulva.

We have pried her apart, divided her again, discarded the center portion, given her a good soaking. We behave, for what it is worth, with our dicks protruding, as if we were gentlemen.

I have worked pretty hard at this. This has taken me a long time. I expected this to be scratched or chipped by now. I am surprised it isn't.

Diane touched the collar bar you gave me. People must think it is a sin for me to wear this.

She said, "What is this?"

I said, "I found it. Somebody gave it to me. I found it." She said, "Which? Did you find it? Or did somebody give it to you?"

I said, "Both!"

Now you listen, I do not do anything too strenuous. People say I did not leave the garden. That is not true. This is a lie.

My clothing was described. Only what a woman wears is this interesting.

Mary, I spoke to Diane as frankly as I speak to you. I thought Diane was doing fine. There was a fluttering. I felt a tickling. I was stung.

I said, "I was stung." I said, "Would you look, Diane?" I said, "Diane, dear, Olga wouldn't mind it if you fished around inside of my trousers."

"Diane, you have been here forever," Olga said, "haven't you?"

"No," Diane said, "just for two years."

A woman asked us if we had seen Diane. The woman said, "That one wasn't Diane."

I said, "It wasn't?"

"No," the woman said.

We were so surprised. Janet said, "That wasn't Big Gretch."

"It wasn't?" I said.

Janet said, "No, no, that wasn't Big Gretch."

I said, "Where in the world does Big Gretch go?" "

Up and around," Buster said, "that way."

I have a terrible tale I could tell you about that. That that is. Oh, my Mary!—I can tell you anything!

I behave myself.

I use simple words that you can understand—*the vagina of Diane, the children of Mary.* There isn't any puzzle. I could have caught sight of you I realize.

I felt as if they were doing your fucking for you when I saw some people fucking.

Can you remember my exact words out here in the blue? You should receive my instructions today. I apologize, Mary, for hurting your vagina. I apologize, Mary, for being so clumsy with your vagina.

My worry is, is Buster fine now? Uh, the doctor spoke to Buster. The doctor said, "Good job, Buster."

Buster hasn't been that careful and I have had to say to Buster, "Please be careful!"

What will Buster do for me? is what I ask myself. What do you think that Buster will do for me?

Will Buster help out? Buster can be so clever. Mother is clever. It is no surprise, I suppose, that we are clever. I spoke to Buster as frankly as I speak to you, honey.

I don't think I will ever speak so frankly again. Buster can do anything within reason with Diane and Diane agrees with me about this.

I cannot tell you how wonderful I feel when Diane tells anyone, "You are right."

Mary, I wonder what you would have done. One day you will tell me. We have another hard week next week. It will be one thing after another.

To put it another way, it is not too difficult for us to get up into an asshole, and yet it makes some of us say our knees hurt to just think of going up there.

In driblets, we execute our duties toward Diane. We have promised to carry her, to collect her, to distribute her, to fully dispose of her and her name. Daughter of William, second daughter of William. Born 1946. Helpful, tactful, genial—hasn't she often tried to bring herself back in?

She had gone off into the kitchen to get the dessert, to bring it back to us. We were waiting for her. No one was with her in the kitchen.

We might feel a dessert is too scratched up or too cheap, that it is cheap. We could think it is thick.

Diane has to throw herself into bringing us some dessert. "What happened to her?" we said. "Is she coming back?" Boy! She should take every opportunity to come back.

That was her in the window. We could tell by how she was hunched. At last she peeped in.

Diane said, "Fuck me. Touch my breasts." She comes forward. She greets you. She does not go backward. She says hello. Isn't it strange she does not go backward when we walk forward?

We make an effort to avoid getting angry with her. We try not to talk to her in a loud tone. We try not to interrupt her. We try to understand a girl when she speaks to us. We say, "Would you mind going over that again? Will you be kind enough?"

Diane doesn't have your confidence or your courage, but Mary, she is a good person.

Now Mary, Thelma is designed as my new friend. Mr. Cohen said that I should never bring Thelma to London because they beat up people who bring Thelma to London. If she is in it, they will even burn a store to the ground in London. I can bring Thelma to Paris. Paris is fine. Mr. Cohen does not know anything about Prague. Vienna is fine.

I said I have been so careful of Thelma. I said I have never taken her anywhere. I have not fully enjoyed Thelma for all these years. I said I really wanted to take Thelma to Europe. Mr. Cohen said, "Not in the snow! because the skin cracks!"

I am aware of the risks.

I do not want people to gossip about me. You said, "I understand they question you."

We are not the only ones here.

We found a sexual one, but we do not have enough wisdom to take care of so many full-fledged girls and their vulvas. That we still love those girls gives us some reassurance.

A girl should be entertaining and instructive in life. Will it ever be different? Marjorie said she didn't think so.

We can celebrate in the old style. Ahead of time, we prepare. We push our tongues, some of us, into some of them, into their anuses.

"You are pretty, too!" they said.

They were the biggest, the most beautiful batch of people we have ever seen!

"Is there something we should be jealous about?" we said. They said, "No."

We said, "How do you know?"

The eldest of our girls was the fiercest. We don't care. We hope she does come over. Something better comes along.

She was pure gold, Ma'am. We have always said she should have lived in a fairy kingdom, fitted snugly into the fairy kingdom.

It takes us so long to believe what we are saying.

Nominated by Boston Review, Melissa Pritchard

THE POOR ANGEL

by RAY GONZALEZ

from DENVER QUARTERLY

•

One morning I noticed someone passed by.
she looked like the poor woman from across the street,
her family had been destroyed in the earthquake.
Her house is nothing but adobe dust,
straw and wooden beams broken into the first forms
of the cross I recognized outside of any church.

•

Beside the beggar's knife,
I will rejoin the dove.
Beside the wine that is
the blood of the gang leader,
I will fill the bottle with quarters.
Beside the car painted with graffiti,
a street sign that says "One Way."

•

*Tacho prays a lie. He believes in the devil. The tattoo on
    his arm proves it.*
Tacho prays a lie. He wears a hat and sunglasses.
*He used to be in the navy. He used to be my father before
    I was born.*
He used to love my mother before the divorce.

400

Tacho prays a lie.
He cut himself with a razor trying to erase the horns and
tail from his skin.

•

Once I saw a dark mouth.
It played in the air of the night.
It spoke of love and the heart conditioned to believe
our love is the mark of the hair turning gray,
the arms holding each other to say
there is a whisper interpreted as a way to begin again,
a moment of shouting inside the leg,
a loose manner of sweating so we can believe
there are praises that will never go away,
a bite in the dark changing the blackness of security
into the oncoming collision with shoulders,
arms, and legs that have waited too long
for something to invisibly change in that blackness.

•

Asking for the pomegranate to dissolve in my mouth, I spit two or
three seeds out, the red juice marking me as the one who told the
truth, the slowly decapitated piece of fruit turning redder in my
open palm, the seeds rolling out, some of them falling to the floor
for me to step on and crush into red stars that splash farther than
I can imagine. Taking the pomegranate means there is a bare tree
that lied to me, made up a story about how a man and wife remain
perfect, the seeds of the pomegranate hiding on their tongues to be
taken out by each other's soft hands. Sucking on the tiny seeds
means there is a nub, a nipple, a promise to grow old beyond the
tree that escaped the year of the moss, the year of the fungus, the
year of the purple streaks that invaded the earth and changed the
fruit into the sweetest joy and lie enjoyed by the few men able to
identify and pick the pomegranate at the right weight, the correct
fullness, the hardness of red becoming a globe they can never hang

between their legs like the sharpest fantasy they have carried about being mutated, transformed into the red scrotum waiting to be plucked by the lover's hand.

·

Tacho on fire.
Tacho hosting the party.
Tacho and his sandals.
Tacho and his moustache.
Tacho and the hidden bag of sensimilla buds.
Tacho and the cross on the wall.
Tacho and the glowing cross on the wall at night.
Tacho in his bed looking up in the dark at the glowing
    Christ.
Suddenly, something gets in the way.
Something blocks the glow.
Tacho on fire.
Tacho hosting the party.

·

A man was given one chance.
He turned it into a kiss that outburned the blade on the
    car hood.
He turned his chance into escape.
He followed his shoes beyond the city lights.
He saw the river and knew it was true.
The radiance of tomorrow was the mud on his shoes.

·

A man was given one chance to copy the sun and try to build a house out of a dead horse lying in the field, build a farm out of a soil that wouldn't turn black, change his house into the remnant of an old dream where his son came running, the ex-con hiding from the latest crime, the body builder grunting in the backyard, dropping his weights when the rattlesnake struck his leg from behind, dropping the last dumb-bell to flatten the thing that made his father come running for the first and last time.

·

The poor angel's name is Antonio.
He hovers over the poor and the forgotten dogs.
He plays timbales in the ghost band.
He eats thunder and lightning and the rotten shells of
    discarded eggs.
The poor angel has been driven from heaven
and has often invaded hell.
Antonio wanders over the cemetery of the barrio.
He knows where everyone sleeps,
why the young boy standing before the gravestone
of his great-grandmother knows there is a secret down
    there.
The poor angel wants to share it.
It is why it rains when the boy brings flowers in a
    rusted can.

It is why it rains when the boy looks up at the sky.
It is why the poor angel's name is Antonio.
He flooded the cemetery in the storm.
He made the boy find shelter by the gate.
He was the angel who opened the tomb.
He was the black cloud that gave the boy an idea.
He was the rain that watered the flowers over the graves.
The poor angel has more to say,
but the objects the boy finds in the open grave
are things his great-grandmother left him
when he was five years old,
a secret will no one told him about,
his mother and grandmother not wanting him to know
the bright red rosary she left is his,
the crucifix of mahogany was brought from San Luis
    Potosi,
the faded drawing of a man standing by a church tearing
    to shreds,
a second sketch of a woman with long hair sending an odor
across the cemetery grounds,
the poor angel wanting to tell the boy what it means,
why the tiny box of tin the boy can't pry open
is the real find, the testament from the land,

403

the thing it traps inside made for only one boy,
the finger bone clattering inside the box
making noise as the boy gathers the objects,
looks to the sky and runs when he sees
there are poor angels wanting to guide him,
poor angels without hands stretching their arms

•

Tacho came back. He hid in the back of an old 56 Chevy his father left
in the dirt lot next to their house. Tacho tried to sleep it off, but heard
a noise in the middle of the night. He rose from the torn back seat of
the car, looked through the broken window to see that the black pig
had returned. The animal stood looking up at him, its fat greasy skin
shining in the night, its low grunts telling him the sign of the black pig
was good and bad luck and it was time to jump out of the car and go
inside the house, beg his father for a place to sleep.

•

I'm more than the man who gives up,
who says yes I was the one who ran away,
I was the holder of the candle
and the maker of the clay.
I'm more than the whisper
the family finds when they sit down to eat.
They recognize me in time to scold me,
tell me I can't be told anything
because my eyes have been blinded
by the last star that fell in the desert,
my eyes have been altered to fit the story
and get rid of the father.

I'm more than the man who gives up,
who wants to wear a bead around his neck
that means nothing more than I found it
shining on my walk across the hills,
the blue and orange glass hovering
over the thorns, waiting for me to retrieve it
before I could go home.

404

I don't want to be told wearing it
is a sign of belief in something else,
a true mirror of the nightmare and
the coyote transfixed and waiting for me
to share the moon with him.

I'm more than the man with the name Ramon.
I'm more than the man with too much weight.
I'm more than the man who is too silent.

I'm more than the man who dreams of a claw
holding him down, not letting him breathe.

I'm more than the man who believes
in the heat of arrivals when the savior comes down
to cut the claw and let me go.

I'm more than the man who left the desert.
I'm more than the man who fingers the rosary.
I'm more than the man hiding in the cottonfield of the
    Rio Grande.

I'm more than the man who can lead you to the adobe
    ruins.
I'm more than the man who knows what is hidden there.
I'm more than the man who can read the graffiti on the
    cracked walls.

I'm more than the man who gives his life to the wings
that scatter the seed across the river and sows one or two
    floods
that won't allow anything to grow.

I'm more than the man who let Tacho go without a hug.
I'm more than the man who creates his father out of
    loneliness.
I'm more than the man who can show any boy.

I'm more than the man whose future is sequined with
    permission.
I'm more than the man who knows the language of
    heat, sun,
and the myth of the snake and eagle devour each other

until there is nothing left for those who survive
with the presence of strong old women
who will hate you if you say no, if you cross them,

if you talk back, if you tell the truth, if you pray to the
    wrong god,
if you tell them they are wrong, if you invent your own
    family
with the presence of a male to show you how men who
    are more than men

don't need a tree, a long piece of wood, one or two
    timbers, hammers and nail, a
sacrifice—they don't need the great arch to allow
    themselves to survive and still be more
than the men willing to be mounted on the bloody cross.

Nominated by Denver Quarterly

A PARTY ON THE WAY TO ROME

by CHRISTOPHER HOWELL

from POETRY NORTHWEST

In rouge of the night lanterns
I saw four of them rise, one trailing
a blanket, and steal to a bunk near
where I pretended sleep.
Beyond bulkheads and decks the sea
was a rushing dirge by which they cast
that blanket over the man there and began
to hit, hissing "How's this you fucking
faggot bastard!"

Most of us little more than boys, taken off
to war in the usual way, lay listening
to the curses and the cries.

When they were done, Chuck, the leader, saw me
watching and could not clear his face of angry, shamed
confusion, a man caught between what was
and what was wrong. Meanwhile
the beaten one began to scream, "You let them
do it, you just let them!" Then he went weeping
and bleeding up the ladder, the compartment behind him
quiet as an empty church.

When the MAA, taking his time, came among us,
his flashlight could not wake a single witness
so he left, shrugging, promising Justice.

Aeneas endured the distant smoke he knew was Dido
burning. Poor wench. But nothing could sway him
from the path appointed. That is, the free
right life, even the very fruits of empire, was not
so far or difficult to reach, we knew, if one held
steady, unnoticed and on course, if one obeyed
necessity's goddess and could pay
with the kind of fear that pleased her. So smoke
drifted
beyond horizon's palpable secret and nothing more
came of it. So on our very own ship a man
had dared not to sail
from whatever called him down to what he was.
So he had loved men,
it was more than you could say
for the rest of us.

Nominated by Vern Rutsala, Poetry Northwest

WHAT THEY DID

fiction by DAVID MEANS

from OPEN CITY

WHAT THEY DID WAS COVER THE STREAM WITH LONG SLABS OF
reinforced concrete, the kind with steel rods through it. Maybe they
started with a web of rods, then concrete poured over, making a sand-
wich of cement and steel. Perhaps you'd call it more of a creek than a
stream, or in some places, depending on the vernacular, a narrow
gorge through that land, a kind of small canyon with steep sides. They
covered the cement slabs with a few feet of fill, odds and ends, cement
chunks, scraps, bits of stump and crap from excavating the foundation
to the house on the lot, which was about fifty yards in front of the
stream. Then they covered the scraps and crap with a half foot of sandy
dirt excavated near Lake Michigan, bad topsoil, the kind of stuff that
wiped out the Okies in the dust bowl storms. Over that stuff they put
a quarter foot of good topsoil, rich dank humus that costs a bundle,
and then over that they put the turf, rolled it out the way you'd roll out
sheets of toilet paper; then they watered the hell out of it and let it
grow together while the house, being finished, was sided and prepped
for the first walkthroughs by potential owners. His nesting instinct, he
explained, shaking hands with Ingersol, the real estate guy. Marjorie
Howard rested the flat of her hand on her extended belly and thought
due in two weeks but didn't say it. A few stray rocks, or boulders, were
piled near the edge of the driveway and left there as a reminder of
something, maybe the fact that once this had been a natural little glen
with poplars and a few white birch and an easy slope down to the edge,
the drop-off to the creek or brook or whatever it is now hidden under
slabs of concrete—already sinking slightly but not noticeable to the

building inspector who has no idea that the creek is there because it's one of those out of sight out of mind things, better left unsaid so as not to worry the future owners who might worry, if that's their nature, over a creek under reinforced concrete. So all one might see from the kitchen, a big one with the little cooking island in the middle with burners and the wide window, is a slope down to the very end of the yard where a tall cedar fence is being installed, a gentle slope with a very slight sag in the center—but no hint, not in the least, of any kind of stream running through there. In the trial the landscaper guys—or whatever they are—called it a creek, connoting something small and supposedly lessening the stupidity of what they did. The DA called it a river, likened it to River Styx, or the Phlegethon, the boiling river of blood, not citing Dante or anything but just using the words to the befuddlement of the jury, four white men and three white women, three black women, two male Hispanics. Slabs were placed over the creek, or river, whatever, on both adjacent lots, too, same deal, bad soil, humus, rolled turf, sprinkled to high hell until it grew together but still had the slightly fake look that that kind of grass has years and years after the initial unrolling, not a hint of chokeweed or bramble or crabgrass to give it a natural texture. And the river turned to the left further up, into the wasted fields and wooded area slated for development soon but held off by a recession (mainly in heavy industry), pegs with slim fluorescent orange tape fluttering the wind, demarcating future "estates" and cul-de-sacs and gated communities once the poplars and white birch on that section were scalped down to the muddy tire-track ruts. What they did was cover another creek up elsewhere in the same manner, and in doing so they noticed that the slabs buckled slightly upward for some reason, the drying constriction of concrete on the steel rods; and therefore, to counterweight, they hung small galvanized garden buckets of cement down from the centers of each slab on short chains, a bucket per slab that allowed a slight downward pucker until the hardening—not drying, an engineer explained in the trial, but setting, a chemical change, molecules rearranging and so on and so forth—evened it out. So when the rescue guy went down twelve feet sashaying the beam of his miner's lamp around, he saw a strange sight, hardly registered it but saw it, a series of dangling buckets fading out into the darkness above the stream until the creek turned slightly towards the north and disappeared in shadow. What they could've done instead, the engineer said, was to divert the stream to the north (of course costing big bucks and also involving impinging on a railroad right-of-way owned by Conrail, or Penn Central), a process that involves trenching out a path, diverting the water, and allowing the flow to naturally erode out a new bed. What they could've done, a different guy said, an environmental architect who turned bright pink when he called himself that, ashamed as he was of tooting his own horn with the self-righteousness of his title—or so it seemed to Mr. Howard, who of the two was the only one able to compose himself enough to bring his eyes forward. Mrs. Howard dabbled her nose with a shredded Kleenex, sniffed, caught tears, sobbed, did what she had to do. She didn't attend all of the trial, avoiding the part when the photos of the body were shown. She avoided the diagrams of the stream and lot, the charts and cutaways, cross sections of the slabs. Nor could she stand the sight of the backyard, the gaping hole, the yellow police tape and orange cones, and now and then, bright as lightning, a television news light floating there, a final wrap-up for the eleven o'-clock, even CNN coming back days later for a last taste of it. What they could have done is just leave the stream where it was and buffer it up along the sides with a nice-looking, cut-stone retaining wall because according to one expert, the creek, a tributary into the Kalamazoo River, fed mainly by runoff from a local golf course and woods, was drying up slowly anyhow. In the next hundred years or so it would be mostly gone, the guy said, not wanting to contradict the fact that it might have been strong enough to erode the edges of the slab support and pull it away or something, no one was sure, to weaken it enough for the pucker to form. The pucker is what they called it. Not a hole. It's a fucking hole, Mr. Howard said. No one on the defense would admit that it was one of those buckets yanking down in that spot that broke a hole through. Their side of the case was built on erosion, natural forces, an act of God. No one would admit that it had little or nothing to do with the natural forces of erosion. Except silently to himself Ralph Hightower, the site foreman, who came up with the bucket idea in the first place, under great pressure from the guys in Lansing who were funding the project, and his boss, Rob, who was pushing for completion in time for the walkthroughs in spring. Now and then he thought about it, drank a couple of beers and smoked one of his Red Owls and mulled over his guilt the way someone might mull over a very bad ball game, one that lost someone some cash; he didn't like kids a bit, even innocent little girls, but he still felt a small hint of guilt over the rescue guy having to go down there and see her body floating fifteen yards downstream like that and having to wade the shallows in

411

the cramped dark through that spooky water to get her; he'd waded rivers before a couple of times snagging steelhead salmon and knew how slippery it was going over slime-covered rock. Other than Ralph Hightower and his beer, guilt and blame was distributed between ten-odd people until it was a tepid and watered-down thing, like a single droplet of milk in a large tumbler of water—barely visible, a light haze, if even that. All real guilt hung on Marjorie Howard, who saw her girl disappear, vanish, gulped whole by the smooth turf, which was bright green-blue under a clear, absolutely brilliant spring sky. All that rolled turf was just bursting with photosynthetic zest, although you could still tell it was rolled turf by the slightly different gradient hues where the edges met, melded—this after a couple of good years of growth and the sprinkler system going full blast on summer eves and Mr. Howard laying down carefully plotted swaths of Weed & Feed (she'd just read days before her girl vanished in the yard that it was warmth that caused dormant seeds and such to germinate, not light but simply heat). Glancing outside, her point of focus was past the Fisher Price safety gate, which was supposed to mind the deck stairs. She saw Trudy go down them, her half-balanced wobble walk, just able to nav-igate their awkward width (built way past code which is almost worse than breaking code and making them too narrow or too tall, stupidly wide and short for no good reason except some blunder the deck guy made, an apprentice deck kid, really). She was just about halfway across the yard, just about halfway to the cedar fence, making a bee-line after something—real or imagined, who will ever know?—in her mind's eye or real eye, the small bird bath they had out there, perhaps. What they did was frame the reinforcement rods—web or just long straight ones—in wooden rectangles back in the woods, or what had been woods and then was just a rut-filled muddy spot where, in a few months, another house would come. Frames set up, the trucks came in and poured the concrete in and the cement set and then a large rig was brought in to lift the slabs over to the creek, or stream, or what-ever, which by this time was no longer the zippy swift-running knife of water but was so full of silt and mud and runoff from the digging it was more of an oozing swath of brown substance. Whatever fish were still there were so befuddled and dazed they'd hardly count as fish. Lifted them up and over, guiding with ropes, and slapped them down across the top of the stream—maybe twenty in all, more or less depending on how large they were. Then more were put down when they moved up to the next lot, approved or not approved by the inspector who never really came around much anyhow. Then the layers of crappy soil stuff and then the humus and then the rolls of turf while the other guys were roofing and putting up the siding, and the interior guys were cranking away slapping drywall up fast as they could with spackling crews coming behind them, then the painters working alongside the carpet crews with nail guns popping like wild, and behind them, or with them, alongside, whatever, the electricians doing finishing fixtures and the furnace and all that stuff in conjunction with the boss's orders, and the prefab window guys, too, those being slapped into preset frames, double-paned, easy-to-clean and all that, all in order to get ready for the walkthroughs the real estate guys, operating out of Detroit, had lined up. Already the demand was so high on account of the company which was setting up a new international headquarters nearby. This was a rather remote setting for such a venture, but on account of low taxes (an industrial park) and fax machines and all the new technology it didn't matter where your headquarters were so long as they were near enough to one of those branch airports and had a helipad on the roof for CEOs' arrivals and departures. Housing was urgently necessary for the new people. The walkthrough date was in the spring because the company up-and-running date was July first. What the ground did that day was to open up in a smooth, neat little gape— which wasn't more than thirty pounds, maybe less but enough to spur forces already at bay, but that doesn't matter, the facts, the physics, are nothing magical, as one engineer testified, and if this tragedy hadn't've happened—his words—certainly the river itself would have won out, eroded the edge, caused the whole slab to fall during some outdoor barbecue or something, a whole volleyball or badminton game swallowed up in a big gulp of earth. There one second, gone the next was how someone, best left unsaid who, but most likely CNN, described what Marjorie Howard saw—or sensed, because really the phrase seems like a metaphysical poem or maybe a philosophical precept (bad choices on the part of the contractors, no, not choice, nothing about choice there, or maybe fate of God if that has to do with it, one local news report actually used the phrase Act of God, if it's a phrase). But it was an accurate account because standing in the kitchen it was like that, seeing her go, watching her vanish, and all the disbelief that she had seeing it, the momentary loss of sanity and the rubbing of her eyes in utter, fantastical disbelief, would burgeon outward in big waves and never go away no matter what, so that between that one second she was there and the one where her little girl was gone was a wide

413

opening wound that would never be filled, or maybe finished is the word. What they did was guide the slabs down, doing the whole job in one morning because the crane was slated to be used on a project all the way over in Plainwell, and then think while eating lunch from black lunch tins afterwards, feet up on a stump, Ho Hos and Twinkies at the end, looking at the slabs, the river gone, vanished, the creek gone, vanished, nothing but slabs of still-damp cement swirled with swaths of mud—the buckets hanging beneath them out of view—we did a good morning's work, nothing more, nothing less.

Nominated by John Allman

DIARY

by SUSAN WOOD

from THE GETTYSBURG REVIEW

Memory is the diary that chronicles what never happened and couldn't have happened.

Oscar Wilde

Twenty years ago, a spring
    like this one, azaleas spilling
        over the lawns, the color of blood,

of hearts, of fire, a few the color
    of snow, of eggs, white as the blank
        pages of a diary. And our daughter

was like that, about to bloom,
    delicate, lovely as an azalea,
        a tiny bud in her red school uniform.

She was ready to burst
    into blossom that spring day
        we picked her up after school

and she couldn't wait to tell
    what she'd learned. This
        was knowledge and she thought

415

she was giving it to us, a gift,
  making a circle with her thumb
    and forefinger, poking another

finger through it. Do you know
  what this is, she said, do you, do you
    know what happens sometimes at night

when the woman is sleeping,
  that the man puts his penis inside her
    like this and that's how they get their eggs?

She thought it had nothing to do
  with us, and I tried to tell her, to say
    no, wait, it's not like that, not like that

at all, not the woman asleep,
  open, as though she were merely
    a receptacle, like a flower drinking in

pollen, that they both must
  desire it. But she sank back
    in her seat, she was satisfied

then, she didn't care.
  This was mystery, mystery
    explained. And all these years

later you still come to me
  in dreams, and again I'm ready
    to receive you, ready again to make

another child as perfect
  as this one. In one dream
    we're flying, our naked bodies

winging through air,
  and I believe that we'll crash,
    but we don't. And every time

I believe I'm caught
        like a bee in a flower
                that closes around it or that

it never happened at all,
        that I never did what I did,
                never left. And what does she

think now when she thinks
        of another day, the day when
                she opened the door of my closet

and found only the ghosts
        of my dresses, the shadows
                of my shoes dim as footprints

in the moist earth? It was
        winter then, gray and cold.
                Perhaps she thinks of me

then as someone who never
        lived, who never could have
                lived, a woman like a diary lying

open in the rain. Perhaps
        she thinks that this never
                happened, that it never could

have happened, that memory
        is only the blurred and fading images
                of ghosts, the echo of someone's footfall

on an empty stair, a cold pocket of air
        in a room, that this is mystery, a diary's
                ink-stained pages, ruined, indecipherable.

Now she is trying to write
        the story over, in her own hand,
                a diary of a life that has no room

for one like her. She is so like me
        sometimes I believe you had no part
                in her conception, and always I wonder

what she thinks now of that
        mystery, what she thinks when she
                opens and turns to the lover lying open

beside her. This is the life
        I would have had without her,
                and I envy her, I do, the red flower

of envy blooms in my chest, envy
        of mothers for daughters, the way
                my mother must have envied me too,

the first time we turned to each other
        in the long-ago dark and the night closed
                around us. Of course, I haven't forgotten it,

the blossoming of desire, how much
        we wanted to make this child together,
                this child, this bud, this blossom, this flower.

Nominated by Philip Levine, Rosellen Brown

BASHA LEAH

memoir by BRENDA MILLER

from PRAIRIE SCHOONER

> *. . . You are here to kneel*
> *Where prayer has been valid . . .*
> — *T.S. Eliot*

I

In Portugal I walk slowly, like the old Portuguese men: hands crossed behind my back, head tilted forward, lips moving soundlessly around a few simple words. This posture comes naturally in a country wedded to patience, where the bark of the cork oak takes seven years to mature, and olives swell imperceptibly within their leaves. Food simmers a long time—kid stew, bread soup, roast lamb. Celtic dolmens rise slab-layered in fields hazy with lupine and poppies.

It's very late. I've drunk a lot of wine. I don't sense the cords that keep my body synchronized, only the sockets of my shoulders, my fingers hooked on my wrist, the many bones of my feet articulating each step. I'm flimsy as a walking skeleton; a strong breeze might scatter me through the eucalyptus.

A few days ago, in a sixteenth-century church in Évora, I entered the "Chapel of the Bones." Skulls and ribs and femurs mortared the walls, the bones of 5,000 monks arranged in tangled, overlapping tiers. A yellow light bulb burned in the dank ceiling. Two mummified corpses flanked the altar. A placard above the lintel read: *Nos ossos que aqui estamos, Pelos vossos esperamos.* "We bones here are waiting for yours . . . " Visitors murmured all around me, but not in prayer; none of us knelt in front of that dark shrine. What kind of prayer, I wondered, does a person say in the presence of so many bodies, jumbled into mosaic, with no prospect of an orderly resurrection? A prayer of terror, I imagined, or an exclamation of baffled apology.

II

On Shabbat, the observant Jew is given an extra soul, a *Neshama Yeterah* that descends from the tree of life. This ancillary soul enables a person to "celebrate with great joy, and even to eat more than he is capable of during the week." The Shabbat candles represent this spirit, and the woman of the house draws the flame toward her eyes three times to absorb the light.

In California, one rarely heard about such things. We grilled cheeseburgers on the barbecue, and bought thinly sliced ham at the deli, ate bacon with our eggs before going to Hebrew School. Occasionally we visited my grandparents in New York; they lived in a Brooklyn brownstone, descendants of Russian immigrants, and they murmured to each other in Yiddish in their tiny kitchen. They reflexively touched the mezuzah as they came and went from their house. When I watched my grandmother cooking knishes or stuffed cabbage, I imagined her in *babushka* and shawl, bending over the sacred flames while her husband and daughters gazed at her in admiration. So I assumed my mother must have, at some time, lit the Shabbat candles and waited for the *Neshama Yeterah* to flutter into her body like a white, flapping bird.

But when I ask my mother about this, she says no, she never did light the candles. "I didn't really understand," she says. "I thought the candles were lit only in memory of your parents, after they died." She remembers her mother performed a private ceremony at the kitchen counter every Friday evening, but didn't call for her daughters to join in the prayers. My grandfather worked nights as a typesetter; he might have worked on Shabbat, doing whatever was necessary to feed his family in Brooklyn during the Depression, and so my grandmother stood there alone, in her apron, practicing those gestures that took just a few moments: the rasp of the match, the kindle of the wick, the sweep of the arms. She did this after the chicken had roasted, the potatoes had boiled, and the cooking flames were extinguished. But my mother, this American girl with red lips and cropped hair, was never tutored in the physical acts of this womanly ritual.

The *Neshama Yeterah* departs with great commotion on Saturday night. To revive from the Shabbat visitation, a person must sniff a bouquet of spices "meant to comfort and stimulate the ordinary, weekday soul which remains." The ordinary, weekday soul? Does he pace through the arteries and lungs, hands behind his back, finding fault with the liver, the imperfect workings of the heart? "Some cinnamon is all I get?" he mutters. "Some cloves?" In my family, the word soul was rarely mentioned, but my mother and my grandmother chanted the Jewish hymn, "eat, eat," as if they knew our ordinary, everyday souls were always hungry. As if they knew we had within us these little mouths constantly open, sharp beaks ravenous for chicken liver and brisket, *latkes* and pickles and rolls.

III

Outside the spa town of Luso, in the Buçaco woods, in a monastery built by the Carmelite Monks, the shrine to Mary's breast flickers inside a tiny room. I open the cork door, sidle in sideways, and face a portrait of the sorrowful Mary who holds her naked breast between outstretched fingers, one drop of milk lingering on her nipple. The baby Jesus lies faceless in her arms, almost outside the frame, the lines of focus drawn to the exposed breast and the milk about to be spilled. Hundreds of wax breasts burn on a high table, and tucked among these candles are hundreds of children—faded Polaroids of infants in diapers, formal portraits of children with slicked-back hair, stiff ruffles, and bow ties. The children's eyes, moist in the candlelight, peer out from among the breasts and the bowls of silver coins.

The tour guide describes the shrine in Portuguese, using his hands to make the universal symbol for breast. I catch the word *leite;* of course the milk is worshipped here, not the breast itself, that soft chalice of pleasure and duty. I want to ask: what are the words of the prayer? Is the prayer a prophylactic or a cure? But my language here is halting and ridiculous. Whispers linger in the alcove, *Por favor, Maria, Obrigada, Por favor.*

I want to kindle the wick on Mary's breast, but I don't know the proper way—how much money to drop in the bowl, or the posture and volume of prayer.

At home, in Seattle, I volunteer once a week on the infant's ward at Children's Hospital. I hold babies for three hours, and during that time become nothing but a pair of arms, a beating heart, a core of heat. I'm not mindful of any prayer rising in me as we rock, only a wordless, off-key hum. Most of these children eat through a tube slid gently under the skin on the backs of their hands; pacifiers lie gummy on their small pillows as they sleep. I'm sure there's a chapel in the hospital where candles stutter, and a font of holy water drawn from the tap and blessed. Maybe a crucifix, but more likely secular stained glass illuminated by a wan bulb. Mary's breast will not be displayed, of course—the distance between these two places is measured in more than miles—but the succor of Mary's milk might be sought nonetheless.

It will be quiet. The quiet is what's necessary, I suppose, and an opportunity to face the direction where God might reside. I imagine there are always a few people in the chapel, their lips moving in various languages of prayer, including the tongue of grief.

IV

Our synagogue was near the freeway in Van Nuys, California, and it looked like a single-story elementary school, with several cluttered bulletin boards, heavy plate-glass doors, gray carpet thin as felt. White candles flickered in the temple; the Torah was sheathed in purple velvet; gold tassels dangled from the pointed rollers. Black letters, glossy and smooth as scars, rose from the surface of the violet mantle. When the rabbi, or a bar-mitzvah boy, brought the Torah through the congregation, cradling it in his arms, I kissed my fingers and darted out my hand to touch it, like the rest of the women.

In Hebrew School, we learned the greatest sin was to worship a false idol. "God is not a person," my teacher said, "but God is everywhere." The Torah, though we respected it, was not God. The alphabet, though it was a powerful tool, was not God. Abraham and Isaac and Moses were great men, not God. "God is everywhere," my teacher said. "Like the air." I learned about Exodus. I learned about Noah's ark. I learned about the Burning Bush. These miracles were played out by faceless figures smoothed onto the felt board. The twenty-two letters of the alphabet paraded like amiable cartoons across the top of the classroom wall, and I was called by my Hebrew name—*Basha Leah*, which over time was shortened to *Batya*. I preferred the ele-

422

gance of *Basha Leah,* enfolded by lacy veils, while *Batya* turned me into a lumpy dullard, dressed in burlap, switching after the mules.

In the temple, the drone of the prayers rose in a voice close to anger from the men, nearer to anguish from the women, then ebbed into a muttered garble of tongues. I tried not to look too hard at the rabbi, lest I should worship him. I averted my eyes from the face of the cantor. I ended up staring at my feet, squished and aching in their snub-nosed shoes. My mother's hand fell like a feathery apology on the back of my neck, and I swayed uncomfortably in place. The ache in my feet rose through my body until it reached my eye sockets.

"I've had it up to here," my mother sometimes cried, her hand chopping the air like a salute at eye level, grief and frustration rising in her visible as water. In the synagogue, waters of boredom lapped through my body, pouring into every cavity, like a chase scene from "Get Smart." I imagined my soul as a miniature Max, scrambling away, climbing hand over hand up my spine to perch on the occipital ridge until the waters began to recede.

V

There's another kind of soul that enters the body—a *dybbuk,* "one who cleaves." A *dybbuk* speaks in tongues, commits slander, possibly murder, using the body of a weak person as a convenient vehicle. If roused and defeated, this soul will drain out through the person's little toe.

The word *dybbuk* is in me, part of my innate vocabulary, though I don't know how. Perhaps from the murmured conversations of my relatives in Brooklyn and their neighbors, the women with the billowing housedresses and the fleshy upper arms. I was only an occasional visitor to these boroughs saturated with odors of mothballs and boiled chicken, soot and melted snow. I may have heard the Yiddish words in the exchanges between my paternal grandmother and the customers in her knitting shop; I blended into a wall of yarn, camouflaged by the many shades of brown, in a trance of boredom, as the women clustered near the cash register. "That one's a *golem,*" they might say, nodding in the direction of a simple-minded man in the street. A *golem* meaning a zombie, a creature shaped from soil into human form, animated by the name of God slipped under the tongue. Or, "He's possessed of a *dybbuk,*" they might whisper of a neighbor's child gone bad. They gossiped about *nebiches* and *schlemeils,* the bumbling fools who never quite got anything right, swindled from their money or parted from their families through ignorance or bad luck.

Sometimes I sat next to my grandfather after he woke in the afternoons, and he explained the transformation of hot lead into letters, the letters into words, the words into stories. I held my name, printed upside down and backwards on a strip of heavy metal. My grandmothers pinched my cheek and called me *bubbala*—little mother. They cried "God Forbid!" to ward off any harm. On Passover I opened the front door and hollered for Elijah to come in; I watched the wineglass shake as the angel touched his lips to the Manishevitz. I closed my eyes in front of the Hanukkah candles and prayed, fervently, for roller skates.

VI

In the central chapel of the Carmelite monastery in the Buçaco woods, dusty porcelain saints enact their deaths inside scratched glass cases. Above each case the haloed saint, calm and benedictory, gazes down on the lurid scene below: a small single bed, a man's legs twisting the bedclothes, his thin arms reaching out in desperation. The witnesses (a doctor called in the middle of the night? A maid, nauseated by the bloody cough of her master? A scribe, summoned to write the last words?) recoil from the bed in a scattered arc.

And the saint? Somehow he's beamed up and transformed into the overhanging portrait, the eyes half-closed, the halo pressing into place the immaculately combed hair. One finger touches his lips as if to hush the tormented figure below. His arms have flesh; the lips are moist; the background is lush and green.

We have our heaven, too, though I don't remember the mention of Paradise at Temple Ner Tamid. Paradise, I thought, was for the Gentiles; when my Christian friends asked me if I would go to heaven, I sorrowfully shook my head no. They looked at each other, and then at me, touching my shoulder in sweet-natured commiseration. "We don't believe in Jesus," I said, my voice trailing off. I thought our religion was about food. It was about study, hard work, persecution, and grief. But I've since learned there is a Paradise for the Jews; it is, in fact, the Garden of Eden, where the Tree of Life grows dead center. "So huge is this tree that it would take five hundred years to pass from one side of its trunk to the other." We even have a hell: *Gehinnom*, where "malicious gossip is punished by hanging from one's tongue, and Balaam, who enticed the Israelites into sexual immorality, spends his time immersed in boiling semen." Of course, such things weren't mentioned when I was a child.

But my mother covered the mirrors with black cloth when her father died. She sat in mourning, with her mother, for seven days. She may have even spoken the Kaddish for twelve months, since my grandfather had no sons. Certainly she lit the Kaddish candle on Yom Kippur. But I was a child. I didn't listen, or I didn't understand, that the soul remains attached to the dead body for seven days, and takes twelve arduous months—ascending upward, flopping downward, cleaning itself in a river of fire—to enter Paradise. I didn't realize the soul needs our help, in the form of many and repeated prayers.

Before me now, a saint is dying in his rectangular case, on a narrow bed covered with a single woolen blanket. I surreptitiously cross myself, the way I've seen people do. The gesture, so delicate, touching the directional points of my body—my head, my heart, my two arms—seems far removed from the passion of Christ. It doesn't feel like a crucifix I inscribe on my body, but the points of a geometrically perfect circle. I curl one fist inside the other, and I kiss my knuckles, I bow my head. I don't know if I'm praying. It feels more like I'm talking to myself.

VII

Swaying in prayer is "a reflection of the flickering light of the Jewish soul, . . . or it provides much-needed exercise for scholars who spend most of their day sitting and studying." I get out my yoga mat; I sway down into a forward bend and stay there a long time, breathing, and then roll up, one vertebra on top of the other until I stand perfectly straight, aligned. I think about moving a little, and I do, like the oracle's pendulum that swings to and fro in answer to an unspoken question.

VIII

When I was sixteen, I became president of my Jewish Youth group, and we set out to create *meaningful* Shabbat ceremonies, feeding each other *challah* on Friday night, reading passages from Rod McKuen, holding hands in a circle and rapping about our relationships. We petitioned for and received permission for a slumber party, properly chaperoned by our counselors—college students in their early twenties. The minutes from the planning meetings illustrate our real concerns: "It was decided no one under the age of twenty can sleep on the couches." "Challah will be split equally before anyone begins to eat." "Ronnie says no wine. So Mike's in charge of the grape juice." We rented spin-art machines. We got a ping-pong table. We decided to give Ronnie a bar mitzvah.

Ronnie had a black mustache and dreamy brown eyes. He wore tight jeans and read Dylan Thomas. When he confessed that he'd never been bar mitzvahed, we clucked over him like a gaggle of grandmothers. We made plans in the bathroom. We took out every prayerbook we could find. We found him a yarmulke and a dingy tallis to drape across his shoulders. *"Baruch Atah Adonai,"* we chanted in unison, *"elohanu, melach ha'olum . . ."* We closed our eyes, and the prayers trailed off when we didn't know the words; we moved our lips in the parched, desperate way of the old people in synagogue. We swayed back and forth; we felt mature, and very wise. Someone gave a speech enumerating all of Ronnie's strong points. Ronnie gave a speech telling us how he expected to improve in the coming years. We improvised a Torah with pillows, and we made him walk among us, beneath an arch made of our intertwined hands.

I think he cried then, his lips scrunched tight together, a Kleenex in his hand. I remember his thanks, and I remember us sitting in a circle around him, our eager hands damp with sweat, our satisfied faces aglow.

IX

I call home from a post office in Lisbon. My booth, number four, is hot and dusty, my hands already clumsy with sweat, and I dial the many numbers I need to connect me with home. Like the Kabbalists, manipulating the letters of the alphabet, I work this dreary magic. Travel has not agreed with me. I have a fever, and I want to lie down, but my pension has a dark, steep staircase and soggy newspapers in the windows holding back the rain.

My mother answers the phone. I picture her at the kitchen counter: the long wall of photographs tacked together on a bulletin board—all the children, my two brothers and I, peering out at my mother from our many ages. She sits in the green vinyl chair, reflexively picking up

426

her ballpoint to doodle. The lace *shalom* hangs motionless in the entry. A red clay menorah sits on the mantel, the candle holders shaped like chubby monks, their hands uplifted.

"How's everything?" I ask. We talk in a rush. "How are *you*?" she asks again and again. Not until I'm almost ready to hang up does she mention: "Well there is a little problem."

"What?"

"Everything's a little *meshuga*" she says, and her voice gets that catch; I can see her biting her lower lip, pushing her hand up into the hair at her forehead. "I'll put your father on," she says, and I hear the phone change hands.

"Your mother," he says.

"What?"

"Your mother had to have a hysterectomy. They found some cancer."

"What?"

"She's okay," my father says. "Everything's okay."

"A hysterectomy?"

"They got it all, the cancer. They found it early enough. Don't worry."

I'm breaking out in a damp sweat across my face, under my arms. I can't think of anything to say but, "Why didn't she tell me herself?"

"Don't worry," my father says. "Everything's fine."

I decide to believe him. After a few more distance-filled exchanges, our voices overlapping with the delay, I hang up. I push my way past the people waiting for my booth, I pay my *escuedos,* I walk out on the Avenida Da Liberdade among the taxis and the buses. I start walking to the north, but I don't know where I'm going, so I turn around and head to the south along the busy, tree-lined boulevard. I stumble past the National Theater, past a vendor selling brass doorknockers the shape of a hand. What am I looking for? A synagogue? Or another shrine, this one to Mary's womb?

"In the womb a candle burns," the Kabbalah tells us, "the light of which enables the embryo to see from one end of the world to the other. One of the angels teaches it the Torah, but just before birth the angel touches the embryo on the top lip, so it forgets all it has learnt, hence the cleavage on a person's upper lip."

I want to light a candle, the flame sputtering in a bed of salt water and blood. If I had the lace scarf my grandmother gave me when she died, I might slip into a stone synagogue, cover my head and follow the words of the Torah. But I don't know how. I don't know to whom I'd be praying; I thought we weren't allowed to worship a human God, so

I eradicated the concept of God entirely. *It was all a mistake,* I want to say now. *I wasn't listening.* I don't know how to take the alphabet and assemble the letters into a prayer.

There is a Kabbalah tale about an illiterate man who merely uttered the Hebrew alphabet, trusting that God would turn the letters into the necessary words. His prayers, the story goes, were quite potent. But I can hardly remember the alphabet. *Alef, Gimmel, Chai . . .* I don't remember the Hebrew word for please. I remember the words *Aba, Ima.* Father, Mother. I remember the letters tripping across the ceiling, the letters minus their vowels, invisible sounds we needed to learn by heart.

X

A touch of the angel's finger, and knowledge ceases. I touch my lip, the cleavage. *Do you remember?* I ask myself. *Do you?* Something glimmers, like a stone worn an odd color under the stream, but my vision is clouded by a froth of rushing water. Perhaps knowledge exists in the amnion; the fluid is knowledge itself, and the angel's fingernail is sharp; his touch splits the sac, and drains us dumb.

The *mikveh* is a gathering of living waters—pure water from rain or a natural spring. This public bath was the center of any Jewish village; the water refined the body, washed off any unclean souls residing there. A woman stepping into these baths purified herself before marital relations with her husband; on emergence the first object she spied determined the kind of child she might conceive. If she saw a horse, this meant a happy child. A bird might equal spiritual beauty. If she saw an inauspicious omen—a dog, say, with its ugly tongue, or a swine—she could return to the bath and start again.

"The Talmud tells how Rabbi Yochanan, a Palestinian sage of handsome appearance, used to sit at the entrance to the *mikveh,* so that women would see him and have beautiful children like him. To those who questioned his behavior, he answered that he was not troubled by unchaste thoughts on seeing the women emerge, for to him they were like white swans."

What do I see when I step from my tub? My own body, lean and young in the mirror, kneeling to pull the plug and scrub the white porcelain. What do I see when I step from the baths of the Luso spa? Water arcing from the fountain, and all the Portuguese women gathered round its many spouts: bending forward, kneeling, holding out cups and jugs to be filled. A grandmother—in black scarf, wool skirt, and thick stockings—turns to me and smiles.

XI

At my cousin Murray's house, brisket and matzoh balls and potato kugel lay heavy on the oak table. The curtains were drawn; I think of them as black, but they couldn't have been. They were probably maroon, and faintly ribbed like corduroy. I remember an easy chair; and my cousin in the easy chair looking too tense to be reclined; he should have been ramrod straight, the murmur of relatives lapping against him. My memory is hazy with the self-centered fog of childhood, the deep boredom, my eyes at table height, scanning the food.

"If only she'd gotten the dog," someone murmured, not to anyone in particular. This must have been a funeral. I remember my cousin Anita being "found." I didn't understand what that meant, but my cousins were sitting in the living room, covering their faces with their hands. Their yarmulkes slipped sideways off the crowns of their head. I remember the gesture, that's all—three grown men, slumped in chairs, their hands covering their eyes as if they couldn't bear to see any longer. As if they had already seen too much.

I don't think I went to the service. All I remember clearly is the food on the table: platters of chicken, congealing; baskets of knotted rolls; tureens of yellowish soup. And the men in the living room, so contorted in their grief. When I think of my cousins, I see them framed between the legs of adults, in a triangle of light, frozen. No one ate. All that food: for the extra souls, the one extra soul who wouldn't leave the room, even though the burial must have taken place according to Jewish Law, as soon as possible. Someone must have washed the body, anointed her with oil, wrapped her in a shroud. But a soul hovered in the corner of the room, a darkness smudging the corners of my vision. Eat, someone said, it is good to eat, and a plate was brought into my hands.

XII

"One who cleaves." The definition of the word "cleave" is two-fold and contradictory: to cleave means both to split apart and to adhere. Perhaps one is not possible without the other. Perhaps we need to break open before anything can enter us. Or maybe we have to split apart that to which we cling fast.

In yoga class, my teacher tells us to "move from the inner body." We glide our arms and our legs through a substance "thicker than air, like deep water." We swim through the postures. The Sphinx pose. Sun Salute. Tree. I generate intent before the muscles follow. I breathe deeply, I stretch sideways, I reach up, I bring my hands together at my heart. *Namasté,* I whisper. *Namasté.* I know my access to composure is through attention to the pathways and cavities of my body, so I sit cross-legged, my forehead bent to the ground in a posture of deep humility. Sometimes, then, I feel whatever *dybbuks* cling inside me loosen their hold; they begin the long slide down my skeleton to drain out through my little toe.

XIII

I have a snapshot taken of me when I was eighteen. I've got long straight hair, and I'm wearing a Saint Christopher medal around my neck. It falls between my breasts. On another, shorter chain, I wear a gold *chai,* the Hebrew letter for "life." It clings to the bare skin between my collarbones.

The medal was given to me by my first boyfriend—a boy I cleaved to, a boy by whom I was cleaved, split apart. I was *crazy* for him. I wanted the medal because I had seen it on his chest; I had gripped it in my fingers as we made love. He draped the pendant over my head, and kissed me between the eyes.

Eighteen years later, I still have Saint Christopher—a gnarled old man carrying a child on his shoulder, a knotted staff clutched in one hand. He dangles off the edge of my windowsill, next to a *yad* amulet inset with a stone from the Dead Sea. I have candles on the windowsill, their flames swaying to and fro, like little people in prayer.

A Catholic friend tells me that Saint Christopher is no longer a saint; the Vatican has declared him a non-entity. His life is now mere fable about the Christ child crossing a river on the ferryman's shoulders, growing so heavy he became the weight of every bird and tree and animal, the combined tonnage of mankind's suffering. But the ferryman, being a good man, kept at his task, his knees buckling, his back breaking, until he had safely ferried the small child to shore. "It's just a story," my friend says, but I don't understand how this tale differs from

430

the other Biblical accounts: the walking on water, the bread into body, the wine into blood. "It is different," my friend assures me. "Saint Christopher never existed."

But I know people still pray to him. They believe he intervenes in emergency landings, rough storms at sea, close calls on the freeway. Words of terror and belief form a presence too strong to be revoked. I still take him on the road; *it couldn't hurt,* as my grandmother used to say, with the small Jewish shrug, an arch of her plucked eyebrows. All this, whatever you call it—superstition, religion, mysticism—do what makes you happy, *bubbala.*

XIV

Alef, Gimmel, Chai . . . I recite the letters I know, and they grow steady as an incantation, a continual flame. The Kabbalists manipulated the letters into the bodies of living animals and men. They know an alphabet behind the alphabet, a whisper that travels up the Tree of Life like water.

White swans. I dream I am wrapped only in a white sheet, and the Chasidic men turn their square shoulders against me; they will not touch me, they will not talk to me, because I am a woman. I am unclean and dangerous. If I do not follow the law—if I do not light the Sabbath lamp, if I touch the parchment of the Torah, if I look at a man while I'm menstruating—I will be punished by death in childbirth. Punished when I'm most vulnerable, during the act that makes me most a woman. But what about Miriam? I plead. What about Rachel, and Leah, and Ruth? They were women. They saved us. It is a woman who brings the Sabbath light into the home. It is a woman who resides as a divine spirit in the Wailing Wall. But the men, in their black coats, their black hats—the men turn away. They ignore me. I grip the white sheet tighter against me as the men file into the synagogue, muttering.

XV

I'm staying in a pink mansion on a hill overlooking Luso. It used to be the residence of a countess, and the breakfast waitress makes fun of my halting Portuguese. *"Pequeno Leite,"* I say in my submissive voice as she raises the pot of warm milk. I only want a little, but she drenches my coffee anyway, laughing.

431

In the evening I stroll down a winding street, past two women waiting at their windows, their wrinkled elbows resting on the sill. I don't know what they're waiting for: children to come home, or perhaps the pork to grow tender in the stew. They wave to me, amused. Another woman splashes bleach outside her doorway and kneels to scrub the already whitened stone. Bougainvillea, bright as blood, clings to her windowsill. Men are nowhere in sight; this appears to be a province maintained entirely by women. I make my way to a stone bridge and watch the sun sink beyond fields of flowering potatoes.

In the distance, women harvest vegetables in a field. I think they are women, but I can't be sure; all I see are the silhouettes of their bodies bending, and lifting, and bending again. These women—are they the ones who walk to the monastery and tuck pictures of their children between Mary's breasts? Do they pray before that altar? I don't know; they seem always to be working, or resting from their work.

Back in the square, the Portuguese men emerge to sit in clusters, wearing hats and wool vests; they walk down the lanes, their hands behind their backs, or they stand together, leaning on wooden canes. I sit on a bench facing the fountain, and the men converse around me, all inflection and vowels, grunts and assents. I'm silent as a hub, turned by words without meaning, without sense.

XVI

The *luz* bone is a hub, unyielding. "An indestructible bone, shaped like an almond, at the base of the spine, around which a new body will be formed at the Resurrection of the Dead." The *luz* bone feeds only off the *Melaveh Malkah*, the meal eaten on Saturday night to break the Sabbath. It's a bone without sin, taking no part in Adam's gluttony in the garden; so our new bodies on the day of judgment will be sweet and pure.

For proof of its durability, three men in a Jewish village tested a *luz* bone. (Like magpies, did they pluck the bone out of the rubble of an old man? or of a woman dead in childbirth? or of a child?) They smuggled the *luz* bone to the outskirts of their village, to a blacksmith's shop, the fires glowing red in the stove. They thrust the vertebra in the coals; they plunged it under water; they beat upon it with sledgehammers. I can see them, these men dressed in ripe wool, sweating, their black hats tilted back on their heads. They hold it up to the light of the moon, the bone glossy from its trials, but intact. It's smooth as an egg, oval and warm.

XVII

" . . . those who bow to God in prayer are thought to guarantee themselves a resurrected body, because they stimulate the *luz* bone when they bend their spine."

Downward-Facing Dog: the sit-bones lifted upward. Forward bend. Triangle. Warrior I, II, III. Sphinx. Cobra. Cow. These words come to me like directives, and my body twists and bends and turns, gyrating in a circle around the *luz* bone.

The Tree. I balance on one foot, the other pressed into my thigh. I put my hands together in front of my chest. I breathe. I look past my reflection in the window; I focus my gaze on the trunk of a holly. I grow steady and invisible. The alphabet hangs from my branches like oddly-shaped fruit.

Child's pose. I curl into a fetal position on the mat.

Nu? I hear my mother's voice across a great distance. *Nu, Fay-galleh?* She pats one hand on her swollen abdomen, and holds it there. I want to answer, but from my mouth comes a watery language no one can understand.

Nominated by Prairie Schooner, Nancy Richard

FOR BRIGIT IN ILLINOIS

by RENÉE ASHLEY

from THE VARIOUS REASONS OF LIGHT (Avocet Press Inc)

Dear Brigit,
          (Come back.) Here the quiet moon burns
like hayfire over the mountain; the lush rose,
wild as milkweed, burgeons in the dark on the roadside
where, in daylight, you saw yourself in the stark yellow eye
of the grackle. (I never really thought you'd leave.)
Now, your words, dusky as bird wings, rise; you

reckon the distance between our lives—I can hear you
thinking. (What I know is: the good sober will burns
in you like insatiable fire. You never lost it.) The leaves
in May (do you remember?) burst from their delirious twigs and rose
sharp as sawteeth in the generous sky. I
thought god had made his glorious point right there, outside

the body, in the visible heaven where the new green sighed
and the air shimmered like the coruscating pond. You
spoke of angels with bodies, the soul focusing its bright eye
on substance, the solace of a promised resurrection, the burning
need for the coming together again (I believed every word). We rose
like spirits ourselves, two souls glad of understanding—the leaves

about us, above us like dreams. We thought: no one ever really leaves.
In this life we were wrong. In this life the issue of where you reside
matters. (I miss you—the house finch, hungry and rose-
colored, takes his thistle like alms; he is humble and strong. You

434

would like that.) Now, all around me the bright tongue of god
    unfurls and burns
—you must see it in the plains: the gold light of morning, the violet
    dusk. I

trust we still share the vivid heavens; the idea of the mountains, I
leave that to recall: the way they rise beneath god's feet, the way the
    leaves
that crown them catch the vast, explosive light, and burn
around and around the countless birds who live invisibly on the
    mountainsides.
(Nothing is the same. The landscape is too big without you.)
I imagine the flat land where you live: linear, predictable,
    innumerable placid rows,

inexhaustible greens, lush golds keen as the level eye of the grackle
    as he rose
and you saw yourself go with him. (We never understood the birds,
    their cold eyes
like small stones, or like glass. The ambivalent fires rage inside their
    hollow bones—you
must understand that now, the way I understand, or think I do, the
    taking leave
of a place you love and the way sorrow, its quiet shadow ebbing, one
    day subsides.)
Nothing is forever. (Come back. Tonight the night burns

in the thousand treetops and the fire leaps even from the pale rose,
    its leaves,
its fine, myriad thorns; it springs from the eyes of the dark sleeping
    birds, from the undersides
of their dark wings. You must close your eyes. Come home—we'll
    watch the red finch burn.)

Nominated by Molly Bendall

HARRY GINSBERG

fiction by CHARLES BAXTER

from PLOUGHSHARES

As a Jew, I am drawn in a suicidal manner toward the maddest of Christians. Kierkegaard, being one of the craziest and most lovable of the lot, and, therefore, dialectically, possibly the most sane of them all, is of compelling interest to me. All my life, I have tracked his ghost doggedly through the snow. Lonely, eccentric, and deranged, the man Kierkegaard (1813–1855) was drawn to philosophize about matters concerning which one cannot acquire *any* certainty whatsoever. Kierkegaard worried continuously about the mode in which one might think, or could think, about two unknowns: God and love. These were for the hapless Kierkegaard the most compelling topics. They bound him in tantalizing straps. Of the two vast subjects about which one can never be certain and should therefore perhaps keep silent, God and love, Kierkegaard, a bachelor, claimed especial expertise. Kierkegaard's homage to both was multifarious verbiage. He wrote intricately beautiful semi-nonsense and thus became a hero of the intellectual type.

I learned Danish in order to read Kierkegaard. His picture is on the wall in my study. I cannot write a word without his image up there, looking down at me.

As a member of the bourgeoisie, which is what I am, I live quietly in Ann Arbor, Michigan, a city of ghosts and mutterers. Everywhere you go in this town, you hear people muttering. Often this is brilliant muttering, *tenurable* muttering, but that is not my point. All these mini-vocalizations are the effect of the local university, the Amalga-

436

mated Education Corporation, as I call it, my employer. It is in the nature of universities to promote ideas that should not be put to use, whose glories must reside exclusively in the cranium. Therefore the muttering. There are exceptions, of course. The multimillionaire lawyers and doctors and engineers—how did they get into the university in the first place?—live here among us in their, to quote Cole Porter, *stinking pink palazzos*, and motor about in their lustrous sleek cars massive with horsepower. The warped personalities, like myself, like my prey Kierkegaard, walk hunched over and unnoticed, or we wait at the bus stops, managing our intricate and tiny mental kingdoms as the rain falls on our unhatted heads. We wait for the millennium and for Elijah.

I live next door to Bradley W. Smith. I see him walking his dog, also called Bradley. What is this, that a man should name his dog after himself? The man runs a local coffee franchise, a modest achievement, in all truth. Megalomania can strike anywhere, I suppose is the point.

After he lost his second wife to another man, I decided to explain to him about Kierkegaard. In doing so, I first used the example of myself.

My wife is Esther, a tough bird, the love of my existence. She works as a biochemist for one of the local drug companies. It was Esther who years ago found out that the wonder medication Clodobrazole deformed babies in the womb, gave them unnatural shapes, took away toes and fingers and entire arms. If Esther's mother hadn't joined the Party as a young woman (and who else but the Reds were trying to desegregate the public beaches in those days? who else had a *single* social idea worth implementing?), and hadn't dressed Esther in red diapers, and hadn't signed Esther up for the Party as a child, she would have been proclaimed, my Esther, from the rooftops. But somehow, in the shower of publicity, some measuring worm looked up her background, and, though Esther as a youngster was blameless, and not a Leninist but a reader of Trotsky, that was that.

We live, in all truth, a tranquil domestic life. We have a year or two to go before retirement. Mondays, Wednesdays, and Fridays, I cook dinner. My specialty is beef burgundy, very tasty, you have to remember to cook it slowly, covered, of course, in the liquids so that the meat and the onions and the potatoes become tender. Tuesday and Thursdays are the nights when Esther cooks. We read, we talk, we play canasta and Scrabble. We feed the two goldfish, Julius and Ethel. *They must live.*

As is proper, the children—all grown—have left home. We have three. The oldest, our beautiful daughter, Sarah, is, like her mother, a biochemist. She is successful but, so far, unmarried. She would be a handful for any man. I mean this as praise and description. The middle one, Ephraim, is a mathematician and father to three wonderful little ones, our grandchildren. I have pictures here somewhere. Of the youngest, Aaron, who is crazy, I should not speak. And not because he blames me for the mess in his head. No: he deserves to be left alone with his commonplace lunacies—he calls them ideas—and given peace. He lives, it goes without saying, in Los Angeles.

After Kathryn, Bradley's first wife—a woman I never met, I should add—left him, Bradley became a manager of a local coffee shop and subsequently bought the house next door. He became our neighbor. He moved into the haunted house adjacent to ours, haunted not by ghosts but divorce. There was a divorce dybbuk living inside the woodwork. Young couples would purchase that property, they would take up occupancy, they would quarrel, the quarreling would escalate to shouting and table pounding, they would anathematize each other, and, presto, they would move out, not together, but separately. They would scatter. Then back it would go onto the real estate market. *Three couples* we saw this happen to.

I should explain. At first sight, each time they arrived, they were fine scrubbed American pragmatists you might see photographed in a glossy magazine. Blond, blue-eyed Rotarians, fresh owners of real estate, Hemingway readers, they would unload their cheerful sunny furniture from U-Haul vans. By the time they moved out, they would have acquired mottled gray skin and haggard Eastern European expressions. Even the children by that time would have the greenish appearance of owl-eyed Soviet refugees stumbling out of Aeroflot. Well, of course domesticity is not for every taste, but these young families emerged from that house bent and broken, like vegetables left forgotten in the crisper.

So, when Bradley arrived, alone except for his dog, we thought: The curse is over. The dybbuk will have to locate itself elsewhere. That was until Bradley met and married Diana. But I am getting ahead of myself.

This Bradley, an interesting man, invited Esther and me to dinner the second week he was installed in that house. A courageous gesture. He was not afraid of Jews. He served veal, which Esther will not eat. In the dining room, she picked at it delicately. She left small scraps of it distributed randomly around her plate. I said later, At least no ham, no pork, no shrimp mousse, no trayf. But Harry, she said, veal to me is like a frozen scream. I can't eat it. So don't eat it, I said. So I don't, she said. So?

The man, Bradley, had a certain hangdog diffuseness characteristic of the recently divorced. But he was trying against certain odds to be cheerful. He asked me about my work, he asked Esther about *her* work, and he listened pleasantly while we did our best to explain. These topics do not provide good conversation. He listened, though. He had large watchful eyes. I was reminded of an extremely handsome toad, a toad with class and style and good tailoring. He seemed to be living far down inside himself, perhaps in a secret passageway connected to his heart. Biochemistry does not scintillate at the dinner table, however, nor do neo-Kantian aesthetics. Only when I mentioned Kierkegaard did Bradley perk up. From behind a locked bedroom door, his dog simultaneously barked. I assumed that the dog had caught sight of the dybbuk or was interested in Kierkegaard.

Prompted by his interest, I said that Kierkegaard, the Danish philosopher, had been both unlucky and boorish in love. He had fallen in love with an attractive girl, Regine Olsen, and then he had concluded that they would be incompatible, that the love was mistaken, that he himself was complex and she was simple, and he contrived to break the engagement so as to give the appearance that it was the young lady's fault, not his.

He succeeded at least in breaking the engagement, in never marrying her. Cowardice familiar to many young men was probably involved here. Kierkegaard wished to believe that the fault lay with the nature of love itself, the *problem* of love, its fate in his life. From the personal he extrapolated to the general. A philosopher's trick. Regine married another man and moved away from Copenhagen to the West Indies, but Kierkegaard, the knight of faith, carried a burning torch, in the form of his philosophy, for her the rest of his days. This is madness of a complex lifelong variety. He spent his career writing philosophy that would, among other things, justify his actions toward Regine Olsen. He died of a warped spine.

Esther says that when I am seated at a dinner table, plates and food in front of me, I am transmogrified into a bore. Yak yak, she says. At the table she adjusted her watchband and raised her eyebrows to me. I felt her kicking me in the shins.

Still I pressed on.

439

Søren Kierkegaard maintained that everyone experiences love, everyone knows what it is intuitively, and yet it cannot be spoken of directly. Or distinctly. It falls into the category of the unknown, where plain speech is inadequate to the obscurity of the subject. Similarly, everyone experiences God, but the experience of God is so unlike the rest of our experiences that there, too, plain speech is defeated. According to Kierkegaard, nearly everyone intuits the subtlety of God, but almost no one knows how to speak of Him. This is where our troubles begin.

At this point I noticed Bradley's attention flagging somewhat. Esther kicked me again. She glanced toward Bradley, our new neighbor. Don't lecture the boy, she meant.

I raised my voice to keep his attention. Speaking about God is not, I said, pounding the dinner table lightly with my fist for emphasis, the same as talking about car dealerships or Phillips screwdrivers. The salt and pepper shakers clattered. The problem with love and God, the two of them, is how to say anything about them that doesn't annihilate them instantly with the wrong words, with untruth. In *The Philosophical Fragments,* Kierkegaard points out that the wrong words destroy love in a way that waiting for one's lover, delaying consummation, never can. In this sense, love and God are equivalents. We feel both, but because we cannot speak clearly about them, we end up—wordless, inarticulate—by denying their existence altogether, and, pfffffft, they die. (They can, however, come back. Because God is a god, when He is dead, He doesn't have to *stay* dead. He can come back if He chooses to. Nietzsche somehow failed to mention this.)

Both God and love are best described and addressed by means of poetry. Poetry, however, is also stone dead at the present time, like its first cousin, God. Love will very quickly follow, no? Hmm? Don't you agree? I asked. After God dies, must love, a smaller god, not follow?

Uh, I don't know. I'll have to think about it. Do you want some dessert, professor? Bradley, our new neighbor, asked. I got some ice cream here in the refrigerator. It's chocolate.

A very nice change of subject, Esther said, breathless with relief. Harry, she continued, I think you should save Kierkegaard for some other time. For perhaps another party. A party with more Ph.D.'s.

She gave me a loving but boldly impatient look, perfected from a lifetime of practice. Esther does not like it when I philosophize about love. She feels implicated.

Okay, I said, I'm sorry. I get going, and I can't help myself. I'm like a man trying to rid himself of an obsession. Actually, I *am* that man. I'm not *like* him at all.

Esther turned toward Bradley Smith. Harry, she said, is on the outs in his department. He does all the unfashionable philosophers, he's a baggage handler of Bigthink. What do you do, again, Mr. Smith? You explained, but I forgot.

Well, he said, I've just bought into a coffee shop in the mall, I have a partnership, and now I'm managing it.

This interested me because I've always wanted to open a restaurant.

Also, he continued, I'm an artist. I paint pictures. There was an appreciable pause in the conversation while Esther and I took this in. Would you like to see my paintings? he asked. They're all in the basement. Except for that one—he pointed—up there on the living room wall.

Esther appeared discountenanced but recovered herself quickly.

The artwork he had indicated had a great deal of open space in it. The painting itself covered much of the wall. However, three quarters of the canvas appeared to be vacant. It was like undeveloped commercial property. It hadn't even been compromised with white paint. It was just unfulfilled canvas. Perhaps the open space was a commentary on what *was* there. In the upper right-hand corner of the picture, though, was the appearance of a window, or what might have been a window if you were disposed to think of it representationally. Through this window you could discern, distantly, a patch of green—which I took to be a field—and in the center of this green, one could construe a figure. A figure of sorts. Unmistakably a woman.

Who's that? I asked.

The painting's called *Synergy #1,* Bradley said.

Okay, but *who's* that?

Just a person.

What sort of person? What were you thinking of?

Oh, it's just an abstract person.

Esther laughed. Bradley, she said, I never heard of an abstract person before. Except for the persons that my husband thinks of professionally. Example-persons, for example.

Well, this one is. Abstract, I mean.

It looks like a woman to me, Esther said. Viewed from a distance. As long as it's a woman, it's not abstract.

441

Well, maybe she's on the way to becoming abstract.

Oh, you mean, as if she's all women? *A symbol for women?* There she is, not a woman but all women, wrapped up in one woman, there in the distance?

Maybe.

Well, Esther said, I don't like *that.* No such thing as Woman. Just women, and *a* woman, such as me, for example, clomping around in my mud boots. But that's not to say that I don't like your painting. I do like it.

Thank you. I haven't sold it yet.

I like the window, Esther continued, and all those scrappy unpainted areas.

It's not quite unpainted, he informed us. It's underpainted. I splashed some coffee on the canvas to stain it. Blend-of-the-day coffee from the place where I work. It's a statement. You just can't see the stains from here.

Ah, I said, nodding. A statement about capitalism?

Esther glared at me.

You want to see my pictures in the basement? Bradley asked.

Sure, I said, why not?

Only thing is, he said, there're some yellow jackets nesting in the walls—or wasps—and you'll have to watch when you get down there. Careful not to get stung.

We'll do that, I said.

About this basement and the paintings residing there, what can I say? I held Esther's hand as we descended the stairs. I feared that she might stumble. Wasps, likewise, were on my mind. I did not want to have her stung and would protect her if necessary. Bradley had located his paintings along the walls, as painters do, on the floor, leaning. Each painting leaned into another like derelicts reclining against other derelicts. He had installed a fervent showering bath of fluorescent light overhead. A quantity of light like that will give you a headache if you're inclined, as I am, toward pain. The basement smelled of turpentine and paint substances, the pleasant sinus-clearing elemental ingredients of art, backed by the more pessimistic odors of sub-surface cellar mold and mildew.

One by one he brought out his visions.

This, he said, is *Composition in Gray and Black.*

He held up, for our inspection, images of syphilis and gonorrhea.

442

And this, he said, is called *Free Weights.*

Very interesting, Esther said, scratching her nose with a pencil she had found somewhere, as she contemplated our neighbor's abstract dumbbells and barbells, seemingly hanging, like acorns, from badly imagined and executed surrealist trees, growing in a forest of fog and painterly confusion that no revision could hope to clarify.

And here, he said, lugging out a larger canvas from behind the others, is a different sort of picture. In my former style. He placed it before us.

Until that moment I had thought the boy, our neighbor, a dumb bunny. This painting was breath-snatching. What's this called? I asked him.

I call it *The Feast of Love,* Bradley said.

In contrast to his other paintings, which appeared to have been slopped over with mud and coffee grounds, this one, this feast of love, consisted of color. A sunlit table—on which had been set dishes and cups and glasses—appeared to be overflowing with light. The table and the feast had been placed in the foreground, and on all sides the background fell backward into a sort of visible darkness. The eye returned to the table. In the glasses was not wine but light, on the plates were dishes of the brightest hues, as if the appetite the guest brought to this feast was an appetite not for food but for the entire spectrum as lit by celestial arc lamps. The food had no shape. It only had color, burning pastels, of the pale but intense variety. Spooky magic flowed from one end of the table to the other, all the suggestions of food having been abstracted into too-bright shapes, as if one had stepped out of a movie theater into a bright afternoon summer downtown where all the objects were so overcrowded with light that the eye couldn't process any of it. The painting was like a flashbulb, a blinding, cataract art. This food laid out before us was like that. Then I noticed that the front of the table seemed to be tipped toward the viewer, as if all this light, and all this food, and all this love, was about to slide into our laps. The feast of love was the feast of light, and it was about to become ours.

Esther sighed: Oh oh oh. It's beautiful. And then she said, Where are the people?

There aren't any, Bradley told her.

Why not?

Because, he said, no one's ever allowed to go there. You can see it, but you can't reach it.

Now it was my turn to scratch my balding head. Bradley, I barked at him, this is not like your other paintings, this is magnificent, why do you hide such things?

Because it's not true, he said.

What do you mean, it's not true? Of course it's true, if you can paint it.

No, he said, still looking fixedly at his creation. If you can't get there, then it's not true. He looked up at me and Esther, two old people holding hands in our neighbor's basement. I'm not a fool, he said. I don't spend my time painting foolish dreams and fantasies. Once was enough.

I could have argued with him but chose not to.

And with that, he picked up the painting and hid it behind the silly ugly dumbbells growing like acorns on psychotic trees.

What a strange young man, Esther said, tucked in next to me, several hours later, sleepy but sleepless in the dark. Her nightgown swished as she tossed and turned. He seems so nondescript and Midwestern, harmless, and then he produces from the back of his basement a picture that anyone would remember for the rest of their lives.

Oh, I said, you could say it's imitation-Matisse or imitation-Hockney. Besides, I said, light as a subject for contemporary paintings is passé.

You *could* say that, Esther whispered, but you *wouldn't,* and if you *did*, you'd be *wrong*.

She gave me a little playful slap.

I only said that you could say that, not that you would.

You didn't actually say it.

No. Not actually.

Good, Esther said. I realized that she was agitated. I turned to her and rubbed her back and her neck, and she put her hands on my face. I could feel her smiling in the darkness. I could feel her wrinkles rising.

Harry, she said, it was a recognition for me, a moment of beauty. How strange that a wonderful painting should be created by such a seemingly mediocre man. Our neighbor, living in the Dybbuk House. How strange, how strange. Then she sighed. How strange, she said again.

Then the phone rang.

Don't answer it, Esther quickly said. You mustn't. Don't, dear, don't, don't, don't.

No, I must, I told her. I must.

I picked up the telephone receiver and said hello. From across the continent, on the West Coast, my son Aaron began speaking to me. In

444

a voice tireless with rage, he cursed me and his mother who lay beside me. Once again I was invited to hear the story of how I had ruined his life, destroyed his soul, sacrificed him to the devils and angels of lost ambition. In numbing fashion he found words to batter my heart. Indictment: I had expected more of him than he could achieve. Indictment: I had had hopes for him that drove him, he said, insane. Indictment: I was who I was. Crazy, sick, and inspired with malice, he described his craziness and his sickness in detail, his terrible impulses to hurt others and to hurt himself, as if I had not heard this story many times before, several times, innumerable times. Razors, wire, gas. He called me, his father, a motherfucker. Then he broke down in tears and asked for money. *Demanded* money. From the nothingness and everlasting night of his life, he demanded cash. I, too, was weeping with sorrow and rage, holding the earpiece tightly to my head so that not a word would escape to be audible to Esther. Cupping my hand around the mouthpiece, I asked him if he had hurt anyone, if he had hurt himself, and he said no, but he was thinking about it, he planned every single minute in advance, he planned monstrous personal calamities, he needed help, he would ask for help, but first he had to have money *now*, this very minute, *my* money, superhuman quantities of it. Don't make me your sacrificial lamp, he said, then corrected himself, sacrificial lamb, don't you do that now, not again. I said, against my better judgement, that I would see what I could do, I would send him what I had. He seemed briefly calm. He breathed in and out. He pleasantly wished me goodnight, as if at the conclusion of an effective performance.

To have a son or daughter like this is to have a portion of the spirit shrivel and die, never to recover. You witness the lost soul of your child floating out into the ethers of eternity. Ethics is a dream, and tenderness a daytime phantasm, lost when night comes. Esther and I, eyes open, held each other until dawn broke. My darling wept in my arms, our hearts in ruin. We live in a large city, populated only by ourselves.

Kafka: *A false alarm on the night bell once answered—it cannot be made good, not ever.*

Nominated by Ploughshares, Rosellen Brown, David Jauss, Lee Upton

THE SKY-BLUE DRESS

by CATHY SONG

from THE KENYON REVIEW

The light says *hurry* and the woman
gathers the perishables to the table, the fish
thawed to a chilled translucency, the roses
lifted out of a sink of rainwater, the clean hunger
on the faces of her husband and children faithful
as the biscuits they crumble into their mouths.
Hunger is the wedge that keeps them intact,
a star spilling from the fruit
she slices in a dizzying multiplication of hands
wiping a child's mouth of butter, hands
wiping a dishrag across a clean plate.
She stands at the door waving the dishrag—
ready, set, go!—calling the children in, shooing
the children out, caught in a perpetual
dismantling, a restlessness she strikes the rag at
as if she could hush the air invented by flies.

The light says *hurry* and the family
gathers at the table, the tablecloth washed through countless
fumblings of grace, its garland hem of fruits clouds
into blue pools, faded as a bruise or a reckless tattoo or the roses
the woman hurried that morning into the house,
rushing to revive the steaming petals out of wet
bundles of newspaper the roses traveled in
up the mountain from the market by the sea,
flowers more precious than fish

she left spoiling in the backseat of the car.
Petals and flesh are perishable as the starfruit
a friend of the family climbed the tree to save,
tossing to earth what the sun, the birds, the insects
were days, hours, minutes from rotting.
The roses, stems cut at a slant under rainwater,
breathe cool nights into the air thick with biscuits.
On the table beside the roses a dish of butter disappears
as each knife swipes
its portion, its brightness, its wedge of cadmium lemon.

The light says *hurry* and the man
begins to paint roses while his wife tosses in her sleep
and dreams of a dress she wore long before
she was married, a dress that flowed to her feet
when her hair swirled at her knees, swirled
even when she was simply standing under a tree.
The man who was just a boy then remembers
the first time he saw her, she was standing in a river of hair,
remembers this as he begins to paint roses.
She dreams of the sky-blue dress,
how she once filled it with nothing but skin.
Flesh does not fill it.
Neither does wind.
The girl who wore it left it
pinned like a hole in the sky
the woman passes through, sleep
pouring out of her into water,
all the broken water that leaves
the dress empty, simply hanging from a tree.
She throws off the covers and the moon
washes her in a light that is disturbing,
lifts her into a restlessness
that coincides with the appearance of flies
earlier in the week dragging a net of buzzing,
blue and claustrophobic,
forcing her to examine the roses.

The light says *hurry* and the boy
who came to the man and the woman late in marriage

447

slips his tooth under his parents' pillow.
In this way he knows they will remember to wake up.
He fills the night with his sweet breath,
breath unimpeded, flowing out of the space
once blocked by the tooth.
Behind the rock there is a cave.
Behind the moon there is simply dark space.
His mother will find the tooth when she makes the bed.
She will save it with all the other teeth hidden under pillows—
broken and intact, smooth and milky—
petals and buttons,
slices of the star-shaped fruit,
shells found nesting in the crevice of pools.

Nominated by Arthur Sze

LOVE OR NOTHING

by HUGH COYLE

from ART AND UNDERSTANDING

for A. Caston

I call our house a hive, not for the wasps
that hover along the eaves on hot days
or the honeybees darting from lilac
to apple out back, but for ourselves:
Bradley, Ben, and me, William—
three men with HIV, a housing grant,
and Medicaid subsidies. The windows
of our four-bedroom building
look east into urban sprawl, west
toward a cemetery where deer drift about
in the evening, peaceable spirits.
The tallest monuments rise in the middle,
cracked granite phalluses. Around them
cluster lesser stones, plain white slabs
and sunken markers. With binoculars,
I can squint to make out carved crosses
and inscriptions, last names mostly,
never Christian names or dates.

I'm the one who's lived here
longest, the one whose wheelchair
hums down ground floor hallways

449

to answer the doorbell, the phone, the call
of nature. Bradley and Ben have rooms
above mine, but mostly spend days
downstairs with me. They sometimes sleep
in the fourth upstairs bedroom,
the empty one we've come to call
"Hope." Some days my friends drop
by with casseroles, might stay for a quick
round of Hearts. They ask me about Ben,
the most recent resident, and his progress
with protease cocktails. I tell them he's fine,
no signs of resistance, but they really want
to know if he sleeps in the nude, if his cock
swings right or left, if he still has unprotected sex.

Some nights our living room is crowded
with Bradley's activist friends, thick with
the pungent stink of their magic markers
and spray paint. Our tongues get all sticky
and dry with the minty adhesive
of envelopes. Loud music pulses
around us, mostly dance mixes.
"Adrenal enhancers," Ben likes
to call them. "Sonic stimulants."

I love Ben.
I love the way he slips his pills
into tapioca, winks and licks his lips
as he raises the spoon. I love the fact
that he walks around naked each morning
and practices kick-boxing while watching
the TV talk shows. I love his pierced nipple,
the thin hoop of gold his dead lover
left there. I love that he lets me
wheel him around in my lap, that we dance
that way when we're alone and feeling
all cooped up and crazy. I love seeing him
as a killer queen among drones, strong
in spite of adversity, the one sting
I'd die for.

I may be senseless below the waist, but I believe
in the generosity of gods, in life
after death, in love despite affliction.
When I close my eyes and listen
intently, I can hear the bees upstairs
building their combs, cell by cell in the walls.
I can see Ben sleeping beside them, and send
my soul up to curl and settle like smoke
in the curve of his stomach. It spreads across
his chest, between the thin brown hairs
that cover his heart, and trembles slightly.
I believe that dreams do outlive us, do last
beyond the body. Even as my spirit lifts
above him and dissipates, some trace
will linger. It's love that keeps it there.
It's either that, or it's nothing.

Nominated by Michael Collier

SELF KNOWLEDGE

fiction by RICHARD BAUSCH

from FIVE POINTS

T HAT MORNING Allan Meltzer had an asthma attack and was taken to the hospital. It disrupted the class, and Miss Porter, the teacher, felt herself edge toward panic. Her husband was in Seattle trying to save things. A once-big man in the airline industry, was Jack—gone a lot these days, even when home: money troubles, drinking through the evenings to calm down. She too. They drank separately, and he'd been abusive on occasion. They were going to pieces.

A wonderful word—cordials. She'd drink cordials in the nights, bouncing around alone in the house. She felt no bitterness, considered herself a fighter. They were in serious debt, living on cash only, bills piling up. This month's cash was gone. The house was empty of cordiality. She had no appetite, to speak of, and nothing to drink. A terrible morning.

But she got herself up and out to work. And Allan had the asthma attack.

Pure terror. No one had ever expressed how *physical* thirst could get, how deep it went down into the soul.

Some days, Allan Meltzer's parents prevailed on her to give the boy a ride home. They lived a hundred yards from her, on the other side of a stand of sycamores. Allan was a quiet kid. She had heard the boy's loud father outside, calling him "stupid." Names like that. She would think about Allan's big eyes in class, how he stared. She'd tried being especially kind—this kid with asthma, allergies, a fear of others. The other children were murderously perceptive, and pecked at him.

All this lent urgency—and guilt—to the fact that he was gone to the hospital with asthma. Urgency because she feared for him; guilt because she planned to use his absence. No sense lying to herself.

She had such an awful dread in her.

When the day ended—the long, damned day—she got in her car and started for the hospital, planning to check on Allan. The Meltzers would be there, both of them. They saw her as a kindly childless woman, Miss Porter, who had nurtured the schoolchildren—a whole generation. Well, it was true. And they trusted her. She had a key to their house, for those times she took the boy home.

No, she would not deceive herself. A drink was necessary before she faced the Meltzers.

She drove to their house and let herself in. Mr. Meltzer kept only whiskey. She ransacked their kitchen looking for it. Vaguely, she resolved to fix everything when she got to a level, when she could think straight again, out of this shaking. It was simple. She was contending with something that had come up on her and surprised her.

She drank most of the bottle, slowly and painfully at first, but then with more ease, gulping it, getting calm. She wasn't a bad woman. She loved those kids, loved everyone. She'd always carried herself with dignity, and never complained. She had a smile and a kind word for everybody. Once, she and Jack had made love on the roof of a Holiday Inn, while fireworks went off in another part of the city where she went to college. On their fifth anniversary they had pretended to be strangers in a hotel bar, and gone racing to their room on the sixth floor, laughing, filled with an illicit-feeling hunger for each other.

Now she did what she could with the kitchen, reeling. Her own crashing-down fall startled her, as if it were someone else. "Jack?" she said. Oh, yes—Jack. Her once-friend and lover, a world away. But all would be well. She could believe it now. She went out into the yard, looked at the trees, the late afternoon sun pouring through with breezes, life's light and breath. The great wide world. She felt good. She felt quite reasonable. Nothing out of order. Life would provide.

She started across the span of grass leading to the trees. It was confusing, where home was. She sat down in the grass, then lay back. When they returned, the Meltzers would see. They would know everything. She would have to find some way to explain, show them the necessity. "Honesty is what we owe each other." She'd always told the

453

children that, hadn't she? She had lived by it. Hadn't she? "Be true, my darlings," she had said. "Always, always tell the truth. Even to yourself." That was what she had said. She was Miss Porter. That was what she was known for.

Nominated by Gary Fincke, Joyce Carol Oates, David Jauss

SON OF STET

by JOHN KISTNER

from THE COLORADO REVIEW

> stet - *n*. the word used as an indication to the printer that
> an instruction to delete is to be ignored.
> —*New Webster's Dictionary*

never mind how it was. let me tell you about now.
I am a small black and white lesbian boy and I loved my mother.
no, take that back. maybe it was my mother who loved me.
but I know we both loved time. we would sit together on the couch
and listen to the preaching of the second hand.
it was funny, at age six, I told mom
the clock had two hands like us. no, mother said.
there was a third hand. she asked me if I wanted to see it
and I was afraid. no, X that, I was not afraid.
no. maybe a little. she showed me what she meant. she talked about
every lover I would have, the carrot-fed air, the orthodontic grief,
the haircuts underneath their brains. the lovers that
talk about me the way they do now, the liars.
let me say that again. I'm the liar. I'll allow that.
but I can't stop picking at it. my mother told me about how
to drink my water and wash my hands, but mostly she told
about things my father did wrong. what a forest,
a clear cut of bad lots, misgivings and false premises,
the first falling down the first drunk. some were big, kicking a dog
    down
a flight of stairs. some small, his habit of building home

stereos from spit and linoleum, forgetting her for days, weeks.
he wanted to open up a bar. no, strike that. he studied
for the bar. he waves to me now in that old joke,
beard curling under the sturdy tug of his cold hands.
my mother dried me off after baths, two green
smiley-faced pitchers to clean that bitter
soap from my hair. ears she never forgot. listen,
she said it is important for you to be an editor, to catch
people in their wrong words and to shine in the face of cheap soft-shoe
from the skies. it's important that you do not change your
mind or go back on your word or miss a beat. steal what you fancy
but don't call for a fiat and don't talk at your fellow
man about sin with clenched fists. no one's anyone to talk.
I remember mother well. no, that's not exactly true. I made her
up the way she made up her face in the morning, one color
at a time. one brush, another dab. the smell of sleeplessness and
    rosewater.

Nominated by Mark Irwin

THE SEA IN MOURNING

by EDUARDO URIOS-APARISI

from *SHARDS OF LIGHT* (TIA CHUCHA PRESS)

THERE, OUTSIDE YOUR WINDOW, Adela, the mourning sea. The short waves carry black crests. You turn away and look inside; your room, its sheets so white, the light raving through the curtains, from the dressing room mirror, in the white caps of the bed. Blue rises up the hushed ceiling. A stoic hour, midday on the dot. The sea approaching as a court wears mourning for the living, those who greedily drink even the salt from the day, salt from before happiness, from before finding you and looking in your eyes. Your eyes are so big, your smile so beneficent, so preciously eternal. The sea is in mourning, and you can't watch it from sorrow.

J.F.

De tu ventana, Adela, se ve la mar de luto. Las olas pequeñas llevan crestones negros. Vuelves tu mirada hacia dentro, tu habitación, sus sábanas tan blancas, la luz delirando por las cortinas, por el espejo del vestidor, en las palomas de la cama. Azul se alza el techo arrullado. Una estoica hora, el mediodía en punta. La mar en cortejo lleva luto por los vivos, aquellos que voraces beben aún la sal del día, la de antes de ser felices, la de antes de encontrarte y mirarte a los ojos. Tus ojos son tan grandes, tu sonrisa tan benéfica, tan preciosidad eterna. La mar está de luto y tú no quieres ni mirarla de pena.

Nominated by Tia Chucha Press

THE WEDDING JESTER

fiction by STEVE STERN

from THE NEW ENGLAND REVIEW

> *As for me, who called myself a sorcerer or angel, I have now returned to the earth,*
> *with a duty to look for and a rough reality to embrace. Peasant!*
>
> —Arthur Rimbaud

AS HE DROVE HER toward the wedding in the Catskills, Saul Bozoff's aged mother told him yet another of her stories.

". . . So Lolly Segal wouldn't go with the girls to see *Chorus Line* at the Orpheum last week . . ."

While Saul, who wondered why he should care, withheld as long as his conscience allowed a half-hearted, "Why not?"

"I don't know," Mrs. Bozoff expressed her own bafflement. "She said her nipples ached."

Saul glanced at the crepe-hung little woman, her bosom like a sat-upon ottoman, and tried to blame her for his life. Hadn't he adopted his own rueful nature as a protest against her relentless sanguinity?—which he knew to be only skin-deep.

Her he blamed for his feeling that, at fifty-three, he was not even successful at failure. An author, the books of his middle years (there had been no books of his youth) had earned him a small audience in what he considered "the ghetto." His fiction, full of exotic Jewish legends translated to contemporary settings, had been well received among a generation that was already half legend itself, and a handful of a generation that was tediously born again. Among his peers Saul Bozoff had no currency at all.

Of course, if he were honest, Saul would have to admit it served him right. Sometime in his early forties, after a protracted and largely fruitless literary apprenticeship, he'd been seduced by "heritage." But for a handful of short-lived absences (school, wanderjahre, artists colony), he'd spent his life in an unlikely town in the Mississippi Delta, wishing he were somewhere else. He'd taken a job—one in an endless series of temporary positions—doing clerical work at a local folklore center, transcribing interviews with Baptist preachers who'd taught their hogs to pray, blind blues singers with half a dozen wives, a pawnbroker who'd sold the young Elvis Presley his first guitar. During this latter interview the retired usurer had alluded to a transplanted Old World community on North Main Street where he was reared; and Saul, recalling that he too was Jewish, made a pilgrimage to take a look.

What he found was a desolate street of crumbling buildings and weed-choked lots, a junkyard, a bridge ramp, an old synagogue converted into a discotheque of ill repute. But blink and there were ghosts—the immigrants crying hockfleish and irregular pants, pumping their sewing machines like swarming hornets in the tenement lofts, braiding Yiddish curses into their yellow challah bread. Not ordinarily given to ecstatic transports, Saul was as struck by the timelessness of his vision as was another Saul on the road to Damascus. Never much at home among the living (in whose company he'd managed only to botch a marriage and squander an education), he resolved to take up residence among the dead, whose adventures he was convinced made good copy.

Saul reported their picturesque antics in a book of stories that earned him a modest reputation, which he parlayed into a teaching job at a small New England college. (North Main Street being portable, Saul was hardly aware of the change of scene.) Noted for its Jewish studies program, the college was a place where Saul felt he could go native, immersing himself in a tradition he'd previously ignored. No longer confined to his Mississippi River outpost, or attached to any particular moment in time, he dwelled in the place where history and myth intersected; he was the contemporary of prophets, martyrs, and exiles, whom his spirit (he felt) had expanded to accommodate. From that vantage he sent back dispatches in the form of two subsequent books, each more saturated in Jewish arcana than the one before. Heedless of the tradition's rational ethos, he populated his tales with every species of its folklore, every manner of fanciful event—a labor that kept him occupied for about ten years. Then, just as abruptly as the spell had come over him, it lifted: Saul's vision of Yiddishkeit ever-lasting reverted back to rubble and unsaleable real estate.

"What possessed me?" he wondered, astonished to find himself in his sixth decade the author of books catalogued as *Fiction/Judaica*.

Still, he mourned the loss of his *yenne velt,* his other world. It was cruel that spiritual afflatus should have abandoned him at an age when he had also to suffer so many other desertions: like muscle tone and a formerly thick head of wavy auburn hair. (Saul would have liked to draw a parallel with Samson, but such references now seemed distant echoes of a once joyful noise.) And things better abandoned, such as libido, had begun after a dormant period to reassert themselves. So, when his eighty-something-year-old mother asked him to accompany her to a wedding at a Catskills resort, Saul surprised himself by say-ing, "Why not?" Maybe a trip to the buckle of the Borscht Belt, the famed Concord Hotel itself, would be just the thing to revive his lost inspiration.

He'd forgotten, however, his mother's gift for reducing him to a childish petulance with her gossip, which Saul judged a poor substi-tute for an unlived life.

"So Wednesday night the women are playing canasta in Harriet Fleish-man's apartment when Millie Blank can't get up from the table. . . ."

His moody silence giving way to surrender, "Why not?"

"Oh, honey," replied his mother, "she was dead."

Mrs. Bozoff had flown into her hometown of Boston from Ten-nessee, where she'd remained despite the passing of her husband two decades before. Picking her up at Logan Airport, Saul had driven the Mass Turnpike into "the Mountains" of southern New York, wonder-ing: What mountains? Because Sullivan County, heart of the Jewish Catskills, was nothing but gently rolling hills. The renowned autumn foliage had already flared and expired, leaving a scorched landscape of gray and tobacco brown. Then there were the towns, which in their heyday had supported conspicuous Jewish populations, boasting scores of kosher butchers and delicatessens; not to mention the hemlock-shaded boarding houses, bungalow colonies, cochelayns. Now their fa-cades, where intact, were mostly boarded up, strangled in wisteria vines: providing backdrops for the local unemployed, who loitered in front of them as on blighted city streets.

Spotting a single hoary Hasid beside an ashcan, Saul thought to him-self, Reb Ben Vinkl: he went to sleep in the golden age of the Moun-tains and woke up to this. "Looks like we're too late," he observed.

"What?" The battery of his mother's hearing aid was conveniently rundown.

"I said it looks like we're too late, all the Jews are gone."

Mrs. Bozoff smiled in serene denial.

The hotel was no less a disappointment. A good forty or fifty years out of fashion, the Concord was a cluster of boxy buildings, their rusting exteriors as forbidding as the Pentagon. Once inside, there was the sense of corridors measureless to man, though the acres of oriental sofas in flammable fabrics, the showy fixtures out of Belshazzar's salon, were faded, the enormous mirrors as shot through with cracks as with veins of gold. None of this was lost on Saul as he lugged their bags in a snail-like progress alongside his mother; while she, preceded by the clanking third leg of her metal cane, exclaimed, "It's like another world!"

Here and there you saw a woman with cat's-eye glasses and flashy jewelry, her husband in plaid pants, sporting the hairpiece that could double for a yarmulke; but these were far exceeded by the decidedly gentile presence of a regional convention of Emergency Medical Technicians. They were welcomed by a banner that spanned the lobby and eclipsed the bulletin board, which announced (among other weekend functions) the Supoznik-Shapiro wedding. Identifiable by their insignias, the paramedics also shared a generosity of girth—men and women alike wearing T-shirts bearing life-affirming logos stretched across medicine-ball midriffs. Parking his mother on a circular sofa surrounding a fountain, Saul resented her fixed smile, the rheumy eyes whose vision was as selective as her hearing. Had she even noticed the mixed clientele, which in this kosher-style establishment were the equivalent of mingling dairy with meat?

But he'd no sooner checked them in than Saul turned to find that his mother had become a rallying point. She was beset by what must have been *mishpocheh*—a host of relations she had perhaps not laid eyes on since migrating south with Saul's father over half a century before. Each was protesting that the others hadn't changed a bit.

Approaching them, Saul could hear Mrs. Bozoff unburdening herself: "You know I lost my husband," as though the event had occurred only yesterday; and one or two of her listeners looked about as if Mr. Bozoff, a weary merchant who'd gone much too gently into his good night, might only have been misplaced.

Saul was introduced to a pint-sized character in bubble spectacles whom Mrs. B referred to as Uncle Julius, and his wife Becky, a head

461

taller though bowed by a sizable dowager's hump. There were a trio of thick-ankled maiden ladies with a neutered-looking fellow in tow, his trousers hoisted to the level of his pigeon breast. These were relations once, twice removed, hailing from places like Larchmont and New Rochelle, names that for Saul had a fabled resonance. And judging from the way they greeted him, making a perfunctory show of civility before dispersing wholesale, his name must have had some significance for them as well.

Back home, owing to his fecklessness, Saul had enjoyed the reputation of a confirmed (if harmless) black sheep. Writing books had only aggravated the perception, since most assumed without reading him that he'd merely graduated from private to public disgrace. That his notoriety should have preceded him to such far-flung parts was in some way flattering, lending a slightly outlaw cast to an otherwise lackluster career.

"Help me up," his mother was entreating, sunk in the sofa's upholstery like a reclining Michelin man. Saul gripped her pudgy fingers and made a token effort to raise her, complaining that his back was sore from the drive. But even as he warned her she might have to sit there the entire weekend, a woman unsolicitedly grasped Mrs. Bozoff's other hand. Together she and Saul hauled his mother to her feet.

"Thanks," muttered Saul under his breath, "I thought I might need a forklift."

"Wiseguy," replied the woman, whom Saul noted was nevertheless sizing him up with a heavily mascara'd eye.

"Thank you so much," panted Mrs. B with the excessive gratitude of a person pulled from the jaws of a beast. "I'm Belle Bozoff and this is my son Saul," who perhaps needed further explaining, "the author."

"Oh?" said the woman, circumflexing a plucked brow. The information seemed to have rung a bell. "Haven't I heard of you?"

"See," kvelled Mrs. Bozoff to her son, "everybody knows you," and to the woman: "He thinks he's a failure."

Clucking her tongue in sham sympathy, she introduced herself as Myrna Halevy and offered her hand.

Saul took it reluctantly, avoiding her eye. "Any kin to Judah?" he inquired in a pedantic reference to the Hebrew poet famous for declaring, "The air is full of souls!"

"Whodah?" asked Myrna. "Myself, I'm from the Great Neck Halevys. You maybe heard of Halevy's Fine Furs? That's my papa, the retired fur king, that dashing character over there—Isador, short for

Is adorable." She pointed to an ancient party in a sport coat the hue of a putting green, his ginger-gray hair back-combed over a freckled pate. Tall and ramrod-stiff, he was prominent among his cronies in their various stages of decrepitude.

As for his daughter, Saul thought he could read her history at a glance, though she was a type he'd seldom encountered outside of books and film. She was a "girl" in her early forties trying hard to hide the fact, no doubt divorced and living on generous alimony. Her painted face was somewhat vulpine, her snuff brown hair (highlighted with henna) puffed high and as sticky with spray as candy floss. She was thin to the point of appearing malnourished, probably due to a diet of white wine and pills, though her breasts, which proffered themselves as on a platter, were disproportionately large. She wore an ocelot top and a tight leather skirt, below which—Saul had grudgingly to admit—her legs in their patterned stockings and heels were good.

She gave him a sidewise smile as if to ask if he was finished looking, and Saul flushed, adjusting his collar. A decade's hermetic devotion to dreams and outré texts had left him sensitive in the area of desire, and he resented that this aging princess, bracelets clattering like a Kristallnacht, should chafe him there.

"Is your mama with you?" Mrs. Bozoff was asking, to which Myrna replied that her mother had passed on some years ago; and accepting Mrs. B's condolences with a dismissive wave, she assured her she'd always been Daddy's girl.

Saul's mother sighed. "You know my husband, Mister Bozoff . . ."

But Saul intervened, having realized that his mother, like the Ancient Mariner, might never stop button-holing wedding guests to tell her tale. Clearing his throat, he piped, "I don't like to break up the party, but there's a tired old bellhop waiting to take up our bags."

Myrna Halevy gave him another appraising look, from which Saul recoiled. "Are you in the bride's party or the groom's?" queried Mrs. Bozoff, and when Myrna said the groom's, Mrs. B pooched her lip to signal an incorrect answer. "We're in the bride's," she stated with regret, "but it was nice to meet you anyway."

With his mother safely installed in her room for an afternoon nap, Saul was free to inspect the premises looking for ghosts. This was what he'd been anxiously waiting for. He strolled out under a leaden sky past a drained swimming pool the size of an inland sea, venturing onto a desert golf course called the Monster. Everything seemed to suggest

463

that a race of giants had once walked these hills. But the visionary gift that had served him so well on North Main Street remained inactive on this brisk afternoon.

"Come back Eddie Cantor singing 'Cohen Owes Me Ninety-Seven Dollars'," Saul beckoned softly. "Come back Sophie Tucker, Sid Caesar, Fat Jackie Leonard, Danny Kaye né David Daniel Kaminsky; come back Mister Wonderful, Little Farfel, Eddie Fisher, Totie Fields . . ." Come back the mamboniks, the mothering waiters named Shayke ("Boychik, you want heartburn? Go ahead and order chop meat"), the bungalow bunnies, the busboys from City College chasing the garment czar's daughter, the porch clowns doing Simon Sez. Saul could call the roll of all the talents that had their start in the Mountains, the gangsters and boxers and nabobs who'd watered there—he'd read the literature; he could trace the lineage of Yid personalities from the lion-tamers, conjurers, and strong men of the Old Testament through the wedding jesters of the Diaspora, the shpielers and singing waiters of Second Avenue, right down to this late chapter in the long-running pageant, entitled "the Catskills."

What hadn't he missed growing up in the Delta? Poverty and diseases notwithstanding, he coveted the Lower East Side; Nazis, he'd missed, and Cossacks, Inquisitors, Crusaders, Amalekites. At least there would have been some compensation in summers spent hustling tips in the Mountains, oppressed by flighty hoteliers and drunken chefs. But no: born at the wrong place and time, Saul Bozoff had been forced to abuse himself these fifty odd years.

Later on, trudging beside his mother (through a herd of paramedicals) toward the rehearsal dinner, Saul wondered why he'd agreed to come. What did this tacky terminus to the dream of a golden America, this Jewish wasteland, have to do with him—a lover of the "old knowledge"? Life prior to the discovery of North Main Street—the dead-end jobs, the brief dead-end marriage to a woman he scarcely remembered, who'd blamed him (as he blamed her) for its barrenness—had been a largely somnambulant affair. He'd had to wake up in order to dream. But now, bereft of the company of his wonder rabbis and hidden saints, Saul deplored his banishment to the ordinary world. What identity did he have beyond that of a dilettante, all passions spent? A bachelor professor of a certain age, squiring his mother to a faded resort half a century past its prime.

"So Kitty Dreyfus wouldn't go to her husband Moey's funeral," Mrs. Bozoff informed him to the beat of her clanking cane. (All her gossip was home-grown within the walls of Ploughshares Towers, a geriatric high-rise wherein the Angel of Death—Saul surmised—kept his own efficiency.)

Said her son, reflexively: "Why not?"

"She said he wasn't her husband; sixty-five years they never, what you call it, consommé'd the marriage."

On their way past the neglected closet of a hotel chapel, mother and son were abruptly halted by the sight of a young woman leaving the Ladies Room in disarray. In completing her business inside, she had carelessly tucked the hem of an indigo cocktail dress into the waistband of her underpants. The panties, Saul could not help but notice, were a satiny eggshell white, scarcely visible (but for the tic-tocking cleft at their center) against the cream of her perfect tush. "Oo oo!" exclaimed Mrs. Bozoff, pointing. "Saul, tell her before she makes an embarrassment."

"*I* can't tell her!" he objected. "It's not my place."

"Excuse me, dear!" his mother had begun to shout at the girl, when Saul clamped his palm over her mouth. At that moment the girl was met by several others, one of whom saw the problem and corrected it discreetly with a sweep of her hand. A crushed velvet curtain dropped over the girl's bottom, concealing the stockings that made her look as if she waded in blue water to the thighs.

Her friend whispered, giggling, to the girl, who turned to see who might have observed her: only a trundling old woman and her round-shouldered, middle-aged escort, neither of them apparently worth wasting a blush on. So why was it that Saul, removing his hand from his mother's sputtering mouth and assuring her he didn't know what had come over him—why did he feel as agitated as an elder who'd spied on Susanna? And why, even more than her fanny, should her face—distinctive for its cameo pallor among the artificial tans of her sisterhood—set his vitals vibrating like a tuning fork?

The cavernous Calypso Room, with its undulant walls and glittering terrazzo floors, reverberated with the noise of happy reunions. Every-where families and friends reclaimed prodigal members and long-lost acquaintances to draw them into the larger fold. To insure his own exclusion from such scenes, Saul had contrived to leave his name-tag in his room. At his mother's request that he go back for it, he complained to her much tested patience that such badges invoked for him bitter racial memories. It was in any case a relief to see how his mother, once again an object of warm regard, drew the attention away from him.

Seated next to her at their appointed table, Saul had assumed an expression so arch as to forbid anyone's attempting to engage him in conversation. The strategy was effective enough that he began in a while to feel sorry for himself; nor was he heartened by the notice of the Halevy woman, who fluttered her fingers at him from a nearby table. He nodded without altering the set of his jaw, and inwardly groaned. She was a cultural cliché, wasn't she?—the spoiled New World Jewess, her life organized around excursions to boutiques. The room was lousy with her tribe. Still, as a caricature, she seemed to Saul slightly larger than life—a condition in the face of which he was duly humbled.

Mrs. Bozoff was confiding to a lady with hair the blue of a pilot light (something about a nonagenarian neighbor no better than she should be), when a tinkling of silver on crystal was heard from the head table. A youthful rabbi with a neatly trimmed VanDyke was begging indulgence to perform, as it was Saturday evening, a brief havdalah service. Pushing back the cuffs of a sharkskin jacket as if to show he had nothing up his sleeves, he lit the candle, tasted the wine, and thanked the Lord for holding the line between the secular and the sacred. The guests amen'd, some with mouths full of chopped liver salad, then pitched in to the beef flanken a l'anglaise and the roast stuffed breast of veal with peach garni. They were gnashing asparagus spears, slathering baked potatoes in sour cream, when the crystal tinkled again.

This time a prosperous-looking gent, his spun silk suit shooting asterisks of light, had risen to his feet. He introduced himself (unnecessarily for most) as Irving Supoznik, father of the bride. Deeply tanned, he was endowed with a regal nose and a two-tone head of hair—sandy on top and fluffy gray at the temples, like an inverted cotton boll. Observing him, Saul was troubled to note that, for one thing, he and the bride's father were approximately the same age, and that the daughter seated next to him was none other than the glimmering girl of the visible tush. Saul realized he'd been leering at her all along.

"You're probably wondering why I asked you all here," said Supoznik, waiting for the laugh. Someone called out, "A tummler you'll never make!" to which he replied, "Very cute. Who let Milton Graber in here? Will the ushers please escort that man from the hall?" Then confidentially, "Milt's still p.o.'d about last night's pinochle game. Anyway, I hope you're enjoying your nosh because I'm in hock to the eyeballs over this little soiree." Again polite laughter, while their benefactor assured them that, really, the house of Supoznik was in no immediate danger.

466

"Now if Nate Pinchas there can stop stuffing his face for a minute—I know the kishke is good, Nate, but this is my moment, OK? Gertrude, control your husband! But seriously, I'd like to thank you for traveling so far for this shindig. Everybody told me, who has weddings in the Catskills anymore? So call me sentimental, but when Ilka and I got married here thirty-two years ago, the place was lucky for us, and I'm betting some of that luck will rub off on these kids." With his pocket handkerchief he dabbed the corner of an eye.

Graber, the wag, shouted, "Shmaltz we had already from the herring!"

"You didn't blubber like a baby at your Tracy's wedding last spring?" challenged Supoznik, to which Graber:

"That's because she married a bum," knuckling the burr-head of the lad beside him, who good-naturedly shook a fist.

"But all kidding aside," continued Supoznik, "I'd like you to join me in a toast to the happy couple." He lifted his glass. "Have I got *naches* or what? You young people maybe don't know *naches?*—that's when your daughter brings home a fine, clean boy like David Shapiro . . ." He bestowed a smile on the bridegroom at his left, a curly-haired, fresh-faced youth with a Clark Kent forelock, his blazer displaying a fraternity crest. ". . . who's about to graduate Yale Law School with a job waiting for him already at the firm of Klein, Klein, Klein . . ."

"Goes the trolley," sang Milton Graber.

". . . and Levine!" proclaimed Supoznik, ignoring his heckler. Young David, showing ivory teeth, clenched his hands in mock-triumph over his head. Irving Supoznik then turned to his daughter, his tone becoming worshipful. "And now I give you our doll, our treasure, our Shelly—mwhaaa . . . !" He kissed his fingers, which inspired more needling from Graber. Saul asked himself if the literature of the day hadn't already *done* these people. Shouldn't they have been retired like old stage props? But for all that, he couldn't take his eyes off Irving Supoznik's languid daughter. Her fine-boned beauty seemed a bit out of place amongst the solid, aerobically contoured girls of her circle, her tranquil features opposing their constant animation. Her blue-black hair, whose lustrous profusion she'd tried to arrest with ribbons, tumbled over a milky brow. Occasionally she parted the tendrils to peer with dark eyes from behind them, but, the pert tilt of her head notwithstanding, she seemed drowsily unimpressed by what she saw. Here, thought Saul, was the meeting in one girl of Marjorie Morningstar and Trilby; for Shelly Supoznik appeared as if under an enchantment, her secret inaccessible even to one who'd spied the secret of her bottom drawer.

467

Having divested himself of platitudes ("Like they say, love is sweet but better with bread"), Irving Supoznik offered a health to the bride and groom. Saul sighed, trying to remember the last time he'd been intimate with a woman. During his driven years abstinence was never an issue; so sated was his spirit that his physical self was a virtual irrelevancy. But now that his spirit had flagged, hadn't his flesh begun to go the same way? Though a restlessness in his pants argued to the contrary, he needed further assurance. What he needed was some fey creature like Shelly Supoznik to help him achieve, through the medium of his baggy body, the restoration of his soul.

"What am I thinking?" Saul asked himself, feeling that he ought to be ashamed. But while others fed on sponge cake, halvah, and petit fours, he nourished himself on fantasies of stealing the bride away.

Then Myrna Halevy, in a form-fitting, strapless tube dress that seemed to be made of mirrors, approached the table shadowed by her plank-like father, whom she introduced to Mrs. Bozoff. Mrs. B, for her part, removed the napkin from under her chins and—a touch coquettishly if Saul weren't mistaken—invited Mr. Halevy to sit down. Myrna said they were on their way to the Imperial Room to see the bygone teen idol Frankie somebody, whom Saul had supposed long dead.

"Maybe you," she turned briefly from his mother to give Saul what he wanted to believe was an involuntary tic, but was clearly a wink, "maybe you and your son would care to join us?" He lowered his eyes, only to see himself dizzily multiplied in the scales of her gown.

"Oh, Saul," shrilled his mother, "Let's go! It'll do you good."

Still preoccupied with thoughts of romance, Saul nonetheless wondered what she meant by "do him good." More curtly than he'd intended, he told her, "Go ahead, you'll have more fun without me," then conceding to universal objections, agreed to join them later on. First he needed a little air.

He made a wrong turn outside the Calypso Room and ended up in a dimly lit cul-de-sac. A dumpy couple plastered in paramedical emblems were in mid-tryst beside a faux-marble cherub, rubbing noses Eskimo-fashion. As it was too late to back off unnoticed, Saul asked them foolishly, "How do you get outside?" The man scratched his muttonchops: "You mean this place has an outside?", his moonfaced companion bursting into titters.

Eventually he found an exit that delivered him into an uncomfortably chilly night whose fine mist was turning to drizzle; though insulated by his visions of Shelly Supoznik, what did Saul care? But out there in the elements it wasn't so easy to pick up the thread of his imaginings. Still he tried: reviewing precedents from *Blood Wedding* to *The Graduate,* Saul endeavored to picture himself snatching the girl from the altar; but who was he kidding? What he felt had more in common with a pedophile attraction than heroic passion. He turned up his coat collar against the October wind, cursed the rain pelting his unprotected head, and supposed he ought to be inside among the guests. But inside he would doubtless want to be out. After all, what did he have to say to the young go-getters and their fathers who had already gone and gotten? From the worldly world Saul had long since decamped for the society of his phantom Jews. Now, excluded from their number, he was neither here nor there, inside or out. Neither past nor present were hospitable, and his people were not his people, and there was nowhere on earth that Saul Bozoff belonged.

He decided it was time to go and check on his mother, since what reason did he have for being here other than looking after her? Suddenly Saul was resentful that others should have presumed to usurp his role. But as he was about to enter the lobby under a massive porte cochere, who should he encounter but La Myrna leaning against a stucco'd column. With a scarlet lambskin jacket draped like an opera cape over her scintillating dress, a cigarette wedged between talon-like nails, she was a thing of smoke and mirrors. "The Dragon Lady," thought Saul, hoping to get past her with some minimal courtesy, but the question she posed brought him up short.

"So, are you getting good material or what?"

He uttered a querulous, "Come again?"

"Admit it, we're all just kitsch for your mill."

Saul thought he caught her implication: she was confusing him with writers of a more acerbic bent, the kind that made satirical hay out of affairs such as these. Not wishing to disabuse her, however, he replied mysteriously, "The mills of kitsch grind slow but exceedingly fine."

"What's that supposed to mean?" she asked.

Saul shrugged his shoulders. "You tell me. Look, I'll level with you, Miss . . . ?" He pretended to have forgotten her name but sensed she wasn't fooled. "I never draw from life."

"Then what do you draw from," Myrna exhaled a plume of smoke with all the éclat of the caterpillar in *Alice*, "death?"

Saul coughed. "You never heard from the imagination?" he said with undisguised condescension. Myrna was thoughtful. "The what nation . . . ?"

"Now who's the wiseguy?" asked Saul, irked with himself for having been lured into an exchange with this ridiculous person.

Then Myrna abruptly changed the subject. "Your mama's enjoying herself," she said, taking—as it seemed to Saul—credit for Mrs. Bozoff's good time.

"My mother always enjoys herself. She doesn't know any better," he apprised her, then attempting to beg off, "If you'll pardon me . . ."

"You got something against enjoying yourself?" asked Myrna.

Said Saul: "I have a very low fun threshold."

"I think you've seen too many Woody Allen movies," she submitted.

"Oh, very astute," replied Saul—was there no end to the woman's presumption? "Look, Miss . . . Halevy was it?" summoning patience, "you might think you know me, but you don't know me."

Then came what was probably supposed to pass for a sibylline remark: "Everybody's disappointed, sweetheart."

Sweetheart?

"You want disappointed, you should see the crowd in the Imperial Room," continued Myrna, upon which she threw down her cigarette and ground it with studied precision under a spiked heel. Suddenly frisky, she stepped forward to take Saul's arm. "C'mon, I'll show you."

"I'm not disappointed," Saul lied, reclaiming the arm. "I'm just damp from walking in the rain. I want to get out of these clothes and go to bed."

Myrna arched her brow, and Saul feared for a second she might offer to help him undress. "Naughty boy," she accused him, "you made a rendezvous with some college cutie, didn't you? Your type doesn't waste any time."

Would it were so, thought Saul, who allowed himself for the briefest instant to believe he was a ladies' man. Of course, Myrna Halevy was only teasing him, wasn't she? She had about her, seasoning her character of the Long Island parvenu, a touch of the demoness. Shelly Supoznik, he knew, would never tease him; though Shelly Supoznik might not have the wit. In any case, rather than give the woman the pleasure of witnessing his chagrin, Saul adopted what he imagined was a roué's demeanor. He smiled enigmatically, made a careless little salute, and swept back into the hotel alone.

He woke the next morning wracked with guilt over his mother whom he'd neglected to see to her room the night before. To get even with her for having deserted him, never mind that the opposite was true, he'd gone straight to bed. There he tried again to conjure erotic scenarios featuring himself and the spectral Shelly, though images of Myrna Halevy kept intruding. Oddly, Saul had been none the less aroused. In vain he'd attempted to defuse his lust by recalling Hasidic folktales, a proven remedy for insomnia in recent years. There was the one, for instance, about Rabbi Elimelech, whose seed, spilled in his effort to resist the temptations of the she-devil Lilith, turned to glow-worms at his feet.

Dressing on the run, Saul hurried to his mother's room, separated from his own by two flights of stairs. (The hotel had been unable to provide adjoining rooms, for which Saul was much obliged.) He knocked at her door, called her name, and receiving no answer, began to pound. Had she died in her sleep or—unthinkable prospect—spent the night somewhere else? Aware that neither circumstance was likely, Saul still couldn't shake his unease, and as there remained no response from within, made a dash for the elevator. The lobby was full of medical conventioneers, to whom Saul in an irrational moment considered appealing, when he saw his mother shuffling toward the dining room. She was flanked by the Halevys, father and daughter, which gave him the impression she was being abducted.

Catching them up, Saul had it on the tip of his tongue to exclaim "Thank God I found you!" but got hold of himself in time to utter a glib, "Remember me?" Myrna turned to greet him with a wry and knowing, "Hello, sleepyhead!"

Said Mrs. Bozoff, "We didn't want to wake you, tateleh," and Saul wondered who was this *we?*, but vowed to keep his own counsel until he'd had his coffee.

At breakfast he was still wrought up. Why was he so wrought up? After all, his mother was well taken care of—she was regaling Mr. Halevy (who nodded either from compassion or palsy) about a friend's uterectomy and subsequent malpractice suit. They were in the common dining room where the wedding guests, though legion, were outnumbered by paramedics. Many of the latter said grace before eating, ending their devotions with "in Jesus' name, amen," but none of the Jews seemed aware of any menace. Instead, beyond an air of mutual tolerance, there was even a shared preference of attire among wedding guests and medical fellowship alike—namely, the nylon warm-up suits as brilliant as jockeys' silks. Dining, it appeared, was a friendly athletic competition.

Puerto Rican waiters brought groaning trays of food to the table, excess having remained a constant over the years. There were Danishes,

471

jelly blintzes, bagels with lox, nova, and whitefish, baked herring, cream cheese omelets. In light of such abundance Saul had ordered, perversely, a poached egg and toast. When it arrived, Myrna, wearing a shoulder-padded jumpsuit that looked like commando issue (but with spangles), leaned over to shovel some of her bounty onto his plate.

"Essen un fressen," she invited, taking the further liberty of unfolding a napkin and tucking it into his collar. Saul removed it, flinging it down like a gauntlet.

"That's it, isn't it?" he asked rhetorically. "That's all that's left, *essen un fressen?* The language of Mendele, Peretz, and Sholem Aleichem, Halpern and Leivick—poor consumptive Leivick, who came to the East Side via Siberia, and had to check his paperhanger's ladder at the box office before attending the debut of his play, *The Golem.* The language of Itzik Manger, Moishe Kulbak, and Israel Rabon, who crawled out of the corpse-strewn trenches at the Polish front to write *The Street,* then hung on long enough to be slaughtered by Nazis and tossed in a mass grave. The world's most resilient language, it survives every worst calamity of the past ten centuries only to dribble its last on the lips of a pampered Long Island minx at a Catskills hotel. O *essen un fressen,* yourself, and despair!"

Myrna batted her fake lashes the size of bats' wings. "I also know *gai kuckn in yam . . .*"

He stared at her with a sanctimony that crumbled in the face of her taunting admiration, then lowered his eyes. They lit on the lavender kerchief round her neck. Myrna followed his gaze, touched her throat, its tendons taut as bowstrings.

"You like the scarf?" she asked. "It's got sentimental value. I strangled my first husband with it."

Saul took a breath, odors of stewed prunes and cologne vying in his nostrils, taking him to the brink of a sneeze which he suppressed. "Myrna," he said—it was the first time he'd used her given name, "can I ask you a question?"

"I'm all ears, kiddo," replied Myrna, bending an ear from which dangled a pendant like a loaded keyring.

"With all due respect, just what is it you think you're doing?"

She gave him a kittenish smile. "I'm throwing myself at you, can't you tell?"

Saul's mouth must have been hanging open, because Myrna took the occasion to stuff into it a thick piece of whitefish. He chewed tentatively, eyeing her like she might be Lucrezia Borgia, then succumb-

472

ing to its savoriness, swallowed the fish, and took up his fork to skewer another piece from her plate.

Mrs. Bozoff was struggling to rise from her chair. "I'm gonna plotz," she jovially announced, and, suggestible, Saul had a brief panicked vision of his mother's exploding. "Let me help you," offered Myrna, getting up to take Mrs. B's free arm, and together they made their way toward the powder room.

Left alone at the table with Mr. Halevy, Saul felt obliged to break the heavy silence between them—while on the other hand, given the paces his daughter was putting him through, why should he pay court to her tight-lipped old man? If this was a standoff, Saul was damned if he'd be the first to fold.

Though you had to hand it to the geezer: he was certainly fastidious—his hair spread like tortoiseshell tines over a sun-speckled poll, his close-shaven cheeks (thanks to cracked capillaries) in perpetual blush. His safari jacket was complemented by a Hawaiian print shirt whose collar was tucked neatly outside the wide lapels. It was a nattiness, though, that didn't quite conform to Mr. Halevy's mummy-like deportment; and it dawned on Saul that the old guy's spruce aspect might be owing to the fact that his daughter dressed him.

Then Mr. Halevy's mouth had started working, distorting the stony dignity of his features—his fierce eyes asquint, face twisted from the effort, noises that scarcely resembled speech burbling up from his diaphragm.

"Your m-m-m-m, m-m-m-mah . . ."

"My ma?" guessed Saul. "My mother?"

The old man nodded. " . . . is whhh, a w-wha . . ."

Saul found himself mouthing the syllables by way of encouragement. "W-whaaa . . ."

A Watusi? This was awful. "A woman?"

Again a nod; two out of two. "My mother is a woman . . . ," Saul restated what he'd gleaned thus far, but just as he felt he was getting the hang of it, the game was over: an ancient engine, Mr. Halevy's voice had apparently required a few false starts.

"Your mo-ther," he said, the words coherent if agonizingly deliberate, "is a whole lot of w-woman." And with what sounded slightly tinged with hoarse reproach, "K-character she got, and heart."

Then it was Saul's turn to nod, wondering was this an idiot or a madman? Or more sinister, were the alleged fur king and his daughter some kind of confidence team, gigolo and gigolette, who worked weddings and bar mitzvahs to fleece the unsuspecting? If so, it was clear that Mrs. Bozoff had fallen into their clutches past redemption. This was unfortunate, and while Saul wished he could help her, already lost, she would surely want him to save himself.

"Excuse me," he said, rising from the table and pointing to his slightly distended belly, "the fish isn't sitting too well." The phrase sounded inscrutable in his own ears.

The wedding was not until late afternoon, but according to the handouts there were meanwhile no end of activities to amuse and distract. There were organized water aerobics in an indoor pool with someone called Gilda, a cosmetic makeover workshop with Carol, a hair replacement lecture, a lecture on "the sensuous spine," shuffleboard and horseshoe pitching tourneys. There were gold clinics, investment clinics, bingo, duplicate bridge, instant art with Morris Katz, complimentary tango lessons with Mike Terrace on the promenade. . . .

What, wondered Saul, no practical kabbalah with Rabbi Naftali? Still nursing the distress he'd brought away from the breakfast table, he felt disoriented to the point of nausea, whose antidote (he decided) lay in the pursuit of boredom.

He nosed about the shops, wandered past the solarium where off-season sunbathers lolled behind glass as in a human zoo. Leery of running into Myrna, he nevertheless tried to comprehend why the woman, any woman, should have set her coif for him: a mediocrity manqué. Though hadn't he once been a kind of poor man's Prospero? They were probably wondering where he was at that very moment, Myrna soothing his mother's worries by offering to go and look for him; and Saul supposed there were worse things than being found. But after a time it came to him that he wasn't so much eluding Myrna as seeking the sylphlike Shelly Supoznik. She too might be wandering aimlessly, entertaining second thoughts. He would come upon her lingering before a wall of celebrity photos—Red Buttons, Jerry Lewis, Jan Peerce—and step up to recite their pedigrees: "Aaron Chwatt, Jerome Levitch, Pinky Perlmut . . ." They'd chat, establishing their distant cousinhood, and once he was technically no stranger, the girl would begin to confide in him. "The future seems so predictable," she'd admit, and Saul would delicately suggest it didn't have to be. She'd insist that she wanted the life her husband wanted, and Saul would ask who was she trying to convince, him or herself? Then he'd tell her of the timeless world he'd discovered and lost, but might locate again with her help; and she would lift her Dresden face, open wide her sleepy eyes to behold a man . . .

When he came back to himself, Saul had strayed beyond the confines of the hotel proper; he was outside under a breezeway connecting the main building with the covered tennis courts. Entering on impulse, he was thrust into the bigtop atmosphere of the Emergency Medical Technicians' showroom. Here was an even greater density of conventioneers than he'd seen at large in the hotel. Scores of them milled about the exhibits of helicopters and streamlined ambulances with computerized instruments for monitoring every vital sign. Sirens sounded, some in ear-splitting squawks, some in arpeggios like Good Humor-mobiles. Broad-beamed men and women modeled the latest in emergency medical fashion, from insignia'd windbreakers to double-knit fatigues, their hips girded in utility belts worn with a military flair. Like stage magicians they demonstrated their ventricular fibrillators and blood/gas apparatus on live volunteers. A few diehards clung to hands-on procedures: artificial resuscitation and Heimlich maneuvers; but the majority seemed to glory in the use of their whirring and blinking machines. It was a technology, to judge from the reverence the paramedical community paid it, that put miracles in the shade; that rendered outmoded the devices of a Prophet Elijah or a Baal Shem Tov when it came to raising the dead.

Moving furtively among them, Saul felt like a trespasser who'd penetrated some forbidden holy of holies; he was thankful, once he was out of there, to have escaped (as he saw it) with his own wounds still unstanched. Making for his room, he dove between the covers of a recent translation of the mystical text *Palm Tree of Deborah*, but couldn't fathom it. For a couple of hours he alternated between dozing fitfully and longing for Shelly Supoznik, until it was almost time for the ceremony; though why he should bother to attend he didn't know. But knotting his tie—a task he hadn't performed since his own nearly forgotten wedding day—Saul experienced a vague twinge of anticipation, which he had actively to dispel. On the way he stopped by his mother's room, knocked fatalistically, and was surprised to find her in.

"Isador?" she called, a name Saul didn't answer to.

"Oh Saul!" Mrs. Bozoff greeted upon cracking the door, delighted to see him. She had a sense of time like a house pet, her zeal as fervent after an hour as a year. "I don't know why I thought you might be Mister Halevy—he said they would save us a seat at the wedding. Oh, we had a lovely day; we played bingo and I won seven dollars, and

Mister Halevy . . ." She clucked her tongue, shook her head in fond sympathy. "The poor soul, you know in Great Neck they won't let him sit in a minyan."

Saul heaved a sigh, "Why not?"

"They say he had too many insides replaced with artificial—he's not a man anymore but a machine. So can you tell I'm wearing a girdle?"

Her dress, its material shimmering like an oil slick, was shapeless; it looked as though, to fill it, she'd been inflated to nearly life-size. Punch her and she might reel backward only to bob up again still smiling. Her rouged cheeks stood out like strawberry stains in oatmeal.

"You look fine," said Saul.

"So tell me, what did you do all morning? Myrna was worried you weren't enjoying yourself. I told her you never let yourself relax. You know she's crazy about you, don't you?"

Under his breath Saul muttered, "She's just plain crazy."

Mrs. B tapped her hearing aid. "What's that?"

"I said Myrna Halevy has got a screw loose!"

"Oo oo," exclaimed Mrs. Bozoff, who could not abide unpleasantness.

Saul fairly shouted that he hadn't meant to shout, which elicited one of his mother's conciliatory non sequiturs.

"You know, Saul, we're more like good friends than mother and son."

Downstairs, as they inched along the corridor, Mrs. B, but for the clanking of her cane, was unusually quiet. She seemed to be pondering something, though since when did she ponder? When at last she spoke, it was to inquire experimentally of her son, "So how would you like a new papa?"

Saul ceased his forward progress. Incredulous, he would have liked to borrow her tactic of pretending she hadn't heard, but the question wouldn't go away. "You must be kidding!"

Mrs. Bozoff hunched her shoulders as if to say maybe she was and then again maybe she wasn't.

"But you only just met," gasped her son, thinking surely he could do better than this.

"Sometimes," replied his mother, reciting from what seemed the only available script, "these things happen." And on further consideration, "Maybe it's this place—don't you think it's sort of, I dunno, magical?"

"Magical?" The bite of his fingernails into his palms would leave fossil-like traces till doomsday. "This is the place where magic died!" Then making what he deemed a superhuman effort to control his emotions, Saul adopted a breezy tone: "OK, fine, if you want to be the bride

476

of Frankenstein, go ahead. So what if my father's not even cold . . ." His father was twenty years in the grave, but who was counting?

Then it pleased him to see how readily his mother acquiesced. "You're right," she said, her lower lip beginning to quiver, face clouding over, "I was just being selfish." Her eyes behind their fishbowl lenses were already aswim with tears, and pulling a tissue from her purse, she gave herself up to sobbing.

Having unmasked her for the forlorn thing she was, Saul tried to savor his triumph. The punishment, he told himself, fitted the crime. For, after all, hadn't she betrayed their unspoken contract, that they should each remain solitary and disconsolate throughout their days? But as he watched her brittle smile collapse before the deluge, Saul's victory began to turn hollow, and ashamed of himself, he wanted to take it all back.

"I didn't mean it," he declared, "It's just so . . ." discarding *ludicrous* and its fellows ". . . sudden."

More to conceal their spectacle from the guests than to comfort his mother, Saul steered her between a potted rubber tree and the wall. There he enfolded her with arms whose circumference at first barely touched her. Then bracing himself, he put a hand in Mrs. Bozoff's crisp, silver hair and pressed her injured face to his chest.

The unsettling warmth of her tears seeped through his shirt. Patting her back, Saul asked himself why, after her years of carrying tales, shouldn't she be allowed to become an item of gossip herself. Just because he lived with ghosts didn't mean she had to as well. But the truth was, he didn't live with ghosts, and he couldn't live without them, and but for the fact that his narrative fund had dried up while hers remained bottomless, he was every inch his mother's son. Her misery having awakened his own, Saul too surrendered to a quiet blubbering.

At length he managed to swallow the lump in his throat (it sank into his heart, increasing its burden) and make an effort to humor his mother: "Mama, why don't you tell me a story."

Still snuffling, Mrs. B disengaged herself from her son's embrace, corrected her lopsided glasses, and blew her nose. Her pout dissolved the moment she began to talk. "Did I tell you Sally Blockman asked to be buried in her apple green nightie, but her husband Myron, the momzer, said not on your life . . ."

"Why not?" asked Saul, wiping an eye with his jacket sleeve.

But before the mystery of Sally's nightie could be disclosed, they were apprehended by Myrna Halevy, nudge extraordinaire. "Where have you two been?" she said, appearing as if out of the mushroom cloud of her own hair. "Do you want to miss the show?" She hooked her arms through those of Saul and his mother, coaxing them in the direction of the converted nightclub.

As they entered, Myrna quipped, "Look at us, we just met and already—"

"—we're strolling down the aisle," Saul dryly coopted her remark; and to further cover his vulnerability, when Mrs. Bozoff exclaimed "Oh, isn't it beautiful!" he responded:

"Sure, if you like beauty."

Transformed yet again, the Calypso Room was a bower, its capaciousness reduced to almost cozy by the long wine-red curtain dividing it. Rafts of flowers in unnatural shades of yellow, pink, and blue decked the walls and trimmed the stage that doubled as an altar; flowers overwhelmed the wedding canopy like a garden gazebo, suffusing the air with their sickly perfume. It was a scent made audible by the cloying strains of a Broadway musical that Mrs. Bozoff identified as "Phantom of the Opera." She allowed that she'd always loved the music of Andrew Lloyd Wright.

Ignoring the business of bride's side versus groom's, Myrna conducted the Bozoffs into an aisle where her father sat poker-stiff beside three empty chairs. Mrs. B was deposited next to Mr. Halevy, Saul plunking himself down beside her, while Myrna took the folding chair to his right. Thus hemmed, Saul was interested to see how his mother took the furrier's hand in her own: how, laced together, their gnarled fingers looked as if they held between them a liver-spotted brain.

In his ear Myrna buzzed unrelentingly, "Don't they make a nice couple?"

"Yeah," said Saul, "like the Trylon and the Perisphere."

"I bet that's very witty," replied Myrna, and gave him a playful elbow in the ribs.

Saul made a face at the woman, her shoulders and glossy legs left exposed by her bustier'd jack-o-lantern of a frock, and thought she didn't look half bad. Then he wondered was he losing his mind, or had the generations of love matches inaugurated at the Concord contaminated the atmosphere? How else account for the ease he'd begun to feel in his adversary relation to this impossible female?

"Myrna," he said, to try and sink their intimacy, "why me? This place is full of millionaires."

She narrowed her eyes in a burlesque of indignation. "So that's what you take me for, a gold-digger? Well, I can assure you, sweetie," lifting a hand to let the bracelets rattle down her forearm, "I don't have to dig."

Saul back-pedaled, lowering his voice in the hope that Myrna would do the same, for heads had turned. "All I'm asking is, what the hell do you see in me?"

She looked at him as if amazed he didn't know. "You're the *author*," she informed him, giving the word the romantic dash of, say, *scourge of the Spanish Main.*

Saul struggled to keep from glimpsing himself through her eyes—God forbid she should lend him any unwonted self-esteem—and remembered that he knew her type: hadn't his wife been one of them? Women who believed the cure for what ailed him was to show him a good time. Well, he didn't want to have a good time. He was about to give her reasons why the title of author no longer applied, but when he opened his mouth, she put a finger to his lips and said "Shah!" The theme from "Exodus" had started up over the public address, which was apparently the cue for the wedding procession to begin.

First the groomsmen then the bridesmaids marched in in double-file, their full-dress ensembles repeating the pastel floral scheme. A crinolined toddler strewing rose petals waddled behind them, herself followed by a boy in a Tom Thumb tuxedo bearing a ring on a cushion. In their wake came the bride, escorted by her father—and the sight of her gliding over scattered petals, her breasts nestled dove-like in the empire bodice of an alabaster gown, her face tantalizingly obscured by a chiffon veil, chased every other consideration out of Saul's mind.

Her intended waited on the altar, imperially handsome, his slender frame flattered by the white cutaway with its crimson boutonniere. Beside him stood his own flushed father, potbelly corseted in a silk cummerbund, looking either smug or pickled in his capacity as best man. Giving his daughter a melancholy kiss, Mr. Supoznik handed her up the steps to the altar before taking a seat next to his wife. There the girl was greeted with a wink by Rabbi Lapidus, rocking on his heels at the center of the chupeh. Smart in a madras dinner jacket, the rabbi clutched something Saul at first took for a staff of office, but turned out to be a hand-held microphone; for once the participants were in place under the canopy, the wedding suite fanning out behind them like a choir, the rabbi brought the mike to his mouth with a practiced panache.

"Barchu haba ha-shem adonai . . . ," he crooned, while Saul wondered why such a show-biz production should bother paying lip-service to tradition. Of course, he didn't know Hebrew himself, nor had he set foot inside a synagogue since the confirmation of his sixteenth year—an ecumenical affair that in the reform movement replaced bar mitzvah. Saul had not been bar mitzvah'd: his Jewishness, like his connection to his mother's family, was several times removed. But for a brief bibliography of fables he felt increasingly had been written by someone else, Saul regarded himself an artificial Jew. So what made him think that his presence among this company should have anything to do with providence?

The first sign that something was wrong occurred after the second benediction, when the rabbi invited the couple to drink alternately from a goblet of wine. The Shapiro kid took a modest sip, but the bride, when her turn came, upended the cup and greedily slaked its contents to the dregs; then she emitted a most unladylike belch and wiped her mouth with the back of her hand. A shocked murmuring rose up among the guests, subsiding only after they'd assured one another (at least those in Saul's hearing) that Shelly was just a little high-strung.

The ceremony proceeded on a note of tension, which relaxed a bit as the groom began to recite, after the rabbi, the marriage formula: "Blessed art Thou, O Lord our God, Who hast made man in Thine image . . ." Vows were exchanged, the bride's with an especially breathy deliberation; then the groom, receiving the ring from his father (who, to the delight of the crowd, rifled his empty pockets before remembering the ringbearer), tried to place it on the tapered finger of his betrothed. But before he could succeed in this, the girl snatched the ring from his hand. She threw back her veil, disarranging a complicated black braid, and examined the stone through the loupe she made of her fingers; then wresting the mike from Rabbi Lapidus, she blurted in a Yiddish-inflected voice that bore no resemblance to her own,

"You say rock, I say shlock—let's call the whole thing off," nevertheless dropping the ring into her bodice.

The wedding guests collectively forgot how to breathe.

Turning toward them, Shelly Supoznik appeared for all the world like some callow ingenue with stage fright, though the words that came out of her conveyed no hint of trepidation.

"Maybe you heard about this fellow started a line of maternity wedding gowns?—un iz geshvoln zayn gesheft!" The room was deadly silent. "I said, you should see how his business is growing!" Not a sound, though the girl, or rather the voice that had borrowed her, remained undismayed. "It's not every line can bomb twice," it declared. "So Ethel and Abie are discussing Einstein's theory of relativity. Explains Abie to Ethel, 'All this means, everytink is relative. It's like this but it's also like that, it's different but it's the same, farshteyst?' 'Neyn,' says Ethel, 'give to me an example.' 'OK, let's say I shtup you in the fanny. I got a prick up the fanny and you got a prick up the fanny. It's different but it's also the same. Now you understand?' 'Ah,' says Ethel, 'but I got only one question: from this Einstein makes a livink?'"

The party on stage, but for Mr. Shapiro who guffawed, remained frozen in place, while the only movement among the folding chairs was from seniors reaching for pills.

"The doorbell rings at a nafkeh byiss," continued the bride who was not herself: her body rigid, a helix of hair dangling over one eye. "You know nafkeh byiss, dear? A whoorhouse. So the madame answers and finds there a poor soul with no arms or legs. 'What do you think you can do here?' she asks him. The cripple says, 'I rang the doorbell, didn't I?'"

Standing on either side of her, the groom and the rabbi traded glances of stunned bewilderment, both of them afraid to touch the girl. A susurrus of murmurs was again heard throughout the cabaret.

"Don't laugh so loud, you'll start a landsleit, I mean startle the landslide, a nechtiker tog . . ." None of the mordancy escaping Shelly's lips was expressed in her face. The bridal veil trailed like vapor from her inky tresses which—though she'd yet to move a muscle—seemed to have grown even wilder; her gown had fallen off a pale shoulder. "Gornisht helfn," said the voice, "we got here tonight the undead. So what should I say to make friends? I want to sleep with each and every one of you, and I mean sleep! I ain't had a moment's rest since I croaked . . ."

The murmuring had swelled in volume to the hum of an aerodrome.

"But seriously," the voice went on, "it's great to be here in the bosom of Shelly Supoznik—and such a lovely bosom it is. Forty years I'm in the cold, I can't find shelter to save my soul, and believe me, I wasn't so young when I died. When I was a boy, the Dead Sea was only sick. I'd go to the doctor, he'd tell me, 'Romaine, I need from you a specimen urine and samples of your blood and stool.' 'So I'll show you my underwear,' I'd say . . . " The hand she lifted to quell the laughter that wasn't forthcoming looked as if raised by a puppeteer. "But this one, this maidele, so delicate, so graceful like a gazelle, so . . . empty. I mean, hello?" The girl knocked mechanically at her temple as the voice echoed from within. "Is anybody home-mome-ome . . . ? But don't think I ain't grateful. Who else can accommodate a whole extra person without doing a time-share? Oy, Shelly Supoznik, such a princess! Ever see her eat a banana?"

Pretending the microphone was a banana, the bride made-believe she was peeling it, then placed a hand behind her head to force her open mouth toward the fruit.

Gasps of revulsion greeted the pantomime, the bridal party beginning to break ranks. Mr. Supoznik, having mounted the altar, appealed to the rabbi to for God's sake do something; while Rabbi Lapidus, checking his watch, replied that the episode was outside his jurisdiction, then screwed up his face as if to ask himself what he meant. Infuriated, Supoznik gave him a shove, which jarred the rabbi into asking if there were a doctor in the house.

A half-dozen or more men and women got officiously to their feet and began to make their way toward the altar spouting conjectures: "Cataleptic dementia," "paraconvivialis," and "Trepuka's syndrome" among the infirmities heard bandied between them. Consequently, before they'd reached the foot of the stage, the neurologist, the psychoanalyst in her stretch-velour original, the hidebound osteopath dredging the bowl of a pipe—each identifiable by their respective theories—were at an impasse. Fixed on diagnoses peculiar to his or her own area of expertise, they were stalled by their differences, quarreling before any had bothered to examine the girl.

As other guests weighed in with their theories ("Her mouth you should wash it out with soap!"), Mrs. Bozoff turned to her son and said, "Nu?" Saul shifted in his seat and conceded that they were certainly witnessing a one-of-a-kind event. On his right hand Myrna Halevy leaned a spongy breast into his shoulder, the teasing tone as ever in her voice.

"This is up your alley, no?"

"No," Saul denied unequivocally, then sheepish: "What makes you think so?"

"Your mama gave me one of your books."

Saul didn't know which was more surprising, that his mother carried around his books or that Myrna could read. Moreover, he was aware that she was aware he was lying: for wasn't he familiar enough with the sources, both canonical and apocryphal?—S. Ansky's classic drama and Paddy Chayevsky's heretical spinoff; he'd read Scholem and Steinsaltz, *The Path of the Name, The Booth of the Skin of Leviathan.* He might be a dunce when it came to observance, but ask him about King Solomon's necromancy or the properties of an herb called *flight of the demons* from Josephus' *Antiquities,* and he'd give you an earful. He understood, for instance (though he was much too agitated to say so), that the girl was possessed of an alien essence, a *dybbuk,* and that this one was the restless spirit of a dead Borscht Belt comedian—whose name, as it introduced itself following the gangbusters opening, was Eddie Romaine.

"My parents changed their name to Rabinowitz when I went into show business." Eddie's voice waxed nostalgic. "Ach, I played them all, Kutscher's, the Nevele, the Concord, the Pines—this was back in the days when you came up from the City by the Derma Road. I started in the Mountains eighty years ago at a place called the Tamawack Lodge. This was a bungalow colony run by a Jewish farmer famous for mating a Guernsey cow with a Holstein to get a Goldstein—instead of moo it said 'Nu?' The Tamawack was just thirty miles from here, and look how far I came in this business," nostalgia giving way to resentment, "thirty farkokte miles! This is the end of a career, ladies and gentlemen; on your way out leave a stone afn meyn kop . . ."

Under the canopy David Shapiro, his forelock dripping sweat, pleaded with his bride to admit she was having a joke—wasn't she? (Though not even her father, in his recital of her virtues at last night's banquet, had counted among them a sense of humor.) Chastised by Supoznik, David's dad had buried a rufous nose in the bib of his shirt, trying unsuccessfully to choke down his wheezing laughter—this while his counterpart Irving Supoznik tore the hairpiece from his own head and, inconsolable, stood wringing it in his hands as if strangling a rodent.

"Anybody helps her can have her!" he cried out in his desperation, which brought his wife in her yards of sequins and tulle to her feet.

"Irving, what are you saying?"

Again Myrna tickled Saul's ear with the feather of her breath. "Go ahead, Mister You-Don't-Know-Me, I dare you."

Saul turned to her in annoyance—she had a nerve! Though on the other hand, with all his yearning after the supernatural, wasn't he at least partially to blame for this visitation? Wasn't Eddie Romaine in a sense Saul's guest, and therefore, in a manner of speaking, his ghost to lay? Though he fought it, his vexation with Myrna fizzled into gratitude; he was beholden to her for calling his bluff.

Still he sat chewing his lip, emotions battling in his heart like cats in a bag. Who, after all, was Saul Bozoff, flash in a pan whose sheen had since rusted, to imagine himself the hero that saves the day?—to say nothing of a fundamental conflict of interests: because how could he not help feeling a certain sympathy for the dybbuk, who like himself was stuck between this world and another? Wavering, he asked himself where he got off even contemplating such a trespass, or for that matter even believing that this could happen. But somewhere between not wanting to seem a coward to Myrna and the growing conviction that he'd been elected, that no one else could release the girl from her spell, Saul stood up.

And instantly he felt it was too late to sit down. Exactly what he was going to do he didn't know, but excusing himself to his mother and Mr. Halevy ("Nature calls"), he slid past them, hearing nothing but the hammering of his heart in his ears. Between him and the girl the physicians debated, Mrs. Supoznik, breaking a heel, stumbled to all-fours as she clambered onto the stage—all of which appeared as in a dumbshow to Saul. He was conscious of little else but the babbling bride and his stinging left buttock, where Myrna had pinched him to speed him on his way.

"The Concord, gottenyu," repined Eddie Romaine from his situation inside the girl. "Today I don't know, but forty years ago the Concord was swank, the barbershop so deluxe you had to shave before entering. I said, *you had to shave before entering,* badabum. You would eat like there's no tomorrow, check in to the hotel as people and check out as freight. We had a waiter in those days, Shmuel— a k'nacher. 'Shmuel,' you'd say to him, 'what do you get with the brisket?' 'Severe vomiting and diarrhea,' he'd tell you. Ask him, 'Shmuel, you got matzoh balls?', he'd say, 'No, I walk like this from my arthritis.' Ask for Russian dressing, he'd bring you a picture of Stalin putting his pants on . . ."

Under cover of the general disorder, Saul passed virtually unnoticed up the aisle, taking the stairs to the altar at a couple of stealthy bounds. Mr. Supoznik was busy dragging his rumpled wife to her feet, David Shapiro handing over his father—whose hilarity was now indistinguishable from sobbing—to the long-suffering Mrs. Shapiro, who'd come up from the floor to lead her squiffy husband away. Solacing one another as at a graveside, some of the bridesmaids wept openly, as Saul warily approached the girl.

Possessed by another, she appeared to him more desirable than ever. Her ebony eye, the one not hidden behind her hair, remained moist but unblinking despite the fingers he waved in front of it. Her gown had slipped low enough on one side to reveal a breast, the aureole of a nipple just visible above the lace of her wonder bra. Attempting to cover her, Saul gingerly lifted the strap of the gown to her shoulder, though it instantly slipped down again. Sighing aloud, he made a mighty effort to subdue the tremor in his voice and address the dead comic inside her.

"Mister Romaine," Saul greeted respectfully, and was ignored.

". . . Oy, it was a regular sexpool in those days, the Concord. We had this house dick, you'll excuse the expression—Glickman; he was all the time kicking in doors. He hears shouts: 'Murder! Fire! Police!' so he kicks in the door. How's he to know it's only Sadie shouting 'Furder, Meyer, p'lease!'"

Clearing his throat to summon what was meant to pass for forcefulness, Saul tried again. "Excuse me, Mr. Romaine."

"You got to love a wedding," declared Eddie, who began pensively recalling his own wedding night. "I'm strutting my stuff in the buff in front of my new wife: 'Look by me,' I say, 'one hundred fifty pounds pure dynamite!'"

"Mr. Romaine, you have to leave this girl."

"'That's right,' says the wife, 'and with a three-inch fuse . . .'" Then Shelly's head swiveled in Saul's direction, the movement drawing with it the attention of the entire room—upon which the commotion died down.

"What is this, audience participation?" The dybbuk's delivery was arch. "Did I ask for a volunteer? Do I look like Mezmar the Great? All right, you're in my power: quack like a duck. No? Then quack like a chicken, I don't care." The voice becoming oily, "Gib a keek on this nice gentleman, so young, God bless him, he's just getting his hair. Nice gentleman, buttinsky, what's your name?"

Saul cautioned himself to stay on his guard, but for all his shuddering saw no reason why he shouldn't tell her, or him, or it, who he was.

"Okay, Mister Bozo, buzz off," said the dybbuk, "but first repeat after me: 'The sight of her behind . . .' What are you waiting? 'The sight of her behind . . .'"

"Pardon?"

"C'mon, be a sport. 'The sight of her behind . . .'"

Hesitating, Saul was nonetheless conscious that this was a beginning: he was involved in a dialogue with an un-disembodied spirit; it was a step. Gathering courage, he forced himself to look past the violated beauty of the bride to the job at hand. He even found the temerity to propose a condition. "If I repeat, will you leave the body of this girl?"

"Sure, sure," replied the dybbuk. "Now say it," holding the microphone up to Saul's jaw: "'The sight of her behind . . .'"

Uneasily, "The sight of her behind . . ."

"Forces Pushkin from your mind. Then you say: 'Forces Pushkin, Mister Romaine?'"

"Forces Pushkin, Mister Romaine?"

"Pushes foreskin, Mister B."

Shelly's expressionless head swiveled back toward the guests, some of whom chuckled only to be met by a barrage of angry "Shah's!"

"How do you like that?" said the voice. "We're a double act—Weber and Fields, Sacco and Vanzetti . . . Of course our people ain't had a pipputz, what you call a foreskin, for three thousand years, which reminds me of a story. A guy's watch has stopped so he goes into a shop with a giant watch hanging outside . . ."

Saul was squeamishly aware of his kibbitzers. The groom and the Supozniks, man and wife, had edged close to him and the girl, themselves pressed from behind by members of the bridal suite on tiptoe. Wiping the incipient grin from his face (for God help him, he'd taken pleasure in the exchange), Saul made an attempt to dispel any hint of complicity, exhorting the dead jester, "Now will you leave this girl?"

"Was that the shortest partnership in history or what" remarked Eddie Romaine. "Anyhoo, the guy asks the shopkeeper to fix his watch. Shopkeeper says, 'I don't fix watches.' Guy says, 'But you got a big watch hanging outside . . .'"

"Will you leave her?" Saul reiterated with warmth.

"Shopkeeper says, 'I know, but I don't fix watches—I'm a mohel, a circumcisor.' 'So why do you have a watch outside?' 'Tahkeh,' says the mohel, 'what should I have?'"

Saul started again. "Will you . . . ?"

"No!" roared the dybbuk, its attention once more engaged, then sweetly, "but you can come in too if you like—there's plenty of room."

"What about our deal?" asked Saul, who knew better than to ask.

Said Eddie: "I lied."

No longer able to contain themselves, Mr. Supoznik and the bridegroom erupted simultaneously: "What do you think you're doing!"/ "Shmuck, get away from her!"

Saul held up a placating hand and tried to explain that he was there to help.

"Help? You call this funny business helping?" said Supoznik, mopping his brow with the rug which he flung down in disgust. His wife begged him to remember his blood pressure.

"Listen to me," pleaded the intruder, "I'm Saul Bozoff," which made no impression whatever, and grasping at some straw of a credential, added, "the author." Then speaking hurriedly lest he be interrupted: "Your daughter Shelly has been occupied, that is possessed, by the spirit of a dead comedian. What she needs is . . ."

Inserted Eddie Romaine, ". . . an enema."

"What she needs," insisted Saul through gritted teeth, "is an exorcism."

Voices of outrage and disbelief were raised from all quarters, the shrillest emanating from the girl herself.

"Nisht gedugedakh!" shrieked the dybbuk, mimicking the shock of the assembly, "We shouldn't know from it!"

In the hush that followed Eddie's outburst, Saul tried to reassert himself. "With all due respect, I believe that with your help," steering a tricky course between humility and resolve, "I can expel the uninvited spirit from Shelly's body." Again a stirring in the room. "Rabbi," appealed Saul in an effort to curry favor, "you know better than I what's required." Rabbi Lapidus, though he raised his anointed head, showed no signs of having a clue, nor did he seem especially disposed to indulge Saul on the subject.

"A rabbi?" asked the dybbuk, perhaps repeating Lapidus's own thoughts, "this is a job for a nice Jewish boy?"

"Of course," continued Saul with forced optimism, "we'll need a quorum."

"Nonsense!" barked Supoznik, and through Shelly's coral lips the dybbuk voiced its hearty accord.

"I know what I'm talking about," argued Saul, though he was frankly riddled with doubts; had an unexpected party not come forward in his defense, he might have been persuaded there and then to give up the cause.

"Irving," submitted Mrs. Supoznik, tiara askew, "my mama from the Old Country and all of them, they believed in dybbuks and the evil eye. Who knows but this Bozoff is maybe right?"

Saul lifted his weak chin like a prow.

Others from among the gathering, all admittedly in their twilight years, began to mutter their solidarity with Mrs. Supoznik: Bozoff should be given a chance. Her husband rolled his eyes. "Ilka, you're playing dice with our daughter's welfare," he warned, but moved by the urgency of her plea and otherwise stymied, he asked the rabbi if it wasn't worth a try. Rabbi Lapidus remained sullenly unresponsive, but from the floor the stretch-velour psychoanalyst opined that, in some cases, ritual could have dramatic results; though she cautioned it should only be used in the last resort.

"If the Concord ain't the last resort," shouted the joker Milton Graber (without irony) from his third-row seat, "I don't know what is."

In the meantime a dwarfish old man with one blind and one basilisk eye, whom Irving Supoznik greeted as "Papa," had begun a slow ascent up the steps to the altar. He was aided by an equally aged peer, head bald and veined as a marble egg, the two of them followed in turn by an assortment of antiquated gentlemen. Among them, in defiance of the Great Neck interdict, was Mrs. Bozoff's suitor Isador Halevy. Why his presence should've mattered so much, Saul couldn't say, but at Mr. Halevy's arrival he felt a surge of confidence—the kind he suspected sorcerers must feel upon creating a golem.

Still it was daunting how these alter kuckers, constituting a quorum and then some, had so readily placed themselves at his disposal. What if he should disappoint them? But once he'd recovered his tongue, Saul impressed himself with the poise he now seemed to have at his command.

"We'll need the Torah scrolls and the ram's horn from the little chapel, the shtibl," he advised, "and also some black candles—I think I saw some in the gift shop . . ."

A couple of the old men relayed these requests to the floor—"Eric! Kevin! Kimberly!"—whereupon a gang of eager grandchildren bolted from the room in pursuit of the specified items. One of the doctors petitioned Rabbi Lapidus to put his foot down, but the rabbi was absorbed in the study of his oxblood shoes; and besides, the whole place now seemed galvanized by the sense that something was finally being done. Scarcely believing what he'd set in motion, Saul began to think he might actually be equal to the dreadful responsibility he'd shouldered.

Meanwhile the dybbuk kept up its tireless monologue: "Back in the thirties I'm dating this shikse—you know *shikse?* a girl who buys retail. So she calls me, the shikse, says, 'Eddie?'" Shelly held an imaginary receiver to her ear. "'Who is this?'" Eddie waxed falsetto: "'This is Matilda.' 'Matilda?' I say, 'Which Matilda I'm having the pleasure?' 'This is the Matilda which you already had the pleasure.' 'Oh, that

Matilda. I remember you and that wonderful weekend we spent together. Oy, what a weekend! And did I forget to tell you what a good sport you were?' 'That's why I'm calling, Eddie. I'm pregnant and I'm going to kill myself.' 'Say, you *are* a good sport.'" Shelly hung up the receiver. "But seriously . . ."

Shepherded by Milton Graber, the children's crusade returned bearing ritual objects. Further heartened at having been so quickly deferred to, Saul thought he should try and consolidate his authority.

"Irving, David," waiving the formalities since they were all united in a common cause, "why don't you light the candles and arrange them in a circle under the chupeh."

Clearly of two minds, the groom hung back with Rabbi Lapidus, but Supoznik, having placed his wife in the care of the maids of honor, began dispensing black candles. He kindled them one by one with his monogrammed Zippo, releasing their incense, as Saul called to the back of the house for someone to turn down the lights. The star-studded ceiling expired and the flames grew brighter, making goatish masks of the old men's faces. There was a crackling of joints as they bent to plant the candles in the puddles of dripping tallow—until the bride and minyan were circumscribed and all others banished to the dark periphery.

Skull caps and prayer shawls having also been issued, the men began putting them on, and Saul followed suit. He pulled a yarmulke over his bald spot, a tallis over his yarmulke like a cowl. Then, though he hadn't asked, Mr. Halevy presented Saul with the scrolls of the Law in their velvet mantle, the silver breastplate mirroring the old gold of the surrounding flames. Cradling the Torah, Saul imagined that in the darkness beyond the candles lay a courtyard instead of a nightclub; and in the courtyard the guests held cocks and hens and garlands of garlic, and were accompanied by the ghosts of ancestors on furlough from paradise.

Filling his lungs with all the righteousness conferred upon him, Saul was more than himself; he was exalted as he hadn't been since his decade mirabilis, back when he was a fine-tuned instrument for the telling of tales. Intoxicated by an energy that cleared his head of any lingering reverence for the dead comedian, he set his sights exclusively on saving the girl. "Spirit," pronounced Saul, "in the name of all that's holy, leave this child!"

Replied the dybbuk: "So this Jewish lady's on the subway when a pervert opens his raincoat. 'Feh,' she says, 'you call that a lining?' Then there was the time I asked my wife, 'How come I never know when you're having an orgasm?'"

"With the power of the Almighty and with the authority of the sacred Torah . . . ," said Saul, taking his text from S. Ansky who'd taken it from the ancients.

"'Because you're never around,' she tells me," continued the dybbuk.

". . . I, Saul Bozoff son of Belle, do hereby sever the threads that bind you to the world of the living and to the body of the maiden Shelly, daughter of . . ." In a whispered aside to Supoznik, "Ilka?" Supoznik nodded.

". . . daughter of Ilka . . ."

"Not until I get a spot on the Sullivan show," interrupted the dybbuk, Shelly's head having rotated once again toward Saul.

He stopped in mid-invocation. "Come again?"

"You heard me, I don't leave the girl till I get a spot on the Ed Sullivan Show, which is my deepest regret that I never had in my life."

"Eddie," Saul was consolatory; he knew that unfinished business was a common reason for a spirit's inability to find eternal rest. "I hate to have to tell you but Ed Sullivan is dead."

"So give him an enema."

"He's dead over twenty years," said Saul, "it wouldn't help."

"Nu, so it wouldn't hurt."

Realizing he'd walked into that one, Saul attempted to regain lost ground. "What's the matter, Eddie," he asked, "didn't anybody say kaddish for you when you passed away?" Because the old wisdom had it that failure to say the prayer for the dead over a corpse could result in an insomniac soul. To the circle Saul proclaimed, "Let us recite the mourner's kaddish."

"V'yish gadol v'yish kadosh sh'may rabo . . ." the men chanted inharmoniously along with Saul, loudly reciting one of the few prayers he had by heart. "May His great name be magnified and sanctified throughout the world . . ."

While Eddie proceeded: "It's Abie and Ethel's wedding night, and Ethel—she's old-fashioned, you know; so the groom goes down to the hotel bar while she gets ready . . ."

". . . Yisborach v'yishtabach v'yispoar v'yisromam v'yisnaseh . . ."

". . . In the bar Abie has a couple of drinks then returns to the room, where he finds his bride in bed with three bellhops . . ."

As the kaddish seemed to be having no effect, Saul called for Psalm 91, known as the anti-demonic psalm. "O thou dwellest in the

490

covert of the Most High and abideth in the shadow of the Almighty . . . ," which was all he could remember, though he mumbled along as others carried the tune.

". . . 'Ethel,' says Abie, 'how could you!' Ethel's got a little something in every orifice, see, so she lets loose a bellhop from her mouth mit a—" Shelly stuck her thumb in her mouth to make a popping sound, then said via Eddie as Ethel, " 'Well, you know I've always been a flirt.' But seriously . . ."

Rather than discouraged, Saul welcomed the opportunity to employ yet another item from the repertoire. "All right," he bellowed, "let's take off the gloves. Blow the ram's horn!"

With the help of his son the elder Supoznik raised the spiral horn (double-twisted and as long as he was tall) to his bearded lips, but could make only the feeblest farting noise. He passed the horn to one of his brethren, whose lungs proved no stronger than his own. It was then that Rabbi Lapidus began to come around. Apparently offended by the out-of-key bleating and tired of his supernumary role, he shook off his funk; he picked up his trouser legs to step over the candles, borrowed a tallis to cover his head, and prized the shofar from crooked fingers. Lifting the horn, he ballooned his cheeks and brought forth a long unbroken note that ended abruptly. Then he sounded the note again.

This was *tekiah,* whose echoes Saul could trace back to his childhood: the first chilling blast of the shofar sounded the Days of Awe, it was guaranteed to chase demonic intruders back to the other side.

"Which reminds me of the lady," said the dybbuk, "who during the Yom Kippur penance, the *al chet,* she beats herself below the pipik instead of on the chest. 'Why do you beat yourself there?' I ask her. 'Dezookst mir vi ich hob gezindikt,' she tells me. 'That's where I sinned.' "

"Give it up already, Eddie," demanded Saul, doubly reinforced now that the rabbi had come on board. "Don't you know you're dead?"

"So it wouldn't be the first time—but give me a minute, I'll warm this bunch up."

Again the ram's horn, and Eddie adopted a minstrel dialect: "Dem Jewish folk got curious customs; on dey holidays de head ob de household, he blow de chauffeur . . .' "

"Rabbi," said Saul, still feeling his oats, "blow *shevarim,*" and Rabbi Lapidus, wielding the horn like a virtuoso, trumpeted a short series of three unbroken notes. Then Saul pressed the dybbuk in a voice so withering he hardly recognized it as his own: "Face it, Eddie, you're just not

491

funny," notwithstanding those maverick members of the audience in stitches; "Don't you know when you're not wanted anymore?"

Once again the shofar, and Eddie: "Ach, didn't nobody ever want me. I couldn't get booked for love or money, and then I dropped dead. Sometimes I wish I was never born—but tell me, who should be so lucky? Not one in a hundred."

Saul wondered if it was his imagination or had the dybbuk's voice grown more subdued. Had the hectoring perhaps struck a nerve? Then girding himself against pity, he seized the advantage: *"Teruah!"* Saul clamored for the traditional climactic flourish: a succession of bloodcurdling staccato blasts alternating with eldritch trills.

A slightly winded quality was now detectable in the dybbuk's locution: "Guy goes to the doctor, tells him, 'Doc, I got five penises.' Doctor says, 'How do your pants fit?'"

"Like a glove," answered Saul, still the bully. "I heard it already, your material's stale."

"Gay avek, go away from me why don't you," said Eddie Romaine in exasperation. "I got my memoirs yet to write." And attempting to bargain, "You could be my whatsit, my ghost-writer; we'd split the royalties. I'd call it *The Catskills and Beyond.*"

"Memoirs?" scoffed Saul, satisfied that of the two of them his own will was the stronger. "You've got no memories, Eddie, only stale jokes. You're a cheap, two-bit Borscht Belt tummler, which is what you are for all eternity, so die already and let live. Leave the girl!"

"What do you expect from what I got to work with?" complained the dybbuk, its anger mocked by a throaty delivery. "By which I don't mean the shtik but the shtiff. Look at me, or rather *her*—a shaineh maidl? This is a beautiful girl? Look at her eyes, like railroad tracks they cross." Shelly tossed her hair to reveal crossed eyes. "This is not Miss America but *Meis* America. Lips like petals? Like bicycle pedals, gib a keek."

Here, as if to defend the honor of his bride, David Shapiro stumbled into the circle, then in lieu of throttling his frail intended, lowered his fists and donned a yarmulke.

"Beautiful teeth? A kolyerah, such buck teeth she's got, she could eat watermelon through a picket fence." The girl manufactured an overbite. "Body like a treasure?" Shelly slumped, allowing the gown to slip to her waist, exposing lace-cupped breasts and the creamy hollow of her abdomen. "It should have been buried already five hundred years. Let me be, a nechtiker tog—this totsie's no great loss."

492

Such rancor toward the vessel it occupied was a fair enough sign to Saul that the dybbuk was on the ropes. And oddly, the more abuse Eddie heaped on the head of his host, the more comely appeared the girl in Saul's eyes. All that was left was for him to deliver a swift coup de grace, and then to hell with Eddie Romaine!

"Leave the body of the maiden Shelly," he commanded, the borrowed lines become his own in the saying, "or be cut off forever from the community of Israel!"

Another, more violent reprise of the ram's horn.

Though reduced to mere curses, the dybbuk fought back: "You should wear out an iron shivah stool, you should fall into an outhouse just as a regiment of Cossacks finishes their prune stew and twelve barrels of beer . . . ," its voice losing volume with every syllable.

"In the name of the most holy, submit to the will of this congregation!" cried Saul.

"May your son meet a nice Jewish doctor."

"Dybbuk, submit!"

"What do you call it," Eddie's utterance was profoundly weary, "when a Jew has got only one arm?"

Student of exotic lore, Saul reckoned himself no stranger to the popular. "A speech impediment!" he crowed, tearing the mike from the girl's hand to speak into it himself: "Now do you submit?" Electronic feedback rivaled the wail of the horn.

The dybbuk was barely audible: "Why do Jewish women do it with their eyes closed?"

"Because God forbid they should see their husbands having a good time," replied Saul, who—inspired—ordered his minyan to "Snuff out the candles!"

One by one the flames were extinguished, permitting the throng of gawking faces to become discernible once more in the dim cabaret.

So faintly was the dybbuk speaking that Saul muffled the mouth of the shofar with his hand; he leaned near enough for Shelly's lips to brush his ear. "What happens," peeped Eddie, his words souring the girl's ragged breath, "when a Jew walks into a wall . . . with a hard-on?"

"He breaks his nose!" Saul shouted triumphantly, as the last candle was put out.

"In alle shwartz yor," moaned the dybbuk, "my time has come. Ach un vey, what a world, what a world!" Then the bride crumpled to her knees.

Her father and David, along with several old men, lurched forward to take hold of her arms. For a moment the girl sagged between them like washing on a line, her loose gown pooling at her feet. But as they started to lift her, her knees went rigid, her limp body snapped back to attention, and flapping her arms to rid herself of would-be samaritans, she spoke again through the medium of the deceased,

"Had you going there, didn't I?" Eddie's voice was restored to its caustic vitality. "So where was I? Oh yeah, this swinger walks into a barroom . . ."

Saul trembled from a rage that made the room swim before him as in the eyes of a drowning man. He wanted to grab hold of something, as for instance the girl's swanlike throat; he wanted to strangle her for the sake of expelling the spirit. But with the candles out, he was once more aware of the size of the assembly on stage, never mind the mob of guests on the cabaret floor. Dumbstruck by the magnitude of the task he'd undertaken, amazed at his own presumption, Saul shrank accordingly.

And deflated, he was his old familiar self, ready to take up the theme of failure again—when he remembered a trump card he'd yet to play.

". . . He's all farputst, the swinger, dressed to the nines," continued the irrepressible Eddie; "he's got the diamond stickpin, the Cuban cigar, the cathouse aftershave; when he sees this kurveh, this whoor sitting on a barstool, her legs crossed high, y'know, the garters showing . . ."

Saul knew the risks involved in what he contemplated, that only perfect masters should attempt so advanced a technique; all others would be in peril of their lives—which, in his case, seemed little enough to lose. Returning the Torah scrolls to Mr. Halevy, the microphone to Rabbi Lapidus, he gazed on the drooping but still luminous Shelly Supoznik.

"So the swinger, call him Marvin—his name's Mikey Bloom of Mosholu Parkway, the Bronx, but let's call him Marvin—he saunters up to the whoor, asks her, 'What would you say to a yentz, y'know, a little fuck?' Whoor gives him the once-over head to toe, from his single slick strand of hair to his Doctor Scholls," at which point Saul took Shelly in his arms, "says mmphm . . . ," and stifled the voice from inside her with a kiss.

He kissed her hard with what the kabbalists called *kavannah*, deep intent, and clung to her with the cleaving called *devekut*. Straightaway a force invaded his body: a black bird seemed to have entered his chest, searing its wings in the heat from his heart till they melted like wax. Hot liquid filled his lungs to overflowing and gathered in his loins, so that his spine became a wick dipped in oil. A spontaneous flame at

494

the base of the wick shot up its length and flared like a roman candle in his skull. Saul could have wished that the fever was mutual and would fuse them in their embrace; but instead the jolt to his brain pried his lips from the girl's, and with a cry of exquisite pathos—"Hello, little fuck!"—he plummeted into oblivion.

Then I'm hovering just under the wedding canopy. Below me is pandemonium: Irving Supoznik, steadied by his father (himself supported by others), is holding up his swooning daughter, while his wife Ilka fans the girl's cheek with the castoff toupee. A tousled David Shapiro is trying on and rejecting a variety of solicitous expressions to greet his slowly reviving bride. Meanwhile Rabbi Lapidus entreats the still debating specialists to help the fallen man—who is myself, evidently not breathing. A couple of doctors do finally break from their huddle and step onto the stage, where they lean over my horizontal body swapping opinions. Nobody seems to know basic CPR.

But somehow the paramedics have been alerted, because a team of them is lumbering down the aisle with apparatus in tow. Mounting the altar, they push past indecisive physicians and set straight to work looking for vital signs. Having hoisted their machines onto the stage, they turn switches that start them whirring and blinking, attach wires to various parts of my lifeless form. Like pachyderms come to the aid of a fallen ape man, they hunker around me, their trousers dipping to show toches cleavage in back.

Fresh from the disbanded minyan, Mr. Halevy is stationed beside my mother, attempting to still her fidgeting with a withered hand. His daughter has left him to join those bending over me under the chupeh, where she practically rides the backs of the paramedicals. "Hooray!" she bawls once the fibrillations have restored a pulse to my body, which the monitors had shown to be technically kaput. A funny thing, though; for while I recognize this as the moment when I ought to be sucked back into my sad sack of bones, it doesn't happen, nor do I feel the least pang of regret. In fact, I don't know when I've been so relieved.

The one I'll hereafter refer to as Saul Bozoff, breathing but still unconscious, is lowered from the stage onto a gurney, which the EMTs, under Myrna's gratuitous direction, begin to wheel up the aisle. Then in another interesting development (though I confess my level of interest is beginning to wane) the suspended marriage ceremony resumes. This is doubtless due to a collective amnesia: since the preceding events have not figured in any rational categories of understanding, they've conveniently dropped from everyone's mind. The rabbi, picking up where he left off, pronounces the final benediction; the groom stomps the goblet and, to salvoes of flashbulbs and resounding "Mazel tovs!", kisses the bride. Vacantly she receives the kiss, which does little to rekindle in her cheek the bloom that was never there.

When the stretcher has been rolled as far as the hallway—whose high windows are ablaze with a burnt orange dusk—Saul opens a furtive eye, then closes it. He snakes an arm about the waist of Myrna's rustling pumpkin gown, and abruptly pulls her down on top of him. She screams in a fright that dissolves into giddy laughter, which Saul chokes off with a kiss. This is not the beatific Kiss of Moses, which only I could've inspired him to perform, but judging from Myrna's ardent response it will do. The paramedics, though impressed, remind Saul he's suffered a trauma and should lie back down; he's too weak for such shenanigans. But against their advice, only halfheartedly seconded by Myrna, he rises from the gurney. He agrees that, pending the results of a battery of tests, his discharge will remain unofficial; he promises them in addition a testimonial and a photograph.

By the time Saul and Myrna reenter the Calypso Room, it's been converted yet again. A brigade of waiters have struck the canopy, removed and stacked the folding chairs; they've parted the curtain bisecting the erstwhile altar to reveal a space as large as the original on the other side. In it, laden with steam trays and the centerpiece of a seven-tiered wedding cake, the smorgasbord trestle meanders along a wall. Dining tables surround the parqueted dancefloor, and a paunchy, middle-aged orchestra in mambo shirts with ruffled sleeves, dragging fiddles, concertinas, and music stands, have taken over the stage. They are launched into the overture from "Hello Dolly."

Posed beside her husband for the ritual cutting of the cake, the new Mrs. David Shapiro, herself a wilted lily, flings her bridal bouquet. It falls short of the assembled maids of honor, who dive for it like scavengers. In the ensuing scuffle the blossoms are so mangled that no single girl emerges with enough to comprise a bouquet. When they sulkily disperse, Mr. Halevy abandons his sentinel post to creep forward; and in an act of unexampled agility, he approximates a deep kneebend to retrieve a sprig of baby's breath from the floor. He returns to Mrs. Bozoff and, bowing from the waist, deposits the stray sprig in her lap; but before he can straighten, she's stuck it in his buttonhole. Then the band breaks into an obligatory "Hava nagilah," and in a nod to (or parody of?) tradition the bride and groom are lifted in their chairs by spirited youths. Carried in a wild ride around the dancefloor, the couple hang on apprehensively to either end of a lace paper napkin.

Following Myrna's lead, Saul loads a platter with potted meat in mango sauce, gefilte fish in honeydew, noodle pudding with smetana, poppyseed strudel; then he and Myrna approach the table where their parents are seated. Mrs. Bozoff smiles absently at her son to acknowledge the food, then picks up the thread of her discourse. She's relating to Isador the predicament of one Minnie Horowitz—who, during a fit at a Hadassah meeting, began to speak in the voice of a girl kidnapped from a Russian shtetl three centuries ago.

"We were gonna try and give her a whaddayacallit?" says Mrs. B.

Suggests Saul: "An enema?"

"No," replies his mother, who wasn't supposed to have heard, "one of those things like what you did with the Supoznik girl—only the dybbuk was better company than Minnie."

Saul knits his brow, rummaging his brain for a memory that won't come. (Because it's *my* memory, though I hereby relinquish it forever.) Giving up the search with a shrug, he inquires of his mother, "Would that be Minnie Ha-Ha-Horowitz, the Indian maidele, to whom you refer?" Then he tenderly assures her, "Mama, you're a stitch, I'm gonna put you in a book one of these days." He stoops to kiss her forehead— he's a regular kissing fool tonight—and Mrs. Bozoff, absorbed again in her story, touches the spot as if to dab a drop of rain.

The orchestra has begun playing a bubbly version of "Never My Love," to which the bride and her father are waltzing, somewhat shakily, alone in the limelight. Having stepped to the edge of the dance floor, Saul watches the ethereal Shelly Supoznik Shapiro with a philosophical appreciation, as if he rather than her father had given the bride away. Then a hand tugs at his sleeve and he turns to face a barrel-shaped matron wearing what looks like a vintage prom gown, who introduces herself as his aunt, or cousin, Rosalie.

"I was just talking with your mama, she's such a love," she informs him, "and I wanted to meet her son, the author."

"Ah, my mama, God bless her," sighs Saul. "Y'know, we may be here next year for *her* nuptials. Can you believe this is the same woman who last week went to the doctor? Doc says, 'How do you feel, Mrs. B, sort of sluggish?' 'If I felt that good,' says Mama, 'I wouldn't be here.'"

There's a moment when the woman's broad face seems perplexed, her eyes closed as if in pain, just before she gives way to a loud, braying laughter. Some of her intimates bustle over to see what's so funny.

"She's got three sets of dentures, my mama," Saul persists, "one for milchik, one for fleishik, and one for Chinese."

His little circle of admirers cackle like a henhouse, attracting a larger audience.

"She's a card all right—what am I saying, she's the whole fershlogener pack. She gives me a pair of neckties, and when I wear one she asks me, 'What's a matter, you don't like the other?' A shnorrer comes up and complains to her he hasn't eaten for days. 'You should try and force yourself,' she tells him. I ask her how's the champagne and caviar; 'The ginger ale was fine,' she says, 'but the huckleberries tasted from herring.' She says she feels chilly, so I tell her, 'Close the window, it's cold outside.' 'Nu,' she replies, 'if I close the window, will it be warm outside?'"

He's surrounded now by a knot of hilarious wedding guests, including Myrna Halevy who's sidled up next to him. In a motion that appears to be second nature Saul hooks an arm about her shoulders and pulls her close; he leans toward her to accept her nibbling at his earlobe, and continues talking.

"When my father was dying, I asked him if he had any last wishes. 'All I want is you should fetch me a nice piece of your mother's coffee cake from the sideboard downstairs.' Then I have to tell him what my mama tells me, that it's for after . . ."

As you see, he was never a serious person, Saul Bozoff; I was the only thing that kept him in line. I tried my best to restrain his high spirits lest he squander them in the pursuit of happiness, and for a while it worked: the lost cause of his sorry self was found. But it didn't last; it wasn't enough he had me and the run of a Yid Neverland. He got lonely just the same.

Well, no hard feelings: may he be as at home in his shambling body as I am to be out of it. Anyway, I've stuck around long enough. A vagabond now, I'm content to let the winds of fancy blow me north or south, forward or backward in time. It's all the same to me. And if I sound a little wistful, I can assure you it'll pass; I've already as good as forgotten the container I came in. Still I suppose I ought to look for another—a worthier that can manage, with grace, to live in two worlds at once; though I'm in no hurry, savoring as I do the life (so to speak) of a solitary wanderer. Of course, you couldn't exactly call this flying solo; I'm not really in any immediate need of companions, since the air is as full of souls as falling leaves.

Nominated by Debra Spark, New England Review

SWAN

by OLEH LYSHEHA

from AGNI

My God, I'm vanishing . .
This road won't guide me anymore . .
I'm not so drunk . .
Moon, don't go . .
I appear from behind a pine—you hide . .
I step into shadow—you appear . .
I run—already you are behind me . .
I stop—you're gone . .
Only the dark pines . .
I hide behind a trunk—again, you're alone . .
I am—you are elsewhere . .
Absent . .
Absent . .
I am . .
Elsewhere . .
I am . .absent . .
I can't pass by so brightly! . .
Wait a while . .I want so much
Just to have you above me . .
Perhaps, you don't notice me? . .
Look: here is my foot—
Doesn't the copper lace gleam on my shoe? . .
Doesn't a bare bone whiten inside it? . .
I need a smoke . .
Bending, I find nothing on the ground . .
It hasn't been too long since

People walked home from a night train—
Someone might've dropped something . .
I'll smoke it after anyone . .
Look: I'm bending low again
And again I touch the dirt . .
No, an empty paper sheath . .
Something fragile again . .
Someone's moldering bone . .
Why don't you send someone? . .
Why doesn't night's bicycle give a ring? . .
Here you are—I'm stepping aside . .
Your road's free now . .
I stand out of the way . .
Here once, under the pines
I found a glass shard . .
Farther on, the road forked—
The shard lay just in the middle . .
I simply took it . .I smelled it . .
Someone might have poured it up for me . .
Fine . . faceted . .
At first, I wanted it, but no . .
Here, once at midnight, I hauled out
A dry pine with roots, dragged it home,
And very near the village, drops of rain caught me . .
Suddenly, I was stopped by a quiet song . .
Somebody stood, swaying slowly on the road,
In the darkest shadow by a puddle,
And low above it a small tree grew . .
It might've been a wild cherry tree . .
He kept singing, watching the puddle fill . .
I dragged the pine through the water,
And with my other hand steadied my sack,
Where a bottle of red vino dangled . .
He didn't move, but kept on singing . .
Should I have stopped there
And joined his singing? . .
Had he found
The one happy tree? . .
No one knows where it grows—
Or what it looks like . .

And who is allowed to recognize it? . .
I never stood under it,
Even to wait for rain to pass
Or watch between the drops
The silent froth appear . .
Swaying, he kept on singing . .
Otherwise, he would have fallen
And the rain stopped . .
He danced his own rain
Under that tree . .
I can't do such things . .
Perhaps it was a wolf? . .
And once among the pines
A woman ran, looking around nervously—
Plump legs were still hers,
And hugging her neck
And hanging over her shoulders,
Hiding them loosely,
Was an armful of irises
Lulled on her breasts . .
Dusted with pollen, eyelids of the flowers
Blinked heavily, nodding off . .
She was floating, a huge light cloud,
And sinking into that fervent dream
I rocked gently on those breasts . .
She ran carefully as if carrying
Something intimate, a last treasure;
She plunged into shadow,
Harboring the small, weak lungs
From the deep incisions
Of this raw world . .
And it seemed at that moment,
When she came out, she ran from my heart,
Disappearing suddenly, with the whole world
Waiting on this deserted road . .
Last winter, I wasn't here . .
I could escape . .
Just a little farther on—over there,
Beyond the tallest pine,
Under the Great Bear

Where the impetuous Venus,
Head down, descends . .
That winter, she burned violently,
Hurrying me farther westward . .
In Danzig I didn't find any shoes . .
Look here: this one's tied with a copper wire . .
There's a hole near the big toe,
And though I entered all
The carved and heavy doors with crystal rings,
What can satisfy this foot? . .
At last I entered your bright museum
Over the river channel
Just to get warm. The cold rain
Seemed not to stop,
And no one was there . .
But in the corner, under glass
A pair of tall boots was drying
After lying idle somewhere
In a peat bog or a swamp . .
The feet that owned them
Are stones now
Under rippled laces,
With sharpened toes . .
I couldn't stop staring . .
Near there, stood burial urns—
Such dark pots,
With eyes painted and small ears, etched,
Perhaps, with a bone awl . .
And rough bronze rings hung from them . .
The urns seemed one large family
Settled in forest meadow,
Feasting on wild boar . .
Astonished, I looked,
Each to each . .
Fine . . truly fine . .
And each wore a string of cloudy amber
Small, split like mice fangs . .
And these were the urns with souls
Of very young girls
Sacrificed after their meal . .

Each one suddenly swollen . .
Does anyone believe
I have been there? . .
That my feet felt so comfortable
In those shoes? . .
After such a museum
There is nowhere to go . .
It grew cold toward evening . .
Winter was winter without snow,
Only that pungent rain . .
I waited until it died,
Then I left . .
Darkness was falling . .
I passed under low, twisted pines . .
Under the trees, mines were dug
And maybe, in a few,
There once lay a seam of amber,
And a few perhaps
Were deepened by foxes,
And I came close to falling into one . .
Then I was past them . .
It was night
When I came up to the shore . .
I saw no one . .
Only the damp sand . .
I sat a long time, looking out . .
Such quiet . .
Then from the thick mist
The swan appeared on the water,
Turned its head,
Then began to fade again,
Its high neck lifted
Was the last ray . .
Did that attendant let me go? . .
What an odd glare it gave! . .
And afterwards, with no one there,
I took off my clothes and went in . .
There was no tide,
All receded, lugging me out . .
Suddenly, the floor gave way, crumbling beneath my feet

And I went under . .
Turning my eyes from the bottom,
I embraced the whole sea at once . .
Our eyes opened to endlessness,
No sky, no ground . .
And now, coming back
On this night road,
I can't seem to close those eyelids . .
Who waits for me
Behind a pine? . .
Drunk again, with empty hands . .
Oh, take my eyes—
I can step aside . .
Tell me, how does one return? . .
Just step into the shadow of a pine? . .
Like that? . .
Won't it be forever? . .
Is it me? . . Have I come back? . .
But then, who has returned? . .
And that day . . no, a little later,
When at last I pushed the wicket gate
And asked for an egg
And had a hundred rubles to my name,
And Maria went to the hen coop
And brought me three eggs,
And took nothing . .
Only looked at me,
Telling how our one-armed neighbor
Left his house
And now begs alms in the trains . .
How regretful . .
So self-assured, his gray eyes, like a child's . .
This road is calling me farther and farther
But I must leave . .
To what place can a man return
After the sea at night? . .
What is left for him? . .
Mountains, perhaps . .
How tedious the walk is, up and down . .
I feel the road under me,

Finding only the shadows of pines again—
Again and again the same shadow . .
Were these the mountains? . . Have they begun to rise? . .
Was it the swan
Lifting its neck . .
It overshadowed even the sky over the sea . .
I don't know . . I've just entered the sea and am departing now . .
Look at me—
—I am spreading my arms
And rising to you . .
My God, I'm falling . .

Translated from the Ukrainian by the author and James Brasfield

Nominated by Agni

DAUGHTER-MOTHER-MAYA-SEETA

by REETIKA VAZIRANI

from PRAIRIE SCHOONER

To replay agonies was the necessary terror
the revolving door of days
Now it's over
There's no one point thank god in the turning world
I was always moving
tired too but laughing
To be a widow is an old
freedom I have known
vidua paradisea a bird
Singly I flew trespassing on silence
and synergy was happiness my giraffe
in the face of Africa
not the clenched teeth of a mythical exile
but me among daughters
and my son at work
me pregnant with them
taking in the glamour days
town and country mirabella elle vogue
cosmopolitan We have made this world
brown these beautiful women
the laughing and crying till we cleared the dining table
In hotels men asked my girls to fetch them more towels
In restaurants they asked us for bread

Today I'm a civil servant on the Hill
my children are with me

From the Mall what colorful sarongs
they bring me to drape my tiny ankles
the gifts we give
to Mina a necklace of Mikimoto pearls
Tara a Paloma purse for cosmetics
Lata a pair of lime shoes for the miles
Devi gives me her eclectic lit eyes
the glamour of our wilder regions
and with Bombay weavers on the twenty-four-hour looms
shocking pink is the navy of India

Listen I am listening
my mind is a journey
I took its English ships
I flew over oceans
I flew in the face of skies
orienting my loss of caste in a molting nation
my dark complexion
the folly of envy
wishing all my life to be fair
My jealous god leaves and I'm no longer lonely
Hello son this is your mother
Here daughters take this energy
these maroon saris and these maroon bras
I am proud to have borne you
When you gather around me
newness comes into the world

Nominated by Rita Dove, Marilyn Hacker, Dorianne Laux

LIVING TO TELL THE TALE

memoir by GABRIEL GARCÍA MÁRQUEZ

from ZOETROPE: ALL-STORY

MY MOTHER ASKED me to go with her to sell the house. She had come that morning from the distant town where the family lived, and had no idea where to find me. She asked around among my acquaintances and was told to look for me at the Mundo Bookstore, or in the nearby cafés, where I went every day at one o'clock and at six to talk with my writer friends. The one who suggested this warned her: "Be careful, because they're all certifiable." She arrived at twelve sharp. With her light step she made her way among the tables of books on display, stopped in front of me, looking into my eyes with the mischievous smile of her better days, and before I could react, she said:

"I'm your mother."

Something in her had changed, and this kept me from recognizing her at first glance. She was forty-five, and we hadn't seen one another for the past four years. Adding up her eleven births, she had been pregnant for almost ten years and had spent at least another ten nursing her children. She had gone gray before her time, her eyes seemed larger and more startled behind her first bifocals, and she wore strict, somber mourning for the recent death of her mother, but she still preserved the Roman beauty of her wedding portrait, dignified now by an aura of authority. Before anything else, even before she embraced me, she said in her customary, ceremonial way:

"I've come to ask you to do me the favor of going with me to sell the house."

She didn't have to tell me which one, or where, because for us only one existed in the world: my grandparents' old house in Aracataca, where I had the good fortune to be born and which I left, never to return, not long before my eighth birthday. I had just dropped out of the Faculty of Law after six semesters devoted in their entirety to reading and reciting from memory the unrepeatable poetry of the Spanish Golden Age. I had read, in borrowed translations, all the books I would have needed to learn the novelist's craft, and had published four stories in newspaper supplements, winning the enthusiasm of my friends and the attention of a few critics. The following month I would turn twenty-three, I had passed the age of military service and was a veteran of two bouts of gonorrhea, and every day I smoked, with no foreboding, sixty cigarettes made from the most barbaric tobacco. I divided my leisure between Barranquilla and Cartagena de Indias, on Colombia's Caribbean coast, living like a king on what I was paid for my first journalistic pieces, which amounted to almost less than nothing, and sleeping in the best possible company wherever I happened to be at night. For reasons of poverty rather than taste, I anticipated what would be the style in twenty years: untrimmed mustache, wild hair, jeans, flowered shirts, and a pilgrim's sandals. In a darkened movie, and not knowing I was nearby, a girl I knew told someone: "Poor Gabito is a lost cause." Which meant that when my mother asked me to go with her to sell the house, there was nothing to keep me from saying I would. She told me she didn't have enough money, and out of pride I said I would pay my expenses. An impossibility at the paper. They paid three pesos for a brief daily article, four for an editorial when one of the staff writers was out, but it was barely enough to live on. I tried to borrow money, but the managing editor reminded me that my debt amounted to more than the equivalent of one hundred articles. That afternoon I was guilty of an abuse that none of my friends would have been capable of committing. At the door of the Café Colombia, next to the bookstore, I approached don Ramón Vinyes, the old Catalonian teacher and bookseller, and asked for a loan of ten pesos. He had only six.

Neither my mother nor I, of course, ever imagined that this simple two-day trip would be so determinative for me that the longest and most diligent of lives would not be long enough to finish telling about it. Now, with more than seventy years behind me, I know it was the most important of all the decisions I had to make in my entire career as a writer. That is to say: in my entire life.

I hadn't been to Aracataca in fourteen years, not since my maternal grandfather died and I was taken to live with my parents in Barranquilla. Before adolescence, one's memory is more interested in the future than the past, and so my recollections of the town had not been idealized by nostalgia. I remembered it as it was: a good place to live, where everybody knew everybody else, on the bank of a river of clear water that ran along a bed of polished stones which were white and enormous prehistoric eggs. At dusk, above all in December, when the rains had ended and the air was like a diamond, the Sierra Nevada de Santa Marta with its white peaks seemed very close to the banana plantations across the river. From there you could see the Arawak Indians moving in lines like ants along the cliffs of the sierra, carrying sacks of ginger on their backs and chewing pellets of coca to make life bearable. As children we dreamed of shaping balls of perpetual snow and playing war on the parched, burning streets. For the heat was so incredible, in particular at siesta time, that the adults complained as if it were a daily surprise. From the day I was born I had heard it said, over and over again, that the rail lines and camps of the United Fruit Company were built at night because during the day the sun made tools too hot to pick up.

The only way to get to Aracataca from Barranquilla was by dilapidated motor launch through a narrow channel excavated by slave labor during colonial times, and then across La Ciénaga, a vast swamp of muddy, desolate water, to the mysterious town that was also called Ciénaga. There you took the daily train that had started out as the best in the country, and traveled the last stretch of the journey through immense banana plantations, making many pointless stops at hot, dusty villages and deserted stations. This was the trip my mother and I began at seven in the evening on February 19, 1950—Shrove Sunday— in an unseasonable rainstorm and with thirty-two pesos that might just be enough to get us home if the house was not sold for the amount she had anticipated.

The trade winds were so fierce that night that I had trouble convincing my mother to get on the boat at the river port. She was not being unreasonable. The launches were rudimentary imitations of the steamships out of New Orleans, but with gasoline motors that transmitted an intolerable vibration to everything on board. There was a small salon with large prongs for hanging hammocks at different levels, and wooden benches where people elbowed their way to a seat with all their baggage, bundles of merchandise or crates of chickens, and even live pigs. There were a few suffocating cabins with two army cots, almost always occupied by threadbare little whores who offered emergency services during the trip. Since by now none of the cabins were free, and we hadn't brought hammocks, my mother and I took by storm two iron chairs in the central passageway, and there we prepared to spend the night.

Just as she had feared, the squall lashed the foolhardy ship as we crossed the Magdalena River, which has an oceanic temperament so close to its estuary. In the port I had bought a good supply of the cheapest cigarettes, made of black tobacco and a paper that could have been used to wrap packages, and I began to smoke the way I did in those days, using the butt end of one cigarette to light the next, as I read *Light in August* by William Faulkner, who was the most faithful of my tutelary demons. My mother clung to her rosary as if it were a capstan that could raise a bulldozer or hold a plane in the air, and, as always, she requested nothing for herself but asked for the prosperity and long life of her eleven orphans. Her prayer must have gone where she sent it, because the rain became gentle when we entered the channel, and the breeze was almost too calm to keep the mosquitoes away. Then my mother put back her rosary, and for a long while she observed in silence the clamoring life around us.

She had been born to a modest family but grew up in the ephemeral splendor of the banana company, from which she had at least retained her rich girl's education at the Academy of La Presentación de la Santísima Virgen, in Santa Marta. During Christmas vacations she would embroider with her friends, play the clavichord at charity bazaars, and with an aunt as chaperone, attend the purest dances given by the timid local aristocracy, but as far as anyone knew she had no sweetheart until, against her parents' wishes, she married the local telegraph operator. Since then her most outstanding virtue had been a sense of humor and an iron constitution that the sneak attacks of adversity would never defeat during her long life. But her most surprising trait, and also the least suspected, was the exquisite skill with which she hid her tremendous strength of character. A perfect Leo. This had allowed her to establish a matriarchal power whose domain extended to the most distant relatives in the most unexpected places, like a planetary system that she controlled from her kitchen, with a quiet voice and almost without blinking, while the pot of beans was simmering.

Seeing her equanimity during that brutal trip, I asked myself how she had been able to overcome, with so much speed and mastery, the injustices of poverty. That awful night tested her to the limit. The bloodthirsty mosquitoes, the dense heat reeking from the mud in the canals churned up by the launch as it passed, the frantic back and forth of sleepless passengers who could find no place to sit in the crush of people—it all seemed intended to unhinge the most even temper. My mother endured everything, sitting motionless in her chair, while the girls for hire reaped the night's harvest in the nearby cabins. One of them had entered and left her room, which was right next to my mother's chair, several times, and always with a different man. I thought she hadn't seen her. But the fourth or fifth time in less than an hour that the girl went in and came out, my mother followed her with a pitying eye to the end of the passage.

"Poor things," she said with a sigh. "What they have to do to live is worse than working."

This is how matters stood until midnight, when the constant vibration and dim lights in the passageway made me tired of reading, and I sat down beside her to smoke, trying to free myself from the quicksands of Yoknapatawpha County. I had left the university the year before with the rash hope that I could earn a living in journalism and literature without any need to learn them, inspired by a sentence I think I read in George Bernard Shaw: "From a very early age I've had to interrupt my education to go to school." I wasn't inclined to discuss this with anyone because I felt, though I couldn't explain why, that my reasons might be valid only to me.

Trying to win my parents over to this kind of folly, when they had placed so many hopes in me and spent so much money they didn't have, was a waste of time. My father in particular would have forgiven me anything except my not hanging on the wall the kind of academic degree he could not have. Our communication broke off. Almost a year later I was still planning a visit to explain my reasons to him when my mother appeared and asked me to go with her to sell the house. And yet, she didn't mention the subject until after midnight, on the launch, when I sensed as if by divine revelation that she had at last found the opportune moment to tell me what was, beyond all doubt, the real reason for her coming, and she began in the manner and tone and with the precise words she must have thought out in the solitude of sleepless nights long before she undertook the trip.

"Your father is very sad," she told me.

So there it was, the inferno I feared so much. She began as she always did, when you least expected it, in a silken voice that nothing

512

could agitate. For the sake of the ritual, since I knew very well what the answer would be, I asked:

"Why's that?"

"Because you've left your studies."

"I didn't leave them," I said. "I only changed careers."

The idea of a thorough discussion raised her spirits. "Your father says it amounts to the same thing," she told me. Knowing this was false, I said: "He stopped studying, too, to play the violin." "That was different," she replied with great vivacity. "He only played the violin for parties and serenades. If he left his studies it was simply because he didn't have enough money to eat. But in less than a month he learned telegraphy, which was a very good profession back then, especially in Aracataca."

"I earn a living, too, writing for newspapers," I lied.

"You say that so as not to mortify me," she said. "But anybody can see how bad it is just by looking at you. I didn't even recognize you when I saw you in the bookstore."

"I didn't recognize you either," I told her.

"But not for the same reason," she said. "I thought you were a beggar." She looked at my worn sandals, and added: "Not even any socks."

"It's more comfortable," I said. "Two shirts and two pairs of undershorts: you wear one while the other's drying. What else do you need?"

"A little dignity," she said. But she must have said this without thinking, because she softened it at once in a different tone: "I'm saying this because of how much we love you."

"I know," I said. "But tell me something: wouldn't you do the same if you were in my place?"

"No, I wouldn't," she said, "not if it meant upsetting my parents."

Recalling the tenacity with which she had broken down her parents' opposition to her marriage, I said with a laugh: "I dare you to look me in the eye." But she was unsmiling as she looked away because she knew all too well what I was thinking.

"I didn't marry until I had my parents' blessing," she said. "Unwilling, I grant you, but I had it."

She interrupted the discussion, not because my arguments had defeated her, but because she wanted to use the toilet and didn't trust its cleanliness. I spoke to the bosun to find out if there was a more sanitary place, but he explained that he himself used the common lavatory. And concluded, as if he had just been reading Conrad: "At sea we are all equal." And so my mother submitted to the law of equality.

Contrary to what I had feared, when she came out it was all she could do to control her laughter.

"Imagine," she said to me. "What will your father think if I come back with a social disease?"

Some time after midnight we were held up for three hours because clumps of taruya growing in the channel fouled the propellers, the pilot lost control, the launch ran aground in a mangrove thicket, and many of the passengers had to get out and pull it free with the cords of their hammocks. The heat and mosquitoes became excruciating, but my mother got around them with her instantaneous and intermittent catnaps, famous in our family, that allowed her to rest without losing the thread of the conversation. When we started up again and a fresh breeze began to blow, she was wide awake.

"In any case," she said with a sigh, "I have to bring your father some kind of answer."

"Don't worry about it," I said with the same innocence. "In December I'll go myself and explain everything to him."

"That's ten months from now," she said.

"Well, after all, it's too late this year to arrange anything at the university," I told her.

"Do you really promise you'll go?"

"I promise."

For the first time I detected a certain tension in her voice:

"Can I tell your father that you're going to say yes?"

"No," was my categorical answer. "You can't."

It was clear she was looking for another way out. But I didn't give it to her.

"Then it's better if I tell him the whole truth once and for all," she said. "Then it won't seem like deceit."

"All right," I said. "Tell him."

We stopped there, and someone who didn't know her very well would have thought it had ended, but I knew this was only a pause to recharge her energy. A little while later she was sound asleep. A light wind blew away the mosquitoes and saturated the new air with the fragrance of flowers. Then the launch acquired the grace of a sailboat.

We were in the great swamp, La Ciénaga Grande, another of the myths of my childhood. I had crossed it several times, when my grandfather Colonel Nicolás Ricardo Márquez Mejía took me from Aracataca to Barranquilla to visit my parents. "You shouldn't be afraid of La Ciénaga, but you must respect it," he had told me, speaking of the un-

514

predictable moods of its water, which behaved like either a pond or an untameable ocean. In the rainy season it was at the mercy of storms that came down from the sierra. From December to April, when the weather was supposed to be calm, the trade winds charged at it with so much force that each night was an adventure. My maternal grandmother, Tranquilina Iguarán, would not risk the crossing, except in cases of dire emergency, after a terrifying trip when they'd had to seek shelter and wait until dawn at the mouth of a river.

We were lucky. That night it was a still water. From the windows at the prow, where I went for a breath of air a little before dawn, the lights of the fishing boats floated like stars in the water. There were countless numbers of them, and the invisible fishermen conversed as if they were paying a call, for their voices, enclosed in the night, had a ghostly resonance. Leaning on the railing, trying to make out the line of the sierra, the first onslaught of nostalgia took me by surprise.

On another night like this, as we were crossing La Ciénaga Grande, my grandfather had left me sleeping and gone to the bar. I don't know what time it was when, over the drone of the rusted fan and the clattering metal laths in the cabin, the shouting of a crowd woke me. I couldn't have been more than five years old, and I was very frightened, but it soon grew quiet again and I thought it must have been a dream. In the morning, when we were already at the dock in Ciénaga, my grandfather stood shaving with his straight razor, with the door open and the mirror hanging from the frame. The memory is exact: he hadn't put on his shirt yet, but he wore his eternal elastic suspenders, wide and with green stripes, over his undershirt. As he shaved, he talked to a man I would recognize at first glance even today. He had the unmistakable profile of a sheep, a sailor's tattoo on his right hand, and he wore several solid gold chains around his neck, and bracelets and bangles, also of gold, on both wrists. I had just gotten dressed and was sitting on the bed, putting on my boots, when the man said to my grandfather:

"Don't doubt it for a second, Colonel. What they wanted to do with you was throw you into the water."

My grandfather smiled and kept on shaving, and with a haughtiness that was typical of him, he replied:

"Just as well for them they didn't try."

Only then did I understand the uproar of the previous night, and I was very shaken by the idea that anyone would have thrown my grandfather into La Ciénaga. So much so that I can evoke it now in all its visual detail, and see him lifted onto the shoulders of the crowd, thrown up and

515

down like Sancho Panza being tossed in a blanket by the mule drivers, and then hurled overboard. But at the time it was erased from my memory and didn't come back until twenty years later, when it returned sharp and clear, without warning and for no reason, while I was eating lunch with my uncle Esteban Carrillo in Riohacha, during the period when I was going from town to town in La Guajira selling encyclopedias and medical tracts. By then my grandfather had died, and I recounted what I remembered to Uncle Esteban because I thought it was amusing. But he leaped up from his seat, enraged because I hadn't told anyone as soon as it happened, and eager for me to identify the other man so he could find out who had tried to drown his father. My uncle could not understand why my grandfather hadn't defended himself, since he was a good shot who was almost always armed, who slept with a revolver under his pillow, had often been on the firing line during the civil wars, and who, when peace was restored had killed an attacker in self-defense. In any case, Esteban said, it would never be too late for him and his numerous brothers to punish the offense. It was the law of La Guajira: an affront to one member of the family had to be paid for by all the males in the offender's family. Uncle Esteban was so determined that he pulled his revolver out from under the pillow and placed it on the table so as not to lose any time while he finished questioning me. From then on, whenever we met in our wanderings along the Caribbean coast, his hope was renewed that I might have remembered. One night he came to my cubicle at the paper, during the time when I was researching the family's past for a first novel I never finished, and proposed that the two of us investigate the attack together. He never gave up. The last time I saw him in Cartagena de Indias, when he was old and his heart was battered, he said goodbye to me with a sad smile:

"I don't know how you've been able to be a writer when your memory's so bad."

Well: the recollection of this unexplained episode took me by surprise on the night I was going with my mother to sell the house, as I contemplated the sierra snows gleaming blue in the first rays of the sun. From then on, from that day to this, I have been at the mercy of nostalgia.

The delay in the channels allowed us to see in the full light of day the narrow bar of luminous sand that separates the sea from La Ciénaga, where there were fishing villages with nets laid out to dry in the sun, and thin, grimy children playing soccer with balls made of rags. It was astounding to see on the streets the number of fishermen whose

516

arms were mutilated because they hadn't thrown their sticks of dyna-mite in time. As the launch passed by, the children began to dive for coins the passengers tossed to them. It was after eight when we dropped anchor in a pestilential marsh a short distance from the town of Ciénaga. Teams of porters, up to their knees in mud, took us in their arms and carried us to the dock, splashing through the wheeling turkey buzzards that fought over the unspeakable filth in that quagmire.

We ate an unhurried breakfast at the tables in the port, where they served delicious mojarra fish from La Ciénaga with slices of fried green plantain, and my mother used the occasion to mount a new of-fensive in her personal war. Sitting next to me, and without looking up, she ambushed me with a question:

"So, tell me once and for all: what am I going to say to your father?"

I tried stalling for time:

"About what?"

"The only thing he cares about," she said with some impatience. "Your studies."

It was my good fortune that an impertinent fellow diner, intrigued by the intensity of our conversation, wanted to know my reasons. My mother's immediate response not only intimidated me, but was also a surprise coming from her, a woman who kept jealous watch over her private life.

"He wants to be a writer," she said.

"A good writer can earn good money," was his thoughtful reply. "Above all if he works with the government."

I don't know if it was discretion that made my mother change the subject, or fear of the arguments offered by this unexpected partici-pant in the conversation, but the two of them ended up sympathizing with one another over the unpredictability of my generation, and shar-ing their memories of the past. At last, following the trail of names of mutual acquaintances, they discovered we were doubly related through the Cotes and the Iguaráns. In those days this happened with two out of three people we met along the Caribbean coast, and my mother always celebrated it as a family event.

We drove to the railroad station in a one-horse victoria, perhaps the last of a legendary line already extinct in the rest of the world. My mother was lost in thought, looking at the arid plain ashy with nitrate, which began at the mudhole of the port and stretched to the horizon. For me it was a historic spot: one day, when I was three or four years old, my grandfather had taken me by the hand and crossed the burning

517

wasteland, walking fast and not telling me where we were going, and then, without warning, we found ourselves facing a vast extension of green water belching foam, where an entire world of drowned chickens lay floating.

"It's the ocean," he said.

I was disappointed and asked him what was on the other shore, and without a moment's hesitation he answered: "There is no shore on the other side." Today, after seeing so many oceans front and back, I still think that was one of his great answers.

I don't remember when I heard about the ocean for the first time, or what anticipatory image of it I had formed from the stories of adults. My grandfather had wanted to show it to me in the muddled pages of his old, tattered dictionary, but couldn't find it. When he recovered from his chagrin, he remedied the situation with an explanation that deserved to be true: "There are words that aren't there because everybody knows what they mean." It was because of this mishap that he had an illustrated dictionary brought from Santa Marta, with a picture on the cover of Atlas holding the vault of heaven on his shoulders. This was the first of the countless dictionaries about everything that I've had in my life, and in primary school I read it like a novel, in alphabetical order, understanding almost nothing. In it my grandfather found the definition of the ocean that he had missed in the other one: "A great extension of salt water covering most of the globe." With that kind of vagueness, of course, I never would have recognized the ocean if my grandfather hadn't told me I was looking at it. None of my earlier images corresponded to that sordid mass of water with its nitrate-encrusted beach, where the tangled branches of rotting mangroves and sharp fragments of shell made it impossible to walk. It was horrible.

My mother must have had the same opinion of the ocean at Ciénaga, for as soon as she caught sight of it through the coach window, she said with a sigh: "There's no ocean like the one at Riohacha." That was when I told her my memory of the drowned chickens, and, like all adults, she thought it was a childhood hallucination. Then she continued her contemplation of each place along the way, and I knew what she thought of each one by the changes in her silence. We passed the red-light district on the other side of the tracks, with its little painted houses with rusty roofs and the old parrots from Paramaribo that sat on rings hung from the eaves and called out to clients in Portuguese. We passed the watering site for the locomotives, with its immense iron dome where migratory birds and lost seagulls took shelter to sleep. We passed the sinister house where Martina Fonseca was murdered. We circled the city without going in, but we saw the wide, desolate streets and the former splendor of one-story houses with floor-to-ceiling windows where endless exercises on the piano began at dawn. Then my mother pointed.

"Look," she said. "That's where the world ended."

I followed the direction of her index finger and saw the station: a building of peeling wood with sloping tin roofs and continuous balconies, and in front of it a dry little square that couldn't hold more than two hundred people. It was there, my mother told me that day, where in 1928 the army had killed an undetermined number of banana workers.

The information amazed me, because I always thought the massacre had taken place at the station in Aracataca. Often, when I went with my grandfather to wait for the train, I relived the horror of that imaginary moment: the soldier reading the decree in which the striking laborers were declared a gang of lawbreakers; the three thousand men, women, and children motionless under the barbaric sun after the officer gave them five minutes to leave the square; the order to fire, the clattering machine guns spitting in white-hot bursts, the crowd trapped in panic as it was cut down, inch by inch, by the methodical, insatiable blades of shrapnel. My grandfather could not have been uninvolved in my false memories, because I once asked him in the Aracataca station where the murderous guns had been placed. He was reading a letter he had just received, and without looking at me he pointed toward the roofs of the cars. "There," he said. Then he finished reading the letter, and as he tore it into tiny pieces to be sure it would never be read by his wife, he asked me, perplexed:

"What was it you wanted to know about myrtles?"

My ability to visualize certain events as if I had in fact experienced them, above all during my childhood, has caused many confusions in my memory. But none could compare to my belief that the massacre had occurred at the Aracataca station. My mother's certainty, however, left no room for doubt. And when I asked her how many had been killed, she answered with the same assurance: "Seven." Though she went on to warn me not to take this number as literal fact, because on the day of the massacre the number was said to be more than a hundred, and later the figure kept decreasing until it reached none at all. And so the only issue on which reality and my memory agreed was that the soldiers had fired from the roofs of the cars.

519

My mother's account had such meager numbers, and so poor a setting for the grandiose drama I had imagined, that it produced a feeling of deep frustration in me. Later, I spoke to survivors and witnesses, and went through newspaper archives and official documents, and realized that the truth was not to be found anywhere, but that my mother's version was the most probable. Conformists said, in effect, that there were no dead. Those at the opposite end of the spectrum stated, their voices firm, that there had been more than a hundred, that they had seen them bleeding to death on the square, and that the victims had been taken away in freight cars and dumped into the ocean like spoiled bananas. And so the truth was lost forever at some improbable point between the two extremes.

My false memory was so persistent that in one of my novels I told about the massacre with the same precision and all the horror I believed I had seen in Aracataca, for I could not describe any version other than the one that had incubated for so many years in my imagination. This was why I increased the number of dead from seven to three thousand: to maintain the epic proportions of the drama. Real life lost no time in proving me right: not long ago, on one of the anniversaries of the tragedy, the speaker asked for a minute of silence in memory of the three thousand anonymous martyrs slaughtered by the forces of law and order.

The train was supposed to reach Ciénaga at eight in the morning, pick up the passengers from the launches and those who had come down from the sierra, and leave for the interior of the banana region a quarter of an hour later. My mother and I reached the station after nine, but the train had been delayed. Still, we were the only passengers. She realized it as soon as she went into the empty car, and exclaimed with festive humor:

"What luxury! The whole train just for us!"

I've always thought it was a false gaiety to hide her disillusionment, for the ravages of time were plain to see in the condition of the cars. They were old second-class cars that had been converted to a single class, but instead of cane seats or glass-paned windows that could be raised or lowered, they had wooden benches polished by the warm, unadorned bottoms of the poor. Compared to what it had been before, not only that car but the entire train was a ghost of itself. The train had once had three classes. The poorest people rode in third, the same boxcars made of planks used to transport bananas or cattle going to slaughter, and modified for passengers with long benches of raw wood.

Second class had cane seats and bronze trim. First class, where government officials and executives of the banana company traveled, had carpets in the passageway and upholstered seats, covered in red velvet, that could change position. When the head of the company traveled, or his family, or his distinguished guests, a luxury car was coupled to the end of the train. It had tinted glass in the windows and gilded cornices and an outdoor terrace with two little tables for drinking tea on the journey. I never met a single mortal who had seen the inside of this unimaginable coach. My grandfather had twice been mayor, and had a frivolous idea of money, but he used second class only if he was with a female relative. And when asked why he traveled third class, he would answer: "Because there's no fourth." The most memorable aspect of the train, however, was its punctuality. Clocks in the towns were set by its whistle.

That day, for one reason or another, it left an hour and a half late. When it began to move, slowly and with a mournful creaking, my mother crossed herself, then made an immediate return to reality.

"The springs on this train need oil," she said.

We were the only passengers, perhaps in the entire train, and so far nothing had been of any real interest to me. I sank into the lethargy of *Light in August*, smoking without pause, but with occasional rapid glances to identify the places we were leaving behind. With a long whistle the train crossed the salt marshes of La Ciénaga and raced at top speed along a bone-shaking corridor of bright red rock, where the deafening noise of the cars became intolerable. But after about fifteen minutes it slowed down, and entered, with discreet silence, the shadowy coolness of the plantations, and time grew heavy and you could no longer feel the ocean breeze. I didn't have to interrupt my reading to know we had entered the hermetic kingdom of the banana region.

The world changed. Stretching away on both sides of the track were the symmetrical, interminable avenues through the plantations, where oxcarts loaded with green stalks of bananas were moving. Without warning, in uncultivated spaces, there were red-brick camps, offices with wire grating on the doors and windows and fans hanging from the ceilings, and a solitary hospital in a field of poppies. Each river had its village and its iron bridge that the train crossed with a blast of its whistle, and the girls bathing in the icy water leaped like shad as it passed, unsettling travelers with the flash of their breasts.

In the town of Riofrío several Arawak families got on the train carrying packs filled with avocadoes from the sierra, the most delicious in

521

the country. They made their timid way up and down the car looking for a place to sit, but when the train started up again the only people left were two white women with a baby, and a young priest. The baby didn't stop crying for the rest of the trip. The priest wore an explorer's boots and helmet and a rough linen cassock darned in square patches, like a sail, and he spoke at the same time the baby cried, and always as if he were in the pulpit. The subject of his sermon was the possibility that the banana company would return. Ever since it left nothing else was talked about in the region, and opinion was divided between those who wanted it to come back and those who didn't, but everyone believed it would. The priest was against it, and expressed his position with so personal an argument that the women thought it was nonsense: "The company leaves ruin wherever it goes." It was the only original thing he said, but he wasn't able to explain it, and in the end the woman with the baby confounded him by saying that God could not be in agreement with him.

Nostalgia, as always, had wiped away bad memories and magnified the good ones. No one was safe from its onslaught. Through the window in the car you could see men sitting in the doorways of their houses, and you only had to look at their faces to know what they were waiting for. Women washing clothes on the stony beaches watched the train go by with the same hope. They thought every stranger who arrived carrying a briefcase was the man from the United Fruit Company coming back to reestablish the past. At every encounter, on every visit, in every letter, sooner or later the sacramental sentence would make its appearance: "They say the company's coming back." Nobody knew who said it, or when, or why, but nobody doubted it was true.

My mother thought herself free of those ghosts, for when her parents died she had cut all connections to Aracataca. But her dreams betrayed her. At least, when she had one interesting enough to recount at breakfast, it was always related to her memories of the banana region. She survived the most difficult times without selling the house, hoping to quadruple the price when the company came back. The irresistible pressure of reality had defeated her at last. But when she heard the priest on the train say that the company was about to return, she made a gesture of despair and whispered in my ear:

"What a shame we can't wait just a little longer."

While the priest was talking, we passed a town where a crowd filled the square, and a band played a lively concert under the oppressive sun. All those towns always seemed identical to me. When my grandfather would take me to don Antonio Daconte's brand-new Olympia Cinema, I noticed that the railroad depots in cowboy movies looked like our train stations. Later, when I began to read Faulkner, the small towns in his novels also seemed like ours. And it was not surprising, for ours had been built under the messianic inspiration of the United Fruit Company, and in the same provisional style of a temporary camp. I remembered them all, except Aracataca, with the church on the square and little fairy-tale houses painted in primary colors. I remembered the gangs of black laborers singing at twilight, the shanties on the estates where field hands sat to rest and watch endless freight trains go by, the ditches where morning found macheteros with their heads hacked off in drunken Saturday night brawls. I remembered the private cities of the gringos in Aracataca and Sevilla, on the other side of the railroad tracks, surrounded like enormous electrified chicken yards by metal fences that on cool summer dawns were black with charred swallows. I remembered their slow blue lawns with peacocks and quail, the residences with red roofs and wire grating on the windows, and little round tables with folding chairs for eating on the terraces among palm trees and dusty rosebushes. Sometimes, through the wire fence, you could see beautiful languid women, in muslin dresses and wide gauze hats, cutting the flowers in their gardens with gold scissors. And then, like a fleeting apparition, the head of the banana company rode through the streets of the town one afternoon in a sumptuous open car, beside a woman whose long blonde hair blew in the wind, with a German shepherd sitting like a king in the backseat. They were momentary glimpses of a remote, unimaginable world forbidden to mortals like us.

In my childhood it was not easy to distinguish some towns from others. Twenty years later it was even more difficult, because in the station porticoes the boards with their names had fallen down: Tucurinca, Guamachito, Neerlandia, Guacamayal. And they were all more desolate and dusty than in memory.

At about ten in the morning the train stopped in Sevilla for fifteen interminable minutes to change locomotives and take on water. That's when the heat began. To make matters worse, when we began to move again, at each bend in the track the new locomotive sent back a blast of soot that blew in the paneless windows and left us covered in black snow. The priest and the women had gotten off in some town without our even realizing it, and this heightened my feeling that my mother and I were traveling all alone in a train going nowhere. Sitting across from me, looking out the window, she had nodded off two or three times, but all of a sudden she was wide awake and asked me the dreaded question again:

"So, what shall I tell your father?"

I thought she would never give up her search for the flank where she could break through my decision. Earlier she had suggested a few compromises that I rejected out of hand, but I knew her withdrawal would not last long. Even so, this new assault took me by surprise. Prepared for another long, fruitless battle, I answered with more calm than I had shown before:

"Tell him the only thing I want in life is to be a writer, and that's what I'm going to be."

"He isn't opposed to your being what you want to be, but he wants to see you graduate," she said.

She spoke without looking at me, pretending to be more interested in the life passing by the window than in our conversation.

"I don't know why you insist so much when you know very well I won't give in," I said to her.

Then she looked into my eyes and asked, intrigued:

"Why do you think I know that?"

"Because you and I are just alike," I said.

The train stopped at a station that had no town, and a little while later it passed the only banana plantation along the route that had its name written over the gate: MACONDO. This word had attracted my attention ever since the first trips I had made with my grandfather, but only as an adult did I discover that I liked it for its poetic resonance. I had never heard it before, no one ever said it, and I didn't even ask myself what it meant. I had already used it in three books as the name of an imaginary town when I happened to read in an encyclopedia that it is a tropical tree resembling the ceiba, that it produces no flowers or fruit, and that its light, porous wood is used for making canoes and carving cooking implements. Later, I learned in the *Encyclopædia Britannica* that in Tanganyika there is a nomadic people called the Makondos, and I thought this might be the origin of the word. But I never confirmed it, and I never saw the tree, for though I often asked about it in the banana region, no one had anything to tell me. Perhaps it never existed.

The train used to pass the Macondo plantation at eleven o'clock, and stop ten minutes later in Aracataca. On the day I went with my mother to sell the house, it ran two and a half hours late. I was in the lavatory when the train began to accelerate, and a dry burning wind came in the broken window, mixing with the din of the old cars and the terrified whistle of the locomotive. My heart pounded in my chest and an icy nausea froze my belly. I rushed out, driven by the kind of fear you feel in an earthquake, and I found my mother, imperturbable in her seat, reciting out loud the places she saw passing by the window like instantaneous flashes of the life that once was and never would be again. "That's the land they sold my father with the story that there was gold in it," she said. The house of the Seventh-Day Adventists passed like a sigh, with its flower garden and a sign over the door: *THE SUN SHINES FOR ALL.* "That was the first thing you learned in English," my mother said. "Not the first thing," I told her, "the only thing." The cement bridge passed by, and the muddy waters of the irrigation ditch from the days when the gringos diverted the river to bring it to the plantations. "The houses with their easy women where the men spent the whole night dancing the cumbiamba and lighting rolls of bills instead of candles," she said. "The little Montessori school where I learned to read." For an instant, the total image of the town on that luminous Tuesday in February shone through the window. "The station," my mother exclaimed. "How the world has changed if nobody's waiting for the train." Then the locomotive stopped whistling, slowed down, and came to a halt with a long lament.

The first thing that struck me was the silence. A material silence I could have identified blindfolded among all the other silences in the world. The reverberation of the heat was so intense that you seemed to be looking at everything through undulating glass. In the little cobblestone square not even a compassionate memory was left of the three thousand workers massacred by the forces of law and order. For as far as the eye could see there was no recollection of human life, nothing that was not covered by a faint sprinkling of burning dust. My mother stayed in her seat for a few more minutes, looking at the dead town laid out along empty streets, and at last she exclaimed in horror:

"My God!"

That was the only thing she said.

Nominated by Zoetrope: All-Story

DEER TABLE LEGS

by KATAYOON ZANDVAKILI

from DEER TABLE LEGS (University of Georgia Press)

THIS IS WHERE YOU live with no further patience for Chess: the etiquette of fan and smile, sloping back.

The men I met fell from the tops of sentences. They promised hot-air balloon rides, would've stolen sheep. On the way up the mountain, they held silent. (Silence is power, the book said.) And in the winter of my young year, when I was desperate as wind, they laughed. It cannot be, I thought (am thinking still)—but I talked to them, one by one, and they laughed. In the same way perhaps that they didn't know about what had gone on before—like the rupture, burst—didn't know about the guide; it happened often enough. So I granted them interviews; they came to my photo shoots.

———

We enter houses in fields ringing with thistles and impatiens (home, moody). Death comes later, in public: the smatter of white pavement, classic boots. Long arms in dark jackets. Monday follows Thursday. You leave the elevator and kiss me hard for good measure: step away like a faint red leaf—
Night carves out toy bridges.

———

I saw her leave the book, saw the sun on the tabletop, knife on the bread. "Bagel" became "bread." I was writing for all time.

I am going to hold your baby. A sunny, clear picture. I want to under-
stand the different waves of his head and body, the smiling eyes, the
other riding out of me.

———

he says he has never seen the ocean
and looks around the room nervously as Christopher Robin would
climbs out of the car and says he'll be right back
he pours coffee in a thermos and I watch like mermaids breathing
a leg of weight draped over me (: in the attic, a paperboy hat)
he calls people to say he's made love—oh no, they groan in
Chicago—when all he has done is kiss my hand like a stolen statue,
dropping to his knees as at deepest wood
the round of his white shoulders
at twilight we were on the bleachers by the river
        he was learning to run

———

But what of macadamia nuts/salt/a television producer/public battles
in South/Carolina and baths
This man and woman/kissing/at our shared table are/not married. She
is/plain and he is/rich. They/kiss again.
The woman/at the other table has/on the same exercise/socks I have
in a drawer at home./
He leaves. I am working, I really am. His pants sag.
The rest of the day is accustomed exhilaration: spins.

———

You give1p2.5 me your money because you love me. We enter each
other at night. Sometimes, we don't want to but we do anyway.
We could've left it for another time. Hands trail.

———

You scoffed at Grace Cathedral, the lamp overhead. Felt your teeth
grow, the fine hair.

527

I was 27 and you were 28. We touched (afternoon teapots, deer table legs) in profile, startled by the word "we."

I wanted to make a film about cab drivers in other cities—not really, I wanted to want to.

In Europe, they wear wedding rings on the other hand.

The men I met, each one, an unspoken name living in a house on a beach. I made blue glass-cathedral slivers in a cone of tangerine night. No man could take that sort of life away, and no woman. Dog noses, like moose, were okay.

Nominated by The University of Georgia Press

LOVE LETTERS

by MICHAEL BURKARD

from AMERICAN POETRY REVIEW

In some less than willful way the boy snaps to.
This is the time of the sea: he must pretend to be
doing much better than he is doing. His aunt
is about to marry a man who has the name of a dog.
This is not funny to anyone and the sea is a place
to drown.

Endlessly, I see the boy collapsing into war with
himself, but because he is young he is strong, and
a secret place inside begins to burn like some birthday
candle. Someone he knew swims awkwardly and nervously
out to a raft in the middle of a large pond, and this
someone is very out of breath.

The daughter-in-law of a famous judge dies a very early
death. A student our boy-as-a-secret-man taught befriends
the woman months before her death, but the dye is cast.
Another woman in another city about the same time has
the green eyes a deer would have and borrows a copy
of Auden's *The Dyer's Hand* from a novice at the job

but a coworker nonetheless. Rumors have green eyes taking
much too much speed—wonderful copywriter. Much too much
speed. She puts her face just an inch or two from his.
He wants to kiss her eyes, but tells her to keep the book,
it's a gift, he didn't need it anyway ("I am through with it.").
The sun knows you are through with it also.

Her green eyes know. A student knows. Our boy-secret
and his aunt and even the namesake dog know. One fact loops
into another like the ripples in the silly but dangerous pond.
Something planetary is sinking in the sky at 4 a.m. He is
letting the cat out. He is thinking the shredded turkey in
the canned cat food is a terrible sounding fact, and it, like
the others, might be horsemeat, and there will be no more of that!

Nominated by Agha Shahid Ali, Susan Wheeler

SPECIAL MENTION

(The editors also wish to mention the following important works published by small presses last year. Listing is in no particular order.)

POETRY

Upon Being Asked My Opinion About An Autopsy—Robin Behn (The Iowa Review)
Captive Music—Patricia Dobler (Nightsun)
Fish Tea Rice—Linda Gregg (TriQuarterly)
Daughter-In-Law—Cynthia Huntington (Cafe Review)
For the Roses—Dorianne Laux (Talking River Review)
Last Night—Gail Mazur (Agni)
Sleepwalkers—Judith Minty (Luna)
Free Radicals—Harryette Mullen (Hambone)
A Star Is Born in the Eagle Nebula—Marcia Southwick (Gettysburg Review)
Sanctuary—Larissa Szporluk (Grand Street)
Finitude—Patricia Traxler (New Letters)
Borrowed Love Poems—John Yau (Boston Review)
The Erotic Philosophers—Carolyn Kizer (Yale Review)
Enough—Eamon Grennan (Yale Review)
Letter To My Bed—Linh Dinh (Watermark)
Eva Sitting On The Curb With Pen And Paper Before The Torturers Came to Get Her—Luis Rodriguez (*Shards of Light,* Tia Chucha Press)
Paragraphs From A Day Book—Marilyn Hacker (River Styx)
Epistle—Mark Jarman (Five Points)
Stones—Ann Lauterbach (Avec)
First Fire—Amiri Baraka (Hunger)

A Geology—Brenda Hillman (American Poetry Review)

Two Men Find A Place Known Only to Deer—Cyrus Cassells (James White Review)

For The Twentieth Century—Frank Bidart (Threepenny Review)

After Han Yu—Sam Hamill (BOA Editions)

Adiós Again, My Blessed Angel of Thunderheads And Urine—Adrian C. Louis (Ploughshares)

Hospital In Oregon—Marilyn Chin (The American Voice)

Cervical Jazz: A Girl Friend Poem—C.D. Wright (American Letters & Commentary)

Early Saturday Afternoon, Early Evening—Charles Wright (Paris Review)

Abaude—Louise Glück (American Poetry Review)

ESSAYS AND MEMOIRS

Kismet—Floyd Skloot (Boulevard)

Distance and Direction—Judith Kitchen (Georgia Review)

Skill—Scott Russell Sanders (Georgia Review)

Portrait of A Pseudonym—Hortense Calisher (American Scholar)

The Storekeeper—Otis Haschemeyer (Missouri Review)

How To Write A Personal Essay—Mike Moxcey (Georgia Review)

What Was So Beautiful About the Father—Connie Voisine (Western Humanities Review)

Where We Do Our Work—Frederick Busch (Zoetrope)

Ralph Ellison In Tivoli—Saul Bellow (Partisan Review)

The Third Servant—Margot Livesey (Five Points)

Emmet's Canyon—John Smolens (Grand Tour)

Matthew Arnold and T.S. Eliot—Adam Kirsch (American Scholar)

A Marriage Disagreement—Alix Kates Shulman (Dissent)

Love, War and Deer Hunting—John Hales (Creative Nonfiction)

The Insomniac—Bill Hayes (Speak)

The Wilderness North of the Merrimack—Jane Brox (Georgia Review)

Reading With Diana—Kathleen Hill (Yale Review)

Further Questions?—John Barth (Michigan Quarterly Review)

The Summit on the Summit—Christopher Merrill (Orion)

Avesnes: Reading In Place—Kathleen Hill (Michigan Quarterly Review)

A Long Day's Night—Discovering The Mississippi—Paul Gruchow (Ascent)

Marine Air: Thinking About Fish, Weather and Coastal Stories—
Theresa Kishkan (Mānoa)
Life Itself—Louis Simpson (Black Moon)
"David Castleman"—David Castleman (Mandrake Poetry Review)

FICTION

Lau The Tailor—Charles Philipp Martin (Mānoa)
The Gates Are Closing—Amy Bloom (Zoetrope)
Friends: An Elegy—Alyce Miller (Witness)
Ground—Gordon Lish (Salmagundi)
The Visiting Privilege—Joy Williams (Conjunctions)
Watching Girls Play—W.D. Wetherell (Georgia Review)
Port De Bras—Melissa Pritchard (Southern Review)
The Girl Everything Was Done To—Ian MacMillan (The Sun)
Among the Missing—Dan Chaon (TriQuarterly)
The Hearts of Men—John Griesemer (Fish Stories)
Slumming—Nicholas Montemarano (Puerto del Sol)
War Games—Karen Bjorneby (Nebraska Review)
Here I Am—Kirby Gann (Bananafish)
Tempest-Tossed—Alana Ryan (Sycamore Review)
Mollusks—Arthur Bradford (McSweeney's)
Poachers—Tom Franklin (Texas Review)
Consummation—Peggy Shinner (River Styx)
Hernando Alonso—Alan Cheuse (North American Review)
Close Enough—Becky Hagenston (Witness)
Exchange Students—Robin Hemley (The Sun)
The Woman Who Married Her Garden—Alvin Greenberg (Ascent)
Kuyashii—Eric Miles Williamson (Notre Dame Review)
Mercy—R.D. Skillings (Notre Dame Review)
The Prodigal Son—Karenmary Penn (Gulf Coast)
Interpreter of Maladies—Jhumpa Lahiri (Agni)
Milk, Blood, Bone, Moon—Lex Williford (Quarterly West)
A Nurse's Story—Peter Baida (Gettysburg Review)
Legal—Brian Evenson (Weber Studies)
Riptide—Kathryn Trueblood (*The Sperm Donor's Daugher*, Permanent Press)
The Burning Room—Thomas E. Kennedy (Mediphors)
Salad Girls—Jean Harfenist (Crazyhorse)

PRESSES FEATURED IN THE PUSHCART PRIZE EDITIONS SINCE 1976

Acts
Agni Review
Ahsahta Press
Ailanthus Press
Alaska Quarterly Review
Alcheringa/Ethnopoetics
Alice James Books
Ambergris
Amelia
American Letters and Commentary
American Literature
American PEN
American Poetry Review
American Scholar
American Short Fiction
The American Voice
Amicus Journal
Amnesty International
Anaesthesia Review
Another Chicago Magazine
Antaeus
Antietam Review
Antioch Review
Apalachee Quarterly
Aphra
Aralia Press

The Ark
Art and Understanding
Artword Quarterly
Ascensius Press
Ascent
Aspen Leaves
Aspen Poetry Anthology
Assembling
Atlanta Review
Autonomedia
Avocet Press
The Baffler
Bakunin
Bamboo Ridge
Barlenmir House
Barnwood Press
The Bellingham Review
Bellowing Ark
Beloit Poetry Journal
Bennington Review
Bilingual Review
Black American Literature Forum
Black Rooster
Black Scholar
Black Sparrow
Black Warrior Review

Blackwells Press
Bloomsbury Review
Blue Cloud Quarterly
Blue Unicorn
Blue Wind Press
Bluefish
BOA Editions
Bomb
Bookslinger Editions
Boston Review
Boulevard
Boxspring
Bridges
Brown Journal of Arts
Burning Deck Press
Caliban
California Quarterly
Callaloo
Calliope
Calliopea Press
Calyx
Canto
Capra Press
Caribbean Writer
Carolina Quarterly
Cedar Rock
Center
Chariton Review
Charnel House
Chattahochee Review
Chelsea
Chicago Review
Chouteau Review
Chowder Review
Cimarron Review
Cincinnati Poetry Review
City Lights Books
Clown War
CoEvolution Quarterly
Cold Mountain Press
Colorado Review
Columbia: A Magazine of Poetry
and Prose

Confluence Press
Confrontation
Conjunctions
Connecticut Review
Copper Canyon Press
Cosmic Information Agency
Countermeasures
Counterpoint
Crawl Out Your Window
Crazyhorse
Crescent Review
Cross Cultural Communications
Cross Currents
Crosstown Books
Cumberland Poetry Review
Curbstone Press
Cutbank
Dacotah Territory
Daedalus
Dalkey Archive Press
Decatur House
December
Denver Quarterly
Domestic Crude
Doubletake
Dragon Gate Inc.
Dreamworks
Dryad Press
Duck Down Press
Durak
East River Anthology
Ellis Press
Empty Bowl
Epoch
Ergo!
Exquisite Corpse
Faultline
Fiction
Fiction Collective
Fiction International
Field
Fine Madness
Firebrand Books

Firelands Art Review
First Intensity
Five Fingers Review
Five Points Press
Five Trees Press
The Formalist
Frontiers: A Journal of Women Studies
Gallimaufry
Genre
The Georgia Review
Gettysburg Review
Ghost Dance
Gibbs-Smith
Glimmer Train
Goddard Journal
David Godine, Publisher
Graham House Press
Grand Street
Granta
Graywolf Press
Green Mountains Review
Greenfield Review
Greensboro Review
Guardian Press
Gulf Coast
Hanging Loose
Hard Pressed
Harvard Review
Hayden's Ferry Review
Hermitage Press
Hills
Holmgangers Press
Holy Cow!
Home Planet News
Hudson Review
Hungry Mind Review
Icarus
Icon
Iguana Press
Indiana Review
Indiana Writes
Intermedia
Intro

Invisible City
Inwood Press
Iowa Review
Ironwood
Jam To-day
The Journal
The Kanchenjuga Press
Kansas Quarterly
Kayak
Kelsey Street Press
Kenyon Review
Latitudes Press
Laughing Waters Press
Laurel Review
L'Epervier Press
Liberation
Linquis
Literal Latté
The Literary Review
The Little Magazine
Living Hand Press
Living Poets Press
Logbridge-Rhodes
Louisville Review
Lowlands Review
Lucille
Lynx House Press
The MacGuffin
Magic Circle Press
Malahat Review
Mānoa
Manroot
Many Mountains Moving
Marlboro Review
Massachusetts Review
Mho & Mho Works
Micah Publications
Michigan Quarterly
Mid-American Review
Milkweed Editions
Milkweed Quarterly
The Minnesota Review
Mississippi Review

Mississippi Valley Review
Missouri Review
Montana Gothic
Montana Review
Montemora
Moon Pony Press
Mr. Cogito Press
MSS
Mudfish
Mulch Press
Nada Press
New America
New American Review
New American Writing
The New Criterion
New Delta Review
New Directions
New England Review
New England Review and Bread Loaf Quarterly
New Letters
New Virginia Review
New York Quarterly
New York University Press
Nimrod
9 × 9 Industries
North American Review
North Atlantic Books
North Dakota Quarterly
North Point Press
Northern Lights
Northwest Review
Notre Dame Review
O. ARS
O·Blēk
Obsidian
Obsidian II
Oconee Review
October
Ohio Review
Old Crow Review
Ontario Review
Open City

Open Places
Orca Press
Orchises Press
Orion
Other Voices
Oxford American
Oxford Press
Oyez Press
Oyster Boy Review
Painted Bride Quarterly
Painted Hills Review
Paris Press
Paris Review
Parnassus: Poetry in Review
Partisan Review
Passages North
Penca Books
Pentagram
Penumbra Press
Pequod
Persea: An International Review
Pipedream Press
Pitcairn Press
Pitt Magazine
Ploughshares
Poet and Critic
Poetry
Poetry East
Poetry Ireland Review
Poetry Northwest
Poetry Now
Prairie Schooner
Prescott Street Press
Press
Promise of Learnings
Provincetown Arts
Puerto Del Sol
Quarry West
The Quarterly
Quarterly West
Raccoon
Rainbow Press
Raritan: A Quarterly Review

Red Cedar Review
Red Clay Books
Red Dust Press
Red Earth Press
Red Hen Press
Release Press
Review of Contemporary Fiction
Revista Chicano-Riquena
Rhetoric Review
River Styx
Rowan Tree Press
Russian *Samizdat*
Salmagundi
San Marcos Press
Sea Pen Press and Paper Mill
Seal Press
Seamark Press
Seattle Review
Second Coming Press
Semiotext(e)
Seneca Review
Seven Days
The Seventies Press
Sewanee Review
Shankpainter
Shantih
Sheep Meadow Press
Shenandoah
A Shout In the Street
Sibyl-Child Press
Side Show
Small Moon
The Smith
Solo
Solo 2
Some
The Sonora Review
Southern Poetry Review
Southern Review
Southwest Review
Spectrum
The Spirit That Moves Us
St. Andrews Press

Story
Story Quarterly
Streetfare Journal
Stuart Wright, Publisher
Sulfur
The Sun
Sun & Moon Press
Sun Press
Sunstone
Sycamore Review
Tamagwa
Tar River Poetry
Teal Press
Telephone Books
Telescope
Temblor
Tendril
Texas Slough
Third Coast
13th Moon
THIS
Thorp Springs Press
Three Rivers Press
Threepenny Review
Thunder City Press
Thunder's Mouth Press
Tia Chucha Press
Tikkun
Tombouctou Books
Toothpaste Press
Transatlantic Review
TriQuarterly
Truck Press
Undine
Unicorn Press
University of Georgia Press
University of Illinois Press
University of Iowa Press
University of Massachusetts Press
University of Pittsburgh Press
University of North Texas Press
Unmuzzled Ox
Unspeakable Visions of the Individual

Vagabond
Vignette
Virginia Quarterly
Volt
Wampeter Press
Washington Writers Workshop
Water Table
Western Humanities Review
Westigan Review
White Pine Press
Wickwire Press
Willow Springs
Wilmore City

Witness
Word Beat Press
Word-Smith
Wormwood Review
Writers Forum
Xanadu
Yale Review
Yardbird Reader
Yarrow
Y'Bird
Zeitgeist Press
Zoetrope: All-Story
ZYZZYVA

CONTRIBUTOR'S NOTES

ELIZABETH ALEXANDER is the author of *The Venus Hottentot* and *Body of Life*. She lives in New Haven.

JULIAN ANDERSON's first novel, *Empire Under Glass,* was published by Faber and Faber in 1996. She has been a Bread Loaf Fellow.

RENÉE ASHLEY's collection is *Salt* (University of Wisconsin Press). She has won many awards for her poetry and is the assistant poetry coordinator for the Geraldine R. Dodge Foundation.

TOM BAILEY once taught at Harvard and now teaches at Susquehanna University. His new book, *On Writing Short Stories,* is just out from Oxford University Press.

RICHARD BAUSCH has published eight novels and five books of stories. He was recently inducted into the Fellowship of Southern Writers.

CHARLES BAXTER's most recent book of fiction is *Believers.* He is also the author of *Burning Down the House.* He lives in Ann Arbor.

BRUCE BEASLEY is the author of three collections of poems, most recently *The Creation* (winner of the 1993 Ohio State University Press/Journal Award) and *Summer Mystagogia,* winner of the 1996 Colorado Prize. He teaches at Western Washington University.

ROBERT BOSWELL has published six books of fiction, received two NEA Fellowships, a Guggenheim, the Iowa Prize and the PEN West Award for Fiction. He lives with his wife, the writer Antonya Nelson, and their children in New Mexico.

FREDERICK BUSCH's has written, most recently, *A Dangerous Profession* and *The Night Inspector.* He lives in Sherburne, New York.

MICHAEL BURKARD's poems will appear in issues of *Conduit, Fence* and *The Louisville Review*. His books include *Entire Dilemma* (Sarabande), *My Secret Boat* (Norton) and *The Fires They Kept* (Metro Book Co.)

DAN CHAON is the author of *Fitting Ends and Other Stories* (Tri-Quarterly Books). His new collection is due out soon from TriQuarterly. He lives and teaches in Cleveland.

JANE COOPER was the New York State Poet recently. Her fifth book is *The Flashboat: Poems Collected and Reclaimed*, just published by W. W. Norton Co.

ROBERT COOVER's most recent book is *Ghost Town*. He teaches at Brown University.

HUGH COYLE lives in New York City and Vermont, where he serves on the board of Bread Loaf Writers Conference. His novel in progress is *Magnetism*.

ROBERT CREELEY won the Bollingen Poetry Prize in 1999. He has taught for many years at SUNY, Buffalo. His most recent collection is *Life and Death* (New Directions).

THEODORE DEPPE is the author of *Children of the Air* (1990) and *The Wanderer King* (1996), both published by Alice James Books.

PAULA FOX has been writing and publishing for almost four decades starting with *Poor George*, her first novel. She lives in Brooklyn, New York.

FORREST GANDER is the author of *Science & Steepleflower* (New Directions, 1998) and other titles. He is the editor of *Mouth to Mouth*, an anthology of contemporary Mexican poets (Milkweed, 1996).

AMITAV GHOSH is the author of three novels and two nonfiction works. His novel, *The Shadow Lines*, won two prestigious Indian prizes—the Sahitya Akademi Award and the Ananda Puraskar prize.

RAY GONZALEZ is the author of five books, including *The Heat of Arrivals* (BOA). He won the PEN-Oakland Josephine Miles Award.

SUSAN HAHN is the editor of *TriQuarterly* magazine and co-founder/editor of TriQuarterly Books. Her poetry collections are published by the University of Chicago Press.

GAIL N. HARADA was born and lives in Honolulu and has been published in *Bamboo Ridge, Breaking Silence: An Anthology of Contemporary Asian American Poets* and elsewhere.

DANIEL HENRY lives with his wife and son in a house they built themselves on a remote shore of Lynn Canal, the deepest fjord in North America. He teaches at Haines High School, Haines, Alaska, and his work has appeared in numerous journals.

BOB HICOK's third book, *Plus Shipping,* was published by BOA Editions in 1998. He lives in Ann Arbor.

EMILY HIESTAND is a writer and visual artist. Her most recent book is *Angela The Upside-Down Girl* (Beacon, 1998).

BRUCE HOLLAND ROGERS has twice won science fiction's Nebula Award. He lives in Eugene, Oregon.

PAM HOUSTON is the author of *Cowboys Are My Weakness, Waltzing the Cat* and *A Little More About Me,* all from Norton. She is a horsewoman and licensed river guide, and lives in Colorado.

TONY HOAGLAND's poems have appeared in *Pushcart Prize* XVI and XVIII. He lives in Las Croces, New Mexico.

CATHY HONG has published in *Mudfish* and many other journals. She lives in Brooklyn, New York.

ANN HOOD is the author of seven novels, most recently *Ruby.* Her work has appeared in many journals and she lives in Providence, Rhode Island with her husband, son and daughter.

CHRISTOPHER HOWELL is editor of *Willow Springs* and director of Lynx House Press. His *Memory and Heaven,* collected poems, was published by Eastern Washington University Press in 1997.

JOHN KISTNER informs us that "Son of Stet" was composed on his grandmother's 1920 Sterling manual typewriter. He lives in Seattle, where he works as a word processor. His poetry has appeared in *Whiskey Island, Ambergris, Uno Mas* and elsewhere.

JAS. MARDIS is the author of the chapbooks *Southern Tongue* (1990), *Hanging Time* (1992) and *The Ticking and the Time Going Past* (1995). He lives in Dallas.

OLEH LYSHEHA was a Ukrainian dissident in the 1970s. All his work was banned from publication by Soviet authorities until his first book,

Great Bridge, was published in 1989. A collection of his selected poems is forthcoming from Harvard University Press.

GABRIEL GARCÍA MÁRQUEZ is the author of *One Hundred Years of Solitude* and other novels.

HARRY MATHEWS is a long-time member of Oulipo. He composed "Dear Mother" by the Oulipian compositional process of combining works by Tate and William Cullen Bryant.

ALICE MATTISON has written three books of short fiction and her third novel, *The Book Borrower,* is just out from Morrow. She lives in New Haven.

DAVID MEANS wrote *A Quick Kiss of Redemption,* stories. He lives in Upper Nyack, New York.

LEONARD MICHAELS lives in Kensington, California and has appeared in *The Pushcart Prize* several times, most recently with "Tell Me Everything" (PPXVIII).

MÔNG-LAN is a writer and visual artist. Her work has appeared in *Watermark, Iowa Review, Kenyon Review* and *Manoa.* She lives in Tucson.

BRENDA MILLER's collection of essays, *A Thousand Buddhas,* won a Utah Arts Council Award. Her work also appears in *The Sun, Willow Springs,* and *Seattle Magazine.*

RICK MOODY lives on an island in Long Island Sound. He is the author of *Purple America, The Ice Storm* and *Garden State,* winner of Pushcart's Editors' Book Award.

CHARLOTTE MORGAN has published stories in *Thema, Pearl* and *Phoebe.* Her novel, *One August Day,* was published in 1998 by Van Neste Books.

ALICIA OSTRIKER lives in Princeton, New Jersey. She previously appeared in *Pushcart Prize IV.*

STACEY RICHTER lives in Tucson and her story collection, *My Date With Satan,* is just out.

LAURIE SHECK's poetry collection, *The Willow Grove,* was published by Knopf in 1996. She teaches at Princeton.

REGINALD SHEPHERD's third book is due out from the University of Pittsburgh Press, which also published his first two books. He teaches at Cornell.

ELISABETH SIFTON has been a book editor for many years and is now senior vice president at Farrar, Straus and Giroux.

PETER MOORE SMITH's first novel will be published by Little, Brown in 2000. His short fiction has appeared in *American Literary Review, Folio, The Journal, South Dakota Review* and elsewhere.

CATHY SONG is author of *Picture Bride* (Yale, 1983). *Frameless Windows, Squares of Light* (Norton, 1987) and *School Figures* (Pittsburgh, 1994). She lives in Honolulu.

STEVE STERN's most recent collection of fiction is just out from Graywolf Press. He lives in Saratoga Springs, New York.

JOSEPH STROUD poetry collections have been published by Copper Canyon, Capra, and BOA. He lives in Santa Cruz, California.

ADRIENNE SU comes from Atlanta and lives in Iowa City. Her book of poems is *Middle Kingdom* (Alice James).

ALEXANDER THEOROUX appeared in the very first Pushcart Prize with "Lynda Van Cats" and later re-appeared here with "A Note On the Type" (PPXVII). He is the author of two novels and two essay collections, and lives in West Barnstable, Massachusetts.

EDUARDO URIOS-APARISI was born in Spain and now studies at the University of Illinois, Chicago. He is director of the journal *Abrapalabra*.

REETIKA VAZIRANI's poetry collection, *White Elephants,* was published by Beacon in 1996. She is a contributing editor to *Shenandoah.*

KATE WALBERT's first novel will be out soon from Scribner. She is the author of *Where She Went,* linked stories, and she teaches at Yale.

MARY YUKARI WATERS lives in Los Angeles. Her work has appeared in *TriQuarterly, Glimmer Train Stories* and elsewhere.

LIZA WIELAND's novel, *The Names of the Lost* (Southern Methodist University Press, 1992), was named Best First Novel of the Year by *The Dictionary of Literary Biography. Discovering America,* a fiction collection, was published by Random House in 1994.

DIANE WILLIAMS' *Excitability: Selected Stories* is out from Dalkey Archive Press. "Very, Very Red" appeared first on Ben Marcus's webzine, Impossible Object.

SUSAN WOOD's book *Campo Santo* was a Lamont selection in 1991. She teaches at Rice University.

KATAYOON ZANDVAKILI's poems have appeared in *Five Fingers, Hawaii Review* and most recently *A World Between: Poems, Short Stories and Essays by Iranian-Americans.* She is at work on a novel and lives in Piedmont, California.

CONTRIBUTING SMALL PRESSES FOR THIS EDITION

(These presses made or received nominations for this edition of *The Pushcart Prize*. See the *International Directory of Little Magazines and Small Presses*, Dustbooks, P.O. Paradise, CA 95697, for subscription rates, manuscript requirements and a complete international listing of small presses.)

A

The Acorn, see Hot Pepper Press
Acorn Whistle, 907 Brewster Ave., Beloit, WI 53511
Affair of the Mind, 8 Mare Lane, Comack, NY 11725
Affirmative Publications, Inc., P.O. Box 24471, Detroit, MI 48224
Afterthoughts, 1100 Commissioners Rd. E, P.O. Box 41040, London, Ont., CANADA N5Z 4Z7
Agni, Boston Univ., Boston, MA 02215
Alaska Quarterly Review, Univ. of Alaska, Anchorage, AK 99508
Alma Publishing Co., 6823 N. Michigan, Gladstone, MO 64118
American Jones Building & Maintenance, see Missing Spoke Press
American Letters & Commentary, 850 Park Ave., ste. 5b, New York, NY 10021
American Literary Review, Univ. of North Texas, Denton, TX 76203
American Poetry Review, 1721 Walnut St., Philadelphia, PA 19103
The American Voice, 332 W. Broadway, Louisville, KY 40202
American Writing, 4343 Manayunk Ave., Philadelphia, PA 19128
Amherst Writers & Artists Press, P.O. Box 1076, Amherst, MA 01004
The Amicus Journal, 40 W. 20th St., New York, NY 10011
Angst Productions, P.O. Box 508, Calumet, MI 49913
Antietam Review, 41 S. Potomac St., Hagerstown, MD 21740
Antioch Review, P.O. Box 148, Yellow Springs, OH 45387
Arctos Press, P.O. Box 401, Sausalito, CA 94966

Art and Understanding, 25 Monroe St., Albany, NY 12210
Artisan, P.O. Box 157, Wilmette, IL 60091
Artword Quarterly, 5273 Portland Ave., White Bear Lake, MN 55110
Ascent, 901 S. 8th St., Moorhead, MN 56562
Atlanta Review, P.O. Box 8248, Atlanta, GA 30306
The Aurorean, P.O. Box 219, Sagamore Beach, MA 02562
Avec Books, P.O. Box 1059, Penngrove, CA 94951
Avocet Press, Ste. 400, 635 Madison Ave., New York, NY 10022
Axe Factory Review, P.O. Box 40691, Philadelphia, PA 19107

B

Baacchor Magazine, 2555 Huntington Dr., ste. 235, San Marino, CA 91108
The Baffler, P.O. Box 378293, Chicago, IL 60637
The Baltimore Review, P.O. Box 410, Riderwood, MD 21139
Bamboo Ridge Press, P.O. Box 61781, Honolulu, HI 96839
bananafish, P.O. Box 381332, Cambridge, MA 02238
Barrow Street, P.O. Box 2017, Old Chelsea Sta., New York, NY 10113
Bathtub Gin, P.O. Box 2392, Bloomington, IN 47402
Baybury Review, P.O. Box 462, Ephraim, WI 54211
Belletrist Review, see Marmarc Publications
Bellingham Review, Western Washington Univ., Bellingham, WA 98225
Beloit Poetry Journal, 24 Berry Cove Rd., Lamoine, ME 04605
Berkeley Fiction Review, Univ. of Calif., 201 Heller Lounge, Berkeley, CA 94720
Bitter Oleander, 4983 Tall Oaks Dr., Fayetteville, NY 13066
Black Moon, 233 Northway Rd., Reistertown, MD 21136
Black Warrior Review, P.O. Box 862936, Tuscaloosa, AL 35486
Blue Collar Review, P.O. Box 11417, Norfolk, VA 23517
Blue Light Press, P.O. Box 642, Fairfield, IA 52556
Blue Satellite, see Sacred Beverage Press
BOA Editions, Ltd., 260 East Ave., Rochester, NY 14604
Boston Review, E53-407, Massachusetts Inst. Of Technology, Cambridge, MA 02139
Bottom Dog Press, c/o Firelands College, Huron, OH 44839
Bottomfish, De Anza College, Cupertino, CA 95014
The Briarcliff Review, Briarcliff College, Sioux City, IA 51104
Bridge Works Press, P.O. Box 1798, Bridgehampton, NY 11932
Brilliant Corners, Lycoming College, Williamsport, PA 17701
Brouhaha, see Green Bean Press
Burning Deck, 71 Elmgrove Ave., Providence, RI 02906
Burning Press, P.O. Box 585, Lakewood, OH 44107

C

Calyx, Inc., P.O. Box B, Corvallis, OR 97339
Cambridge Book Review Press, Box 222, Cambridge, WI 53523
Canio's Editions, P.O. Box 1962, Sag Harbor, NY 11963
Capra Press, P.O. Box 2068, Santa Barbara, CA 93120
Caprice, P.O. Box 439, Ripley, TN 38063
The Caribbean Writer, Univ. of Virgin Islands, RR02, Box 10,000, Kingshill, St. Croix, USVI
    00850

The Carolina Quarterly, Greenlaw Hall, Univ. of North Carolina, Chapel Hill, NC 27599
Cassowary Press, 15550 Wyandotte St., Van Nuys, CA 91406
The Chariton Review, Northeast Missouri St. Univ., Kirksville, MO 63501
The Chattahoochee Review, 2101 Womack Rd., Dunwoody, GA 30338
Chelsea, Box 773 Cooper Sta., New York, NY 10276
Chelsea Green Publishing Co., P.O. Box 428, White River Junction, VT 05001
Chicago Review, Univ. of Chicago, 5801 S. Kenwood Ave., Chicago, IL 60637
Chicory Blue Press, 795 East St. N., Goshen, CT 06756
Chiron Review, 702 N. Prairie, St. John, KS 67575
City Lights Books, 261 Columbus Ave., San Francisco, CA 94133
Clackamas Literary Review, 19600 S. Molalla Ave., Oregon City, OR 97045
ClampDown Press, P.O. Box 7270, Cape Porpoise, ME 04014
Cleveland State Univ. Poetry Center, Euclid Ave. at E. 24 St., Cleveland, OH 44115
Coffee House Press, 27 N. 4th St., Minneapolis, MN 55401
Colorado Review, Colorado State University, Ft. Collins, CO 80523
Communities Magazine, P.O. Box 169, Masonville, CO 80541
Confrontation, English Dept., C.W. Post of L.I.U., Brookville, NY 11548
Conjunctions, Bard College, Annandale-on-Hudson, NY 12504
Connecticut Review, English Dept., So. Connecticut St. Univ., 501 Crescent St., New Haven, CT 06515
Consafos Press, P.O. Box 931568, Los Angeles, CA 90093
Converge Magazine, see Affirmative Publications, Inc.
Copper Canyon Press, P.O. Box 271, Port Townsend, WA 98368
Coracle, 1516 Euclid Ave., Berkeley, CA 94708
Cottonwood Magazine, Box J, Kansas Union, Univ. of Kansas, Lawrence, KS 66045
Crab Orchard Review, English Dept., So. Illinois Univ., Carbondale, IL 62901
Crescent Review, P.O. Box 15069, Chevy Chase, MD 20825
CutBank, English Dept., Univ. of Montana, Missoula, MT 59812
Cynic Press, P.O. Box 40691, Philadelphia, PA 19107

D

Dancing Moon Press, P.O. Box 832, Newport, OR 97365
John Daniel, Inc., 23030 W. Sheffler Rd., Elmira, OR 97437
Delaware Valley Poets, 111 Taylor Terrace, Hopewell, NJ 08525
Denver Quarterly, Univ. of Denver, Denver, CO 80208
The Distillery, English Dept., Motlow College, P.O. Box 88100, Tullahoma, TN 37388
DoubleTake, 1317 W. Pettigrew, Durham, NC 27705

E

The Ear, Irvine Valley College, 5500 Irvine Center Dr., Irvine, CA 92620
Eclectic, English Dept., State Univ. of West Georgia, Carrollton, GA 30118
Eidolon Editions, 78 Niagara Ave., San Francisco, CA 94112
Ekphrasis, see Frith Press
Enterzone, 1017 Bayview, Oakland, CA 94610
Epoch, 251 Goldwin Smith Hall, Cornell Univ., Ithaca, NY 14853
Eureka Literary Magazine, P.O. Box 280, Eureka, IL 61530
Event, Douglas College, P.O. Box 2503, New Westminster, B.C. CANADA V3L 5B2
EWU Press, Eastern Washington Univ., 526 5th St., Cheney, WA 99004
Exit 13 Magazine, P.O. Box 423, Fanwood, NJ 07023

F

Faultline, P.O. Box 599-4960, Irvine, CA 92716
Fence, 14 Fifth Ave., Apt. 1A, New York, NY 10011
Fiction International, 5500 Campanile Dr., San Diego, CA 92182
Field, Oberlin College, Oberlin, OH 44074
The Figures, 5 Castle Hill, Great Barrington, MA 01230
Finishing Line Press, P.O. Box 1016, Cincinnati, OH 45201
First Intensity, P.O. Box 665, Lawrence, KS 66044
Fish Stories, 3540 N. Southport, #493, Chicago, IL 60657
Five Points, English Dept., Georgia State Univ., Atlanta, GA 30303
The Florida Review, English Dept., Univ. of Central Florida, Orlando, FL 32816
Flyway, 206 Ross Hall, Iowa State Univ., Ames, IA 50011
The Formalist, 320 Hunter Dr., Evansville, IN 47711
Fourteen Hills, see The SFSU Review
Free Lunch, P.O. Box 7647, Laguna Niguel, CA 92607
Freedom Daily, 11350 RandomHills Rd., ste. 800, Fairfax, VA 22030
Frith Press, P.O. Box 161236, Sacramento, CA 95816
Fugue Magazine, English Dept., Univ. of Idaho, Moscow, ID 83844
Futures, 3039 38th Ave. S, Minneapolis, MN 55406

G

Gargoyle, 1508 U St., NW, Washington, DC 20009
George & Mertle's Place, P.O. Box 10335, Spokane, WA 99209
The George Washington Review, 800 21st St., NW, Washington, DC 20052
Gettysburg Review, Gettysburg College, Gettysburg, PA 17325
Glimmer Train, 812 S.W. Washington St., Portland, OR 97205
Gorrión Press, P.O. Box 1013, New York, NY 10040
Green Bean Press, P.O. Box 237, Canal St. Sta., New York, NY 10013
Green Hills Literary Lantern, P.O. Box 375, Trenton, MO 64683
Green Mountains Review, Johnson State College, Johnson, VT 05656
The Greensboro Review, English Dept., P.O. Box 26170, UNCG, Greensboro, NC 27402
Gulf Coast, English Dept., Univ. of Houston, Houston, TX 77204
The GW Forum, 764 Rome Hall, George Washington Univ., Washington, DC 20052

H

Haight-Ashbury Literary Jounal, 558 Joust Ave., San Francisco, CA 94127
Hampton Shorts, P.O. Box, Bridgehampton, NY 11928
Hannacroix Creek Books, 1127 High Ridge Rd., #110, Stamford, CT 06905
Happy, 240 E. 35th St., New York, NY 10016
Hart, P.O. Box 46, Newburgh, NY 12550
Harvard Review, Harvard College, Cambridge, MA 02138
Hayden's Ferry Review, Box 871502, Arizona State Univ., Tempe, AZ 85287
Helicon Nine, P.O. Box 22412, Kansas City, MO 64113
Heliotrope, P.O. Box 9517, Spokane, WA 99209
The Higginsville Reader, P.O. Box 141, Three Bridges, NJ 08887
High Plains Literary Review, 180 Adams St., ste. 250, Denver, CO 80206
Hip Mama, P.O. Box 9097, Oakland, CA 94613

Hot Pepper Press, P.O. Box 39, Somerset, CA 95684
Hubbub, 5344 SE 38th Ave., Portland, OR 97202
The Hudson Review, 684 Park Ave., New York, NY 10021
Hunger Magazine, P.O. Box 505, Rosendale, NY 12472
Hutton Publications, P.O. Box 2907, Decatur, IL 62524

I

The Ice Cube Press, 205 N. Front St., North Liberty, IA 52317
The Iconoclast, 1675 Amazon Rd., Mohegan Lake, NY 10547
Illumination Arts Publishing Co., P.O. Box 1875, Bellevue, WA 98009
INK, 11 Spring Hill Terrace, Somerville, MA 02143
International Quarterly, P.O. Box 10521, Tallahassee, FL 32302
Iowa Review, Univ. of Iowa, Iowa City, IA 52242
Italian Americana, 52 Kirkland St., Cambridge, MA 02138

J

The Journal, English Dept., Ohio St. Univ., Columbus, OH 43210
Journal of African Travel-Writing, P.O. Box 346, Chapel Hill, NC 27514
Journal of New Jersey Poets, County College of Morris, 214 Center Grove Rd., Randolph, NJ
   07869

K

Kalliope, Florida Community College, 3939 Roosevelt Blvd., Jacksonville, FL 32205
Karamu, English Dept., Eastern Illinois Univ., Charleston, IL 61920
Kelsey Review, Mercer County Community College, P.O. Box B, Trenton, NJ 08690
The Kenyon Review, Kenyon College, Gambier, OH 43022
Kestrel, Fairmont State College, 1201 Locust Ave., Fairmont, WV 26554
Kings Estate Press, 870 Kings Estate Rd., St. Augustine, FL 32086

L

Latin American Literary Review Press, 121 Edgewood Ave., Pittsburgh, PA 15218
The Laurel Review, Northwest Missouri State Univ., Maryville, MO 64468
The Ledge, 78-44 80th St., Glendale, NY 11385
Licking River Review, Northern Kentucky Univ., Highland Heights, KY 41099
Lit Rag, P.O. Box 21066, Seattle, WA 98111
Literal Latte, 61 E. 8th St., New York, NY 10003
Livingston Press, UWA sta. 22, Livingston, AL 35470
Lone Stars Magazine, 4219 Flinthill Dr., San Antonio, TX 78230
Lost Roads Publishers, 351 Nayatt Rd., Barrington, RI 02806
The Louisville Review, Spalding Univ., 851 S. Fourth St., Louisville, KY 40203
Lynx, P.O. Box 1250, Gualala, CA 95445
Lynx Eye, 1880 Hill Dr., Los Angeles, CA 90041

M

The MacGuffin, Schoolcraft College, 18600 Haggerty Rd., Livonia, MI 48152
Main Street Rag, P.O. Box 25331, Charlotte, NC 28229
Mandrake Poetry Review, P.O. Box 792, Larkspur, CA 94977
Manoa, English Dept., Univ. of Hawaii, Honolulu, HI 96822
Many Beaches Press, 1527 N. 36 St., Sheboygan, WI 53081
Many Mountains Moving, Inc., 420 22nd St., Boulder, CO 80302
The Marlboro Review, P.O. Box 243, Marlboro, VT 05344
Marmarc Publications, P.O. Box 596, Plainville, CT 06062
The Massachusetts Review, Univ. of Massachusetts, Amherst, MA 01003
Medicinal Purposes Literary Review, 86-37 120th St. #2D, Richmond Hill, NY 11418
Melic Review, 700 E. Ocean Blvd., #2504, Long Beach, CA 90802
The Metropolitan Review, P.O. Box 26470, San Francisco, CA 94126
Michigan Quarterly Review, 3032 Rockham Bldg., Ann Arbor, MI 48109
Mid-Amerian Review, Bowling Green State Univ., Bowling Green, OH 43403
Mid-List Press, 4324 12th Ave. S., Minneapolis, MN 55407
Mike and Dale's Younger Poets, 2925 Higgins St., Austin, TX 78722
Milkweed Editions, 430 First Ave. N, Minneapolis, MN 55401
Mind in Motion, P.O. Box 1701, Bishop, CA 93515
mind the gap, 119 N. 11th St., Brooklyn, NY 11211
Missing Spoke Press, P.O. Box 9569, Seattle, WA 98109
Mississippi Review, Univ. of So. Mississippi, Box 5144, Hattiesburg, MS 39406
Missouri Review, 1507 Hillcrest Hall, Univ. of Missouri, Columbia, MO 65211
mm Review, see Finishing Line Press
The Montserrat Review, P.O. Box 8297, San Jose, CA 95155
Moon Pony Press, 740 30th Ave., #78, Santa Cruz, CA 95062
Mortco, P.O. Box 1430, Cooper Sta., New York, NY 10976
Mudfish, 184 Franklin St., New York, NY 10013
Muse, 116 Green Knolls Dr., #D, Rochester, NY 14620
Mystery Time, see Hutton Publications

N

Nassau Review, Nassau Community College, One Education Dr., Garden City, NY 11530
The Nebraska Review, UNO Writers Workshop, FA212, Univ. of Nebraska, Omaha, NE 68182
Nerve Cowboy, P.O. Box 4973, Austin, TX 78765
New American Writing, 389 Molino Ave., Mill Valley, CA 94941
New College Writers, c/o J. Koch, 8907-A Trone Circle, Austin, TX 78758
New Delta Review, English Dept., Louisiana State Univ., Baton Rouge, LA 70803
New England Review, Middlebury College, Middlebury, VT 05753
New England Writers, Vermont Poets Assoc., P.O. Box 483, Windsor, VT 05089
New Letters, 5101 Rockhill Rd., Kansas City, MO 64110
New Millenium Writings, P.O. Box 2463, Knoxville, TN 37901
The New Orphic Review, 1095 Victoria Dr., Vancouver, B.C., CANADA V5L 4G3
The New Renaissance, 28 Heath Rd., #11, Arlington, MA 02474
New Rivers Press, 420 N. 5th St., ste. 910, Minneapolis, MN 55401
New York Quarterly, P.O. Box 693, Old Chelsea Sta., New York, NY 10113
Newton's Baby, 788 Murphey St., Scottdale, GA 30079
Nightshade Press, P.O. Box 76, Troy, ME 04987
North American Review, Univ. of Northern Iowa, Cedar Falls, IA 50614
NorthLife, 5302 Ramsey St., Duluth, MN 55807
Northern Lights, P.O. Box 8084, Missoula, MT 59807
Notre Dame Review, English Dept., Univ. of Notre Dame, Notre Dame, IN 46556

O

Octavo, 7381 Swan Point Way, Columbia, MD 21045
The Ohio Review, 344 Scott Quadrangle, Ohio Univ., Athens, OH 45701
Old Crow Review, P.O. Box 403, Easthampton, MA 01027
One Trick Pony, P.O. Box 11186, Philadelphia, PA 19136
The Onset Review, P.O. Box 3157, Wareham, MA 02571
Ontario Review, 9 Honey Brook Dr., Princeton, NJ 08540
Open City, 225 Lafayette, #1114, New York, NY 10012
Orchises Press, P.O. Box 20602, Alexandria, VA 22320
Osiris, P.O. Box 297, Deerfield, MA 01342
Other Voices, 601 S. Morgan St., Chicago, IL 60607
Owen Wister Review, P.O. Box 3625, Laramie, WY 82071
Oxford Magazine, Miami Univ., Bachelor Hall, Oxford, OH 45056
Oyster Boy Review, 191 Sickles Ave., San Francisco, CA 94112
O!! Zone, 1266 Fountain View, Houston, TX 77057

P

Palanquin Press, English Dept., Univ. of South Carolina, Aiken, SC 29801
Pangolin Papers, Box 241, Nordland, WA 98358
Papier-Mache Press, 627 Walker St., Watsonville, CA 95076
Papyrus Publishing, P.O. Box 144, Upper Ferntree Gully, Victoria, 3156, AUSTRALIA
Parnassus: Poetry in Review, 205 W. 89th St., #8F, New York, NY 10024
Partisan Review, 236 Bay State Rd., Boston, MA 02215
Paterson Literary Review, One College Blvd., Paterson, NJ 07505
Pearl, 3030 E. Second St., Long Beach, CA 90803
Pendragonian Publications, 407 W. 50th St., #16, Hell's Kitchen, NY 10019
Penny Dreadful, see Pendragonian Publications
The People's Press, 4810 Norwood Ave., Baltimore, MD 21207
Peregrine, see Amherst Writers & Artists Press
Perihelion, c/o J. Ley, 7 Ernst Ave., Bloomfield, NJ 07003
The Permanent Press, 4170 Noyac Rd., Sag Harbor, NY 11963
Perugia Press, P.O. Box 108, Shutesbury, MA 01072
Phoebe, 4400 University Dr., Fairfax, VA 22030
Pif, P.O. Box 538, Dupont, WA 98327
Pine Grove Press, P.O. Box 85, Jamesville, NY 13078
Pivot, 250 Riversdale Dr., #23, New York, NY 10025
Plains Press, P.O. Box 6, Granite Falls, MN 56241
Plainview Press, P.O. Box 33311, Austin, TX 78764
Pleiades, Central Missouri State Univ., Warrensburg, MO 64093
Ploughshares, 100 Beacon St., Boston, MA 02116
Poems & Plays, English Dept., Middle Tennessee State Univ., Murfreesboro, TN 37132
Poet to Poet, see Medicinal Purposes Literary Review
Poetry, 60 W. Walton, Chicago, IL 60610
Poetry Northwest, Univ. of Washington, Seattle, WA 98105
Porcupine, P.O. Box 259, Cedarburg, WI 53012
Pot Shard Press, P.O. Box 215, Comptche, CA 95427
Potato Eyes, see Nightshade Press
Potomac Review, P.O. Box 354, Port Tobacco, MD 20677
Potpourri, P.O. Box 8278, Prairie Village, KS 66208
Prairie Schooner, 201 Andrews, Univ. of Nebraska, Lincoln, NE 68588
Press, 35 W. 69th St., 1-F, New York, NY 10023

Primavero, Box 37-7547, Chicago, IL 60637
Puerto del Sol, Box 3001, Dept. 3-E, NMSU, Las Cruces, NM 88003

Q

QECE, 406 Main St., #3C, Collegeville, PA 19426
Quarterly West, Univ. of Utah, Salt Lake City, UT 84112

R

Raritan, 31 Mine St., New Brunswick, NJ 08903
Rattle, 13440 Ventura Blvd., #200, Sherman Oaks, CA 91423
Reader's Break, see Pine Grove Press
Red Hen Press, P.O. Box 902582, Palmdale, CA 93590
Red Moon Press, P.O. Box 2461, Winchester, VA 22604
Red Rock Review, English Dept., J2A, Community College of S. Nevada, N. Las Vegas, NV 89030
Redfruit, P.O. Box 475, Fairfax, CA 94978
Rhyme Time, see Hutton Publications
Ridgeway Press, P.O. Box 120, Roseville, MI 48066
River King Poetry Supplement, see River King Press
River King Press, P.O. Box 122, Freeburg, IL 62243
River Oak Review, P.O. Box 3127, Oak Park, IL 60303
River Styx, 3207 Washington, St. Louis, MO 63103
Rosebud, P.O. Box 459, Cambridge, WI 53523
Russian Hill Press, 3020 Bridgeway, #204, Sausalito, CA 94965

S

Sacred Beverage Press, P.O. Box 10312, Burbank, CA 91510
Salt Hill, Sycamore Univ., Syracuse, NY 13244
Sarabande Books, 2234 Dundee Rd., Louisville, KY 40205
Satire, P.O. Box 340, Hancock, MD 21750
Scripsit, Eastern Kentucky Univ., Richmond, KY 40475
Scrivner Creative Review, 853 Sherbrooke St. W, Montreal, Que. CANADA H3A 2T6
Seal Press, 3131 Western Ave., #410, Seattle, WA 98121
Seneca Review, Hobart & William Smith Colleges, Geneva, NY 14456
Seven Days, P.O. Box 1164, Burlington, VT 05402
SFSU Review, College of Humanities, SFSU, 1600 Holloway Ave., San Francisco, CA 94132
Shenandoah, Washington & Lee Univ., Lexington, VA 24450
[sic] Vice & Verse, P.O. Box 27635, Los Angeles, CA 90027
Sidewalks, P.O. Box 321, Champlin, MN 55316
Skylark, Purdue Univ. Calumet, 2200 169 St., Hammond, IN 46323
Slipstream, P.O. Box 2071, Niagara Falls, NY 14301
SlugFest, Ltd., P.O. Box 1238, Simpsonville, SC 29681
Snowy Egret, P.O. Box 9, Bowling Green, IN 47833
Solo, 5146 Foothill Rd., Carpinteria, CA 93013
Somersault Press, 404 Vista Heights Rd., Richmond, CA 94805

South Carolina Review, English Dept., Clemson Univ., Clemson, SC 29634
Southern Humanities Review, 9088 Haley Center, Auburn Univ., Auburn, AL 36849
Southern Methodist University Press, P.O. Box 750415, Dallas, TX 75275
The Southern Review, Louisiana State Univ., Baton Rouge, LA 70803
Southwest Review, P.O. Box 750374, Dallas, TX 75275
Sou'Wester Magazine, Southern Illinois Univ., Edwardsville, IL 62026
Speak, 301 8th St., ste. 240, San Francisco, CA 94103
Spectacle, 101 Middlesex Turnpike, ste. 6-155, Burlington, MA 01803
Spindrift, 1507 E. 53rd St., #649, Chicago, IL 60615
Sport Literate, P.O. Box 577166, Chicago, IL 60657
Story, 1507 Dana Ave., Cincinnati, OH 45207
Story Quarterly, P.O. Box 1416, Northbrook, IL 60065
Sulphur River Literary Review, P.O. Box 19228, Austin, TX 78760
The Sun, 107 N. Roberson St., Chapel Hill, NC 27516
Sweet Annie Press, 7750 Highway F-24 W, Baxter, IA 50028
Sycamore Review, English Dept., Purdue Univ., W. Lafayette, IN 47907

T

Talking River Review, Lewis-Clark State College, Lewiston, ID 83501
Talus and Scree, P.O. Box 832, Newport, OR 97365
Tampa Review, UT Box 19F, 401 W. Kennedy Blvd., Tampa, FL 33606
Tar River Poetry, English Dept., East Carolina Univ., Greenville, NC 27858
Thema, Box 8747, Metairie, LA 70311
Third Coast, Western Michigan Univ., Kalamazoo, MI 49008
The Threepenny Review, P.O. Box 9131, Berkeley, CA 94709
Tia Chucha Press, P.O. Box 476969, Chicago, IL 60647
Tintern Abbey, 7724 Big Bend Blvd., Apt. 1W, St. Louis, MO 63119
Tractor, 2022 X Ave., Dysart, IA 52224
TriQuarterly, 2020 Ridge Rd., Evanston, IL 60208
Two Rivers Review, 215 McCartney St., Easton, PA 18042

U

Universities West Press, P.O. Box 22310, Flagstaff, AZ 86002
University of Georgia Press, Athens, GA 30602
University of Massachusetts Press, Amherst, MA 01003
University Press of New England, 235 Main St., Hanover, NH 03755
University of North Texas Press, P.O. Box 311336, Denton, TX 76203
University of Pittsburgh Press, Pittsburgh, PA 15261
University of Wisconsin Press, 2537 Daniels St., Madison, WI 53718
The Uphill House, P.O. Box 135, Eaton, NH 03832

V

Verse, English Dept., Plymouth State College, Plymouth, NH 03264
Victory Park (Journal of New Hampshire Inst. of Art), 148 Concord St., Manchester, NH 03104
Vincent Brothers Review, 4566 Northern Circle, Riverside, OH 45424

W

Washington Review, P.O. Box 50132, Washington, DC 20091
Watermark: Vietnamese-American Poetry & Prose, c/o B. Ivan, 469 2nd St., Apt. 7, Ann Arbor, MI 48103
The Waterways Project, 393 St. Pauls Ave., Staten Island, NY 10304
West Anglia Publications, P.O. Box 2683, LaJolla, CA 92038
Whelks Walk Review, 37 Harvest Lane, Southampton, NY 11968
Whetstone, Barrington Area Arts Council, P.O. Box 1266, Barrington, IL 60011
White Eagle Coffee Store Press, P.O. Box 383, Fox River Grove, IL 60021
Wild Duck Review, 419 Spring St., ste. D, Nevada City, CA 92038
Wild Earth, P.O. Box 455, Richmond, VT 05477
Wildco Inc., Rt. 6, 3127 Wild Mountain Rd., Tulsa, OK 74127
Wildheart Press, P.O. Box 1115, Jamaica Plain, MA 02130
Willow Springs, Eastern Washington Univ., 526 5th St., Cheney, WA 99004
Wired Hearts Magazine, P.O. Box 1012, West Palm Beach, FL 33402
Witness, 27055 Orchard Lake Rd., Farmington Hills, MI 48334
Wordcraft of Oregon, P.O. Box 3235, La Grande, OR 97850
Writer's Forum, English Dept., UCCS, P.O. Box 7150, Colorado Springs, CO 80933
Writing For Our Lives, 647 N. Santa Cruz Ave., ANNEX, Los Gatos, CA 95030

X

The Yale Review, Box 208243, New Haven, CT 06520
Yemassee, Univ. of South Carolina, Columbia, SC 29208

Z

Zoetrope, 260 Fifth Ave., New York, NY 10001
ZYZZYVA, 41 Sutter St., San Francisco, CA 94104

INDEX

The following is a listing in alphabetical order by author's last name of works reprinted in the *Pushcart Prize* editions.

561

563

567

571

575

581